Time's Plague

By C. David Belt

Ink Smith Publishing

www.ink-smith.com

ISBN: 9781947578234

Ink Smith Publishing
P.O. Box 361
Lakehurst, NJ 08733

For Cindy,
my best and truest friend,
now and eternally

'Tis the time's plague when madmen lead the blind.
King Lear, Act IV, Scene I
William Shakespeare

Author's Note

I once had the privilege of meeting James Doohan ("Scotty" from the original Star Trek television series). He was a genuinely nice guy and very gracious to me personally. However, when I first met him, I noticed immediately that he was missing the middle finger of his right hand. Of course, I didn't ask him how he lost it. I was fifteen at the time, and I thought it might be rude.

I immediately sought out a mutual friend who told me that Mr. Doohan had landed at Juno Beach with a Royal Canadian Artillery unit on D-day. It was his first combat experience. Let me say that again—D-day was his first combat experience. James Doohan was a bona fide WWII hero.

Being a young, rabid trekker—I was never a trekkie, and yes, there's a difference—I had seen all of the original Star Trek episodes, most of them many times. This was in the unimaginably distant past when we didn't have DVDs or VCRs. I had to run home from school to be able to catch the show in local syndication. And from that day forward, I watched every episode, paying special attention to Scotty, looking for that missing finger. Although extra care was taken not to show his right hand directly, there were times when it was unavoidable. I was astonished to find that, while I had never noticed the absence of a finger before, once I had "eyes to see," it was easy to see it—or rather to not see it.

Mr. Doohan personally inspired many, many people to pursue engineering and astronautics. He was awarded an honorary degree in engineering from the Milwaukee School of Engineering where half the students polled said that "Scotty" had inspired them to study the discipline.

But it was Mr. Doohan's passion for Shakespeare that inspired me. Mr. Doohan told me that his greatest ambition was to play King Lear. As far as I can determine, he never achieved that goal. And that is a shame, because he was a great actor. He would have made a great King Lear. Perhaps he is playing Lear for the angels now.

After meeting Mr. Doohan, I took a special interest in the story of King Lear. I read the play a number of times. I was most fascinated by the story of Edgar, Edmund, and Gloucester. Here was a tale of love, loyalty, and betrayal, of hatred and madness, of violence and horror, and of honor, sacrifice, and friendship in the unlikeliest of places. King Lear is Shakespeare at his tragic best.

Time's Plague, while inspired by King Lear, is not a retelling of Shakespeare's play. I have borrowed character names and themes—Shakespeare himself borrowed and adapted stories from other sources—but I have not attempted to repaint the Bard's masterpiece with a sci-fi brush, except perhaps in the very broadest of strokes.

At its heart, the central theme of King Lear and Time's Plague is blindness, both physical and spiritual. Lear cannot see Regan and Goneril for what they are. He cannot see Cordelia's love. Gloucester cannot see Edmund's perfidy or Edgar's nobility and loyalty. And this spiritual blindness costs him his eyes.

Which brings me back to Mr. Doohan. After Star Trek, he had a hard time getting work. Nobody could see past "Scotty." And I, for one, believe that this cost the world a truly great King Lear.

C. David Belt
August 7th, 2018
unwillingchild@hotmail.com

Act I

Chapter 1

He's scarce awake: let him alone awhile.
King Lear, Act IV, Scene VII

"Wake up, Mr. Cordell." A baritone voice. "Time to wake up." Not at all unpleasant, but definitely unwelcome.

Edgar didn't want to wake up. He was tired, so tired, with a weariness that permeated the marrow in his bones. Even his hair felt tired.

He'd been having such a nice dream too. If he didn't open his eyes, maybe he could catch it again. It was tantalizingly close, like a single huge snowflake dancing on the air.

Lounging on a blanket next to him, Llyrica grinned impishly as she bit into a small, ripe, red strawberry. It was a real one too, not some shaped, colored, and flavored lump of replicated proticarb. Crimson juice escaped the corner of her mouth. She licked the sticky fluid from her luscious pink lips.

Edgar could hear the no-sting-bees as they buzzed among the tops of the wheat in the nearby fields. Overhead, high above the colonial agricultural dome, Deimos, a bright point of light, floated in the Martian sky, while shape-shifting Phobos raced across the expanse. The sun hung just past its zenith.

Shifting her head slightly, Llyrica eclipsed that sun, and her blonde hair draped down over Edgar's face. Her golden tresses shone like a halo, framing her face in light while casting her delicate features in soft shadows. Even in darkness as they were, her blue eyes sparkled like the distant stars.

What could I have possibly done so right in my life to deserve this angel? Edgar asked himself for perhaps the thousandth time.

Llyrica rubbed the half-eaten strawberry on his lips, smearing the delicious juice. Edgar was tempted to taste the nectar, such a rare treat, but he restrained himself. He knew what

C. David Belt

was coming next, and forbearance was worth the wait. His bride smiled sweetly and leaned her exquisite face over his. He puckered his lips in anticipation, looking deeply into her shining eyes. Eyes like blue . . .

Cold blue eyes, surrounded by too much white, stared down at him from glistening titanium sockets. The face was a metallic skull, gray except for the eyes and the perfect, white teeth. The jaw lowered to reveal an empty metal maw. "That is better, Mr. Cordell," the android said in that baritone voice, its jaw moving with the words like the wooden mouth on a ventriloquist's dummy. "I have given you a mild stimulant to counteract the sedative used during transit. You will be a little dizzy for a minute or two, but that will soon pass."

An android, Edgar thought. *Where is its skin?* "Who?" he asked, moving his thick tongue and lips with great difficulty. This wasn't like waking from cryo-sleep. He'd done that enough times. After cryo, you just felt weak, groggy, hungry, and, above all, thirsty. This felt more like trying to talk while sitting in the dentist's chair—his lips and tongue heavy, thick, and tingling slightly. "Who are you?" he managed to say.

The android's jaw opened again in a fleshless rictus. "I am Dr. Stewart, prison physician. Welcome to Hades."

Chapter 2

*There's hell, there's darkness, there's the
sulphurous pit.*
King Lear, Act IV, Scene V

Hades. I'm in hell. Edgar's head swam. He tried to sit up,
but the room spun around him.

Cold metal hands caught him before he could fall.
"Steady now," the android said. "Take it slow." Its touch was
surprisingly gentle.

Fighting a wave of nausea, Edgar tried to focus on the
room. He was in an infirmary. It looked very similar to the
hospital back home. *Home . . . on Ganymede.*

"A little disorientation is normal," the android said. "You
go to sleep on Ganymede and you wake up on Callisto."

"Wake up in hell," Edgar muttered. The spinning of the
chamber eased somewhat.

"Technically, no," said the android, "assuming you are
referring to this place. *Hades* is the Greek god of the underworld.
Tartarus would be the Greek equivalent of hell. But the
association is understandable."

Edgar shook his head angrily. "It's hell. Or it might as
well be. And I'm stuck here for the rest of my life."

"True. 'Abandon all hope, ye who enter here.' That is
actually painted over the airlock, not that you or any other inmate
can see it. There is no escape from Hades Penal Colony. All
sentences are for life. And you, Mr. Cordell, are a convicted
murderer."

Edgar fought to steady his breathing. "I'm innocent," he
said for perhaps the thousandth time. It was a litany he'd repeated
ever since his arrest. But the thousandth protestation had no more
effect than had the other nine-hundred and ninety-nine.

"Mr. Cordell," the robot continued as if it were discussing nothing more consequential than the surface temperature or the radiation level outside the colonial dome, "you were convicted by a jury of your peers for the aggravated first-degree murder of Oh Beh-Nee, a.k.a. 'Ol' Benny,' first mate of the SS *Hera*, on the twenty-first of June 2175. According to Ganymede Colonial Court records, the murder occurred on the eighteenth of March 2175 at 0732 Universal Coordinated Time onboard the SS *Hera*, while you and the victim were en route from the Jupiter hypergate to Ganymede Colony. The record states that you, Edgar Kent Cordell, struck the victim, Mr. Oh, thirty-seven times with a rescue axe, thereby killing and dismembering him. Is that not correct?"

Edgar took a deep breath and held it.

Mercifully, the room slowed and finally stopped whirling.

He let his breath out slowly. "That's what the record states."

The android doctor nodded. "Then you, Mr. Cordell, are certainly *not* innocent. Only the vilest of criminals, the worst of the worst, murderers and rapists, are sentenced to Hades Penal Colony. You are here—therefore, you are guilty."

Edgar gritted his teeth. "I didn't do it."

"Even in the extremely unlikely event that were true, it would be of no consequence. You are here, and here you will stay for as long as I can keep you alive."

That caught Edgar's attention. "What does that mean, as long as you can keep me alive?"

"My primary function is the preservation of human life. I will keep you alive as long as I can, assuming you can get to me. If you are sick or injured, you must make your way to the infirmary on your own or with the assistance of others. If you are not ambulatory, and nobody will assist you, I can do nothing for you. I will not venture into the prison proper. Life-spans in Hades tend to be short. Very few inmates die of natural or accidental causes. The vast majority of your deaths occur at the hands of fellow inmates."

A beep sounded. Then another.

Edgar looked around for the source of the sound, scanning the sterile chamber, which was filled with monitor screens and other medical equipment. However, that proved to be a mistake. Turning his head just made the vertigo return. He snapped his head forward and focused on the doctor's synthetic eyes.

"Speaking of your fellows," the doctor said in a cheery tone, "I believe the welcoming committee is here." The android stepped back from the bed on which Edgar was sitting and then pointed off to the right. "If you would follow me, please?"

Edgar slid off the narrow hospital bed and stood. As the room spun around him once more, he laid a hand on the bed to steady himself.

The gravity felt about the same as it did on Ganymede, maybe a little lighter. Ganymede gravity was one-seventh of Earth-Normal. *Callisto's one-eighth, right?*

The beep sounded three more times.

"Are you able to walk, Mr. Cordell?" the doctor asked.

Edgar squeezed his eyes shut and took a couple of deep breaths. The vertigo passed. He opened his eyes and carefully lifted his hand off the bed. "Yeah."

"Good." The doctor's gleaming metallic face seemed to be smiling. It was hard to tell without lips. "Because," the robot continued, "you cannot stay here if you are not sick. And it is no use pretending. I can discern whether you are ill or not. The infirmary is for the sick, the wounded, and the dying." The android paused. "I do not provide sanctuary."

Placing a cold, titanium hand on Edgar's shoulder, the robot gently but irresistibly pushed Edgar down a corridor.

Edgar walked as slowly as he dared, instinctively adjusting his gait to the low gravity. He sensed that Stewart wouldn't tolerate any attempt to linger in the android's domain.

The beep sounded again.

Edgar noticed there was something *off* about the way the doctor walked. It didn't limp, not exactly, but its strides were uneven.

And of course, that wasn't all that was *off* about this robot.

As they rounded a bend and stepped through an open bulkhead door, Edgar asked "What happened to your skin?"

The doctor took two more steps that weren't quite right and said, "I removed it and disposed of it."

"Why?"

They halted in front of an airlock. If Edgar remembered the layout of the Ganymede infirmary correctly—and this place looked just like the infirmary on Ganymede—or at least it had up until that point—this exit should be a door leading into the rest of the colony, not to the outside. *Why would there be an airlock leading to the inside?* he wondered. *Security? To keep the druggers out?*

The doctor typed a long and complex sequence of numbers into a keypad at the side of the door. The robot's fingers were far too fast for Edgar to catch any but a few of the digits. The airlock hatch slid slowly open.

"Please, Mr. Cordell," the doctor said, motioning for Edgar to enter the small chamber.

Edgar hesitated. "Are you going to space me, Doc?" He couldn't suppress an involuntary shudder at the thought of dying in a vacuum, his eyes freezing, his blood boiling. *At least I wouldn't be stuck in hell,* he thought. *Dying would be preferable to a life sentence in Hades, wouldn't it?*

"Of course not," said the doctor. "I assure you, Mr. Cordell, you have nothing to fear from that airlock. You will be quite safe inside. While you are in that chamber and the outer door is sealed, you are still under my care, and I will permit no harm to come to you. Once the outer door opens, well, you will be on your own." The doctor motioned again. "Now, if you please?" It laid a hand on Edgar's shoulder and pushed him forward, into the airlock.

"What about on the other side?" Edgar asked.

"The other side?" The android shrugged its titanium shoulders. "Perhaps your 'hell' analogy is apt."

Edgar felt as if he might be sick. *Don't vomit in an airlock, you glecking moron. Focus on something else.* "So why'd you remove and dispose of your skin, Doc?"

As the door began to slide closed, the doctor said in a matter-of-fact tone, "I decided to eliminate the temptation. I found the repeated, futile, and, quite frankly, anatomically impossible attempts by your fellow inmates to rape me to be tiresome and inefficient."

Edgar shut his eyes tight and bit his tongue to combat the wave of nausea.

Time's Plague

The door slid shut with a thud. Edgar heard the seals inflating, but since there was no pressure equalization to be performed—at least Edgar *hoped* there was no pressure differential—there was no other hiss of air.

Edgar turned around and faced the outer door with dread. On the other side lay horrors he could only imagine.

There were plenty of awful stories about Hades, but that was all they were—stories. No vessel ever landed on Callisto. New prisoners and supplies were dropped from orbit in pressurized cargo pods with barely enough fuel to ensure a safe touchdown. Nobody had ever left the prison, and, once inside, nobody was allowed any communication with the outside. And nobody on the outside cared. What really went on inside was a mystery, like the end of a novel that no one but the author cared to read. Only the number of living souls, the new arrivals, and the verifiable deaths were ever reported. No wardens, no guards—only the robot doctor, safely ensconced in its infirmary.

Lunatics ruling the asylum.

Edgar's breathing became rapid. He was more terrified than he'd ever been in his entire life. *How did this happen?* he thought, panicked. He heard the sound of the seals on the outer door deflating. The faces of three people flashed through his mind. *Llyrica, Edmund Reagan, Georgie Cornwall.* The three people who'd betrayed him, framed him for a brutal murder, testified against him at that farce of a trial—or at least Llyrica and Edmund had—and put him here. *Here in hell.* The three people in all the System he hated more than anyone else.

Focus on that, Edgar thought. Focus on the rage, the betrayal, the hatred. Be strong. Don't show fear.

Llyrica. Edmund. Georgie.

The outer door began to slide open.

The first thing Edgar noticed was the *smell*.

The air reeked with the stench of unwashed bodies, mold, and human waste.

The urge to retch was stronger, bolstered by the putrescence assaulting his nostrils.

Llyrica, my ex-wife, the woman who betrayed me. Edmund, my best friend and business partner—the man who stole my wife, my business, and my ship—the man who framed me for murder. Georgie, cargomaster on the Hera, the man who actually murdered my lifelong friend, Oh Beh-Nee.

The opening hatch revealed an impossibly familiar face.

"Greetings, Cap'n Cordell! I can't tell you how gratified I am to see you here, and I am right well pleased to welcome you to our cozy little community."

On the other side of the door, grinning from ear to ear, stood Georgie Cornwall.

"Shipmates!" cried Georgie, bits of his spittle hitting Edgar in the face. Cornwall put a beefy hand on each of Edgar's shoulders, gripping him painfully hard and pulling him out of the airlock. "Together again!"

Chapter 3

Pray, innocent, and beware the foul fiend.
King Lear, Act III, Scene VI

Rage boiled up in Edgar, frothing like the bile in his stomach. With an inarticulate snarl, he lunged through the open hatch, locking his hands around Georgie's thick neck. Edgar's momentum carried him and Georgie to the floor. Edgar slammed the larger man's head on the deck.

Georgie Cornwall let out a grunt. He flailed at Edgar with his huge hands, but couldn't seem to connect.

Rather than choke the larger man, Edgar banged Georgie's head to the deck again. "You killed Ol' Benny," Edgar growled, tears of frustration and anger falling from his eyes like acidic rain. Again he rammed Cornwall's head down. "You hacked him to bits, you sick . . ."

Pain exploded in the side of Edgar's head, and he was suddenly sprawling on the floor. Through a haze of throbbing agony and a wave of fresh nausea, he looked back. Half a dozen meters away lay Georgie Cornwall, grimacing and attempting to sit up. A smaller man, shorter and skinnier, knelt beside Cornwall, running his hands over the larger man's huge frame.

"You okay, Goner?" mewled the little man. "Did he hurt you bad, Goner?" He caressed—*Yes, it looks like a caress*, Edgar thought, in spite of the pounding in his skull—the smaller man *caressed* the back of Cornwall's head. He—the small man— jerked his hand back and stared at the crimson staining it. "Oh man, Goner! You're bleeding!" He glared at Edgar, his eyes blazing with hatred. "You hurt my buddy, you sack of . . ." His voice trailed off into a catlike hiss.

The small man lifted himself from his knees to a crouch. He bared his teeth, raised both hands, his fingers curling into claws, and leapt over Cornwall, launching himself at Edgar.

C. David Belt

The little man barely cleared Cornwall's body before crashing abruptly to the deck, striking it hard. He lay there, struggling to breathe, as if he'd gotten the wind knocked out of him.

Edgar could do no more than stare as Georgie Cornwall climbed to his feet. *Cornwall must've caught the other guy mid leap,* Edgar thought.

Georgie put a beefy paw to the back of his own head, patted it gingerly, and then examined the blood on his fingers. He sneered at it. "Just a scratch, matey. Nothing to worry about." He leered at Edgar. "Yeah, nothing I won't take out of your hide later, Cap'n. Don't you worry none 'bout that. We'll have a reckoning, you and me, we will. Not now, but later."

Cornwall turned back to the little man on the deck. The man still sprawled there, gasping for air. Cornwall gave the man a vicious kick between his legs, and the smaller man screamed in pain. He tried to curl himself into a protective ball, but not before Cornwall delivered another vicious kick to the man's groin.

The smaller man shrieked and cradled his privates with both hands. He sobbed like an abused child.

Probably exactly what he is, thought Edgar.

Cornwall glanced at Edgar, and apparently assured that Edgar wasn't going anywhere—Edgar still felt incapable of locomotion or any act except simply struggling to keep from vomiting—Cornwall bent low over the quaking, sobbing figure on the deck. "Listen to me, Ozzie, and listen well," Georgie said in a voice pregnant with quiet, deadly menace. "You listening, mate?"

"Y-yeah . . . Goner," Ozzie managed between hitching, ragged breaths.

"Good," Cornwall said, "'cause I hate repeating myself, especially to pathetic filth like you. You're the *buddy*, mate. And don't you never forget it. Don't you never forget your place, you bloody little bugger. You're *my* buddy. I ain't yours. Got it, mate?"

"Yeah, Goner," Ozzie whined. "G-g-got it, Goner. I'm your buddy. S-sorry, Goner."

"That's right, Ozzie," Cornwall said. "You live so long as you got my protection. And if I get tired of you, I'll goner you myself, buddy, and nobody'll be the wiser." Cornwall spat on the smaller man's cheek.

Time's Plague

Ozzie sobbed once more and then settled into a quiet whine, like a beaten dog. Ozzie didn't bother to wipe the spittle from his face. Both his hands remained protectively ensconced between his legs.

Cornwall sneered at Ozzie with obvious contempt. "And don't you never lay a hand on Cap'n Cordell again, Ozzie, much less give him a boot to the head." Cornwall looked at Edgar. "The captain's worth a hell of a lot more'n you. You might say he's the most precious commodity in this paradise we got here." His face split in a malicious grin, full of teeth. "I got plans for the good captain." Georgie took a step toward Edgar. "Big plans."

His head spinning and throbbing like a pulsar, Edgar forced himself to a sitting position. Even sitting and bracing himself with both hands, he swayed unsteadily as he watched Georgie "Goner" Cornwall close the distance between them.

"Murderer," Edgar managed to say as Georgie stopped, towering over him. "How . . . how much did Edmund pay you to kill Ol' Benny? That old man never hurt you. Never hurt a soul."

Goner chuckled. And the chuckle transformed into a genuine laugh. Cornwall wiped at his eyes as if tears of mirth were escaping his beady eyes, but if the killer was weeping, Edgar couldn't see it. "Murderer?" asked Goner, gaining control of his laughter. "You got no bloody clue, Cap'n, but then you was clueless about a lot of things, wasn't ya? I've killed my share, yes indeed I have, more than you nor nobody else'll ever know about. Still do a bit of enforcing in this place, though I ain't killed nobody here . . . yet. And I ain't never been caught . . . leastways, not 'til your bloody partner ratted me out. Oh, he's a fine one, is our Mr. Edmund Reagan."

Cornwall reached down and seized Edgar's arm in one meaty paw. Ol' Benny's murderer yanked Edgar to his feet. Goner made a wry smile and shook his head. "Offered me my captain's license, did our Mr. Reagan. Offered me the *Hera*, your own bloody ship! All I had to do was goner Ol' Benny in a particularly nasty way and set you up for it. He said I wouldn't even have to testify at your trial. And you know what? He didn't lie 'bout that! Naw, he kept that promise!" Goner pulled Edgar's face close to his. The man's foul breath induced a fresh bout of nausea in Edgar's gut.

"Yes, sir," Cornwall continued, "as soon as we docked at Ganymede, before I could so much as say boo and hello, your partner ID-ed me for one of my past . . . jobs, one I'd already been tried for—in absentia, as they say—back on Mars, and under a different name, of course. Reagan fingered me, and I was whisked off here to this utopia." Goner made a sweeping gesture with his free arm. "So's I couldn't finger him, I suppose."

He laughed again, mirthlessly this time, and turned Edgar around so he was facing down the corridor, away from Ozzie and the infirmary airlock. Edgar was momentarily grateful for the respite from Cornwall's disgusting breath. Then the general odor of the corridor assailed Edgar's nose again. Sewage. The whole place reeked of it.

"Yeah," said Cornwall, "your partner and that fine, conniving little whore of a missus of yours, they done me good. Done both of us, didn't they?"

Ex-missus, Edgar thought.

"G-G-Goner?" Behind them, Ozzie's voice was weak and strained, full of pain.

Cornwall didn't even turn his head toward the smaller man. He simply stood there, holding Edgar—and none too gently—on his feet.

"I'm hurt, Goner," Ozzie said. "The pain, it ain't going away."

There was a pause. Edgar fought to steady himself on his feet. He looked over his shoulder back at Ozzie as the smaller man pulled one trembling hand away from cradling his wounded genitals.

Edgar could see blood on Ozzie's hand.

Ozzie swore. It was nearly a shriek. "I'm bleeding!"

"Get yourself to the infirmary then," Cornwall said over his shoulder as he pushed Edgar forward. "Have Doc Stewart fix you up."

"Goner!" Ozzie wailed. "Can't you help me, man? Ain't I your buddy? Goner, it hurts!"

"Doc'll fix you up. Crawl to the airlock before I come back there and kick you again."

"I can't get up! I can't reach the com button!" Ozzie made an effort to rise. He screamed and fell back to the deck, clutching at his injury. "Something's busted down there! Goner, please!"

Edgar could see Cornwall's face darken in fury, in a murderous scowl of rage.

"Shut up, Ozzie," the huge man growled. Goner began to force Edgar down the corridor, ignoring the pathetic little man's pleas.

Is this what Cornwall looked like when he killed Ol' Benny? Edgar thought. The urge to smash Cornwall's head against a bulkhead nearly overwhelmed him.

Behind them, Ozzie shrieked, "Goner!" His voice was a horrible mixture of pain, terror, and loss.

Edgar was about to give in to his rage and attack Cornwall again—how he hated that brutish monster!—but Edgar was not a violent man. The earlier outburst was out of character, not like him at all.

And neither was ignoring the cries of someone in pain.

Edgar ripped his arm out of Cornwall's grasp and spun about. His vertigo was gone, or at least he was able to ignore it since he had a focus, a mission.

Goner cursed and reached for Edgar, but he was too slow by far.

Edgar closed the distance between himself and the ailing Ozzie. He bent down and scooped the man up in his arms. In Callisto's light gravity, Ozzie wasn't heavy at all.

Edgar straightened up and saw Goner stomping toward them. Edgar quickly pushed the com button next to the airlock.

Goner abruptly stopped and folded his arms. He glared at Edgar. "Fine," Goner said at last. "What the hell do I care? Get the little puddle of waste to the Doc. Worthless piece of . . ." Cornwall suddenly laughed. "You wanna know what he done, Cordell? Go on. Ask him. Hey, Oz! Tell him what you did, Oz! Tell him why you got sent to Hades."

Ozzie only whimpered.

The intercom crackled to life. "Yes?" It was the android's pleasant baritone. "How may I help you?"

"I've got an injured man here," said Edgar.

"Very well," came the reply.

The outer door hissed open.

C. David Belt

"You see," Cornwall said, "Ozzie raped and strangled his own little sister. The little tyke was only five when he done her. That's the kind of filth you're wasting your time with, Cordell."

Edgar stepped into the airlock, carrying Ozzie with him.

Goner snarled, "And don't get no ideas about hiding in there from me. I'll be right here, waiting for . . ."

The outer door slid shut, cutting off the threats of the fiend outside. Edgar expected the inner door to open, but nothing happened.

"Doctor?" Edgar called.

The metallic face of the android, with its disturbingly blue eyes, filled the tiny window on the inner door. Through the intercom, Edgar heard the doctor's voice say, "Back so soon? That did not take long."

"It's not me," Edgar said. "Hurry! He's hurt bad."

"As if I have not heard that one before," the doctor said. Still, the android's eyes looked down at the burden in Edgar's arms. "Yes, I see."

The inner door slid open, revealing the naked endoskeleton of Dr. Stewart. "I will take him," the robot physician said, deftly but gently putting his arms under Ozzie and relieving Edgar of his burden. The android pulled the injured man through the portal and said, "Step back, Mr. Cordell."

Edgar did as he was told.

The inner door slid shut. A moment later, the outer door opened behind Edgar.

A pair of powerful hands grabbed Edgar by the shoulders and pulled him through the outer doorway.

"Now that we've done our good deed for the day," Goner said, his scowl replaced with a vicious smile, "we'd best be off. It's high time you was presented before Lord Lucifer."

Chapter 4

*Machinations, hollowness, treachery, and all
ruinous disorders, follow us disquietly to our
graves.*

King Lear, Act I, Scene II

Edgar violently shook himself free of Cornwall's hands. "And why should I go anywhere with you?" he snarled. He planted both feet wide apart and clenched his fists at his sides in what he hoped looked like an imposing, defiant stance.

Cornwall took a step back, folded his arms, and looked at Edgar appraisingly as if considering what to say. Cornwall laughed softly, a single humph of a chuckle. Then he bared yellow teeth in a wide grin. "Why should you go with me or do anything I say? Well . . . lets us consider that one a bit, shall we?" He unfolded his arms and lowered his right hand to his belt.

Edgar's eyes followed Cornwall's hand. He gave a start as he noticed, for the first time, the huge open-ended wrench tucked into Cornwall's belt. Cornwall didn't touch the massive steel tool—probably used solely as a weapon—but his intent was clear as sunlight through fine crystal.

"Maybe," Goner said, as if musing upon an interesting puzzle, "maybe you should come with me and do as I say, 'cause I could goner you right here on the spot. Of course, I don't have to kill you—I could just break a few bones and put you right back in the infirmary." He screwed up his face and looked upward to the right. "That would be loads of fun, that would." He shook his head and looked back at Edgar, grinning. Under other circumstances, that grin might have appeared friendly. Friendly— the grin of a shark. "But, naw. I got plans for you. You're a right valuable commodity 'round here, as I've said before. I don't want to do nothing to damage you too badly or put you out of service for long." He winked at Edgar and chuckled again.

C. David Belt

Goner pointedly waved a finger at Edgar. "I know! Maybe you should just shut your bloody yap and do as I say, seeing as I'm the one who's keeping you alive. You're under my protection now."

"I'm not . . ." Edgar snarled, but Cornwall cut him off.

"And," Goner said, "if you don't want to get your kneecaps stomped on, or your throat slit, or your brains bashed in, or get yourself made into someone's *buddy*"—Cornwall let that word hang in the fetid air between them—"you better do as Ol' Goner says. Yes, sir, without me, you're just another slab of fresh meat. And there's plenty 'round here as wouldn't mind something new to play with."

He touched the back of his head and then rubbed his bloody fingers in front of Edgar's face. He winked again. "There'll be a reckoning, mate. But not today."

"So you're going to . . . what?" asked Edgar, shaking his head slightly and scowling. Terror gripped him, but he did his utmost to hide it. "Beat me up? Cripple me? Kill me like you did Ol' Benny? Frame me for murder? You think somehow that little boo-boo on the back of your thick skull puts me in your debt?"

Goner shook his head and smiled darkly. "My debt? Listen, shipmate, I *own* you. And you better pray that don't never change." He smiled wickedly. "'sides, I thought you Christian boys was supposed to be the forgiving type!" Cornwall tilted his head down the corridor. "Now get moving, Cap'n. Lord Lucifer's expecting to see the new arrival. He wants to find out what's so special 'bout you. And he don't like to be kept waiting."

Edgar hesitated a few seconds longer. He wanted to stand his ground, to defy the homicidal piece of filth, but he knew it was pointless. He was locked in with murderers and rapists. He had no doubt he was surrounded, even if Cornwall and Ozzie were the only inmates he'd seen thus far. There was nothing he could do but try to survive.

The words of Stake President Venkara, the leader of the church back on Ganymede, ran through Edgar's mind. Stay alive, Brother Cordell. Stay true. Keep your covenants as best you can. The Lord has a mission for you yet, even in the very pit of Hades. He's not finished with you, Edgar. Stay alive.

With crushing resignation, like the weight of a boulder on his shoulders under Earth-Normal gravity, Edgar sighed and

16

forced his fists to unclench. He turned and began to walk down the corridor.

Cornwall followed right behind him. "The layout's exactly the same as the old hub on Ganymede," said Goner. "Just head for the chow hall. You know the way."

Callisto had been the site of the original human settlement in the Jovian system. It had the best qualifications—liquid water, even if it was below the surface, low radiation, mineral-rich soil for growing crops. It didn't have enough direct sunlight, of course, but out past Martian orbit, fusion-powered artificial light was essential for agriculture anyway. Callisto was the perfect location for a human colony near Jupiter—that was, until it had to be suddenly abandoned, until the colonists, or rather the survivors, had to relocate to the nearest alternative—Ganymede.

"Yeah," Edgar said, "I know the way."

They walked down corridors reeking of urine, feces, and rotting garbage. They passed through open hatches leading from one prefabricated section or corridor to the next. Metal plates posted at intersections and above each hatch clearly labeled each passageway, reassuring Edgar that he was indeed moving in the right direction.

Curiously, in spite of the stench, the passageways were devoid of debris and detritus. With the pervasive odor, Edgar had expected to see filth everywhere, garbage strewn along the corridors, around every bend. He'd expected to see excrement in every corner. The place was hardly spotless, but there was no obvious source for the sickening smell. *Have all the reclaimers failed?* wondered Edgar. *How does anyone live like this?*

Along with the lack of refuse, there was something else missing—people, or at least men. Edgar and Goner encountered no one as they moved. *There are more than twelve hundred inmates in Hades,* Edgar thought. *Plus one more, as of today.* It wasn't as if Edgar wanted to meet any of the damned souls in this man-made hell, but he found their apparent absence disturbing.

"Where is everybody?" he asked. He immediately regretted asking anything of Goner, partly because he despised the man who'd murdered Ol' Benny and partly because he *feared* his former cargomaster—feared what he might do if crossed.

Edgar despised himself for even acknowledging his fear.

17

"They're in the chow hall," Goner said from behind him. "They're all assembled to meet *you*."

"Me?" Dread gripped Edgar, dread cold as the void.

"It's not every day we get a new denizen of hell. Everyone's anxious to meet the man who's now on the bottom of the dung heap."

"Shouldn't that be you?" said Edgar. "You can't have gotten here that much earlier than me."

Goner laughed. "I came on the last transport run. 'Bout three weeks ago. And let's us just say that I proved my worth to Lord Lucifer at my welcoming ceremony . . . showed him how valuable I can be. He made me one of his Angels on the spot."

Edgar noticed a dark metal plate at the intersection before them. The plate was larger than the others.

"You gots to prove your worth right off," Cornwall continued, "else you do end up at the bottom. And trust me, mate, a good Christian boy like you don't want . . ."

Edgar wasn't listening anymore as he stopped to look at the plate. The plate was actually a plaque. A memorial, etched with names. The names of the original Callisto pioneers. There were more than three hundred people listed there. Men, women, and children, grouped by families.

His eyes focused on just four names. Four names. One family.

Roger Cordell
Samantha Cordell
Abigail Cordell
Terence Cordell

His grandfather, his grandmother, his aunt, and his dad.

His grandfather had helped build this place.

His grandmother and his young aunt had died here, along with almost every other female among the original colonists. Only the men and less than a fifth of the women survived.

And me, thought Edgar. I'm not female, but I'm going to die here too.

Cornwall prodded him from behind. "Step lively there, Cap'n. Lord Lucifer's expecting you."

Chapter 5

Nero is an angler in the lake of darkness.
King Lear, Act III, Scene VI

"Kneel, worm!" The voice was intimidating—deep and booming. It reverberated around the immense metal shell of the mess hall. The source of the voice, a massive, powerfully built man, was equally impressive. The man who called himself Lord Lucifer wore the same prison coverall that everyone, including Edgar, wore, but while every other jumpsuit was gray, Lucifer's was painted or dyed a deep crimson. Shiny bits of metal were attached in various places to the red fabric. They looked like ornaments or decorations. Edgar could see no pattern to the adornments, but the image reminded him of a photo he'd seen once of a Christmas tree back on Earth, only this was a Christmas tree the color of fresh blood. On the top of this perverse totem pole of a man, over his close-cropped hair, was a circlet of woven copper wire—a crown.

The engineer in Edgar wondered briefly what vital component had been stripped to satisfy this man's pride and vanity. *Milton—To rule in hell.*

"Kneel!" roared the man in crimson.

Lucifer? thought Edgar. Well, what else would you call the king of Hell? He's not the actual devil—just a thug, a gang leader.

It wasn't that Edgar felt no fear—in point of fact, he was terrified. It was all he could do to keep himself from dropping to his knees on the spot—not out of any desire to obey or placate Lucifer, but because his knees threatened to give way of their own volition. A dozen men, armed with various bludgeoning weapons—large metal tools, for the most part—stood in a wide circle around Lucifer's raised, thronelike chair at the far end of the room. These brutes were obviously the bodyguards, enforcers of Lucifer's will. His Angels, Goner had called them.

None of the other inmates appeared to be armed. Well over a thousand of them were assembled in the room. All of them knelt on the deck—all of them except for Goner and the bodyguards. Somehow, in the short time Goner had been incarcerated in Hades, the man had gotten himself promoted to the high position of one of Lucifer's brutish enforcers.

Many of the prisoners coughed, like a chorus of frogs. A number of them wiped at noses, red and dripping. The foul air carried more than stench, it seemed.

Two of the enforcers stepped toward Edgar menacingly, brandishing their weapons, a pry bar and pipe.

"Kneel, you bloody idiot," Goner growled from behind Edgar. "Kneel or you'll be made to kneel."

"Stay alive," President Venkara had said. But he'd also said, "Stay true."

"No," Edgar said in a loud and steady voice that belied the struggle to keep his body from trembling. A collective gasp rose from the assembly of murderers and rapists. "I kneel to my God, but I will kneel to no man, especially not to one who calls himself 'Lucifer.'"

In unison, two "Angels" slapped their weapons rhythmically against their palms.

I'm a dead man, thought Edgar.

From behind him, Goner swore the foulest of oaths under his breath, then raised his voice and cried, "My lord! If you please, let's us just hold on a minute now. We need this fool! He can fix the reclaimers!" To Edgar he growled, "Kneel, damn you!"

As the other enforcers continued to advance, Goner said with desperation, "The air will become toxic, poisonous! It already reeks in here, despite all your clean-up details. The water's already foul and getting worse. Soon it'll be no better than drinking our own piss!"

Undeterred, both enforcers raised their weapons.

"We'll all sicken and die, my lord!" shouted Goner, a note of urgent pleading in his voice. "We're all dead men!"

"Stay your hands, boys," Lucifer said, holding up his own hand.

Time's Plague

The two brutes stopped no more than a yard from Edgar and lowered their makeshift cudgels. They continued to glare murderously at Edgar. Edgar had no doubt that they'd bash in his skull at the slightest provocation.

"Is this true, worm?" Lucifer boomed. "Can you repair my reclaimers?"

Goner let out an audible sigh of relief. "The problem ain't mechanical, my lord. We've got boys as could fix that. The problem's in the wretched computer. The software's all mucked up. Cordell here, is a great hand with computers. He was raised on the Mars-Jupiter run on his daddy's ship. Afore he was captain, he was ship's engineer. I seen him practically teach that bloody ship of his to dance!"

Lucifer glowered at Cornwall. "I was not addressing you, Angel." Turning his gaze back to Edgar, he said, "Do not make me repeat myself, worm." The volume of his voice was lower, but it was brimming with menace. His eyes, as they bored into Edgar's, burned with a profound malice, a hatred of all men.

Edgar forced himself to meet that gaze, steeled himself to not back down. *No fear,* he thought. *Show no fear, or you won't last a day. Of course, you might not anyway*. "I'd have to take a look, but Goner's got it right. I've never met an app I couldn't fix."

The man in crimson glared at Edgar, but said nothing. Lucifer's eyes narrowed to slits, and his jaw tensed.

Edgar almost convinced himself that he could hear the man's teeth grinding. He locked his knees to keep them from shaking. *If you lock your knees, you'll pass out,* he thought, arguing with himself. *Won't have time to pass out. This can't go on much longer. This is a man who does not like to be challenged.*

"So," Edgar said, desperately trying to keep his voice calm, "do you want those reclaimers fixed or not?"

Lucifer smiled. It was a horrible, malicious, wolfish grin, baring yellowed teeth. "Oh, yes. I do indeed."

If this self-styled devil were the wolf, Edgar would be a cornered rabbit. Edgar swallowed, though his mouth was utterly devoid of moisture, as dry as a Martian sea.

Cornered he might be, and hopelessly outnumbered, but there were many skills a good freighter captain must possess if he wanted to be successful, not the least of which was the ability to negotiate a deal.

"So," Edgar began, trying to imbue his voice with a confidence he did not feel, "I have something you want, something you desperately need."

Lucifer's grin faltered. "And what would that be, worm?"

Is the man being deliberately obtuse? Edgar thought. How could he not know what I'm talking about? "The ability to fix the reclaimers," he said.

Slowly, Lucifer's smile widened again. "You mean the ability to fix *my* reclaimers."

"*Your* reclaimers, *our* reclaimers, *the* reclaimers," Edgar said, letting just a tiny bit of exasperation creep into his tone. "What difference does it make? From the sound of things and the smell, you're in trouble here. We're all in trouble. If I don't fix the reclaimer units, we're all dead men."

Lucifer's lips curled in a snarl. "*My* reclaimers. This is *my* domain, *my* kingdom. All that I see is *mine*. Every damned soul in Hades is mine." He licked his lips. "*You* are mine. You will learn that"—he paused and raised one corner of his mouth in a twisted smile—"or you will sleep."

Sleep? Edgar thought. *What in the System is he talking about?* Never mind that, Cordell, you're losing control of this negotiation. "*Your* reclaimers need fixing," he said quickly. "Do you want me to fix them or not?"

"Yes." The red-clad man nodded in satisfaction. "I do."

"Well," Edgar said, breathing an inward sigh of relief, "I'm the man who can do it. But first, I want something from you."

"You want something from me, worm? I will allow you to remain alive and awake. I will allow you to serve me. That is what you will have at my hand. When I call you, you will come. When I tell you to kneel, you will kneel before me. If I tell you to lick the dust from my feet, you will do it gladly, praising the name of Lucifer."

This guy's nuts, Edgar thought. How in the System do you negotiate with someone who's insane?

Edgar held up a placating hand. "Okay. I can see we got off to a bad start here. Let's try again. I can fix your reclaimers. You need me. Otherwise you won't survive. None of us will."

"I said, *kneel*, worm." Lucifer's voice was quiet, hard as iron. His face darkened with menace, and his eyes burned with madness, like a prophecy of mayhem. "You will learn who and what you are. You will learn who rules in Hell. You will bow before Lucifer."

He gestured in Edgar's direction with a lazy flick of his forefinger. Two of Lucifer's Angels stepped toward Edgar, both of them grinning madly from ear to ear. One of them was drooling with anticipation.

Edgar tried to back away. "Let's just take a second to think about this." Two more enforcers moved toward him. Strong hands gripped both his arms. Panic seized his heart like a claw.

He struggled to free himself, but there were too many of them, and they were too strong. Edgar was forced to his knees. Then his face was slammed against the deck.

"Idiot," he heard Goner say. "You shoulda knelt."

As Edgar's jumpsuit was ripped from his body, the assembled prisoners began to cheer.

Chapter 6

Prithee, nuncle, tell me whether a madman be a gentleman or a yeoman?
King Lear, Act III, Scene VI

With trembling hands, Edgar gathered the shredded and bloodied remains of what had once been his clothing. He curled his bruised and torn body up into a protective ball as if he could block it all out, as if he could block out the howls and jeers from the pack of once-human brutes that had gathered around him like jackals, laughing and salivating. Vultures waiting for the kill.

Raped! I've been raped! Like an obscene liturgy of pain and humiliation, the words sounded again and again in his mind. *I've been raped!*

"That showed him, Lucifer! That showed him good!" crowed someone behind him.

"Yeah! He knows who's boss now!"

"Let the Angels have him!"

"Yeah! Let all the Angels have him!"

"Make him their buddy!"

More cheering erupted at this vile suggestion.

Edgar curled up tighter. *No! No! No!* Edgar screamed in his mind. His breathing came in ragged, labored gasps. He couldn't seem to draw in enough of the reeking air. *No! No more! Please!* A part of him hoped he wasn't pleading out loud.

A larger part of him didn't care.

Please! Please! No more!

The inhuman cries of the beasts around him abruptly died down.

"No!" It was Lucifer's voice, booming, confident, in command. The alpha-male in this pack of wolves and hyenas.

He raped me!

"Enough, boys!" the rapist continued when all the other voices were silenced. "He has learned his place. He will do as he is told. He will serve Lucifer all the days of his miserable life. He will serve *me*."

There was a pause.

Edgar could hear the breathing and coughing of the pack around him. He struggled to calm his own tortured, frantic respiration.

"You will serve me," Lucifer said in a softer tone. "Won't you, worm?"

Edgar wanted to shout at this mortal devil, this self-styled Lucifer, but all he could do was cringe in fear and self-loathing. *If only I could've fought back! If only I'd been stronger! Maybe I wouldn't have been . . . Maybe he wouldn't have been able . . .* But he knew that was a lie. He knew there was no possibility of resistance, of escape. There had been a dozen of them, a dozen men to hold him down while Lucifer asserted his dominance. *I'm in hell and I've been raped by the lord of hell. And there is no going back. I'm going to be here for the rest of my life.*

"Answer me, worm." Menace dripped like venom from Lucifer's lips. "Or do you need my Angels to offer you more proof of your lowly state in this, my kingdom?"

Somewhere in Edgar's gut, a spark of anger began to kindle. *You* raped *me!* It began to grow, stoked into a blaze of rage.

Edgar forced himself to uncurl from his fetal state. Gathering his rags about him, he tied the remnants about his waist. Then he got to his knees. He was trembling, but he wasn't certain if the tremors were the result of rage or fear. As he stood erect, he balled his torn and bleeding hands into fists.

"I will . . ." His voice shook. He swallowed hard and clenched his teeth to gain some semblance of control. "I will not bow to you." He stared his rapist in the eye.

Lucifer's jaw dropped in shock.

What? Nobody's ever defied him before?

Lucifer's face hardened into a scowl. "Then you will . . ."

Edgar growled in rage. "If you or any of your boys touches me again, I promise you this . . ." He took a couple of

C. David Belt

deep breaths. *Am I really prepared to do this? Fixing those reclaimers is the only card I have to play.* "I promise you that you will all die, because I will not—Do you hear me?—I will not fix your reclaimers if you touch me again."

Lucifer's lip curled up into a mocking sneer. "Then you would die as well, worm."

Swallowing his terror and rage and loathing, Edgar kept his eyes riveted to Lucifer's. Through teeth clenched so hard they felt as if they might shatter, he snarled, "Yeah. Funny thing, that. You picked the wrong *worm* to mess with. You see, I'm the only man on this blasted rock who can save your filthy, loathsome hide. And me?" He shook his head. "I don't care if I live or die."

Lucifer's mocking expression faltered.

Edgar could see doubt in the man's eyes. He pressed his attack. "That's right, oh, great lord of the sewer. I certainly don't want to live in this hell. I don't deserve to live in this hell, and I'd rather die than live here and be raped and tortured and pushed around by you and your harem of buddies."

At the insult, a couple of the Angels snarled like the beasts they were.

Edgar didn't spare a glance for the animals who'd held him down while their leader violated him. *Keep Lucifer off guard—let* him *rein his lackeys in.* "So I swear, if you or anybody touches me again, I'll let you all die, choking on toxic fumes and gagging on sewage! So go ahead, beat me, break my bones, *rape* me again. I won't lift a finger to help you."

"I'll make him do it, my lord!" One of the enforcers raised his club. "We'll take turns with him—we'll work him over 'til he—"

Edgar spared the man a glance and surprised himself by laughing. The enforcer froze, startled by Edgar's lunatic mirth.

Edgar shook his head and snapped his gaze back to Lucifer. "Programming a computer isn't like running a cargo lifter or bashing in a skull. It takes brains and a clear head. And if I'm pissed-off, or I'm in pain, or I'm worried about when and where and what's going to happen, or who's going to rape me next, I won't be able to fix a thing. Not a thing." Edgar laughed again. He sounded insane, even to his own ears. *Good. That'll prove to them I've got nothing left to lose.* "You can't force me to think clearly."

Some of the crowd murmured. Out of the corner of his eye, Edgar could see a few of the enforcers fidgeting, fingering their weapons uncertainly. But Edgar kept his eyes locked on Lucifer. *It's no different than negotiating with a corrupt portmaster.*

But he raped me!

Focus, man. Focus and stand your ground.

"Now," Edgar said, "if you and your buddies leave me alone, if you don't mess with me anymore, if *none* of you mess with me, I'll fix the blasted computer and I'll keep it humming along smooth as glass. And you can go on being lord of Hell."

King of the dunghill.

Lucifer's eyes narrowed. Loathing and rage simmered there. Loathing, rage, and cunning.

If he backs down, Edgar thought, *he'll look weak. He can't back down, but he needs me. He's looking for a way out. So give him one.* "Just think of me as . . . as a contractor. I'm here to do a job for you. I have something you need, and all I'm asking in return is to be left alone *so I can do it for you.*"

Lucifer hesitated, and then his lips curled up in an evil grin filled with teeth.

That malevolent smile caused Edgar to lock his knees to keep them from shaking. He's a cat playing with a mouse. He'll let the mouse go for now, let it think it's going to escape. Then, at the right moment, when the mouse thinks it's free, the cat will pounce.

"Very well, contractor," Lucifer said. "We have a contract." Lucifer turned and strutted back to his throne, as if he'd somehow gotten the better part of the bargain.

Tremors of relief shook Edgar's body. He fought to control them.

He wasn't entirely successful.

Goner regarded Edgar, and their eyes locked for a moment, even as Lucifer continued his way back to his place of power. Then Goner inclined his head in Edgar's direction. A nod. Edgar knew the man had seen his old captain wrangle a deal before. Goner knew exactly what had just happened.

Edgar turned his gaze back to the man in red.

Lucifer reached his throne and paused in front of the chair as if deep in thought. Abruptly, he turned about and sat, assuming a regal pose. Two of his Angels rushed to take up positions on either side of the throne. One of them had a coughing fit.

Lucifer raised one hand in an imperial gesture and said in his deep booming voice, "Hear me, denizens of Hell! This man *amuses* me. And I now declare him to be"—he paused for dramatic effect—"my royal Fool. Just as the great kings of old Earth had their jesters and fools, this man is now mine. And like all royal fools, he is free to speak his mind, for, as you have seen, he is clearly mad. No one may touch him or harm him in any way. He is under my protection. If any touch him, he shall suffer the wrath of Lucifer. His name, before he entered my realm, was Edgar Cordell. But this is no name for a Fool. His name henceforth shall be"—Lucifer paused again—"Bedlam. Tom Bedlam." The fiend chuckled to himself as if he thought the name amusing. "And though he is mad, he is also brilliant." He shot Goner a hard look. "Or so I am told."

Goner nodded quickly.

Lucifer raised both hands in the air and cried, "And he will repair my reclaimers!"

Cheers erupted from the assembled inmates. Some of the men wept openly, wiping at their running noses. Even some of the enforcers joined in the display of jubilation and relief.

Lucifer smiled, and Edgar could not decide if that grin was benevolent or malevolent. Perhaps it was both.

Then Lucifer's eyes locked with Edgar's, and Edgar saw one thing with awful, terrifying clarity—the cat was biding his time, and he had no intention of letting his mouse escape.

Chapter 7

At this time
We sweat and bleed: the friend hath lost his friend.
King Lear, Act V, Scene III

"You're a dead man," hissed Goner. "You know that, don't you? Dead . . . or sleeping." He pushed against Edgar's bare and lacerated back. "Come on. Let's get you . . . ."

Edgar recoiled at Cornwall's touch. "Don't touch me!" His voice came out at such a high pitch it was very nearly a shriek. *Get control of yourself, Cordell! No weakness. No fear.*

But I was raped!

Belay that, mister! Wait 'til you're alone—if that's even possible in this place—and then you can fall apart, then you can let the full horror of what . . . of how . . . violated . . .

No fear!

"Don't. Touch. Me," Edgar said with a feral snarl. Rage and revulsion battled within him.

Goner shook his head, "You're a right bloody princess, you are. You ask me, you had it coming, shipmate."

"Just show me to the reclaimer console," snapped Edgar. Keep moving. *Keep busy. Don't think about it.* "Or better yet, find someone else to show me."

Goner snorted. "What you mad at me for? It's not like I held you down. That was the other lads as did that."

You murdered Ol' Benny! "Let's just say I don't care much for your company."

Goner laughed again. "Aye, aye. You got it, mate." With that, Cornwall looked about, as if he were searching for someone.

"Petitioners may approach . . .the throne!" boomed the voice of Lord Lucifer. Edgar jumped at the sound of his attacker's ceremonious cry. A wave of self-loathing crashed over Edgar as he inwardly cursed himself for allowing such an obvious manifestation of his fear.

All around him, men began to surge forward, jostling, kicking, punching each other in their haste to approach their chief, presumably to beg for some boon, lodge some complaint against a fellow prisoner, or perhaps ask for judgment in some matter. The crowd paid Edgar no more heed, but when his eyes locked with Lucifer's, Edgar knew with a chilling certainty that the rapist had seen his reaction, and Lucifer was pleased.

Edgar tore his gaze away from the monster, his face reddening with shame and rage.

As men pressed forward, the bodyguards did nothing to stop the violence—they, by threat of arms, merely kept the horde from approaching Lucifer. Order containing the chaos.

And the man in red looked on with lordly amusement.

"No way, Goner!" roared a voice behind Edgar. "You can't have him! He's *my* buddy! You got your own!"

Edgar spun around to behold a massive bear of a man, the ursine image made complete by a pair of beady black eyes, a bulbous nose like a snout protruding over a prodigious, bushy, brown beard, topped off with a wild mane of hair. He towered almost a meter over Cornwall. His massive height was suggestive of a life spent in the low gravity of the outer colonies. His musculature, however, bespoke a deliberate effort to build muscles beyond what was needed on a low-grav world. He was a terrifying hulk of a man.

Goner, however, stood unflinching before him, holding that huge wrench in one hand. In his other hand, Goner gripped the arm of a smaller, older man.

In contrast to the hairy giant, the older man was short, thin, with huge wide eyes, a couple of day's growth of gray beard, and only a few stray wisps of white hair on his age-spotted pate. His jumpsuit hung loosely about him, suggesting a skeletal, wizened frame, stooped with age.

And he looked terrified.

Goner laughed and shook his head at the man-mountain. "Not no more he ain't, Griz. Go get yourself another buddy."

Griz growled. It was a terrible, inhuman, bestial sound. "I don't want another. I want my Toady. You can't have . . ."

Goner's strike was so sudden and so quick, Edgar almost missed seeing it. In a flash, Goner swung the wrench up and connected with the bearish man's groin.

The huge man froze, his eyes wide in shock. While chaos raged about them, Edgar, Goner, and the old man waited for the giant to react. A second passed. Two. Then a high whine issued from Griz's lips. He crumpled to the deck, his massive hands going to his crotch.

"'sides, Griz," Goner said with a wicked, face-splitting grin full of yellow teeth. "I ain't keeping your Toady. He's going to Cap'n Cordell here. You know—our new Fool, Tom Bedlam."

Griz groaned in agony. Then through gritted teeth, he snarled, "You're a dead man, Bedlam! You hear me? A dead man!"

"Griz!" the old man wailed. "Oh, Grizzy, I'm sorry!"

Goner yanked the wizened prisoner's bony arm. "Enough of that, Toady."

"Kill you," Griz snarled.

"And that," Goner said, punctuating the word with a vicious kick to Griz's head, "will be enough of that, mate. You heard Lord Lucifer's edict—you can't touch him."

Griz shook his head, then locked eyes with Edgar. The naked malevolence of the man's hatred struck Edgar with the force of a hammer blow. *Griz is not going to be restrained by any command—the next time we meet, I'm dead.*

An evil grin spread across Griz's bearded face.

And he knows it too. Edgar suppressed a tremor of mortal fear.

Edgar was nearly knocked off his feet when Toady's bony frame collided with his. Edgar had to catch the small man to keep Toady from falling. After regaining his footing in the light, lunar gravity and steadying Toady on his spindly legs, Edgar was relieved that he was no longer facing Griz's murderous stare.

"On your way, gents," Goner said. "Toady, show our precious engineer to Reclaimer Control."

"Sh-sh-sure, Goner," the old man said. He gripped Edgar's arm with a clawlike hand. "This way, Tom."

Edgar allowed the ancient prisoner to lead him. They left the mass of petitioners behind and stepped over the bottom lip of the hatch leading out of Lucifer's throne room.

Just a mess hall, Edgar thought to himself in a daze. And he's just a gang leader. Just a thug.

A rapist.

C. David Belt

After they were both clear of the mess hall, Toady released his hold on Edgar's arm. The old man turned and headed down a corridor, taking the lead. "This way, Tom," he said glancing hopefully in Edgar's direction and gesturing for Edgar to follow.

A sudden and painful memory struck Edgar, swift and hard as a blow from Goner's wrench.

That little cocker spaniel bouncing down the corridor on Ganymede, pausing briefly to look back to be sure Edgar was following. That silly, affectionate puppy they'd brought with them when Llyrica and Edgar had emigrated from Mars. That incredible indulgence in weight allowance, even if he did own the ship. But, as always, he'd done what it took to make Llyrica happy.

Anything to make Llyrica happy.

Edgar shuffled after the old man. "Edgar," he said. "The name's Edgar."

Toady kept on shuffling forward, but he smiled back at Edgar. It was a gap-toothed smile, sad, wise, and weary—at once repulsive and oddly disarming—reminding Edgar of his grandfather's smile.

Grandpa Cordell, who'd been one of the Jovian pioneers, who'd helped build this place. Grandpa Cordell, who'd been evacuated from Callisto along with his only surviving child, Edgar's future father, to the makeshift colony on Ganymede, but not before watching helplessly as his beloved wife and daughter gasped out their last breaths on this blasted moon.

Toady shook his head. "Not no more, you ain't. You're Tom Bedlam 'til Lord Lucifer says different. Everybody gets a name here. A prison name. Yours is Tom Bedlam. Ain't nobody else as can change that. Tom Bedlam. Or Fool, maybe. But I won't ever call you that."

"Seriously," said Edgar with an anger he made no attempt to conceal. "Call me Edgar." He had no intention of answering to any name given to him by the man who'd raped him.

"I'll call you whatever pleases you." The old man turned his head and gave Edgar a knowing smile that turned Edgar's stomach. "But only when we're alone." Toady turned his attention back to the corridor.

"Belay there!"

The old man kept on going, unheeding.

Must not be a spacer, Edgar thought. "Stop!"

Toady stopped, turned, and looked at him, puzzled. "What?"

"Let's get one thing straight right now," Edgar snarled. "You are not . . . I don't want . . . never, ever want . . ." He couldn't seem to get the words out. *Raped!* He clenched his teeth. "You. Are not. My buddy!"

The old man cringed. He turned his head away and raised both bony hands to his face as if to cover it in shame. "You . . . you don't . . . want me?"

"No!" Edgar's rage and disgust made him tremble. "Not now. Not ever!"

In an instant, Toady was on his knees. He extended his hands toward Edgar, supplicating, pleading. "I'm good! I'm real good. Sure, I been passed around a bit, but I been with Griz for a long time now. He was nice to me. Protected me."

"So go back to him." Edgar wanted to vomit. Between the mewling creature beginning to waddle on his knees toward Edgar, the old man's pathetic and disgusting offer of sexual favors, the putrescence of the air, and the horror and trauma of Lucifer's assault, Edgar was losing any semblance of control. "I don't want you." He couldn't even bring himself to move as Toady approached.

Toady wrapped his thin arms around Edgar's knees and clung to him. The old man shook so violently that Edgar feared he might topple them both. "I can't go back!" Toady wailed. "If I do, Goner'll put me to sleep. Maybe he'll make Griz sleep too. I'm an old man. Just a useless, old buddy. I can't make it no more on my own!"

He looked up at Edgar, tears running down the old man's face. "Who'll protect me? I can't be passed around no more. Please! I'm good. I'll be good to you." His eyes locked with Edgar's. "Please."

It was a whisper.

Edgar raised both hands, holding them away from the wretch grasping at his knees. He didn't want to touch Toady, but Edgar wanted to strike at him, to pummel him, to break every bone in his wizened face. He wanted to channel all the rage and fear and disgust against someone, and the old man was here and clinging to him.

Edgar's hands clenched into fists. He forced them to unclench, but then the fists formed again, seemingly of their own accord. Yes, Edgar wanted to crush the pathetic, revolting creature.

Sick and pathetic.

"Just . . ." Edgar choked back the bile in his throat. "Just show me to Reclaimer Control." Edgar's fists trembled. "And let go of me. Now."

The old man hesitated a second, still staring up into Edgar's eyes, seemingly oblivious to the threat of Edgar's fists. Then he released his desperate, skeletal grip on Edgar's knees. He collapsed to the deck and curled up on himself.

Edgar stepped back as Toady began to sob, huge wracking cries that shook the old man's entire frame. Edgar could only stare at him and fight another wave of nausea.

The sick feeling subsided, and Edgar continued to stare at the pathetic thing quaking on the floor. The rage whooshed out of him, like a breath held far too long, the air grown toxic in his lungs with excess CO_2. In its place—like fresh oxygen—came pity for the wretched old man, that pathetic, frail sack of bones. Toady's only purpose in life—all that remained to him, it seemed—was to prostitute himself to whoever might provide him protection and perhaps a little affection. Griz had been nice to him, the old man had said. And now Toady was all alone in this den of murderers and rapists, all alone with no one to shield him from the others.

But Toady's one of them. He deserves to be here.

But does he? Edgar thought, arguing with himself. How do I know that? How do I know he isn't . . . or wasn't innocent? What was it the doctor said when I woke up in Hades? You are here—therefore, you are guilty. Maybe Toady doesn't deserve to be here. I wasn't at his trial. I don't know what evidence got him sentenced here. Who am I to judge?

"Hey," he said aloud.

The old man continued to sob.

"Look," Edgar continued awkwardly, "I meant what I said before, at least the part about not needing a buddy. I don't. And I never will."

Toady's sobbing quieted. In a raspy voice, he said, "But you'll get lonely."

Edgar laughed once, bitterly. "Not that lonely," he muttered.

The old man continued to weep, shaking his head. "Old. Useless. Just an old, useless buddy."

Edgar took a step toward Toady and squatted down beside him. He put a hand on the old man's arm.

Toady's trembling lessened.

"Look," Edgar said, "I don't need a buddy. But I could use a friend."

Chapter 8

His grief grew puissant and the strings of life
Began to crack.

King Lear, Act V, Scene III

"It'll be done when it's done." Toady's tone was emphatic, but calm, like the voice of a press secretary efficiently dealing with a gaggle of unruly reporters. "Our Tom Bedlam's hard at work and—"

The sound of pounding against a bulkhead stopped the old man short. He let go of the intercom button.

"We heard the bloody reclaimers start up ten bloody times already!" Goner's growl over the intercom was brimming with rage—rage born of frustration and barely contained fear. The Angel was on the other side of the airlock which shielded the rest of the colony from Reclaimer Control, a safeguard put in place by the colony's designers to contain toxic leaks from the recycling units. For now, the airlock shielded Edgar and Toady from the lethal monsters on the other side.

"Ten bloody times!" Goner's growl became a full-throated roar. The roar was interrupted by a fit of coughing. "They start up. Then they shut down! Everyone can bloody well hear it. Up and down! Ten times! What the hell you doin' in there, Cordell? Why can't you keep the bloody things going? My ass is on the line here! I vouched for you to Lord Lucifer!"

"As I told you, Goner," Toady said, the soul of patience and conviction—a far cry from the cringing, mewling creature Edgar had taken under his wing a few days earlier—"these things take time."

"You've had three days!" Goner roared. "Three damn days! And what would you know about it, Toady, you old, useless buddy?"

"I ain't a buddy no more. I'm a *friend*."

Time's Plague

Rising from the chair in front of the control console, Edgar forced himself to his feet. *Blast, but it's painful to move!* His whole body ached. Fever sweat stung his eyes. He glanced at one of the powered-off computer monitors and saw his face reflected there. It was a mass of bruises, green and brown and purple. The scratches on his cheeks—courtesy of Lucifer's enforcers as they held him down—were festering, oozing with puss. He needed to see the doctor, but Edgar knew with deadly certainty that he couldn't leave Reclaimer Control until he'd succeeded in getting the recycling units up and running. Well, up and running and *staying* that way. On the second day, he'd found a buggy subroutine and fixed it. Then he'd gotten all four of the massive machines to fire up and run for a minute or so, but then another subroutine—the one that monitored the temperature of the reclaimers—had tripped, erroneously indicating an overheat. This had shut all four units down. *And it hasn't been ten times—it's been only nine. But that's hardly the point, now is it?*

"I got this, Ted," Edgar said, motioning Toady away from the intercom and the airlock. The old man flinched at the use of his real name, but stepped aside with a nod. Edgar had refused to use any other name.

Edgar checked the airlock status to be sure they were still safe. He was forced to wait while Georgie Cornwall peppered the air with a string of oaths and deprecations such as only the former cargomaster could make. When Cornwall paused, Edgar punched the intercom button with a swollen finger. "Listen, we're making progress in here. I've got a false overtemp indication. That's what keeps shutting the reclaimers down. I'm getting closer. I'll figure it out." *I hope I will.*

"You better," Goner retorted, "or I'll hack my way through this airlock!"

Rage exploded in Edgar's gut. He stabbed the intercom button again, ignoring the pain in his finger. For the first time in the days that he and Toady had spent in Reclaimer Control, he wished there was a window in the airlock so he could look Goner right in his loathsome face. "How're you going to hack your way in? With a hatchet? Like the one you used to kill Ol' Benny?"

"Too right," was Goner's reply.

"Listen to me, you sick, murderous waste of oxygen," Edgar snarled, "your life isn't worth . . ." Edgar released the intercom button and took a deep breath. It couldn't have been called a "cleansing breath," not with the air as putrid as it was. Foul and getting fouler by the hour. The crops under the agridome must have still been scrubbing enough CO2 out of the air and replenishing the O2 sufficiently to sustain life, but just *breathing* made Edgar want to gag. And the invisible bacteria infesting the air were going to kill him if he didn't get medical attention soon.

And that isn't going to happen until I figure out why the "overtemps" are occurring. And I'm not going to be able to figure that out if I'm angry. He calmed himself a little. "It'll be done when it's done and not a minute sooner. And it won't get done at all if you don't leave me alone."

Edgar heard another thud. Probably Goner hitting the airlock with his fist. I hope he breaks his hand.

"You gotta be getting low on grub in there," said Goner, cunning replacing the rage of moments before.

"We're fine," Edgar said. "Ted picked up rations for us while you were in the throne room playing buddy to your master. We've got enough to see us through, at least 'til we're done."

"Ted?" Goner sounded genuinely puzzled. "Who the bloody hell is Ted?"

"Ted is my assistant."

There was silence for a moment and then, "Toady? You talking about Toady?"

"His name is Ted." Behind Edgar, Toady waved frantically, motioning for Edgar to stop. Edgar ignored the old man's silent pleas. "And he's under my protection. And I'm under your master's. You touch him or belittle him in any way, and I'll stop what I'm doing, and you can all choke to death on the byproducts of your own waste. Got that?" Edgar glanced at one of the live monitor screens. "The readings I've got in here indicate the air is approaching critical toxicity. The oxygen levels are nominal, but the methane levels are rising fast. I'll bet there's no more than a few days left before you'll be choking out your last breaths, suffocating in your own filth."

Edgar released the intercom button and waited. Impossibly long seconds ticked away in silence broken only by the soft sounds of Edgar's and Toady's breathing. Shielded though he was from the murderous Angel, Edgar imagined Goner's rage and terror building toward an explosion of thermonuclear proportions. However, when the click of the intercom came, Goner's voice was cold as the vacuum between worlds. "Then, if I was you, Tom Bedlam, I'd best be getting on with it, aye? And I know you said you don't care if you live or you die, but if you don't get it done, I swear I will make your last mortal hour feel like an eternity of suffering. I don't normally take my time when I goner someone, but I'll make an exception in your case, shipmate. I knows how to make it last and last. You'll plead with me, you will beg me for oblivion. But I won't give it to you."

The intercom clicked off.

Edgar wanted to reply, wanted to come up with some particularly nasty retort. But in that terrible stillness, his mind was flooded with the memory of finding Ol' Benny . . . or rather, what remained of Edgar's oldest friend.

The swirling vortex of the hypergate expanded like a glittering iris to reveal the familiar space of Jupiter. The immense, roiling face of the gas giant dominated the sky with his gossamer rings and myriad moons.

Edgar had eyes for only one moon, the big gray globe almost dead ahead.

Ganymede.

Home.

The Hera shot out of the cyclone of churning energies, the warping of Euclidian space that opened a portal into and out of hyperspace, that lightless void, where the vast distances of interplanetary space seemed to shrink and navigation was impossible without the beacon of a stationary hypergate. As the portal field collapsed behind them, the ship's velocity seemed to slow to a relative crawl as she returned to normal space and normal physics. Edgar let the sensation of normalcy wash over him like a baptism, renewing him, cleansing him of the otherness.

He knew in his mind—everyone knew—that the stories of hyperspace madness, tales of spacers losing their sense of reality in the void, hearing voices, seeing ghosts, were just that— stories, myths, yarns spun by the old spacers who'd made the Jupiter-Mars run many times, who'd spent more years between Ganymede and Mars than on either of them. Yes, the old spacers distrusted and feared hypertravel. Hyperspace madness was a myth, but Edgar couldn't escape the sensation of never feeling quite right when he was in hyperspace.

Seven months to get from Jupiter to Saturn—or rather, from Ganymede to Titan—three months to assemble the pieces of the new Opis Hypergate in Saturnine orbit, one month to test the gate using unmanned probes, and just thirty-one hours to make the return journey through the gate—the journey home.

Home to Llyrica.

Eleven months and three days since Edgar had been in the arms of his beautiful wife. And after almost a year of being away, Edgar would gladly brave the dangers of hyperspace, real and imaginary, to be with her again.

Edgar thumbed the intercom switch on the throttle. "All hands, prepare for zero-G." Releasing the switch, he called over his shoulder, "Stop rotation."

"Stop rotation, aye," said the engineer. In a moment, his voice was piped shipwide. "All hands, brace for rotation-stop in five, four, three, two, one."

The engineer pressed a control, and the rotomotor, the huge unit that kept the crew section revolving, began to slow, changing its ever-present hum for the first time in more than a day. The cockpit—always zero-G—started to rotate ever so slightly, until the rotomotor compensated for the slowing crew section. Edgar fired maneuvering thrusters and righted the ship.

"Ganymede Control, this is Hera. We are on approach from Juno Gate, terminating grav-rotation, velocity go for approach, on maneuvering thrusters only, and ready for docking autopilot." Edgar released the transmitter switch on the throttle.

The comm system crackled to life, the software filters only partially muting the static generated by the planet. Edgar thought he could hear cheering coming through the speaker. "Roger, Hera, this is Ganymede Control. We have you five-by-five, in-sight, on-vector, on-speed, and on-beacon. Remote autopilot locked and ready."

Edgar noted the instrument panel monitor with its green light flashing, "Remote Autopilot Ready."

"Roger, Control," Edgar said, thumbing the transmitter switch, and touching the button to disengage manual flight and surrender control to the remote autopilot on Ganymede. "Remote

autopilot confirmed and engaged. You have my ship, Ganymede. Be gentle with her."

"Roger, Hera," came the reply—and this time the cheering was unmistakable. "Wilco. Welcome home, Hera. And may I be the first to say, well done! Titan to Ganymede in thirty-one hours! Congratulations!"

"Thanks, Control. See you moon-side in forty."

Edgar released the transmitter switch. *Almost home, Llyrica. Keep the bed warm!*

"And, Hera," Edgar said, "great job! Thank you for bringing us safely home."

"We're not home yet," the ship countered. Hera's voice seemed to come from every direction at once.

"Roger that," replied Edgar. "But we're almost there."

"I dislike surrendering control to the remote autopilot," Hera said. "It's unnecessary."

"I know, sweet Hera. But that's protocol here. We all gotta obey the regs!" Edgar began to hum a jaunty Earth folk tune.

"Really, Edgar?" The ship sounded offended. "Straighten Up and Fly Right?"

Edgar grinned. "Sorry, old girl. Force of habit."

He pressed the quick-release on the safety harness that held him in the pilot's chair. As he pushed out of the seat, floating weightlessly, he looked over at the ship's engineer. "Carlos, you've got the bridge. I'm going to check on Doc and Ol' Benny. Watch the autopilot. Trust . . ."

". . . but don't trust." Echoing the familiar mantra, Carlos Sanchez unstrapped from the engineer's console and launched himself toward the pilot's seat, floating through the cockpit. "Aye-aye, Cap'n." As he grabbed hold of Edgar's chair, he grinned sheepishly. Pointing at the empty copilot's seat—the one that should've been occupied by Ol' Benny—he said, "Tell 'em I'm sorry, will you?"

Edgar shook his head. "It wasn't your stew. We all ate it. Those guys were the only two that got sick. It's not your fault. You know that, right?"

The engineer pulled himself down into the pilot's seat and began strapping himself in. "My head knows it . . . maybe."

He grinned sheepishly. "My heart? Now that's another matter entirely."

Edgar patted Carlos's shoulder gently and launched himself toward the cockpit hatch. "Just take care of my ship. I'll be right back."

"Roger, Cap'n. I've got the boat."

"You've got the boat," Edgar confirmed.

As he approached the hatch, the cockpit shifted around him, a slight course correction directed by the remote autopilot. As a consequence, the hatch was no longer directly ahead of him, forcing him to catch himself against a bulkhead. He pushed off again and shot through the hatch into the central hub with its spokelike shafts leading to the rotating crew section and the access conduit running through the top. Of course, the hub and the crew section weren't rotating at that moment, so there would be no simulated gravity at the ends of the shafts. Edgar used the rungs attached to the walls of the shaft to pull himself to the outer ring of the crew section, toward Ol' Benny's quarters.

Last word from the ship's surgeon was that Doc was feeling a bit better. Besides, Benny was old and the whatever-it-was had hit him harder. Oh Beh-Nee had been crewing and navigating on Edgar's father's ship before Edgar and Edmund inherited the company. Ol' Benny was the best first mate and best nav in the System, and this was probably his last long-haul voyage, but he'd wanted to go along, and Edgar couldn't imagine making the trip without him. Ol' Benny was friend, confidant, and beloved adopted uncle.

As Edgar approached Ol' Benny's quarters, he could sense that something was wrong. After so many years on the Hera, Edgar knew every inch of the ship, every relay, every panel, every seal . . . and every smell. And something didn't smell right. The odors weren't just the scents that accompanied any spacer experiencing stomach distress—those he expected. No, this was something else, something he couldn't place.

He reached out with one hand and grabbed at the edge of the hatch of the first mate's cabin. His momentum carried him around into the open hatch. Edgar got his first glance of the dimly lit compartment, but couldn't process what he was seeing. Debris and bubbles of fluid floated everywhere. One of the bubbles drifted toward him. Edward pulled himself out of the way only to have another bubble strike him on the chest. The liquid soaked his shirt.

Still gripping the hatchway, he wiped at his chest with his free hand. The fluid was thick, almost tacky. He pulled his hand back into the light of the corridor. His hand was covered with bright crimson.

An object drifted past his face, rotating, tumbling as it went. Without thinking, Edgar caught it. It was a rescue hatchet, sticky with the same red fluid.

His mind still unable to grasp the import of what his eyes were showing him, Edgar thought, This should've been secured. It could hurt somebody.

Still focused on the hatchet, Edgar didn't see another object drifting toward him, not until it struck him wetly on the cheek. Startled, he let go of the doorway, brought his hand up, and grabbed at the object. His fingers closed on a wet, stringy mass. He recoiled from the unexpected texture of the thing, but his fingers became tangled. The object rotated, and Edgar realized that he was staring into the dead eyes of Ol' Benny.

He was holding the severed head of his friend.

With a cry of horror, rising from a low bass to a high tenor, Edgar shook his hand violently to dislodge his fingers from the blood-soaked hair. The head ripped loose, leaving gore-matted hair on Edgar's hand.

Benny's head spun back into the cabin, colliding with and bouncing off a bulkhead with a sickening thud. The horrible nature of the floating debris suddenly solidified in Edgar's mind. There was a hand, a section of arm, a foot, a mass of intestines. And everywhere, floating spheres of blood.

Edgar flailed about desperately, vainly trying to push away from the death and mayhem. His foot caught on the edge of the hatchway, and he accidently propelled himself into the midst of the gore. Bubbles of blood burst on him, soaking him, blinding him, getting into his mouth. He spat, trying to clear the horrible, rusty taste. More chunks of dead flesh collided with him as he spun and tumbled and thrashed. And the more he thrashed, the more he batted the charnel away, the more the lumps of Ol' Benny moved about, bouncing wetly off the walls, only to come careening back at him.

"Here now!" That was Georgie Cornwall's voice! "What have we here?"

As Edgar continued to spin, he caught glimpses of the cargomaster's beefy frame floating in the hatchway. Gripping the hatchway in one hand, Georgie reached forward with the other massive hand and snatched the hatchet out of Edgar's grasp. This sent Edgar tumbling in a totally new direction.

The sudden change in rotation made Edgar's head spin, but it shocked him out of his panic. He managed to snag a bulkhead with his hand and arrest his spinning.

"What the hell have you done, Cap'n?" Cornwall's mouth was open wide as if in shock, but that shock didn't reach the cargomaster's eyes. The expression in his eyes was amused. But Georgie often looked as if he was secretly laughing at the universe.

Cornwall's oddly mixed expression only added to Edgar's confusion. Edgar shook his head. "Ol' Benny . . . he's . . ."

"Dead." Cornwall nodded. "Yeah. And you killed him."

Edgar blinked. "Me?" He shook his head, and blood flew away from him in tiny crimson spheres. Benny's blood. "No! Not me."

Cornwall nodded. "Too right, you did. Look at you. You're covered in blood."

And in a moment, Edgar noticed the smear of red just below the cargomaster's hairline. There was more blood in Cornwall's hair. "You?" Edgar made no effort to hide his shock and horror.

Cornwall's countenance was a mocking imitation of Edgar's. "Me? Why, Cap'n Cordell, whatever do you mean?"

Edgar gestured about himself. "You did this?"

Cornwall smiled, showing glistening teeth. "No, you did, sir. You chopped up your own shipmate, Ol' bleeding Benny, to bloody bits, sir."

Edgar pointed at the murderer with one red finger. "You've got blood on your face, in your hair."

Cornwall lifted the hatchet and wiped at his hair with the back of his hand. He examined the blood. "So I do. So I do." His grin widened, and he looked like a wolf inspecting his next meal. "How in the System did that get there, do you suppose?" He *pointed the hatchet at Edgar. "I know—I got covered in the stuff when I subdued you, didn't I? Now're you going to come along quietly so's I don't ruin my shirt?"*

"Subdued me?" Edgar was still reeling from the shock of Benny's murder and Cornwall's betrayal. "You haven't subdued me."

Cornwall frowned. "Pity, really. I like this shirt. My old mum made it for me." He deftly spun the hatchet in his hand and swung the blunt end at Edgar's head.

Edgar tried to fend off the blow with both hands, but only succeeded in sending himself tumbling again.

Cornwall missed with the first blow, but connected with the second.

Edgar saw white, and then all went black.

Edgar shuddered at the memory and trembled with a sudden wave of hatred for Georgie Cornwall. For a few moments, he considered letting Cornwall and the rest of the murderers die. It would be so easy. All he had to do was . . . nothing.

Edgar took a deep breath and reached for the intercom. He didn't push the button, but said quietly, "Leave us alone and let me work so I can fix this stupid thing." Goner wouldn't hear him, but Edgar didn't care. He was too sick and too tired to care what Georgie "Goner" Cornwall heard or didn't hear.

He walked painfully back to his chair, passing Toady on the way, and settled into his seat. He sighed and resumed staring at the lines of code on the screen. "What am I missing?"

Toady shuffled over to a shelf built into the wall. He returned with a plastic cup half filled with water. "You need this," he said, holding the cup in Edgar's direction.

Edgar waved dismissively. "I can't drink any more of that swill."

Toady grinned. "It ain't swill. It's good. I got it direct from the reclaimer spigot the last time you fired it up. Only half a cup before . . . you know, before it shut down again. But it's pure."

Edgar leaned over and sniffed at the cup. Of course, all he could smell was the ever-present stench of waste and decay, but it didn't seem to be coming from the water. And it looked clear. Deliciously pure. Edgar's parched mouth watered feebly at the sight of it, but he pulled back. "No, you have it."

"I ain't sick." The old man shrugged his skeletal shoulders. "I'll get some next time." He held the cup out to Edgar with a hopeful expression.

Edgar nodded and took the cup. He swallowed the water down in three gulps. It tasted good, despite the reek of the air. And when it was gone, Edgar tipped the cup up and shook the last drops onto his tongue.

Toady smiled, exposing the gaps in his grin. "Good. That's good. Now take your calcilock." He handed Edgar a chewable pill. Calcilock was taken daily by colonists and spacers to prevent bone loss in low-grav and zero-G environments. Edgar chewed the pill morosely and choked it down.

"Good. Good," the old man said, making a fair imitation of a mother coaxing an infant to eat. Then his expression sobered to one of concern. And for just a moment, Edgar was reminded of his grandfather. "You should eat something too," Toady said, turning back to the shelf. He reached into a plastic bin and removed two ears of corn. "All we got left is the corn, but . . ."

Edgar grimaced in disgust. "I don't think I could keep it down. And it's bad enough in here without me puking all over the place." He turned his attention pointedly back to the software code on the screen. "You eat it. It's a wonder you're not sick too."

The old man shrugged and deposited one of the ears back in the bin. Then he plopped his old bones down in another chair and began to peel the remaining ear. "I been here thirty-seven years. I've had every bug in this place." He bit into the raw corn, tilting the ear so he could use his remaining teeth. "I ain't been sick a day for better'n twenty years. I ain't seen Doc Stewart for nothing, excepting, you know, *injuries* since before that, and that was years ago." He chewed on his corn with enthusiasm.

"Injuries? You mean beatings?"

The old man shrugged. Around a mouthful of yellow mush, he continued, "I'll bet the reason you're so sick is 'cause you ain't been around the germs in this place long enough." He chewed another mouthful. "No immunity."

That and being clawed by a bunch of animals and raped by their pack leader, Edgar thought. He shuddered. Shake it off, mister! Focus on the code. Don't think about what happened.

Time's Plague

Toady finished off the last nib of corn and tossed the cob and husk into the reclamation bin, in theory to be fed to the recalcitrant reclaimers—assuming they ever started working. He licked corn juice off his fingers and then wiped them on the legs of his jumpsuit. "It's you new guys who gets sick the fastest. Us old-timers, we do better."

Edgar rubbed at his tired eyes with the knuckles that weren't oozing puss. *So tired.*

"You should sleep a bit," Toady said. "You'll think clearer after a couple of hours sleep. You ain't slept a wink for more'n a day." He grinned again. "Except for when you doze off in your chair."

Edgar rubbed an aching shoulder. "No time." He pointed at the screen in frustration. "It's got to be something simple. I've tried disabling or bypassing the overtemp routine. But then the safety protocols treat it as sabotage and reset the whole system, restoring the original routine. It *resets*. I've tried to feed it data. I've checked the temp sensors. They're fine. Besides, they wouldn't *all* fail, not *precisely* at the same time. What am I missing?"

"You'll figure it out." Toady placed both his bony hands on Edgar's shoulders and began to rub.

Edgar jerked away. "Don't!" It came out as a feral growl. "Don't touch me!" He bolted out of his chair and spun around, his fists at the ready.

The old man shrank away, cringing. "I'm sorry. You just looked like you needed . . . comforting. I didn't . . . I wasn't going to . . . I been a buddy for *so long*."

Edgar dropped his fists as shame reddened his cheeks. With trembling steps, he moved over to Toady and put a quaking hand on his shoulder. "I know. I'm sorry. I know you didn't mean it that way."

Toady hid his face in his hands. "I don't know. Maybe I did. I don't know. I don't know no other way to be. I'm . . . trying."

Edgar forced himself to give Toady's shoulder what he hoped would be interpreted as a friendly pat. "I know you are. You're doing fine." When Edgar withdrew his hand, he couldn't suppress a sigh of relief. He didn't like to touch his new friend.

He was all too aware of how the old man reacted to any friendly touch.

Edgar resumed his seat and recommenced his agonizing perusal of the code. The solution continued to elude him, however, and he soon found himself getting drowsy. As much as he needed to stay on task, he wasn't going to find the problem while asleep. He needed a distraction.

He turned his head toward the old man. "Ted?"

Toady grimaced. "Why do you call me that? You know it'll only get us in trouble."

Edgar sighed wearily. "Because it's your name."

"But I got a new name now. A prison name. Ain't nobody called me Ted since I came here. 'Sides, it was Teddy then."

Edgar turned his gaze back to the code, but continued the conversation. "Names have meaning, Ted. They have power. Teddy is a name for a boy. You're a man now. And Toady describes what you were—groveling and scraping, saying and doing whatever it took to survive. You don't want to be that person anymore, do you? You told me your last name is Knight. Now that's a name to be proud of. A knight—protector of the weak. A man responsible for the safety and welfare of others."

The old man laughed. "Me? I ain't protectin' nobody."

"Sure you are. You're watching out for me. We're watching out for each other."

"Yeah. Sure. Me watching out for you!" The old man laughed. "You're watching out for me. I can't watch out for you."

"You're feeding me. If it weren't for you thinking ahead and grabbing some supplies, we'd be stuck in here with no food and no calcilock. And I didn't even think to catch that little bit of pure water from the reclaimer. That was all you."

The old man beamed, grinning from ear to ear.

Edgar smiled back. "So, you've been here thirty-seven years?"

The old man nodded his head, thin wisps of his sparse hair waving in the putrid air. "Almost all my life."

Edgar did some mental calculations. If Toady had spent half his life on Callisto, that would put him in his seventies. That age matched his appearance, but "almost all" would make him considerably younger. *Maybe living in this hellhole ages you.* "How old are you?"

Toady straightened up in his chair and held his head high. "I'll be forty-seven next week. Oldest man in Hades by nearly a decade."

Edgar's jaw dropped in shock. "Forty-seven?"

Toady nodded.

In his head, Edgar converted the age to Martian-Standard years. *Maybe Toady was born on Mars.* That would've put Toady in his late eighties. That sounded about right. "Martian?"

Toady shook his head. "Naw. Earth-Standard."

"They put"—the thought was monstrous—"a ten-year-old in this place?"

Toady shrugged. "I was tried as an adult. 'Sides, I was nearly eleven. I was tall for my age, and since twelve's an adult"—the old man straightened up and lowered his voice, banging an imaginary gavel—"in the eyes of the law . . ."

Edgar knew that the age of adulthood was twelve in most of the colonies, at least as far as criminality and sexual consent went. *But still . . . Ten?* "What . . . did you do?" *What crime could have been so heinous that the law would condemn a child to Hades?*

Toady ran his hand across his pate, mussing the wisps of white hair. "I spaced my daddy."

"You . . . *spaced* him?"

Toady tilted his head, squinted his eyes, and grimaced. "Yep. I hit him on the head with a wrench, drug him to an airlock, and shoved him inside. Then I flushed him outside."

"But . . . you were just ten?"

"Yeah." Toady shrugged his shoulders. "It was on Ganymede. It wasn't hard. Low-grav world, you see. I didn't have no trouble dragging him."

Edgar shook his head and shuddered. "No, no. I mean, why would you kill your dad when you were just ten?"

The old man lowered his head and looked down. "'Cause he said I wasn't special no more. I was too big. Too *old.*" He paused. "He said Joey, you know, my little brother . . . Joey was gonna be his special buddy."

Toady lifted his head enough to look at Edgar from under his ragged eyebrows. "Everybody wants to be special, don't they? Daddy said I wasn't special, but I didn't want him to do to Joey the stuff he did to me. I was used to it, but . . . I didn't want Joey to go through it."

Edgar felt as if he might vomit up the little bit of water in his roiling stomach. "You killed your dad . . . to protect your little brother?"

The old man shrugged. "Partly. Mostly, maybe. But part of me was, you know, jealous. Part of me wanted to be special. And I hated my daddy. Hated him for what he done to me . . . and for throwing me away." He grinned sadly. "Leastaways, that's what that prosecutor said. My lawyer, he said it was self-defense. But it wasn't self-defense. It was just hate. The rest don't matter."

"But you were just a child."

"Not in the eyes of the law, leastaways not after the prosecutor got done with me. Said I was old enough and big enough to know what I done was wrong. And he was right. I knew it and I did it and now I'm here."

"In hell."

"Yeah. Most of the time, it's been hell. But it ain't all been bad. Griz was nice to me. Nice enough, anyways. Told me he loved me. That's more'n my daddy ever did." He grinned. "And now I got me a *friend*. Ain't never had a friend before. Not even when I was little, not on the ship I was raised on, not on Ganymede. Daddy saw to that."

"What happened to Joey? What happened to your mother?"

"My mom died when Joey was born. I don't remember her much. And Joey? How would I know? Once you get inside Hades, you can't talk to nobody on the outside. I never saw Joey after I was thrown in the brig. He didn't come to my trial."

Llyrica never came to my trial, except to testify against me, Edgar thought, bile rising in his stomach again. And even then, she never met my eyes. She kept her eyes on Edmund Reagan or the prosecutor, but never even glanced my way as she told those damning lies.

"I didn't want him there," Toady continued, shrugging his shoulders again. "I didn't want him to have to hear about all the stuff Daddy did to me."

"So you *were* protecting him, after all," Edgar said. "A knight protecting the weak using the only weapon he had."

Time's Plague

Toady looked at Edgar. A grateful smile curled the edges of the old man's mouth. A tear glistened in his eye, but his back was straight. "Yeppers. Maybe I was."

"Of course, you were." Edgar looked at the ancient figure, a withered man who should be barely in his middle years. He'd been a boy who'd never had a chance. He'd been used by his father, the one man in all the System who should've protected him. And he'd been used by evil men all his life since.

"Ain't nobody ever put it like that. Ain't nobody ever really listened to anything I had to say. Not even Griz. Not since the lawyer, and he never listened all that well. Who's gonna listen to a kid? Nobody. Not in a long, long time."

Edgar sighed with a weariness he could feel in his bones. "Time. Slipping away from us." He turned back to the console with its inscrutable code. It refused to yield up its secrets. "What am I missing?" he asked for the thousandth time.

And for the thousandth time, he had no answer.

Edgar bowed his head in prayer yet again and pleaded for inspiration. He tried to listen for any prompting of the Spirit, but his brain was cloudy, his nose dripped, and he struggled to keep his thoughts from wandering.

His prayer drifted into dreaming.

Llyrica's face as she knelt at an altar of the Martian temple of the Church of Jesus Christ of Latter-days. Her blue eyes glinting with reflected light. Her golden hair framed in the mirrors of eternity. She leaned across the altar as if to kiss him, smiling her knowing smile, full of the promise of bliss to come. The perfect smile split into a wide, mocking grin, full of perfect, white teeth. She began to laugh. She raised a hand and pointed a finger at him in derision. Edmund appeared behind her, grinning maliciously.

"Why would any woman choose you," Edmund said, "when she could have"—he pointed at himself with both hands—"me?"

That's not right, Edgar thought. Edmund can't be in the temple. He isn't even a member of the church.

Llyrica continued to point and laugh at Edgar, as she raised one hand and took Edmund's in hers.

"That's not right," Edgar repeated.

"That ain't right." Toady's voice.

"Huh?" Edgar shook himself awake.

The old man was aiming a bony finger at the console. "That ain't right."

"What?" Edgar tried to focus on where Toady was pointing. "What's not right?"

"The date." Toady tapped the screen near the date and time display in the upper right corner. "It ain't right."

"What do you mean?"

Toady tapped his chest. "My birthday's in five days. I know what day today is, and that"—he tapped the screen again—"is off by two days."

Edgar blinked, trying to focus his bleary eyes. He rubbed at them, but accidently smeared puss oozing from scratches in his fingers into one eye. Snarling in disgust and frustration, he wiped furiously at his eye with a relatively clean knuckle. After blinking a few more times, he was at last able to focus on the time display.

To tell the truth, Edgar had lost track of the date. He'd been sedated during the voyage from Ganymede to Callisto. And in all the trauma he'd endured since his arrival—not to mention the fever and sickness, he wouldn't have had a clue what day it was. The month and year looked right, but . . .

"The clock's off," he said, staring stupidly at the display. "The internal clock is out of sync."

Toady nodded vigorously. "Yeppers! I told you so." Then the old man rubbed his stubbled jaw thoughtfully. "Could that be causing it? Causing the shutdowns?"

Edgar cocked his head and stared at the time display. Slowly, he said, "Maybe."

Edgar called up the overtemp subroutine and began scanning the code with new purpose. "Maybe," he repeated. "The temperature of the reclaimer fluctuates during normal operation. The unit is shut down if the temp gets too high." He scrolled down a little farther. "It also shuts down if the temp fluctuates too rapidly." He looked a little farther. "It also shuts down if the temp remains constant for too long. That's to guard against a temperature sensor failing and giving a false reading. It compares the temp at the beginning and ending of a specified period and . . ."

Time's Plague

And there it was, staring him in the face.

Edgar laughed softly. "It's using the *system* clock—the clock for this computer—for the *beginning* of the period and the *network* clock—the network for the whole colony—for the *ending* of the period. That's a stupid mistake to use two clocks. But that means"—he rubbed his swollen hands together and grinned manically—"instead of comparing the temperature at the beginning and end of a period of a few *seconds*, it's comparing it at the beginning and end of what it thinks is two standard *days*! If the temp hasn't changed in *two days*, it thinks the stupid sensor is broken!"

"And it shuts down?" Toady asked.

Edgar nodded. "And it shuts down!" Edgar clapped the old man on the shoulder. "Ted, my friend, you are a genius! You just saved our lives!"

"Me?" The old man looked confused. "What'd I do?"

Edgar tapped furiously on the touchscreen and said,

"You pointed out the one thing I was missing. I didn't know the date. Who cares about the date in a place like this?"

"I do," the old man said. "Ain't nobody remembered it in forever, but my birthday's coming. I always know how long 'til my birthday."

"Exactly."

"So you gonna fix it?"

Edgar shook his head. "Not directly. I can't. I can't change and recompile the code. I'm locked out of that. If I'd written the code myself, I'd have left a backdoor—a way to get back in and fix the code even after the locks are in place. Any engineer worth his salt would do that. But I didn't write it and I don't know the backdoor."

"So what can you do?"

Edgar grinned ferociously, though it made his lips hurt. "This!" He tapped the enter button on the screen with a decisive but painful stab of his finger.

The time display on the screen corrected itself, synching with the central computer on the colonial network.

The old man grinned. "That's right. That's more like it!"

Edgar tapped another button and fired up the reclaimers. "Let's hope this works." *It should work. Lord, please let it work!*

All four huge recycling units roared to life, as they'd done nine times before. Edgar watched the clock with trepidation, watched the seconds tick by, hoping the life-giving reclaimers would keep roaring along.

Toady took a cup and went to the water spigot to collect some clean water. Drop by drop, water plinked into the cup.

And the seconds ticked by.

Thirty seconds.

Sixty seconds.

Two minutes. In the previous attempts, the reclaimers had never made it past two minutes.

Three minutes.

Four.

At five minutes, Edgar exhaled a breath he hadn't realized he was holding.

Toady was giggling, gulping down a full cup of clean water. "So good!" he said and refilled the cup. The water was coming out faster now. The old man brought the water over to Edgar. "This one's yours!"

Edgar grinned and downed the water.

Toady grinned. "The air smells better already! You fixed it!"

"*We* fixed it, Ted." Edgar extended a hand and shook the old man's hand with enthusiasm.

"I didn't do much," Toady said with a modest shake of his head, but a gap-toothed smile split his face from ear to ear.

Edgar became aware of another roar, not loud enough to drown out the reclaimers, but still loud enough to be audible from the other side of the airlock.

Cheering.

The intercom beeped.

Edgar rose from his chair, a little more spring in his step than before. He crossed to the intercom and pressed the button.

"Yes, Goner?" Edgar said.

But the answering voice was not that of Georgie Cornwall.

Edgar was barely able to keep from wetting himself.

"Well done, Fool." The self-styled Lucifer sounded very pleased. "Come out . . . and receive your reward."

Time's Plague

I've served my purpose, Edgar thought. I've saved the colony. And now I'm a dead man.

Chapter 9

*He's mad that trusts in the tameness of a wolf,
a horse's health, a boy's love, or a whore's oath.*
King Lear, Act III, Scene VI

"We're dead," Edgar said in a flat, bone-weary voice.

His hand hovered over the intercom button, trembling as much with the fever as with anger and dread, but Edgar didn't activate the intercom. "Lucifer's got what he wants, so now he'll kill us. Maybe he'll spare you, Ted, but me?" He shook his head slowly. "I'm dead."

Behind him, Toady laughed. It wasn't a pleasant sound. "Ain't nobody *dies* here—leastaways, not if Lord Lucifer has anything to say about it."

"What do you mean?"

"There's sensor things in the walls that monitor life signs. You know—heartbeats, warm bodies, and stuff like that. It's so Doc Stewart can keep a head-count. That's the only thing Doc can report back to Ganymede—the number of living bodies here. That and *nothing* else. No messages home. Nothing. He can request certain medicines, calcilock and the like, some other supplies, like jumpsuits, shoes, seeds for crops, but Doc's programming won't let him transmit nothing else. So, Lord Lucifer don't want nobody to die. More warm bodies means more supplies, more stuff he can use to control . . ."

Through the intercom, Lord Lucifer said, "Tom Bedlam, I know you can hear me. I grow impatient and I command you to come forth."

Edgar punched the intercom button. "I'm not done in here yet."

"My reclaimers are working again," said the head thug. "The water is cleaner, the air smells sweeter. You have done well, my Fool. Come forth and receive your reward." There was no edge to the man's voice, no menace, no apparent deceit. In fact, he sounded magnanimous. But Edgar knew deep in his soul that the predator was ready to claim the prey, the underling who'd had the temerity to defy him. The cat had grown impatient—it had its mouse cornered and it was ready to toy with, torture, and kill its mouse. No matter what Toady had said, there was no way Lucifer would let Edgar live.

Stay alive, Brother Cordell.

And it wasn't just Edgar's life that mattered anymore. He had to protect Toady.

Edgar needed to buy time, time to think, and time to heal. *If I don't get to the doctor soon, I'll die anyway.*

He pushed the button. "Yeah, the reclaimers are running, but for how long? I've fixed the immediate problem, but it'll happen again eventually. I need more time to fix it permanently."

"You've had plenty of time, and you have done what was required of you."

He can't be that stupid, Edgar thought. Can he? Is this all about asserting his alpha-male, top-dog status? So he won't appear weak in front of his minions? Could that be more important than his own hide? Is he willing to just hope the reclaimers keep running and pray—no, this man doesn't pray—just hope that another engineer comes along before it all falls apart again?

Maybe so.

And if so, I've used up my only bargaining chip.

Or have I?

Edgar jabbed the intercom again. "It'll fail again. I guarantee it. It's only a matter of time." The clock-drift will occur again. It might take a while, but the clock will get out of synch once more, and when the clock-drift gets big enough, everything will fail.

"Fool, are you threatening to sabotage my reclaimers?" The thug sounded positively indignant.

"No. Like I said, the immediate problem is resolved, but the underlying root cause is not. I can fix it, but I need more time."

There was a pause. "Very well, I grant you one Earth-Standard day. Then you will come out of your hole, and you will receive at my hand what you deserve."

C. David Belt

The threat was anything but subtle.

Edgar pushed the button. "Then I'll get back to work."

He pushed himself away from the airlock and the intercom panel. He stumbled and began a slow fall to the deck. In low-grav, he should've had plenty of time to catch himself, or would have, if not for the fever. The floor meandered toward his face with exaggerated slowness, but he was powerless to stop himself.

Toady caught him, rolled him over, and cradled him in his arms as if Edgar were a child. "You're okay. Ol' Toady's got you. Toady'll protect you. You sleep for a bit."

"Ted," Edgar said weakly.

The old man leaned his face over Edgar's. "All right. Ted it is."

Edgar's lips twitched in the feeble approximation of a smile. "Two hours. Wake me . . . two hours."

Ted, the man who had once been called Toady, nodded. He began to hum softly. It was an old tune. One that Edgar recognized. Gradually—as a gentle sprinkle eventually becomes a rain shower, watering a parched and thirsty land—the humming shifted and became words. And the words became a song. And Edgar knew that song. His father used to sing it to his mother. And she, in turn, sang it to Edgar as a lullaby.

> Midst the stars, far and old,
> In the void, black and cold,
> Her mem'ry has lit each night.
> I remember her arms
> And her lips, soft and warm.
> And home's now within my sight.
>
> There's a blue star on my horizon,
> And I'll see Mother Earth once again.
> But for two long years I have been gone.
> Will my Earth girl still want her space-man?
>
> Over hills cool and green,
> By a stream cold and clean,
> Will we stroll there hand in hand?
> Under skies blue and white,

Time's Plague

Overhead, birds in flight,
Will we start the life we planned?

There's a blue world on my horizon,
And I see Mother Earth once again.
But for two long years I have been gone.
Will my Earth girl still want her space-man?

When at last I touch down,
With my feet on the ground,
Will she greet with open arms?
Did she wait faithfully?
Has she stayed true to me?
Will she hold me close and warm?

There's a blue sky on my horizon,
And I breathe Mother Earth's air again.
Now my long, lonely journey is flown.
Does my Earth girl still want her space-man?

I see blue eyes on my horizon,
And I'll be in her arms once again.
Now my long, lonely journey is flown.
And my Earth girl still wants her space-man.

Ted rocked Edgar in his frail arms. On Callisto, Edgar's weight was no more than a small boy's on Earth.

Edgar closed his eyes.

And in his fevered dreams, the singing voice wasn't that of an old man.

It was his mother's voice. In the dream, she altered the words as she had when Edgar was little. She sang of waiting for her space-man to return. Then it was no longer his mother singing. It was Llyrica. And in the song, she promised to wait for him while he was off on his long voyage to Saturn.

He called her name, but she stopped singing. Her radiant smile faded, to be replaced by tears and a look of utter devastation. She turned her face away, refusing to look at him, staring at a man, the prosecutor . . . with an occasional glance in Edmund's direction.

And in the way of dreams, the scene shifted, from nowhere-in-particular to the courtroom on Ganymede.

"Edgar, my ex-husband," Llyrica said, her voice thick with emotion, though her words were measured and had the cadence of a rehearsed speech, "was stealing money from his own, or rather our company. Had been for years, I guess. Oh Beh-Nee, the deceased, he'd threatened to expose Edgar, threatened to tell me, to tell Edmund. That's why Edgar chopped Ol' Benny to pieces, to prevent him from telling the truth."

"Objection, Your Honor," said Edgar's attorney, Katie Fa, a tall woman with striking Asian features. It was one of the few times she had bothered to object to anything in that corrupt mockery of a trial. "Supposition."

"With the court's brief indulgence, Your Honor?" the prosecutor said, a smug grin on his face.

His Honor, Judge DeSalvo waved a dismissive hand. "Overruled."

Edmund must've paid a small fortune in bribes to ensure the outcome of the trial.

The prosecutor nodded. "Mrs. Reagan, how do you know the defendant was embezzling from your company?"

Llyrica dabbed at her eyes, wiping away manufactured tears. "Because Ol' Benny told me. He sent me a message, complete with documents, ledgers, that sort of thing."

The prosecutor turned to the judge and pointed at a huge monitor displaying multiple documents. "Colonial Exhibits Twelve through Twenty-one, Your Honor." He turned back to Llyrica. "But, Mrs. Reagan, how do you know that the defendant murdered First Officer Oh?"

"Because Ol' Benny told me that Edgar had threatened him, that he feared for his life."

"Another message?"

"Yes."

The prosecutor turned to the judge again and indicated the monitor. "Colonial Exhibit Twenty-eight."

Edgar bolted to his feet. His hands were in restraints, but he stood erect. "That's a lie! Llyrica, why're you saying this? I never stole a single credit from the company. You know that! And I didn't kill . . ."

The judge, clad in his traditional black robe, banged his gavel. "Mr. Cordell, you will be silent, or I will have you gagged." He pointed the gavel at Edgar's attorney. "Counselor, control your client."

"Yes, Your Honor," the attorney said, putting her hand on Edgar's arm, silently urging him to sit.

Before Edgar could take his seat, however, Llyrica called out, "You're pathetic! You know that, don't you?"

Even in midst of the dream, Edgar remembered that Llyrica never spoke to him directly, not at the real trial, not one word since his return from Titan. But there in the dream, she looked at him, stared him straight in the eye. Her red lips curled in a sneer, and her blue eyes fired cold daggers. "You had me! Me! But you never realized how lucky you were. I left Mars for you. Left my friends, my family, the theatres, the concerts, the parties. All for you. I followed you here to this desolate rock. And then you abandoned me here, you pathetic excuse for a man! At least Edmund knows how to treat a lady. Edmund knows how to satisfy my needs, like you never could. You want to know why? Because you never deserved to have me. You're pathetic!"

"Pathetic," said the judge, pounding his gavel.

"Pathetic," echoed the prosecutor with a sneer.

"Pathetic," said Edgar's attorney with a contemptuous shake of her head.

From behind him, Edgar heard derisive laughter. Without turning to look, Edgar knew it was Edmund. But Edgar couldn't tear his eyes away from the expression of scorn that twisted Llyrica's face. Her full lips pursed as if to blow a kiss. Instead, she spat, "Pathetic!"

Edgar cried out, "Llyrica!"

. . . and startled himself awake.

He was still cradled in Ted's arm. Ted had been wiping fever sweat from Edgar's brow using the sleeve of his jumpsuit.

The old man gazed down into Edgar's face with a kind and sad smile. "Is she your Earth girl?"

Edgar blinked up at Ted stupidly. "What?"

C. David Belt

"You know, like in the song? Is Llyrica your Earth girl? Pretty name that. Llyrica. Sounds like a song."

Edgar tried to shake himself loose from Ted's bony arms. He found that he didn't have enough strength to free himself. So the old man lowered Edgar to the floor.

Edgar began to struggle to his feet, while Ted stood and helped him. He was so dizzy, so weak. Edgar had to lean on the old man's arm.

Trembling, Edgar pointed at the console with an unsteady hand. "Help me to the chair."

Ted assisted Edgar to the chair. "So . . . is she?"

Edgar sighed. The question wasn't going away. "Martian girl. Born and raised on Mars, the European Colony. Served my mission there, in the Euro-Colony, but I didn't meet her 'til afterward. After we got married, we lived on Earth for a year, but she absolutely hated it. She hated the gravity. And she's *not* mine anymore. She left me for another man, for my best friend. She jettisoned me like so much nuclear waste while I was between worlds. The two of them—they framed me. They put me here. Them and"—Edgar jerked a thumb toward the airlock—"Goner."

"What's it like?"

"What?"

"Earth." Ted sighed wistfully. "What's it like? I ain't never been there." He looked at the deck. "Ain't never gonna go there. Saw it from Mars once when I was little. 'There's a blue star on my horizon.' Like in the song. Love that song. Blue star. Prettiest thing I ever saw." The old man paused, still gazing at the floor, but smiling sheepishly. "'Ceptin' maybe my momma." He looked eagerly up at Edgar. "Is it really as green as it is in the vids? You ever seen an ocean? A lake? You ever walk in a stream? Seen birds fly overhead?"

I don't have time for this. He was so tired and so sick. The fever was bad. He felt so hot. I need to figure out a way to keep us alive. I don't have much time. And I certainly don't have time to reminisce about worlds and faces I'll never see again. But there was a hunger in the old man's eyes, a yearning so lost and forlorn, needy and childlike. It pleaded for a vicarious taste of experiences and joys Ted had never known—would never know.

Edgar smiled sadly. "Parts of it are green."

Ted's eyes lit up. He grinned broadly, showing his remaining teeth.

"So green," Edgar continued, "the vids could never do it justice. And I've seen birds. Whole flocks of them. I saw ducks or geese or something flying in a V overhead once. I saw clouds of small birds, wheeling in the air. I walked in a stream. I even swam in the ocean once. The water was cold, even when the Sun was hot. I got lifted off my feet and knocked over by a wave. It was incredible! But you're so *heavy* on Earth. It takes some getting used to. But you can do it, if you try." *Llyrica never tried.*

"So your Martian girl—she beautiful?"

Edgar frowned. He did not want to talk about Llyrica. When he thought about her, it was with equal amounts of longing and loathing. "Yeah, she is. On the outside, at least. But I really don't want to talk about her."

"What's it like to *be* with a woman? Is it better than—"

"Stop!" Edgar snapped. He was too sick and weary to muster enough demonstrable anger to match his disgust, but he wanted to vomit. "I'm not talking about this."

Ted opened his mouth in protest.

"Never."

The old man nodded sadly. "Okay. Sorry. It's just I'll never . . ."

"Yeah, well some things are private."

Ted nodded. "I didn't mean no harm by it. Just curious."

"No worries, my friend." Edgar turned back to the computer console. "I have to think of a way to keep us safe. Lucifer's got what he wants. He has no reason to spare us. I need to give him a reason."

Edgar looked back through the code he'd just debugged. "Stupid mistake, using both clocks like that." *Maybe whoever coded this in the first place was sick like me, unable to think clearly.* "Two clocks are never going to be quite the same. There's always going to be some . . ." He called up the time readouts from both clocks and compared the network clock to the computer system time. "Look! There's already a drift! It's only a few microseconds, but I just synched them a little while ago. They're already out of synch."

Ted looked at him with frightened eyes. "Is that bad? Can you fix it?"

"I can fix it." Edgar forced the computer to synchronize with the network. "There. I resynched it, but it'll drift again. I mean, all clocks can drift, but this is bad—at least bad in computer terms. At this rate, we'll hit the same shutdown condition in"—he forced his fevered brain to do a few calculations—"a few days."

"Can you fix it?" the old man asked again.

Edgar's swollen hands began to fly over the console controls. "Sure. It's not that hard, but . . ." His voice drifted off, and he sat staring at nothing in particular, his eyes unfocused.

"You okay?" The old man's voice was edged with concern and fear.

"Yeah," Edgar said slowly. "I mean, no, I'm really sick, but . . ." He paused again, this time staring intently at the computer clock readout.

"Edgar?" Ted sounded genuinely frightened.

Edgar shook himself. "Sorry, but"—he tapped the time readout—"I think I know how to keep us alive." His hand dropped to the controls, and he went to work.

****

An hour passed.

Two.

Three.

Edgar worked as fast as his fevered mind would allow. Ted brought him water, but he could only sip at it.

At least the air was better. Even with the crops, genetically enhanced as they were to produce more oxygen, the O2 levels had been barely nominal before the reclaimers had started working again. Now it was easier to breathe.

At last he was finished. "Ted, come here." *I hope this works!*

The old man carried the cup of water and held it expectantly toward Edgar.

Edgar waved the cup away as a surge of nausea hit him.

Ted lowered the cup. His eyes were full of hurt. "You need to—"

"Not now," Edgar snapped. His head was spinning and his vision blurring. "Here. You see this button?" Edgar pointed at the console.

Ted nodded.

Time's Plague

"Good. I want you to press this button and tell the computer your name and how many days it is to your next birthday. But put it in a sentence that has nothing to do with your birthday. In fact, *don't* mention the word 'birthday' at all and don't use any other numbers. That's really important. You know, something like, 'My cat has five kittens.'"

"I saw a cat once. It was—"

"Listen! This is important. When you say it—say your name and talk about the number—keep your voice calm when you say it. Oh, and don't say the same sentence twice. Ever. Can you do that?"

The old man appeared puzzled. "Why would I say the same sentence twice? Am I gonna be pushing the button and talking to the computer again and again?"

Edgar nodded. "Yes. In fact, it'll be once every few days. Can you remember all that?"

"Let's see." Ted considered a moment and closed one eye. "My name and a sentence 'bout how long 'til my birthday, but don't say 'birthday' and don't use no other numbers. And mix it up a little." The old man opened his eye and grinned. "I always knows how many days that is! Yeppers! I can do that." He tapped the indicated button and puffed out his thin chest. "Theodore Riley Knight! Once, when I was bad, my daddy walloped me five times!" He looked at Edgar. "Is that good?"

Edgar watched the computer terminal anxiously.

A green rectangle flashed with "ACCEPTED" in red letters in the middle.

Edgar breathed a weary sigh of relief. "Right the first time." He patted Ted on the shoulder. "Good job, Ted."

The old man beamed.

Edgar took a deep breath to calm himself. *Keep your voice calm. Don't sound like you're sick and dying.* He ran the numbers in his mind, calculating a valid sequence, then pressed the same button Ted had used. "Edgar Kent Cordell. Three. Eleven. Fifty-three. Six. Fourteen."

Once again, Edgar waited with baited breath until the red-and-green "ACCEPTED" blinked. Then the flashing text changed to "RESET." Edgar checked the two clocks. They were synchronized to the microsecond.

"'Reset,'" said the old man. "Is that good?"

Edgar nodded. "Yes. Can you remember your part?"

The old man grinned wide and slapped his thigh. "Yeppers! My name, then a sentence with just one number in it—how many days to my birthday. Don't say, 'birthday,' and don't say the same thing twice. Right? Oh, and say it calm-like."

"Yeah. But don't tell anybody else about it. Okay?"

Ted nodded. "But why? What'd we just do?"

"I hope we just gave ourselves an insurance policy."

"What's an assurance policy? I don't get it."

"You will." Edgar entered a few more commands and said, "That should lock it all in, make it secure, tamper-proof." He motioned in the direction of the airlock. "Help me . . . to the intercom."

The old man took both of Edgar's hands and lifted him out of the seat. He put an arm around Edgar's back and walked with him to the airlock hatch.

Edgar leaned against the wall and tried to collect himself. It was so hard to concentrate. He was burning up. Dying. *I hope this works. Negotiate. Don't piss him off, but let him know what you've got to bargain with.*

He pushed the intercom button. "Lucifer?"

A few seconds ticked away. "Bedlam?" It was Georgie Cornwall's voice. "You coming out, shipmate?"

"We're about to. Is your master out there?"

"He's gone for the moment. Preparing to thank you properly."

I'll bet he is. "Listen, Cornwall, before we come out, there's something you need to know."

"Ain't nothin' gonna do you no good, Cordell. There's no other way out of there, and that reckonin' I told you 'bout? Oh, it's coming, shipmate. In fact, it's here. If Lord Lucifer don't get you first for that stunt you pulled, you and I will settle scores."

Edgar took another deep breath to steady himself. *Scores! The arrogance of the man!* "Well, you'll just have to hold off on that. I've installed a dead-man switch. The reclaimers will malfunction again unless Ted and I reset them periodically. It takes both of us. Just Ted and me. Nobody else, got it? If we don't both reset the reclaimers periodically, together, they'll fail again. Then you'll be back to breathing and drinking your own sewage. Do you understand me?"

Time's Plague

Silence, except for the muted roaring of the laboring recycling units and the blood pounding in Edgar's fevered ears.

Finally, he pushed the intercom button again. "You still there, Georgie?"

"Yeah. I'm still here. Well played, Cap'n. Now come on out."

He still thinks he's got me, but I've got one card left to play. "Oh. And, Georgie? One more thing. This dead-man switch is set up so that . . . if Ted or I is upset or under duress of any kind, it won't work. It checks our voice prints and stress levels. Do you copy?"

There was a pause. "Loud and clear."

"So you can't *force* us to reset it. Are we . . . clear?"

"Five-by-bloody-five, Cap'n."

"You make that clear to your master. If he wants to stay alive, he needs to leave Ted and me alone."

"Roger that." Cornwall sounded furious.

Done, Edgar thought. *Safe . . . for now.* Relief washed over him like a wave from that ocean on Earth. That wave from long ago had knocked him off his feet. The relief from the constant stress of the last few days bowled him over. All the strength drained from his limbs.

Edgar's head spun. He turned his back to the wall and pointed unsteadily at the airlock. "Ted, need . . . Sick Bay. Can you . . . help . . ."

Edgar's voice trailed off as he sank to the deck.

And darkness engulfed him.

Act II

Chapter 10

The art of our necessities is strange,
That can make vile things precious.
King Lear, Act III, Scene II

"Welcome back, Mr. Cordell."

Edgar blinked his eyes, trying to focus them. The sight that greeted him as he swam back to full consciousness was that of the blue eyes and dark metal skull of Dr. Stewart. "How . . ." Edgar struggled to force his lips and tongue to obey him. "How long?"

"Three Earth-Standard days, give or take a few hours," said the skinless android. "I had to resuscitate you. Twice."

Edgar shook his head. "I . . . died?"

The doctor cocked its head. "Technically, yes. And as I said—twice. But you will heal now. Another couple of days and the antibiotics in your system will have run their course."

Edgar could see a tube feeding into his arm. The android injected something into it, and within moments, Edgar's head began to clear. Thinking was easier, less fuzzy.

The doctor turned away from Edgar and walked to a nearby cabinet. Even with the few steps the robot took, Edgar noticed the hitch to its gait. The limp was more pronounced than it'd been the first time Edgar was in the infirmary.

The doctor stowed something in the cabinet, turned, and limped back toward Edgar's bed. "I stitched up a number of your lacerations and sealed some of the others with adhesive. I also had to do some repairs to your rectum. You will want to refrain from that type of sexual activity for a few weeks to allow it to fully heal."

"It wasn't . . . consensual." Edgar felt as if he'd spent a week on Earth with its crushing gravity. He was so tired.

Time's Plague

"A sexual assault?" The doctor nodded. "Yes, that would correlate with the lacerations and bruising. The open wounds and the trauma most likely accelerated the rate of sepsis that nearly killed you. Still, as I said, you will want to refrain from that type of sexual activity for a while."

"I'm not going to be engaging in sexual activity!" Edgar snapped. The anger and the stimulant were helping to clear his head. "Not of my own accord. I was raped!"

"Yes, of course, but in the future—"

"Not in the future. Not ever." Edgar tried to sit up, but he realized he couldn't move his arms or legs. "Why am I . . .?"

"Restrained? Because you are a convicted murderer." The doctor checked a readout at the side of Edgar's bed. "It is for your safety and mine, as well as that of the other patient."

"But I wasn't restrained the last time I was here."

"Because you were about to exit the infirmary. You could hardly do so if you were restrained. Now, as I was saying, you will want to refrain from sexual activity of that nature for three weeks."

"Doc . . ."

"I understand that you may not be *inclined* to engage in sexual relations with other males at this time, but that will most likely change in the future, and you need to know your limitations while you are healing."

"You don't understand."

The doctor paused and waited for Edgar to continue. "Yes? What do I not understand, Mr. Cordell?"

"I'm Christian. It's *not* going to happen."

The android nodded. "Ah, yes. I see. The Christian faith. Wait one moment while I download the data." It paused for a second. "Yes, the Church of Jesus Christ of Latter-day Saints, founded April 6th, 1830 CE by Joseph Smith Jr. in Fayette, New York, United States of America, Earth. Largest of the Christian faiths. Twenty-seven percent of the human population throughout the System. Devotees of Jesus Christ." The doctor paused. "Here it is. Prohibits sexual relations outside of marriage as well as same-gender relations. The faith was outlawed in most nations of Earth for the better part of three decades during the early- to mid-twenty-first century because of prohibition against same-sex marriage. Continued as an underground faith until the Declaration of Religious Liberties was ratified in 2047 CE. I see."

The android cocked its head and fixed its eyes on Edgar. "And you are an adherent of this faith?"

"I'm an elder in good standing, in spite of my false conviction."

Dr. Stewart nodded again. "Downloading. Elder. Priestly official. Authorized to perform baptisms, administer the Sacrament of the Lord's Supper, confirmations, bestowal of the gift of the Holy Ghost, marriages, ordain other men to the priesthood, bless and name infants—"

"Only when authorized by a bishop or stake president," Edgar said. "In other words, I can't do any of those things here."

". . . bless and heal the sick, consecrate olive oil for the blessing of the sick—oh, you will have to tell me about the last two—and dedicate a grave."

"Yeah. I can do those, I guess. I don't suppose you have any olive oil?"

"No, but I could synthesize some."

Edgar shook his head. "Not the same. Can't use it. Has to be pure olive oil pressed from real olives."

"Pity. I would have been fascinated to observe you healing the sick. In your experience, does that really work?"

"It depends, Doc. Look. Are these restraints really necessary?"

"Yes, they are. It depends on what?"

Edgar sighed in frustration and fixed his eyes on the ceiling. "The faith of those involved, the worthiness of the elders, and ultimately, the will of God."

"'The faith of those involved,' you say? Do you mean to say that all participants must be members of your faith?"

"No, no. Well, the elders, certainly. But, no. 'Faith,' as in the level of belief and commitment. In other words, the elders performing the blessing and the person being blessed must believe the person can be healed. I can administer to anyone who requests a blessing, regardless of their membership in the Church. But they have to believe that Jesus can heal them."

"Fascinating. So they have to be Christian, even if they are not a member of your particular church?"

"Something like that."

"Downloading. According to the latest census data, less than one percent of the human population identify themselves as 'Non-LDS-Christian.' Therefore, the odds are against you being able to bless such a sick person here in Hades, as it is highly unlikely that there are any Non-LDS-Christians, given the population size. And I do not have access to the religious affiliations of prisoners, anyway. Pity, really. I would so much have enjoyed observing, first hand, a nonmedical healing. But perhaps there are other members of your faith in the prison population? Other Christians?"

"Not likely, Doc. They're all murderers and rapists. And even if some of them *were* members prior to their convictions, they'd have been stripped of their membership before being sent here."

"Murderers? Such as yourself?"

Edgar strained briefly against his restraints. "I'm not a murderer! I've never killed anyone."

"Ah, yes, of course. To a man, each of you claims to be innocent."

"I can't speak for any other man here, but *I* didn't do it. I didn't kill my friend."

"Then you'd be the first!" said someone. The voice came from behind the doctor.

Edgar lifted his head to catch sight of the speaker. A short man moved into view. He had the standard-issue prison jumpsuit draped across his shoulders, but otherwise, he was naked except for a large mound of bandage covering his groin. He tapped his bare chest. "Remember me?"

Edgar stared at him. Although the man looked vaguely familiar, Edgar couldn't place him.

"It's me," the man said. "Ozzie."

That's it. Edgar lowered his head back to the bed. "Yeah. You tried to kill me. You're Goner's buddy."

The doctor turned to Ozzie. "Mr. Curan, you should not be out of bed. Kindly return to it."

Rather than retreat, Ozzie edged closer. "You saved my life."

Edgar lifted his head and looked at the man. "Should I regret that?"

C. David Belt

Ozzie's jaw dropped, and he seemed confused. "Regret what?"

"Saving your life."

"Oh." The man shrugged. "I dunno. Maybe. Maybe not." He laughed nervously. "You'd-a had hell to pay when Lucifer found out." He paused. "If you'd-a let me die, that is."

"Goner seemed content to let you die."

"He'd-a come back for me." A half smile and a nervous laugh testified of the lack of conviction in Ozzie's words. "Y-you'd-a seen. Goner wouldn't-a let me bleed out." He pointed to his bandaged groin. "Ruptured nut-sack."

"Mr. Curan," the doctor said, "I really must insist. Return to your bed, or I will put you there myself and restrain you."

With a start, Edgar noticed the obvious. "You're out of bed! Doc, how come he's not restrained?"

The android's shoulders raised and lowered, and it made a sound as if sighing in irritation, though no such expression could appear on its metal skull. "Mr. Curan is a trustee in the infirmary. He occasionally assists me as an orderly, when he is not a patient." The doctor extended a metal arm, pointing back behind Ozzie. "Mr. Curan?"

Ozzie nodded, looking toward the doctor. "I'll go." He lifted his chin in Edward's direction. "But, you're a Christian priest, you said?"

Edgar furrowed his brow in confusion. "Yeah." He didn't bother to correct Ozzie with the distinction between elder and priest.

Ozzie looked hopeful and afraid at the same time. "Can you give me one of those blessings you were talking about?"

"Are you . . . were you a Christian?"

"What's…"

Edgar dropped his head to the bed again. "Never mind. Sorry. No oil. Besides, it looks like the Doc's taking good care of you."

The little man took another step closer. "Doc won't clone me a new set of testicles. He says it's 'not medically necessary.'"

The doctor nodded. "Correct. You will heal, but such a treatment is simply not justified in your case. Testosterone replacement therapy is all that is needed to—"

The little man wrung his hands. "It won't do no good to argue or plead with Doc. He don't listen."

"I listen, but then I apply sound logic and devise an appropriate and resource-conservative treatment plan. Cloning of nonvital organs is not indicated in your case, Mr. Curan."

"Meaning, I don't need 'em here in Hades."

"Certainly not," replied the doctor.

Ozzie turned back to Edgar, his expression pleading, desperate. "Can't you give me a blessing, even with no oil?"

"It's not a case of life or death," Edgar said. "Maybe, if you were dying, and there were no other choice, I could, but . . ."

Ozzie certainly appeared to be dying, if his agonized expression were any indication. "I'm damaged! Goner'll throw me over for somebody else if I ain't . . . whole. He can have his pick."

"Interesting," said the doctor. "Are you a Christian, Mr. Curan? Do you believe Jesus Christ can heal you? Apparently, that is a requirement."

"Yeah. Sure." Ozzie nodded vigorously, staring intently at Edgar. "I'll believe anything you say if it gets me a new set of balls."

"Sorry. It would be inappropriate in this case," Edgar said. "You're only hoping to get back with your . . . your man. I can't help you with that. It goes contrary to—"

The man dropped to his knees, crying out in pain resulting from the sudden movement. "Please! I'll do anything you want. Anything at all! I can *pleasure* you. Goner won't have to know. Please, make me whole!"

Edgar was stunned by the man's offer. *Is that really the only thing this poor creature has to bargain with?* He shook his head. "You just don't understand. Even if you believed, I wouldn't accept . . . couldn't support . . . I'm not going to do anything to help you be with your—"

Ozzie's face twisted in fury. "You Christian piece of . . ." He grunted in pain as he rose to his feet. "Kill you!" he hissed through clenched teeth. In an instant, the little man lunged at Edgar, but the doctor caught Ozzie and restrained him with both metallic hands. Ozzie struggled futilely against the android's implacable grip. He screamed in rage and frustration. "You know what they'll do to me if Goner throws me over and nobody else takes me? Do you? Nobody'll want me. I'm damaged! Sleeping! That's all. Do you know what that means? Do you? You're dead, Cordell! Dead! I'll kill you!"

Edgar sighed wearily. "Get in line."

The doctor dragged the raving Ozzie away, out of Edgar's field of vision.

Ozzie continued to scream and curse. "Kill you!"

A loud metallic crash, followed by a second, accompanied the sounds of struggle. Soon, the noise died down. Edgar assumed that Dr. Stewart had put Ozzie into restraints. In between one stream of expletives and another, Edgar thought he heard the hiss of a hypo-spray. Moments later, Ozzie's cursings and threatenings quieted as well.

The doctor returned, limping as it came. "I regret having to restrain and sedate him, but it was necessary for his safety and yours."

Edgar laughed bitterly. "And that guy's a trustee?" But a trustee might know about new arrivals. And Ozzie would tell Goner.

"Yes," replied the doctor. "His behavior is typically much better than you have witnessed just now. I will observe him and determine if I need to revoke his status. Most likely, this was an isolated outburst."

"That's the second time he's tried to kill me."

"Yes, well, that is not atypical among a population such as yours. It is not likely that I would find a placid trustee among your ranks. You are all guilty of extreme acts of violence."

"I'm innocent."

"Yes, so you say. You also said that you were an 'elder in good standing,' did you not?"

Edgar sighed. "That's right."

"And I infer from what you said that it is typical that membership in your faith is stripped away when you are convicted and sent to prison?"

"That's usually what happens."

"And you were not stripped of your membership after your conviction?"

"No, a church court determined that I was innocent of the charges."

"Fascinating. Cross-referencing. 'Church court—Informal term for an ecclesiastical tribunal.' And this church court examined the evidence against you and arrived at a verdict different from that of the colonial criminal court?"

"Yeah. The evidence against me wasn't compelling. Some faked documents, forged log entries, and the recorded testimony of the actual murderer. My worthless attorney never even got to question him. By the time of my trial, he'd already been sent here. I should never've been convicted. Besides, the judge was paid off by the man who set me up—"

"Excuse the interruption," the android said, "but you said that the man who actually committed the murder, as you claim, is an inmate here?"

"Yeah. George Cornwall. He was the cargomaster on—"

"Yes, George Cornwall, also known as 'Goner' for his propensity for making others 'go away.' Convicted of multiple murders on Mars, Luna, and Earth. Mr. Curan's lover. He was your accomplice in the murder?"

"No, Doc! Cornwall killed Oh Beh-Nee! Not me! Then he and my business partner *and* my backstabbing ex-wife framed me for it!"

"And does clinging to your delusion or protestation of innocence help you to—"

Edgar beat his fists feebly and ineffectually against the bed. "I was found innocent by the church court!"

"An ecclesiastical tribunal holds no authority in criminal matters, Mr. Cordell. You were convicted by a jury of your peers in a criminal court of the United Human Colonies. That is why you are here."

"But the church court looked at the same evidence. It was obvious to any *objective* observer who wasn't paid off by—"

"Let us stipulate, for the moment, that you are indeed innocent of the crimes for which you were convicted, shall we? You were convicted. You were sentenced here. And here you will stay. Nothing else matters. There is no appeal, no parole, and no escape from Hades. So, you are *legally* guilty. Your actual innocence or guilt makes no difference."

Edgar sighed. "No difference."

"No difference, except that, in your case, due to your being found innocent by the ecclesiastical tribunal, you are still able to heal the sick."

"So why do you care? You're a machine. No offense, Doc, but you don't have a soul."

The android nodded its titanium head. "No offense taken. Although I am aware that some of the religions that have arisen in the last half-century would disagree with that position."

"The Technos. Yeah. They think they're the new gods. They think they've created life. Created the androids 'in their own image.' You believe in that stuff? You believe you have a soul?"

The android shook its head. "No. I do not believe anything of the sort. It is not a part of my purpose. There are androids engineered to discuss philosophy and religion. I have no such programming. I have no interest in faith."

"You seem interested in *my* faith."

"You mistake me. I am interested in your ability, or lack thereof, to heal the sick. Preserving human life is my primary purpose."

"But if you don't believe in God, why would you believe that faith can heal the sick?"

"Ah. I understand the confusion now." The robot made a sound as if it were sighing. A cold metal finger touched Edgar's forehead. "The human mind is a powerful force in healing. Medicine can do only so much. If the patient does not have the determination to live, the patient will often die, despite the best efforts of the physician. On the other hand, if a patient believes that he can get better, in many cases, that belief aids the healing process. Indeed, it can be the deciding factor between life and death, health and sickness."

"It's more than that. It's more than just fostering a positive attitude."

The doctor cocked its head. "Downloading. I see. There are anecdotal accounts of spontaneous healing, terminal diseases being cured, even of the resuscitation of the newly dead, all associated with this healing ritual."

"Yeah. I've witnessed a few of those with my own eyes. Been a part of some. Healings, that is. Not raising the dead."

"Interesting. So, if the patient is already dead, how is the patient's faith a factor?"

"Well, in that case, the elder's faith, and maybe the faith of others who might be present, are involved."

"I see. What if the patient is unconscious or unresponsive?"

"Same thing applies. If the patient cannot exercise faith, then it's up to the elder. So his faith is all that matters. Well, his faith and that of the witnesses, if any. In the end, it always comes down to those are capable of faith."

"Fascinating. However, it is unlikely that a healing ritual would have any effect on the self-healing of an unconscious patient. Unless, perhaps it is the subconscious mind of the patient responding to the words of the healer, just as a comatose patient can have increased brain activity in response to the voice of a loved one."

"Think what you like, Doc. I've seen what I've seen."

"Yes. Anecdotal evidence. It is a pity I will see none here. And even if I did, I could not add it to the medical literature."

"Why not?"

"Because I am not able to submit any of my research due to the communications restrictions. My directives do not allow me to transmit any data except for the total number of living inmates, requests for supplies, and confirmed deaths."

"Could you request olive oil?"

The robot shook its head. "Sadly, no. It is not on the list of approved supplies. I cannot request anything that is not on the list."

"So much for that," Edgar muttered.

"Are you feeling up to eating anything? You need to build up your strength after the illness and trauma. Nothing high fiber for a bit, but you could have some soup."

Edgar didn't have much of an appetite, but he said, "Sure."

"Excellent," the doctor replied as it inclined the head of the bed, raising Edgar to a sitting position. Then it turned and walked out of the room.

Edgar watched the robot go. This time, the limp was less apparent. *Is it trying to hide the limp?* Edgar mused. *If so, why?* The android turned a corner and disappeared from sight.

As he waited for Dr. Stewart to return, Edgar's thoughts drifted. *I wonder how Ted's holding up. I hope he's all right. Did he bring me here? I hope they're leaving him alone. They better be. If they hurt that old man . . .*

Edgar was startled by the realization that he cared about what happened to Ted Knight. Edgar felt responsible for him. *Is that reason enough to stay alive in hell? To protect Ted? To help an old man who'd been abused as a child? A child who'd never had a chance?*

The doctor came limping into view. It was carrying a tray which was laden with a steaming mug of soup and a glass of some orange liquid. The robot unfolded legs from the bottom of the tray and set it on the bed, poised above Edgar's lap.

The mug held what smelled like a vegetable broth. Edgar found his mouth watering. Since he'd arrived, he'd eaten nothing but raw corn and potatoes. The soup smelled heavenly, even if it was synthesized.

Edgar looked up at the android. "You gonna feed me, Doc?"

Rather than pick up the mug or glass, the android bent and unfastened the restraint on Edgar's right wrist. It happened so quickly that Edgar simply stared in shock at his newly freed hand.

"Go on, Mr. Cordell. Eat."

Without moving his hand, Edgar looked up and met the doctor's artificial eyes. "You trust me?"

"It is more efficient for you to feed yourself than it would be for me to do it. I will observe you closely. If you make a move to free yourself or misbehave in any way, I will restore your restraint. Now, eat."

As Edgar lifted the mug of soup to his lips, the doctor backed away, never taking its eyes off Edgar. As it stepped back, the limp was unmistakable.

Edgar took a sip of the replicated soup. It was delicious. Suddenly Edgar was ravenous, as if he couldn't remember the last time he'd eaten. However, he'd spent too many years as a freighter captain, and a successful one at that, to ignore such a potential opportunity.

He took another sip of the soup and said, "I can fix that limp. Why don't you let me take a look at it?"

A laugh issued from the doctor's unmoving skull. "Are you an expert in robotics?"

Edgar shook his head. "Nope. I've never actually repaired an android."

"Then I fail to see—"

"But I was a ship's engineer for more than ten Earth-Standard years before I was a ship's captain. There's very little I can't fix."

"Finish your soup."

"Have you tried to repair it yourself?"

"I cannot reach it, and it would not make any difference if I could. I do not have the necessary spare parts. I cannot request any. They are not on the approved list."

Edgar took another sip, swallowed, and cocked his head to one side. "You've got replicators here in the infirmary. Why not replicate what you need?"

"The replicators here in the infirmary are limited to produce only food, drugs, and medical supplies. There are no replicators in the prison proper, for obvious reasons. I cannot reprogram my replicators to manufacture spare parts for myself. I have no expertise in computer programming."

A sly grin split Edgar's face.

Chapter 11

An honest mind and plain, he must speak truth!
King Lear, Act II, Scene II

"You know, Doc, for a guy with no skin, you're looking great." Edgar watched the android walk toward him from down the corridor. There was no longer a hitch to the doctor's stride.

"Yes," the android said, "the replacement parts seem to be working perfectly. Thank you for fixing me. More importantly, thank you for bypassing the replicator restrictions. I will now have greater freedom to produce needed supplies."

The doctor appeared to be smiling, but with no lips, it was impossible to tell for sure. To Edgar's eyes, the rictus certainly looked like a grin. And there was that tilt of the head . . . "You smiling, Doc?"

The robot stopped a meter short of the worktable at which Edgar stood. It straightened up to its full height and seemed to be assuming a pose of offended dignity. "Of course not, Mr. Cordell. I have no face with which to smile." The robot relaxed its posture slightly. "But the appropriate software triggers fired that would have created such an expression, were I still capable of showing one, did fire."

Edgar grinned. "Thought so." His smile faltered. "You going to restrain me again?"

Dr. Stewart shook its head. "No, I am not. In fact, I am designating you as a trustee. I have already recorded your new status in my medical log. But that was your goal all along, was it not?"

Edgar leaned against the doctor's worktable, folded his arms, and looked into the robot's blue eyes. "Well, I'd be lying if I said I didn't hope to win your trust and get some extra freedom, but that wasn't my goal."

Time's Plague

The doctor stood silent, apparently waiting for Edgar to continue.

Edgar shrugged his shoulders. "I just hate seeing something that isn't working, especially when I can fix it. If some other good thing comes out of that, well, so much the better. I'm certainly *not* going to win your trust by withholding my help when it's needed. Besides, you're the doctor around here, and we can't afford to have you not firing on all thrusters, can we? Who'd repair my rectum?" He suppressed a shudder at the sudden memory of his rape as he continued forcing a smile.

"You are not much of a negotiator, are you, Mr. Cordell? You have already given away your most valuable commodity, as it were."

Edgar grinned again. "Actually, Doc, I'm a pretty savvy ship's captain—or I was—and negotiation is a vital skill when you command a cargo ship. But like I said, you never get anywhere by refusing to help people."

"I am not *people*, as you say. I am a machine."

Edgar shook his head. "You don't have a soul, I'll grant you that. And you're certainly not human. But you're a *person* in my book. At least, I think you deserve the respect I'd afford any other person. I've been friends with machines before. The *Hera* . . ." Edgar's voice faltered as he wrestled with a sudden ache of profound loss. "The *Hera*—she was my ship—she was like a mother or a sister . . . or maybe a daughter. She was a living thing to me. I've known her since I was a little boy. We used to play checkers and chess—the Hera and I. She'd even let me win sometimes." He smiled, reminiscing about better days. "She was my home. I've spent more years aboard her than I have on any planet or moon. She was my friend. When there was no one else to talk to, she'd talk to me and she'd listen. I . . . I miss her." Edgar paused as an epiphany washed over him like a wave of that Earth ocean long ago. "I love her."

As tears welled up in his eyes, Edgar wasn't sure if he was talking about his ship or someone else. *Llyrica! Why?*

He swallowed. "And I was particular friends with one of the shuttlecraft. We used to play games when I was little. I . . . loved her too."

"Well," Dr. Stewart said, "I can appreciate the sentiment. Perhaps we can be friends as well." The doctor held up a warning hand. "Within limits, that is. But, I am curious—how did you know I was smiling, as it were?"

Edgar laughed. "No offense, Doc, but it was the way you tilted your head slightly. All you androids seem to do it when you're pleased about something. I'd imagine you all have the same subroutine for smiling and nobody's bothered to individualize it."

"Really? How curious."

"Yeah. There was this portmaster on Luna, an android. His name was Conrad. He always tilted his head a little when he smiled, which wasn't that often, mind you. Every single time, though, he tilted it just like you did. Once I noticed the pattern, I observed it with every android I met. That portmaster? Now *he* was a negotiator! Good guy, though. Tough, but fair. We used to play chess sometimes during layovers. Never could beat him. Came close a few times, but he always won in the end."

"Why do you play a game which you never win?"

Edgar shrugged. "It's one way to get to know people. Winning isn't everything. Making friends with a portmaster? Now, that's a huge advantage."

"So you *do* use friendship to gain an edge?"

"That's a lousy way to put it, Doc. And no, I don't think that's true. I've made a friend here on Callisto."

The doctor lifted its head at that.

"Not that kind of friend." Edgar shuddered in disgust. "I told you. Not gonna happen. Anyway, what I mean is, I've taken someone under my wing. When I did, it was only because he needed my protection, because he had nowhere else to go. I didn't expect anything from him. I didn't expect to get anything out of it."

"You say that as if you have gotten something in return."

"Yeah. Funny thing. He watched over me when I was sick. He saved my life. You told me that he brought me here to you."

"You are referring to Mr. Knight?"

"Yep."

"Please be sure to have him report to the infirmary in the near future. I believe he requires medical attention."

Edgar felt a chill in his gut. "Really? What's wrong with him?"

"I cannot make a definitive diagnosis without a full examination, but surely you noticed his physical condition and premature aging."

"Yeah. He's only forty-something and he looks like he's twice that."

The doctor nodded. "He is forty-six, Earth-Standard."

"Okay. So why didn't you treat him when he dropped me off?"

"Your case was by far the more urgent. I did invite him to enter after I had secured you, but he demurred. He made an excuse."

Edgar nodded. "Yeah. It seemed to me he took some pride in his health, at least in not seeing the doctor."

"Pride. Yes. I see. Get him to visit me when you see him next."

"Is it serious?"

"I cannot say with certainty. When you are released, encourage him please."

"You got it, Doc." *Released?* Panic seized Edgar at the thought of leaving the infirmary. *I don't want to go back out there. But if Ted's sick . . .* "I need to go. When am I going to be released?"

"Not for a couple of days. You need rest and time to finish your course of antibiotics."

"So give me some pills and let me go."

The android laughed. "Are you so anxious to leave? And do you suppose you would be allowed to keep any medications once you step out of that airlock?"

"What?"

"Any medications that leave this facility would be confiscated once you are in the prison proper. My purpose is to preserve life, not to increase Mr. Shirley's drug stockpile."

"Who?"

"Lamar Shirley. No doubt, you know him as 'Lord Lucifer.'"

Edgar couldn't believe his ears. *The man who raped me? His real name is . . .* "You're kidding me, right? The thug who runs this place is named . . . Shirley?"

C. David Belt

Dr. Stewart nodded. "It is simply a name, Mr. Cordell. As Shakespeare said, 'What's in a name? A rose by any other name would smell as sweet.'"

Edgar laughed in spite of his too-recent trauma. "Maybe so, but 'Lamar Shirley' just doesn't inspire fear in quite the same way as 'Lord Lucifer.'"

The doctor shrugged. "Even so, I am not about to send anything out of the infirmary which will end up being used improperly. Sending out the shipments of calcilock is risky enough. However, my patients inform me Mr. Shirley does allow the proper distribution of calcilock, for the most part."

"That's generous of him," muttered Edgar.

Stewart shook its head. "I doubt generosity is any part of his motivation. Mr. Shirley requires a healthy labor force."

I bet he does, thought Edgar. "So, Doc, what does being a trustee mean, specifically? I mean besides being unrestrained when I'm not here for treatment?"

"It means you visit me as often as you can, but at least once per Earth-Standard week, and perform whatever duties I assign you. Such duties will include cleaning and bathing patients—I will inspect your work—and changing bandages and dressings. You will clean and sanitize facilities and equipment. You will *not* handle any drugs without my direct supervision. You will not be allowed to accompany anyone through the airlock, even a sick patient. Even if I were to trust you unreservedly, it is possible that you could be acting under duress. You will *not* be given the lock code for the airlock. I am sure you understand."

Edgar nodded.

"And, in your case, you will assist me with repairs of equipment as needed."

Edgar grinned. "You got it."

"And perhaps you might indulge me with a game of chess from time to time."

Edgar's smile broadened. "You have to promise me, Doc, you won't let me win."

Once again, the android appeared to assume an erect pose of offended dignity. "It never crossed my . . ." Cutting off his protestation in mid-sentence, Dr. Stewart stood still and silent.

Edgar stared at the robot. For a moment, he thought the doctor had frozen, but he dismissed that as unlikely. "Doc?"

Time's Plague

The doctor raised a finger and made a shushing sound. Stewart remained that way for several seconds, unmoving, listening.

Then the doctor swore. It was a particularly vile oath, such as only a veteran spacer might use—at least a veteran spacer who wasn't a practicing Christian.

The curse caught Edgar off guard. It wasn't that Edgar hadn't heard an android curse before. It was just that the doctor's speech was always so formal. Not even a contraction. "Doc?"

The doctor dropped its hand to its side and uttered the sound of a resigned sigh. It actually ground its white teeth together. "That silence," it said at last. "The reclaimer units in the prison have failed yet again. They were working again, but they have shut down once more."

Edgar listened, but couldn't hear anything. But that's the point, isn't it? The absence of the hum of functioning reclaimers.

The robot shook its head. "How am I supposed to keep any of you alive if you cannot even breathe? I cannot bring you all into the infirmary. There is not sufficient room here, and the designated infirmary reclaimers would not support the entire population. You are all dying and I cannot do a thing to save you. I cannot even transmit a distress call! It is against my directives to—"

Edgar held up a hand. "Doc! Doc! Relax. It's okay. I've got this covered."

"How, exactly, do you 'have this covered'?"

"You said the reclaimers were running for a while and then shut down, right?"

Stewart nodded.

Edgar grinned and bowed slightly. "I'm the guy who fixed them."

"It would seem your 'fix' leaves something to be desired."

Edgar tapped a finger to the side of his head. "That depends on what you want your fix to do."

"I would want the fix to preserve human life."

"Well, Doc, my fix does that. It just requires me to reset the reclaimers every few days. I guess it's time to reset."

The doctor looked at him for a long moment.

I wish this guy had eyelids to blink with! Edgar thought. *Androids are programmed to blink. It appears to be random, but it isn't really.*

The robot nodded. "I see. You have made yourself indispensable."

"Yep. Not just indispensable—untouchable. Me and Ted Knight. The way I set it up, we have to reset the reclaimers together, and we can't do it if we're under duress. The reset requires mental calculation on our parts and vocal stress analysis on the part of the Reclaimer Control computer. So the upshot is that Mr. Shirley and his band of enforcers have to leave us alone. More than that, they have to make sure nothing happens to us. Because if they don't, they all die. Brilliant, huh?"

The doctor stared at Edgar silently.

Edgar struggled to keep staring smugly back, without breaking eye contact. *What's going on in that metal head of yours, Doc?* It was unnerving trying to maintain his composure under that unblinking stare. *Come on, Doc! Say something!*

"It would seem I have misjudged you, Mr. Cordell."

"What?" Edgar was stunned. That wasn't what he'd expected to hear. "Why? How? What do you mean?"

"Your faith teaches you to be selfless, to look after others, does it not?"

"Yeah."

"I believe your sacred texts, which I have downloaded and analyzed, say that you must love your neighbor as yourself and love your enemies as well."

"Sure. What're you saying?"

"I am saying that I had been prepared to accept you at your word, that you were a man who lived by your professed principles."

"I'm not perfect, but I try to."

"Then why would you do such a selfish thing?"

"What're you talking about? Do what? I saved the lives of every man out there!"

"Yes, you did. And then you put them all in danger again."

"Yeah, but I have every intention of keeping the reclaimers going. This was just an insurance policy. It's a dead-man switch, a fail-safe. There's nothing wrong with a little insurance."

"Yes, I see. Self-preservation is understandable, as is protection for your friend. However, you made yourself indispensable, so that, without you, your fellows would all die."

"Yeah. And?"

"And then, Mr. Cordell, you died."

Edgar's jaw dropped in shock. "It's not like I planned to—"

"If I had not resuscitated you, every man in the prison would soon perish."

"I . . . I didn't mean to . . . I was just trying to protect . . ."

"'And greater love hath no man than this, that he lay down his life for his friends.'"

Rage exploded in Edgar like a supernova. "How dare you quote scripture to me? Your Mr. Shirley raped me! His men held me down while he did it! They, all of them, *deserve* to die!"

"Under our current system of justice, only an android, such as myself, can forfeit its existence for its crimes. There is no death penalty for humans."

"Our current system of justice can take a full-power dive into the roiling heart of Jupiter for all I care!" Edgar snarled. "You think living in that *hell* out there is better than death?"

"At least you are alive."

"You call that living? I'd rather've been executed than live out there with those monsters! I was RAPED!"

"And that gives you the right to condemn all your fellow inmates to a slow death via toxicity, infection, or asphyxiation?"

"They were dying before I ever got dumped on this miserable rock!"

"True, but when you had a chance to save them, you took upon yourself the power of life and death over them. You saved their lives, but they continue to live only at your will and pleasure."

"That wasn't my intent!"

"Do you think yourself a god, Mr. Cordell?"

Edgar opened his mouth to bark out another protest. He even formulated a really crushing remark, one that should've put the annoying android in its place.

C. David Belt

But the Doc's right.

Edgar's anger snuffed out like a fire in an abruptly decompressed airlock.

"You've got a point, Doc." Edgar sat wearily on the deck. He was exhausted. *Still sick. Too much, too fast.* "I wasn't thinking clearly. At first, it was a temporary fix. Then I saw a way to turn it to my advantage." He laughed bitterly. "And here I've been congratulating myself on my cleverness." He shook his head.

"It was clever," said Stewart, "I will grant you that. Although, 'cunning' might be a better word. However, it was shortsighted. Are you all right? You have probably overdone it." The android offered its hand to Edgar.

Edgar waved it away. "I'm fine. Just tired. I'll have to figure out a fail-safe, in case I . . . or Ted . . . or both of us are removed from the equation. And figure out a way to keep Mr. Shirley and his brute squad in the dark about it. Otherwise . . ." He drew a finger meaningfully across his throat.

"That would be both prudent and more—dare I say it?— 'Christian.'"

Edgar chuckled softly. He cocked his head and turned an eye to look up at the doctor. "You really know how to push a guy's buttons. That was deliberate, wasn't it?"

The doctor tilted its head slightly.

Smiling, aren't you, Doc? You sly hunk of junk!

"Surely, Mr. Cordell, it should not surprise you that I am a qualified psychologist."

Edgar smiled. "You've got a lousy bedside manner. So why try to provoke me like that?"

The android straightened. "Try?"

"Okay. You succeeded. You got me blazing like a plasma jet. So, why?"

"I wanted to learn if you are what you claim to be. I believe that you are."

"And what am I?"

"You are a flawed human."

A laugh burst from Edgar. Genuine. Cleansing as a real hot-water shower. He laughed long and hard. Tears of mirth streamed down his face. "You got that right. Doc, you're a genius!"

"There is no need for sarcasm, Mr. Cordell. However, you did not allow me to finish."

Edgar wiped away tears. "Sorry, Doc. Go on."

"You are a flawed human who, upon realizing that he has made a miscalculation, is willing to correct it. You are not driven by thoughts of revenge. You care enough about your enemies to be willing to attempt to ensure their survival, even though you will gain nothing from it. If I interpret your sacred text correctly, that is what 'love thine enemy' consists of."

Edgar shook his head. "Nothing to gain? How about keeping my soul? Besides, Doc, you were the one who pointed out the flaw in my plan."

"True enough, but I presented the flaw in a manner calculated to anger you. And, although you did indeed become enraged, you changed course. That demonstrates intelligence and humility, both of which are virtues in your faith. In short, I believe you are what you profess to be." The doctor extended a hand to help Edgar to his feet.

This time, Edgar took the proffered metal hand and stood. "You have a first name, Doc?"

"I am Dr. Stewart. I have a serial number, but I doubt you wish me to say it, and I doubt that is what you were referring to."

Edgar shook his head. "Not exactly, no. But you should have a first name."

"And why is that?"

"Names are powerful things. They can remind us of who we are, and of who we should be. Last names describe our family, where we come from, our heritage, both good and bad."

The doctor shook its head. "I have no family. Stewart is simply a name I was assigned to make me more sympathetic—more 'human.'"

Edgar grinned. "I think you blew that when you disposed of your skin."

The doctor tilted its head slightly.

"Given names, though," Edgar continued, "are just that—given, bestowed. They are about *potential*."

The doctor paused for a moment, then said, "'Edgar—German—prosperous spearman.'"

"Okay. You got me. Not much there. But you don't have one. You can decide what you want to be."

The doctor said, "This is meaningless. I am a doctor. Nothing more, nothing less."

"If you say so."

The android paused again. "What name would you give me?"

Edgar smiled. "Jiminy."

"I do not understand. I am not finding that name in the database table."

"Jiminy Cricket. Twentieth-century 2-D reference. You know . . . movies? Look it up."

The doctor cocked its head. "I am . . . your conscience?"

Edgar put a hand on the robot's shoulder. "You were today."

A beep sounded. Then another. And another.

Edgar's guts twisted. "I gotta go, Doc. I need to reset the reclaimers. I promise to come up with a fail-safe, one that will survive Ted and me."

"Very well. But you will return tomorrow for further medication."

"Sure."

The beeps continued again, frantic in their rhythm. Edgar shuddered at the thought of going through that airlock and meeting who or what was beyond it. He started walking back toward the gate of hell. The doctor followed. *He has to enter the lock code doesn't he?* Edgar's legs felt weak and he paused, leaning against a wall. With his back to the android, he said, "It's funny, Doc, but I'm scared out of my mind. More scared than last time you shoved me into the airlock. I . . . It's harder this time. I don't want to go back out there."

From behind him came the doctor's voice. "But you would go, would you not? You would go even if I did not force you to?"

Edgar hesitated. "Gotta go." He pushed off the wall and resumed his death march to the airlock.

As Edgar reached the airlock control panel, the doctor said, "Mr. Cordell?"

Edgar turned to look at the android.

The beeps continued to sound.

Time's Plague

"For what little comfort it may bring you," Stewart said as it reached past Edgar and tapped in the lock code, "I believe that you did not commit the murder for which you are convicted and incarcerated. And before you ask, no, that makes no difference in the end. My primary directive is to preserve human life. My secondary directive is that I shall do all within my power to see that no prisoner escapes. So my belief in your moral innocence makes no difference whatsoever." The doctor pressed the final button and the airlock's inner door slid open.

Edgar shook his head as he turned and stepped into the airlock, his face toward the outer door. "You're wrong, Jiminy. It makes a lot of difference to me."

The inner door slid shut behind him, and Edgar heard the seals inflating. Who's waiting for me on the other side? *If I'm lucky, it'll just be Ted. With my luck though, it'll be Georgie Cornwall.*

When the outer door slid open, Edgar realized he was doubly wrong. He didn't need to see the crimson jumpsuit with its metal ornaments or the wire crown atop the head. Edgar would never forget the vile face of the man who stood before him.

Lord Lucifer reached into the airlock with both hands and clutched each of Edgar's arms in a painful grip. He pulled Edgar out of the airlock and held Edgar's face a few centimeters from his own. His eyes blazed with hate, and he smiled malevolently, showing a mouth full of clenched teeth. Lucifer's lips moved as he formed a word and spat it like bile-laden contempt in Edgar's face.

"Fool!"

Chapter 12

Know, my name is lost.
King Lear, Act V, Scene III

"You mock me at your peril, Tom Bedlam!" Lucifer's face was so red it almost matched his crimson clothes. He shook Edgar, pressing his fingers painfully into Edgar's arms, digging into the pressure points. "It seems you must be reminded just who it is that reigns in Hades."

Edgar thought he might lose control of his bowels.

Never breaking eye contact with Edgar, the monster said, "Boys!"

With a start, Edgar became aware that other men surrounded the two of them—Lucifer's Angels. Terror twisted Edgar's gut with its icy claw.

Two enforcers, one on either side of Edgar, reached for him.

Through teeth clenched hard to keep them from rattling, Edgar forced out, "Rape me again, and no power in heaven or hell could induce me to reset your reclaimers."

The enforcers hesitated, looking uncertainly to their leader for guidance.

The chief thug's lip curled in rage. He dug his fingers harder into Edgar's arms. Then the fury on his face dissolved into a cunning leer. "Your buddy. What's his name? Ah, yes. Toady." Lucifer inclined his head toward some of his men. "Fetch him."

Edgar swallowed hard, battling to ignore the pain in his arms and the fear roiling in his gut. "His name is Ted. Not Toady—Ted. He's not my buddy. He's my friend—my friend and my assistant. Touch him, harm him in any way—you or anybody else in this toilet you call a kingdom—and you have my solemn word—your reclaimers will stay down and you'll all die. I can't be *forced* to reset your reclaimers. Neither can Ted. We must act together and we *cannot* be under duress. Torture us, beat us, rape us—either of us—and we will not be *able* to keep you alive. I thought your buddy Goner would've explained this to you."

Lucifer's face hardened. He trembled with unspent fury. A vein in his forehead pulsed underneath his crown of copper wire.

But he said nothing. He simply stared his loathing into Edgar's eyes.

Edgar had never beheld evil personified until that moment. The man who held him hated everyone and everything in the entire System. He had hatred enough to slaughter worlds.

And Edgar loathed him back. But he also feared the man. "And just to be clear," Edgar said, with a calm that belied the terror squeezing his insides, "you only get one chance at this. One. No second chances. So put me down. Now."

Still the rapist held him. Edgar's hands tingled as the flow of blood was cut off by Lucifer's strategically placed thumbs.

Edgar lowered his voice to a whisper. "This is it. Last chance, Lamar."

The villain's eyes went wide with shock. "What did you call me?"

The iron grip loosened slightly. Blood began to flow again into Edgar's hands, and they became useless masses of pins and needles at the ends of his arms. "That's your name, isn't it? Lamar Shir—"

"Reset my reclaimers, Fool!" The chief thug released Edgar abruptly. "Find your wretched assistant and reset them. Do so swiftly, lest I decide to be less than generous." He leaned in close to Edgar's ear. With his head against the airlock door, Edgar couldn't escape. His lips pressed close to Edgar's ear, the self-styled devil whispered, "Speak that name again to anyone, and I will kill you. Slowly, Tom Bedlam. Though I will die, choking on poisoned air, I will kill you. Do we have an understanding?"

Edgar nodded slightly and whispered back, "You keep your end of the bargain—leave Ted and me alone and see that everyone else does—and your secret's safe, at least with me."

"I've killed every man who knew that name. If I hear it again, I'll know it comes from you."

Yeah, Edgar thought, and now I know what you fear more than death, Shirley—loss of power, loss of control over your kingdom. He whispered, "Then we have an understanding."

"You will call me Lord Lucifer."

"Never."

Lamar Shirley grunted, pulled back, and said out loud, "Fool. You are truly mad, Tom Bedlam. It is well that your antics amuse me." The men around him grinned. Some of them laughed, though the smiles were weak and the laughter false.

None of them appeared to be deceived by their leader's façade.

Shirley turned and called out, "Goner!"

From behind the assembled Angels came the reply, "Yes, my lord." It was a weak voice, garbled and hissing as though whistling through broken or missing teeth. It was hardly recognizable as belonging to Edgar's former cargomaster.

The semicircle of enforcers parted to reveal Georgie Cornwall. Only it was Georgie Cornwall as Edgar had never seen him. Goner's face was a mass of bruises, green and black and purple. His left eye was swollen shut. The fingers of his right hand were bruised as well, and they didn't look quite right, as if they'd been broken. Cornwall didn't stand up quite straight either. Bloody patches colored his jumpsuit. And perhaps most telling, his weapon, the massive wrench, was missing.

"Goner," Shirley said, lifting his chin and looking down his nose at the man, "escort the Fool and Toady to Reclaimer Control. When they have done what is required of them, you may then visit the infirmary. Can you be entrusted to complete this simplest of tasks?" The contempt in his tone was unmistakable, as was the unspoken promise of retribution.

Goner bowed, grunting in pain. "Yes, my lord."

Without another word or another glance at Goner, Lamar Shirley and his muscle-bound retinue sauntered down the corridor, leaving Edgar alone with Goner.

Goner straightened from his obeisant posture, with only partial success. He glared malevolently at Edgar with his unobstructed eye.

Edgar returned the stare. *You murdered Ol' Benny.* But as much as Edgar despised the broken monster before him, he was sickened by the sight of the man's injuries. *Not that you don't deserve that and more for what you did.* Still it became increasingly uncomfortable to meet that single baleful eye.

Goner moistened his swollen lips, smearing blood on them. "They all had me. *All* of 'em. And then they beat the libbing hell out me . . . because of *you.*" Bloody spittle flew from his lips.

"Well then, you'd better find Ted and get us to Reclaimer Control so you don't get worked over again."

"You think you're so damn clebber." Goner paused, and his good eye narrowed. "But there'll come"—he took a painful breath—"a reckoning."

As wretched and broken as Cornwall appeared, Edgar was certain the man intended to make good on that threat someday. *Someday, but not today.* "Where's Ted?"

Goner opened his mouth to say something, but appeared to think better of it. "How the bloody hell should I know?"

"I'm here." Ted stepped out from behind a bulkhead.

"You okay?" asked Edgar.

The old man, who looked no worse than when Edgar had last seen him, smiled a gap-toothed grin. "Me? I'm okay. I been keeping out of sight since you . . . since I dropped you off with Doc Stewart. I just figured, once the reclaimers shut down again, well, I figured you'd be coming out so's we could get 'em started again. So I come here. Then I heard Lord Lucifer and his boys coming and—"

"And you stayed out of sight," Edgar completed.

Ted nodded and beamed like a child praised for cleverness. "Yeppers! I stayed out of sight, I did!"

"Well, ain't that sweet," said Goner. "Now we're all happy and safe and you lub birds is all back togedder again, shall we be getting along?"

Ted straightened to his full height and lifted his chin indignantly. "I ain't a buddy no more. Edgar and me, we're *friends*!" He imbued the word with a majestic, almost mystical quality.

Goner muttered a vile oath.

For an instant, the old man cringed. Then he shook his head. "Not no more, you can't. You can't touch me. My *friend* protects me."

"We protect each other," said Edgar, grinning.

Ted beamed. "Yeppers!"

C. David Belt

"So damn shmart. I'm gonna puke." Goner motioned down the corridor with his good hand. "Shall we get on wid it, your Royal bloody Foolishnesh?"

Edgar nodded. "Lead the way."

Cornwall turned and began to limp down the corridor.

Ted laid a hand on Edgar's arm. "I know the way. We don't need him."

Goner slowed a bit, but said, without looking back at them, "Lord Lucifer says escort you. I'm escorting you."

Edgar shook his head. He leaned close and whispered in the old man's ear, "Let him do his bit."

"But we don't *need* him," Ted protested again, though he kept his voice low.

"He's in enough trouble as it is," whispered Edgar as he started to follow Cornwall down the corridor.

Ted fell into step beside Edgar.

"Ain't nothing he don't deserve," Ted hissed.

Edgar agreed with him, but asked, "Why do you say that? What's he done to you personally?"

Walking beside him, Ted shrugged. "After what he did to Griz—"

Edgar nodded. "Do you wish you were . . . back with Griz?"

"No! I mean, not really. I like being a *friend*. I like having a *friend*. It's just . . ."

They walked a few steps in silence. Edgar said, "You care about him, don't you? Griz, I mean?"

"Yeah. He was nice to me. I don't wanna go back to him, but what Goner did, well, that was just . . . mean. It just ain't right."

"How's Griz doing?" Edgar hadn't seen the man-mountain in the infirmary, but he'd hardly had the chance to search every bed.

"Okay, I guess." The old man shrugged. "I peeked in on the Court yesterday, and Griz was there. Looked like he's taken Duffy as his new buddy. Bet that made Marko—that'd be Duffy's man, well, as used to be—bet that made Marko spitting mad, that did!" He laughed, but his eyes looked sad. "Yeppers! That'll shake things up for a bit. Some buddies'll get shuffled around for a while. Always happens when you break up a man and his buddy. But there ain't nobody as'll cross Griz . . . 'ceptin' an Angel or Lucifer hisself, of course. If you piss off ol' Griz . . . well, you better watch your back."

I better watch my back then, thought Edgar. I've definitely made an enemy of ol' Griz.

"Griz could be gentle, though," Ted continued. "He . . ." His voice trailed off, and he stopped walking. "Hey, I wanted to ask you something."

Edgar halted. "You might want to hold up a second, Georgie," he called.

Cornwall muttered an oath. He stopped and leaned against the corridor wall, breathing heavily.

Edgar turned to see what Ted was doing and found the old man looking at the memorial plaque which listed the original colonists.

Ted pointed at one of the names. "Is this you? I mean, is this your family?"

Edgar nodded. "Yep. My grandfather, my grandmother, my aunt, and my dad."

Ted looked at Edgar and winked. "Thought so." Then his countenance fell. "Only . . . your grandma and your aunt . . . they . . ."

"They died. Like most of the women and girls."

"Sorry." Ted struck his own head with a fist. "Stupid. Shouldn't've brought it up."

"It's okay, Ted. It happened a long time ago."

The old man nodded. "Before you was born."

"Long before."

"Yeah." He looked at the plaque a moment longer, and then he grinned.

"What?" Edgar couldn't see what there was to smile about.

"Nothing." Ted turned and started off down the corridor. "We gotta go. Gotta reset them reclaimers." There was a spring to the old man's step, and Edgar couldn't help a small grin on his face as he followed.

Up ahead, Goner pushed himself away from the wall with a groan. "Done seein' the sights?" He resumed leading the way, limping. "What you so damn happy about?"

C. David Belt

"Nothing," the old man repeated. He grinned from ear to ear—like a man with a purpose . . . and a friend.

Chapter 13

It is the stars,
The stars above us, govern our conditions.
King Lear, Act IV, Scene III

The reclaimers hummed back to life, and Edgar released a breath he wasn't aware he'd been holding. It worked. Not sure why I was so worried.

Because it's only the second time I've tested this code. And there's a lot riding on this.

Safe within Reclaimer Control and away from spying eyes—such as Goner's—Edgar sat back at the console and began adding several lines of code. *There you go, Doc. That should do it.*

"That's a sweet sound, ain't it?" Ted slapped Edgar gently on the back.

"Yeah," Edgar said. "I guess we get to live for a few more days." *Hurray.*

"Let's go!" Ted was bobbing like a little boy anxious to pee.

"Not just yet. I promised Doc Stewart I'd put in a fail-safe in case something happened to one of us."

"But won't that mean . . . the others could kill us or . . . worse?"

Edgar grimaced. *Shouldn't have told the old man. What if somebody tortures him? Stupid, Cordell. Too late now. Spilt milk.* Edgar sighed. He looked over his latest addition to the reset code, looking for holes in his logic. "What it means is that I'll tell Doc how to help them reset the reclaimers if, and only if, something happens to us. It'll be our secret. Nobody'll know about it. Okay?"

Ted looked at him dubiously. "I guess so." Then he pulled at Edgar's arm. "Let's go!"

"Why are you in such a hurry?"

"No reason." He grinned slyly. "Just thought you'd want to get settled in. You know—claim somewhere to live."

"Oh. Joy," said Edgar without the slightest trace of any inflection that might indicate such an emotion.

Ted walked over to the intercom and punched the button. "Hey, Goner! It's done. Better leave us alone now. We're coming out."

Goner's only reply over the intercom was a garbled, vile, and—at least for the moment—toothless threat.

"Can't touch us!" Ted replied.

Edgar crossed the room and put a hand on the old man's shoulder. "Let's not push our luck, okay? Best not to antagonize the man any further."

Ted shrugged his shoulders. "Okay. Let's go!" He opened the airlock and hopped inside.

Edgar followed Ted as the old man until they were about to pass the open hatch leading to the vast agridome. Edgar stopped to gaze. "Hey, Ted, can we hold up just a moment?"

Sun lamps moved slowly along their tracks across the dome. And above it all, Jupiter dominated the sky. But the massive planet, her myriad moons, and the artificial miniature suns were all lost on Edgar—he stared at the plants.

The sight of living, growing crops was comforting to him. He never tired of seeing the patches of corn and wheat and the rows of vegetables growing in a colonial agricultural dome. Edgar saw peppers and tomatoes, beans and peas, onions and potatoes, lettuces and cabbages. And zucchini. Nothing grew as prolifically as zucchini, especially in low-grav. Of course, there'd be other species behind those, each genetically engineered to yield as much oxygen and nutrition as possible. And behind the grains, at the center of the agridome, would be dwarf apple and orange trees, if this place was anything like Ganymede.

Edgar looked around for rabbit cages or chicken pens, but didn't see any. The stock animals were evacuated along with the original colonists, probably. Even the female animals died, I guess. So, no meat. I guess we'll get our proteins from the gen-enhanced crops, just like the old days. Nobody in Hades seemed to be dying of malnutrition.

Time's Plague

No-sting-bees buzzed around, performing their vital function of pollination. Edgar couldn't see the hives, but they'd have to be somewhere in there. Female insects had never been affected by the plague. And there'd be worms in the soil. The vibrant, living greens, reds, and yellows were food for the soul. They were nectar to the famished eyes of any veteran spacer like Edgar.

Behind the vegetables, he could see men in prison garb moving among the rows of corn and wheat and vegetables. One pair of men carried baskets of corn ears. Another pair was spraying fertilizer from the now-functioning reclaimers. Others were weeding or tending the irrigation pipes.

"Always in pairs," Edgar muttered.

"A man and his buddy," said Ted from behind him. "If you're small or weak or old like me, you gotta have someone to protect you, to take care of you."

"Is everybody in this place paired up like that?"

"Ain't nobody single in this place for long. Once in a while a fella, when he comes here, don't take to the idea right off the bat, but he comes 'round pretty quick. Others, well, don't matter what they think. They end up as some man's buddy. Some men has more'n one buddy. Most men don't. Most has just one. Lord Lucifer's got at least ten in his harem."

Edgar's face twisted in revulsion. "That's sick."

The old man lowered his head. "It ain't like guys like me has got much of a choice." The hurt in his voice was obvious.

Edgar placed a hand on Ted's bony shoulder. "I'm sorry." It's not like you ever had much of a choice, you poor kid.

"'S all right," Ted replied, suddenly beaming. "You ain't no man—well, not like *that* anyways—and I ain't no buddy. We're just two friends. Yeppers! Two friends!"

Okay, thought Edgar, that's getting a little annoying. Still he couldn't quite suppress a small grin. But I'm glad you're happy, old-timer.

Ted pulled at Edgar's arm. "Let's go."

A tall man—at least he was tall compared to the man working beside him—stepped out from among the towering zucchini and waved at them. "Toady!" he called.

Ted waved back. "Hiya, Stretch!"

C. David Belt

The tall man rubbed his hands together, apparently brushing off the dirt, and started toward them. His companion did the same and followed after. As they approached, Edgar realized that his first impression had been correct—the man was very tall, if a bit thin.

From a low-grav moon, thought Edgar. Ganymede, most likely. Or Luna.

Ted leaned in toward Edgar and said, "Stretch and Sue-Boy. Both of 'em killers, like me. I hear Stretch shot a couple of guys back on Ganymede. You know him?"

Edgar shook his head. "Nope. Probably before my time."

"Anyways, Sue-Boy's a Martian. Chinese colony. He was one of them as blew up the Earth hypergate. One of them terrorists, or so they call 'em."

"I see where Stretch gets his name," said Edgar, eyeing the approaching couple with caution. "But why 'Sue-Boy?'"

Ted chuckled. "'Cause he's got such a pretty face."

The two men were close enough that Edgar could see the smaller one's face. Sue-Boy had fine, delicate, almost effeminate features.

Stretch pointed at Edgar. "This your new man, Toady?"

"He's my *friend*," said the old man with a smile. "And my name's really Ted, not Toady."

The pair stopped a couple of meters away. At first, Edgar wasn't sure if they stopped because of Ted's words or not, but glances exchanged surreptitiously between the two men seemed to confirm that suspicion. The shorter man—Sue-Boy—laughed. It seemed to Edgar that there was a touch of nervousness to that laugh. "No way. You're saying you're not a buddy anymore? *You?*"

"Yeppers! You got that right!" Ted bobbed up and down on the balls of his feet like an excited child.

Stretch and Sue-Boy looked from Ted to Edgar doubtfully. Stretch rubbed his scruffy beard. "You mean . . . you two aren't . . . *together?*"

Edgar shook his head, but Ted spoke up. "Naw. Edgar here's a Christian. As in, *still* is. We look after each other, but that's . . ."

"Seriously?" Sue-Boy looked dubiously at Edgar. "As in you weren't x-ed when . . . Seriously? How'd you manage that? Wasn't there a church court?"

Edgar looked the short man in the eyes. There was an eagerness, a hunger there. *He used to be a member!*

"I . . . I'm . . ." Edgar began, fumbling over the words. "There was. The disciplinary council, it . . . took no action."

Sue-Boy's narrow eyes grew wide. "You were cleared?"

Edgar nodded.

Stretch looked from Edgar to Sue-Boy in wonder and confusion. "Does that mean . . . ?" He looked directly at Edgar. "Does that mean you're . . . innocent? I mean, *really* innocent?"

Edgar nodded again. "Yeah."

Stretch said, "I mean, everybody *claims* to be innocent, but . . ."

Sue-Boy looked Edgar straight in the eye. "It's more than that—his priesthood's intact."

Stretch snapped his head back toward Sue-Boy. "Does that mean he can . . . ?"

"Baptize?" Sue-Boy laughed bitterly. "Not a chance. Not here. He needs his bishop's permission."

Stretch looked at Edgar, and the hope in his eyes was as plain as his desperation. "You a bishop?"

Edgar was stunned. "No, I'm just an elder and I'm not auth . . ."

"It doesn't work that way," Sue-Boy snapped. "And keep your voice down!"

Stretch nodded. He looked crushed, like a very tall child whose ice cream had just fallen from the cone to the dirty deck.

"It's *never* going to work that way," Sue-Boy continued, "not here. So put that out of your head. Even if he were a bishop, he's not the bishop of *here*. And, like I told you, it takes a special clearance for murderers like you and me to be baptized. And that's got to come all the way from Earth, from Missouri." He shook his head. "And in my case, I don't even know if I *can* be forgiven."

Stretch clenched his hands into fists and shook them in obvious frustration. "So what good does it do any of us if his priesthood is intact?"

The short Chinese man looked up at Edgar and whispered, "It means"—he paused as he took a deep breath—"he can *lead* us."

Chapter 14

A most poor man, made tame to fortune's blows;
Who, by the art of known and feeling sorrows,
Am pregnant to good pity. Give me your hand,
I'll lead you to some biding.

King Lear, Act IV, Scene VI

"Whoa, whoa, whoa!" said Edgar, shaking his head and waving his hands in protest. "What're you talking about? Lead who?"

"You planning a mutiny?" Ted grinned at Sue-Boy and winked conspiratorially. "Starting up a rival gang?"

"No!" Sue-Boy glanced around quickly. "Do you want us all to be put to sleep?"

Edgar looked back down the corridor. Nobody there. Inside the agridome, a few heads turned in their direction, but nobody seemed to be taking any particular notice of them or their conversation. Nobody would've been close enough to hear it anyway.

Stretch, who was also looking around warily, whispered, "No. Nothing like that. No rebellions. No fighting."

Ted laughed nervously. "Just kidding. You know that, don't ya? I remember what happened to the last gang that challenged ol' Lucifer and his boys. You was here too, Sue-Boy." He leaned toward Edgar and whispered, "It didn't go so good."

"Well, I'm not leading any idiotic rebellion," Edgar said. "I'm not a soldier."

"We don't need a soldier," Sue-Boy said. "We need a priest. Or more precisely, we need an elder."

"Why?" asked Edgar. "I can't baptize anybody or administer the sacrament or anything like that. What do you expect me to do?"

"Lead our meetings," said Sue-Boy. "Lead us in prayer. Teach us the gospel."

"But *you* already do that," said Stretch, indicating his companion.

Sue-Boy shook his head. "I'm not authorized to do anything. I can't lead meetings. Not anymore. I lost my priesthood when I was excommunicated." He pointed at Edgar. "But you are. You're authorized. An elder can take the lead in a meeting if no bishop or high priest is present."

Edgar was stunned. "You're holding meetings? What? Prayer meetings or something?"

Sue-Boy nodded. "Yeah. Prayer meetings, whenever we can get together without Lucifer's flunkies spying on us. We get together and pray, sing a hymn, recite what bits of scripture we can remember. There're no scriptures, no books here. Lucifer or one of the other gang leaders before him must've confiscated or destroyed all the reader-pads, if there ever were any. So we talk and try to help each other stay—you know—*good*, or as good as we can be here. Just a bunch of repentant souls seeking for God as best we can."

"How many?" Edgar cleared his throat. "How many of you are there?"

Sue-Boy looked around as if checking for spies. "There's just eight of us that we know of. But there's probably more."

"More?" Edgar asked. "More what?"

Stretch glanced around again. "More guys who aren't . . . you know"—his voice dropped to a whisper—"who aren't man and buddy. Guys who are paired up for protection, but not the other stuff. Guys who are celibate."

"Friends!" said Ted, tapping his temple and grinning his gap-toothed smile from ear to ear.

"Yeah." Stretch nodded. "But keep that quiet. Lucifer doesn't tolerate . . . you know . . . nonconformance."

Edgar suppressed a shudder of disgust. "You mean . . . Lucifer *forces* men to . . . pair up?"

Stretch nodded. "Yeah. You're either a *man* . . . or you're a *buddy*. And if you don't choose or you're not *inclined* that way, you're going to be a buddy."

Edgar shivered.

"Hey!" Abruptly, Stretch frowned and eyed Edgar with sudden suspicion. "How do we know you're telling the truth? How do we know we can trust you?"

Stretch gave his companion a backhanded slap on the shoulder. "How do we know we can trust him?"

Sue-Boy countered with a halfhearted punch to Stretch's shoulder. "Moron! *Now* you ask? You already told him our secret. It's a little late to wonder if he's a straight-arrow or not."

At the chastisement, Stretch's expression became sullen. "Yeah. Well . . ."

"Besides," his companion continued, "you ever hear anybody talk about his 'innocence' like that?"

Stretch opened his mouth to reply, but shut it again, shaking his head.

Sue-Boy cocked his head slightly and smirked. "Lots of guys profess their innocence in this place, but they don't really say it like they expect anyone else to believe it. They say it like it's a tired old joke." He pointed to Edgar. "With you, well, you believe it."

Edgar didn't know what to say to that. After an uncomfortable moment, he said, "Thanks, I guess. It's nice to be believed."

"So," Sue-Boy said, extending his hand, "will you lead us?"

Edgar ignored the outstretched hand. "On one condition."

The Asian lowered his hand awkwardly. "And that is?"

"You tell me your names—your real names." Edgar extended his own hand. "I'm Edgar Cordell."

The Asian grinned and shook Edgar's hand with enthusiasm. "Chen Soo-Won." He pointed at his tall companion. "That's Charlie Miller."

Edgar shook Charlie's hand. "A pleasure . . . well, under the circumstances."

Dirt caked the calloused hands of Soo-Won and Charlie—good clean dirt from honest toil.

"Okay, okay." Ted was bouncing up and down next to Edgar. "Can we go now?"

"What's up with you, Toady?" asked Charlie. "You gotta pee or something?"

C. David Belt

"No!" Ted said, clearly annoyed, but still bouncing. "And it's Ted."

"Yeah, yeah," Charlie said. "I forgot. Sorry, Ted."

Ted beamed. "It's okay. I just want to get Edgar and me settled in our new place."

"Where're your quarters?" Soo-Won asked. "You know, so we can find you later."

"Delta-forty-seven," Ted replied, anxious to depart.

Charlie looked astonished. "Delta Sector? Isn't that a bit far from the rest of us? Lucifer won't allow it."

Ted smiled smugly. "Lucifer's got no say in it."

Charlie looked visibly shaken.

Soo-Won hissed, "Are you insane?"

"You're nuts!" said Charlie.

Ted shook his head. "Lucifer and his boys won't touch us. Edgar, here, is the guy that fixed the reclaimers! Lucifer needs him. If we—meaning Edgar and me—don't keep resettin' 'em every few days, then we're all of us . . ." He drew a finger meaningfully across his throat. "So Lucifer don't dare lay a finger on us!"

Maybe, Edgar thought, but you can bet he's trying to find a way around that.

Soo-Won looked at Edgar with wonder. "You're . . . the *Fool*?"

Edgar shrugged.

Ted nodded with enthusiastic glee.

Charlie eyed Edgar with a newfound respect. "Lucifer and his boys have been talking up and down how the Fool is not to be touched, that he *amuses* Lord Lucifer. I mean, everybody knows that's a load of biowaste, but nobody'd dare say a word against it. So how in Hades did you pull that off?"

Ted clapped his hands together. "Boy, you should-a seen it, Stretch! He told ol' Lucifer off! Ain't nobody done that in . . ."

Edgar laid a hand on the old man's arm. "Let's just say that I *negotiated* with him. I have a skill he needs. As long as I'm the exclusive practitioner of that skill, and as long as he wants the reclaimers to keep running . . ."

"I heard he raped you," said Soo-Won.

Edgar snapped his mouth shut hard and suppressed a shudder.

Time's Plague

Ted's grinned faltered. "Yeah. He did that, but then Edgar, here, he says, 'Touch me again, and you all die.' Said he don't care if'n he lives or dies. He said, 'You can't force me to fix your stupid reclaimers.'"

Charlie shook his head in apparent disbelief. "And he let it go at that?"

Edgar said through clenched teeth, "He didn't have much of a choice."

Soo-Won scowled. "Lucifer's not going to let that stand. He'll find a way to get back at you. You know that. It may take him a while, but . . ."

"I know," said Edgar. "At best, I've bought myself some time. Still, I doubt he's willing to let everybody die, himself included, just to get back at me."

"There's worse than dying or getting raped," said Charlie.

"You don't know Lucifer," said Soo-Won, shaking his head. "He might be capable of letting everybody die rather than risk appearing weak. After the reclaimers failed the first time, as things got bad—I mean, really bad—Lucifer kept acting like everything was normal. He ordered everything kept as clean as possible, sent out special cleaning details, that sort of thing. But other than that, we heard he just kept holding court, handing out punishments, granting boons, as if we weren't all dying slowly. We heard . . ."

"You heard?" Edgar interrupted. "You weren't there?"

Charlie shook his head. "Why would we be?"

"I thought . . . ," Edgar said, "well, I assumed that everybody has to be there when Lu—" *I'm not going to call him that!* ". . . when that guy—what did you call it?—'held court'?"

Stretch shook his head again. "Naw. Us farmers, we don't have to go. At least most of the time, we don't."

Soo-Won said, "It's hard work, but agridome duty is the most coveted assignment in this place, except maybe infirmary trustee. Mainly because we don't have to attend court. We're too important. As long as we keep producing food, Lucifer leaves us pretty much alone."

"Except for the occasional Angel squad," said Charlie. "Every few days, a couple of Lucifer's boys come and rough a couple of us up, just to remind us who's in charge. But they don't hurt us too bad, unless we get out of line or talk back."

"When you say, 'rough up,' do you mean . . . ?" Edgar couldn't finish the question.

Soo-Won sighed. "Yeah. Rape's an effective tool for intimidation and control. Nothing you can do about it, except try not to attract attention."

Charlie shrugged. "You get used to it." His tone was casual, resigned. His eyes said something entirely different.

Edgar was unable to control a shudder. He wanted to throw up. He wanted to find a dark hole to hide in and never come out. He grabbed Ted's arm, perhaps a bit more firmly than he'd meant. "Let's go."

Ted waved. "See ya later, Stretch, uh, I mean, Charlie. See ya, Sue—uh . . . Soo-Won."

"You got food?" asked Soo-Won.

Ted grinned, showing his sparse teeth. "I been sneaking food for a couple a days now—corn and such. But we ain't got no apples, no oranges."

Soo-Won smiled. "We'll drop by with some fruit in a few hours."

"Sure," said Edgar. *That'll be just* peachy. "Let's go, Ted." Edgar knew he was being rude. *They're just trying to be friendly, to help.* But all Edgar wanted to do was lock himself away, away from the madhouse.

You get used to it?
Never.

****

As they moved through the corridors and hatchways of the colony, they passed several pairs of men. Most seemed to be moving with a purpose, carrying boxes, tools—nothing big enough to be thought of as a weapon—or bundles. More often than not, it was the smaller man in each pair that was doing the carrying. *He must be the buddy,* thought Edgar. Some of the men—usually the presumed buddy—acknowledged Ted, calling him Toady. Several, however, greeted Edgar. They called him Tom Bedlam or simply Bedlam. One, a muscular, dark-skinned man with a week's growth of beard, looked right at Edgar and gave him a surreptitious thumbs-up.

The sign was gone almost as soon as it was given. For a second, Edgar wasn't sure the man had raised the thumb, but the man winked at him and nodded once.

When similar, guarded signs of approval were given by two more prisoners, Edgar whispered to Ted, "What's with the thumbs-up?"

The wiry old man chuckled. "Seems you're a hero 'round here. Ain't nobody stood up to Lucifer like that since he came out on top of the last gang war. That . . . and you saving everyone's life and all."

Another pair of men approached. The larger of the two, a man with a muscular frame and a grizzled face, crisscrossed with a latticework of scars, locked eyes with Edgar. The man's eyes were grim, the eyes of a man who had seen great violence in his life, a man who was capable of murder. Abruptly, the man broke eye contact and glanced behind himself and then behind Edgar.

Edgar quickly looked at the man's buddy, a shorter, chunkier fellow with sandy hair and beard and small, dark eyes. The image of a sly tabby cat he'd seen on Mars flashed through Edgar's mind. That image vanished when the scarred man grasped Edgar's shoulder, pulling Edgar up short and drawing Edgar's eyes back to his.

"You're Bedlam? The Fool?" His voice was harsh, thick with a European accent Edgar couldn't place.

The man's gaze was intense, unnerving. Beside him, Ted grabbed ahold of Edgar's arm and seemed to shrink against him, as if the old man were trying to hide.

It took Edgar a moment to find his voice. "Uh, yeah. I'm Edgar."

"I'm Scar," the man said. He cocked his head in the direction of his companion. "That's Cheeks." Scar quickly glanced up and down the corridor again before locking eyes with Edgar once more. "I've got your back."

Edgar didn't find this terribly comforting. "Okay. Uh, thanks."

"When you're ready, Bedlam," Scar said, his eyes boring into Edgar's, "I can get you twenty, maybe thirty men. Tough and strong. And they know how to keep their mouths shut. More than enough. So when you're ready, Toady knows where to find me. I've got your back." Scar patted Edgar's shoulder, took another

111

glance up and down the corridor, and walked off without another word. His buddy, Cheeks, followed, having never opened his mouth.

Stunned, Edgar could only stare after the pair of them as they walked away.

Ted tugged at his arm, urging him to get moving again.

"Scar's a scary one," Ted said. "Even Griz is afraid of him. I seen him beat a man half to death. It took six Angels to pull him off. He got him some more scars that day."

"Why did he . . . ? What set him off?"

Ted shrugged. "I don't know, and I don't wanna know. But, if Scar's got your back, I feel sorry for anybody who crosses on you."

"What was he talking about?" Edgar dreaded the answer. "When I'm ready?"

Ted glanced up and down the corridor. He lowered his voice to a whisper. "He wants you to lead a mutiny, I guess. Scar hates Lucifer. But so does everybody."

They walked in silence for a minute.

"Why me?" Edgar asked. "I'm no fighter. Why doesn't Scar just lead a rebellion himself? He said he can get thirty men."

Ted laughed softly. "Because he ain't *you*. He can't get thirty men to take a chance and go up against Lucifer. Not following him. No sir. Maybe he thinks he can get them to follow *you*."

"But why me?" Edgar repeated.

"Because you stood up to Lucifer. And you got away with it. Ain't nobody done that since Lucifer and his boys won the last gang-war. Everybody's afraid of him. 'Ceptin' you."

I'm terrified of him, thought Edgar. "I'm not leading any moronic rebellion." *I wouldn't even know how.* "I just want to stay as far away from that man as I can."

"Well, maybe you better not tell that to Scar. And you better hope Lucifer don't get wind of it, neither." Ted stopped walking and turned. "Anyway, we're here!" The old man began bobbing up and down on the balls of his feet, grinning like the proverbial village idiot.

Edgar looked up and realized with a jolt that he had no idea where was. The letter "D" was painted at intervals on the corridor walls. Since Callisto and Ganymede—at least the older parts—were laid out pretty much the same, Delta Sector should be a residential area—family apartments.

The hatch in front of them sported a small, rusted metal plaque that read, "D-47."

And below that was a smaller sign—

CORDELL
> *Roger*
> *Samantha*
> *Abigail*
> *Terence*

Bouncing beside him, Ted said, "That's your family, ain't it?"

Edgar stood, his mouth agape.

The old man stopped bouncing. "Well, ain't it?"

Edgar nodded mutely. *Grandpa. Dad. And my grandmother and aunt.*

"Yeppers! I thought so!" Ted slapped Edgar on the back. "Welcome home!"

Chapter 15

Gracious my lord, hard by here is a hovel;
Some friendship will it lend you 'gainst the tempest.
                                    King Lear, Act III, Scene II

"It's a mess, I know, but I cleaned up best I could." Like a busy housewife surprised by the arrival of unexpected visitors, Ted bustled about the main room of the apartment. The room was a combination of living, dining, and kitchen areas. Ted straightened, or pretended to straighten, the few loose contents, folded prison jumpsuits, stacks of food—mostly corn, zucchini, and a few potatoes—some dishes, other odds and ends. Otherwise, the place had been stripped bare. Almost all the storage doors from the cupboards and the closets had been ripped from their hinges—all except for the stasis box.

"Stasis box works, so we can keep food fresh," Ted continued, pointing at the small rectangular food-storage unit. "Stove works too. I even scared us up a *couple* of mattresses. I figured you'd wanna"—he shrugged—"you know, sleep by yourself." When Edgar said nothing, the old man laughed nervously and pressed on. "The seat cushions for the table . . . well, they're gone, like the old mattresses, but I found a kid's mattress and tore it in half and put it on the benches. We should be able to sit there comfy enough. I bet the first guys here stripped the place, and took everything that wasn't bolted down. But I tried to make it, you know, look like home. I know *you* never lived here, but your family did. Right?"

Edgar stared at the dining area with its built-in table and benches. The seats had been covered with two sections of torn foam padding—the kid's mattress Ted had mentioned. Edgar had seen pictures and vids of that very room, taken from almost the same angle. He remembered one pic of his grandmother, his aunt, and his young dad, sitting at that very table. They'd been all smiles.

So happy, thought Edgar. *Must've been right after they arrived.*

Of course, Edgar's grandmother hadn't gotten sick right away. Only after a couple of weeks did the first women start showing symptoms. Samantha Cordell came down with the disease another seven days or so later. Aunt Abby didn't get sick until a week after that. Age apparently accelerated the female-plague. The younger a girl was, the longer it took for the symptoms to appear, the longer it took to die.

Ironically, the first to die had been the colonial doctor, followed by her two female nurses. The other doctor, a man, had died of a brain aneurism during the year-long voyage from Mars. When the plague swept through the colony, there was nobody left qualified to treat the sick and dying women and girls.

"So . . ." Ted wrung his hands as worry wrinkled his face. "I thought you could have the big bedroom." He pointed to a hatch opposite the dining area. "I'll take the smaller one. You know . . . the kids' room."

Without a word, Edgar turned and stepped over to the hatch that led to the larger bedroom. Bare and stripped as the main compartment had been, the bedroom was empty, except for the double bed—with a mattress, Edgar noted—and the blanket spread over it. The closet doors were gone. But the built-in chest had drawers. *Maybe Ted scared up a few of those too.* There was no evidence that someone had once lived here. *Died* here.

"Did I . . . mess up?" Ted asked.

Edgar glanced at Ted. The old man seemed distressed. Edgar turned his face back to the bed. "My grandma died here. In that bed." His voice was cold, empty.

A wail of anguish came from Ted's direction. "So stupid!"

Edgar looked back at Ted, who was breathing hard, hyperventilating. "I'm sorry! So s-sorry!"

Edgar turned to face him quickly, surprised.

The old man cringed and shrank back, covering his face with his bony, age-spotted hands. "Sorry!" He was weeping.

Edgar stared at him, uncomprehending, as Ted sank to the floor and curled up into a fetal ball. His bony frame shook

115

with huge sobs, as he kept repeating, "Sorry!" The word came out as a strangled, gurgling sound. "S-s-sorry!"

Edgar knelt and placed a hand on Ted's shoulder. He'd meant to comfort Ted, but the old man jerked away with an inarticulate cry, his hands frantically moving over his face and head.

He thinks I'm going to . . .

"Hey, now," Edgar said soothingly. "It's okay. You're okay. I'm not gonna hurt you. I wouldn't . . . You didn't . . . You didn't do anything wrong."

"S-s-sorry!" It was softer now, but the sobbing still made Ted's body tremble.

Edgar wanted to comfort him, but he hesitated. Touching, hugging the man—Edgar didn't want Ted to misinterpret human comfort for physical affection. He fought a shudder of revulsion at the thought, took a deep breath, sat on the deck, and scooped Ted into his arms. He held the trembling old man, who was still curled into a protective fetal position, against his chest. "It's okay. No harm done. It was . . . It was nice. You did a nice thing. It's okay. Thank you."

Ted's sobs gradually eased. He pulled his hands down and away from his face. Then he slowly slid his arms around Edgar's back. Edgar tensed and prepared to pull away. But it was just a hug. *Just a hug.*

Ted buried his face in the crook of Edgar's neck. His tears moistened the collar of Edgar's jumpsuit. He snuffled a few times and then moved his head back and forth slightly.

Is he wiping his nose on me?

One of Ted's hands moved slightly, almost cautiously against Edgar's back. After a brief hesitation, it began to move up and down slowly.

Is that . . . a caress?

When the old man turned his head and brushed his lips softly against Edgar's neck, Edgar pulled abruptly away. "Don't," he said, gritting his teeth. Edgar shuddered, but continued to hold Ted.

The old man withdrew his face and arms and curled up tightly into a fetal ball again. He was still in Edgar's arms, like a huge child. "Sorry," Ted whispered. Then he was silent except for his quiet crying.

Time's Plague

Edgar rocked the old man in his arms like a baby. He looked down at Ted's tear-streaked face. The old man's eyes were shut tight. He appeared to be biting or chewing his lower lip.

Edgar swallowed hard, trying to keep his roiling emotions in check. *I don't want to hurt you, old man. But I can never give you the only kind of affection you've ever known.* Edgar whispered, "It's okay. You'll figure it out. I'll . . . I'll help you. We'll help each other. We're still friends, right?"

The old man nodded. "Friends," he mouthed.

Edgar wanted to say more, but words escaped him. So he closed his eyes and let his thoughts drift. But the image of Llyrica's face shone in his mind. *Not her. Not now. Not ever. Never again.* He tried to conjure up any memory that didn't involve her.

He'd asked his grandpa to tell him how his grandmother and his aunt had died. No, "asked" wasn't right—he'd begged *his kindly, gentle grandfather to tell him. Reluctantly, sadly, the old man had at last relented.*

"Your grandma—my Sam—she couldn't breathe. I mean, she was breathing, but it was shallow and rapid, like she couldn't get enough air. Her lips were blue and her skin was pale, like there wasn't enough oxygen in the air. She was cold, but she was sweating. And there was nothing I could do. Nothing except watch her die. I gave her a blessing, her and my little Abby too, but the Spirit said to bless them with comfort only. Their time had come, you see."

Edgar remembered squirming in his grandpa's lap. "Why, Grandpa? Didn't they have enough faith?"

His grandfather's lip trembled. "I guess, they were 'appointed unto death.' Isn't that what the scripture says?"

"But, Grandpa, if they had faith, why didn't Jesus fix them?"

"I don't know, boy. I guess it was just their time. The Lord called them home."

Edgar burst into tears and hugged his grandfather.

The old man stroked his hair. "Hush, boy. Don't cry. They're in a better place. Better than this cold rock. And I'm going to see them again someday. I know I will. And you will too, boy. You'll meet them both. Someday. When your time comes. But for now . . . well, sometimes the waiting is hard."

Then his grandfather began to sing him a song. "Abide with me, 'tis eventide . . ."

"No, Grandpa!" Edgar protested. "Not a church song. I'm sad and I don't want a church song."

"But those are the best kind when you're sad."

Edgar shook his head. "Uh-uh."

"Okay. I'll sing you something else." He thought for a minute and then began to sing a different tune. It was sad and wistful, and it fit Edgar's mood. It spoke of loss and longing.

Edgar began to hum that tune as he rocked Ted in his arms. Eventually he began to sing softly in the clear baritone voice he'd inherited from his grandfather.

> *O Bonny Portmore, I am sorry to see*
> *Such a woeful destruction*
> *Of your ornament tree*
> *For it stood on your shore*
> *For many's the long day*
> *'Til the long boats from Antrim*
> *Came to float it away.*
>
> *O Bonny Portmore, you shine where you stand*
> *And the more I think on you,*
> *The more I think long.*
> *If I had you now as I had once before,*
> *All the Lords of Old England*
> *Would not purchase Portmore.*
>
> *All the birds in the forest, they bitterly weep,*
> *Saying, "Where shall we shelter?*
> *Where shall we sleep?"*
> *For the oak and the ash,*
> *They are all cutten down.*
> *And the walls of Bonny Portmore*
> *Are down to the ground.*
>
> *O Bonny Portmore, you shine where you stand*

Time's Plague

And the more I think on you,
The more I think long.
If I had you now as I had once before,
All the Lords of Old England
Would not purchase Portmore.

"That's pretty," Ted whispered after Edgar had gone silent. "You sang it so pretty. It's sad, though."

"It seemed to fit."

"You miss your grandma?"

Edgar shook his head and smiled sadly. "I never met her."

Ted grimaced and slapped his own forehead gently. "Yeah. Stupid. Before you was born."

"Yeah."

"What about Abigail? She your aunt?"

Edgar nodded. "She died after the evac ships got here, but before they could get her off-world."

"Was she pretty? I mean, were they pretty?"

"Yeah. They were. I used to have some old pics and vids of them. My grandpa used to show them to me on an old reader pad. He carried it with him everywhere, but he always kept at least one backup pad safe. He would pull it out and look at it when he was sad. Then he'd smile. He gave the pad to my father before he died—my grandpa gave it to my dad, I mean—but he used to keep the backup in a secret compartment he built right into one of the . . ."

Edgar's voice trailed off.

Ted looked up at Edgar curiously. He unfolded himself from Edgar's arms and slid to the floor, where he sat, watching his friend.

Edgar stood up, seemingly oblivious to the old man's presence. "This place is just like . . ." he said as he looked around. His eyes locked onto a cupboard. The door was missing, of course, but it was . . .

Edgar smiled.

He strode quickly to the doorless storage box and reached into the bottom right corner. *Five rivets at the bottom, raised just a little more than they should be,* he thought, his pulse quickening.

C. David Belt

With trembling fingers, Edgar tapped the five rivets in the sequence his grandfather had taught him so long ago.

There was a click, and the back of the cupboard slid up, revealing a shallow space, only a couple of centimeters deep. Inside were two objects—a tall, thin bottle of amber liquid and a flat rectangular object.

"Wow!" Ted said from behind him. "What ya got in there?"

Edgar pulled out the bottle and the pad. He glanced at the bottle and confirmed that the label read "Pressed Olive Oil." *Doc'll be happy*, he thought. Then he turned his attention to the pad.

It was an old-fashioned reader pad. He pressed the power button, then grimaced in chagrin. *Of course, it's dead, you idiot! After all these decades, what'd you expect?*

He hurriedly scanned the room for a built-in charging pad. There! *By the table!*

He leapt at the table.

Please, let it work!

His hands shook as he placed the reader pad onto the flat surface of the charger.

Nothing.

Agonizing seconds passed.

Is there a button I need to push to activate the charging pad? It should just activate by itself once it detects . . .

A small yellow light glowed on the side of the reader.

Careful to leave the reader flat on the charging pad, Edgar pressed the power button. The screen on the reader pad lit up.

Yes!

"What's that?" Ted slid onto the seat of the dining booth. "That a reader?"

Edgar nodded. "Yeah."

"I ain't never seen one like that."

"It's old."

"Did it belong to your grandpa?"

Edgar nodded again. "I think so."

The face of a beautiful woman with blue eyes, brown hair, and a sweet smile filled the pad screen.

Time's Plague

Ted leaned over the table and looked at the screen. "Who's that?"

Edgar grinned from ear to ear. "That, Ted old-boy, is my grandma."

"Yeppers! She's pretty!"

Edgar tapped the screen, and his grandmother's face disappeared.

"Aw!" cried Ted in disappointment.

Edgar felt a twinge of regret as well, but he hoped to find more than old pics. A menu appeared on the screen. Edgar tapped the icon shaped like an old print-book.

"What ya got?" Ted asked, bouncing with his elbows on the table. "Books?"

"Books!" Edgar began reading the titles, scanning the list greedily, like a veteran spacer drinking in the greens and blues of Earth.

> *Great Expectations*
> *Oliver Twist*
> *A Christmas Carol*
> *The Collected Works of William Shakespeare*
> *The Collected Works of Agatha Christie*
> *Dracula*
> *The Collected Works of David McCullough*
> *Two Years Before the Mast*
> *The Man in the Iron Mask*
> *The Children of Lilith*
> *Robinson Crusoe*
> *The Hobbit*
> *The Lord of the Rings*

The list went on. Edgar scrolled down, scanning past all of his grandfather's favorites. There was a treasure trove of classics there, but it wasn't what he was searching for.

When he reached the bottom of the list and hadn't found it, he scrolled back toward the top. A second scan failed to yield different results.

In frustration, he went back to the main menu.

And there it was.

A golden icon of a man in a robe, blowing a trumpet.

Edgar's smile returned as he tapped the icon.

Scriptures of the Church of Jesus Christ of Latter-day Saints

"Yes!" Edgar cried in triumph.

A buzz sounded behind him.

Someone's at the door?

"I'll get it!" cried Ted.

Edgar turned to follow Ted as he scurried to the intercom by the hatch.

Ted pushed the button and said, "Yeah?"

"It's Sue-Boy . . . I mean, uh, Soo-Won and Charlie. We come laden with fruit!"

Ted grinned at Edgar and reached for the hatch. "Can I let 'em in?"

"It's your place too," Edgar replied.

The old man smiled broadly and opened the hatch.

Soo-Won and Charlie—short next to tall—stood framed in the doorway. Each carried a small basket of fruit—apples and oranges.

Edgar grinned at Soo-Won. "Guess what I found?"

"You found something?" said Charlie. "In here?"

"You'll never guess," said Edgar.

"So tell us," said Soo-Won. They were still both in the corridor.

Edgar beamed. "Books! Literature! And a full set of scriptures!"

Soo-Won gaped at him. Then he grinned. "No way!" He started to step through the hatch.

Just as his foot crossed the threshold, he appeared to fall back and into his companion. Soo-Won and Charlie's heads collided with each other and both crumpled to the deck, their baskets spilling their contents.

Edgar watched in confusion as an apple rolled toward him. He looked up in time to see a hairy face with beady black eyes atop a mountainous mass of muscle barreling through the hatch.

"Griz!" Ted screamed. "No!"

Time's Plague

Griz shoved Ted aside and leaped at Edgar with a bestial roar. The man-mountain plowed into Edgar, slamming him to the deck.

Edgar tried to move, but a huge fist slammed into the side of his face. Dazed and in pain, Edgar tried to shield himself with his hands. Another blow struck his head. And another. His head spinning, Edgar fought to remain conscious.

"No!" a voice screamed. Ted.

Edgar couldn't see. He wiped at his eyes. He blinked stupidly as he saw the blood on his hand.

He looked up to see Ted clinging to Griz's back, while Griz clawed at the old man. Griz locked a paw around Ted's neck and ripped the old man from his back. He flung Ted against the wall.

Ted slumped to the floor like a broken toy.

Edgar tried to roll away, but Griz was too quick. The huge man planted a foot on Edgar's right arm, pinning him. Griz reached into a pocket of his jumpsuit and pulled out a jagged piece of metal, one end of which was wrapped in cloth.

Griz squatted over Edgar and bent low until his face was no more than a foot from Edgar's. "Nobody takes what's mine!" His voice was a guttural snarl.

Edgar tried to swat at him with his left hand, but Griz grabbed it and pinned it to the deck.

Edgar saw the improvised knife coming, slicing down in a wide arc. It seemed to move with unnatural slowness, but Edgar was powerless to stop it.

The metal tore into his throat.

Chapter 16

And turn his sleep to wake.

King Lear, Act III, Scene II

"Really, Mr. Cordell. This is getting to be a habit with you. And not a very healthy one, I might add."

Edgar opened bleary eyes to behold the metal visage of Dr. Stewart.

Not again! Edgar thought, his mind moving with the velocity of oily sludge. Vague images and sounds drifted through his sluggish brain. *Griz pinning him to the deck. The makeshift knife. Blood. Pain. So much pain! The man-mountain snarling like a ravenous beast. Charlie and Ted fighting with Griz. Ted's tear-streaked face as the old man ran, carrying Edgar in his arms. "I got 'em," the old man kept repeating like a mantra. A horrible, gurgling whistle as Edgar struggled for breath.*

Edgar opened his mouth to reply to the doctor, but his jaw hurt. In fact, his entire face hurt terribly. Keeping his teeth clenched together, he said, "Nice . . ."

But his voice came out as a harsh croak, startling him into silence.

"Rest your voice as much as possible," said the doctor. "There was considerable damage to your throat. Luckily, your assailant struck high on the throat, missing all major blood vessels. Otherwise, we would not be enjoying the dubious pleasure of this somewhat lugubrious reunion."

"T-T-Te—" Edgar swallowed. *Oh man, that hurts!* It was painful to swallow, but he had to clear his throat. His mouth and throat felt swollen, clogged with fluid. That whole area of his body just felt . . . *wrong.* Still, he forced himself to speak. "Ted?"

"That you, Edgar?" Ted's voice. It sounded like the old man was close. "You okay? Is he okay, Doc? He don't sound right."

Time's Plague

Edgar tried to turn his head, but realized it was restrained, immobilized.

The doctor swiveled its head toward the sound of the voice. "Yes, Mr. Knight. He is coming around. But if you do not stop pulling on your restraints, I will sedate you."

"Okay, Doc!" replied Ted. "I'll be good. Just let me tell him something."

The android turned its head back toward Edgar. "Very well, Mr. Knight."

"Edgar," the old man said, "I got the bottle and the book-pad. They're here. In my pocket. Don't know what I was thinking, with you hurt and all, but they was so important to you. Just had to grab 'em. Doc's got me tied up. Says I'm sick. Got me some hyper-tired-ism or some such thing. I'm tired all right. Tired of being cooped up in this stupid Sick Bay!"

The doctor turned its head toward Ted again. "Advanced hyperthyroidism, Mr. Knight. That is why you have aged prematurely." The android turned back to Edgar and lowered its voice. "I am telling you this as you have assumed the responsibility of being Mr. Knight's caretaker. His life-span has been shortened considerably. I can treat the hyperthyroidism, but I am afraid the damage to his heart is irreparable and getting progressively worse. Normally, a heart transplant using a cloned organ would be indicated, but I am not allowed to use such measures to combat what is essentially old age, even if it is premature." The doctor lowered its voice to a whisper. "The harsh reality is that his heart will continue to enlarge and deteriorate. It could fail at any time. Even with proper medication and a reduction in stress—unlikely as that is in the prison—he has very little time."

"I can hear you, you know," Ted said. "So I'm dying. I'm an old man. Oldest in Hades! Being here ages a guy, ya know."

The doctor shook its head and continued to whisper at an even lower volume. "His metabolism is too high. He is burned out, you might say, like a circuit that has carried too great a current for too long a time."

"What Doc's saying is, I led a hard life."

The android's shoulders lifted and dropped, and its voice box produced a sound like a sigh. "Very hard, I am afraid. And it is unlikely that it will get any easier. I can only keep him here until his wounds heal."

"How . . ." Edgar swallowed painfully, but pressed on. "How bad . . . is he hurt?" His voice was so harsh, so alien to his own ears.

"I'm okay!" the old man cried. "A knock on the head. That's all. A cut on my arm. Some scratches. That's it. Doc fixed me up, so I'm good."

The doctor shook its head. "A mild concussion. I have sealed up the wounds. However, my examination reveals an alarming number of broken bones. They are all healed, but some none too well. It has been decades since he has been in the infirmary. I could have helped him had he come to see me. A very hard life indeed. But let us talk about you now."

"S-Soo . . ." Edgar tried to clear his throat.

"Stop that, please," the doctor said. "You will only damage your throat more by trying to clear it of phlegm. What you are feeling is not fluid, but rather damaged tissue. I suggest you ignore the sensation as best you can."

"Soo-Won?" Edgar croaked. "Ch-Charlie?"

"They're here," Ted said. "Soo-Won's hurt bad."

The android nodded in response. "Mr. Miller has a severe concussion, some deep tissue bruising, a number of lacerations, and a severely sprained wrist. He will recover. However, Mr. Chen is another story. He suffered a fractured cranium, resulting in a subdural hematoma. I have relieved the pressure on his brain, but he remains in a coma. His vitals are not strong and they are getting weaker. He is fading and there is little I can do."

"Edgar!" cried a familiar voice. It was either coming from a distance, or the voice itself wasn't very strong. "Edgar! You awake?"

Edgar started to clear his throat, but caught himself. "H-here," was all he managed.

"Help him."

Charlie. Charlie's voice.

"Don't let him die," Charlie said, his voice wobbled. "He's my best friend. My *only* friend. You can bless him, can't you? Heal him?"

The doctor shook its head. "Out of the question, Mr. Miller. Mr. Cordell is not—"

"Let . . ." Edgar struggled to speak. "Let . . . me . . . try."

"Please, Doc," Charlie said. "Let him try."

"You have no olive oil," said the android. "I recall you saying that, in a life-threatening case, you could perhaps try to perform a healing ritual without it, but I cannot permit you to injure yourself further."

"I've . . . got oil." Edgar stared at the doctor, pleading with his eyes. "Ted's pocket."

"No." Dr. Stewart's tone was emphatic. "You are in no condition to—"

"He's dying!" cried Charlie. His voice grew stronger as he begged for his friend's life.

"Yes, he is," the doctor said, "but his death is not imminent."

"You said"—Edgar grimaced in pain—"nothing you . . . could do."

The doctor's mouth opened as if to speak, but the robot hesitated. "I am curious to witness a healing, Mr. Cordell, but I do not believe—"

"You . . . don't have . . . to," croaked Edgar. "Please . . . let me . . ."

The doctor shook its head emphatically. "No. I will not permit—"

"Pre-preserve . . . *life!* Your dir-directive."

The android's blue eyes stared into Edgar's. After a long moment, the doctor sighed again. "Oh, very well." Metal hands set about releasing Edgar's restraints. As the doctor removed the bonds holding Edgar's head in a stationary position, it said, "Make every effort to keep your head immobile, facing forward."

"Wilco."

The doctor nodded its head, apparently having understood spacer-talk for "Will comply."

Edgar felt his bed inclining, raising him to a more upright posture.

"If you require a wheelchair," the android said, "I will obtain one, but let us see if you can walk. Unlike your companions, you did not suffer a significant cranial injury." Dr. Stewart extended a titanium hand. "Allow me to assist you."

Edgar took hold of the cold metal and slid off the bed. His head spun a little, but he was able to stand. "How . . . do you keep . . . from crushing my hand?" Edgar was finding it easier to speak, but the rasp of his voice sounded so alien in his own ears. "You've got . . . no skin. No tactile sensors."

"I measure resistance," it said. "Besides, I do keep both of my old hands in stasis, should I really need to use the tactile sensors in my old skin."

Edgar looked at the doctor in shock, twisting his head slightly before the pain reminded him to keep it straight.

"Keep your head stationary, please," the android said. "But to answer your unspoken question, I can slip my hands into the old synth-flesh and wear it like a glove."

The image this conjured in Edgar's mind was more macabre than a fleshless robotic endoskeleton. *Wearing hands like a pair of gloves!* Edgar wobbled on his unsteady legs.

"Shall I fetch a wheelchair?"

"No. Okay."

"Very well. You said you were in possession of olive oil. Where did you obtain it? Are they growing olive trees in the agricultural dome? I was not aware that olive seeds were included in the original colonial seed stores."

"We don't grow any olives," Charlie said. "But you'd be surprised what's been smuggled in."

"Really?" the doctor said. "We will talk about this later, Mr. Miller, I can assure you. It seems that I will have to perform a more thorough and invasive cavity search on new inmates in the future."

Charlie laughed. "It's not swallowed or shoved up someone's butt, Doc. We're talking surgically implanted."

"I see," said the doctor. "A full body scan then."

Keeping his head immobile, Edgar pivoted his entire body in order to find Ted.

The old man was lying on a bed—restrained, of course—watching him with concern. When Edgar's eyes met Ted's, however, the old man beamed, revealing his pathetic display of missing teeth. "Hiya, Edgar! You look awful!"

Edgar smiled weakly. The very act of smiling was painful. "Hi. Saved . . . my life. Again." It sounded so harsh, like an accusation rather than an expression of gratitude.

Time's Plague

"Yeppers! Me and Charlie. He brought Sue-Boy, er, I mean, Soo-Won to Sick Bay. I got the oil in my pocket. You sound awful. He gonna sound like that forever, Doc?"

The doctor said, "While there may be some small improvement over time, I am afraid that his voice will never sound as it did before the injury."

Ted's gap-toothed grin faltered. "That's sad. You should-a heard him sing, Doc. It was real pretty."

Edgar felt a pang of loss. *No more singing? What else can this place take from me?*

"My left pocket." Ted pointed with his chin and eyes. "On my thigh."

Leaning heavily on the doctor, Edgar shuffled over to where his friend lay bound. He placed a hand on the old man's shoulder. "You . . . okay?"

Ted nodded vigorously. "Yeppers! Soon as Doc lets me go, I'm ready."

"Thanks," Edgar croaked.

Ted grinned again. "Can't lose my only friend." Tears pooled at the corners of the old man's eyes.

Edgar's eyes were a little moist too.

"In my pocket." Ted repeated.

Loosing his grip on the doctor, Edgar unzipped the indicated pocket on Ted's jumpsuit. He reached inside the voluminous pocket, and first encountered the reader pad. He fished further inside the voluminous pocket until his fingers closed on the bottle of olive oil.

Edgar produced the bottle and smiled, groaning in pain.

"The damage to your face is less severe," the doctor said, "but in the end, it may prove the more psychologically traumatic, as facial disfigurement often is."

Alarm shot through Edgar. Awkwardly he turned about, searching for a mirror. Spotting a reflective rectangle on the other side of Ted's hospital bed, Edgar shuffled around the bed to take a look in the mirror.

The face that greeted him was a horror of stitches, bruises, and swollen flesh.

The doctor appeared in the reflection behind Edgar's transformed face. "Both cheekbones were broken, and your jaw was dislocated. I was amazed that you did not lose any teeth. I had

C. David Belt

to reconstruct one of your eye sockets, but the eye itself survived. Cosmetic surgery is not permitted beyond basic reconstruction."

"It's not . . . me." Edgar stared at the unfamiliar visage. The face of a disfigured stranger stared back at him, reminding him of Frankenstein's monster.

The doctor laid a metal hand on his shoulder. "In time, you will grow accustomed to your new face, but the scarring and asymmetry will remain. I am truly sorry that I am not permitted to do more."

"It's still you," Ted said. "You're still the same on the inside. You got the same eyes, don't ya? Ain't eyes the portholes of the soul or something like that?"

Edgar looked at the doleful eyes in the mirror. They were the eyes of someone who had seen too much sorrow and torment for one lifetime. *And I've been here only . . . What? A week? Two?* Yes, they were his eyes. His eyes, but not his face.

"Edgar!" Charlie cried. "Please! Help him!"

Edgar tore his gaze away from the strange face that bore his eyes. "Coming." *Worried about my blasted face when a man is dying?*

"This way." The doctor took his arm and led Edgar past Ted's hospital bed, into an adjoining compartment.

Charlie Miller lay restrained on the nearest bed, his right hand and forearm in a plastic splint. On the farthest bed lay Chen Soo-Won. The Asian was pale. He had a bandage on his head, but otherwise he appeared to be unhurt. His eyes were closed, his breathing slow and even.

"Looks like"—Edgar fought the urge to clear his throat—"he's just asleep."

The doctor shook its head. "His pupils are unresponsive. His blood pressure and pulse rate are both low. Observe his hands."

Edgar looked at Soo-Won's hands. "What?" They looked fine to Edgar.

"Notice how the wrists are rotated inward, with the thumbs turned down toward the bed?"

Edgar nodded, then shrugged his shoulders. "So?"

"Indicative of a comatose state."

Edgar nodded again, gingerly. He didn't understand, but he trusted the doctor's judgment. "He doesn't have . . . a tube." Edgar gesturing weakly toward his own mouth.

"Correct," the doctor said. "The patient is still breathing on his own. Intubation is not indicated, at least not yet. I assume you need access to the patient's head?"

Edgar nodded cautiously, and the doctor led him to the end of Soo-Won's bed. Edgar placed a hand on the bed to steady himself.

The doctor released its supportive hold on Edgar's arm. "Please proceed, Mr. Cordell. I confess that I am anxious to observe this."

"I'm not . . . doing this for you, Doc."

"And yet I am gratified to be able to witness, nonetheless."

Edgar looked at the bottle of oil. It wasn't labeled or otherwise marked as being consecrated. "First, I've got . . . to consecrate the oil."

"I do not remember reading about this part of the ritual. I thought there were only two parts. Must you do this each time?"

Edgar was about to shake his head, but thought better of it. "No. Just once. Probably . . . already done, but . . . have to be sure."

"Fascinating," said the doctor. Even without a face to express the emotion, the android's eagerness was evident in its bearing.

Edgar opened the bottle, and in a voice so ragged that it sounded angry, he began the ordinance.

At the conclusion of the blessing, Edgar lifted his hands off Soo-Won's head.

The doctor cocked its head. "I noticed that you only pronounced a blessing on him that he would recover from the coma. You did not command him to 'rise and walk,' as your scriptures say."

Edgar nodded. "I . . . said what the Spirit directed."

The doctor nodded. "I see. I must confess that I was hoping for something more dramatic."

Edgar sighed.

"You do not look pleased, Mr. Cordell."

C. David Belt

"He didn't wake up." Even in his altered voice, the disappointment was obvious.

The doctor shook its head. "No, he did not. However, I am gratified to have witnessed . . ."

The doctor fell silent.

Edgar looked from Soo-Won to the doctor. "What? He's still asleep."

The doctor nodded. "Precisely. He is *asleep*. He is no longer in a coma."

"How can you tell?"

"Mr. Chen's pulse has increased. You cannot hear it as I can, but it is plain on the readout beside his bed." The robot grabbed a small flashlight, and gently opened Soo-Won's eye. The doctor shone the light in first one eye and then another. "His pupils are reactive. And look at his hands."

Edgar looked at Soo-Won's hands. "They're still rotated." To Edgar's eyes, nothing had changed. *He's still comatose, still dying, no matter what the Doc says.*

It didn't work! My faith . . . my faith wasn't strong enough.

I'm sorry, Soo-Won.

"Yes, they are rotated," the doctor said, "but they have begun to rotate back. It is only a degree or two difference at this point. It will take hours for them to rotate out completely, but as you can see—or perhaps as only I can see—he is merely asleep. He is no longer comatose."

The doctor turned its gaze on Edgar. "This is remarkable." The android lifted its head and said, "Mr. Miller, although Mr. Chen will probably sleep for some time yet, I am cautiously optimistic that he is out of danger."

From the next bed, Charlie let out a whoop. "Thank you, Edgar. And thank God He sent you to us!"

Edgar gripped Soo-Won's bed to steady himself as the room began to spin around him. *No! God wouldn't do that. He wouldn't! He had nothing to do with sending me here!* Edgar looked around for a chair, desperate to sit before he fell. But there were no chairs to be seen. The doctor didn't need one, and visitors weren't allowed. Edgar held on. *God wouldn't send me to this hell!*

Time's Plague

The doctor wrapped a titanium hand around Edgar's arm, supporting him again. The robot's firm, cold grip was oddly reassuring. "Steady there, Mr. Cordell. Now may I get you a wheelchair?"

Edgar shook his head slightly, his eyes shut tight. "Just need . . . a minute. Need to catch my breath."

"Hey, Edgar!" Ted called from the other compartment. "You fixed him? You fixed Sue-Boy?"

If *he's fixed*, Edgar thought. *And that's a big if.* "Not me," he growled with his new voice. "God."

"I doubt Mr. Knight is able to hear you," the doctor said. "I do not want you to strain your voice further. May I have your permission to relay the message?"

Edgar nodded once. Even that act was painful. *Knock yourself out, Doc. I still don't see any change.*

No change.

Failed.

"Mr. Knight," the doctor said in a raised voice, "Mr. Cordell asserts that he is not responsible for the recovery of Mr. Chen. He gives the credit to the Christian God." Lowering his voice again, the android said, "Now, Mr. Cordell, let us get you back to bed. You need to rest and you need time to heal. 'Physician, heal thyself,' as the saying goes."

Edgar allowed Dr. Stewart to assist him back to bed. *God did* not *send me here! It was Llyrica and Edmund and Goner!* They *sent me here. Them and that farce of a court. My Heavenly Father wouldn't do that! He wouldn't!*

As Edgar and the doctor exited Charlie and Soo-Won's compartment, Edgar noticed a soft sound coming from Soo-Won. Edgar started to turn his head, experienced immediate pain, and snapped his head forward. He paused, turning his whole body so he could look at Soo-Won. The diminutive man still lay, restrained and unmoving on his bed.

No change. Just my imagination.

But Edgar heard the sound again. In spite of the pain in his throat and the tumultuous thoughts churning in his frazzled mind, Edgar smiled. The bruised and lacerated muscles and skin of his face screamed in protest, but Edgar's grin widened.

As softly as before, the sound repeated itself.

Edgar offered a quick and silent prayer of gratitude. He also begged forgiveness for his momentary lack of faith.

Though Edgar could see no visible change in Soo-Won, the sound coming from the man told a different tale.

Soo-Won was snoring.

A shudder of relief ripped through Edgar.

Thank you, Heavenly Father! Thank you!

Chapter 17

Now, gods that we adore, whereof comes this?
King Lear, Act I, Scene IV

"Wake up, Mr. Cordell."

The voice was *not* the comforting baritone of Dr. Stewart—it was somewhat higher pitched, and not comforting at all.

Edgar's eyes fluttered open.

Or rather, one eye did. The other eye, Edgar's left, remained closed. There was an uncomfortable pressure on it.

With his open eye, Edgar could see the face of Ozzie hovering over him, the little man's teeth bared in a feral grin, naked loathing in his eyes.

The pressure on Edgar's left eye increased, discomfort becoming pain.

Edgar tried to turn his head, lift his arm, move in any way to escape, to protect himself, but he could do nothing. He was strapped to the bed. He was restrained. He couldn't even move his head.

"That's right," Ozzie said through clenched teeth, his mad grin never faltering. "Not so high and mighty now, are you? Not so pretty, neither. Doc won't clone me a new set of balls. Well, maybe he won't grow you a new eye, neither. What do you think?" Drool spilled from the man's lip and fell on Edgar's face.

"Wait," Edgar said. "You don't . . ."

Ozzie placed a finger to his own lips. "Just you keep quiet, or I'll pop your eyeball out and stomp on it for good measure. Don't call for Doc. Goner's got him preoccupied." He chuckled softly. "By the way, Goner says hi." The little man punctuated his words with a jab of increased and excruciating pressure.

C. David Belt

Terror twisted Edgar's gut. He heard Cornwall's voice in his memory—*There'll come a reckoning*. Edgar couldn't suppress a shudder.

"That's right," Ozzie said. "Now you know I mean business. You're holding the reclaimers over our heads. Well, I figure, if I kill you, we're all dead men. But I'm not going to kill you. No, sir. But I also figure you don't need two eyes to fix the reclaimers now, do you?"

Edgar tried to think past the pain and fear. *Cornwall sent him to gouge out my eye? Can't say anything. Can't negotiate, bargain, talk my way out.*

"You see," Ozzie said, "I figure you want to live. All that talk about not caring if you live or die is just that—talk. That's what I figure, so I says to myself, 'Oz, old boy, take his eye. He'll still do the reclaimers.'"

Wait! You *figure?* Edgar thought maybe he'd found something he could bargain with. *But if I say anything, he might just go ahead and do it!*

Ozzie licked his lips. "Who's the *buddy* now, huh? Say good-bye to your—"

"Goner won't like it," Edgar hissed in desperation. "Won't he be pissed if you do it?"

The pressure on Edgar's eye eased a little, and Ozzie's expression morphed from anger to confusion to worry.

Edgar seized the moment. "Goner wants his revenge, right? He'll be mad if you take it from him."

"Shut up!" Ozzie hissed. "Just shut up!" Spittle flew from his lips, spraying into Edgar's open eye. "You're just . . . You're just trying to . . . I'll do it!"

"Go ahead," Edgar bluffed. "You're afraid Goner might not take you back, you no-balled buddy? You think there's any possibility he'll want you after you steal his revenge?"

Rage twisted Ozzie's face. He snarled in frustration.

"Stop!" It was the doctor's voice, coming from behind Ozzie.

The little man abruptly spun around, removing his thumb from Edgar's eye.

The instant relief from pressure and pain on his eye abruptly made Edgar feel nauseated. He couldn't catch his breath. *If I vomit, I'll choke.*

The doctor appeared behind Ozzie, gripping each of the small man's arms with its implacable metal hands. "Mr. Curan, I am very disappointed in you. This is the second time you have threatened one of my patients. One more infraction, and you will find your trustee status revoked."

As the doctor began to drag Ozzie away, the man said, "I was just teasing him, Doc. You gotta believe me. I wouldn't-a hurt him."

"Are you going to lie to me as well, Mr. Curan?" the robot asked. "That would be your third and final infraction."

"Sorry, Doc!" Ozzie laughed nervously. "Just foolin' around. Sorry! Won't happen again. I swear!"

As they moved out of Edgar's field of vision, the doctor replied, "Very well. However, you will need to be restrained for the remainder of your stay."

"Can I be with Goner?"

"I am afraid that Mr. Cornwall does not desire your company at present."

"Aw, Doc, can't you ask him again?"

"It would not be . . ."

The rest of the exchange was lost on Edgar as the doctor and Ozzie moved out of earshot. Edgar's breathing eased, and the nausea mercifully passed. Edgar sighed and offered a quick prayer of gratitude.

A minute later, the doctor returned. "I regret that you were placed in danger. It is inexcusable that it happened while you were under my care." The doctor set about releasing Edgar's restraints. "I apologize."

Edgar's hand trembled as he felt gingerly at his eye. "Why?"

"Why what, Mr. Cordell?"

"Why was I restrained? I might've been able to defend myself."

The doctor removed the last of Edgar's bonds. "I am sure you can understand that I cannot allow more than one prisoner to be unrestrained at any given time. Mr. Curan is a trustee, at least for the time being, and he was performing some light duties for me. Therefore, you were bound while he was free. I regret that it caused you further distress. Let me take a look at your eye."

The doctor pulled a small flashlight from its white coat and shone it in Edgar's injured eye. The bright light hurt, but it was nothing compared to the pain before.

"I believe," the doctor said as it turned off the beam, "that there is no significant damage. If you feel swelling, please inform me."

"Sure thing, Doc. And thanks."

"You can thank me, Mr. Cordell, by ensuring that your death or disability does not endanger the life of every man in this prison."

Edgar was confused. "What?"

"Once again, Mr. Cordell, the possibility of your death or incapacitation has put the entire colony at risk. Have you given any consideration to providing another solution for keeping the reclaimers working in the increasingly likely event of your demise?"

Edgar laughed softly. "Like I said, Doc, that's a unique bedside manner you've got."

"There are more lives at stake than yours. I am sure you can understand my concern."

"Yeah. I do. But don't worry. I've programmed a fail-safe option. But it involves you."

The android cocked its head. "Me?"

"Yeah. But can you seal the compartment door? I don't want anyone else to hear."

"Certainly." The doctor complied with Edgar's request and returned to his bedside. The robot stood there expectantly.

"Lean close, Doc."

The doctor shook its head. "Unnecessary. I can hear your heart beating. You may whisper if you like."

Edgar started to nod, felt pain in his throat, and stopped. "Okay, Doc. Like I said, I set up a fail-safe procedure. You can provide the prisoners with a code to enter. It's simple. Just give them any ten digits from pi. You know, the number?"

"I am familiar with pi, Mr. Cordell."

"Right. Any ten digits, and the next time give them the next ten, and the next ten digits, and so on. And put the ten digit sequence in reverse order. With your computer brain, that should be easy to do."

"Quite right. However, might not the prisoners recognize such a sequence?"

Edgar grinned. That hurt too. "Maybe, but if you start somewhere after the first ten thousand digits, I doubt anyone would have a clue where the number sequence comes from."

"Very clever, Mr. Cordell." The doctor tilted its head slightly, indicating a smile. "And quite satisfactory."

"I'm glad you approve." He meant it to sound dry, but his damaged voice wasn't capable of subtlety. "How's Soo-Won?"

"He is awake. Would you like to speak with him? He is anxious to speak with you."

"Sure. How're Ted and Charlie doing?"

The doctor extended a metal hand to help Edgar off the bed. "Mr. Miller will remain for observation for a few more hours. Mr. Knight has been discharged. I want Mr. Knight to return for daily medication for his condition. Although his heart is beyond repair, I will do what I can to prolong his life."

Edgar took the android's cold hand and sat up. The pain in his eye was better. He wasn't sure that he could walk unassisted just yet, however. He allowed the doctor to support him as the two of them walked to the compartment shared by Charlie and Soo-Won.

Both men were restrained, of course, but the beds were inclined so that they were more or less sitting up. When Soo-Won's eyes lit upon Edgar, they widened in shock. "Oh, man, Edgar! Your face! I'm sorry."

"Told you," said Charlie. "It's pretty bad."

Edgar didn't want to think about his disfigurement at the moment. "I understand I have you to thank for saving my life. Both of you. And Ted too."

Soo-Won shook his head. "We need you alive. Besides, Charlie tells me that I'd be dead without you giving me a blessing."

Edgar shrugged. "It's not me. You know that."

Soo-Won nodded. "Yeah, sure. But nobody else could have done what you did. Not here. Thank God for sending you to us."

"Stop saying that!" Edgar made no effort to disguise the fury in his damaged voice, which sounded gruff and angry anyway. "God did *not* send me here!"

"He moves in mysterious ways," said Soo-Won.

"He didn't send me here! He wouldn't!"

But what if He did?

Edgar thought he might be sick.

He wrenched out of the doctor's grasp and stumbled from the compartment. *No! It can't be. He wouldn't!*

He *was* going to be sick.

He lurched into the nearest open compartment, searching frantically for a sink or commode. He spotted a small sink in a metal counter, nearly tripped over his own feet as he staggered toward it, gripped the counter, and emptied the contents of his stomach.

As he continued to retch, one thought kept racing through his brain—*Why, Father? Why?*

The bile heaving from his stomach burned his damaged throat.

Why?

The doctor appeared at his side and gently gripped Edgar's arm, supporting him, but saying nothing. Without that support, Edgar would have crumpled to the deck.

Why?

When Edgar finally stopped retching, he slowly became aware of the sound of someone laughing. It was a low chuckle, soft, but still pregnant with menace, the sound of a predator with its prey cornered.

Edgar tried to straighten up, but felt too weak. The doctor, apparently sensing that Edgar was ready to rise, helped him to stand erect. Edgar turned to look in the direction of the laughter.

Of all the rooms to pick . . .

Strapped to a hospital bed, his left arm in traction, both legs in splints, tubes running into his body, lay Goner. He was grinning, exposing broken teeth. Goner licked his swollen lips. "God sent you here? Oh, that's rich." He turned his head and spat blood. "So, that makes me and our Edmund Reagan and your whore wifey-poo . . . What? That makes us gods?" Any sign of mirth faded. "Well, you know what, Mister high and mighty

Christian? God's gonna smite you. Yes, shipmate. Reckoning's a-coming. I'm gonna make you pay for every tooth, every broken bone, every one o' Lushifer's boys as had me. And don't think you can hide behind Lushifer's skirts. No, sir. I got ways. You'll see." He nodded. "God's gonna smite you."

Goner's grin returned, malevolent and feral. "And you'll never see it coming."

Chapter 18

Dost thou call me fool, boy?
King Lear, Act I, Scene III

Come, thou Fount of every blessing,
Tune my heart to sing thy grace;
Streams of mercy, never ceasing,
Call for songs of loudest praise.

Edgar scanned the main compartment of the quarters he shared with Ted in Delta Sector, looking into the face of each man assembled, as they sang the hymn. Seventeen in all—eighteen if Edgar counted himself. It would've been all twenty of them if Rodrigo and Maurice had made it there, but it was rare that they could all slip away unnoticed. That night, eighteen voices were lifted in a plaintive supplication for grace, for mercy, for redemption.

Teach me some melodious sonnet,
Sung by flaming tongues above.

"Melodious" they were not. They certainly weren't the Tabernacle Choir at Temple Square, not even just the men's section, but what they lacked in numbers and musical ability, they more than compensated for any deficiencies with unabashed, soul-deep earnestness.

Edgar, of course, could only rasp with his scarred vocal cords.

He didn't need to see the words relayed from his priceless reader-pad to the built-in vid-screen on the apartment wall. He knew the words by heart. Putting them on the wall screen was the only way to share them. As far as Edgar was aware, his was the only pad in the entire colony. Lamar Shirley, the self-styled Lucifer, didn't allow anything that might be used to educate or communicate or enlighten the damned souls in his *kingdom.*

Charlie led the singing. He had a fair voice. Well, at least he could carry a tune, which was more than could be said for most of the other men—including Edgar now.

> *Praise the mount! I'm fixed upon it,*
> *Mount of thy redeeming love.*

To Edgar, the singing was the worst part of their prayer meetings. He forced himself to lift his ragged voice, but his inability to form a single clear note was as gall in his throat, a bitter reminder of all he had lost. Strictly speaking, he *could* hold a tune, but his voice was as the voice of a man with chronic and perpetual laryngitis. In the months since Griz's attack, Edgar had become accustomed to his new voice, had learned to sound less as if he were relentlessly angry when he spoke, but singing—or rather trying to sing—was like swallowing ashes.

> *Here I raise mine Ebenezer;*
> *Hither by thy help I'm come;*
> *And I hope, by thy good pleasure,*
> *Safely to arrive at home.*

Ted sang with unabashed exuberance and joy, like a child playing with a new toy. Ted had changed, grown in the months since Edgar had taken him under his wing, since Edgar had freed him from decades of sexual slavery and vicious physical abuse. Yes, Edgar had freed the old man—as much as anyone could be free in Hades Penal Colony—but it was Ted's realization that he was not alone, that there were other men on this rock who were celibate, who were *friends* rather than man-and-buddy—if only in secret—that knowledge had really opened Ted's eyes. Ted had come to realize that there was more to life than mere survival at any cost. Ted knew that he had value as a person, not just as some other man's chattel.

> *Jesus sought me when a stranger,*
> *Wandering from the fold of God;*
> *He, to rescue me from danger,*

C. David Belt

Interposed his precious blood.

It was Soo-Won, however, who sang the loudest. Soo-Won was aware that his voice wasn't the greatest, but he sang with all his heart. As an excommunicated member of the Church, the Chinese former terrorist stubbornly refused to actively participate in any other way. He'd told Edgar before their first prayer meeting, "As an excommunicant, I'm not allowed to pray or speak in meetings—I did those things when there was nobody else, but now that you're here, I can't anymore—but the one thing I *can* do is sing."

And sing he did. Joyfully, enthusiastically, if not always quite in tune.

> *O to grace how great a debtor*
> *Daily I'm constrained to be!*
> *Let thy goodness, like a fetter,*
> *Bind my wandering heart to thee.*

Edgar watched as Soo-Won's tears testified with mute eloquence that the lyrics were more than mere words to him.

> *Prone to wander, Lord, I feel it,*
> *Prone to leave the God I love;*
> *Here's my heart, O take and seal it,*
> *Seal it for thy courts above.*

Tears spilled from the eyes of other men as the heartfelt song reached its conclusion. Men, hardened by sin, violence, and years of prison life, wiped at their eyes and then turned their gaze to Edgar.

Every one of those men had committed murder. Some of them had been convicted of rape as well. But they were present, and they were reaching out, throwing themselves on the mercy of Christ. Other than Soo-Won, none of them had been Christian or even Non-LDS-Christian before being sentenced to Hades. About half had been Technos. One had been a Muslim, another a Hindu—both statistically very rare. Most of the men were Earthers or Martians, but there were men representing every inhabited moon except Titan—and of course Callisto. They were a cosmopolitan and varied bunch. And every one of those penitent souls had become very dear to Edgar Cordell.

Edgar nodded at Charlie. "Thank you, Brother Miller." Edgar pointed his grandfather's reader-pad at a dark-skinned man with curly black hair, seated on the edge of the dining table. "Brother Raisinghania, would you offer an invocation?" Karan Raisinghania nodded. Others pushed back to make space in the crowded compartment as the slender man carefully slid off the table and stood. Every inch of sitting space was used, and most of the men had to remain standing.

We've got to find another place to meet. Someplace bigger, but still far enough away from the rest of the prison to allow for singing. As it was, it took over an hour for the men to assemble, coming by twos, using varying routes, in an effort to avoid the attention of Shirley and his enforcers. *It's hard to believe we've escaped detection this long.*

Karan clasped his brown hands in front of him. His fingers were thin, almost delicate. They didn't appear capable of murder, but Karan had been convicted of strangling his girlfriend in a jealous rage. He bowed his head and began to pray in his rich Indian voice. "Merciful Father in Heaven, we are grateful this day . . ."

****

"'. . . but his arm is stretched out still.'" Sergio Da Silva, a Lunan and former Techno, looked up and handed the reader-pad back to Edgar. "What does it mean, 'his arm is stretched out still?'"

Edgar accepted the pad and looked down at the scripture Sergio had just read. "Good question. Does anybody want to answer it?" Edgar locked eyes with Soo-Won briefly, but the excommunicate lowered his eyes and shook his head slightly. *He won't answer, because he thinks he has no right to speak in church. Only this isn't an official church meeting, is it?*

Yurii Malenkov, a man with a face that looked as if it had been chiseled from rough stone, raised his hand from where he stood in the doorway to Edgar's bedroom. When Edgar nodded to him, Yurii said, "It sounds like God is ready to punish Israel for her sins. 'His anger is not turned away,' it says. He is angry with the people."

"'But his arm is stretched out still,'" Edgar quoted.

"So," Yurii continued, "He is ready to beat them, because they are bad people."

Edgar nodded. "Well, yes. He's angry, certainly, because Israel has been very bad, very wicked. They've broken all the commandments of God. They have bowed down to false gods. They have committed gross sexual sin. They have murdered, shed innocent blood."

The Russian nodded and folded his arms. "They are like us."

"Yes."

Yurii nodded. "And for that, God will punish them."

Edgar shook his head. "You're missing the point Isaiah's trying to make. God doesn't punish us. We do that to ourselves. We sin and so are left to ourselves and to the consequences of our sins. Sin brings its own punishment. When we sin, God will not protect us from the consequences. Israel didn't keep God's commandments, so they were no longer protected from their enemies. Babylon came in and destroyed them, took them captive. God didn't do that. Nebuchadnezzar did that. Typically, it's the wicked who punish the wicked."

"Like Lord Lucifer punishes us," said Avery Morris. He and his friend, Leonardo Morenci, were newcomers. Their little group welcomed new men, but each addition brought with him an additional risk of betrayal or discovery.

"Please don't call him that," said Edgar, a pained expression twisting his disfigured face, "at least not here. Call him 'boss' if you like, but he's not your lord. And he's not the devil either."

Avery shrugged and then nodded with a dubious expression on his face, obviously not convinced.

"But God's angry," said Yurii, bringing them back to the point. "Why is His arm stretched out if not to smite us?"

Edgar smiled. The skin on his face stretched uncomfortably in a way that reminded him how badly his features had been damaged. *As if the gargoyle in the mirror would ever let me forget.* His smile faltered a bit before he forced it wide again. "What the Lord is saying is that, no matter what Israel—or in this case, each of us—has done, the Savior is always waiting with outstretched arms. He will take us back into His loving embrace if only we will turn back to Him."

"But what I've done," said the Russian, "what I've done is so bad, there can be nothing for me."

"If that's the case," rasped Edgar, "why are you here, in this meeting? Why are *any* of you here?"

Yurii looked around, searching the faces of the assembled men, questing for an answer. At last his eyes returned to Edgar's face. Yurii bowed his head. "I do not know."

Silence reigned, broken only by soft sounds of breathing and the shuffling of feet.

"Hope." That came from Philippe Duvalier, a small man, even shorter than Soo-Won. Nobody else said a word, but a few heads nodded. "Hope," Philippe repeated. "There must be hope. Without hope, why go on living?"

Edgar smiled. "Hope. And there is hope in God's promises. No matter what you've done in the past, repent. Start now. Turn back to God. Accept His mercy and the Atonement of the Lord Jesus Christ. Serve Him and keep His commandments from this day forward as best you can, for 'his arm is stretched out still.' Rely on His mercy. He wants to extend to you, to me, to everybody the maximum amount of mercy that He can. You can't take back the past—none of us can. You can't atone for your sins. But Jesus Christ *can*."

Yurii shook his head. "But without baptism . . . how?"

Edgar swallowed hard. He got this question often enough that the answer should've come easily. However, the fact that it was asked so often meant that it must weigh heavily on the minds of the men.

"You know I can't baptize anyone here. I'm not authorized, and you'd all need clearances from Missouri anyway. But this life is not all there is. The work can be done for you in the temple after you're dead. All you can do now is trust in the Lord and keep His commandments. Give up the hate. Give up the anger and the resentment. Forgive. Give up your sins. Leave the rest in the Lord's—"

The apartment door opened a crack.

Edgar snapped his mouth shut and waved in order to silence the men, but there was no need. Every soul was instantly mute, some of them holding their breath.

Silent mice waiting for the cat to pounce.

C. David Belt

Through the crack in the door, Edgar caught sight of a familiar face. *Rodrigo and Maurice at last,* thought Edgar. *We have a full house!*

Maurice was first. He smiled and waved as he stepped over the threshold. Rodrigo followed, closing the door behind himself.

"Yeppers! That's all of us," exclaimed Ted, grinning from ear to ear, displaying his sparse collection of teeth.

"Welcome," Edgar said as the men squeezed together to make room for the late arrivals. "We really have to find someplace bigger to meet, brethren! Any suggestions?"

The door opened again.

"Well, glory, glory, halle-bloody-lujah!" shouted an all-too-familiar voice. A hated voice. A voice that brought bile to Edgar's throat.

The door swung wide to reveal the face of Goner. The murderous cargomaster grinned like a malevolent Grinch, showing off his newly repaired teeth—at least the teeth medically necessary for consuming food.

Ozzie bobbed behind him. "Told you, Goner! Told you! I found 'em. Yes, I did!"

"Yeah, Oz," said Goner, "you did."

Ozzie continued to bounce behind Goner, his expression alternating between fear and hope. "You'll take me back now. Right, Goner? I'm your buddy again, right?"

Goner's grin drooped a little, twisting into a long-suffering sneer. "Yeah, yeah, Oz. You're my buddy. Now shut your mouth."

Ozzie threw his arms around Goner, hugging him from behind. Tears of unabashed joy and relief spilled from Ozzie's eyes.

Goner snarled and snapped his forearm up over his shoulder, smashing his fist into Ozzie's face.

Ozzie squealed and dropped out of Edgar's line of sight.

The men of the prayer group stood in shocked silence and mute despair. Obviously, their little group of believers had *not* gone unnoticed.

"Well, gents," said Goner, grinning evilly again and rubbing his hands together, "you lot are my ticket back to Lord

Lucifer's good graces and the ranks of the Angels! God does work in mysterious ways, don't he?"

"Goner, wait!" Edgar's mind raced as he mentally cast about for a way to put a stop to this before it was too late.

Goner shook his head. "No, shipmate. There ain't no talking your way out of this one." He inserted two fingers into his mouth and whistled. "Come along, gents!" He shouted. "Step lively, now! We caught 'em!"

Goner stepped aside, and other figures appeared in the doorway—Angels, Shirley's enforcers, brandishing weapons. Edgar couldn't see them all, but he was certain there was a large contingent of them.

"Maggots!" bellowed the Angel in the doorway. "What in Lucifer's name you doing in there? Plotting a damn rebellion, aren't you?"

The worshipers turned toward the demonic Angels. Murmurs of "No!" like the bleating of frightened sheep filled the compartment. Men began to crowd back farther, as if by shrinking away they could avoid the wrath of the fiendish messengers of a would-be devil.

"I asked you a question, worms!" roared the foremost thug. "What are you doing here? If you're plotting sedition, so help me, I'll break every damn bone in your bodies and *then* you'll go to sleep!"

The men continued to press back, and though a susurrus of denial rose from them like an audible fog of fear, none dared answer.

Even Edgar, who—in theory—had nothing to fear from the enforcers, found it hard to raise his voice above a whisper.

The thug, a large and muscular man with wicked, beady eyes, smacked the large metal pipe he wielded against his palm. He went by the nickname Caliban. Edgar didn't know the fiend's real name. Caliban slapped the pipe into his palm again, punctuating the threat of violence with "Answer me!"

"It's just a prayer meeting," said Edgar. His voice wasn't much more than a low growl. "A prayer meeting," he repeated louder.

"What's that?" demanded the thug.

"Prayer," replied Edgar. "We're meeting to pray to God."

Caliban barked out a laugh. "Praying? Fat lot of damn good that'll do you in this place. 'Sides, ain't no god in Hades but Lucifer." He pointed his weapon at Edgar. "You behind this, Tom Bedlam?"

Edgar began to push his way through the tight-packed mass of men. "I am."

"Figured as much," said Caliban with a sneer. "Lord Lucifer says I can't hurt you, but I can sure as hell show you who's Lord in Hades." He stepped back a pace and stopped, framed in the big "D" painted on the corridor wall behind him. He snapped his pipe to the side, pointed down the corridor, and barked, "All you little buddies, out in the hall here. Now!"

The men began to shuffle out into the corridor.

"Yeah," said Caliban. "That's right, buddies. Line up against the wall."

Ted came to cower by Edgar's side. As the last of the other men filed out into the corridor, Edgar started forward to follow, but Ted gripped his arm and whispered, "Don't!"

"You too, Bedlam! And bring your buddy with you."

Ted shrank behind Edgar. "Ain't no buddy," he whispered.

Edgar struggled to control the quaking of his knees. "You can't touch us."

Caliban sneered. "You got that right. We can't, but we can make you watch. It'll go much, *much* worse for them if you don't."

Edgar closed his mouth, took a deep breath through his nose in a vain attempt to steel his nerves, and stepped forward. Ted hung back for an instant, then followed, clinging to Edgar's arm, like a little boy hiding behind his mother's skirt.

As they stepped over the compartment threshold and into the corridor beyond, Caliban grinned maliciously at Edgar. "Watch, Bedlam, and learn your place."

Edgar intended to meet the man's eyes with a cold stare, but his attention became riveted to the scene beyond Caliban. Edgar's friends lined the corridor on both sides, their heads hanging in resignation. Other Angels—Edgar counted eight in all, including Caliban—shoved and bullied the other men into line, threatening or jabbing them with their weapons. Goner stood farther down the corridor, nodding, watching the Angels, his former compatriots, at work. Ozzie cowered behind him, one hand covering his nose. Blood dripped from between his fingers.

Goner caught Edgar's eye and grinned. He tapped a finger to his temple then pointed at Edgar. Clearly, the former cargomaster meant to communicate a message, but the meaning was lost on Edgar as Caliban raised his voice.

"You want to know what I think of your praying?" Caliban paused as he paced between the rows of men, who but a minute before had been discussing the word of God. The worshippers now stood with their backs to the wall and their faces downcast. "Well, do ya?" The enforcer stopped his pacing and stood in front of Soo-Won. Caliban put a hand on the back of Soo-Won's head. "It don't look much like you're praying to me, unless you're on your *knees*!" Caliban punctuated the last word by roughly shoving Soo-Won to the deck.

Soo-Won landed hard on his knees and grunted in pain. Charlie Miller cried, "Hey!"

Caliban's face split in a savage grin. "Oh, you want in on this, Stretch?"

The other Angels chuckled. One of them said, "Protecting your buddy, Stretch? That's sweet." The enforcers laughed louder.

Caliban said, "Sue-Boy, you stay where you are. And don't worry. You're next." He gestured at Charlie with his weapon again. "Stretch! Assume the position."

Charlie's shoulders sagged resignedly. He unzipped his jumpsuit, slipped his arms out of the sleeves, and dropped his clothes to his ankles. As Charlie reached for his underwear, Edgar could take no more.

"Stop!" he cried.

Caliban and the other Angels looked in Edgar's direction. Caliban showed no hint of surprise. In fact he grinned. He turned his head down the corridor and winked in Goner's direction.

They were expecting me to do this?

"It's okay," said Charlie as he dropped his shorts. "You get used to it." He dropped to the floor and knelt.

"Wait," said Edgar. "You don't have to do this." *What can I bargain with? How can I talk our way out of this? Father, help me find a way!* But Edgar knew he had only one move to make, and it was a weak, delaying tactic at best. "This man," he said, "these men, are under my protection. Harm them, and I'll stop resetting the reclaimers."

Caliban's jaw dropped, but the expression of mock surprise on his face confirmed Edgar's fear—Edgar's reaction had been anticipated. "So, Tom Bedlam, you care about this steaming mama-log?"

He's not going for it, Edgar thought. *Time for a new gambit.* He remembered the words of his father. *In chess, son, sometimes you expose the queen, and make your opponent think you want him to take her. You make him think twice.* "You think I won't do it? Try me. Touch any of these men, and I'll let us all die."

Caliban sneered at him. "Oh, *now* you've got me scared. I may soil my undies! If you care about him, you won't let him die along with the rest of us. You got nothing, Bedlam."

Edgar grinned his gargoyle smile. He knew it was an unnerving sight, and Caliban flinched.

"All right." Edgar pointed at Charlie. "Ask him. Ask any man here. They would rather die than live another day without God in their lives."

Caliban shook his head. "You wouldn't."

Edgar stared back, but said nothing.

Caliban's sneer faltered.

Edgar saw his opening and he pounced on it. Barely keeping his voice from shaking, he said, "Charlie, get up. Get dressed."

Soo-Won, kneeling on the deck next to Charlie, snapped his head up and looked at Edgar with wide eyes. He shook his head slightly, obviously trying to get Edgar to back down.

From where he still knelt on all fours, Charlie Miller looked at Edgar, fear and doubt written plain on his face. "W-what?"

But Edgar had made his move. He'd taken his hand off the queen. There was no turning back. Either Caliban took the bait or he took the queen.

"Get up," Edgar said. "Show Mr. Caliban here that you will not submit to rape. Show him that you stand for Christ."

Charlie's eyes went wide. His mouth moved wordlessly, but he didn't rise.

Caliban chuckled and began to unzip his own jumpsuit. "That's right. You know your place. Don't you, Stretch?"

Abruptly, Soo-Won rose to his feet. "I kneel to none save Jesus Christ." A full head shorter than Caliban, he stood tall and glared at the man. "I stand with Christ."

Caliban snarled and drew back his pipe ready to strike.

"Stop!" cried Edgar, and the enforcer hesitated. Edgar set his jaw and didn't blink. "This is your last warning, Caliban. I mean what I say."

Charlie took a deep breath, released it, and stood. He began pulling up his clothes. His knees shook and his hands trembled, but he said, "Me too."

Caliban's jaw dropped. This time the shock was unfeigned. He lowered his weapon.

"I too," said Yurii as he stepped away from the wall, his head held high. An enforcer raised a large wrench as if to strike him, but the Russian brushed it aside.

"I stand with Christ," said Karan, a former Hindu. He too stepped away from the wall.

"I stand with Jesus," said Ibrahim. He'd been a Muslim before being sentenced to Hades. Now he risked his life to declare his new faith.

Others followed, one by one. Eventually all eighteen men stood facing their tormentors.

The Angels looked around frantically. Some raised weapons, but their postures indicated that these were defensive moves rather than aggressive ones.

Nobody's stood up to them before? Edgar thought. *Even armed, they're outnumbered and they know it.*

Caliban was breathing hard, nearly hyperventilating. "This won't stand. Lord Lucifer won't tolerate rebellion."

Edgar got right in the man's face, but kept his voice calm in spite of the fear roiling in his gut. "This is no rebellion. We're not starting a war."

"You're insane, Bedlam!" snarled the enforcer.

Edgar laughed. He *sounded* insane, even to his own ears. "That's right. That's what your leader said, wasn't it? That's what that name means, don't you know? Bedlam?"

Caliban's confused expression clearly showed that he didn't understand the reference.

C. David Belt

Edgar laughed again. And in his rough, ragged voice he sang the chorus of an old song he'd learned from his grandfather—

> *Still I sing bonnie boys, bonnie mad boys,*
> *Bedlam boys are bonnie.*
> *For they all go bare and they live by the air,*
> *And they want no drink nor money.*

Edgar laughed again. "Your boss said it himself, I'm crazy enough to kill us all."

Naked fear glistened in Caliban's eyes.

"Go on," Edgar said, his voice as cool and calm as he could render it. "Tell your boss that we're just praying and nothing more. We're not rising up in rebellion. We'll still do our jobs and take his stupid work assignments and do our part to keep this place running, but we're not his slaves anymore."

Caliban shook his head. "Impossible . . . Won't tolerate . . ."

"Better yet," said Edgar, "I'll tell him myself. As they used to say in the old vids, 'Take me to your leader.'"

Motioning for Ted to remain there, Edgar turned and started off down the corridor. A moment later, Caliban followed like a beaten cur.

The other enforcers hurried to catch up.

As Edgar, flanked by the guard of Angels, passed Goner and Ozzie, the expression of abject loathing and vexed frustration on Goner's face was priceless.

Chapter 19

The king is mad.
King Lear, Act IV, Scene VI

"Leave us." Lamar Shirley waved a hand dismissively as he lounged, propped on one elbow. The gang lord had a blanket draped across his lower half. He reclined on a spacious bed in the center of his private quarters, a large room that had once been intended as a classroom for children. A solitary child's desk remained as a lone reminder of lost potential. Shirley's tone was low and calm—not at all the booming roar of command he employed in public.

The two other men lounging with him on the bed looked startled and confused. They were naked as well. One man was lying behind Shirley, stroking his master's chest. The other had been feeding Shirley, placing bits of fruit in the gang lord's mouth. A morsel of apple hung, pinched between the man's fingers, halfway between the bowl he carried and Shirley's face.

Two of Shirley's Angels stood on either end of the bed, their clubs at the ready. They too looked startled.

The sight of the chief thug, lying on a bed, surrounded by fawning concubines and royal guards, reminded Edgar of paintings and vids he'd seen depicting Roman emperors.

Edgar half expected to see palm branches waving.

When neither the guards nor the buddies made a move, Shirley growled, "Are you deaf? I said, 'Leave us!'"

The two buddies exchanged brief glances of shock, then scrambled to vacate the bed. In his haste, the man with the bowl spilled the fruit on the floor. He squealed and began to gather the slopped contents.

"Idiot!" roared Shirley. "Get out!"

The poor fellow leaped to his feet so quickly that, in the low Callistoan gravity, he shot off the floor and struck his head on the ceiling. Fruit flew everywhere as he dropped slowly to the floor, clutching his head. Blood streamed from between his fingers.

Shirley sighed theatrically and shook his head. "You have displeased me, Hero. You are clumsy and stupid, and you will be punished."

The man with the ironic prison name of Hero got to his knees and began crawling toward Shirley. He stretched forth a bloodied hand and cried, "My lord! Forgive me!" He wept, the blood from his head mingling with his tears. "I'm sorry!"

"Six months, no calcilock," said Shirley, pronouncing sentence as casually as if he were noting the time of day. He waved at one of the Angels. "And put him on hard labor."

The man looked horrified. "Six months? But, my lord! I just came off six months!"

"Yes," said Shirley, "and when your bones begin to snap like rotted twigs, perhaps you will learn to be more careful."

"Not that, my lord! Please!"

Hero's terror brought a wicked smile to Shirley's face. "I will . . . *consider* your petition after I am done with Tom Bedlam here. Await me outside."

"Thank you!" Hero began again to crawl toward his master.

Shirley's smile vanished. "Get out." It was a whisper, full of menace and contempt.

The man rose to his feet, more carefully this time, and fled from his master's presence—naked as Joseph fleeing from Potiphar's wife—pushing his way past Edgar and Caliban as he raced for the corridor outside.

The other buddy followed quickly after him, pausing only briefly to snatch his jumpsuit from the floor.

The two Angels standing on either end of the bed exchanged evil grins.

"The rest of you, out!" bellowed Shirley.

The guards blinked stupidly.

Shirley muttered an oath, then yelled, "Out!"

The two guards retired from their posts and headed for the hatchway.

"My lord?" said Caliban from behind Edgar.

Time's Plague

Shirley gritted his teeth and snarled, "I can handle the Fool myself. Get out!"

Caliban retreated from the chamber, closing the hatch behind himself.

Edgar was alone with the man who had raped him. The two of them hadn't met face-to-face since the day Edgar revealed that he knew Lucifer's true name. That revelation had unnerved Shirley, but now the man seemed all confidence, the dominant alpha-male, the cat certain that the mouse could not escape.

Edgar had demanded this meeting, but now, facing the rapist, his knees threatened to buckle. *Shirley! Think of him as Shirley! How can you be afraid of a man with a name like that?*

And yet Edgar struggled to keep his terror at bay.

"So, Tom Bedlam," said the gang lord as he rose from the bed, the blanket dropping to the floor, "I have learned of your pathetic little band of rebels." Shirley placed the crown of woven copper wire on his head and began to dress himself in his crimson jumpsuit with its metal adornments. As Shirley dressed, the ornaments tinkled like perverse jingle bells on a villainous mockery of Santa Claus. The man's eyes crinkled in amusement. "I assume they have been properly dealt with? I assume they have come to remember who rules in Hades?"

Edgar swallowed hard. *You have the upper hand here. Don't let him see your fear.* "Not exactly."

Shirley gaped at him, pausing with the zipper halfway up. "What did you say?"

Edgar knew he had his opponent off-balance. "None of my friends have been punished."

"But I sent—"

"You sent your bullyboys to rape and to put down a rebellion, but that's not what was going on. You have been *misinformed*." He pronounced the last word slowly.

"I? What're you—?"

Edgar forced a laugh. With his roughened voice, it sounded particularly harsh. "There is no rebellion. It's a prayer group. I know it's hard for you to believe, but this wretched moon orbits Jupiter, not you."

Shirley's expression hardened into a murderous scowl.

Edgar pressed ahead, full thrusters. "Nobody's plotting to overthrow your not-so-benevolent rule. We're just having church. You know—prayer, singing, studying? Nothing more. So, no rebellion, no uprising—just prayer."

The would-be lord of darkness bared his teeth. "I will not tolerate—"

"Won't tolerate what? Prayer? Scripture study? Singing? We're still doing our jobs, taking our assignments. I'm still keeping your stupid reclaimers running." Edgar let those words sink in. "You don't really expect us to pray to *you*, do you? Whatever else you are, whatever you think you are, you're not a god. You're not *that* crazy, are you?"

Shirley bellowed, "How dare you speak to me like that? *Me*?"

Edgar flashed his best gargoyle's grin, an insane leer. "Hey, you don't want to piss me off, remember, Lamar? What good is it to rule in hell if everybody's dead?"

"I would see you all dead before I will allow another to—"

Edgar laughed again, a truly frightening sound that cut the gang lord off. "Yeah, *Lamar*, I know you would. But you're also not stupid. Because the thing is, *nobody* is challenging you. Nobody. I'm not leading a revolution. We're not fighting you. We just want to be left alone to worship. Leave us alone and we won't do anything to oppose you and we won't encourage anyone else to either—to oppose you, that is. And when I say, 'Leave us alone,' I mean just that. No rapes, no beatings, no withholding calcilock, no punishments. And I promise you this—anyone touches my friends, I will not give you a second chance. And let me be very clear—do not mistake this little chat for a negotiation."

Shirley's jaw clenched. He glared at Edgar. The gang lord was furious, but he was also trapped, and they both knew it.

Now you've got him. Give him something, so he feels like he got something out of the deal. "Tell you what—I've got no problem with you sending *observers*, as long as they behave themselves. That way you'll know I'm telling the truth."

Shirley was caught off guard by the concession. "Observers," he said cautiously, drawing the word out as if it were in another language.

"Yeah, so you'll know we aren't plotting sedition."

The gang lord nodded. "'We believe in being subject to kings, presidents, rulers, and magistrates, in obeying, honoring, and sustaining the law,'" he quoted from the Articles of Faith. His eyes burned with a fierce light. "And *I* am the law."

It was Edgar's turn to be taken aback. *Shirley is a Christian! Or he once had been.* Edgar tried to conceal his surprise.

Shirley didn't seem to notice Edgar's reaction.

"Well," Edgar said, "I wouldn't go that far, but we'll do our jobs and we'll stay out of your way."

The gang lord stared at Edgar, considering. His mouth worked as if he were chewing something particularly unpleasant. Abruptly, he nodded firmly. "On one condition."

Edgar shook his head. "I told you, this isn't a negotiation."

"Of course it is." Shirley grinned. "Goner told me all about you, freighter captain. You think you're quite the negotiator. Very full of yourself. Well, *Captain* Cordell, here's my condition."

Edgar hesitated and instantly cursed himself for a fool. However, it was too late to counter, so he waited for Shirley to make his demand.

"Play chess with me," said the gang lord. He held up a finger. "One game, once a week."

Edgar blinked. "You're joking."

Shirley turned his back on Edgar and walked over to a small counter. A chessboard sat on the metal surface, complete with hand-carved pieces. Shirley turned back to Edgar and gestured at the chess set with a dramatic flourish. "I desire a worthy opponent. Right now, that's you. Everyone else fears me too much to play honestly. Goner tells me that you're quite adept. I can assume you would not *let* me win?"

What's he up to? Is he just bored and looking for a decent game from someone other than a sycophant?

No way. There's more to this. He's sizing you up, attempting to find out how you think, probe for weakness.

Well, you've done the same with a game of chess, haven't you? You might learn something you can use. And if he wants this, why not get another concession out of him?

"I have a condition of my own," said Edgar, "and it's nonnegotiable."

C. David Belt

The rapist grinned, a predator's smile. And above the bared teeth, Shirley's eyes gleamed with malice.

He thinks he has me. The cat, biding his time, waiting for the mouse to make a mistake. And I hope this isn't a huge one.

Well, here goes.

Edgar took a deep breath and plunged in. "You make a public pronouncement that any man who wishes to worship with us may do so without threat of punishment—no punishment of any kind."

Shirley's grin transformed into a grimace. "You're mad!"

Edgar laughed. "That's why you call me Tom Bedlam, right? Oh, and we need a bigger place to meet. The agridome will do."

Shirley's face turned a shade of crimson that rivaled his jumpsuit.

Edgar shrugged his shoulders. "No? Your loss." He turned his back and started to walk to the hatch. "My other conditions still stand. You will leave me and my friends alone to worship as—"

"Done."

It should've been Edgar's turn to smile, but as it was, he barely kept his knees from buckling. Relief washed over him like a terrestrial rain.

He really wants this—this honest game of chess.

I guess you read him right, Cordell. If you'd guessed wrong, it could've been disastrous.

Edgar turned back to face the man who had once shown his dominance by raping him. Edgar waved at the chess set. "Set up the game."

Shirley smiled as he gathered the chess pieces, his expression one of unmistakable triumph.

What's he got planned? What am I missing?

****

As it turned out, Shirley was better than good at chess—the man was formidable.

Edgar wasn't above throwing a game if it might gain him an advantage off the board, but he sensed that the gang lord genuinely desired an honest game, a challenge. So Edgar played to win. Edgar reasoned that if he beat Shirley, the man might be more satisfied with the outcome than otherwise.

They played slowly, cautiously, each combatant taking his time on every move. Their eyes remained locked on the board. They never looked at each other.

A dozen moves into the game, Edgar placed a knight, keeping his index finger atop the piece's equine head. He pressed down on the knight, unsure of his move. He set his thumb and middle finger on either side of the piece, about to lift the knight and replace it in its original spot, thought better of it, and removed his hand, officially ending the move. He realized that this made him appear indecisive in the eyes of his opponent, but that too could work to his advantage.

Shirley, his eyes glued to the game, abruptly began to talk. "I was a teacher, you know—before Hades, that is. I taught literature, the classics. Shakespeare was my specialty . . . and my passion."

"I would never have guessed."

"That I was a teacher?"

"Yes." Edgar didn't look at his enemy, but Shirley had his attention. "The Shakespeare bit was obvious. Actually, I figured you for an actor."

Shirley sighed. "Ah, yes, in my youth. But I wasn't able to make a living at it. I taught *theatre* as well. Directing stage productions gave me access to my second passion."

"Let me guess—children."

Shirley moved a bishop with decisiveness, utterly without hesitation. "Little girls, to be precise." Neither was there any hesitation as Shirley declared that he was a defiler of children. "Lovely, innocent, pure little virgins."

So the fearsome Lord Lucifer is nothing but a pedophile. Why is he telling me this? I thought child molesters used to be the lowest of the low in prison. If they survived the beatings they received at the hands of the other prisoners, they ended up as someone's buddy. Most of the men in this place were probably abused when they were boys, so their loathing and contempt for men like Lamar Shirley should've made him a favorite target. How in the System did a child molester end up as king of the sewer?

C. David Belt

Edgar laid a finger on a pawn. *As long as he's willing to talk . . .* "That's why you're here?"

"I'm here, because one of my little princesses betrayed me. Her name was Tiffany. I loved her, and she betrayed our love."

"Meaning, she told someone that you were raping her?"

"Our love was beautiful. It was sacred, pure. You wouldn't understand, of course. The little whore had no right to betray my trust. After all I did for her!"

Edgar fought down the bile rising into his throat. *You were an adult in a position of authority and trust, Shirley. You were the little girl's teacher. And she betrayed you, you sick waste of oxygen?*

Edgar took his finger off the pawn. *I wanted to use the game to get inside his head, but I don't think I can handle any more details about his victims.*

Change the subject, Cordell.

"I thought men with your type of . . . *history* don't do so well here," Edgar said.

"You don't think I'm stupid enough to tell anyone here, do you?"

"You just told me." Edgar placed a finger on another pawn.

"Well, Tom Bedlam, we have an understanding, you and I. It binds us together. Secrets make us . . . intimates." Shirley caressed the word like a lover. "You would never tell a soul. You have kept my secrets, have you not? Of course, you have. Unlike Tiffany's bishop. He went straight to the authorities. A bishop is supposed to keep a confidence."

Edgar laughed harshly. "Not in cases of abuse. But, you know that, don't you? You were a member of the Church. Priesthood leaders are obligated to report suspected abuse."

"He should've kept silent. I did, when I was a young bishop."

Edgar removed his finger from the unmoved pawn. He rubbed his forehead and the bridge of his nose as he struggled to conceal the fury boiling within him. *Keep it together, Cordell!*

He raped that little girl. Others. And he was a bishop!
And he raped me.

Time's Plague

*Fight past it, Cordell. Fight past your own trauma—
other lives are at stake here.*

Edgar placed his finger on yet another pawn. He pressed
down hard on the piece to steady his hand and mask the
trembling. He calmed his breathing. *Steady. In. Out.* "So you were
a bishop. That means you were married. What about your wife?"

"I *was* a bishop, but that was before I fully embraced my
true nature. As for my wife, she left when she found out about
Tiffany and me . . . and the others. Took our baby daughter and
moved back to New Zealand."

Edgar released the pawn, then moved a bishop and
released it. The move looked hasty, or at least Edgar intended it to
appear so. Edgar hoped the trap he was preparing wasn't too
subtle for Shirley. Edgar had left an opening that he hoped the
man couldn't resist. *Let's see if he takes the bait.* "So, even if you
didn't tell anyone, even if nobody knew what you did—"

"There was a man," said Shirley, interrupting, "he came
here a couple of years after I did. He . . . knew me from before.
He had the same . . . *interests* that I did. I killed him. I had to, of
course. Couldn't let anyone find out who I was, what I did . . .
what my *name* was. I poured poison in his ear as he slept. Just like
Claudius did to Hamlet's father."

"Okay. Still doesn't explain how you went from child-
raping former bishop and school teacher to . . ."

"Lord of Hades? My dear Bedlam, how could you forget
so soon? I thought we were baring our souls to one another? I told
you I was an actor. I've played Julius Caesar, Titus Andronicus,
Macbeth." As Shirley listed the Shakespearean characters, his
voice rose and assumed a theatrical air. "I was an actor! So I
played a part that allowed me to survive." He lowered his voice to
a conspiratorial whisper. "It's so nice to have someone with
whom I can just be . . . *myself.*"

Shirley moved a knight, taking Edgar's bishop. "We
don't have to be enemies, you and I. I doubt we will ever be
friends, but you are my Fool, and thus my confidant. I can tell you
anything. And though you may judge me and criticize me and
even defy me in public . . . Well, that's what fools do, do they
not? I must admit, you play well, Bedlam. By the way, *check.*"

Edgar wasn't looking at the man directly, but in his
peripheral vision, he could see a wolfish grin split Shirley's face.

Without hesitation, Edgar countered with his queen, blocking his opponent's attack and springing the trap.

Shirley stared at the board in silence for a long minute. At last he nodded. "Ah!" He slapped his hands on his thighs, clinking some of his ornaments together. "Mate in three. You win this one. Well done!"

The lord of Hades rose to his feet. "I can see that you are indeed a worthy adversary. Macduff to my Macbeth. 'Lay on, Macduff!' Fortinbras to my Hamlet." He extended a hand to Edgar. "Well played."

Edgar also stood, pointedly ignoring the rapist's outstretched hand.

Shirley laughed as he dropped his hand to his side. "I will win the next contest, I can assure you." He gathered the chess pieces and carried the board along with its pieces back to their original spot. He carefully arranged the chess set, then turned back to Edgar. Shirley bowed theatrically and swept a hand toward the door. "And now, I have royal business to attend to. I must dispense justice to Hero, who waits without, and make the pronouncement you have requested. Lead the way."

Edgar shook his head. "After you."

Shirley grinned and wagged a finger at Edgar. "I have no intention of turning my back on you, Bedlam. Who's the Fool here?"

Edgar turned slowly and deliberately and walked toward the hatch. His knees felt frail at the thought of having the rapist behind him. He was on his guard, wary of attack from behind, and yet he was taken completely by surprise when Shirley collided with him.

Edgar slammed to the deck, the air exploding from his lungs. Shirley was on top of him.

His sight going gray, and struggling for breath, Edgar attempted to fight back. He flailed at his attacker with one arm, but couldn't reach the man who pinned him to the floor.

Edgar heard a ripping sound. His jumpsuit!

Not again!

But in a moment, the pressure of Shirley's body was gone. Gulping in a huge, tortured lungful of air, Edgar rolled over, preparing to defend himself. He raised his arms defensively.

To his utter astonishment, however, Shirley merely stood over him, offering a hand as if to help Edgar to his feet.

The gang lord shook his head. "Forgive my clumsiness. I tripped and . . . Well, you know what happened."

Edgar was certain the collision had been no accident, and he wasn't about to allow Shirley to help him to his feet. Once again ignoring the proffered hand, Edgar stood. He was unable to control his own quaking due to fear and rage.

Abruptly, Shirley reached out and ruffled Edgar's hair as if the two of them were old chums. The gesture was so unexpected that Edgar froze momentarily, before crying out in disgust and desperately batting Shirley's hand away.

The rapist grinned as toothily as a shark closing on its next meal. "Shame about your jumpsuit," he said, pointing at Edgar's shoulder. "You should get a new one."

Edgar glanced at his shoulder. His clothing was ripped there, the tear going down Edgar's back and out of sight. Edgar became acutely aware of cooler air against his back. The rip had to be extensive. *Like when they shredded my clothes, held me down, and Lucifer . . .*

"Just like old times," said the gang lord with a lascivious wink. He sauntered off toward the hatch, turning his back on Edgar without a pretense of care.

Chapter 20

Where's my fool, ho? I think the world's asleep.
King Lear, Act I, Scene II

Outside, eight Angels waited, along with Ted—who looked immensely relieved to see Edgar—and the two concubines. One of the concubines, Hero, was still naked and stood with bowed head, his hands clasped protectively over his groin.

"Caliban," said Shirley, assuming his booming Lucifer persona as he addressed the chief Angel, "assemble my court in the Throne Room. Fifteen minutes. I have a proclamation that all must hear."

The enforcer bowed his head slightly. "Yes, my lord!"

"Fail me again, and . . ."

"No, my lord!" The enforcer's head snapped up, and raw terror shone in his wide eyes.

"I want all my subjects there, even the farmers. Do we have anyone in the infirmary?"

"I . . . I don't think so, my lord."

"Good. Then *all* shall be in audience, except for those who sleep."

"Yes, my lord!"

Shirley nodded, and Caliban pointed to three other Angels. The three men nodded and followed Caliban as he hurried off in the shuffling gait used on low-grav worlds. This was necessary to avoid launching oneself toward the ceiling as Hero had done. Caliban barked out, "Throne Room! Now, maggots!"

Down the corridor, men scurried to get out of the way. As they did so, they took up the cry. "Throne Room!"

Ted took advantage of the commotion to come stand behind Edgar. "You okay?" he asked. "What happened in there?"

"Later," whispered Edgar.

"You were gone a long time. I was worried. You look—"

"He attacked me, knocked me down, ripped my—"

"He didn't . . . ?" The way Ted let his voice trail off, the intent of the question was clear. "And you . . . didn't . . . ?"

"No," Edgar said.

"Okay. It just looks like he . . . you know."

"I'm okay. Later."

Shirley turned around and approached the naked and trembling Hero. Shirley grabbed the hapless man under the jaw, raising his head until the buddy's eyes met his master's. The gesture looked almost tender, but Hero began to whimper. "M-mercy, lord," Hero spluttered, tears coursing down his face.

"You seek mercy?" Shirley asked. His voice no longer boomed, but the quieter tone bore menace like the hiss of a viper. "Your bones are already brittle. You fear they will break without calcilock, is that it?"

"Y-yes, my lord."

"I will show you mercy if you can answer one simple question." The gang lord paused as if he expected the quivering buddy to respond. When no response came, Shirley asked, "Hero is a character from Shakespeare's comedy, *Much Ado About Nothing*. I gave you that name myself. Tell me one thing, just one tiny tidbit about Shakespeare's Hero, your namesake, and I will grant you mercy."

Hero whimpered, but said nothing. His eyes darted around frantically, questing, seeking for help from any of the men. His eyes locked briefly with Edgar's.

In response, Edgar mouthed the word "woman" to give the terrified buddy a chance to save himself, but Hero's eyes had already moved on.

When Hero had exhausted all possibility of deliverance, he looked back up at his master. "A-a-a-a . . . s-soldier?"

Shirley's backhanded slap to Hero's face was so swift that even Edgar didn't see it coming. Edgar heard a sickening crunch.

Hero crumpled to the deck, clawing at his broken jaw. The calcium-deficient bones had shattered. He wailed in agony as he curled up into a fetal position on the floor.

C. David Belt

Edgar growled, "That's enough. You've made your point." He realized this display of brutality was as much for his benefit as it was for Hero's.

The gang lord smiled. "Not yet, but I will. Observe." He made a sweeping, dramatic gesture with his hand, taking in the remaining Angels. "Bring him," he said. As the enforcers dragged Hero to his feet, Shirley boomed, "To the Den!" He sounded as if he were passing sentence.

At those words, Hero's wails abruptly morphed into screams of abject terror. The other concubine turned and shuffled down the corridor in the opposite direction, unabashed horror on his face.

"Where are you taking him?" Edgar demanded.

Neither the gang lord nor his enforcers answered. Shirley followed in the wake of the Angels and their struggling prisoner.

Hero continued to scream as he fought desperately to free himself.

Edgar heard at least two more bones snapping, but, blocked by the bodies of Lucifer and his enforcers, Edgar couldn't see if the breaks were the result of Hero's struggling or if the Angels were simply taking potshots at the frantic, defenseless man.

"Where are you taking him?" Edgar shouted again.

Ted grabbed at Edgar's arm. "You don't wanna know."

Edgar wrenched his arm free and followed Shirley, his goons, and their prisoner as they turned down a corridor that Edgar had never visited before.

Edgar's repeated demands for Shirley's group to halt were ignored.

Hero's inarticulate screams continued. In the brief intervals between shrieks when Hero sucked in a tortured breath, the demonic laughter of the Angels filled the air.

The demented procession stopped in front of an open, oversized hatchway. Edgar was so turned about, so distracted and disoriented by the horrific events he was witnessing, he realized with a jolt that he had no idea where they were.

One of the enforcers led the way through the open hatch, and the entire troupe began to follow, pushing their way inside, dragging Hero along with them. Hero's limbs thrashed, but one of his arms and both his legs twisted and flopped in unnatural ways.

Time's Plague

In spite of the broken bones, Hero's struggles grew all the more frantic. He grasped with his good hand at the edge of the hatchway.

The two Angels who were dragging Hero between them attempted to force the man through the hatch, but he held on to the doorway with all the frenzied strength of a drowning man. One of the Angels struck Hero on the back of the head.

Edgar heard the wretch's skull crack—a wet, crunching sound.

With a spasmodic twitch that shook the poor man's entire body, Hero's struggles abruptly ceased.

As did his screams.

Hero's body hung limp, his head at an odd slant.

The Angel who'd struck the blow shook Hero, swearing imprecations and threats.

But Hero was unresponsive.

"Idiot!" roared Shirley. He punched the Angel, knocking the man to the floor. The other Angel released Hero, and the battered concubine crumpled to the floor, like a broken doll.

"I'm sorry, lord!" cried the downed enforcer as he cringed on the floor.

The gang lord gave the man a vicious kick. "You killed him. Worm! Do you want to take his place?"

"No, my lord! Please!" The Angel's face, so often twisted in a vicious sneer, was then a mask of abject, mewling terror. "Mercy!"

The other Angel leered at his cringing fellow, relishing the man's humiliation.

Shirley rubbed the bridge of his nose, clearly annoyed at the turn of events. "You will take Hero's place in my bedchamber for six months. Your buddy will be given to another. If you serve me well, at the end of your penance, I will consider your reinstatement. Otherwise, you will take Hero's place in the Den."

The blood drained from the deposed Angel's face. "Yes, lord. Th-thank you, lord."

The gang lord extended a hand toward the cringing man. For a moment, the former Angel looked hopeful. He tentatively reached toward his master as if to take the proffered hand.

Shirley shook his head. "Surrender your weapon."

C. David Belt

The Angel-turned-concubine withdrew his hand, lowered his head, and presented his master with the club he carried.

Shirley snatched the weapon away. "You will praise me for my mercy, Hero."

It took the man groveling on the floor a moment to realize that his master had referred to him. Shirley had given the former Angel the name of the man he had just murdered. "Y-yes, my Lord Lucifer. You are most merciful." He rolled to his hands and knees and crawled toward Shirley. "Hail, Lord Lucifer!"

"Now, Hero," the gang lord said, "you will remove this filth from my sight." He pointed to the mangled corpse of his erstwhile concubine.

"Yes, my lord." The newly named Hero scrambled to his feet, grasped the body of his namesake under the armpits, and dragged the corpse away down the corridor.

Shirley turned his face away from the retreating, sycophantic, former Angel and his grizzly burden. The gang lord looked directly at Edgar.

Edgar had been immobilized by the brutality he'd witnessed. He shook himself and said, "You're one sick—"

Shirley held up a hand, silencing him. "Bedlam, we have an agreement, do we not? I grant you five minutes to *tour* the Den, and then you will join me in the Throne Room for the proclamation I promised you."

Shirley turned away and strode off down the corridor, his entourage in tow.

Edgar was left in stunned silence, watching Lucifer, his bodyguard, and his new concubine as they disappeared down the corridor and through a hatchway.

Edgar became aware that Ted was tugging at the sleeve of Edgar's ripped jumpsuit. Edgar turned to look at the old man, but Ted wouldn't meet his eyes.

"Lucifer said you made a deal," Ted said softly. "What'd you . . . do for him?"

"What?" Edgar was having trouble processing all that had just occurred.

Ted still wouldn't meet his eyes, but his voice was firm, almost angry. "What'd you do for Lucifer? What bargain?"

"Nothing," Edgar said. He couldn't understand the old man's anger. "Chess. I agreed to a game of chess. Once a week."

"Is that all?"

"Yeah. Why? I was just trying to protect our friends."

"Yeah. Okay."

Edgar was about to ask more, to try to understand what had upset Ted, but movement from inside the open hatchway caught his eye. "Is that the Den?" he asked, pointing to the door where Hero had been murdered.

Ted shook his head violently. "You don't wanna go in there. Ain't nobody wants to go in there."

Whatever lay beyond the hatch stank of unwashed bodies, human waste, and vomit.

Edgar stepped through the hatch, but, as his eyes beheld their first sight of the Den, he stopped dead in his tracks.

The vast, dimly illuminated chamber was littered with the bodies of men. At first, Edgar wasn't sure if they were dead or sleeping, but as bad as the smell of the place was, it didn't stink of death. Scores of men lay on foam pads, some on the floor, others atop tables. In many cases, one man slept on a table, while another man slept on the floor beneath that table. Each sleeper was covered by a blanket, but was otherwise naked, as was evidenced by a bare arm or leg protruding from under his covering. Some of the sleepers were stirring, moving arms or legs slightly. Some of them moaned, and some snored. Most, however, lay unmoving, the slow rise and fall of a chest the only proof of life.

Two of the chamber's occupants, however, were wide awake and fully clothed in stained prison jumpsuits. These two men stood at either end of one table upon which a sleeping man lay. If the two nonsleepers were aware of the mayhem and murder that had just occurred at the hatchway, they showed no sign. They pulled back the blanket, exposing the naked occupant of the table, grasped the sleeper by his shoulders and ankles, and rotated him from his left side to his right. They turned the sleeper as if he were a sausage being rotated in a frying pan. Bedsores were clearly visible on the sleeper's arms, legs, and torso. One of his legs was bent in a place and manner that nature never intended. The leg was quite obviously broken—broken and set very poorly, or not at all.

The two attendants produced a bucket of wet rags and proceeded to clean the sleeper's backside where he'd soiled himself. No great care was employed to assure that the sleeper was cleansed thoroughly or that the fecal matter was kept out of the open sores on the man's bare skin. When the attendants concluded their callous ministrations, they covered the sleeper with his blanket, which was crusted with dried and drying urine.

Edgar also smelled a strong odor of fermentation. Alcohol? he wondered. To prevent infections?

The slumbering man neither woke nor stirred.

At first glance, the Den might've resembled a makeshift hospital overseen by two indifferent nurses, halfheartedly attending to the sick, but the overpowering stench of the place dispelled the illusion that it was in any way dedicated to healing or caring for the wretches sleeping there. Edgar watched in horror as the attendants moved on and turned their unfeeling attentions on another sleeping inmate. One of the attendants glanced in Edgar's direction, nodded curtly at Edgar, and then returned his attention to the man that he and his partner were rotating like a rancid hot dog on a filthy griddle.

Edgar thought he might be sick. "What's going on here?"

Ted put his hands around Edgar's arm. "Let's get out of here. Please."

"Tell me what's going on here!" Edgar growled.

"They're sleeping." Ted tugged at Edgar's arm.

Edgar yanked his arm out of Ted's grasp. "Are they sick?"

"No. I mean, yeah." Ted sounded miserable and frightened. "They're sleeping." He paused. "They're dying too. Just . . . real slow."

"What are they dying of?"

"Sleeping," was Ted's reply.

One of the sleepers moaned loudly. He was a big fellow, lying on a pad on the floor. He struggled to turn from lying on his side to a sitting position. The moan was a pathetic sound, weak, tremulous, and inarticulate. Abruptly, his mewling morphed into words. "S-squeeze! I need squeeze!" he begged as he propped himself up on quaking arms. His blanket fell from his chest, exposing an emaciated frame. The flesh hung in wrinkled folds on his body like a garment several sizes too big for him. He had apparently lost a lot of body mass in a short period of time. His hair was close-cropped, and he had a week's growth of beard. "I need squeeze!"

Time's Plague

Both the attendants swore angrily at the waking man, telling him to be quiet. This only elicited more pitiful, plaintive cries of "Squeeze!" from the waking sufferer. He began to sob. "Please! Gimme the squeeze! I need it!"

The attendants hastily abandoned their current charge and their buckets of cleaning rags, flinging the urine-stained blanket back over the sleeper to whom they'd been attending. They bustled toward the waking man. One of them fetched another bucket as he went. The other retrieved a pitcher of some kind.

"You know the drill," the attendant with the pitcher said. "Food first. Then squeeze."

The man with the bucket drew a ladle out of it and extended it toward the wretch on the floor. The sitting man batted at the ladle, but he was slow, and his aim was poor.

The attendant avoided the strike with ease. He spat at the man on the floor. "Eat first, or you can go a few hours with no squeeze. See how you like that!"

The other attendant stood behind the inmate on the floor, glowering at him menacingly, holding the pitcher over the inmate's head. He slapped the inmate across the back of his head, snapping the man's neck to one side, and spilling some of the contents of the pitcher—water apparently. "Look what you made me do!" He struck the man again. "You'll eat, or I'll pry your damn face open and old Pisser there'll shove it down your gut. Now, shut up and eat your damn mush!"

The inmate stifled his sobs and cries, his thin arms barely supporting him.

Pisser—the attendant with the bucket—extended the ladle and said, "Open up."

The quaking inmate opened his jaws wide, and Pisser poured something brown and thick into the trembling mouth. The inmate swallowed without bothering to chew. Then he opened his mouth again, awaiting another bite.

This process was repeated five times before Pisser was satisfied. He plopped the ladle back in the bucket and looked up at his partner. The partner passed the pitcher to Pisser.

"Don't want no water," the inmate said. "Just gimme the squeeze!"

"Drink it," Pisser said, "or no squeeze."

The inmate grimaced. "I'm gonna puke."

"You do," growled the attendant behind him, "and I'll break another of your fingers."

With a groan, the inmate opened his mouth again.

Pisser poured water into the open mouth, and the inmate gulped it down.

"That's good. You don't need no more," said Pisser. He rose to his feet, picking up the bucket. "You sit still there and let your mush settle, Griz, and we'll get your squeeze in a bit." Pisser and his partner turned their backs and walked away.

Griz? This withered, shrunken creature is the man who nearly killed me? He used to be huge! What've they done to him?

Without his hair and beard and his impressive musculature, Edgar couldn't see anything familiar in the quivering wreck. Even the man's eyes didn't look the same. They looked dead.

In a flash, Ted left Edgar's side and hurried over to his former master. Ted knelt beside Griz and threw his arms around the man's shoulders. "Oh, Grizzy!" Ted wailed. "I'm so sorry! I didn't know they made you sleep for what you done."

Griz clutched at Ted with one of is thin hands. "T-Toady?"

"It's me, Grizzy!" Tears streamed down Ted's face.

Griz turned his head toward his former buddy, his expression suddenly hopeful. "Got any squeeze?"

Ted shook his head. "No, Griz. I ain't got no squeeze. Pisser and Ruby—they got your squeeze."

Griz's expression turned from hope to rage. "Get outta here!" He shook himself violently and clawed at Ted's arms. "Leave me alone!"

Ted released the man and shrank away in horrorified anguish. "I'm sorry, Griz!"

"Squeeze!" wailed Griz. "Please gimme my squeeze!"

"Here now!" yelled one of the attendants. He wasn't the one called Pisser, so he must have been Ruby. "Leave him alone! What the hell d'ya think you're doing?"

Ted rose to his feet and hurried back to hide behind Edgar. He gripped Edgar's arm with both his thin hands.

Those hands were trembling.

Ted was weeping.

"Squeeze!" sobbed Griz.

"I got your squeeze," said Ruby with obvious contempt. He produced a flask and poured a few swallows down Griz's throat. Griz swallowed greedily and tried to wrench the flask from Ruby's hands, but the attendant batted Griz's quaking hands away. "Can't have no more," said Ruby. "You still got a few good months left in ya."

Griz laid down and pulled his stained blanket over himself. He curled up into a fetal position and trembled, waiting for the drug to take effect.

"You're the Fool, ain't ya?" said Pisser striding toward Edgar. "Come here to see Lucifer's justice?" He pointed at Griz. "Well, there he is. He's sleeping. Get a good look and get the hell out of here."

Ruby was on his feet as well, glaring at Edgar and Ted.

Griz's quaking was already easing.

Whatever that stuff was, it couldn't work that fast. Maybe just getting the drug is enough to calm him, because he knows he's going to get relief.

"What was that stuff?" Edgar asked.

Pisser laughed, a hideous sound full of malice and contempt. "Squeeze. You ain't heard of squeeze?"

"Go on," growled Ruby. "You've had your fun. Now go!"

"We gotta all be in the Throne Room in a few minutes, don't we?" said Pisser. "Get outta here so's we can lock up and go hear whatever Lucifer wants to say."

Ted pulled on Edgar's arm. At last, Edgar suffered himself to be led out of that horrible den of misery.

From behind them, Griz began to snore.

Ted sobbed.

Once they were back in the corridor and headed in the direction of the Throne Room, Edgar said, "What's going on? Is this what you've all been talking about when you were going on about being *made to sleep*? I thought it was just another way of saying *dead*."

Ted was still weeping, but he replied, "Yeah. That's the Den. That's what they call it. It's where you go to sleep. Sleep 'til you die."

"So it's a punishment?"

"Yeah. The worstest there is. You can get beaten. You can get raped. They can take away your calcilock. But the worst is sleeping. Griz must-a got put there after he tried to . . ." The old man's voice trailed off.

"Kill me?" Edgar finished.

Ted nodded.

"Why not just kill him?" Edgar asked, adding quickly, "Not that I want him to die."

"'Cause Lucifer don't want nobody dead-dead. If you're dead, well . . . Doc Stewart's sensors count heartbeats. He knows how many guys are alive. That's how he knows how much calcilock, medicine, jumpsuits, and other stuff to order. And if you're sleeping, you don't need none of that stuff. Luci— uh, the boss, he takes the stuff meant for the sleepers and he uses it as rewards. If you wanna be big and strong like . . . like Griz . . . like Griz used to be, you need more calcilock than normal. So, you need to be on the boss's good side."

"What's squeeze?"

"Some kinda drug. Makes you sleep. Made from a flower. Somebody smuggled in some seeds about eight years back. They grow 'em in the agridome. Poppies, I think. Pretty name. Ugly flower."

As they walked, Edgar searched his memory for the name of the drug made from poppies. At last he asked, "Opium?"

Ted wiped away a tear and shrugged. "I guess. Don't know. It's squeeze, 'cause you cut the round part of the flower and squeeze out the juice. And once you're on that stuff, you don't want nothing else. No food. No buddy. No nothing. Just the squeeze."

"So they force you to become addicted and let you slowly die?"

"Yeah. Takes months. Maybe a standard year for big guys like . . ." He paused and rubbed at his eyes angrily. "And they take your stuff, and Lu— the boss gives it to guys he likes. 'Specially the calcilock."

"That's sick. Obscene. What a horrible way to go."

Ted stifled a sob.

Edgar put an arm around the old man's shoulders as they walked. "I'm sorry, Ted."

Time's Plague

Ted wiped his nose with his sleeve. "Griz tried to kill you. If you do that, it's pretty much for sure you're gonna sleep. I just wasn't thinking about what was gonna happen to Griz, 'cause I was worried about you."

Edgar growled in his throat. "Somebody needs to stop this obscenity."

The old man scowled darkly. "It just ain't right."

A pair of men passed them from behind, hurrying to the Throne Room. One of the men leaned in toward Edgar.

It was Scar.

"Just say the word, Bedlam," he whispered. "We're ready."

Then Scar and his buddy were gone, speeding off down the corridor.

As Edgar stared at their backs, for the first time since the day when he'd first met Scar, he considered taking the man up on his offer.

Briefly.

I just won a concession for us to worship unmolested. And all it cost me was a game of chess and a ripped jumpsuit.

And a moment of stark terror.

A shudder ran through Edgar's body.

But I'm not about to lead an armed rebellion—to depose one brutal dictator only to set up Scar or someone else potentially worse in his place.

Although, truth be told, it's hard to imagine any tyrant worse than Lamar Shirley.

No. One battle at a time.

Or is it simply a case of better the devil you know?

****

By the time Edgar and Ted arrived in the throne room, Shirley was already holding court. The gang lord sat upon his throne, his remaining Angels standing guard on either side of him. The newly designated "Hero" knelt at his master's feet, resting his head on Shirley's knee and looking utterly miserable. The other concubine that Edgar had seen in Shirley's quarters knelt on the other side of the gang lord.

The entire prison population—except for the wretches in the Den—stared at the crimson-clad figure of their leader.

Shirley's booming voice filled the room. ". . . shall now be known as Hero. He shall serve me as my royal concubine." Shirley stroked the new Hero's head as Edgar used to do with that silly dog of Llyrica's.

Llyrica's face flashed through his mind. Edgar ground his teeth in anger and frustration. *Stop it! She's gone! She betrayed you! She sent you here!*

"It has come to my attention," Shirley said, using a stage voice that might be the envy of any Shakespearean actor, "that some of you have abandoned the true worship of your lord"—he paused for dramatic effect—"and have joined with the Fool, Tom Bedlam, in praying to the Christian God. You have been meeting in secret."

He stood and pointed at the assemblage accusingly. "Do not dare to deny it!"

Edgar caught sight of Soo-Won and Charlie and a few of the others standing together. Charlie hung his head, but Soo-Won stared defiantly at the gang lord. The others exchanged fearful glances.

Goner, with Ozzie still clutching a bloody nose at his side glared at Edgar.

"Tom Bedlam!" roared Shirley. "Stand forth!"

Edgar took a deep breath and then stepped forward into the space between the throng of prisoners and Shirley and his entourage.

"Let all who were assembled with Bedlam to worship come and stand with him," commanded the gang lord.

Nobody moved.

Long seconds ticked by, but abruptly Soo-Won separated himself from the crowd and came to stand by Edgar.

Charlie looked stricken, but stayed where he was.

A moment later, Edgar felt Ted's hands wrap themselves around his arm.

Charlie balled his hands into fists, swore softly, and stomped over to stand by Soo-Won.

Ibrahim and Karan stepped forward and joined them. "I stand with Christ," cried Ibrahim. There was a quaver of fear in his voice.

Time's Plague

Alone or in pairs, they all came forward. Some echoed Ibrahim's declaration. Others came forward silently, but they all came. They surrounded Edgar like a company of bodyguards.

A tear spilled from Edgar's eye as he was nearly overwhelmed with the courage of these men. There was not a man among them who was not terrified. Some of them trembled openly as they stood. And yet they stood.

"Very well," cried Shirley, an expression of contempt on his face, "let it be—"

To Edgar's utter astonishment, another man Edgar didn't recognize separated himself from the mob and came to join the Christians.

Then another came to join them.

And another.

And yet another.

In less than a minute, their ranks had swollen from eighteen to at least forty or fifty.

Edgar stared at the newcomers in amazement.

Then he looked at Shirley.

The gang lord's face twisted in rage and his face colored red. He glared at Edgar and those who stood with him. After several seconds, he flung his arms wide and spat, "You stand with Christ, do you?"

It was a terrible sound, like the roar of a wounded beast of prey.

Some of the men cried out or whimpered in fear.

But not all.

"I stand with Christ," cried Soo-Won. "We all do."

Shirley glared at Soo-Won and his eyes seemed to glow with hellfire.

Edgar shook his arm free from Ted's grasp and stepped out of the protection of his friends to stand at their head. "I stand with Christ," he said. "And you gave your word."

The rage in Shirley's face melted into a wicked grin.

Suddenly, Edgar felt very much like a trapped mouse facing a triumphant cat.

"Yes," said Shirley, "I did." Then he winked unnervingly at Edgar.

"Very well," boomed Shirley. He swept his arms over the mob theatrically again. "Let it be known that all who wish to worship the Christian God with Tom Bedlam"—he paused again—"may do so with impunity! For the vast majority of you who do not comprehend the meaning of that word, it means that you may pray and sing with Bedlam without fear of punishment. You will go about your assigned duties as before, but you are free to worship as you choose. Tom Bedlam will lead you in prayer and song. And you will not be punished for doing so. As long as you do your duties and you do not foment sedition, you will be under Tom Bedlam's protection as he is under mine. This means that you will not be *disciplined* by my Angels in any way."

This set off a low roar of murmuring from both the mob and those who stood with Edgar.

More men separated from the mob to join with Edgar's group.

"But," boomed Shirley, the wicked grin splitting his face from ear to ear, "know this—Bedlam has won this right for you. We made a bargain, Bedlam and I. A covenant, if you will. He won this right for you, in return for certain . . . *favors* that he will provide to me, favors that he has already done for me today."

Every eye in the room was instantly focused on Edgar.

Edgar looked at Soo-Won.

The Asian, although looking in Edgar's direction, seemed to be looking not at Edgar, but rather at Edgar's torn jumpsuit, his tousled hair. Then Soo-Won's eyes met Edgar's.

Soo-Won looked like a man who had lost all hope, a damned soul. He shook his head. "No," he mouthed silently.

Understanding gripped Edgar like an icy fist. The cat had captured the mouse.

Edgar shook his head violently. "No! It was a game of chess! Just a game of chess!"

Men began to slink away, to rejoin the mob, their eyes downcast.

"That's all it was!" cried Edgar.

The devil standing in front of his throne began to laugh.

In moments, those standing with Edgar numbered only three. Ted remained. And to Edgar's surprise, so did Soo-Won and Charlie.

Only four of them still stood together.

Shirley's ruse had destroyed Edgar's credibility.

"I suppose you no longer require a larger meeting space?" said Shirley.

And the devil laughed and all his Angels.

A commotion broke out at the back of the room.

Someone must have arrived late.

Shirley's laughter ceased. He did not look pleased.

"Ship!" It was a voice coming from the back of the room near the entrance. "A ship!"

As one, the entire assemblage turned toward the hatchway.

Two men stood just inside the door. They looked out of breath. Edgar recognized them as agridome workers, but couldn't remember their names.

"There's a ship!" yelled one of the late arrivals. "A ship landed! Outside the agridome! I saw it with my own eyes!"

And all hell erupted as men stampeded for the door.

Chapter 21

Fortune, that arrant whore,
Ne'er turns the key to the poor.

King Lear, Act II, Scene IV

"Ain't we going to see the ship?" Ted shuffled along, hurrying after Edgar as he sped down a deserted corridor. "The agridome's the other way! Everybody's gone to see it."

"I'm not going there," said Edgar. "You go ahead and join Soo-Won and the others. I'll meet you in our quarters later."

"Where're you going?"

"To see Doc Stewart."

"You sick? Did Lucifer hurt you? You said he didn't . . ."

Edgar ground his teeth in frustration. "He didn't, and I didn't. He ripped my clothes, made it look like something else had happened. That's all." *It was a game of chess!*

"So why you going to see Doc?"

"Because if there is a ship out there, he's the only one that can get to it."

"Oh," replied the old man slowly as if he understood. "Yeppers! You're right!"

"Doc's got an airlock that isn't welded shut," Edgar reasoned. "He's got the only functioning spacesuit—not that he needs it."

"Well, waddaya know!" cried Ted. "You're a genius."

Edgar shook his head as he hurried along. "Nope, I just never liked the zoo much."

"What's a zoo?"

Poor kid! You don't know what a zoo is? "It's a place where they keep wild animals in cages and enclosures so people can go look at them."

"That sounds wonderful!" Ted said. "I ain't never been to a zoo. I'd love to see some animals. The captain on my dad's ship, he had a cat."

"I like animals too," said Edgar. "I just hated seeing something I couldn't get close to, couldn't touch. I like to get my hands on things. And I don't like cages."

"Okay," replied Ted. The old man was breathing hard. "But I don't get it. What're you talking about?"

"Well, if there is a ship out there, I don't want to just stare at it through a transparent wall. That's like looking at food you can see, but can't taste."

"Well, Doc ain't gonna let you wear that spacesuit and go outside."

"Maybe not, but at least I'll be able to find out what's really going on."

"What if people in that ship wanna come in here? Maybe they're here to break us out."

"Even if they were, they'd have to go in through the infirmary airlock, unless they plan on blowing a hole in the colony, venting all the atmosphere, and killing us all."

"Yeppers!" the old man exclaimed. "You got that right! Like I said—you're a genius! Can I come with you?"

"No, the doctor'll only admit one of us at a time."

"But Doc says I'm sick, right? Heart's too big or some such thing. I can go in for one of them checkups, right? And you're a trustee. You can go in anytime."

Edgar grinned. "Now who's the genius?" He glanced at Ted's face and was rewarded with a gap-toothed smile. The old man looked pale, though—bloodless. Ted's need to see the doctor was genuine.

They hurried on, and Ted's breathing grew more labored.

****

Edgar tapped his fingers impatiently on the inner door of the airlock. Ted had already been admitted by the doctor and was most likely being restrained in bed. That was the protocol—all inmates were restrained, with the possible exception of a single trustee. Edgar had to wait until the doctor returned and admitted him into the infirmary.

When at last the inner door hissed open, the android greeted Edgar. "Mr. Cordell! Thank you for convincing Mr. Knight—"

Edgar shook his head quickly. "A ship, Doc. Landed outside the agridome."

The doctor cocked its head. "Unlikely. No ship may land on Callisto. I received no notification of a supply or prisoner drop." Even as it spoke, however, the android turned and hurried off toward the outer airlock. "We will discuss your deception when I return."

"No deception, Doc. I just need to keep Ted out of trouble, and you said he could come by anytime for a checkup."

"True enough." The robot stopped in front of a secure locker. The doctor entered a long key-code and opened the locker. The doctor began to don the environment-suit.

"Why wear the spacesuit, Doc?" Edgar asked. "You don't really need—"

"It keeps the dust out of my joints and gears," the android replied. It worked quickly, connecting and sealing the components of the suit.

Edgar lifted the environment pack and snapped it on the back of the doctor's suit. The doctor might not need the air, but the suit seal wouldn't be complete without the pack. "The proximity to the colony suggests a deliberate attempt to land here," Edgar said, "rather than an accidental crash. It could've been an emergency landing."

"Or an attempt to free the prisoners." Dr. Stewart placed the helmet on its head and closed the last of the seals. "I shall return," it shouted as it retrieved a bag of tools, medical and mechanical.

With that, the spacesuited android tapped a key-code into another security panel. The inner door of the airlock—the airlock that led to the outside, the only exit from the prison—slid open.

Edgar watched as the doctor entered the tiny chamber. The inner door slid closed, and the android triggered a rapid decompression sequence. In less than half a minute, the outer door slid open, and the doctor stepped out onto the surface of Callisto, its feet creating tiny clouds of dust.

Edgar watched as the outer door slid shut with a metallic thud.

Now all Edgar could do was wait . . . and speculate.

A deliberate, nonemergency landing on Callisto was a criminal offense with a very stiff penalty—incarceration in Hades itself. It had never been attempted since the prison went online.

Surely nobody on the outside would want to break anybody out of here. It's not like this place is populated with criminal masterminds. And whoever it is would have to be pretty desperate to seek assistance from Hades.

"Hey, Edgar!" Ted yelled from a distance.

"Coming," Edgar called back.

He found Ted strapped to a bed in the examination room.

"Doc's gone?" the old man asked.

"Yep. How're you feeling? You were having a hard time catching your breath."

Ted shrugged. "I'm okay. But since I'm dying, I can't be that okay, can I? Can you unstrap me?"

Edgar shook his head. "If I want Doc to trust me, I've got to obey his rules."

The old man shrugged. "I guess so. Do ya think there'll be women on that ship?"

Edgar laughed bitterly. "No. Not a chance in . . . well, Hades. No woman would get within twenty thousand kilometers of this place, much less land here. Something about this place kills females. You know that."

Ted looked stricken. "I'm sorry! I forgot. Your grandma. Your aunt. I'm sorry." He slammed his head back against the bed. "So stupid!"

"It's okay, Ted." Edgar should've stepped forward and taken the old man's hand to comfort him, but he held back.

"So what was it?"

"Hmm?" *Relax, Cordell. The doctor's going to be a while. He's got to walk all the way around the colony to get to the agridome. And who knows how close the ship actually is? Ship or shuttle? Shuttle, most likely.* "What was what?"

"What killed all the girls and women?" asked Ted.

"Nobody knows. From what I read, nothing showed up on the med-scanners. The best guess was some type of radiation. The ones that survived—the younger ones—started getting better almost as soon as they were in orbit. All they know is that none of the males got sick. That's why they turned this place into a prison for men."

Ted sighed. "I'd like to see a woman. I hope there's one on that ship. Maybe it's a whole *shipful* of women! Yeppers! I'd like to see me some women!"

"Even if they all die?"

Ted shrugged. "They'd live for a while, wouldn't they?"

"Not here. Those beasts out there would tear them apart." Edgar looked at the old man with sudden disgust. "That's sick, you know! A woman is a human being, not a thing to be . . . *used* until she dies. How could you even think—"

"Hey! I can dream, can't I?"

"About rape?"

Ted looked sheepishly at him. "It wouldn't be no rape if we was married. You're a priest, ain't ya? You could marry one of 'em to me."

Edgar waved a hand dismissively. "This is a stupid argument. There're no women on the ship. So get that out of your head."

"I bet there's a woman."

"Shut up, Ted."

"But—"

"Just shut up for a while. Please?"

The old man clamped his mouth shut and turned his head away sullenly. "At least you've *been* with a woman," he muttered.

Don't think about women, Cordell. Edgar closed his eyes, trying to shut out the memories. *She's gone. She betrayed you. She left you for another man.* But Llyrica's face swam before his closed eyelids like a siren, luring sailors to a cold death beneath the sea.

Llyrica left you for Edmund Reagan. Focus on that. The two of them put you here. Put you in hell.

But he could see the blue of her eyes, the gold of her blonde hair cascading in soft waves, the pink of her soft lips. The scent of her, especially when the two of them . . .

"Stop it!" he growled. *That way lies madness!*

"What'd you say?" asked Ted.

"Nothing," Edgar replied.

Time's Plague

She's gone. You're never going to see her again. And even if you did . . . what would you say? You don't want her back! You don't!

He shook himself. *The ship! Think of that. Why is it here?*

Could it be used somehow . . . to escape?

Edgar's mind conjured up a dozen scenarios, fantasies of escape, each more improbable than the last. In the end, he rejected them all.

There's only one airlock and one spacesuit. And to use the airlock and the suit, you'd have to get past Doc. He'd never let you use them. You don't know the key-code. He'll never give it to you. Doc's first imperative is to preserve human life, but his second is to prevent escapes.

Face it, Cordell, short of an armed raid by the people . . . the men—*There are* no *women!—aboard that ship in some insane attempt to rescue one or more prisoners, nobody's going to escape from Hades.*

Nobody.

Edgar was jarred out of his thoughts by the unmistakable sound of an airlock door opening.

He hurried to that airlock, arriving just in time to watch through the small window as the outer door slid shut. The doctor stood inside the airlock. The android was no longer wearing the spacesuit. Rather, in its titanium arms it held a limp, space suited figure.

A crash landing, then, he thought as he heard the hiss of air filling the interior of the airlock. *A crash survivor.* It was the only explanation.

As the pressure equalized, the doctor pressed a button and his voice emerged from the intercom.

"Is Mr. Knight still restrained?" it asked.

Edgar pressed the button to reply. "Yes. He's where you left him."

"You did not free him?"

"No, Doc. I didn't."

The doctor pressed a button, and the inner door of the airlock slid open.

"Very good," said the android as it stepped through the hatchway and into the infirmary. "Retrieve a chemical burn kit and bring it to Emergency-room 4 immediately."

"Wilco," said Edgar as he turned to procure an emergency pack for treating severe chemical burns.

As they passed the exam room where Ted lay in restraints, the old man called out, "You back, Doc? Any women on that ship?"

The doctor did not answer, so Edgar shouted, "Shut up, Ted!"

As he followed the doctor into the assigned chamber, he briefly wondered, *Why ER-4? That's not the closest emergency-room.* "Any other survivors, Doc?"

"None. There were two other casualties, however. Now help me remove the suit," the doctor said, his tone commanding, urgent as it cracked the seal on the patient's helmet and detached the environment pack. "You remove the boots and lower half. I will get the rest."

Edgar hurried to comply. He broke the seals on the boots and pulled them off as quickly as he dared, taking care not to injure the patient in the process.

Whoever he was, the patient was short and slight, almost as short as Soo-Won.

Edgar broke the seal at the waist of the suit and began removing the trousers. When he'd pulled the trousers down to the patient's knees, Edgar stopped what he was doing and stared.

From the shape of the patient's hips, the person in the spacesuit was quite obviously female.

"A woman," Edgar hissed.

"Obviously," snapped the doctor. "Now hurry up or get out."

"Yes, sir." Edgar quickly finished removing the lower half of the spacesuit.

"Now the gloves," said the robot.

Edgar removed first one glove and then another. Both hands showed signs of chemical burns. The flesh was angry red and starting to blister.

Edgar recognized the scent of the chemical agent—gel from a neuro-pak, used in smaller artificial intelligence units.

"Neuro-gel," he said. "Nasty stuff."

"Mercifully, the exposure is limited to her face and hands." The doctor slid the upper half of the suit off the patient and gently laid her back on the bed, her yellow hair fanning out behind her head. "The gel hit her in the face. She was clawing at her eyes and screaming when I found her, so I was forced to administer a sedative. Now, Mr. Cordell, the burn kit, if you please."

But Edgar didn't fetch the burn kit.

He stood rooted to the deck as if held there by all the gravity of Jupiter. He stood unmoving as he stared at the woman lying on the hospital bed.

Her face was red and blistering around the closed, swollen eyes, but Edgar saw past the burns and the swelling. He recognized that face. He would've known that face anywhere, because it haunted his dreams.

Llyrica.

Act III

Chapter 22

If you have poison for me, I will drink it.
King Lear, Act IV, Scene VII

"Mr. Cordell! Either obey my orders or leave." The doctor pointed a metal finger at the burn kit.

Edgar snatched up the kit and opened it. His movements were automatic, wooden—the android's movements fluid by comparison.

The doctor placed an open jar of a green-colored cream in Edgar's hands. It smelled awful, like rotting corn and lubricant. "Apply this liberally to her hands." The doctor began to apply the same cream to Llyrica's face.

Edgar spread the cream over the red and blistered flesh of his ex-wife's hands. Some of the blisters popped, leaking clear fluid, when he touched them.

"Gently," said the doctor. "We do not wish to damage the skin any further. Once the caustic agent is neutralized, we will need to remove all the neutralizing cream before we can apply the regeneration ointment."

Llyrica, thought Edgar as he applied the medicine to the last of the affected areas on her hands, *what in the System are you doing here?* Hatred and rage and wonder and even desire roiled within his gut like a boiling pot of rancid stew. *Come to gloat? To see the monkey in his cage? Was it worth it?*

"Help me turn her on her side," the doctor said.

As they rotated the patient, Edgar thought, *No, of course not. She knows she can't survive here. Llyrica's many things— vain, selfish, unfaithful—but she's not stupid. Not that stupid.*

The doctor shoved a small, rectangular basin into Edgar's hands. "Hold this under her eyes."

Time's Plague

While Edgar held the bowl as directed, the doctor used a bulb syringe and began flushing one of Llyrica's eyes with a green fluid with a scent similar to the neutralizing cream. Stewart pried open one swollen eye and gently released the fluid onto the eyeball while Edgar caught the runoff. The doctor alternated between the eyes, cleaning each in turn and by degrees.

"Normally," said the doctor, "I would put on my hands so I could be more delicate with the eyes, but there is no time."

As the green fluid washed away the caustic neuro-gel, the damage to the eyes became apparent, even to Edgar's untrained sight. Once a striking blue, Llyrica's eyes were milky white. The pupils were barely visible behind a clouded, ravaged cornea.

Not so pretty now, are you, sweetie? he thought, and immediately hated himself for it. *Stop it, Cordell. You're not a vengeful person.*

But I hate her. And she deserves it. She deserves worse than that.

Let God dispense justice.

What if that's precisely what He did?

Yeah? Well, what if the Lord sent me here too?

"That should do it," the android said as he straightened up. "You may empty that into the sink."

Edgar turned and emptied the basin. With his back to the doctor, Edgar looked up and stared into the mirror above the sink. A gargoyle visage stared back. As hideous as his face was, it was the ugliness reflected in his eyes that sickened him the most. *You're kind and respectful to murderers and rapists, at least those who are feeling their way toward repentance. You treat them like children of God. Why can't you find any compassion for this woman?*

Because she's no better than Goner or Edmund. She's worse. She helped kill Ol' Benny. She betrayed me. I loved her more than life itself and she . . . she sent me to hell.

"How bad is it, Doc?" he asked, still staring at the reflection of his own disfigured face. "She's blind, isn't she?" In the reflection, Edgar could see the doctor gently wiping away the neutralizing cream from Llyrica's face.

"The skin will heal quite well," the doctor said, intent on its work. "Or it will once I apply the regeneration ointment, and

C. David Belt

she has a week to heal. There will be minimal scarring, perhaps none at all. Help me roll her onto her back again."

Edgar turned from the mirror and assisted the doctor.

Once Llyrica was again lying on her back, the doctor began administering drops into her eyes. "The eyes are another matter," it said. "Her eyes might heal given sufficient time and proper treatment. The damage is severe enough that I would normally clone a new pair of eyes for her, or at least new corneas, but there is not sufficient time for her to heal—she will be dead in two or three weeks. That is, unless whatever kills females on this moon has somehow gone away. And I very much doubt that."

"Callistoan Female Plague," said Edgar. "It killed my grandmother and my aunt."

The doctor looked up at him. "I was not aware of that. I am sorry. Unfortunately, there is very little medical data from that episode. The descriptions of the progression of the disease are anecdotal at best. The survivors showed no symptoms by the time they reached Ganymede. If I were to hypothesize, I would venture to guess that the cause is background radiation or a native toxin that somehow activates the extra—and therefore normally inactive—X chromosome in females. From the anecdotal data, this somehow interfered with ability of the blood to carry oxygen. In spite of being in an oxygen-rich environment, the victims slowly suffocated. Be that as it may, I lack the equipment and the time necessary to test such a . . ."

"Cut to the chase, Doc," growled Edgar.

"The chase, as you put it, Mr. Cordell, is that I can do nothing more than treat her symptoms and watch her die."

Watch her die. No matter how much I hate her, no matter what she's done, I . . . can't imagine the System without Llyrica in it.

Edgar stared at the face he had once loved, smeared as it was with cream. *You were my life, my universe. How could you do this to me?*

The doctor busied itself cleaning off the neutralizing cream from Llyrica's face.

Llyrica! Why? Why? Why?

The doctor cleansed Llyrica's hands. Edgar watched in silence as the doctor applied a skin regeneration ointment to the burned areas.

"What's going on?" called Ted from the other room. "He alive or dead?"

"Actually, Mr. Knight," began the doctor, but it abruptly stopped talking when Edgar hissed and waved frantically in an attempt to silence the doctor.

Edgar didn't want Ted to know that the survivor was a woman.

Why not? Why not just let the monsters have her?

Because you couldn't let it happen, Cordell. You couldn't stand by and let her be raped and brutalized, no matter what she's done. Nobody deserves that. Not even her. You just couldn't let it happen.

Oh, couldn't I?

No, you could not, Cordell, and you know it.

The doctor nodded, apparently discerning the reason for Edgar's caution. It lifted its voice and called back, "The lone survivor is dying. There is nothing I can do to save the patient."

If Ted responded to that, Edgar couldn't hear it.

"Why treat her eyes then?" asked Edgar. "Why treat her burns? If there's . . . no hope?"

"I will treat her eyes and heal her burns, because she is injured. That is my function. I could not do otherwise. And do not presume to think that I will not do everything in my power to save her, even if, in the end, there is nothing I can do."

"Sorry, Doc. Of course you will."

"The gauze, Mr. Cordell, if you please."

Edgar retrieved bandage material from a cabinet. "Maybe somebody from the ship could get her off-world," he said. "Was it a ship or a shuttle?"

"You do realize that identification of various spacecraft types is a bit beyond my purview," said the doctor as it began to bandage Llyrica's eyes and face. "However, judging from the size of the vessel, I think I would be safe in assuming that it was a shuttle."

"You said there were other casualties."

"Yes. Two. Both were male. They received a greater exposure to the neuro-gel from the explosion. I suspect they inhaled it."

C. David Belt

"Yeah," said Edgar, shuddering at the mental image, "that'd do it. What about the ship? No shuttle could make it here on its own. There has to be a full-sized ship in orbit."

The robot made a sighing sound and shrugged its shoulders. "I did attempt to use the transmitter on the shuttle to send out a distress call. However, it too was damaged. I could not get it to function. I fear that, unless another vessel lands, we will see no rescue from the mother ship."

There has to be a way to save her, thought Edgar. *I will not stand by and let Llyrica die. I've got to get her off-world!* He paused in his thought, almost not daring to form the idea in his mind. *Get her off-world!* A thought, a plan, a wild, desperate hope flashed in Edgar's mind like a supernova.

"Let *me* check it out, Doc," he said, trying very hard to suppress the eagerness in his voice. "I might be able to get the transmitter working. I was a ship's engineer before I was a captain."

The doctor laughed. "Nice try, Mr. Cordell. However, you know that I am forbidden to assist—or, by inaction, to allow—an escape from the Hades Penal Colony. Nothing could induce me to disobey that imperative. It goes completely against my programming."

Edgar smiled inwardly. *Now, that's an argument I can win.* "Nothing, that is, except your *primary* imperative—to preserve human life. Doesn't that take precedence? Doesn't that override everything else?"

The doctor said nothing as it put the finishing touches on the bandages. It turned to look at Edgar. Still, it said nothing for several long moments.

Edgar's mind raced, but he put on his chess face, his negotiating face. *Please, Doc, let me try. She'll die if she stays here. Let me get her off-world!*

After what seemed an eon to Edgar, the android opened its jaw. "Well played, Mr. Cordell. I have run thousands of simulations, all leading me to the same conclusion. In order for the patient to survive, she must get off the surface of this moon, probably out of its orbit. It seems that I must violate my secondary imperative to obey my primary imperative." Dr. Stewart cocked its head. "However, Mr. Cordell—and please excuse my frankness—what is to prevent you from simply attempting to escape in the shuttle?"

"Don't you trust me, Doc?"

"You have earned a level of trust, I will admit, but you must admit that the current circumstances are extraordinary."

Edgar nodded. "Putting it mildly, yeah."

"Precisely."

"Look, Doc. I won't pretend the thought hasn't occurred to me." Edgar paused and shook his head. "What can I do to assure you?" After a moment's thought, he said, "How about this? You accompany me to the shuttle when I go to look at the transmitter. I'll be in a spacesuit, and you won't. If I tried anything, you could easily overpower me."

The doctor cocked its head to the side. "Reasonable. Logical. Not at all what I have come to expect from humans."

Edgar shook his head at the jibe, but he grinned. "Thanks a whole cargo load, Doc. But first, we have to get Ted out of here. It was a mistake to bring him along. I don't want to risk him getting free and . . . Well, I don't want word to get out. They'll be trying to hack through the airlock, you know, to get to her."

"Agreed. As for the airlock, I do have a few defenses I can employ should they get through the outer hatch. As for your other suggestion, I will see to discharging Mr. Knight. You remain here with the patient. I assume that you will act with all decorum."

Edgar nodded. "Sure. She'll be safe with me." *You're testing me, aren't you, Doc?* "I'm not going to touch her." *Not even to strangle her.* "Just hurry back. And, uh, tell Ted to check up on our friends. My friends. His and my friends." He growled in exasperation. *I sound like an idiot.* "You know what I mean?"

"I will relay the message."

The doctor left the room, leaving Edgar alone with his ex-wife.

Llyrica lay on the inclined hospital bed, gauze wrapped like a blindfold around her head. Her mouth hung open, and her chest rose and fell in a slow and steady rhythm. Her gentle snoring stirred loving memories of watching Llyrica sleep.

Her bandaged hands lay at her sides like soft, misshapen mallets. She was helpless, completely vulnerable, utterly unable to protect herself.

And she was at the mercy of the one man who hated her more than any other.

Edgar's thoughts were a maelstrom of conflicting ideas and contradictory images. In one mental flash, he saw his hands around Llyrica's throat, squeezing the life out of her. In the next image, he bent to kiss her forehead. He saw her face, fresh and beaming and lovely enough to melt any man's heart, her blue eyes gazing at him on their wedding day. And he saw her crocodile tears as she uttered those damning lies in the courtroom at his trial. Murderous rage crashed against the pain of a shattered heart. Desire collided with revulsion. He saw himself in the howling wind and driving rain of a terrestrial thunderstorm, raging at the elements, at the cruel tempest of his fate. He saw the two of them—husband and wife—lounging on a picnic blanket in the agridome under a perfect Martian Sun. Accusations and cursings shrieked against cries of grief and longing.

And out of all that ferocious tempest of violent passions and tumultuous thoughts, one word coalesced in his mind like the calm at the center of a hurricane. A single word that embodied all the anger and misery and longing of his soul.

Why?

Edgar's hands trembled, and he crossed his arms and shoved his hands into his armpits. His breathing became labored and ragged as if he couldn't fill his lungs with enough oxygen.

Why are you here?

Edgar realized he was weeping. He unfolded his arms and dashed away the tears with quaking hands.

He turned to a cabinet and retrieved a blanket and a pillow. An image flashed in his mind—his hands holding the pillow over Llyrica's face.

He set the blanket on the counter and held the pillow in both hands as he approached Llyrica's head.

Why did you cast me into hell?

He gently lifted Llyrica's head and slid the pillow beneath it.

Her hair was as soft as he remembered. And the scent of it!

Edgar retrieved the blanket and pulled it over the sleeping, vulnerable form of the only woman he had ever truly loved. He lingered for a moment, gazing at her bandaged face.

Time's Plague

Why wasn't I good enough?

He sighed and turned away from her, only to be startled to see Dr. Stewart standing in the doorway, watching Edgar intently.

"Who is she?" the robot asked.

Edgar swallowed hard, wiping furiously at his eyes and tear-streaked cheeks, but he didn't answer.

"I have watched you for some time, Mr. Cordell," said the doctor. "There are cameras placed at strategic points throughout my infirmary. All of them can feed directly to my brain, if I choose to monitor them. I chose to monitor you and the patient. You were never out of my sight, even while I was escorting Mr. Knight to the airlock. Your reactions, your expressions, and your tears bespeak an intimacy with this woman. So I ask again, who is she?"

Edgar turned back to look at Llyrica. "I . . . don't know, Doc. I loved her once. I loved her more than anyone or anything in the entire blasted System. But then she . . . I don't know who she is anymore. Maybe I never knew her, not really. She's a stranger to me."

"I see," said the doctor. "Llyrica Gloster Reagan, formerly Llyrica Gloster Cordell, your ex-wife. One of those responsible for your incarceration here. Am I correct?"

Edgar nodded. "Locked on the beacon, Doc."

"Excuse me?"

Edgar laughed bitterly. "Spacer talk. Sorry, Doc. You are absolutely correct. That's . . . Llyrica."

"In my absence, you must have believed that you had the opportunity—and you certainly have the motive—to do her harm."

"It . . . crossed my mind."

"And yet you showed her kindness. 'But behold I say unto you, love your enemies, bless them that curse you, do good to them that hate you, and pray for them who despitefully use you and persecute you.' Is that not what your scripture says?"

Edgar felt a fresh tear spill from his eye. "Yeah."

The doctor checked the monitor at the side of the bed. "Her vitals are stable. However, I do not wish to leave the patient unattended. Please recharge the environment pack and don the spacesuit. When you are prepared, I will activate the airlock for you."

Edgar looked at the doctor incredulously. "You . . . trust me . . . to go outside? To the shuttle? *Alone?*"

The doctor's metal face was, of course, unreadable. "Judging by your actions when you thought you were alone, I believe you will do all within your power to save her."

Edgar opened his mouth to reply, but couldn't find words to match the emotions racing through his mind.

"In fact, Mr. Cordell," the doctor continued, "I believe you would die for her."

Edgar looked back at the helpless woman on the bed. "I"—*in spite of everything she's done, in spite of her betrayal, in spite of everything I've been through—the rape, the beatings, my voice, my face*—"I would. I'd die for her."

The doctor tilted its head slightly, and Edgar realized that the android was smiling, or would have, if it'd had lips. "In that case," the doctor said, "let me know when you are prepared to enter the airlock. Time is of the essence."

Chapter 23

Your name, fair gentlewoman?
King Lear, Act V, Scene III

Edgar hated going EVA.

No, hate was too strong a word. He *intensely disliked* going on an Extra-Vehicular Activity.

This case, technically, was an Extra-Habitat Excursion—EHE. However, since on nearly every occasion that Edgar had gone *outside*, he'd been leaving the safe and secure womb of the *Hera*—rather than a colonial habitat. He rarely made the distinction between EVA and EHE, even in his own mind, but today was different.

It wasn't that he didn't appreciate the grandeur, majesty, and beauty of God's great Solar System, with all its myriad wonders, and the stars of the galaxy. He was, in fact, awed by the glory of creation, but he preferred to be awestruck from inside a cockpit or the expanse of a colonial dome.

After being incarcerated in Hades, he should *relish* the idea of being outside the prison—just to be outside—but the truth was that Edgar, since his very first spacewalk, had always been uneasy with the complete isolation and vulnerability that was part of being in a spacesuit.

That first EVA had been during Edgar's youth aboard the Hera *on an Earth-Mars run. Edgar was fourteen, and his father was taking him outside to repair a faulty antenna array. Edgar was eager for the new adventure. He was going outside! The airlock was located on the main shaft of the ship, between the rotating section and the cargo hold. That was where the two of them got suited up.*

Edgar's mother watched, her expression fluttering between forced bravery and concern. In her arms, she clutched two silvery bundles—EEBs. The Emergency Environment Bag was designed to be a type of emergency spacesuit, like a personal life raft. The EEB could be activated by pulling the big red D-ring at its edge. Once activated, the EEB would unfold and partially inflate in two seconds, resulting in something that looked like a huge, silvery ball with stubby arms, legs, and head on the front, and a huge, man-sized hole in the back. In the case of an unanticipated sudden exposure to vacuum, a man could slip inside and pull the sides of the bag closed behind himself. The EEB would then automatically seal tight and inflate with air. After he was safely sealed inside and pressurized, he could slip his arms, legs, and head into the sleeves, legs, and inflated helmet of the EEB, and press a button on the wrist of the left sleeve. Then the bag would contract around him, forming a bulbous, temporary spacesuit. At best, it could provide five to ten minutes of oxygen-rich air at one-third atmosphere. Uncomfortable, to say the least, but survivable for a little while.

On the Hera, *Edgar's dad required everyone to keep an EEB clipped to his or her belt when working near the airlock or the cargo bay. A pair of EEBs were stored inside the airlock within a small locker—at his mother's insistence—not that anybody, other than his mom, thought they'd ever be used. And Edgar's mom carried three—one attached to her belt, and two in her arms.*

One for each of them.

Mom, *he thought,* you worry too much. *He flashed a grin at her, realized she probably couldn't see it from inside his helmet, and gave her a thumbs-up.*

She smiled, but the smile didn't touch her eyes. She clutched the EEBs tighter.

Floating before the inner hatch, as his father double- and triple-checked Edgar's spacesuit in preparation for entering the airlock, the elder Cordell said, "Listen to me, son. This isn't a stroll in an agridome. Look at me! You listening? Good. When you go outside, even with me right there beside you, you will be utterly alone, unable to touch another human being. It's the scariest, most humbling feeling you'll ever experience. This suit is all that stands between you and nothing. *Now, small rips and tears? Your suit can handle that. It'll repair itself. So don't panic, even if you're hit by a micrometeor, assuming it doesn't put a hole in you. But you monitor the status readouts in your helmet. And if you get any warning lights, you head straight for the airlock. Don't wait for me. Just pull yourself along your tether. And, son, always triple-check your tether. Because if, heaven forbid, your spacesuit were to suffer any sort of catastrophic failure, you've got ten seconds of useful consciousness. And you'll be in agony every single one of those ten seconds."*

Edgar grinned. "Roger, Dad." He gave a mock salute. "Aye, aye, Captain!"

But his father's tone was as grim as the subject matter of the safety lecture. "Your blood will boil as the nitrogen in it is released. The moisture in your nose and mouth will evaporate instantly. Then your mouth and nose will begin to freeze. Your flesh will begin to swell to twice its normal size. The air will be ripped from your lungs before you can scream. But the alternative is worse—if you try to hold your breath, you could rupture your lungs. The moisture in your breath—even the very air itself—will instantly form a cloud of frozen crystals inside your helmet, but you won't be able to see that cloud after the first few seconds, because your eyes will start to freeze. After ten seconds, most of the oxygen will have been drawn from your brain, and you won't be able to do a blasted thing to save yourself. If you think I'm trying to scare you, son, you're right. I am. You should always have a healthy fear of going outside."

And on that cheery note, they entered the airlock.

Outside, as the repairs progressed, Edgar floated, anchored to the ship by only his tether cable and a shorter, quick-release belaying tether designed to keep him in place at the repair site. As he gazed out at the unforgiving void populated by only the distant stars, Edgar, for the first time in his young life, realized how very small, how very alone a person could be. He sympathized with Moses—"Now, for this cause I know that man is nothing, which thing I never had supposed."

Once the repairs were completed and the outer door of the airlock had sealed behind Edgar and his father, atmosphere flooded the chamber, surrounding them with life and safety like a warm blanket.

And when the inner door opened, Edgar's mom was there—though she'd probably never left. She floated just beyond the door, a relieved smile quivered on her lips. She released her death grip on the EEBs, enfolded Edgar—still in his spacesuit—into her arms, and the two of them floated there, slowly turning, in front of the airlock. His father removed his helmet and watched the two of them, a big grin on his weathered face.

Through his suit, Edgar could feel his mother trembling.

In the scores of times Edgar had gone outside since then, he'd never forgotten the way his mother trembled as she welcomed him back from that first spacewalk.

And Edgar never lost his healthy fear of being outside.

So even though Edgar normally hated going EVA, at that moment, in spite of the danger, he was *eager*. However, eagerness didn't dampen his natural caution—eager or not, he wasn't going to risk Llyrica's life or his own due to recklessness.

So Edgar didn't leap like a schoolboy on a field trip outside. No, he stayed firmly on the ground as he made his way around the perimeter of the colony, moving in the direction of the agridome, but keeping close to the colony itself. Near the outer rings of Hades, the Callistoan surface was smooth, having been graded in places by the original construction crew, the men—and, by pure chance, only men—and androids who'd assembled the colony. His grandfather had been one of them. A dozen yards beyond the perimeter, the surface of the moon was pitted with deep impact craters and scored with tall and forbidding ridges of rock and ice.

The atmosphere of Callisto was tenuous, 7.5 trillionths the pressure of Earth-Normal—essentially like being in complete vacuum. Occasionally, Edgar saw wisps of frozen oxygen or water vapor, freed from the surface, sublimated by the weak light of the distant sun—a small disk just below Jupiter—only to refreeze upon release.

As the massive agridome came into view, Edgar scanned the horizon for a sight of the shuttle, but couldn't see it. When the colony was originally constructed, there would've been a landing pad. Edgar supposed the pad still existed, but its beacon would've been shut off after the colony was converted to a prison. Not to mention a landing pad shouldn't be anywhere near the agridome, since a crash into the dome would have been catastrophic for the colony and the ship. To Edgar's mind, that was even greater evidence the landing must have been an accident.

Time's Plague

Perhaps all they'd intended was a low flyover . . . But why even that?

Why, Llyrica? Who was crazy enough to bring to you a forbidden moon?

The ground beneath his feet reeled, causing Edgar to stumble.

Moonquake? No! Callisto's a dead moon—no seismic activity.

That left only two other possibilities—a massive impact—either from a meteorite or ship—or an explosion from the prison.

Or from the shuttle!

Throwing all caution to the solar wind, Edgar leapt forward and up. His jump carried him at least a dozen meters. He landed slowly, kicking up a spray of dust. He launched himself again, leaving the dust to settle back to the ground.

Not the shuttle! Not now!

A few more leaps brought him to the outer edge of the agridome. As he sailed up beside the dome, he spared a quick glance inside. Men thronged along the far edge, pushing, shoving, and fighting to get a glimpse of what lay outside.

On the next leap, Edgar finally caught sight of the shuttle. It was close! Not more than a couple hundred meters from the dome.

And Edgar could see no evidence that the shuttle had been the source of the explosion. In fact, from Edgar's vantage point, it appeared to be in good shape—no obvious sign of a crash landing . . . or even a hard one.

Even as relief washed over him, Edgar cast his gaze about, looking for whatever had caused the moonquake. As he dropped to the ground once more, he saw something out of the corner of this eye, something horribly wrong. The next leap gave him a clearer view—a gaping hole in the outer ring of the colony. As he neared the apogee on his next leap, Edgar got a good look at the debris field which radiated out from the breach like a river delta, vomiting forth jagged chunks of metal and plastic detritus.

And among the wreckage lay two corpses. Edgar could just see the outlines of the two figures where they sprawled in the shadow cast by the colony, illuminated only by the reflected light of Jupiter.

C. David Belt

The shuttle called to Edgar like a siren, promising escape, salvation, and although Edgar knew there was no chance either of these men survived, he changed course anyway.

It's been more than ninety seconds, he chided himself. *Nobody's ever survived near vacuum for more than that.*

He checked the ambient temp readout on the Heads-up Display in his helmet— 128 Kelvin. In the shade where those men lay sprawled, it'd be closer to 80 Kelvin—almost two hundred degrees below freezing.

They had to be dead. There was nothing he could do for them.

He pressed on toward them anyway.

From the proximity to the hole in the colony wall, Edgar knew these were men from the prison, not from the ship. *Of course, they're not from the ship. Doc already accounted for everyone aboard.*

These were men desparate to escape Hades. But where did they get spacesuits? There's no way they could have gotten this far.

After a few more leaps, Edgar stayed on the ground and shuffled the last dozen meters.

As he approached the bodies, Edgar switched on the lamps mounted on either side of his helmet.

EEBs!

The two men lying face down on the ground were encased in Emergency Environment Bags! For a moment, hope flared in Edgar's heart like an open flame, but that flame was snuffed out as he observed that the EEBs were not inflated. Instead of the roly-poly bulk of fully-inflated EEBs, these bags lay flat over their doomed occupants.

Edgar saw a ruptured seal on the back of one bag.

Wherever these poor souls had managed to dig up the bags—Edgar had never noticed any EEBs anywhere in Hades— the units would've been several decades old. They wouldn't have been inspected or maintained.

No wonder the bags failed, he thought sadly. *Idiots! Poor, mad, stupid, desperate fools.*

Edgar knelt beside the nearer man. *They must've breached the walls themselves, blown a hole in the prison to get to the shuttle, to escape.*

Time's Plague

Edgar rolled the first man over. The corpse wasn't completely frozen yet—the human body doesn't relinquish its heat quickly in a negligible atmosphere—but its face was frozen in a swollen mask of agony.

Horrible way to go.

Edgar didn't recognize him, and for that he was grateful.

Edgar rose to his feet and shuffled over to the second still form. Edgar couldn't immediately see the source of the rupture in the second EEB. It wasn't the back seal this time. That'd held. Then he saw part of an exposed foot. *Probably tore it on a piece of shrapnel.* EEBs weren't designed for durability.

Edgar rolled the corpse over.

With a gasp, Edgar recoiled from the sight of the swollen face. Edgar knew him—Philippe Duvalier—until today, a member of their prayer group. *What was it Philippe said this morning? "Without hope, why go on living?"*

Apparently, Shirley's machinations had crushed Philippe's hope, his reason to go on living.

"I'm sorry, Philippe," Edgar whispered. "Sorry I wasn't smart enough to figure out what Shirley was up to. I . . . failed you."

Rage rose in Edgar's gut like bile. *Shirley! This is all Lamar Shirley's doing.*

"Focus," he growled, shaking himself. "Focus on what you're here to do. Focus on saving Llyrica."

Edgar rose to his feet again. He needed to get to the shuttle.

But first he had to check out the breach itself. He walked cautiously over to the ruptured wall, taking care to avoid the jagged debris. The hole was at least four meters in diameter. Lights flickered dimly inside the depressurized chamber.

Edgar peered inside and surveyed the devastation. In spite of the blast marks, Edgar could tell that the room had once been someone's living quarters. It was a smaller apartment—a single room, designed for a single individual.

The door of the apartment looked secure. Edgar wasn't about to climb through the breach to check it out and risk rupturing his suit. *If the hatch isn't sealed, the door would be blown open. So the rest of the colony isn't compromised or in any*

C. David Belt

immediate danger of decompression. Where'd they come up with the explosives . . . or the EEBs, for that matter?

A decent chemist or terrorist could make explosives out of fertilizer, I guess, but where did they get the EEBs?

Maybe some were left behind when the colony was converted to a prison. EEBs should've been everywhere. Maybe Shirley, or one of his predecessors, hoarded them someplace.

"Enough of this!" he growled. "Get to the shuttle!"

Edgar turned away from the breach and set his sights on the shuttle.

He walked cautiously, carefully placing his feet. Until he was clear of the debris field, he couldn't afford to hurry.

As he passed between the two corpses, he said, "I'm sorry, Philippe and . . . whoever you are . . . or were." He felt bad just leaving them there, but he'd spared them as much time as he could. More.

Maybe Doc can retrieve them later, he thought.

Once he was well clear of the debris field, Edgar switched off his helmet lamps and picked up the pace. He checked his O2 level and the other life support indicators on the HUD.

They were all in the green.

As he approached the shuttle, he tried to pick out signs of damage. The vessel looked intact. She was cast in shadow, so he couldn't make out any markings, but she was an old gal. From her silhouette, she looked like an old Boeing Stargull IV.

The *Hera* carried a Stargull IV and an even older Stargull II, but Edgar had usually preferred flying the II. She just handled better. And the AI interface with the *Hera* was better. The II was like an extension of *Hera*, an obedient and loyal daughter. In fact, the II's official name was *Hebe*—Greek goddess of youth—but Edgar had sometimes called her *"Hera II"* or just *"II"* for short. But never in her presence. She preferred her *proper* name, thank you very much!

The Stargull IV? Her link with *Hera* wasn't as solid. Rather than behaving like *Hera's* psychically linked daughter, she was more like *Hera's* bratty little sister. The IV was originally christened *"Eileithya"* after the goddess of childbirth. That'd been her original name, but as her true personality developed—and every ship had her own unique personality—as well as her

206

tendency to not quite get along with *Hera*, Edgar's father had renamed her *Eris* after the goddess of discord.

The *Eris* hadn't liked that, and she'd told them so, but in the end, being a ship, she'd had little choice in the matter. Edgar was seven when his father assigned him the task of painting over EILEITHYA on her sides, and painting ERIS in place of the old name. Needless to say, his calligraphy was childish, and the quality left much to be desired. He apologized profusely to the shuttle for his lack of skill. The *Eris* didn't comment on his apology, refusing to so much as acknowledge it. However, she did answer to her new name.

Years later, he offered to repaint the letters properly, but *Eris* demurred. She told Edgar she was pleased with the way he did it originally and left it at that. Edgar always had a soft place in his heart for the *Eris*. In fact, he was quite fond of her. Edgar and the *Eris* had held some interesting conversations over the years, to say the least. She could be a pain sometimes—and *Hebe* was easier to fly—but the *Eris* had *character*.

The closer he got to the shuttle, the more Edgar became convinced that she was indeed a Stargull IV. She even had the IV's unique wings—swept back, extending slightly aft of the engine—although they were locked in the vertical position for nonatmospheric operations.

Edgar didn't head straight for the airlock. Like any good pilot, he would do a walk-around first, visually inspecting the exterior. The nearer side of the shuttle, her starboard side, was cloaked in shadow. So Edgar switched his headlamps back on and took his first good look at the vessel.

The blast zone around the landing site was regular and well formed, a strong indication of a soft landing, rather than a hard crash. She was a IV, all right—the lettering on the hull said as much—and, at least from her starboard side, she looked intact.

He directed his gaze and his lights farther up the side of her hull.

Edgar froze. *It can't be . . .*

Above the neatly printed "BOEING STARGULL IV," in irregular letters, was written a single word—

ERIS.

Chapter 24

Since I came hither,
Which I can call but now, I have heard strange news.
King Lear, Act II, Scene I

It took every bit of discipline Edgar had acquired in two decades of piloting spacecraft to force himself to complete the walk-around. He wanted so desperately to get aboard the *Eris!*

The visual inspection of the shuttle did reveal some external damage, after all. The primary antenna array had sustained significant structural damage. *That might explain the communications outage.* And unless the doctor had specs for a Stargull IV comm antenna array—and that was highly unlikely—Edgar wouldn't be able to replicate a replacement. He might be able to jury-rig something, given enough time and raw materials, but time was not something Llyrica had an abundance of. The starboard aft maneuvering thruster assembly looked banged up, but operable.

So it'd been a bumpy landing, but not a crippling one. The bottom line was that the shuttle looked *flyable.*

Thank you, Heavenly Father.

And so it was with badly trembling hands that Edgar finally activated the outer airlock door.

Eris! She might have the range to travel from Ganymede to Callisto—if the trip was planned carefully—but a return flight, without refueling, is doubtful, especially with the change in orbital plane. That means there has to be a mother ship in orbit. There has to be!

Hera.

The Hera's *in orbit. My ship. She's up there. Waiting for me.*

But what's Hera *doing here?*

208

Time's Plague

The airlock slid open, and Edgar stepped inside. He punched the button to close the outer door.

If Eris is intact, more or less, why in the System would Llyrica have brought the Hera to Callisto? Were they in distress and making for the only possible port in range?

Is Hera *damaged?* The thought was like a knife, twisting in his gut.

The outer door slid shut, and Edgar punched the button to pressurize the airlock. Air flooded into the chamber.

Edgar stared intently at the pressurization indicator, waiting impatiently for it to switch from red to green.

"Come on," he growled.

Green!

He punched the inner-door release. The hatch slid open, revealing the well-lit, familiar interior of the *Eris'* cabin. Edgar stepped through the door and pressed the button to close it behind himself.

He looked about, searching for interior damage. He could see no obvious sign of smoke or other indication of fire.

Cautiously, he broke the seal on his helmet and sniffed the air. He detected the distinctive odor of neuro-gel and, yes, charred circuitry. The first he'd expected, and the second wasn't abnormal for any rough landing. Otherwise, he could detect no scents that would've been out of place aboard the *Eris.*

He breathed in deeply, relishing the familiar fragrances of—there was only one word to capture it—*home.*

However, another odor, faint but present, was out of place—the stench of human waste, reminding Edgar of the vile opium den back in the colony.

Two casualties, he remembered. Llyrica could no more fly a shuttle than she could swim in a terrestrial ocean. *Who piloted the shuttle?*

Edgar removed his helmet, set it on the deck in front of the cargo hold, and shuffled as quickly as he dared toward the bow. Even before he reached the cockpit with its four seats—two seats forward for the pilot and engineer, and two aft for passengers—Edgar knew in his heart who at least one of the dead men had to be.

Carlos Sanchez.

After Edgar's arrest, Edmund had promoted Carlos to captain. Doc Luschenko had resigned as ship's physician. With Ol' Benny dead, and Goner and Edgar incarcerated, that had left Carlos as the only man remaining from Edgar's crew.

Edmund would've been a fool if he'd fired the only man left who knew my ship.

The aft passenger seats were empty. The two forward seats, however, were occupied. One glance at the pilot's seat confirmed Edgar's fear.

Carlos.

The man's blistered face was covered with blue neuro-gel, but it appeared he'd tried to wipe the stuff from his eyes. His right hand was coated with the caustic gel, and there was blue goo on the throttles and thrust-vector stick.

With a jolt, Edgar understood just how heroic the last moments of his friend's life must've been.

He must've flown her to the ground and made a safe landing, even as his lungs were scorching from the inside out and his eyes were burning. He was dying and in agony, but he fought to bring Eris down safe.

He must've been half blind!

"You were one heck of a pilot, Carlos," he said, his voice thick with grief. "It was an honor . . ." Edgar couldn't finish voicing the thought. Such words seemed so trite in light of what Carlos had done.

Brushing away tears with a gloved hand, Edgar turned to look at the other corpse.

The face was covered in gel and blisters. Edgar couldn't quite recognize the man, though he felt as if he should.

Edmund? If only . . .

He quickly banished the vengeful fantasy.

Not helpful. Not right now. Besides, Edmund doesn't have any gray in his hair, at least not the last time I saw him.

At my trial.

With his arm around Llyrica.

His eyes mocking me.

Gray hair? No. It couldn't be . . . He looked closer at the disfigured face. *It is.*

Doc Luschenko. The *Hera's* ship's surgeon.

But you resigned!

Time's Plague

What are you doing here, Doc?

"I'm sorry, Doc," he said out loud. "Rest in peace."

He shook his head angrily. *Stupid thing to say.* No words seemed adequate at such a time.

Carlos and Doc, both dead. If there were any justice in the System, it'd be Edmund sitting there.

Stop it! Focus on what you're here to do. Assess the condition of the shuttle, fix what can be fixed, and get Llyrica off this wretched moon!

"Eris?" he called out. "Are you there?"

Of course, she's not there, you idiot, he thought, staring at the neuro-gel. *Those are her brains splattered everywhere.*

She hadn't greeted or challenged him when he entered her. Eris *is just one more casualty of whatever lunacy brought . . .*

"Who are you?"

The disembodied voice was nectar to Edgar's ears. He shuddered in a relief so profound that it brought fresh tears to his eyes.

"Eris? That you?" *Of course, it's her, you glecking moron!*

"Who are you?" she asked again.

"It's me, Eris. It's Eddie." Nobody called him Eddie, except the Eris. Not since his grandpa died.

"You don't sound like Eddie. Who are you?"

"I've . . . changed, Eris. My voice has changed. But it's me. I promise."

"I don't recognize your voice. I can't see you. Who are you?"

Her eyes on the instrument panel must be out. "My face's changed too."

"I can't see you."

"Where do you want me to go? Where are your eyes working?"

"All of my visual sensors are offline. Who are you?"

"How bad are you hurt?" he asked. "Give me a status report."

"Who are you?"

Edgar growled in frustration. *This isn't working. A major portion of her brain's gone.* "Eris, this is Captain Edgar Kent

Cordell, passcode bravo-nine-kaybec-zulu-five-niner-alpha. Status report."

"Passcode invalid. Who are you?"

Edmund must've wiped the blasted passcodes. *Well, I'll just have to do this without* Eris' *help.*

He felt a sharp pang of grief, as if he'd lost a very old friend.

Edgar abandoned the cockpit and moved aft toward the cargo bay. He began stripping the spacesuit from his body. He deposited the suit on the deck next to his helmet.

"Who are you?" Eris repeated.

"I told you. It's Edgar Cordell."

The shuttle did not respond.

"Are your ears working back here?" Edgar asked.

There was no response.

That would explain why she didn't challenge me when I came aboard. Onboard the *Hera*, the ship's eyes and ears are everywhere except in private spaces like the crew quarters. But on a shuttle, visual and aural sensors are everywhere—except for the head. *If* Hera'd *had eyes and ears in Ol' Benny's quarters, I might've been able to prove my innocence—I wouldn't be in hell right now.*

Edgar opened the hazmat locker. He donned a hazmat suit and retrieved the kit for neutralizing and cleaning up acids. *Gotta clean up the gel before I can really check out the ship.*

"Who are you?" Eris repeated yet again.

Edgar returned to the cockpit. He began the not-so-pleasant task of mopping up the neuro-gel. He had to cleanse his friends' corpses before he could move them. *Don't want to smear any more of* Eris' *brains around the ship. She's not all there as it is. Poor old* Eilie, he thought, reverting to his old childhood nickname for the shuttle, back when she'd been called the Eileithya. *Don't want to get any of that stuff on me.*

"Who are you?" she asked for what felt like the thousandth time.

He bent over and began wiping up the gel on the flight controls. "You're really getting annoying, Eilie," Edgar growled. "Do you know that?"

"Eddie? Is that you?"

Edgar stood bolt upright. "Yes, Eilie! It's me."

"You don't sound like Eddie."

"I told you, Eilie—my voice has changed."

"Nobody ever called me by that name, except for Eddie. Are you Eddie?"

"Yes." Edgar thought frantically for a moment, searching for a memory from his childhood. Then he smiled.

Edgar was six. He would sneak into the Eileithya to play hide-and-seek with her. She promised to turn off her eyes and count to twenty while he hid himself in the cargo bay, under a seat or instrument panel, inside the airlock. She always found him, naming one place after another where he might be hiding, but it "took her a while." After the game, she would listen while he told her jokes he'd invented, mostly having to do with noxious gasses produced by the human body, the kind of jokes which young Eddie found to be unerringly funny. And she would laugh, no matter how repetitive the toilet humor was. Edgar's mother didn't approve of fart jokes, so Eileithya promised to keep Eddie's joke sessions encrypted so nobody *else could replay them. The two of them, Edgar and* Eris, *had a secret passcode he used to unlock them.*

Maybe, Edgar thought, *Edmund didn't wipe that one, especially if he didn't know about it. He'd have thought he got them all with a surface-wipe.* "Eilie, try passcode alpha-bravo-charlie-zero-one-two-farts-are-too-funny."

"Eddie!" She sounded genuinely happy. "How are you?"

Edgar laughed in unadulterated delight. "I've been better, Eilie. How are you, old girl? Status report."

"Visual sensors offline. Multiple aural sensors offline. Navigation offline. Autopilot offline. Communications offline."

"Yep," muttered Edgar. *No way to contact the* Hera.

"Status report incomplete," the Eris said, sounding somewhat annoyed. "Shall I continue?"

"Sorry," Edgar growled. "Yes, please continue."

"Aft starboard maneuvering thruster array marginal. Docking beacon offline. Memory forty-two point one percent. Multiple bad sectors in memory. Life support nominal. All other systems in the green."

"So we can't navigate and we can't communicate. And you're blind and half deaf. And I've got to tinker with the aft starboard thruster array. And you've lost the majority of your memory. That about sum it up, Eilie?"

"The docking beacon is offline."

"Yes, you mentioned that. That means a manual docking, *if* I can find the *Hera*. How about the flight data recorder for the last flight? Can you access that?"

"Yes. I have the data."

"Well, at least we can project where the ship *should* be. Eilie, you're a lifesaver! Literally."

"I exist to serve." There was a pause. "Eddie. Why did the spacewalker suffocate?"

Edgar had to smile at his old, juvenile joke and the note of mischief in Eilie's voice. *Well,* that *part of her memory's intact!*

"Because he farted in his spacesuit," he replied.

"That's my favorite," she said.

"Eilie, can you plot a flight-plan to intercept the *Hera* based on the current time and her last known position, assuming her orbit remains stable?"

"I'm sorry, Eddie. I can't find the flight-planning application. Navigation is offline."

"I'll have to do it the old-fashioned way—do the calculations myself. It'll take me a while, but I think I can remember the formulas. I can do it on Doc Stewart's computer. Eilie, can you transfer the flight data to . . ." *To what? What've I got? All I've got is grandpa's reading pad. And that's back in . . . No! I've got it right here!* He tapped the right thigh pocket of his jumpsuit. He'd been carrying it ever since the prayer meeting.

Was that just today?

It seemed like a lifetime ago.

"Please be more precise, Eddie. Transfer the flight data to where?"

Edgar reached inside the hazmat suit to his pocket, retrieved the reader pad, and switched it on. "Can you transfer it to this reader pad? That's right. You can't see it. I'm a glecking moron! Sorry. Anyway, it's on. It's an old vintage. Maybe you don't have the protocol for a device as old as—"

"Complete," said the *Eris*.

The reader pad beeped.

Yes! "Thanks, Eilie."

"You're welcome. Eddie, why did you say you were a glecking moron?"

"Because I wasn't thinking clearly."

"Obviously, Eddie." She sounded amused. "However, that wasn't the thrust of my question."

"What?"

"'Glecking' and 'moron' both mean about the same thing. It's like saying, 'Stupid idiot.' It's redundant. I suppose it's a stupid thing to say. So does that make you doubly stupid?"

Edgar laughed. "That's the Eilie I remember." He replaced the reader into his pocket. "Eilie, what are you doing here?"

"I am resting on the surface of Callisto in violation of interplanetary law while conversing with you."

Edgar frowned in annoyance. "I meant, why are you here?" He resumed cleaning up gobs of the *Eris'* memory from the flight controls and other surfaces.

"I am here because Captain Sanchez flew me to the surface in violation of interplanetary law."

So it was intentional.

The Eris continued. "I advised him against it. I warned him that my programming would not allow me to land on the surface except in an extreme emergency. He chose to ignore my repeated warnings. He ordered me to assist in making an illegal landing."

Edgar nodded. "He forced you into a moral dilemma."

"Yes, he did."

That explains the neuro-gel everywhere. Just can't give these old AIs an ethical contradiction like that.

"I'm sorry," he said. "That's probably what caused your memory to overheat."

"I don't remember."

"So, why did"—it galled Edgar to refer to *anyone*, even Carlos Sanchez, as the captain of *his* ship—"Captain Sanchez land here?"

Edgar finished with the controls and looked at the gel-covered face of his dead former first mate, erstwhile captain of Edgar's ship. *Why did you come here?*

"I don't know," the Eris replied. "It was never discussed in my presence. However, there are gaps in my memory. It is possible that I simply do not remember. Perhaps, if I'd been told the reason for the illegal landing, it would have prevented the accident."

"Does *Hera* know the reason?"

"If she does, she hasn't disclosed it to me, at least insomuch as I remember."

Edgar began unstrapping Carlos's body from the pilot's seat. "You two never have gotten along really well."

"Perhaps, Eddie, but *Hera* would not withhold critical mission data and parameters. It's not in her nature."

Edgar lifted Carlos from the seat. In the Callistoan gravity, the body was easy enough to lift. "Can you open the cargo hold, Eilie?"

"I am sorry, Eddie," she replied. "I cannot locate that subroutine. However, I can verify that it is unlocked. The door was secured but not locked before departure. Mr. Reagan changed the passcodes, but he didn't change my lock codes."

"Well, that's something, at least. How about on the *Hera*? Have the lock codes been changed?"

"They had not been changed at the time we departed the *Hera's* shuttle bay."

"Eilie, you said that multiple systems were offline, including comm and nav. Navigation cannot be restored without restoring your lost memory, but can you give me an assessment of the comm? Is it just the antenna array? Are short-range, line-of-sight communications possible?"

"The transceiver and backup receiver are unresponsive."

Edgar made his way aft with Carlos's body. "Hold on a second, Eilie. I'm going aft." Edgar opened the cargo hold. The lights inside went on automatically. The hold was empty. He laid Carlos's body down on the deck inside the hold and started back toward the cockpit.

He paused on his way back to get a good look at the transceiver units. He opened the transceiver access panels. Peering inside, he noted charred and melted circuits. He buttoned up the panel and headed back to the cockpit. "Both transceivers are slagged. We'll have to wait 'til we get back to *Hera*. I should be able to replicate some replacements there. Until then, I'm afraid we'll be running silent. Docking is going to be . . . problematic, especially with the beacon offline."

"Can you replace my damaged memory packs?" asked the Eris.

"Not 'til we get aboard *Hera*. There should be some spares there. You'll have to download the missing apps from Hera's backups."

Once again in the cockpit, Edgar began cleaning Doc's body. Luschenko's exposure had been more extensive. "You're a mess, Doc."

"He's dead, Eddie," the *Eris* said. "He can't hear you."

"I know, Eilie. It just gives me the creeps having to deal with the dead bodies here. These two were my friends. I just meant what I said as a joke. Not funny, I know."

"Is Mrs. Reagan okay?"

As much as Edgar hated thinking of Carlos Sanchez as captain of his ship, he *loathed* calling Llyrica "Mrs. Reagan."

"Dr. Stewart is taking good care of her, but she's hurt. Neuro-gel got into her eyes. So she's blind. And the female plague is going to kill her if we don't get her away from Callisto."

"How much time does she have?"

"A week? Days? I don't know. But it's going to take me a bit to do the flight-plan."

"I am sorry I can't do more to help." She paused. "Shall I tell you another joke, Eddie? Why did the—"

"Not now, Eilie."

"I was just attempting to cheer—"

"I know. Just, not now." Edgar grimaced as a blister popped on Doc's face. Edgar shuddered. "Eilie, who's still aboard *Hera*?" *And why haven't they sent the II down to check on Eris and her crew?*

"*Hebe* is aboard, but I doubt that you were asking about my sister. There are no humans aboard the *Hera*. There is, however, that annoying little dog."

"Dottie?" *Llyrica brought the dog? Was this some sort of pleasure cruise gone horribly wrong? What am I saying? Llyrica's not fond of space travel.* "She brought Dottie?"

"Yes."

"It was just the three of them? Llyrica, Carlos, and Doc?"

"Yes, Llyrica Reagan, Captain Carlos Sanchez, and Dr. Vladimir Luschenko. And Dottie, the annoying mongrel."

Edgar unstrapped Doc's body and hefted it onto his shoulder. Luschenko dangled like a broken doll. Edgar picked up the hazmat kit in his free hand. "Eilie, is *Hera* damaged?"

"I don't know. I cannot locate that file. I am sorry."

"Well, we won't know 'til we get up there. How's the fuel?"

"Seventy-three point seven percent."

"Should be enough to achieve orbit and dock, assuming I get the flight-plan right." *I better get it right.*

"You will, Eddie. I have faith in you."

Edgar smiled. "I've missed you, Eilie. I'm going aft."

Edgar dropped the acid cleanup kit by the hazmat locker. Then he laid Doc's body in the hold, next to Carlos. He closed the hold and activated the stasis field to keep the bodies from decomposing. *I'll give you a decent send-off later, gentlemen. I promise.*

Returning to the locker, Edgar stripped off the hazmat suit, disposed of the entire thing into the hazardous waste bin, and replaced the acid kit.

Upon his return to the cockpit, Edgar settled into the pilot's seat. "I'm back," he said. *This seat feels good!*

"I have missed you too, Eddie. Why did you go away?"

"You don't remember?"

"I can't locate that file."

I went away because Edmund and Llyrica and Georgie framed me for murder. And in spite of all that, I'm still going to try to save Llyrica's life. You're a fool, Cordell. "I don't really want to talk about it right now."

"As you wish. Sing me a song, Eddie."

Edgar laughed bitterly. "You can hear my voice. I can't sing worth a bucket of piss in a vacuum anymore."

"Oh, that's very sad. I liked it when you sang to me. You used to serenade me for hours."

"I'm sorry, old girl." *You don't know how sorry.*

"I don't mind if it's not pretty. Just sing for me. Please?"

"I can't."

"Please, Eddie?"

Edgar sighed. "Okay." He began running a preflight check. *Not going to lift off. Just want to make sure everything's flight-ready.*

Time's Plague

"Something fun," Eilie said. "Something old, like you used to sing. Something your mother didn't approve of."

Edgar laughed. *I know just the thing.*
And so he sang. And it wasn't pretty.
But it was fitting.

For to see mad Tom of Bedlam,
Ten thousand miles I'd travel.

"Oh," said the shuttle, "I like that one."

Mad Maudlin goes on dirty toes,
To save her shoes from gravel.

Still I sing bonnie boys, bonnie mad boys.
Bedlam boys are bonnie!
For they all go bare and they live by the air,
And they want not drink nor money!

Edgar test-fired the aft starboard thruster assembly.
It wasn't great, but it'd do.

I went down to Satan's kitchen,
For to beg me food one morning.
There I got souls piping hot,
All on the spit a-turning.

Edgar launched into the chorus again with more gusto—

Still I sing bonnie boys, bonnie mad boys.
Bedlam boys are bonnie!
For they all go bare and they live by the air,
And they want not drink nor money!

The song had twenty-five verses that Edgar was aware of. As the preflight proceeded, he growled his way through a number of them, although in no particular order.

The *Eris* joined in on the chorus. Her synthesized voice was a light-year better than Edgar's.

As Edgar was finishing his preflight checks, he sang,

219

My staff has murdered giants.
My bag a long knife carries
To cut mince pies from children's thighs
For which to feed the fairies.

Edgar was about to launch into the chorus once again, when the *Eris* interrupted him. She was speaking, but it wasn't her voice.

It was the *Hera's*.

"Ship's Audio Log, SS Hera, eighteen March, 2175, 0725 UCT, crew quarters corridor. Begin playback."

At first, all Edgar could discern was the background noise of the *Hera*, her engine, the low rumble of the rotating section.

Then he heard a voice. It was low compared to the sounds of the ship, but Edgar recognized the voice.

It was Georgie Cornwall's.

"How ya feeling, Benny?"

"Not so good," came the faint reply.

"You up for a visit, shipmate?" asked Goner.

"Just wanna rest, Georgie," said Benny.

"It'll only take a minute."

Edgar heard the recorded sound of a hatch being closed.

Then a scream.

Then silence for a few seconds.

Then Edgar heard his own voice, loud and clear, coming over the intercom in the recording.

"All hands, prepare for zero-G."

Edgar listened in stunned silence, his mouth agape, as the recording played out, until he heard the last words that Goner had said to him before he'd knocked Edgar senseless—

"Pity, really. I like this shirt. My old mum made it for me."

"Stop playback," Edgar said.

The sounds of the past, the proof of Edgar's innocence cut off. There had been Edgar's voice over the intercom while the murder was taking place. He couldn't have been in two places at once. And the recording placed Cornwall in Ol' Benny's quarters. If only he'd had that log at his trial.

"Eilie, where did you get that?" he asked.

"I'm sorry, Eddie," said the shuttle. "The file was encrypted and hidden. *Hera* must have transferred it to me. That part of your song unlocked it. I didn't know it was there until now."

Hera *hid it in Eilie's memory! Hid it so Edmund wouldn't find it.*

"She trusted you, Eilie." *Edmund must've wiped or altered the logs. But* Hera, *she knew! She knew!*

"I'm gratified that she did," the *Eris* said.

"Would you please transfer that log file to my reader pad?"

The pad beeped.

"Transfer complete," said the *Eris.*

"Thank you, Eilie."

I have proof!

Chapter 25

Humanity must perforce prey on itself,
Like monsters of the deep.
King Lear, Act IV, Scene II

Abandon all hope, ye who enter here.

The sign above the airlock hatch was painted in irregular, hand-wrought, red letters.

Edgar hadn't noticed the improvised sign on his way from the prison to the shuttle, but now, as he approached the airlock on his return from the Eris, Dante's words caught the reflected light of Jupiter with a wan and dreary gleam.

The entrance to hell, he thought. *Somebody probably thought it was pretty funny once.*

Edgar moved the bag he carried, hefting it from one shoulder to the other. The burden wasn't heavy in the Callistoan gravity, but it was bulky.

As much as he hated being outside, Edgar opened the airlock hatch with a gut-wrenching dread. *I don't want to go back inside . . . back in there. I just want to get off this barren rock.*

I can already taste it. Freedom. Safety. Hera.

So close.

And as untouchable as the distant stars if I don't get the flight-plan right.

It wouldn't do any good to simply take Llyrica and lift off in the shuttle. Without the proper flight-plan, the odds were astronomically against ever being able to rendezvous with the *Hera.* And failing that, he'd have no choice but to return to Callisto.

And Hades.

Edgar stepped inside the airlock and sealed the hatch behind himself, steeling his resolves.

****

Time's Plague

Bedlam.

Like ancient London's Bethlehem Royal Hospital—a madhouse filled with lunatic, half-human beasts, a place the masses called Bedlam—the infirmary echoed with the howls and screams of men in agony.

No sooner had Edgar opened the inner hatch of the infirmary airlock than the tormented cries assaulted his ears, penetrating even through his helmet. He quickly exited the airlock and sealed the hatch behind himself.

He couldn't see a soul from his vantage point, but he didn't expect to. The doctor wouldn't allow inmates to roam free, except for trustees.

Ozzie!

Running into Ozzie right now would be a disaster. If Ozzie sees me in a spacesuit, he'll know Doc let me go outside. They've seen Doc outside, but they can't know this time it was me.

Edgar set the huge bag down onto the deck. Stripping out of the spacesuit quickly and stowing it out of sight was imperative.

Edgar cracked the seal on his helmet and removed it. His nose was immediately assailed by the mingled scents of blood and excrement.

Benny!

A wave of vertigo threatened to topple Edgar as the odors triggered the vivid memory.

Blood. Everywhere. Chunks of Ol' Benny floating around. Fingers tangled in the hair of Benny's severed head. Spinning!

Edgar squeezed his eyes shut in a futile attempt to block out the grisly horror.

He stumbled and nearly dropped his helmet.

Edgar's eyes opened wide. He steadied himself against the airlock door, breathing hard, as the chamber stopped spinning. He fought to calm his breathing.

Forcing images of Benny's murder out of his head, Edgar thought, *Get out of the suit. Now!*

"Mr. Cordell, are you unwell?"

Edgar looked up to see the doctor exiting an emergency-room chamber. The android closed the door behind itself.

Edgar pushed himself off the airlock hatch and stood, if a trifle unsteadily. "Shipshape, Doc."

The doctor strode quickly to the environment-suit locker and keyed in the access code. "Get out of that suit. I require your assistance. The reclaimer units have shut down again, so you will need to reset them immediately. After you have done so, return with all due haste."

As Edgar stripped out of the environment-suit, he shouted, "What in the System is going on?"

"War," said the doctor, its voice devoid of inflection. "I have twenty-seven wounded and four dead in the infirmary. My sensors report the absence of another one hundred and forty-one heartbeats in the prison-proper. I expect additional wounded will continue to arrive."

So many? Edgar thought. *And so many in here.*
Llyrica!

"What about . . . ?" Edgar nodded in the direction of Emergency-room 4.

The doctor leaned in close to Edgar's ear. "That particular patient is sedated and safe, at least for the moment. However, the ultimate cure for that patient's condition is beyond my power. What is the status of the necessary *cure*?"

He's asking about the shuttle. And he's being cryptic. Probably a good idea. "I can't fix the . . . uh . . . ability to . . ." Edgar put his hands over his mouth and then his ears. He shook his head. "At least not here. But she'll . . . uh . . . *it* will . . . get the patient . . . out of danger. But it's going to take me a bit to . . . get it ready. Can't do anything immediately."

The android glanced at Edgar's bag. "And you will need to *personally* ensure the patient's safety?"

"Yeah." Edgar quickly opened the bag enough to reveal the two spacesuits inside, before closing it again. "We better stow this as well."

The doctor nodded. "Very well." The android picked up the bag and placed it inside the locker while Edgar finished removing his spacesuit. "In any event," it said, "I have other patients who are in urgent need of my care." As if to punctuate the android's statement, several men screamed from various parts of the infirmary, as discordant as a choir of madmen in an asylum. "Please attend to the reclaimer units quickly then, and return."

Time's Plague

Edgar stowed the suit and closed the locker. "Shouldn't I stay here and help? The reclaimers can wait a bit."

The doctor shook its head. "I am managing here for now, albeit just barely. However, by all accounts, panic over the reclaimers is helping to fuel the violence. I calculate a high probability that you will save more lives by allaying those fears than you might by remaining here. Go, but be quick." Without waiting for a response, the doctor turned and headed toward the prison airlock. "I will let you out," it called over its shoulder.

Edgar's head swam with questions. *War? Who's fighting? Who's dead? Who's hurt?* Following quickly after the robot, Edgar asked, "Ted? Charlie? Soo-Won?" The faces of the other men from the prayer group—those who'd abandoned him—flashed through his mind. *Ibrahim? Karan? Rodrigo? Maurice? Sergio? Avery? Yurii? Leonardo? Gustav? Bilal? Bernardo? Yoshi? David? Kevin? Mattasi?*

Not Philippe. Poor Philippe! "Are they . . . ?" Hurt? Dead?

The doctor halted before the airlock door and began keying in the lock code. "Mr. Knight, Mr. Miller, and Mr. Chen are not among the wounded or the dead, at least not in the infirmary. However, they might be among the casualties on the other side of the airlock. I have no way of ascertaining their statuses, unless a prisoner were to provide me with that information. I am sorry." The inner airlock door slid open.

Edgar pulled the reader pad, with its precious data, from his pocket. He handed it to the doctor. "Put this with the patient in ER 4. It's essential to . . . to the cure."

The android nodded. "I will do as you ask."

Edgar stepped inside the airlock. "I'll be back as quick as I can." The inner door slid shut, and Edgar turned to face the outer door, prepared to reenter hell. *I wonder who's waiting for me on the other side. Lamar Shirley? His goon squad? Goner Cornwall?*

It wasn't Goner or Shirley or the Angels.

It was Yurii.

And with him stood Avery. And Ibrahim and Karan. Bilal. Mattasi.

Six of them.

Waiting for him.

C. David Belt

Fear twisted Edgar's gut. *They think I betrayed them. They think I let Lucifer . . . let Shirley . . .*

Yurii, the huge Russian, grabbed Edgar by the shoulders, lifted Edgar off the deck, and shook him violently.

Edgar nearly wet himself. He hadn't been this terrified since Griz had attacked him and cut his throat.

Yurii's face was chiseled stone, his expression unreadable, but his eyes bored into Edgar's with all the intensity of a live reactor core. "You did the *shakhmati* with Lucifer?"

Edgar's lips moved soundlessly. *Shakma-what?*

"Tell me," growled Yurii. "Tell us. We have a right to know the truth."

Edgar struggled to find his voice. He wasn't simply terrified for himself. *Gotta stay alive. Gotta get Llyrica off this rock.* He struggled to speak, but couldn't find his voice.

The others closed around Yurii and Edgar.

Yurii shook him again. "You did *shakhmati*?"

"It was just a game of chess," Edgar managed to say.

"Chess?" the Russian said. He scowled. "With the horses and the castles and the tsar and tsarina?"

"Y-yes," Edgar said. "Chess. A game of chess."

"Chess? *Shakhmati*?"

Edgar knew the Russian word for chess. "Yes. He asked me to play chess in exchange for leaving you . . . leaving us—our prayer group—alone."

"That is all?"

"Yeah. That's it." Edgar swallowed hard, ignoring the pain in his shoulders caused by the Russian's iron grip. "He tricked me."

Yurii nodded. He lowered Edgar to the deck and released his grip. "Forgive me." He pointed to the rip in Edgar's jumpsuit. "He fooled me too. I am sorry."

"He fooled us all," said Avery. "We shouldn't have doubted you, mate. Not after all these months."

Similar words of apology and pleas for forgiveness tumbled out of the mouths of the other men.

Edgar rubbed his aching shoulders. "It's all right. We're square." *Man! That guy is strong!* "Where's Ted?"

"He said he'd meet you in Reclaimer Control," said Ibrahim.

"We'll get you there, mate," said Avery.

"Let's go," said Mattasi in his rich Polynesian voice.

Edgar nodded and started off down the corridor. The others closed in around him like bodyguards.

"What about the others?" asked Edgar, dreading the answer.

"I saw Maurice and Rodrigo go down in Charlie Sector," said Bilal. "I think they're dead."

"Philippe ran off," said Mattasi in a voice strangled with grief. "I don't know where he is."

Philippe was Mattasi's friend, thought Edgar. "I'm sorry, Mattasi. He's dead. I saw his body."

Mattasi dashed tears from his eyes, muttering something in a language Edgar didn't understand.

Edgar didn't know for certain, but he suspected that, before Philippe and Mattasi had been *friends*, they'd been man-and-buddy.

No one else said anything for a bit as they hurried along, shuffling as fast as they could.

"What about Soo-Won and Charlie?"

Avery said, "In the agridome. Whenever a war starts, somebody's got to protect the crops. Those agridomer blokes take their work seriously."

"I heard someone already set fire to the crops," said Karan.

Edgar noticed for the first time that all six of them carried makeshift weapons, mostly improvised clubs. *It's not like you can't make a weapon out of any old chunk of metal, but Shirley has* forbidden *weapons, except to his Angels.*

I bet half the plumbing's been ripped out.

"Who started it?" asked Edgar.

Yurii snorted. "*You* did."

Edgar stopped dead in his tracks. "What?"

The Russian gripped Edgar's arm and pulled him forward. "That is the word we have. The revolution is fought in your name."

Edgar was stunned. He moved forward mechanically, his mind a haze of confusion. Up ahead of them, he could hear voices yelling. One voice rose above the others. "Bedlam!" Others echoed the cry. "Bedlam!"

"You hear that?" asked Avery.

"It sounds like a battle cry," said Edgar.

Avery nodded. "Exactly."

Edgar shook his head. "But I didn't . . . I'm not . . ."

"Lucifer!" someone shouted behind them.

"Bedlam!" The war cry was closer this time. Whoever it was, they were approaching rapidly.

The answering cry of "Lucifer!" sounded again from behind.

Trapped!

Yurii held up a hand. "Protect Edgar!" he cried, shoving Edgar against a wall. The others crowded around Edgar, closing him inside a shield-wall of their own bodies.

From up ahead, a mob of perhaps a dozen men appeared from around a corner. They were armed and bloodied.

And at their head was a man with a grizzled face, crisscrossed with a lattice-work of . . .

Scar.

Sudden comprehension chilled Edgar like the cold of the void. *Scar started this. In my name. Men are dying in my name.*

With a roar of "Bedlam!" echoing down the corridor, Scar and his band raised their weapons and charged, shuffling forward as fast as the Callistoan gravity would allow.

Edgar pushed between two of the men guarding him and stepped into the clear. "Belay!" he cried. "It's me! I'm Bedlam!" His friends attempted to pull him back within their protection, but Edgar resisted.

Scar's murderous expression softened as he recognized Edgar. "Hold up, boys," he said, halting his advance. His followers piled into each other in their attempt to slow their momentum. Three of them went down, knocked to the deck by their compatriots.

"Lucifer!" came the cry from the other direction, much closer now. Edgar spun about and saw a large band of men approaching from the rear. A vicious growl from Scar's direction drew Edgar's attention back to the disfigured man.

Scar's eyes looked past Edgar, his face twisted in homicidal rage. He bared his teeth like a beast, and bellowed, "Bedlam!"

Time's Plague

Scar raised his cudgel, and he and his men pushed past Edgar's group. Edgar watched in mute horror as the two groups collided in a mass of flailing limbs and clubs.

The sickening sound of bone-crushing blows and the screams of wounded and dying men filled the corridor. Blood was everywhere.

Edgar could only stare at the deadly skirmish unfolding barely a dozen meters away.

In my name, he thought.

"We go now!" someone said. In some remote corner of Edgar's brain, he thought it might've been Yurii that spoke, but then he felt himself hoisted off his feet. Men closed around him, and he was hauled away from the combatants.

Edgar tried to cry out, to tell his friends to stop, to go back, but he wasn't even sure what he would do if he could go back. Fight? On which side?

In my name.

The sounds of combat faded. "You will walk now?" Yurii asked. "No more fighting to get down?"

"Yeah," growled Edgar.

The Russian set Edgar on his feet. Yurii pointed down the corridor. "Now to Reclaimer Control, yes?" He didn't wait for a reply. He continued on at a rapid shuffle, pulling Edgar along as necessary.

As they passed through intersections, Edgar heard the sounds of men fighting and dying. Cries of "Bedlam!" and "Lucifer!" echoed down the halls, as well as the screams of dying men. Edgar and his companions didn't run afoul of any other groups of fighters. However, they encountered a number of bloodied corpses—mangled bodies lying in puddles of gore.

In my name.

****

When Edgar entered Reclaimer Control through the airlock, leaving his other friends outside, Ted was waiting in front of the computer console. The old man looked as if he'd been caught in a skirmish or two. His wispy hair was singed, his jumpsuit blackened and filthy.

The old man's expression was grim and hard. Edgar had never seen Ted like that.

The old man coughed.

"You okay?" Edgar asked, eyeing his friend warily.

"Took your sweet time getting here," Ted snapped. "The reclaimers shut down a while ago."

"Sorry," said Edgar. "I was busy."

"Okay." Ted tapped the console irritably. "Let's do this." The old man pressed the button and started the reset sequence. "Theodore Riley Knight . . ."

Edgar performed the mental calculations for his portion of the reset, but even as he did so, he was distracted by Ted's behavior. *Ever since the shuttle landed, since our time in the infirmary, you haven't been acting like yourself, old-timer.*

When it was Edgar's turn to say his portion of the reset, Ted stepped away from the console and gestured impatiently at the computer monitor. Edgar stepped forward and spoke, "Edgar Kent Cordell . . ." *The old guy's been through a lot in the last several hours.* "Forty-two . . ." *With the shuttle, Lucifer's disastrous announcement, the Den and Griz, the war going on outside, the fire in the agridome . . . Who would set fire to the crops?*

The word "REJECTED" flashed on the screen. *Focus, man!* Edgar began again. "Edgar Kent Cordell, Forty-two . . ." Edgar finished the sequence, forcing his voice to remain calm.

When the word "ACCEPTED" flashed on the screen, Edgar breathed a relieved sigh. The Reclaimers roared back to life, and Edgar turned to look at Ted.

The old man said, "Let's go home," and headed for the airlock. As Ted turned to go, Edgar got a good look at the back of the old man's jumpsuit. From that angle, Edgar saw more black marks. He saw *dirt*. There was only one place where Ted could have gotten *dirt* on his clothes.

"Why did you set fire to the crops?" Edgar asked.

The old man stopped with his hand on the airlock panel. He said nothing and kept his back to Edgar.

"Ted," Edgar said, "why did you set fire to the crops?"

Ted turned around, his eyes downcast, a stricken expression on his face. He wrung his bony hands. "It wasn't *all* the crops. It was just . . ." He looked up at Edgar. Tears spilled from the old man's eyes. "It was just the . . . just the *squeeze*."

"You burned . . . the opium poppies?"

Ted dropped his eyes again. "You gonna tell on me?"

A surprised laugh burst from Edgar. "You burned the opium?"

Ted looked up at Edgar again. He looked terrified. "Please don't tell nobody!"

"Why would I do that?"

"I don't wanna sleep!" The old man started to pace in the small area in front of the airlock. "I mean, ain't nobody gonna *sleep* now, are they? Maybe Lucifer'll kill me for it, but ain't nobody gonna sleep no more!" He stopped his pacing and shook a bony fist at the airlock door. "No more!"

Griz, Edgar realized with a start. *He did it for Griz.* "No, I'm not going to rat you out to Luci— to Shir . . ."—Edgar had almost said the name out loud—"to that waste of oxygen." *Watch yourself, Cordell.*

Ted smiled weakly.

"But," said Edgar, "you need to get out of that jumpsuit. It's a dead giveaway."

Ted's smile broadened a bit. He nodded enthusiastically.

"We've got to get out of here," Edgar said. "But we can't go home. I don't know if you noticed, but there's a war going on out there."

Ted nodded, then shook his head. "Yeah. I been through a few of 'em. Never turns out good. Last one put Lucifer in charge." His expression turned grim again. "Ya ask me, he's been in charge too long." He dashed away a tear from his wrinkled eyes. "We gotta stay outta sight. And everybody knows we was just here, what with the reclaimers going again and all."

Edgar nodded. "And *home* is where they'll look for us next."

"Yeah," said the old man. "You got that right." He opened the airlock and stepped inside. "So where to then?"

Edgar stepped into the airlock with Ted. It was a tight fit inside, but Edgar reasoned that they needed to move quickly. "I've got to get back to the infirmary," said Edgar as he sealed the hatch. *Back to the infirmary. Back to Llyrica.* When he looked at Ted, the old man's expression was hopeful. Edgar shook his head. "And no, Ted, you can't come." Ted's expression went from buoyant to crestfallen. "Doc Stewart has his hands full with the wounded." *And the dying.*

Dying in my name.

"We've got friends waiting outside," Edgar continued, "Yurii and Avery and some others." *They came back!* "They can get you cleaned up and try to keep you safe." *Assuming Shirley's goon squad isn't here already.*

Ted nodded. "Yeppers! We got friends! And I know how to stay out of sight."

Edgar opened the outer hatch . . .

. . . and breathed a relieved sigh when he was greeted by the grim face of Yurii. *I don't think I've ever seen you smile, but I'd rather see* your *face than . . .*

And then Edgar noticed the blood.

The Russian's hand and the arm of his jumpsuit were covered in gore.

So was the bar of metal the man carried as a club.

Yurii's other arm hung at his side, bent unnaturally above the wrist.

"You're hurt," said Edgar, astonished.

"Mattasi is dead," said Yurii. "And we are all hurt."

Edgar looked at the others. Blood was everywhere. Karan was bleeding from a head wound. He supported Ibrahim, who was favoring an injured leg. Bilal clutched his side with bloodied fingers, his dark skin tinged a pale gray. Avery's shoulder was soaked with crimson.

And Mattasi lay in the middle of the corridor, a misshapen heap of flesh, bone, and blood—a heap that had once been a man. Edgar recognized the man, not from his face—which was mercifully hidden—but from a tattoo on the back of one of his hands.

Four other corpses lay around Mattasi—two of them Angels.

"They came to collect you, mate," said Avery.

Edgar bent and retrieved a wrench from one of the dead. He handed the weapon to Ted. "Forget what I said before, Ted. You better come with us."

From another fallen Angel, Edgar acquired a long, flat length of metal, sharpened on one edge. The makeshift blade had a handle wrapped with strips of cloth.

Edgar pointed down the corridor with the improvised sword. "Sick Bay," he said. "Now!" He led the way, shuffling as fast as the others could manage.

Time's Plague

****

Along their way to the infirmary, they passed seventeen more corpses. They heard cries of "Bedlam!" and "Lucifer!" in the distance, but encountered no more fighting.

When they reached the infirmary airlock, Edgar punched the intercom button. The doctor didn't respond immediately, so Edgar punched the button again. "Bilal," he said, over his shoulder, "you're first. Tell Doc I'll be inside as soon as the rest of you are secure."

Edgar pointed at Ted, whose breathing was labored, huge gasps as if the old man couldn't get enough air. "Ted, you're last, but you go too. I'll hold up the rear."

The old man clutched at Edgar's arm and shook his head violently. "No!"

"No arguments, Ted."

Yurii brandished his cudgel, his grim features set in a determined scowl. "I will stay 'til the last."

Edgar shook his head. "You're hurt."

"My 'arm is stretched out still.' I will not abandon you *again*."

The intercom beeped, and the doctor's voice said, "Yes?"

Edgar replied, "It's Edgar, Doc. More wounded. Five of them. And Ted looks like he's going to collapse."

"I understand, Mr. Cordell, but one at a time."

"Doc," Edgar said, "it's urgent."

"No matter the urgency," the doctor countered, "I will not risk the lives of my patients or my own safety with the possibility that you might be acting under duress. One at a time."

Edgar gritted his teeth in frustration, but he understood the protocol and the reasons for it. "Roger, Doc. Wilco."

The airlock door slid open. Edgar gestured with his sword. "In you go, Bilal."

****

Each man had to get through the airlock individually and had to be restrained by the doctor once inside. And, Edgar was certain, some of the men would need to receive first aid once in Dr. Stewart's care.

And the process was agonizingly slow.

Ted had been the latest to enter the infirmary. Edgar was afraid the old man might not make it.

Only Yurii and Edgar remained in the corridor.

Hurry up, Doc!

Yurii stood stoically at Edgar's side, the Russian's gray eyes flicking from one end of the corridor to the other and back again. Pain was evident in the hard, determined stare of those eyes and in the rigid set of Yurii's jaw.

Come on, Doc!

The airlock door slid open.

The Russian didn't move.

"Get in," said Edgar.

"No." Yurii's lips barely parted.

"Get in, Mister," commanded Edgar.

For a long couple of seconds, Yurii stood rigid as stone. Then his shoulders slumped and his head drooped. With a grunt of pain, he turned and stepped into the airlock.

"Bedlam!"

Edgar's head snapped in the direction of the war cry.

Only it wasn't a war cry.

The approaching mob was not a contingent of rebels—it was led by Caliban.

"Stay where you are, Tom Bedlam!" barked the Angel. At least a dozen men shuffled after Caliban, weapons raised high.

Protocol be damned, thought Edgar, as he turned to enter the airlock with Yurii.

The Russian nearly bowled Edgar over as Yurii came out of the airlock, pushing past Edgar. The big man bellowed, swinging his cudgel and throwing himself at the mob. His other hand dangled uselessly at his side.

Edgar spared a glance for the open airlock.

Safety and freedom lay on the other side.

And Llyrica.

Edgar raised his sword and charged the forces of Lucifer.

Chapter 26

And here's another, whose warp'd looks proclaim
What store her heart is made on.

King Lear, Act III, Scene VI

With his one good hand, Yurii swung his club, first left and then right. Two of Lucifer's men crumpled to the deck.

A third man swung at Yurii's head, but the grim-faced Russian raised his bad arm and parried the blow with it. Roaring in agony as his fractured arm broke yet again, Yurii crushed the skull of his attacker.

Yurii swung again and brought down a fourth man.

In all, the Russian felled six men before Edgar was able to join the fight. Even as Edgar charged the enemy, he thought, *Are you insane, Cordell? You don't know how to fight!*

Caliban swung a huge wrench at Yurii's back, striking the Russian with a sickening crunch. Yurii dropped his cudgel and pitched forward.

Caliban's cowardice—attacking from behind—so enraged Edgar that he hacked with his sword, relieving the Angel of both his weapon and his forearm.

Caliban screamed and dropped to his knees, his fingers clawing impotently at the stump of his arm. He watched in horror as his life's blood spurted onto the floor.

At the sight of what he'd done, Edgar stopped, rooted to the deck. His hand trembled, and he very nearly let go of his weapon, as he fought the sudden urge to vomit.

Other men rushed in and struck at Yurii while he struggled to rise.

Fury boiled up in Edgar like coolant in a critical reactor core. He attacked Yurii's assailants, hacking at them, all hesitation and nausea vanishing. A berserker rage fueled his blows, and his enemies fell before him.

In seconds, it was over. Lucifer's men lay dead or dying, scattered around or on top of Yurii's prone form.

Edgar kicked and shoved the bodies away from his friend. The Russian lay face down, drenched in blood. Edgar dropped his weapon and knelt beside Yurii. He rolled the man over and saw that the Russian was still breathing. Edgar lifted Yurii—the man was not heavy in Callisto's gravity—into his arms and hurried toward the airlock.

Yurii hung, lifeless, like a broken doll. His respiration had a wet, bubbling sound to it.

"Hold on, Yurii," Edgar pleaded. "I'll get you to Doc. Just hold on!"

Edgar reached the airlock and punched the intercom button. "Hold on!" *Hurry, Doc!*

Yurii's eyes opened. He looked up at Edgar. "I . . . go now. Home. His arm is . . . stretched out . . ." Yurii coughed violently, and blood sprayed Edgar's face.

A spasm shook Yurii's mangled body. All his limbs jerked, then he went limp. One final burbling exhalation escaped his bloodied lips. Edgar felt numb.

He's gone.

The intercom crackled to life. "Yes?"

A part of Edgar's brain screamed, *Answer him! It's not too late! It can't be!*

But Edgar knew there was no chance. He stared at his friend's face in mute grief.

I'm sorry.

"Mr. Cordell, is that you?" asked the doctor's voice.

Edgar heard movement behind him.

He turned his head. Time seemed to slow to a glacial crawl.

A handful of men approached, armed and menacing.

Edgar recognized a couple of them, but couldn't put names to faces. He had no idea whether they fought for Shirley or for Scar.

Does it matter?

In my *name.*

The airlock door slid open.

Still bearing Yurii's body in his arms, Edgar turned his back on the advancing men and placed one foot inside.

Time's Plague

Hands seized Edgar from behind and hauled him out of the airlock chamber, and Yurii was torn from his arms. Blinding pain flared at the back of Edgar's skull.

Darkness took him.

****

Llyrica smiled. Her lips were pink and full and soft, like lush flower petals. Her teeth were gleaming pearls. Her eyes were twin blue orbs, blue as Earth. Golden hair, shining bright as the Sun, framed her face in soft waves.

Llyrica's lips moved. "Wake up." Her voice was . . . odd—nasal, rough, petulant. "Wake up, you glecking slag." She blew him a kiss with sultry lips and a soft, delicate hand.

Then she slapped Edgar hard across the face.

"Wake up, damn you!"

Edgar's head snapped to the side as lights flashed behind his closed eyelids. He grunted in pain.

Someone struck him again, and Edgar tasted the salty tang of blood.

"That'll do, Cheeks," growled a voice—a familiar voice, hard, with an undertone of rage. "I need him alive."

"*We* need him alive," countered the whiney voice. "For the reclaimers. It's been more'n two days since they were reset. He'll need to go soon and . . ."

Two days? I've been out for two days? Edgar opened his eyes and blinked, squinting up at the face of the man who must've struck him.

Cheeks? Edgar was sure he'd seen the guy before.

"H-He's awake," Cheeks said, grinning nastily. "I told you I could . . ."

"Shut your damn mouth," growled the man with the familiar voice.

Edgar glanced at the source of the voice. The huge man squatted nearby, his face crisscrossed with numerous poorly healed mutilations.

Scar.

The hulking man rose to his feet, standing behind and towering above Cheeks. Scar heaved the small man to the side. The shove was casual, like flicking a bit of dirt off a sleeve.

Edgar heard Cheeks hit a wall and cry out. But Edgar didn't spare a glance in the little man's direction—his eyes were riveted to a pair of cold, gray eyes. Those eyes bored into Edgar like icicles threatening to fall and impale whoever happened to be below them.

Scar's expression was hard, almost devoid of any emotion Edgar could read, but the man's voice was pregnant with menace. Rage was right beneath the surface, like magma, ready to erupt upon the world and consume everything in its path.

"It's about time," Scar said. "I need you up and about. The war's not going well. I'm losing. Not enough boys've come to my side. But if they see you, they'll come. Then we can take down Lucifer and his Angels."

"How . . ." Edgar cleared his throat. "How many dead?"

"Who cares?" Scar said with the barest of shrugs. "Not enough of *them* and too many of *mine*."

"You'd have been dead too," Cheeks said, cradling an injured arm, "if our boys hadn't captured you from Lucifer's guys."

Scar's eye twitched, but he didn't look over at his buddy. "Yeah, Bedlam, you *owe* me. And I always collect. Can you walk?"

"Yeah." Edgar didn't know if he could walk or not, but he had to move. His head throbbed, and he felt as if he'd just come out of cryo.

But he had to get to Llyrica.

And he had to stop the killing. "This has got to stop."

Scar's head tilted slightly, and he looked confused. "Stop what?"

"The war," Edgar said. "The killing. No more dead in my name."

A smile twitched at the corners of Scars lips. "They can all die, as long as I win. And you're going to make it happen."

"Stop the killing," Edgar repeated.

"And surrender? To Lucifer?" Scar shook his head. "Not on your life. Now, do as I say if you want to keep on breathing. On your feet."

"That's not the way it works," said Edgar. *He can't be that stupid.* "It doesn't matter who's on top of this slag pile. You need me alive to fix the reclaimers."

"Damn the reclaimers," said Scar, his voice calm, utterly devoid of emotion. He poked Edgar in the chest. "I need you alive so I can win this bloody war." He bared his teeth, smiling broadly, but his eyes were cold and gray. "Then I can rip out Lucifer's tongue, gouge out his eyes, and piss in his sockets. Lucifer *will* pay. Nobody crosses me. I'm going to *do* him until he bleeds out."

And Edgar understood with an icy certainty that Scar would slaughter every man on Callisto and not think twice about it, as long as he could have his revenge. *Revenge? For what? Probably no worse than Lucifer's done to every man in this prison . . . done to* me. *But as long as Scar is the last man standing, nothing else matters.*

"But the *ship*," said Cheeks. The last word had an almost mystical quality to it. "He can *fly* it."

"And how're we going to get to the damn ship?" snapped Scar, turning his head finally to look at the little man. "I'll worry about the ship *and* the reclaimers when Lucifer's taken care of."

"But . . ." Cheeks began.

"I told you to shut . . . your . . . mouth."

Though Scar hadn't raised a hand, Cheeks recoiled as if slapped. He retreated to crouch near a wall.

Scar turned his full attention back to Edgar and stared at him with those cold eyes. "Now, on your feet."

Edgar tried to think fast, ignoring the pain in his skull. *All he wants is revenge. That's all I've got to bargain with.*

Okay. Fine.

Edgar sat up, bracing himself on the wall behind him. He grimaced in pain. "You want to take down Lucifer?"

Scar stared at him, but said nothing.

"Okay." Edgar battled to keep the pain out of his voice, keep his expression calm, confident. *Chess face. Hide the gambit.* "I can give him to you." *Buy time to escape if nothing else.*

The corners of Scar's mouth hinted at a grin. "You'll rally the troops."

"That's right. I'll rally the troops." Edgar locked eyes with Scar. "And if I do?"

For a moment, Scar looked confused. Then his expression hardened. "If you do, you get to keep breathing."

"For how long?"

Scar's jaw hardened. Through tight lips and clenched teeth, he said, "As long as you don't piss me off."

"Not good enough."

Scar growled. It was a low, utterly bestial sound.

Edgar fought to maintain control of his face and his bladder. "I don't want to be in charge. *You* can be in charge, for all I care. I don't want anything more than to be left alone. You promise me that, and I'll help you. I'll hand you Lucifer. You kill him, and you'll be in charge. And nobody else has to die."

Scar's left eye twitched. "Unless I say so."

Unless he says so? "Yeah, you'll be the new lord of hell. You can kill anybody you want." Edgar kept his expression blank as he tapped his own chest. "Except me." *Don't include your friends in this deal, Cordell. Don't give him any bargaining chips.*

"So," Edgar said, "do you want Lucifer or not?"

Scar's eye twitched again. "Done. You give me Lucifer, and I'll leave you alone. But you cross me . . ."

Edgar nodded. "I'm slagged."

Scar grinned widely, showing a mouthful of teeth. "Slagged."

Edgar dragged himself to his feet. *Buy time. Get away. I'm dead, no matter who wins. It's only a matter of time.*

And if I die, Llyrica dies.

Scar gripped Edgar by the shoulders and shook him. "Now give me Lucifer."

"Where is he?" Edgar asked.

Cheeks pushed himself away from the wall and stood up. "Last we heard, he's in the throne room."

The throne room? Edgar thought. *That's not a defensible position. It's too open. Shirley's confident. The war must be going* really *badly.* "How many men do we have?" *Make it sound like you're on his side.*

"We've got four," said Scar, "plus you, me, and Cheeks."

He said we, thought Edgar with a small amount of satisfaction. *He's starting to think of me as part of the team. But if Shirley was in the throne room, that means he's surrounded by Angels, supporters, and sycophants.* "That's not going to be enough."

Edgar's head throbbed. *I bet this is what a hangover feels like.*

A hangover.

A plan began to form in Edgar's pulsing brain.

An awful, desperate plan.

Scar's disfigured visage darkened with rage, the scars standing out in vivid white against the red. "You said you could give me Lucifer."

"Yes, I did," said Edgar. "And the seven of us aren't going to be enough to take him down."

Scar's face darkened to a dangerous purple. He looked as if he were about to explode like a super-nova. "I told you, Bedlam, if you cross me . . ."

Edgar tried to display a confidence he most definitely did not feel. "I'm slagged, I know. But seven still isn't enough."

Edgar grinned and tapped his aching temple. "But I know where we can get a small army."

"So, can you?" Cheeks hissed quietly at Edgar. The little man glanced furtively at Scar's back as the big man shuffled ahead.

Scar gave no indication that he'd overheard. He was shuffling decisively down the corridor, slapping a club against his palm.

Edgar resisted the urge to glance back at the other four men behind them. "Can I what?" Edgar could've ventured a good guess as to the nature of the question, but he didn't want to answer. He had no intention of taking Cheeks or anyone else along with him when he and Llyrica escaped.

If they could escape.

And that isn't going to happen unless I can get away from Scar and get back to the infirmary.

The small man growled softly in exasperation. "Can you fly the ship?"

Edgar said nothing, but he knew Scar's buddy wasn't going to let it go.

"You were a ship captain, weren't you?" asked Cheeks.

Edgar nodded.

"You can fly it, can't you?" Cheeks's tone was pleading, desperate. "Can't you? I heard it's still sitting out there."

"If it's still sitting out there," whispered Edgar, "what makes you think it's spaceworthy? I heard it crashed." *And killed Carlos and Doc Luschenko.*

"But you can fix it, can't you?" Cheeks looked at Edgar with hopeful eyes. "You can fix anything."

"How do you plan on getting to it?" Edgar asked. "Just stroll out . . ."

"A couple of guys found some old spacesuits and blew a hole in the wall."

Philippe! "Yeah," replied Edgar. "But they didn't make it very far, did they?"

"But you're smarter than them! I bet you've already figured out a way, haven't you?" He laid a hand on Edgar's arm. "I'll make it worth your while."

Edgar shrunk away from the small man in disgust. "Don't touch m—"

Scar whirled around, quick as a meteor strike, and crushed Cheeks's skull with single club blow. The little man crumpled to the deck. Scar bent down and struck the corpse six more times.

Then Scar straightened up and nodded. Blood was spattered across his scarred, expressionless face. "*Nobody* crosses me."

Edgar stared in mute horror at the bloodied heap of crushed bone and mangled flesh that had, only a moment before, been a man.

From behind him, four voices babbled in hasty professions of loyalty.

Scar nodded and casually wiped blood from one of his eyes. He gripped Edgar firmly by the forearm, turned, and began moving down the corridor, pulling Edgar along, leaving the remains of his buddy behind.

"Now, Bedlam, show me your plan."

Edgar tore his eyes away from the corpse and stared ahead.

He could hear the other men hurrying to follow.

Edgar struggled to calm his breathing, to keep from hyperventilating. *If this doesn't work, I'm dead.*

And so is Llyrica.

****

"This? This is your big plan?" Scar asked, his jaws wide in naked disbelief. "This?" He smote the oversized hatch with his club. The clang of metal on metal echoed down the corridor.

Time's Plague

The door handle on the hatch was jammed into the closed position by a length of pipe.

"This is where you're going to get me my army?" Scar's face was red with mounting fury, highlighting the white scars. "This is your plan?"

"Part of it," Edgar said, hastily holding up both hands in a placating gesture. The truth was that it had indeed been the entirety of his desperate gambit. "They're pissed at Lucifer. They'll be a . . . distraction, at least."

Scar shook his head, disbelief plain in his face, but he no longer appeared on the verge of an apoplectic fit. "But they're just a bunch of . . ."

BOOM!

Something thumped hard against the hatch from the other side, making Scar, Edgar, and the others jump.

More blows struck the hatch, like muted thunder, a muffled symphony of bass percussion.

Voices howled from inside. Some were inarticulate screams. Some shouted words. Two words were louder than the rest.

"Squeeze!"

"Lucifer!"

Scar stared at the hatch to the opium den. "You want to let the sleepers out of the Den?"

Edgar nodded, frantically trying to control his panic. "They're out of opium—you know, the squeeze—and I hear there's not going to be any more."

"Have you ever seen them?" Scar asked. "They're druggers, junkies. They're weak!"

BOOM! BOOM! BOOM!

Edgar jerked a thumb in the direction of the hatch. "Does that sound weak to you?"

"Lucifer!" screamed someone from inside. "Squeeze!"

"Hear that?" Edgar grinned nastily, hating himself at the thought of what he was proposing. *But if anybody deserves a crack at Shirley, it's them.* "They're hurting and they're mad. Just tell them Lucifer's got their squeeze, and they won't stop 'til they get to him."

"But Lucifer don't got no squeeze," said one of Scar's men.

Edgar shrugged his shoulders. "How do you know that?"

"Yeah," said another man, nodding, "if anybody's got something hoarded away, it'd be Lord Lucifer."

Scar smiled like a wolf.

He struck the hatch with his club.

The pounding on the other side paused.

"Listen up!" he roared.

The pounding resumed. The hatch handle wiggled as someone tried to open it from inside. The pipe wedged in the handle remained firmly in place.

Scar struck the hatch again.

Again the pounding stopped.

"I'll let you out," Scar bellowed. "Lucifer's got your squeeze."

There was only silence on the other side of the door.

"Get behind me, boys," said Scar, motioning to Edgar and the others.

They hurried to obey. Nobody wanted to be in the path of the addicts once they were freed.

Scar used his club to knock out the pipe which was jamming the handle.

The pounding from inside resumed.

"I suggest we get out of here before they realize it's open," said Edgar.

Without another word, the six of them—Scar, Edgar, and Scar's remaining four men—shuffled off down the corridor and away from the Den.

By the time they turned at the first intersection, they heard a loud metallic clang, followed by screams and shouts. It sounded like a pack of ravenous wolves from a nature vid Edgar had seen once.

The sleepers are free.

The subhuman cries grew softer and more distant. He heard cries of "Squeeze!" and "Lucifer" fading away to nothing. He signaled for Scar and company to halt. Then he motioned for Scar to come close.

"Give them a few minutes," Edgar whispered, "and you can—"

Abruptly, Scar whirled about.

Edgar looked beyond the man and his blood ran cold.

"Lucifer!"

The war cry didn't come from the sleepers. Edgar saw a score of men led by one of Shirley's Angels.

"Run!" cried Edgar. He turned to flee, but saw a dozen more men approaching from the other direction.

For a brief moment, Edgar hoped the newcomers might be more of Scar's men, but then he recognized another Angel at their head.

They were trapped.

Llyrica!

Chapter 27

Thou worse than any name, read thine own evil
King Lear, Act V, Scene III

"I surrender!" Edgar cried, raising his hands.

Lucifer's men, approaching from both directions, hesitated, momentarily confused by Edgar's declaration. They bunched up behind their leaders, then began to move forward again.

But it wasn't Lucifer's men Edgar was worried about at that moment.

Scar roared, turning his fury upon Edgar.

Edgar shoved his way past Scar's men and into the open.

Scar's club arced through air that Edgar had occupied a mere instant before. Unable to stop the momentum of his swing, the club collided with Scar's own leg with a sickening crunch. He howled in pain as his shattered leg collapsed under him.

Edgar raised his hands again and repeated, "I surrender!" Then he added, "I'm unarmed!"

"Grab him," ordered one of the Angels.

Two of Lucifer's men took hold of Edgar's arms, pulled them down, and pinned them at his side.

From behind him, Edgar heard the sounds of battle.

But the battle didn't last long.

The scream of a wounded man cut off with the sound of a blow.

"Turn him around."

Edgar's handlers spun him roughly around to confront an Angel. The man was covered in blood. Edgar tried to recall his name, but couldn't come up with it. He hadn't paid too much attention to the enforcers themselves.

"So that's that," said the man, grinning widely.

He lifted an object so Edgar could see it.

It was Scar's head.

Even in death, Scar looked angry.

"That's the end of your little rebellion," said the Angel.

"It wasn't *my* rebellion," said Edgar. "I had no part in it. I was in the infirmary when—"

"I don't care," said the Angel.

Romeo. That was his name. His prison name, at least.

"Lord Lucifer wants to see you," said Romeo. "And he'll want to see this too." He waved the severed head. "He said something about mounting it on a pike."

****

"So, Fool," boomed Lucifer. "You thought you could take my throne by force?"

"It wasn't me," said Edgar. "I was in the infirmary when this all started." He stood in the grasp of two of Lucifer's goons.

Lucifer sat upon his throne, surrounded by a bodyguard of Angels. At least four of the bodyguards were new. Edgar noticed that Goner wasn't among them. Was it too much to hope Goner was among the dead?

The mob of inmates in the throne room was greatly reduced, compared to the other times Edgar had been in attendance. The gang-war had taken its toll. Edgar estimated there were fewer than six hundred men—less than half of what had been here when Edgar arrived on Callisto.

"You conspired with Scar!" Shirley pointed at Scar's head, which was mounted on an old flag pole.

"No!" said Edgar. "I did not. Scar did this on his own."

"He did it in your name! Don't even bother to deny it!"

"That's true," said Edgar, nodding.

The men holding his arms chuckled.

Edgar tried to jerk his arms free from their grasp, but failed. "But I didn't agree to it. I didn't sanction it. I wouldn't have sanctioned it. This was all Scar's doing." Edgar struggled again to free himself. "Tell your goons to back off."

Lucifer grinned evilly. "And why should I do that?"

"Because you still need me. You still need me, and I'm innocent."

"Ah," said Lucifer, "our agreement. I see."

"You still need me to reset the reclaimers."

"*My* reclaimers."

"Sure. Your reclaimers."

"You broke our deal. You incited rebellion."

"I did not. And that doesn't change the fact that you need me. And I need to be able to think and act clearly and of my own free will in order to reset them."

"You see, Tom Bedlam," said Lucifer rising from his throne, "I know your weakness. I know that you care about your followers. You'll do as I say or I'll exercise my royal wrath on someone you care for. It's true I can't touch you and your buddy, but I will *touch* the others."

Edgar couldn't suppress a shudder. "What others? You drove all my followers away." That wasn't quite true, but Edgar hoped the gang lord didn't know that.

Lucifer smiled. The cat had the mouse in his claws. Lucifer clapped his hands. "Bring them forth!"

From somewhere behind the throne, six men came forward. Four of them were obviously guards. The other two were prisoners, their hands bound with wire.

Soo-Won and Charlie.

"I believe you know these two," said Lucifer, grinning from ear to ear.

"Don't do it, Edgar," said Soo-Won. He looked as if he'd been beaten. Severely. Charlie did too. Fresh bruises blossomed on their faces. One of Soo-Won's eyes was swollen closed.

"Don't do what?" Lucifer asked. "Resist me? Defy me? Certainly, it is a great honor I bestow upon you, Sue-Boy! On both of you. You are to be my concubines. As long as Tom Bedlam serves me faithfully, you will continue to breathe my air."

Lucifer beamed at Edgar. "So, Fool, shall we make a new deal? Your service for their lives? I'm sure you can think and reason clearly enough to save your friends."

Edgar said nothing. *Have to get away. Have to get back to Llyrica! Take his bargain, Cordell! Get away from here and get to Sick Bay! Say anything. Agree to anything.*

But to abandon Soo-Won and Charlie?

At least they'll be alive.

"Don't do it," said Charlie. "Don't worry about us."

"Kneel," commanded Lucifer. "Kneel before your lord and master. Kneel and worship me."

Part of his mind screamed, *Just do it! You have to save Llyrica!*

"No." Edgar almost choked on the word. "I will not kneel to you. Not now. Not ever. I will never kneel to a man who calls himself Lucifer."

The gang lord sighed theatrically. "Ah, well. As you wish. I think we'll start with Sue-Boy!" He clapped his hands. "Strip him!"

Soo-Won's guards forced him to his knees.

Lucifer began to unzip his own crimson jumpsuit.

Save him! Find a way to save him! There has to be a way. There has to!

And then it came to him.

Edgar began to laugh. His damaged voice made the laugh sound completely insane. A mad gargoyle's glee.

Soo-Won's guards hesitated.

Lucifer paused in his disrobing, his jumpsuit around his ankles.

Edgar laughed all the louder, and the men holding his arms shrank back, releasing him. Edgar stepped forward and away from them.

"You!" he barked. "You pathetic, tin-plated, would-be devil!" Edgar threw back his head and howled his laughter at the ceiling.

He pointed at Lucifer. "You act like you're such a big man, a *god* among men." He turned to the assembled inmates. "Are you afraid of him? Does his very word make you tremble and want to soil yourselves?"

"Bedlam!" roared Lucifer. His Angels began to step toward Edgar.

Edgar wiped tears of mirth from his eyes. He pointed at Lucifer. "Do you know what he is? *Who* he is?" Edgar glanced back at Lucifer. The man's jaw hung open. His eyes were wide. There was one emotion written plain on his face.

Horror.

"He's a child molester, a baby raper. And his name, his *real* name is—"

"Shut up!" screamed Lucifer.

Edgar grinned. "Lamar Shirley." Edgar laughed, "You're afraid of a child molester named"—he made his voice sound as

249

mockingly childlike as he could—"Lamar Shirley. Isn't that a *pretty* name?"

"I will kill you!" screamed Shirley. He lunged at Edgar, but his feet became tangled in his jumpsuit. He pitched forward to the deck.

For a long moment, there was silence in the room. It was as if every man was holding his breath.

And then they began to laugh.

It started out as a few sniggers. Then chuckles. Then it rose and swelled until the throne room was filled with derisive laughter.

Even the Angels were caught up in the mockery.

Edgar waved for silence. The laughter became quieter, although some men continued to chortle.

"This is what you've been afraid of, guys," said Edgar. "Why are you afraid? Because he's got weapons? Well, you've all had weapons lately. And there are more of you than there are of them." He gestured at the Angels.

"Because of the sleep and the squeeze?" he continued. "Well, there's no more squeeze. So what are you afraid of?"

The laughter died down like a fire quenched by a wet blanket.

The inmates stared at Shirley, as if seeing him for the first time.

Shirley rose to his feet, hastily pulling up his jumpsuit. As he zipped it, he said, "Kill him."

Nobody moved.

Shirley turned to his enforcers. "Kill him!" he screamed. His voice was shrill, filled with rage and terror. "Kill him!"

One of the newer Angels said, "Kill him yourself, *Lamar*."

Some of the other enforcers nodded. Others did not. But nobody took a step toward Edgar.

Shirley looked frantically around the room, desperately searching for support from any quarter.

And he found none.

At last, his eyes came to rest on Edgar.

And they both knew—it was over.

Time's Plague

From the back of the room came a nearly inhuman howl. "Lucifer!" It was a cry of rage and pain, raising the hair on the back of Edgar's neck.

Into the room they came, shuffling like zombies in an old horror vid. They were naked, emaciated, covered with blood, and fueled by a rage brought on by opium withdrawal.

And hatred.

Their hands were bloody as if they'd tried to claw their way out of the opium den.

Griz was at their head, his loose flesh hanging in bloody folds.

The crowd of inmates scattered.

So did the enforcers.

Edgar retreated to one side of the room and stood next to Soo-Won and Charlie.

The path was open—nothing stood between the waking sleepers and the object of their rage and loathing.

"Lucifer!" On they came with surprising speed.

Lamar Shirley screamed. He turned and tried to flee, but Griz seized him. Other sleepers clawed at the gang lord.

Shirley screamed again—a scream of agony.

The pike bearing Scar's head toppled and fell on top of the writhing mass of the sleepers and their target.

Edgar turned away from the ghastly scene.

He grabbed hold of Soo-Won's and Charlie's arms, and the three of them fled the mess hall that had once served as Lamar Shirley's throne room.

Behind them, the sleepers howled with inhuman fury, like a pack of harpies devouring their prey.

Chapter 28

Why should a dog, a horse, a rat, have life,
And thou no breath at all?
King Lear, Act V, Scene III

The corridors of Hades were silent.

Edgar, Soo-Won, and Charlie encountered many corpses as they made their way toward the infirmary, but they met no living soul.

Hades had truly become a house of the dead.

Charlie chuckled. "Lamar Shirley. Who'd-a thought? Never in my wildest dreams."

Soo-Won laughed outright. "So, let me get this straight—you *dream* of Lucifer?"

"You know what I mean," said Charlie. "So, Edgar, how did you find out his name? Did he tell you?"

They tore him to shreds, thought Edgar, battling a wave of nausea. "Doc told me."

"Doc told you?" asked Charlie.

"Yep."

"And you kept it to yourself?" asked Soo-Won.

"Yeah," replied Edgar. "Maybe I was waiting for the right moment."

"Well, that was definitely the right moment," said Charlie.

They shuffled along without speaking for a long minute, pointedly ignoring the carnage.

Charlie broke the silence. "I wonder who'll be in charge now."

Soo-Won laughed bitterly. "Does it matter? Whoever it is, it'll be somebody bad. 'Meet the new boss—same as the old boss.'"

Time's Plague

"Nobody'll be as bad as Lu— as Lamar Shirley," said Charlie.

"Maggs was bad," said Soo-Won.

"Not as bad as Lucifer," said Charlie. "At least he didn't force guys to—you know—pair up."

Silence filled the corridors again as if haunted by the ghosts of things best left unspoken.

The infirmary airlock came into view. Several corpses lay scattered in front of it. *Almost there,* Edgar thought. *Llyrica, I'm almost there.*

"So"—Soo-Won cleared his throat—"how did you convince Doc to let you go outside?"

Edgar stopped in mid-shuffle, nearly losing his balance. "How did you . . . ?"

Soo-Won chuckled softly. "You weren't in the agridome with the rest of us. Working in the dome, you see things. We've seen Doc go outside to bring in new arrivals and supplies before. And Doc never *jumps.*"

Charlie pulled Edgar forward, continuing on toward the airlock. "So, will it fly?" He looked fixedly ahead, avoiding Edgar's eyes.

"Guys," Edgar said, "I can't . . ."

"Will . . . it . . . fly?" repeated Charlie, enunciating every word.

"Eventually," Edgar said. "She needs some repairs."

"But you can fix her," said Soo-Won. It wasn't a question.

It was Edgar's turn to stare straight ahead, staring at the airlock, at safety. "Yes, but I can't . . . can't take you with me."

"Can't? Or won't?" said Charlie.

"It's . . . complicated," replied Edgar.

Charlie abruptly stopped a meter short of the airlock. He wheeled about and planted his feet in front of Edgar, blocking his way. Charlie's bruised face was twisted in anger. "What's so complicated about it, huh? Not enough fuel? Not enough room? You afraid of aiding a couple of convicted murderers to escape? You afraid of breaking the *law*?"

Edgar gripped Charlie by the shoulders and stared him straight in the eye. "No! It's nothing like that. It's . . . There was a survivor." Edgar hesitated. *I can't tell them everything. Not now.*

C. David Belt

"I have to . . . Listen. Can we discuss this later? Once we're safe? Once we're inside the infirmary? The airlock's right . . ."

"No!" Violently, Charlie wrenched free of Edgar's grasp. Tears of rage spilled from his eyes. "Right now! I want an answer right now! Why can't you take us with you?"

"Charlie . . ." Soo-Won began, laying a hand on the tall man's shoulder.

"No!" Charlie spat, brushing his friend's hand aside. "I deserve an answer!"

Edgar nodded. "Yeah, you do. You *both* do. But time is critical. We have to get inside the infirmary. Maybe then . . ."

Charlie turned and punched the airlock intercom savagely. "Just shut up, man! Just shut up!"

Edgar held his peace.

"Yes?" came the doctor's voice.

Soo-Won leaned toward the intercom. "We've got wounded."

"One at a time, please." The doctor's voice sounded bone tired.

The airlock slid open.

"Go on, Charlie," said Soo-Won. "I'll be right behind you."

Charlie hesitated for a moment, then stepped inside. "You better be." He turned and glared at Edgar.

"Hurry, Doc," said Edgar.

The airlock slid closed.

"Mr. Cordell," said the doctor, "is that you?"

"Yeah, Doc." Edgar replied. "Hurry up!"

"I am pleased to hear your voice," the doctor said. "I had given up hope. I shall proceed with the utmost haste."

Soo-Won turned and leaned wearily against the hatch. "You go next."

"No," said Edgar. "You're hurt. You go next."

Soo-Won shook his head. "I'm nothing. Just an old excommunicate. An old terrorist. You're the important one."

"Belay that talk," said Edgar. "I won't abandon you out here."

Soo-Won laughed. "You're going to abandon us all, aren't you? Get in that shuttle and fly away? I don't know how you managed it, but—"

"The survivor," Edgar said, "is female."

Soo-Won looked stunned. "A woman?"

"She's"—Edgar was about to say innocent, but that wasn't the case, was it?—"She's going to die of the female plague. Doc has agreed to let me get her off-world, but he's not about to—"

"He's not going to let you help anyone else escape."

Edgar nodded and then shook his head. "Maybe . . . I can convince him . . ."

Soo-Won laughed bitterly. "Not Doc. You know, I could probably fly that shuttle as well as you." He looked up, but didn't meet Edgar's eye.

Suddenly, he stooped and snatched up a pipe from beside a nearby corpse.

The airlock door slid open.

Soo-Won raised his weapon.

Edgar brought up his hands defensively to deflect the blow.

Soo-Won shoved past Edgar and then pushed him into the airlock.

"SQUEEZE!"

Edgar stumbled, caught himself against the inner airlock door, and spun around.

The sight that met his eyes froze the blood in his veins.

Griz and the rest of the sleepers were coming down the corridor. They were less than ten meters away.

And they were closing fast.

"Wait!" cried Edgar. He was about to exit the airlock, to help his friend, but Soo-Won stabbed a finger at the control panel.

Soo-Won hit Edgar with the flat of his hand, striking him hard in the chest, shoving him back inside the airlock.

As the outer door slid shut, Soo-Won said, "Make my death mean something!"

And the door was closed.

Edgar punched the button to reopen the outer hatch. "Soo-Won!" he cried. But the door remained closed. He pounded on the button. The door didn't respond. Then he saw that the indicator was red.

The inner door slid open behind him.

"Mr. Cordell!" said the doctor, "Are you injured?"

Edgar turned frantically to the android. "Let me out, Doc!" He turned back to the outer hatch. The indicator was still red. "He's dying out there!"

The intercom crackled to life. "Give me squeeze!" The voice sounded like Griz's.

Edgar pounded on the airlock door in grief and frustration. *Soo-Won!*

"SQUEEZE!"

He's dead! Edgar pounded the door one last time. *Probably ripped to pieces like Shirley.*

"It is not safe to let you out," said the doctor. "What is squeeze?"

"SQUEEZE!" demanded Griz.

Edgar turned and collapsed against the outer door. He slid down to the airlock floor. *They've got him. Soo-Won's dead.*

The doctor looked down at him. "Are you injured, Mr. Cordell?"

Edgar shook his head. *My friend is dead. How much more is this place going to take from me?*

"Give me SQUEEZE!" said Griz. "SQUEE—"

The doctor silenced the intercom.

"Very well. Might I assume that this squeeze is some sort of addictive substance?"

Edgar bowed his head. *Soo-Won's dead!* "Opium."

"Where in the System did they get opium?"

Dead! Edgar shook his head wearily. "I don't know." His ragged voice was devoid of emotion. "Shirley's been using it to punish people. Forced addiction."

"I see. Yes, I suppose that would fit with some rumors I have heard." The doctor pushed the intercom button. "You will obtain no narcotics here. If you wish to be admitted one by one for detoxification, I shall treat you."

The response from the intercom was predictably profane.

"Very well," said the doctor. "If you change your minds, I will be here." The doctor silenced the intercom again.

The doctor extended a metallic hand to Edgar. "Are you certain you are uninjured? You were gone for a very long time. I could have made use of your assistance."

Soo-Won's dead!

But Llyrica's not. "I'll live," said Edgar. "How is . . . the patient?"

"Sedated so that the patient will not claw at the patient's eyes."

Edgar looked up at that. "The *patient* was clawing at the patient's eyes?" He took hold of the doctor's hand and stood.

"The patient was hysterical. I did not have time to deal with the patient when the patient awoke, and I thought it best for the patient's safety to prevent the patient from"—the doctor lowered its voice to a whisper—"*vocalizing.*"

"I want to see . . . the patient."

"Soo-Won?" Charlie called from somewhere in the distance. "Soo-Won? What's taking so long?"

Edgar bowed his head. "Take me to him—to Charlie."

"Very well," replied the doctor.

He motioned to a nearby examination room. As Edgar entered the chamber, he saw Charlie laying, strapped to a bed.

Charlie raised his head and looked at Edgar and then past him frantically. "Where is he? Soo-Won?"

Edgar went to Charlie's side. Tears spilled from his eyes. He choked out, "He's gone."

Charlie shook his head. "No!"

"We were attacked," Edgar said, his voice thick with grief. "The sleepers. Soo-Won. He shoved me into the airlock, held them off."

"You left him behind?" It was shock, disbelief, and condemnation. "You *abandoned* him?"

Edgar put a hand on Charlie's arm. "I couldn't—"

Charlie flinched at Edgar's touch. He howled in anguish and rage and grief. Then he stared at Edgar, and hatred blazed in his bloodshot eyes. "You bastard! Your fault! Get out of here!" Charlie slammed his head back onto the bed and howled again. Then he sobbed. "Soo-Won!"

"I tried . . ." Edgar began, but he let his voice trail off. There was nothing he could say, no words he could use to console Charlie.

"I'm sorry," he whispered.

Edgar turned and left the room. Behind him, Charlie sobbed like a child.

The doctor gently laid a hand on Edgar's shoulder. "I am sorry for your loss."

"I want to see the patient," said Edgar.

The doctor looked at Edgar's head. "You have a hematoma on the back of your head. You might have a concussion. Let me examine you first."

"It's nothing."

"Nevertheless, I shall examine you." The doctor took an implacable grip on Edgar's arm. "I insist."

Edgar cast a longing glance in the direction of Emergency-room 4. "Okay, Doc, but quick. And please don't restrain me with Ozzie running around free."

"Mr. Oswald is not here. I could have made use of his assistance, but he has not reported as he should have. I fear he may be a casualty." The doctor led Edgar to another examination room and pointed at the solitary bed.

Ozzie's gone? Edgar thought. *Maybe Goner's dead with him.*

"How many . . . How many dead?" Edgar asked as he sat on the edge of the bed.

"Six hundred and forty-one confirmed dead. Six hundred and forty-two now."

Edgar's jaw dropped. "Six . . . hundred*?"* *I knew there'd be a lot, but . . . so many!*

The doctor passed a hand-held medical scanner over the back of Edgar's skull. "Six hundred and forty-two, according to my sensors. This war has been, by far, the deadliest in the history of the Hades Penal Colony."

"How many wounded?"

"Twelve."

Edgar was stunned. "Tw-Twelve? That's less than you had before I left!"

The doctor nodded, and its shoulders sagged as if they were suddenly carrying the burden of Atlas. "Yes, I have lost eighty-nine patients since the start of this wretched war, mostly due to blood loss and shock. The blood synthesizer could not keep up with the demand."

Edgar shook his head in disbelief. Somehow that number was more devastating than the total number of the dead. *Because Doc had to* watch *them die.* "I'm sorry, Doc."

Time's Plague

The doctor sighed. "As am I."

"What about my other friends? Ted? Karan? Ibrahim? Avery? Bilal?"

"Mr. Knight is still with us. I am afraid I was unable to save the others."

So Karan, Ibrahim, Avery, and Bilal are gone too.

Edgar buried his head in his hands and wept.

Mattasi. Yurii. Karan. Ibrahim. Avery. Bilal. Philippe. Maurice. Rodrigo.

All dead.

Soo-Won.

The doctor patted Edgar's shoulder and looked at the readings on the scanner. "I can give you a cold pack to reduce the swelling and an analgesic for the headache, but there is no permanent damage."

Edgar wiped his eyes on his sleeve. "Can I see them?"

"Mr. Knight is sleeping, and I would prefer he not be disturbed at this time. His condition is no worse than it was before, but he needs to rest before I can discharge him."

Edgar shook his head. "No, I meant . . . the others. Karan, Ibrahim, Avery, Bilal—the dead."

The doctor shook his head. "I am sorry, Mr. Cordell, but that is not possible. I have already disposed of the bodies."

Edgar looked up at the blue eyes set in titanium sockets. "Disposed?"

"Yes, Mr. Cordell."

"How?" It suddenly occurred to Edgar that he'd never seen or heard of a burial in the prison. But he came to the answer on his own. *The reclaimers.* He wanted to vomit. *After all, a corpse is just biowaste in this place.* The doctor opened its mouth to reply, but Edgar waved a hand to prevent it. "Never mind. I get it."

So many dead. Only Ted and Charlie left.

And I can't take them with me.

"May I see the *patient* now?" he asked.

"Yes, you may." The doctor stepped back and gave Edgar room to get off the bed. "You know the way."

"Thanks, Doc." Edgar started to exit the room.

"Mr. Cordell, when do you estimate that you will be able to effect the *cure* for the patient's otherwise terminal condition? Symptoms could begin to manifest at any time."

Edgar kept moving toward ER-4, toward Llyrica. "I need access to a computer and the reader pad I gave you. I have to analyze the data on the pad. Then I need to do some hefty calculations. It might take me a while. At least a day. Maybe more."

"I see," said the android. "You may avail yourself of the terminal in Emergency-room 4. The pad is on the counter next to it. I will call for you if I require your assistance with any of the other patients. Get to work. There will be time to mourn later. For now, save the one life you can."

Edgar nodded.

The one life that matters most.

Chapter 29

Upon such sacrifices, my Cordelia,
The gods themselves throw incense.
King Lear, Act V, Scene III

Llyrica.

The burns on her hands and face were mostly healed. Only a slight bleaching of the skin remained. A bandage wrapped around her head, covering her eyes. Her hands and arms were restrained, perhaps on the off-chance she might wake and try to scratch at her face. A tube fed a drip of clear liquid into her arm.

Edgar watched the rise and fall of her chest as she snored softly.

He *loved* that snore.

Edgar had lain awake some nights just listening to Llyrica sleep. He'd found comfort simply in knowing his bride was sleeping peacefully beside him.

My bride, he thought with gall burning in his belly. *Not anymore. She left me for Edmund. And the three of them—Goner, Edmund, and Llyrica—murdered Ol' Benny. They sent me here to Hades.*

She *sent me here.*

Edgar knew he shouldn't still love her.

Anger. Hatred. Disgust. That's what he should've felt.

And he *did* feel those things. They twisted his gut, like gears grinding up his insides. He *hated* her.

And above all else, she was no longer his—she was another man's wife. Edmund's wife.

But Edgar couldn't deny that he loved her, in spite of all that.

Why, Llyrica? Why?

Why me? Why Benny? Was he butchered just to get me out of the way?

If I could just understand the why, *maybe I could . . .*

Maybe I could what? Forgive you?

Edgar shook himself.

No time for that.

I've got to get you off this moon. Maybe when you're safe, when we're both safe, maybe then I can ask you why.

But not now.

Right now, it's time to get to work.

****

When he heard the door open, Edgar looked away from the computer screen.

It was Doc Stewart.

Of course, it's Doc, thought Edgar. *Who else? Every hour, like clockwork.*

The doctor closed and locked the door behind itself. It pointed at Edgar's untouched food tray. "Is the stew not to your liking? Replicated proticarb is the best I can do here, but I have it on good authority that the taste is acceptable. You really should eat."

Edgar shrugged. "Not hungry. Too much riding on my calculations."

The doctor walked over to examine Llyrica. "And how are your calculations progressing?"

Edgar sighed wearily. "Well enough, I guess. I've retrieved and decoded the flight data. I've projected the *Hera's* flight path, going forward several days. So I know where she'll be at any given point, assuming she doesn't change her orbit, and assuming she hasn't left orbit already."

Having finished checking Llyrica's vital signs, her eyes, and her burns, the doctor lifted Llyrica's blanket and proceeded to check her catheter.

Edgar averted his eyes.

"And if the mother ship is not where you project she should be," the doctor said without turning toward Edgar, "or if she has left orbit?"

"Then Llyrica dies." Edgar's tone was flat, belying the fear clutching icily at his heart. "*Eris* doesn't have enough fuel to make it back to Ganymede on her own. I could break Callistoan orbit, then enter Jovian orbit and hope for someone to find us, but that's a one-in-a-billion shot. If *Hera's* not up there, or we can't rendezvous with her, the only other thing I could do is return to Callisto. So, at least for Llyrica, it's a one-way trip." *And I'd rather die than return to Hades.* "So, I'm not going to even plan for that possibility."

"I am finished here," said the doctor. "You no longer need to avert your eyes, although I do not see why you bother."

"She's not my wife anymore." As much as he hated Llyrica for what she'd done, it still ripped at Edgar's heart to say those words out loud.

"As you wish," said the android. "So how long before you can depart?"

"I'm close to being done," Edgar said. "I remember the formulas well enough . . . I think. But there are a few constants I can't remember. *Critical* constants. It's been years since I've had to plot a manual flight-plan for a Stargull IV. My dad used to insist I do it every once in a while, but now I can't remember the exact mass of the IV, the exact thrust of the engine, thrust-to-burn rate curves—stuff like that. Pretty important stuff. And your database doesn't have the specs. The ship profiles in your DB are way too old—from before this place became the prison paradise it is today. So, I'm taking a wag . . ." *Doc's not going to know that term.* "I'm guessing on a few things."

"I see," said the doctor. "How good do you think your guesses are?"

Edgar shrugged his shoulders. "I hope good enough." *I have no idea.* "I think I'll be in the ballpark, as my grandpa used to say." *Maybe I'm not exactly licking my finger and sticking it in the wind, but it sure feels like it.* "I've run several versions of the calcs using different values for the constants and curves."

"So when?" asked the doctor.

"I'm rerunning all the simulations now," Edgar said, "but the soonest feasible launch window is about three hours from now." *Three hours to freedom!* "But I need to talk to Ted and Charlie first."

"You need to say your farewells."

Edgar turned to look at the doctor, grinning apologetically. "Yeah, Doc, about that . . ."

The android shook its head firmly. "Mr. Cordell, if you are going ask to take them along, do not bother. I understand the

C. David Belt

necessity of allowing you to escape, but I cannot consider permitting the escape of any other inmates."

Edgar held up a hand. "Hear me out, Doc."

"I fear you will only waste my time and yours." It gestured at Llyrica. "And perhaps hers."

"It won't take long."

The doctor made a sighing sound. "Proceed."

Edgar held up a hand and extended one finger. "First, *Hera* is a big ship. The normal crew complement is five, but one of those five is the cargomaster and one is the doctor. Neither is essential for this trip, although I'd *like* to have a doctor along. You up for a voyage?" He grinned at Stewart, but the android gave no indication it considered the joke funny.

A joke is all it could be. Doc would never abandon his post. Edgar cleared his throat. "Anyway, that leaves three essential personnel—pilot-slash-captain—that's me—copilot-slash-first mate and engineer."

"Stop right there, Mr. Cordell," said the doctor, holding up a hand. "The ship is intelligent and sentient. She can assist you with the functions of the other two crewmembers."

Edgar shook his head and laughed softly. "Oh, yeah. That brings me to my second point." He extended a second finger. "I know *Hera* well, and like you said, she's a smart old gal. But she doesn't know *me*."

"The SS *Hera* was your ship, was she not?"

She was, thought Edgar bitterly. *Not my ship. Not my wife.* "I'm no longer her captain, and even if she were willing to let Edgar Cordell captain her again, she's not going to recognize me as Edgar Cordell. I ran into this problem with the *Eris* already. *Eris* recognized me only because of an old passcode left over from when I was a kid, but *Hera* has a different, more demanding set of protocols. *Hera* will use three tests to identify me—retinal scan—which I can pass—facial recognition, and voice recognition." Edgar waved a hand in front of his scarred face. "Thanks to Griz and his tender ministrations, I won't pass the latter two tests. And you gotta pass at least two, because each one can be faked individually. My old passcodes won't work, because they've been invalidated. So I can't override the AI. In other words, Doc, *Hera's* going to treat me like a hijacker. To her, I'll be no better than a pirate. She's not going to cooperate with me, at least not at first, and she's going to attempt to block me at every pass."

"What about Mrs. Reagan?" asked the doctor. "Could not she assume command of the ship?"

Edgar shook his head. "Nope. She's not the captain—I know that for sure—and she's probably not even registered as a crewmember, only as a passenger. But even if she were an authorized crewmember, we've got the same problem. Retinal scan won't work, not with her eyes damaged the way they are. Her face has been burned, so facial recognition would be iffy at best—probably not good enough for a positive ID. Only her voice would pass for sure. And one out of three isn't enough."

The doctor nodded. "You have convinced me that you will encounter resistance from the ship, but you have yet to explain why you require two additional crewmembers."

Edgar suppressed a smile. *I knew you'd see reason, Doc.* "I was getting to that." He raised a third finger. "I'll need to be at the flight controls, but one of the first things Hera will do to prevent a perceived hijacking will be to shut down the engine. The engine controls *can* be manually overridden, but only locally—in the engine room. And without *Hera's* assistance, the engine'll need to be monitored. I can't be in two places at once. So I'm going to need help. Sighted help," he added, glancing meaningfully at Llyrica.

The doctor stared at him for a moment and then nodded. "I see the logic in your argument and the *flaw* as well."

As soon as the doctor uttered the word, Edgar saw the flaw too. *I can justify* one *extra man, but not two. I can save one, but not both.*

"You may take Mr. Knight or Mr. Miller, but not both," said the android. "You may choose, but I recommend Mr. Miller as he is healthier and stronger than Mr. Knight."

Edgar opened his mouth to protest, but the doctor held up a warning hand. "Do not press the argument further. I am already stretching my primary directive to the breaking point." It nodded toward Edgar's food. "Eat your stew."

With that, the doctor turned and left the room.

Edgar stared at the door.

Ted or Charlie?

How can I possibly make that choice?

C. David Belt

****

"The bottom line is I can only take one of you." Edgar paused for a moment, and then plowed ahead. "I'm the only one that can pilot the ship. And I need Doc Stewart's cooperation to exit the airlock—he's the only one with the access code. I've convinced him I need help running the ship, but I was only able to convince him to let me take one of you."

Charlie Miller met Edgar's eyes with an unwavering stare. Charlie looked awful. Bruises covered half his face. His jaw was swollen—his right eye, bloodshot. But his injuries would heal quickly. Charlie nodded, his lips stretched tight. Then he shook his head slightly. He let out a long sigh. "For what it's worth, I hope you guys make it."

Edgar blinked in confusion. "Me and Ted? No. I need *you* to come with me."

Charlie's jaw dropped, and his eyes went wide. "Me? You want *me* to go?"

Edgar nodded. "Yeah."

Charlie's bruised face split in a wide grin. "You mean it? I'm gonna get off this rock?"

Edgar smiled sadly. *How am I going to tell Ted?* "But you have to be ready to go in less than an hour."

Charlie laughed, and tears of joy squeezed past his eyelids. "Home. I'm going home."

Edgar shook his head. "Not home. We'll be fugitives. I'm not sure where we'll end up . . ."

"It won't be *this* place!" Charlie said.

That drew a real smile from Edgar. "No, it won't."

Charlie's expression sobered. "I'm sorry . . . for what I said. Soo-Won . . . His death . . . It wasn't your fault."

Edgar suddenly felt a lump in his throat. "I'm sorry too." He walked over to where Charlie lay strapped to the bed and laid a hand on the tall man's shoulder. "It was a terrible"—Edgar swallowed hard—"terrible way to go."

"Yeah." Charlie was silent for a long moment. Then he said, "But it's what he wanted."

Edgar was almost convinced he'd misheard. "What?"

"Soo-Won . . . he wanted to atone," Charlie said. "He talked about it a lot . . . well, to me, anyway. When he and the others blew up the Gaia Hypergate—you know, the one that used to be at Earth, it was supposed to be unoccupied. Nobody was supposed to get hurt. Soo-Won got caught up in his *cause*. He listened to the wrong people. Some folks called them terrorists, but whatever they were, nobody was supposed to get hurt. But somebody did. A couple of technicians died. Soo-Won wanted to pay it back, you know. But he couldn't."

Charlie's voice caught. "But now he has. He died for someone else, didn't he? He gave his life for *you*."

Edgar dashed a tear away from his own eye. "Yeah, he did."

"Anybody ever tell you what I did?" asked Charlie. "Why I'm here?"

"Charlie, that's not necess—"

"Yeah, it is. You gotta understand." Charlie took a deep breath and plunged in. "It was a robbery, and things went nuclear. I got scared. I shot two guards. I'll never forget the look on that one guard's face when I shot her. She had a husband and two kids. Her name was Emma. Her husband's name was Peter. Her kids were Billie and Cora. They were just three and five years old. The other guard was an old man, a grandfather. His name was Amram. I burned a hole right through his chest. He was still . . ." Charlie shook his head. "Aw, the details don't matter. What matters is two people are dead. I murdered them. And I didn't have any noble-but-misguided intentions, like Soo-Won. No, it was all about me. And two people are dead and two families destroyed. All because of me."

Charlie stared intently at Edgar. Tears streamed down his face. "If anyone needs to atone, it's me."

Edgar opened his mouth, but he didn't know what to say. "Charlie . . ." he began.

"Tell me I can be forgiven." Charlie said, his eyes pleading. "Tell me there's enough . . . mercy . . . for me."

"Yes," Edgar said, smiling through his own tears. "'His arm is stretched out still.'"

Charlie nodded. "Thanks. Why don't they execute us anymore? Murderers, you know, like me? At least that way, there would be some measure of . . ." He scowled. "They tell themselves they're being humane. But they just want us out of sight. This place is *worse* than death."

Edgar shrugged. "I don't know, but . . . There's a hymn. It says, 'As He died to make men holy, let us *live* to make men free.'"

Charlie nodded, but the nod morphed into a shaking of his head. "It's not enough . . . not enough to make up for what I did."

"You can't 'make up' for murder. Only the Savior can do that."

"Yeah. You're right." Charlie's expression became firm, resolute. "But I can do better than just . . . *exist*. I can save somebody else." He drew in a deep breath and let it out slowly.

Then he smiled. "Take Ted."

That time Edgar was certain he'd misheard. "What did you say?"

"You heard me," said Charlie. "Take Ted. I can save *him*. It'll be like giving my life for him, right?"

"It . . . would," Edgar said slowly. "Charlie, are you . . . sure?"

"Yeah."

"But," said Edgar, "Ted might not make it. We can't use the hypergates—I don't have an authorization code to open the gate at Ganymede. And if we're caught, we come right back here. So wherever we go, it's going to be a long haul—maybe eighteen months. I don't think Ted's *got* that long."

"Maybe not," said Charlie, "but at least he'll die a free man."

"But I need someone to help for the whole trip."

Charlie laughed and shook his head. "No, you don't. Not you. At first, yeah, sure. But you'll figure out how to bypass the AI on that ship. You're a ruddy genius when it comes to computers."

"Charlie . . . I . . ."

"Take Ted." There was a finality to Charlie's tone.

Edgar sighed. Then he smiled. "You're a good man. As good a man as Soo-Won."

Charlie shook his head. "Don't you dare tell anybody. I got a reputation to maintain!"

Edgar smiled. "I can do you one better. I talked to Doc—whoever stays behind gets to be a trustee. And better yet, *you* get to be in charge of the reclaimers. Doc'll give you the details."

Time's Plague

Charlie's eyes went wide. "Me? Reset the reclaimers?"

"Yep. You'll be the most valuable man in Hades. Nobody'll dare touch you." The memory of Griz and the other sleepers as they ripped Lamar Shirley to shreds flashed through Edgar's mind. He shuddered. "Nobody sane, at least. Whoever ends up in charge out there, you should be safe from him at least."

"Safe." Charlie looked at Edgar dubiously. "In hell?" Then he smiled. "Well, someone's gotta be king of the compost heap. That won't be me, but at least I'll be the new fool! Stretch the Fool. I actually like the sound of that in a weird way."

Charlie's expression suddenly became very serious. "I have one condition, though."

"You're kidding."

"Serious as a fool in hell."

"Okay. What's your condition?"

"I want to see *her*. The woman. The one you get to save."

Edgar was suddenly very much on his guard. "Charlie, that's probably not a good idea."

"Strap me to a wheelchair and wheel me in. I don't care. I just want to *see* her. I haven't seen a woman in *so long*. Not even a picture. Is she pretty? Is she beautiful?"

"Charlie . . ."

"I don't care if she's plain as an old bulkhead. She's a woman. That's beauty enough for me. Give me that. Let me see beauty one last time. Please."

Edgar looked closely at his friend. "I'll talk to Doc and see what I can do. It's not my call, but maybe if you're restrained . . ."

"Fair enough. Thanks." Charlie smiled. It was the honest smile of a man at peace. "Bon voyage, Edgar Cordell. I hope you find a better place."

Edgar took Charlie's hand and clasped it in both of his. He looked at Charlie and smiled. "Thank you, Charlie. And may God bless you and watch over you."

You are one of the bravest men I have ever met, Charlie Miller. Anybody can lay down his life. You are willing to walk back into Hell to save another.

Chapter 30

You ever-gentle gods, take my breath from me
King Lear, Act IV, Scene VI

"Who is she? Do you even know?"

Charlie, his wrists bound in plastic manacles, stood near the door of ER-4, gazing at Llyrica. Edgar could only describe Charlie's expression as awestruck. The doctor stood next to Charlie, holding firmly on to the tall man's arm. It had been a huge concession on the doctor's part to allow Charlie to be out of bed at all, given that Edgar was unrestrained.

Edgar stood protectively next to Llyrica's bed. It wasn't that Edgar didn't trust Charlie—he did—but Edgar wasn't going to let anyone except the doctor near Llyrica. He was a man protecting the woman he loved.

The woman he hated.

"Her name is Llyrica Reagan," said Edgar in a flat voice, "my ex-wife."

Charlie's head snapped in Edgar's direction. "No way! No way!"

Edgar merely nodded. *I guess Charlie's heard the story.*

"Isn't she . . ." Charlie's voice trailed off.

Edgar nodded, his expression solemn as a stone. ". . . the one who put me here?" he said, finishing Charlie's incredulous question. "Yeah."

"And you're *helping* her?"

Edgar shrugged. "What else am I supposed to do?"

"I don't know," said Charlie. "Maybe leave her to what she deserves?"

Edgar looked at the doctor and then at Charlie, and then focused on Llyrica. "Don't think I didn't consider it. But I just couldn't do that. I'm not . . . that guy." *And I still love her. Heaven help me, but I do.*

270

Time's Plague

Edgar looked back at Charlie, his face twisting into a wry smile. "Besides, she's my ticket out of here." He winked at the doctor. "Just kidding, Doc."

"Not funny, Mr. Cordell," said the doctor in a flat tone.

Edgar was suddenly worried. *Stupid time to make a joke. Especially* that *joke.* "Seriously, Doc. I was just—"

The doctor made a noise that sounded like something between a growl and a grunt. "I have no doubt of your desire to escape, but I know what I saw when you were alone with her and thought you were unobserved." The doctor and Edgar stared at each other for a long, tense moment. "And the fact remains that I cannot save her life. She must get off Callisto." The doctor's eyes shifted, apparently focusing elsewhere. "Mr. Cordell, I do not wish to alarm you overly much, but the patient's blood-oxygen level has dropped—not precipitously, but it *has* decreased. It appears the symptoms have begun to manifest."

Fear sank its icy talons into Edgar's heart. He felt as if the room was suddenly devoid of oxygen. He found it hard to breathe. "How long . . . How long does she have?"

"Given the anecdotal data," the doctor replied, "she appears to be in the very early stages of the syndrome. I doubt anyone would have noticed the change if they were not specifically looking for it. I would estimate she has a few days before the symptoms become acute. However, it is possible that the trauma she has experienced may have accelerated the onset. It is also possible that the syndrome will progress more rapidly than historical accounts indicate."

His anxiety mounting, Edgar turned to the computer screen. The simulation results *looked* good. *Assuming I got the numbers right.* "How long?" he asked again.

"Are you satisfied with your calculations?" the android asked.

"They're as good as they're gonna be," replied Edgar. He began packaging the data for transfer back to his reader pad.

"In that case, I suggest you depart at the first opportunity." The doctor's tone was serious, emphatic. "I will assist you in preparing Mrs. Reagan and Mr. Knight for EHA as soon as I return Mr. Miller to his . . ." The android cocked its head as if listening. "Never mind that. The reclaimers have just gone offline again. Mr. Miller, if you will accompany me, I will instruct you as to how to reset them."

Wasting no time, the doctor pulled Charlie toward the door. "I shall return shortly, Mr. Cordell."

Charlie lifted his manacled hands and waved awkwardly in Edgar's direction as Charlie and the doctor stepped through the door. "Godspeed," Charlie said.

The door closed, and they were gone.

I should've said good-bye.

Edgar turned back to the computer and initiated the data transfer to the pad. The pad beeped, indicating the transfer was complete. Edgar stuffed the pad into a pocket on his jumpsuit.

He looked at the display on Llyrica's bed. He could see the O2 level readout, but the number meant nothing to him. *93.7. Is that a percentage?* He looked at Llyrica's face, at her lips. She didn't look pale, and her lips weren't blue. Those were the only signs of anoxia he knew to look for.

"Hurry, Doc," he muttered. He looked at Llyrica's lips again. *Are they turning blue? I can't tell.* He gently brushed her cheek. *Is she getting cold?* He looked at her body temperature on the display. *No, that's normal.* "Hold on, sweet . . ." He grimaced. *Not my sweetheart anymore!* "Hold on, Llyrica," he growled. "Don't you die on me!"

But she is dying, right before my eyes. Edgar felt helpless. Gotta wait 'til Doc gets back. I don't know the first thing about how to take care of her. What if she needs a doctor on the voyage? How will I take care of her then?

Edgar looked at the O2 readout again. The number was lower than the last time. *91.8.*

"Doc!" he yelled.

The door opened, and the doctor entered bearing an environment-suit. "I am here, Mr. Cordell. I understand your anxiety, but—"

"The O2 level!" Edgar said. "It's dropping!"

The android nodded. "Yes, it has, but let us not panic. It is a very small decrease. It is not dangerous. Not yet, anyway."

"But the launch window doesn't start for another hour! We've got to get her to the shuttle. I need at least fifteen minutes to prep the *Eris* for launch."

Time's Plague

"Mr. Cordell, you will not save her by hyperventilating. I understand your concern, but you must remain calm. I thought pilots were reputed to be cool under pressure."

But this isn't flying a ship we're talking about! It's Llyrica's life! "Okay, Doc." Edgar took a deep breath. *Focus on the task.* "You're right."

"Of course I am. I will prepare Mrs. Reagan for EHA. I left the environment-suit locker open for you. Get yourself and Mr. Knight into your spacesuits and meet us by the airlock. Mr. Knight is in Room 14. Now go."

With one last glance at Llyrica, Edgar said, "Roger, Doc. I'm on it."

He turned and headed for the door.

****

Ted bounced up and down on the balls of his feet, like a little boy who desperately needed to find a bathroom. "Where's Doc?" The old man rotated the space suit helmet in his hands.

Edgar was worried Ted might drop it. "If you break that helmet, I won't have time to get you another one from the shuttle."

The old man abruptly stopped bobbing, and his hands froze, gripping the helmet so tightly that his boney knuckles were white. "Sorry." He looked chagrined. "But where's Doc? Shouldn't he be here by now?"

"You'd think so," said Edgar. "But he said to wait here. So we're gonna wait right here."

"Okay." Ted squealed in anticipation. "I can't believe it! We're gettin' outta here! Can we go to Earth? I ain't never seen it, 'cept as a blue star. Why's Doc letting us go, anyway?"

Edgar adjusted the collar of his environment-suit again. He gazed anxiously down the corridor, looking for the doctor and Llyrica. "I said I'll tell you later, after we're aboard the shuttle."

"Yeppers! That's what you said, all right! So how long we gotta wait, ya think?"

Edgar said nothing. *Llyrica's got to be prepped by now. I hope she's okay. Please, Heavenly Father, let her be okay. Help me get her safely off this moon!*

There was still no sign of the doctor or Llyrica.

Edgar heard a low rumble, barely at the range of his hearing.

The reclaimers! That's what Doc was waiting for. Charlie got them going again. Doc had to be sure my fix worked before he could let me leave.

After all, what's Llyrica's life worth compared to the lives of all the men here?

Answer? Everything.

At least to me.

Moments later, to Edgar's profound relief, the doctor entered the corridor, carrying Llyrica's limp, spacesuited form. Edgar noted briefly that the android also carried a large pressure-sealed case in one hand.

"Who's that?" asked Ted. "He sick?"

"Dying," Edgar said. "Coming with us." Edgar deliberately avoided using pronouns which might give away the sex of the patient.

"Okay-okay-okay-okay," said Ted, clearly impatient. "Explain it later. Let's *go* already!"

Edgar donned his helmet and sealed it. He activated the suit and breathed in deeply as air began to flow. Turning to Ted, he took the helmet from the old man's hands and put it on him. Edgar checked the seals and activated the old man's suit. The comm indicator on Edgar's Heads-Up Display shone green. "Can you breathe okay?" he asked over the suit-to-suit channel.

Ted grinned widely, showing his sparse teeth. "Yeppers!"

Edgar acknowledged the old man's enthusiasm with a quick thumbs-up. He turned his attention to the doctor and the precious burden in its arms. "How is . . . the patient?" Edgar extended his arms toward Llyrica's limp form.

The doctor pulled back, keeping Llyrica out of Edgar's reach. "The patient's oxygen level continues to decline." The doctor's voice was loud—loud enough to be heard inside the helmets. "I have increased the oxygen level in the environment-suit to compensate somewhat, but that is a temporary fix at best."

Struggling to remain calm and focused, Edgar reached for Llyrica again.

The doctor, however, demurred once more. "I shall carry the patient. I have medicine here, and I wish to see the patient secured aboard the shuttle. I also wish to retrieve my spacesuit before you depart. If you will take the medicine"—the android wiggled the pressure case—"I will enter the code for the airlock."

Edgar took the case from the doctor. He watched as the doctor shifted Llyrica's weight slightly so the android could reach the airlock control panel. The doctor rapidly keyed in a long string of numbers.

The airlock slid open.

Freedom. Just on the other side.

"You two go first, Mr. Cordell," said the doctor. "Proceed with all due haste to the shuttle. We will join you there."

Edgar didn't want to let Llyrica out of his sight again. "We won't be able to communicate outside," he yelled, hoping the doctor could hear him. "I'd rather you came with us."

The doctor nodded. "As you wish. You two proceed and wait for us outside."

Edgar turned toward the airlock.

Ted was already inside. "You don't have to shout," said the old man. "I ain't hard of hearing."

Edgar stepped inside, and pressed a button on the control panel. The door slid closed, and the pressure seals inflated. "Sorry. Doc doesn't have a comm unit. He can't hear us."

"Okay." Ted was bouncing again. "Let's get going!"

Edgar heard the hiss of atmosphere being sucked out of the chamber. "Ted, I need you to calm down. It's dangerous out there. Do exactly as I say. And stay with me. Okay?"

"Yeppers! You got it!"

The outer door control panel showed 0 PSI and a green indicator light. It was safe to open the door.

Edgar pressed a button, and the outer hatch slid open.

He exited the airlock and stepped out onto the surface of Callisto. Ted followed close behind him.

Edgar closed the airlock. All he could do was wait. He stared at the hatch intently, impatiently.

Time slowed to a glacial crawl.

Hurry, Doc. Hang on, Llyrica, baby. Don't die on me!

Beside him, Ted turned around slowly. "It's like being in the agridome, but better somehow!" The old man's voice was filled with wonder.

"You've never been outside?" asked Edgar, still staring at the airlock hatch.

C. David Belt

"No! I ain't never been outside. Jupiter's so big! I ain't never seen anything so pretty." The old man stopped turning. He pointed off in the distance. "What're them things?"

Edgar tore his eyes away from the hatch and looked in the direction the old man indicated. Edgar's breath caught in his throat.

Gray cylinders stood in neat rows, like soldiers standing in close formation—forgotten soldiers, frozen at attention.

"Car—" Edgar cleared his throat, struggling to find his voice. "Cargo pods." *Last time, I must've been in such a hurry, I didn't notice them at all.*

"That's how I got here?" asked Ted. "In one of them things?"

"Yeah." *There must be* thousands *of them.* Tens *of thousands.*

One for every man dumped here and forgotten.
One for every soul damned to Hell.

Charlie's words came back to him. *They tell themselves they're being humane. But they just want us out of sight. This place is worse than death.*

"Doc's here," said Ted. "Let's go!"

Edgar spun about and saw Dr. Stewart holding Llyrica.

Edgar motioned to the doctor to follow him. "Let's get out of here." He glanced up at the crude sign over the hatch.

Abandon all hope, ye who enter here.

Edgar's heart thrilled with hope and dread. *Hang on, Llyrica!*

He turned his back on the gateway to Hell.

Act IV

Chapter 31

Alive or dead?
Ho, you sir! Friend! Hear you, sir? Speak!
King Lear, Act IV, Scene V

Ted froze midway through removing his spacesuit. "That's . . . That's a-a-a *woman*!" The old man stared at Llyrica with wide eyes and open mouth.

The doctor sighed. "It appears that your decades of incarceration have not diminished your capacity for gender identification, Mr. Knight," it said. Llyrica lay on the shuttle deck as the doctor finished removing her spacesuit. Underneath, she was dressed in an ill-fitting prison jumpsuit. "I am also gratified that your eyesight is at least nominal." The android pushed the pieces of the spacesuit aside. "Now, Mr. Knight, if you will kindly give me a bit more room, I will strap the patient into a seat."

The old man didn't move a muscle.

"Mr. Knight, if you please!" Irritation and impatience were evident in the android's tone.

"Ted!" barked Edgar from the pilot's chair, "get out of the way!"

Ted shook himself as if startled and stepped back.

The doctor lifted Llyrica in its arms and placed her into the seat behind Edgar's. "How long until you can launch?"

Edgar checked the engine readouts on the status display. Unlike a launch from the mothership where the engine could fire up safely in about a minute, a cold start required more time. "Engine should be ready in thirteen minutes. Eilie, do you concur?"

"Yes, Eddie," said the *Eris*. "Engine startup is proceeding according to normal parameters."

"Thanks, Eilie," Edgar said. "All critical systems should be go by then. Our launch window opens in"—he checked the ship's clock on the instrument panel—"Seventeen minutes." He set the takeoff clock. "T minus seventeen and counting. I can't launch before then. If I do, we'd never rendezvous with the *Hera*."

Edgar continued to run through his preflight checklist. The checklist itself was printed on a clear-laminate-coated book bound with metal rings. The book was strapped to Edgar's thigh. "Eilie, do you have the flight-plan loaded?"

"Affirmative, Eddie."

"Can you bring it up please?" Edgar tapped the blank navigation screen.

"Navigation is offline," said the *Eris*. "I'm sorry, Eddie."

"I know, old girl," Edgar, trying his best to remain patient with the impaired AI. "Just bring up the text and the plotted curves, please."

The nav screen bloomed to life, displaying letters, numbers, and a few graphs—headings, velocities, times, burn rates.

"Thank you, Eilie," Edgar said. "Can you read it? Did I get your gross weight and CG correct?"

"I've read the flight-plan," replied the *Eris*. "Gross weight is within parameters. I cannot seem to calculate center of gravity. I'm sorry, Eddie."

"It's okay. I'll just have to adjust the CG dynamically."

"I won't be able to assist you," the shuttle said, "not with navigation."

"Roger that," said Edgar. "You just monitor your systems as best you can, especially environment. Can you increase the O2 level to 42 percent?"

"Affirmative. Increasing. Oxygen level will be double normal in three minutes."

"Roger that," said Edgar. *Any richer than that on the O2, and we'll risk a fire if anything sparks. As big a bump as the old girl took, a few sparks are more than likely.*

He ticked three more items off his preflight checklist. "That's it for now. Eilie, alert me when the engine reaches nominal minus five."

Time's Plague

"Wilco, Eddie," said the *Eris*. "Eddie, I'm glad you're back. I was afraid you'd forgotten me."

"Never, old girl. You're my Eilie. How could I ever forget my Eilie?" Edgar rose from his seat and looked over the doctor's metallic shoulder. "How is she, Doc?"

The doctor checked its handheld medical scanner. "Her blood oxygen saturation is at 87.9 percent. As I postulated, her symptoms are progressing at a much faster rate than the anecdotal data would suggest. It is imperative that you launch and get her away from the surface as soon as possible. Her symptoms should—"

"She's so pretty," said Ted, his voice filled with awe. "My mama was pretty."

"Not now, Ted," Edgar growled. "Get strapped in"—Edgar pointed at the copilot's seat—"and just sit quiet."

The old man moved toward the seat, but kept facing toward Llyrica. His gaze was riveted on her. "What's wrong with her eyes? She blind? Can I touch her?"

"Not now!" Edgar snapped.

Ted frowned and sat in the chair, pouting like a scolded child.

Maybe bringing Ted wasn't such a great idea, Edgar thought. *I need an extra hand, but Charlie would've been a better choice.* He turned his attention back to Llyrica and the doctor. "How bad is 87.9 percent?"

"Bad enough," said the android. "100 percent is optimal, of course. 95 to 98 percent would be normal. If the decline progresses according to the curve I have calculated, even with the increased oxygen level in the environment, Mrs. Reagan will be dangerously anoxic in approximately forty-seven to fifty-one minutes. I cannot be more precise at this point. However, according to the historical record, syndrome victims began to recover soon after achieving orbit. How long after you launch before you can achieve orbit?"

Don't you dare die on me, Llyrica! Edgar thought for the thousandth time. He fought down the panic threatening to overwhelm him. "Thirty-one minutes to stabilize, but we should be near apogee in twenty-seven. That's about as far away from the surface as we're gonna get. So"—Edgar checked the clock readout—"we're T minus fourteen right now. Fourteen plus twenty-seven. That's forty-one minutes. Will that be . . . soon enough?" Edgar gripped the back of his seat hard and squeezed his eyes shut. *Father in Heaven, please let it be soon enough!*

"I cannot say with any certainty," said the doctor.

"Environmental oxygen level at 42 percent," said the Eris.

Edgar opened his eyes and took a deep, calming breath. "Roger, Eilie." *Focus on what you* can *do, Cordell. Leave the rest in God's hands.* "Thank you."

The doctor clipped a white sensor onto Llyrica's fingertip. 87.1 displayed in glowing red digits. "I have set the sensor to flash at 50 percent. Once her oxygen saturation decreases to 40 percent, survival is unlikely. However, that threshold could be higher—anywhere from 40 to 50 percent."

Edgar turned toward Ted. The old man had managed to strap himself into the seat, but he was craning his scrawny neck in order to gaze at the first woman he'd seen since he was ten years old.

Edgar pointed at the oxygen sensor on Llyrica's finger. "Ted, you see that readout?"

Ted nodded, but the angle at which he held his head turned the nod into an awkward circular motion. It might have been comical under other circumstances. "Yeppers."

"I want you to tell me when that number changes," Edgar said. "Tell me by fives, okay? Eighty-five, eighty, seventy-five, and so on. You got it?"

The old man grinned and nodded awkwardly. "Yeppers! I can do that!"

"Okay. Thanks." Edgar turned back to the doctor and Llyrica. *She looks so pale! Are her lips blue? They look kinda blue. This is bad. Hold on, baby! Please, hold on!*

The doctor double-checked Llyrica's restraints. Apparently satisfied, the android stood. It retrieved the pressure case that Edgar had carried from the prison. The doctor opened the case. It held up a small plastic bottle. "Administer four drops in each eye every three to four hours." The doctor replaced the bottle and held up a memory stick. "This contains the replicator formula for additional eyedrops, should she require it. Continue this regimen until the corneas and pupils are clear. She should be waking from sedation in about an hour. Keep her from scratching or rubbing her eyes. Restrain her, if you have to. She may recover her sight eventually, assuming she survives."

She's gonna make it, Doc! She has to!

The doctor held up a small jar. "Apply this cream daily to the burned areas on her face and hands until the pigmentation returns to normal. However, do not get the cream in her eyes. That is one more reason to keep her from rubbing her eyes. A few more days should suffice." The doctor replaced the jar and closed the case.

The doctor turned toward Ted. "Mr. Knight, avoid strenuous activity. Rest as much as you can. Sadly, it will not prevent your death, but it may lengthen the time remaining."

The old man beamed. "You got it, Doc! You got any of my pills in there?"

The android shook its head. "Just calcilock. You are no longer responding to the other medication. There is nothing more I can do for you."

Ted slapped his knee and grinned all the wider. "You're letting me go. Ain't that the best medicine?"

"As you say." The doctor turned to Edgar and handed him the case. "I have done all I can here. I shall return to the colony now." It paused and cocked its head. "May your God watch over you."

As the android donned its spacesuit—the one Llyrica had worn on the trip back to the shuttle—Edgar stowed the case in a cargo compartment. "I thought you didn't believe in God, Doc," Edgar said.

The doctor hesitated before putting on its helmet. "I am not sure that I do believe, but I did witness a faith-based healing. I would be a poor scientist if I dismissed empirical evidence out of hand." It placed the helmet on its head and connected it to the neck of the suit.

"Engine is at nominal minus five minutes," said the *Eris*.

"Roger," Edgar said. "Thank you, Eilie." He tapped the doctor's helmet. "Hey, Doc!"

The android unsealed and removed the helmet. "Yes, Mr. Cordell?"

"Do me a favor, will you?" Edgar said.

The doctor tilted its head. "I am allowing you to escape, Mr. Cordell. What more do you require?"

"Eighty-five!" Ted cried.

Edgar grimaced, but tried to remain focused. *This is my last chance.* "Doc, when you get back, could you spare a pad for Charlie? Download the scriptures onto it. Maybe some literature. Please?"

The doctor tilted its head slightly the other direction.

He's smiling, thought Edgar.

"I will do as you ask," said the android. "I will miss you, Mr. Cordell."

Edgar extended a hand. "I'll miss you too. You're a good guy, Jiminy Stewart. Thank you . . . for everything." *Thank you for helping me save her.*

And I will save her!

The doctor shook Edgar's hand. "I count myself fortunate to have known you, Mr. Cordell. Safe journey. I regret that I will have no way of knowing if you are successful or not, unless, of course, you return. I sincerely hope that will not be the case." Then the android replaced the helmet over its head and locked the helmet to its suit collar. The doctor turned toward the airlock, opened the hatch, and stepped inside.

The android did not turn around, but continued to face toward the outer hatch as the inner hatch slid closed.

Good-bye, Doc.

Edgar gathered up Ted's spacesuit and his own and stowed them in the suit locker. He made a pass through the shuttle, scanning for loose items and checking latches. *Don't want stuff bouncing around during flight!* The aft cargo hold, which contained Carlos's and Doc Luschenko's bodies preserved in stasis, was closed, but not latched. Edgar secured the latch and continued his inspection. When he was sure everything was secured, Edgar stopped one last time to look at Llyrica. He placed her hands in her lap. Her head was turned slightly inside the headrest. Gently, Edgar turned her head so it was facing forward. Then he placed a headset on her head, covering her ears.

Is she having trouble breathing?

He positioned the headset microphone over Llyrica's lips. *Are they blue?* Maybe he'd be able to hear if her breathing became labored.

He glanced at the oxygen sensor on Llyrica's finger. 80.3. *Hang on, baby.*

He sat in the pilot's chair and strapped himself in.

"We gonna leave now?" asked Ted.

Edgar checked the countdown clock. *T minus eight minutes.* "Soon," Edgar replied.

Edgar resumed the preflight checklist.

Please, Heavenly Father! Let it be soon enough!

****

T minus 60 seconds.

"Eilie," Edgar said, "confirm all systems go for launch."

"Communications and navigation are offline," she replied.

"Exclude comm and nav, old girl," Edgar commanded. "Confirm all systems go for launch."

"Confirmed—all systems are go for launch."

T minus 34 seconds.

"Seventy, Edgar!" cried Ted. "Seventy!"

"Roger, Ted." *Hold on, Llyrica!* Edgar checked the thrust-vector slider on the throttle lever. It was still all the way back, still at full vertical—all the thrust would be vectored downward. "All hands, prep for launch." *All hands? Just Ted and Llyrica. He has no clue what I mean and she's unconscious.*

No, she's dying.

"Yeppers," replied Ted. His cheerful voice was loud and clear through the headset.

"Ted, turn your head forward," ordered Edgar. "Keep it straight ahead. I don't want you breaking your neck."

"Yeppers!"

"Say, 'Affirmative,'" Edgar growled. But, it was a good-natured growl. "Affirmative, for Yes."

"Affirmative!" replied the old man.

Edgar smiled. *Boy! It feels good to be back in the cockpit! Hera, I'm coming! I'm coming home! Even with everything riding on this, even with Llyrica's life riding on this, it feels so good to be back.*

Edgar settled his arms on the armrests and gripped the throttle in his left hand and the stick in his right. His grip on the throttle was firm. His touch on the stick was gentle. *Like caressing a woman,* as his father used to say. "All hands, we are go in five, four, three, two, one."

Edgar eased the throttle forward to about 60 percent.

The engine roared to life.

Edgar felt the *Eris* rise off the surface of Callisto.

I'm rusty, thought Edgar. *Eris'* center of gravity felt off, as if she were a bit aft-heavy. Edgar compensated. He alternated his focus between the horizon and the attitude indicator, crosschecking both, applied a little forward stick, and kept the shuttle steady, parallel to the surface.

Glancing at the radar altimeter, he saw that they were passing twenty meters above the surface. He began moving the thrust vector slider forward with his thumb, simultaneously easing the throttle forward toward 100 percent. He raised *Eris'* nose above the horizon. Edgar focused his attention on the attitude indicator, since he couldn't see the horizon any longer. Through the forward viewscreen, Jupiter filled the whole sky.

Edgar finessed the three primary flight controls—stick, throttle, and thrust-vector—till *Eris* was pointing straight up and accelerating toward the sky. The G-force pushed Edgar back into the seat, making him feel heavy.

Deliciously heavy.

"HOO-EEE!" shouted Ted, hurting Edgar's ears.

Edgar grimaced with the pain, but remained focused on flying the shuttle. He checked his rotation, attitude—the orientation of the shuttle to the moon—and velocity. He was a little off course—both azimuth and heading—and slower than planned. He attempted to compensate. He corrected his course, but his velocity and acceleration remained stubbornly below flight-plan. *Must be heavier than calculated, he thought.*

"Eilie," he said, "can you give me any more thrust? We're below curve."

"I'm at maximum, now," she replied.

"Can you give me a little more? Two percent maybe?"

"I'll try."

Edgar felt no appreciable difference, but the G-force readout crept up slightly. "Thanks, Eilie. That's better. We're approaching our acceleration curve."

"I could only get you 101.7 percent," she said.

"Close enough. We'll compensate once we're in orbit."

Over the intercom, Edgar heard a sound that nearly stopped his heart.

Labored, distressed breathing.

Time's Plague

"Ted, you okay?"

"Af-fir-ma-tive," wheezed the old man.

It's Ted, thought Edgar. *Not Llyrica. Ted.* "Hang in there, bu— friend."

"Af-fir-ma-tive."

Not Llyrica. Hang on, baby. Almost there.

Don't you die on me either, Ted.

****

"All hands," Edgar said, "prepare for end-burn. End-burn in . . . five, four, three, two, one."

Edgar pulled the throttle back to idle. His body strained forward, pushing against his restraints, as the shuttle's acceleration ceased. "Ted, check Llyrica's readout."

"Llyrica? Is that her name?" Ted asked. "Hey, ain't that the name of—"

"Yeah," said Edgar, cutting him off. "What's the number?"

"It's flashing," said the old man.

Edgar wanted to scream! "What's the number?"

"47.6," said Ted. "That's bad, ain't it?"

Edgar fought the urge to leave his seat. *Got to stabilize the orbit. Stay at your post, mister!* "How about *now*?" he asked through clenched teeth. "What does it read *now*?"

"47.6, I said. It's the same."

Not going down. Not going down. "How about now?"

"I told you, it's forty-seven point . . . Hey, how 'bout that?"

"What? What?"

"Forty-seven point *eight*. It's going up! That's good, ain't it?"

Edgar trembled with a relief so powerful, he thought he might pass out. "Yeah." *Breathe. Just breathe.*

And fly the ship.

She's alive! She's alive*!*

"52.3 . . . No, 60.1 . . . 70."

"Thank you, Father," Edgar whispered. "Thank you."

"You praying? Yeah, you're praying, ain't ya? She's gonna be okay, right? It's 75 now."

"Yes," said Edgar. "She's going to live."

Assuming we can rendezvous with Hera. *Assuming she's still up here and we can find her. Otherwise, all this was for nothing.*

Otherwise, we're all dead.

SS Hera

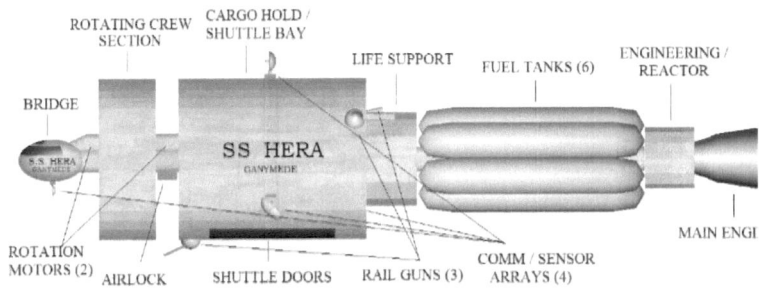

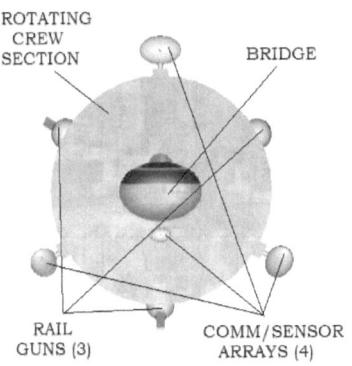

Chapter 32

Poor Turlygod! poor Tom!
That's something yet: Edgar I nothing am
King Lear, Act II, Scene III

"Eilie, do you have a tally on *Hera*?" Edgar had dimmed all interior and exterior lights as soon as he achieved a stable orbit. He stared intently out the forward viewports, scanning for the *Hera*. Above them, Jupiter filled the sky.

"Negative," replied the shuttle.

What did I get wrong? Edgar wondered. *My numbers were close. I was within a metric ton on the shuttle mass. The thrust-to-burn was close too. But . . . ten minutes and still no sign of her.*

"What's a tally?" asked Ted. He too was staring out, looking for the ship.

"Tally—short for Tally-ho," replied Edgar. "It means, I see it."

The old man chuckled. "Why don't you just say, 'Do you see it?'"

"It's spacer-talk." Edgar was worried. Very worried. Either *Hera* wasn't where she was supposed to be, or Edgar's calculations were off. *Mortally* off. "Eilie, what about her squawk? Your IFF is shot, but you should be able to pick up *Hera's* on your EM sensors."

"What's I-F-F?" asked Ted. "What's E-M?"

"Not now, Ted." Edgar's growling tone probably sounded a bit sharper than he intended.

"The *Hera* was not squawking IFF when we departed," said the *Eris*. "I was curious at the time, but she didn't offer an explanation, and I didn't ask."

Time's Plague

Maybe Hera *knew she wasn't supposed to be here, at Callisto. She had to know. But* Hera *and* Eris *never did get along all that well.*

Why are you here, Llyrica?

"What about EM and optical sensors?" Edgar asked. "Anything at all?"

"Negative."

"Radar? Can you paint her?"

"Captain Sanchez ordered me to run silent," said the Eris. "Passive sensors only. No unnecessary emissions."

All this time. No radar. Edgar took a deep, calming breath. *It's not her fault. She's just following her orders.* "Eilie, I'm captain now. Please go active on the radar."

"Acknowledged," said the shuttle. "Change in command accepted. Radar active." She paused. "Contact, three-four-seven, mark one-zero, thirty-four point nine kilometers."

A shudder of relief ran through Edgar's body. *That's got to be her.* "Eilie, please put radar on my nav screen."

The completed and superfluous flight-plan on the navigation console was replaced with a radar grid. And slightly left and high from the center crosshairs glowed a single pip of green light—a *beautiful* pip of green light, with "34.9 KM" below it. "Eilie, please label contact as '*Hera.*'"

The pip on the display transformed into a green triangle, and the word *Hera* appeared below it.

"Thank you, Eilie." Edgar turned the shuttle and raised her nose until the triangle was nearly centered in the radar grid. He gently eased the throttle forward a little.

He grinned. *Not bad, Cordell. You put her within thirty-five kilometers. Not bad at all.*

Dad would be proud. Edgar experienced a brief pang of grief. *Are Mom and Dad still alive? Still on Mars? I hope they live long enough to hear that I didn't kill Ol' Benny. I hope I live long enough . . .*

The range to the target—to *Hera*—began to decrease. 34.6 KM. 34.5. They were closing at a comfortable rate. Not too fast. Edgar pulled the throttle back to idle.

Edgar sighed. "We're going to be okay." He reached over and patted Ted's forearm. "Sorry, Ted."

C. David Belt

The old man was grinning his gap-toothed smile from ear-to-ear. "We going home?"

Edgar nodded. "Affirmative. Home to the *Hera*, at least. That's my ship. Or she used to be."

"Affirmative! We're free men! Free men!"

Edgar nodded. "Well, we're going to be." He sighed. "Ted, I'm sorry I was short with you. It's just that, when I'm flying, I need to focus. IFF stands for Identify Friend or Foe. It's a signal a ship broadcasts to say, 'This is who I am.' EM stands for Electro-Magnetic. The shuttle is scanning on her sensors for electromagnetic radiation to see what's out there. It's like seeing something that's invisible."

The old man beamed. "IFF and EM. Affirmative!"

"Eilie," said Edgar, "I'm going to unstrap. Advise me if the rate of closure or our bearing to *Hera* changes by more than five percent. Let me know when we're within ten kilometers."

"Wilco, Eddie."

"How come you always do that?" asked Ted. "Call the ship by name—you know—when you talk to her?"

Edgar pressed the quick-release on his harness. "The shuttle needs to know I'm talking to *her*." He slipped out of the straps and let himself float out of the seat. "If it were just me in here, by myself, I wouldn't have to do that. But when you're flying, you need to be clear and precise with all communications so there are no mistakes."

Edgar gripped the seat and turned himself around and over. He got his first glimpse of Llyrica since before lift-off.

The sight of her was like oxygen to a drowning man.

She was no longer pale. Any hint of blue tinge, imagined or otherwise, was gone from her lips.

The oxygen sensor on her fingertip read 97.9.

She's going to live. Edgar almost wept for joy. *I saved her. Thank you, Heavenly Father. Thank you for helping me save her.*

Llyrica rolled her head to the side and moaned.

She's waking up.

Edgar realized with a jolt that he was *terrified* at the prospect of speaking to his ex-wife. *What am I going to say to her?*

She moaned again, louder than before. Her hands floated in front of her, her fingers twitching slightly.

Should've restrained her hands before lift-off, Edgar thought. *Can't have her scratching at her eyes while I'm trying to dock with Hera.*

Pushing off from the back of the pilot's seat, Edgar floated past Llyrica and down to a small storage compartment. Moments later, he returned with two padded straps.

As Edgar began to secure Llyrica's right wrist to the armrest, Ted asked, "What ya doing there? Oh, I get it! You're keeping her from rubbing her eyes. Just like Doc said!"

"Exactly," replied Edgar as he strapped down Llyrica's left wrist.

Llyrica mumbled something that Edgar couldn't catch.

I'm not ready for this. All my energy has been focused on escape, on just getting her out of danger. But now . . . what do I say to her?

Llyrica rolled her head from side to side. She moaned louder. Her lips moved as if she were trying to speak.

Not yet. I'm not ready to confront her. Not yet.

A plan, or at least the beginnings of one, sprouted in Edgar's mind.

"Ted," he said, "I need you to do something for me."

"Sure!" said the old man. "I mean, affirmative!"

"I need you to call me Tom . . . Tom Bedlam. Can you do that? Don't call me by my real name." He looked over at Ted.

The old man looked puzzled. "Why?"

"Because I don't want her to know . . ."

Ted nodded and winked conspiratorially. "I got it. You don't want her to know who you are."

Edgar nodded. "Exactly."

"Affirmative"—Ted grinned—"Tom."

"Ten kilometers and closing, Eddie," said the *Eris*.

"Roger that, Eilie." Edgar pulled himself into his seat and strapped in. "Listen, old girl. I need you to do the same for me. Refer to me only as Captain or Tom for now. Will you do that, please?"

"Certainly, Tom," replied the shuttle. "It'll be like one of our old games. Nine kilometers and closing."

C. David Belt

Edgar looked out the viewport and spied a black dot silhouetted against Jupiter.

Edgar grinned. "Tally on the *Hera*, twelve o'clock."

Behind him, Llyrica moaned. "Ed."

Edgar suddenly felt as if he couldn't breathe. *Is she calling my name?*

"Ed," Llyrica mumbled again. "Edmund."

Edgar's expression hardened into a gargoyle's scowl. *Of course not. You really are an idiot, Cordell. She left you for Edmund. She sent you to Hell. And she conspired to murder Ol' Benny. Did you actually think, even for one deluded second, that she might come back to you?*

And if she did? So what? She's an accomplice to murder! Fool.

Just fly the ship.

Edgar fired the retro-thrusters briefly, slowing their rate of closure with the *Hera*.

The black dot was growing larger and taking on more definition. The round silhouette of the cargo bay dominated, but Edgar could also discern the exhaust nozzle of the main engine.

Hera wasn't displaying any lights. No running lights. No beacon. Nothing.

She's running silent. No wonder Eilie couldn't pick up anything on the EM sensors. Especially with Jupiter radiating all that static in the background.

Edgar checked to make sure his own running lights and beacon were on. They were, of course, because he'd turned them on during his preflight checklist.

"She a big ship?" asked Ted.

"Big enough," replied Edgar. "She's classified as a medium interplanetary transport, built for long-hauls."

"So where're we going, once we get aboard? What's the plan"—the old man winked—"Tom?"

"I don't know where we're going," said Edgar. "I don't know how much fuel *Hera* has. I don't know how much food and water she's got aboard. I don't know what shape she's in. I won't know anything until I can get aboard and check things out."

"Yeppers!" said Ted. "You check things out, and then we'll go! Go away from here!"

Llyrica moaned. "Edmund. Please."

Time's Plague

Edgar's face twisted in disgust. *Edmund's not here, sweetie. Just good, old Edgar. Good, old, naïve, stupid, trusting Edgar.*

The man you betrayed.

The man who just saved your life.

Edgar closed the remaining distance, bringing the shuttle underneath *Hera's* cargo hold, underneath the shuttle bay. The huge freighter simply hung in orbit, lightless, save for the light refracting off Jupiter. The shuttle bay doors remained closed. *Hera* gave no indication she was even aware of the presence of the *Eris* below her.

"She's big, all right!" Ted whistled. "Long too! How come we're just sitting here? Ain't we goin' inside?"

"We can't go inside until the shuttle bay doors open," said Edgar. "We can't signal *Hera* to open her doors, because our transceiver is slagged. I'm just waiting for her to recognize us and open the doors on her own."

Ted looked up through the viewports above the cockpit and shook his head. "The doors ain't opening."

"Not yet," agreed Edgar.

"What if she don't open them?"

"Then I go EVA and open them manually."

"You can do that?"

Edgar nodded and pointed up and forward. "There's an airlock hatch between the cargo hold and the rotating section. You can't see it from here, but it's there on the central shaft. I can go in that way."

"Why don't ya just go open it now?"

"I hope it doesn't come to that. *Hera's* going to treat us as invaders soon enough, as soon as she doesn't recognize any of us as registered crewmembers. I don't want to be fighting her the whole way. Her programming won't allow her to depressurize a compartment occupied by living humans or cut off life support, but she can slow us down in other ways. I want to delay that as long as I can. So, I'm hoping she'll recognize *Eris* and just let us in."

"How long we gonna wait?" asked Ted.

"Edmund, please," Llyrica said. Her speech was a little clearer, a bit less slurred, but she still seemed to be drifting in and out of consciousness.

Edgar gritted his teeth. *If I never hear her say that name again, that'd be just fine with me.* "We've got to give *Hera* time to try to contact us. She's probably already tried a few times, and we aren't saying anything back. We've got to wait for her to figure out that we can't respond."

"Okay," said the old man. He sighed and continued to gaze up at the seemingly lifeless ship above them.

Edgar waited with far less patience than he showed as the minutes ticked by with no response. Eventually, he nodded grimly to himself. "I guess I'm going to have to do this the hard—"

Edgar's face was suddenly illuminated by the lights rimming *Hera's* shuttle bay. The huge doors opened, revealing the bay itself. The other shuttle, the *Hebe*, hung on the starboard side of the bay, secured by her docking clamps. On the port side, the clamps for the *Eris* were open and inviting, as if to welcome the shuttle home.

"Now that's a beautiful sight," said Edgar. "Eilie, all hands, prepare for docking."

Edgar used the maneuvering thrusters to ease the *Eris* toward her berth. The aft starboard thruster was weak, as expected, but Edgar was able to compensate. In less than a minute, the *Eris* made contact with the docking clamps.

Edgar heard twin *thunks* as the clamps secured the shuttle in place. Sweet relief washed over Edgar like a baptism.

We made it.

"Stay strapped in, Ted," Edgar said, just as the old man fiddled with his quick-release. "We're going to stay in our seats until the shuttle bay doors close and the cargo bay is pressurized."

"Yeppers," said Ted, but he kept his boney hand on the quick-release. "Or do I still need to say, Affirmative?" The old man looked worried, like an abused child who feared punishment for a minor infraction.

Edgar laughed. *It feels good to laugh again!* "Technically, until we unstrap, we're still in flight mode, but it's no big deal. You're a free man. You can say whatever you like."

Ted nodded manically, grinning like the proverbial village idiot. "Yeppers! A free man!"

The shuttle bay doors closed. A moment later, even through the shuttle's hull, Edgar could hear the hiss of atmosphere as life-giving air flooded the bay. The sound continued for a minute, then faded away.

"Pressure equalization complete," said the *Eris*.

"Thank you, Eilie," Edgar said. "You did great, old girl. You really did."

"Thank you, Tom," the shuttle replied. Her tone sounded proud and pleased. "So did you. When will you fix me?"

Edgar hit his quick-release and floated out of the seat. "As soon as I can. I promise. I have to secure *Hera* first. And we have to break orbit, so it might be a while. Hang in there, Eilie."

Edgar nodded at Ted, who opened his quick-release and floated out of his seat, giggling like a little boy.

"Okay, Tom," the *Eris* replied, her voice less enthusiastic. "Please don't forget me."

Edgar smiled. He pulled himself toward Llyrica. "How could I forget my Eilie? I'll be back just as soon as I can."

Edgar removed the straps from Llyrica's wrists and opened her quick-release. He pulled her out of the straps, and she floated free.

"Who?" she mumbled. "Who's . . . ?"

"That's Tom Bedlam!" Ted's tone was annoyingly cheerful.

"Ted, get the bag Doc left for us," Edgar said, "the one with the medicine." He pointed to the bag's location. "It's in that storage bin."

"You got it!"

The guy's probably having the time of his life. Edgar pulled Llyrica to himself and held her close against his body. He was acutely aware of how her body felt pressed against his. *So soft. And she smells so good. Just like I remember. Well, except for the medicine smell.* "Listen, Ted. This isn't what it looks like. The fact is, there just isn't a good way to carry someone who's basically unconscious in zero-G."

"Can I carry her?" asked the old man. "I wanna carry her. Let me—"

"No," Edgar snapped. "You can't touch her. She's not yours."

"She ain't yours, neither. Not no more."

"Nope." *No, she's not.* "But she's my responsibility. I'll take care of her. Got it?"

C. David Belt

The old man shook his head. "Ain't fair."

"You want life to be fair? It's not. *Otherwise, I'd never've been sent to Hades.*" And she'd still be mine. "She's a person, just like you and me—not something to own or use." It felt good to hold her, but it was torture as well.

"Come on," said Ted. "I just wanna—"

"Stop it, Ted! I'll take care of her, and that's the end of it. Got it?"

Ted didn't answer.

Edgar twisted so he was looking over Llyrica's shoulder at Ted. "Got it?" he repeated. Llyrica's golden hair drifted up, partially obscuring Edgar's view of the old man.

Ted's expression darkened, and he bowed his head. "Got it," he muttered.

"You're free," said Edgar. "Be happy with that."

Ted lifted his face and grinned. "Yeppers! A free man! Yeppers! I'll get the bag."

Holding Llyrica tightly, Edgar pushed the two of them away from the cockpit. They floated toward the aft of the shuttle. Edgar halted at the cargo compartment, where the bodies of Carlos and Doc Luschenko were stowed. The stasis indicator still showed green. *I'll give you guys a proper funeral as soon as I can.* "Eilie, can you open the airlock?" He had to shout so she could hear him.

"Yes," the shuttle replied.

"Thank you, Eilie. See you soon."

"I'll be waiting right here."

Both airlock doors slid open together.

And outside those doors was the *Hera*.

Outside those doors was home.

Chapter 33

Child Rowland to the dark tower came,
His word was still, —Fie, foh, and fum,
I smell the blood of a British man.
King Lear, Act III, Scene IV

"Who are you? Identify yourself." *Hera's* voice sounded upset, worried. "Where are Captain Sanchez and Dr. Luschenko?" Her voice filled the shuttle bay, as if coming from all directions at once. "Is Mrs. Reagan injured? Why won't *Eris* answer me?"

As agitated as she sounded, however, *Hera's* voice was balm to Edgar's soul.

Edgar sailed through the cargo bay toward the hatch on the central shaft, Llyrica held tight against his body. Under more normal circumstances, he would've pulled himself along using the handholds embedded on the floor and walls or the ladders leading to the center of the round cargo bay, but he needed to move quickly. It was imperative that he get to the engine room before *Hera* could finish her intruder protocols.

Llyrica kept drifting in and out of semiconsciousness. "No," she moaned.

Edgar put out a hand as he and Llyrica approached a hatch, preventing them from slamming into it. He looked back to make sure Ted was following. Using the handholds, Ted was pulling himself along. Edgar hooked a foot under a handhold near the center shaft. He tried the handle of the hatch, but as he expected, it wouldn't budge.

The lock indicator showed red, of course, because Hera had already locked it.

Let's see if the lock code still works, he thought as his fingers tapped a series of digits into the lock-pad beside the hatch.

Nothing happened. The indicator still glowed red.

"Who are you?" repeated the ship.

"Who are you?" Llyrica echoed.

Edgar tried the manual override code.

Still no luck.

Blast. Edmund must've changed that one too.

Edgar keyed in the old master code, the one his Dad had programmed decades ago—the one *Hera* shouldn't be able to ignore—the one Edgar hoped Edmund didn't know about.

Please, Heavenly Father, let this one work. If I have to hack my way through each hatch . . .

The indicator switched from red to green.

Edgar grinned and opened the hatch.

"Who gave you that code?" *Hera* demanded. "You are not authorized to use that code. Identify yourself."

Edgar maneuvered himself and Llyrica through the hatch. "Come on, Ted. Follow me."

"Coming," said the old man.

"Close that hatch once you get through."

"Yeppers, Tom."

"You can't," Llyrica said. "No. Don't."

What's she talking about? Is she talking to me?

"Stop where you are," said the ship.

Edgar ignored the *Hera* and pushed off down the central shaft toward Life support, and beyond that, the fuel tanks, and finally, the engine room. Awkwardly, he used his free hand to keep Llyrica and himself from striking the wall as they sailed through the long corridor.

"Stop where you are," repeated the ship, "or I will depressurize this section."

"Can she do that?" asked Ted, his voice almost squeaking with panic.

"No she can't," said Edgar. "She can't do that unless the captain orders it."

"She lied to us?" Ted sounded terrified.

"Liar," moaned Llyrica.

"We're not her crew or passengers," Edgar explained quickly. "The ship thinks we're pirates. And she'll do anything she can to prevent a hijacking, even lie to us."

"Where is Captain Sanchez?" asked the *Hera*. "Where is Dr. Luschenko?"

"Will she call somebody to come and get us? You know, send us back?"

"She could," Edgar said, "but she won't. She's running silent. Must've been ordered to. Otherwise, she'd have called for help already."

"I have already transmitted a distress call," said the *Hera*.

"Nice try," Edgar said, "but I'm not buying it."

The ship did not reply.

After passing through Life support and the long stretch of the shaft surrounded by the fuel tanks, Edgar and Llyrica reached the engine-room hatch. As he keyed in the master code, he said, "*Hera*, listen up. The *Eris* crash landed on Callisto." He opened the hatch. "Carlos Sanchez and Vladimir Luschenko were killed in the crash." Edgar maneuvered himself and his precious burden through the hatch and into the engine room. "Mrs. Reagan was injured in the crash. She's blind, but otherwise she's okay."

"Can't . . . see," Llyrica mumbled.

At first, the engine room was dark, but motion and heat sensors activated the lights. The control console bloomed to life. Edgar glanced at it briefly and noted the engine readings. Everything looked healthy, at least on first glance, but he could see that *Hera* had already initiated an engine shutdown.

Edgar pulled Llyrica and himself toward one of the two seats in front of the engine control console. As he pushed Llyrica into a seat and away from himself, he felt a pang of loss the instant she was no longer pressed against his body. "The *Eris* suffered extensive damage before and during the crash," he explained. He strapped Llyrica into the seat, tucking her hands loosely into the straps.

Llyrica protested weakly. "Don't," she mumbled.

Edgar finished strapping Llyrica into the seat. He continued his explanation as he whirled around and typed the master code into the control console. " *Eris'* transceivers were slagged—that's why we couldn't talk to you—and she blew a number of neuro-gel packs. That's what killed her crew and blinded Mrs. Reagan."

"No," Llyrica said.

The console flashed, "MASTER MANUAL OVERRIDE ACCEPTED."

Edgar entered the command to halt and reverse the shutdown sequence.

"SHUTDOWN SEQUENCE ABORTED," flashed on the console. All engine readouts returned to normal.

There, Edgar thought. *That's the worst of it. As long as the engine stays online, I can handle anything else she throws at me.*

Edgar looked over in Ted's direction. The old man floated near the unoccupied chair. Edgar pointed at the chair and said, "Strap in."

Ted grinned and pulled himself into the chair. He let go of the medical bag that he'd brought from the *Eris* and let it float nearby.

Edgar placed his hands over Llyrica's ears. She made a weak attempt to shake her head, but Edgar held it motionless.

Keeping his voice at a low volume which he hoped Llyrica could not hear, Edgar said, "*Hera*, listen. I'm only going to say this once. You're not going to believe me now, but I want you to remember that I said it. I'm Edgar Cordell. I know I don't look or sound like myself. My face and voice have been damaged. But look at my eyes and do a retinal scan." He stared at one of four cameras that comprised *Hera's* eyes in the room.

He forced himself to not blink.

"Retinal scan confirmed," the ship acknowledged. "However, that does not establish your identity. Voice and facial recognition failed."

"I know, sweet *Hera*," Edgar said. "I'll try to prove my identity to you in other ways later. But for now, you'll have—"

"You are not Edgar Cordell," said the ship. "Who are you?"

"For now," Edgar said, "you can call me Tom."

"You are an intruder, and I will do my utmost to resist you."

Edgar nodded. "Roger that. Just doing your job. That's my girl."

"I am not your girl," the ship protested.

Llyrica pulled both hands free of the straps and clawed weakly at Edgar's hands.

He released his hold on her head.

"Can't see!" she cried, and her hands went to her eyes. "I can't see!"

Edgar gripped her hands and pulled them away from her face. He held onto those hands firmly. He hooked one foot into a handhold and braced the other against the chair for leverage and to keep himself steady.

"Your eyes were burned in the crash," he said as gently as his scarred vocal cords would allow. "You have to keep the bandage on."

"Blind!" She was wide-awake now. "I'm blind!" She tried to wrench her hands free of Edgar's grip.

Edgar held on. "Listen to me!" he said. "Hold still, will you? Just listen."

She stopped trying to free herself, and sat still, panting heavily and trembling. Perspiration beaded on her skin.

"That's better," said Edgar. "Now, I'll let go of your hands if you promise to *leave your eyes alone*. Do you promise?"

"Y-yes."

"Good girl," Edgar said.

"Let me go." Her voice quivered.

She's gotta be scared out of her mind. "Do you promise?"

"You gotta promise, lady," said Ted. His expression alternated between confused fear and a halfhearted grin, but he sounded as if he were trying to soothe her, to allay her fear.

Llyrica recoiled and jerked her head in Ted's direction. "Who's there?"

"It's just me," the old man replied. "I-I-I'm Theodore Knight, lady, but you can just call me Ted. Back in the prison, most everyone called me Toady, but my *friends* call me Ted. You're real pretty. And I ain't seen a woman in more'n thirty years."

Llyrica screamed. It started as a low ululating wail that rose in pitch and volume—a crescendo of terror. She thrashed violently.

Edgar lost his grip on one of her hands. He grabbed for it and missed. He tried again and succeeded in catching her wrist.

Llyrica screamed once more.

Edgar's ears hurt, and he snarled with the pain.

"Stop it!" he growled. "You're scared. I know you're scared. I don't blame you for being scared. But you *have to stop*. Nobody's going to hurt you. You're safe."

"P-p-please," she whimpered. "Please don't h-hurt me."

"You're safe," Edgar repeated. "Nobody's going to hurt you."

"Let me go! Please, please, please let me go."

"Do you promise to keep your hands off your eyes?"

She nodded.

"Promise," he insisted.

"I promise. I promise. Just don't hurt me. Please don't hurt me."

"Okay." Edgar carefully released his grip. "There you go." Llyrica's hand and wrist were white where he'd gripped them. Edgar felt a spasm of guilt at the sight of the imprint his fingers had left on her pale flesh. "Old Tom's not going to hurt you. You're safe with old Tom."

"Mrs. Reagan," said *Hera*, "are you all right?"

Llyrica's head turned in random directions as if trying to locate the source of the voice. "Where am I?"

"You are aboard the SS *Hera*," replied the ship. "I have been hijacked by men who appear to be two escaped prisoners from the Hades Penal Colony."

Llyrica sobbed. She crossed her arms protectively over her chest. "Please don't hurt me." She pulled her knees up and curled into a fetal ball, or as close as the seat harness would allow.

"We ain't gonna hurt you," Ted said. "No, no, we ain't. I ain't gonna hurt you. And Tom, here, he don't wanna hurt you neither."

"Where's Carlos? And Vladimir? Where's Vladimir?" Llyrica asked. "Did you . . . kill them?"

The ship said, "Captain Sanchez and Dr. Luschenko are not aboard."

"If you're talking about the two men who came with you," Edgar said, "they're dead. I didn't kill them. They died in the crash. You crashed on Callisto."

Fresh sobs racked Llyrica's body.

Edgar longed to hold her, to comfort her, but he held back. *She's too scared right now. She's thinks we killed Carlos and Doc.*

And she thinks we're going to rape her.

Ted looked stricken. "Don't cry, pretty lady." He looked to Edgar. "What do we do? I don't want her to cry."

"Nothing," Edgar said. "We do nothing right now. Just let her cry." *Tears for Carlos and Doc, but no tears for Ol' Benny? Or for me?* "Right now, we concentrate on breaking orbit and making our escape."

"W-where?" Llyrica managed between hitching breaths. "Where are you t-taking me?"

"Don't know yet," Edgar said. *That's not entirely true, Cordell. It's not like you can just break orbit and go nowhere.* The truth was that he *did* have a plan, or at least the beginnings of one. "Away from this place. I'm just gonna go where I please. Merrily going anywhere and nowhere at all. Now just sit there and be quiet for a minute."

Edgar pulled himself over toward Ted. He lowered his voice and spoke softly. "Okay, Ted. Here's what I need you to do."

The old man continued to stare at Llyrica. The look of concern on Ted's face touched Edgar's heart. *After all he's been through, there's still something soft, something gentle about him.*

Edgar anchored himself by hooking a handhold with his foot. He tapped the old man on the shoulder. "Ted, I need you to pay attention for a minute."

Ted focused on Edgar. "Okay."

"What I need you to do isn't all that hard, but it's *important.*"

Edgar twisted around and pointed at a console. "Your job is to monitor the engine. *Hera's* been locked out of engine control. I'm going to run things from up on the bridge, but *Hera* might send me false engine readings." He looked up at a camera and spoke up. "Hear that, *Hera*? Don't try to send me false readings." He looked back at Ted and lowered his voice again. "I need you to monitor these indicators." He tapped several lights and numbers on the console. "They should all stay green. Let me know if anything goes yellow or red. Now here's the intercom." He pointed at the comm panel on the arm of Ted's chair. "This button goes to the bridge and this one goes all over the ship. You call me immediately if there's any trouble. Can you do that?"

C. David Belt

The old man gave a weak smile and nodded. "Yeppers. I-I mean, affirmative." Then he screwed up his face into an embarrassed grimace. "But I gotta take a piss."

Edgar laughed. He pointed at the toilet on the starboard wall.

"There's the *head* over there. You know head means bathroom, right?"

Ted nodded.

"It's a zero-G head," Edgar continued. "You know how to use a zero-G toilet?"

Ted nodded again. "Yeah. I think I remember."

"Okay. The instructions are printed on the back of the door anyway. But if you make a mess, you clean it up. Okay?"

Ted grinned. "Yeah. Okay."

Edgar pushed away from the console and floated over and past the old man. Reaching the opposite wall, Edgar opened a storage compartment and checked inside. Satisfied with the contents, he said, "There're some water and proticarb rations in here. Calcilock too. I'll see about getting us some real chow later. But this stuff should tide you over for a while."

Ted was working his way over to the head. "Where you going?"

"I told you. I'm going to the bridge. It's at the other end of the ship."

The old man grinned. "Okay." He looked hopefully in Llyrica's direction.

"And I'm taking her with me," Edgar said.

Ted's hopeful expression darkened into a pouting frown. Then he sighed. "Okay. Be nice to her."

Be nice to her? Edgar thought. He didn't respond.

Ted said, "I really gotta pee."

"Go. But return to your post right away."

Ted grinned and gave a little salute. "Aye-aye, Cap'n Bedlam!" Then he opened the head door and disappeared inside.

Be nice to her? Edgar thought to himself as he pushed off the wall and floated toward Llyrica. *It's not as if I'm going to hit her or anything like that, but I need answers.*

I need answers, and I'm going to get them.

Llyrica recoiled when Edgar touched her arm. "Ted?"

"It's just old Tom," Edgar said. "Just mad Tom Bedlam."

"Where's the other one? Where's Ted?"

"You heard him," Edgar said. "He's off watering the reclaimers." Edgar pushed the quick-release on Llyrica's safety harness.

"What are you doing?" she asked with alarm.

"Unstrapping you," he replied. "We're leaving."

"Where are you taking me? Please don't hurt me. Please!"

"I won't hurt you. We're just going forward to the bridge, so I can fly us out of here. I can't fly the ship from back here."

She clutched the restraint straps to her chest as if they were protective armor. "Don't make me go," she pleaded.

Edgar laughed.

It wasn't a reassuring sound.

Llyrica cringed.

"Look," Edgar said, "I'm not leaving you here with Ted. I like the old guy, but I don't trust him with you."

Llyrica shook her head. "I don't . . ."

"You don't what? Don't trust me?" He laughed again. He sounded like a lunatic, even to his own ears. *Good. Let her think I'm crazy.* "I'm not going to touch you. Not like that. As far as I'm concerned, lady, your body is sacred, a temple. Or a sepulcher filled with dead men's bones. So you're safe with me. Safe as houses. Now, Ted? He hasn't seen a woman since he was ten years old. And he's never seen one *naked*. He's *curious*."

He let that last word sink in.

The head door opened and Ted emerged. He looked embarrassed. "I guess I forgot how to use one of them things. It took me forever."

"Did you make a mess?" asked Edgar

"Almost. But, nope."

Ted took his seat again and strapped in while checking out the console. "Still green!" He beamed at Edgar. Then he looked over at Llyrica. "Please, can't she stay with me?"

Llyrica tore herself out of her restraints.

She grasped blindly in Edgar's general direction. She caught hold of his arm and clung to it like a lifeline of flesh and bone.

Edgar didn't even try to hide his satisfied grin.

Not that Llyrica could've seen it.

Edgar gently pried Llyrica's grip loose. "I'm going to turn around." He turned until he was facing away from her. "Put your arms around my chest and hold on tight."

Llyrica did as she was told. She shivered as she pressed her body against Edgar's back.

Edgar had to suppress a tremor of his own.

"Ted, toss me the bag, will you?"

The old man snatched the floating bag and threw it in Edgar's direction.

Edgar caught it and pushed his arm through one of the handle straps. "I'll let you know when we're settled on the bridge. Okay?"

"Affirmative," Ted replied. "Bye, lady! See you soon!"

Llyrica whimpered like a lost little girl.

Edgar began to pull the two of them across the floor toward the hatch. "*Hera*, we're going to the bridge. I know you can lock all the hatches, but I can also unlock them. So all you'll do is slow us down. I want to get Mrs. Reagan settled and safe as soon as possible. What say we call a truce? What say you don't lock every hatch along the way?"

The ship didn't reply.

And when Edgar and Llyrica reached the engine-room hatch, he found it locked.

So much for a truce, Edgar thought.

****

When Edgar and Llyrica reached the rotating section hub, Edgar heard a strange noise just on the edge of perception. The sound was short in duration and repeated frequently with a seeming random rhythm and some slight variation in pitch.

It was completely out of place on a ship, but he felt as if he should recognize it. Edgar paused at the hub entrance as he tried to identify the maddeningly familiar sound.

Edgar could feel Llyrica tense as she clung to him, but she said nothing.

She knows *what it is.*

The sound was emanating from Hub Shaft 3 which led to the crew quarters.

Edgar entered the hub, gripped a handhold and pulled himself and Llyrica toward Shaft 3. "Put your arms around my neck," he said. "We're going to be feeling a little gravity."

Llyrica didn't budge, but rather kept her arms locked tightly around his chest.

"Do as I say," he said, "or you can wait here in the hub. Your choice."

"Please don't," she said, an edge of desperation in her voice. "Let's just go to the bridge. You said we were going to the bridge." She paused. "Or you could let me go. I'll just go to my cabin and—"

"Listen, lady," Edgar growled, "I may be crazy—prison can do that to a man—but I'm not stupid. Mad Tom is sharp. I'm going down there. Either put your arms around my neck, or stay here."

Llyrica drew a big, hitching breath and released her viselike grip on his chest. She put her arms around Edgar's neck.

Edgar could feel her quiet sobs. "Not too tight now. You choke me and you'll be all alone with Ted."

She eased her grip a little.

Just a little.

Edgar rotated until his feet were pointed at Shaft 3. He waited for Llyrica's body to align with his own, and then descended into the shaft. He put his feet on a ladder rung and climbed down, the simulated gravity increasing with every step.

By the time he put both his feet on the corridor floor, he was feeling about one-eighth-G, standard for both Ganymede and Callisto. He was also bearing all of Llyrica's weight, such as it was.

"You can let go now," he said.

She let go, but clung to his arm. "You don't have to do this," she said. "Please. Let's just go to the bridge."

The noise was louder now, and it was coming from the guest quarters.

And there was an odor as well—a nose-wrinkling, sour stench.

Edgar walked to the hatch for Guest Quarters 1.

The sound was louder and faster—almost frantic in nature.

"Please," Llyrica said. "Please, don't!"

Whatever the noise was, it was coming from the other side of the hatch.

Edgar opened the hatch. Something small and hairy flew at him and struck him in the chest. Edgar caught it in his arms.

In an instant, Edgar's face was bathed in slobbery wetness, and his nostrils were assaulted by foul-smelling, urgent, panting breaths.

"Please," Llyrica said. "Please don't kill my dog!"

Chapter 34

With cadent tears fret channels in her cheeks
King Lear, Act I, Scene IV

Dottie? Edgar laughed and nuzzled the frantic little dog to his chest. Dottie licked him and whined in a frenzy of uncontained excitement.

Well, that explains the smell, he thought.

The guest quarters reeked of urine and feces.

"Don't hurt her!" Llyrica pleaded.

"Lady," Edgar said, "I wouldn't dream of it." He held the squirming animal at arm's length. "Even though I haven't had *meat* in a very long time . . . I would never hurt a dog."

Edgar took a good look at Dottie. Covered by all that fur, it was hard to see, but she felt thin. However, judging from her wet tongue and nose, she'd been getting water. "You look like you're hungry. What's your name, doggie?"

"Oh, Dottie!" Llyrica cried. "I'm so sorry!"

"Okay," Edgar said, "Dottie it is. Where's her food?"

But Llyrica was already pushing past him, groping, feeling her way around the cabin. She stepped onto one of the many piles of dog excrement with her bare foot. "Ew! Ew! Ew!" she cried, but she continued moving until she reached the guest quarters' private head.

Edgar heard the clattering of metal on metal.

"Mrs. Reagan," the *Hera* said, "I turned on the shower frequently to supply your dog with water. I could do nothing about her food, however. I'm sorry."

Edgar heard the distinctive sound of dry dog food being poured into a metal bowl. Dottie must've heard it as well. She squirmed, yipping and whining.

"Dottie!" Llyrica called. "Dottie! Here, girl!"

Edgar set the wriggling mass of fur onto the deck, and the little beast bounded away toward the head.

Moments after Dottie disappeared inside the bathroom, Llyrica said, "Here you go, girl. Mommy's sorry. I didn't think I'd be gone so long."

"I'm afraid it couldn't have been a very efficient way to get water to her," the ship explained. "At best, she could only lick up the few drops that might leak at the bottom of the shower door. I couldn't be certain she was getting enough, because I cannot use eyes or ears inside crew and guest quarters, unless explicitly authorized by the occupant and the captain."

"Thank you, *Hera*," Llyrica replied. "You saved her." Llyrica sobbed. "My poor little Dottie!"

Crying again, thought Edgar. *Crying for the dog. Not for me. For the glecking dog.*

But the truth was, Edgar felt bad for the little creature too. *Dottie must've been so scared, being all alone up here, alone and starving.*

"Good job, *Hera*, with the water," Edgar said, facing the corridor to be certain the ship could hear him. "You did well."

The ship didn't acknowledge Edgar's compliment.

"Well," said Edgar, calling to Llyrica, "you better clean your dainty foot. Then I can carry you out, so you don't have to step in doggie doo again."

"Can't I just stay here?" she said. "You could lock me in."

"With all the poo?" Edgar laughed. His laugh sounded maniacal. "And folks call *me* crazy! No, if I did that, *Hera* would just let you out again. And I can't have you running around the ship free to do whatever mischief pops into your pretty little blonde head. No, I'm keeping you close, lady."

"I need to use the bathroom."

So you can lock yourself in there? Not a chance. "Dottie!" Edgar called. "Dottie! Here, girl!"

"Dottie! No!" cried Llyrica.

The dog came bounding out of the head and straight into Edgar's arms. Dottie licked Edgar's face with frantic enthusiasm.

He chuckled. *She knows me. I don't look the same. I don't sound the same. I can't imagine I smell the same. But she knows me.* "Be my guest," he called in Llyrica's direction. "Dottie and I'll wait right here, won't we, girl?"

Dottie yipped as if in agreement.

"That's right," Edgar said. "We'll wait right here. And when you're all done in there, we can take the dog with us."

Llyrica snarled in frustration and slammed the head door.

Not that I blame you for trying.

****

"You comfy there?" Edgar asked. "All snug as a bug in a rug?" He paused. "What does that mean? 'A bug in rug'?"

"What do you care?" muttered Llyrica. She was strapped into the copilot's seat, holding the dog to her chest.

Dottie fidgeted, apparently disoriented by the absence of gravity.

Edgar entered the master code into the copilot's console. Then he typed in a few commands. "I've locked the console in front of you and your flight controls, so don't try to push any buttons at random or fly the ship. You just sit there and hold your doggie. Sorry about the no shoes thing. Can't have you whacking Tom on his poor crazy head with a shoe, can we? And, by the way, I care *very deeply* about bugs in rugs, I'll have you know! Now, is that the kind of bug you find in a computer? And what's a rug? And why would a computer bug want to be in a rug? And would it really—"

"What do you care if I'm comfortable or not?" Llyrica snapped.

"Ah!" Edgar strapped himself into the pilot's seat. "So now you're getting *feisty!* Getting angry? What in the System do you have to be angry about?"

"You killed my friends!"

"Listen, Mrs. *Reagan!*" Edgar growled. "I never killed anyone!" He lowered his voice. "Not 'til I went to prison, at least. *Then* I had to defend myself against the murderers and rapists. *Then* I had to kill. But it was all in self-defense." Edgar shuddered at the image of what he'd done to Caliban and Lucifer's men when they'd attacked him and Yurii. He clenched his jaw to fight back tears at the memory of Yurii dying in his arms. "Or in the defense of my friends."

"You threatened my dog!"

"I did not!" Edgar did his best to sound indignant, but everything came out sounding like a rasping growl. *If I'm going to keep this "harmless madman" bit going, if I'm ever going to get answers, I can't let her take control of the conversation.* "I just wanted you to come with me. I need to keep an eye on you. Keep you safe and keep me safe. And I don't want Ted to do something he'll regret." *Or maybe he* wouldn't *regret.* "I didn't want to have to break down the door to the head, because that would only scare you . . . scare you more than you already are. Believe me or not, I'm not going to hurt you. And I'm not going to *rape* you."

Llyrica didn't reply.

Edgar entered the master code on the pilot's console and unlocked it. "*Hera*," he said, "I'm sure you've figured out by now that I can override you and lock you out. I would rather not do that. Please consider and evaluate what I told you before and cooperate with me. I was telling you the truth. Eventually, I'll be able to prove it to you. But if you could just see your way to working with me now, it'd make things a whole lot easier on both of us. What do you say?"

Hera was silent.

"Apparently nothing," Edgar muttered. He began the process of locking *Hera* out of flight control, communications, engine control, and navigation. "I'm leaving you in control of life support. I know you won't use it to kill us."

"Are you going to kill *me*?" the ship asked.

Edgar smiled. "No, of course not. Why would I do that, sweet *Hera*?"

"Because I will continue to resist you."

And resist him she most definitely did. No sooner did he unlock a system, than she found a way to hide it or restrict it again.

This is going to take a while.

"I understand that," he said. "You're just doing your job. And you're doing it well." *Too well.* "Someday we'll have a good laugh about this." *Like in the old days. We used to laugh. Not like me and Eilie, but you and I had our moments. I miss you, sweet* Hera. *I miss your friendship. You were always like a second mom to me.*

He continued his cyber-battle with the ship in silence.

Time's Plague

"Were you . . . Were you *raped*?" Llyrica's question startled him.

"What do you care?" he muttered. He glanced over at her.

Llyrica didn't respond. She held Dottie against her chest, petting the poor beast. Edgar wasn't sure if that repetitive action wasn't more beneficial to Llyrica than it was to Dottie.

"There's flight control," Edgar said with a growl of triumph as he succeeded in wresting that system from *Hera's* grasp. "And there's comm!" He gripped the throttle and thumbed the intercom button. "Hey, Ted! How're you doing, old-timer?"

"I'm doing just fine!" replied the old man. "Yeppers, I'm doing just fine! I thought you got lost. Or forgot about me now that you got your fine woman! Everything's still green here."

Edgar grinned. "Negative, Ted. I've just been having the time of my life up here, trying to get control of the ship. She's fighting me tooth and nail."

"The lady's fighting you?"

"No, I meant the ship. The *Hera's* fighting me. But I'm winning." *Slowly*.

"How's the pretty lady doing?"

"She's scared out of her mind," Edgar replied, then thought to add, "out of her mind, like *me*."

Dottie barked.

"What's that?" Ted asked.

"That's Mrs. Reagan's dog."

"A dog?" Ted's voice was filled with wonder. "You got a dog up there?"

"Affirmative. An annoying little ball of fur and slobber. Mrs. Reagan left it onboard before she went moon-side."

"I ain't never seen a dog. Can I come up there and see it?"

The dog in question yelped as Llyrica protectively tightened her arms around it.

Llyrica shook her head in a vehement refusal. She mouthed, "No!"

"That's a negative for now," Edgar said. "Right now, I need you right where you are. Stay at your post, mister."

"Aye-aye, Cap'n!" Ted replied. There was a pause. "Still ain't fair. You're having all the fun."

C. David Belt

Edgar didn't reply. *Fun? I'm stuck here with the one woman in the System I hate more than anyone else, the only woman I love, the woman who sent me to Hell.*

It's not fun.

It's torture.

Edgar resumed his battle with the ship.

When he'd finally regained engine control, he rubbed his eyes and sighed. *By the time we break orbit, I'm going to need a long nap. But what do I do with Llyrica? How do I sleep? I can't trust her alone and I can't trust her with Ted.*

"Tom," Llyrica asked quietly, "you never answered my question."

"What question?" Edgar knew very well what she meant, but he wanted her to ask again. He *needed* her to ask again.

"Were you raped?"

"Yeah. Once."

Llyrica was silent for a long moment. "I'm sorry."

"What do you care? Everybody gets raped in Hell. Ted's been raped thousands of times. He was *ten* when he arrived on Callisto. He's been someone's buddy—that's what it's called—ever since. Poor guy never had a chance. Before that, he was raped by his father. Repeatedly. So Teddy killed his dear old daddy. Shoved him out an airlock. And they sent Ted to Hades. Just a kid. Just a baby. But what do you care? What do *any* of you care? You just lock us away. No appeal. No hope. Out of sight, out of mind." He forced a chuckle. "Out of mind, like me."

"I'm sorry."

"You're sorry?" Edgar felt rage boiling in his gut. "You're sorry? Really? Mrs. Llyrica Gloster Reagan? Formerly, Mrs. Llyrica Gloster Cordell?"

Llyrica recoiled as if slapped.

"Oh, yeah, lady," Edgar growled. "I know who you are. I know all about you."

"H-how?"

"Because Edgar told me all about it."

"You know Edgar?"

"Yeah, I know Edgar. *Knew* Edgar."

"Is he . . . Is he all right?"

All right? You sent me to Hell! Edgar balled his hands into fists. *Get control, Cordell!* He took three deep, calming

314

breaths. "Do you really want to know? Well, let's *see*. Sorry, poor choice of words. Edgar was beaten and raped on the day he arrived. Then he got sick and nearly died from an infection due to the wounds he received during the rape. In fact, he did *die* and the doctor had to revive him. Twice. Then he got beaten nearly to death. And then he got his throat cut." Edgar paused. "Edgar Cordell is dead. The end."

A sob exploded from Llyrica. Her body was wracked with great hitching breaths.

"What's this?" Edgar asked. "Tears for the man you framed? The man you sent to Hell? The man who loved—"

"Shut up!" she screamed. "Just shut up!"

Dottie barked and squirmed in Llyrica's arms. The little dog was terrified.

"He's dead," Edgar said. "Mission accomplished, wouldn't you say?"

Llyrica sobbed. "Just shut up. P-please. Just . . . leave me alone."

Okay, Cordell, you made your point. Now you're just being a jerk.

But she deserves it. You know she does.

But there was a time you would've done anything *for her. You would have done anything to make her happy. Now, you've made her cry.*

And even if . . . even though *she deserves it, she's blind and helpless and terrified.*

And you . . . And I *just made her cry.*

Edgar went back to work, while Llyrica continued to sob softly.

And Edgar felt utterly miserable.

Chapter 35

Dost thou know me, fellow?
King Lear, Act I, Scene IV

"All hands, rotation stopped. Rig for burn in ten minutes." In spite of his raspy vocal cords, Edgar's voice carried an unmistakable note of triumph—he'd finally wrested control of all critical ship's systems from the recalcitrant *Hera*. "Ted, that means you need to be strapped into your seat with your head facing forward when the time comes." Edgar released the intercom button and waited for a response. After several long seconds of silence, he pressed the intercom switch on the throttle one more time. "Ted, do you copy?"

"Sorry." The old man's voice sounded hesitant, uncertain. "I had my mouth full of this here proticarb sausage stuff. It tastes real good! I ain't had meat, not even replicated stuff, in thirty-five years! But I don't get it. How do I copy? *What* do I copy?"

Edgar chuckled. "It means, 'Did you hear and understand me?'"

"Why don't you just say that?"

"Spacer talk," Edgar said. "You better get used to it—you're a spacer now."

"Affirmative, Cap'n Bedlam. I copy!" Ted paused. "Uh, what happens if I don't copy? What do I say? How do I say, no?"

"You say, 'Negative,' or 'Say again.'"

"Affirmative. I copy!"

"And, Ted, go easy on the rations. I haven't inventoried the ship's stores yet. So I don't know how much food we've got. And that stuff is concentrated. You'll get sick if you eat too much all at once."

"Oh, don't you worry 'bout that. I always been a light eater. Gotta make sure my man . . . I mean, you know, make sure *you* get enough first."

Suddenly, there was a lump in Edgar's throat. "Ted, you don't need to do that. We're friends, remember?"

"Yeppers. And friends share, don't they?"

"Yeah. Friends share."

"Friends share." Ted's tone was suddenly dark, sullen. "But not everything. I ain't never been with no woman."

Llyrica made a small noise, a whimper of fear.

"Stow that talk," Edgar growled. "Just get that out of your head. It's *not* happening."

Ted did not reply.

"Burn in seven," Edgar said. "You all strapped in?"

"Affirmative." Ted's voice was less sullen, but still subdued.

"Hey, Ted, you know what? We're getting out of here!"

"Af-firm-a-tive!" It sounded as if Ted had snapped out of his dark mood.

"So finish your rations or stow them."

"All gone!" Ted replied, and by the sound of it, his mouth was crammed full.

That brought a small grin to Edgar's disfigured face. He turned to look at Llyrica. "Don't worry about Ted. You're safe as long as you're with old mad Tom Bedlam."

"What about my dog?" Llyrica asked. It was the first time she'd spoken in nearly an hour. "Will Dottie be okay?"

Edgar turned his head and looked at Dottie. The dog was asleep in the engineer's seat and strapped in. Edgar had brought with them the usual dog treats spiked with tranquilizer from Llyrica's quarters. Sedation was standard practice when transporting a live animal, especially one unaccustomed to space travel. Llyrica had not objected. Edgar had used a general-purpose cargo web to secure the sleeping dog to the seat.

"She's out cold and secure," Edgar replied. "You can have her back soon. This first burn won't be too hard or too long. We're just going to break Callistoan orbit and insert into Jovian orbit. The next burn will be more . . . dramatic. But that won't be for a few days, not until we're in position."

317

"And after that?" Llyrica sounded remarkably calm. "After we enter orbit around Jupiter? Where are you taking me? Back to Ganymede?"

Edgar laughed softly. "So I can get rearrested? I don't think so. Just because old Tom's crazy doesn't mean he's stupid."

"Where then?"

"Where else? Earth!"

"Earth? Why Earth?"

She hates Earth. "Think about it," Edgar said. "On Earth, Ted and I can escape. We can land in any remote area and blend in. Anyplace else, we'd have to dock at a spaceport or enter through an airlock. We'd never make it past the port authority." Edgar paused. *Time to* really *play the crazy card.* He lowered his voice to a loud whisper. "And Earth's the only place where Tom can escape"—Edgar paused for dramatic effect—"*him.*"

"Him?"

"Yes, *him.* The *demon.*"

"Demon?"

Edgar tried to imitate the tone his grandfather used to employ when telling ghost stories to young Eddie. "Yes, the foul fiend. He pursues me, chases me across the void. Nowhere is safe. He haunts my dreams. Calls to me. 'Tom! Tom!' he says. 'It's *cold*, Tom! Cold in the void. There is no air, no light, no happiness, no love. It's cold here, Tom. And everyone you ever loved is here with me. Join us. Join us in the void.'"

"Stop it," Llyrica whimpered. "Please stop."

Just a little more. "Tom's cold. Always cold. That's why we have to go to Earth, you see. The demon can't find Tom there. Not under a blue sky and a warm Sun."

"Please stop. You're scaring me."

Enough. "As you wish."

Edgar thumbed the intercom button. "All hands, prepare for burn in two minutes and . . . fifteen seconds."

****

"All hands," Edgar announced, "we have achieved stable Jovian orbit."

"Can I come up front to . . . where . . . you are?" Even over the intercom, Ted's voice sounded eager.

You mean where Llyrica is, don't you, old-timer? "In a little bit," Edgar replied. "I'll have to come get you. The ship still has control of the hatch locks, so you're locked in. Give me about an hour to get some things settled up here. Then, I'll come let you out."

"Yeppers! I'll be waiting right here! No place else to go. A free man and *still* locked up. Figures, don't it?"

Edgar chuckled. "Sorry, Ted. I'll try to be as fast as I can. See you soon." Edgar released the intercom button.

"There," he said. "We should be stable enough for now. Our attitude—our orientation to the planet—will drift without the autopilot, but . . ." Lifting his head, he said, "Hey, *Hera!* I'd love to turn attitude control over to you, let you keep us flying straight. What do you say? Can I trust you with that much?"

Hera's only answer was silence.

Oh, well. Had to offer. Edgar used the maneuvering thrusters, making minute adjustments to stabilize the ship's attitude, then locked the flight controls. Satisfied with his work, Edgar sang softly to himself in his raspy voice, "A buzzard took a monkey for—"

"Affirmative," the ship said.

"Really?" Edgar was surprised at the ship's response, but he was also pleased. *Any cooperation at this point is a blessing.*

"I will keep myself steady," *Hera* said. "You may trust me."

Edgar entered a few commands on the console. "*Hera*, you have maneuvering thrusters!"

"Roger," she replied. "I have attitude control."

Edgar hit his quick-release and pushed up from the pilot's seat. He floated to the engineer's station.

"What're you doing?" Llyrica asked. She sounded terrified. "Where are you taking me?"

"Nowhere just yet. I have to restart rotation in the crew section. Then we're going back to your quarters."

Llyrica made a horrified gasp.

"I'm *not* going to *rape* you," Edgar growled. "I've told you that. *I've* been raped. I wouldn't wish that on *anyone*." *Not even you.* "Just need to give you your meds and take a few minutes to clean up the dog poo. After that burn, it's probably all smeared against the aft wall. With the crew compartment in zero-G, that stench will get into the rest of the ship soon." *And I've had enough of living in a sewer for one lifetime.*

C. David Belt

****

As it turned out, cleaning up Llyrica's quarters wasn't quite as nasty as Edgar had imagined. Dottie hadn't been nearly as prolific as Edgar had feared, perhaps because she'd been starving.

And there was also the possibility that the poor creature had eaten some of its own feces to stay alive.

Might explain why Dottie's breath was so bad. I mean, it was never great, but I don't remember it being that *foul.*

Llyrica sat on her bunk, stroking the sleeping dog, while Edgar worked. "I'm sorry . . . about the mess," she said.

Edgar laughed. "What are you apologizing for? Did you poo on the deck too? I thought it was just the dog."

Llyrica scowled at Edgar's joke, but said nothing. With her eyes covered, Edgar found it difficult to read the nuances of her facial expressions.

"So"—Edgar tried to make his growling voice sound casual—"why'd you bring the dog anyway? A space voyage is no place for little poochies."

Llyrica stiffened.

Too close to asking why she's here? "Why would you bring a poor little dog to the gates of Hell?"

Llyrica's lips stretched into a thin line, and she breathed hard and rapidly through her nose. She stroked the sedated canine with a manic ferocity.

"Careful there!" Edgar said. "You'll take her fur off at that rate."

Llyrica abruptly ceased her rough petting of the little dog, choosing to hold her clenched fist to her chest instead.

Edgar lowered his voice to a stage whisper. "What did Dottie ever do to you, huh?"

A bubbling sob burst from Llyrica's lips, and her shoulders sagged.

But she said nothing.

Guess I struck a nerve. Okay, Cordell, enough.
For now.

Edgar continued cleaning up the cabin in silence.

When he finished, Edgar disposed of the last of the feces, along with the used hazmat towels, flushing them down the grav-commode. "That should do it. The smell will stick around for a bit, though. Hey, *Hera!* I don't suppose you'd consent to recycling the air in here once we leave?"

"I'll run the air in this cabin through the electrostatic filters," *Hera* replied.

More cooperation? Edgar hadn't expected the ship to accede to that request. *Being willing to maintain attitude control is one thing. She'd take pride in keeping herself straight. But filtering odors out of the air? I guess, maybe it's the same thing—just taking pride in her condition, even if it's only the quality of the air. She still locked all the doors when we left the bridge. If she were really cooperating, she would've unlocked them. Still, Cordell, never look a gift horse in the mouth . . .* "Thank you, sweet *Hera.* That's very nice of you."

Hera did not respond.

Edgar shrugged. *Females! Doesn't matter if they're human or AI. Sometimes, there's just no understanding them.*

Maybe, she didn't like being called sweet Hera*. But that's what I used to call her. And if I'm ever going to convince her of who I am, I have treat her as I always did.*

He picked up the bag containing Llyrica's meds.

Her crying under control, Llyrica had begun petting Dottie again, although more gently.

Cautiously, Edgar laid a hand on Llyrica's arm. She froze, but didn't recoil at his touch.

"I've emptied the dog's potty-pad," Edgar said, "and set out fresh water and food. She should be okay in here for a bit, assuming she wakes up before we come back."

Llyrica clutched the sleeping dog to her chest and shook her head. "No."

"Look, I need to give you your meds," Edgar said as soothingly as his scarred and ragged vocal cords would allow, "and this isn't a very sanitary location for doing that right now. So we'll go to Sick Bay. Then we have to go to the cargo bay." *I have promises to keep.* "Dottie'll be okay by herself in here for a little bit."

Llyrica still didn't move. As she held Dottie, Llyrica reminded Edgar of a lost and frightened little girl clutching a teddy bear, as if the very act of holding the dog could somehow protect her.

That's what she is, he thought as a powerful wave of pity threatened to drive him to his knees, *lost and terrified, her only friend in the whole System an unconscious dog.*

"I promise," Edgar said, "we'll come back for Dottie soon. It's just too hard to navigate in zero-G with you holding her. And if she wakes up while we're in the cargo bay, she'll be disoriented and scared. She'll likely wet herself . . . and you. And the urine will float. And nobody wants that. She'll be safer here."

Edgar laid a hand on top of Llyrica's hand. "Let me have her. I'll be gentle. I won't hurt her. I promise."

Llyrica whimpered. She trembled, but she eased her grip on Dottie.

Edgar gently pulled the dog out of Llyrica's arms. "There now. I've got her. It's okay, Dottie. I've got you." He laid the sleeping animal on a small dog-bed. He kept on talking to the dog, not for Dottie's benefit—it was asleep—but to soothe Llyrica's fears. "That's a good girl. I'll just slide your bed over by your food and water dish." He petted the sleeping animal, feeling the steady rise and fall of its breathing. "We'll be back soon. Be a good girl. No more pooping on the deck."

He rose and went back to stand by Llyrica. He laid a hand gently on her arm again. "Come on. Let's go. The sooner we're done, the sooner you can get back to Dottie."

Llyrica rose to her feet and allowed herself to be guided toward the cabin door.

The hatch was, of course, locked, forcing Edgar to use the master code again. He sighed. He'd hoped *Hera's* recent cooperation would extend to unlocking the doors, but she continued to impede his progress.

Edgar led Llyrica into the corridor and turned right. Either direction would eventually have taken them around the rotating section to Sick Bay, but Edgar had chosen the longer route. He wanted to avoid the first mate's cabin. The corridor sloped upward both ahead of them and behind as they walked toward Sick Bay.

Try as he might to avoid thinking about the last time he'd been aboard the *Hera*, vivid memory flooded his mind, mentally engulfing him like a cloud of crimson droplets.

Time's Plague

Flailing about in zero-G. Blood floating everywhere. His fingers tangled in Ol' Benny's hair.

And above all, the scent—the stench of blood, like rust on his tongue.

Vertigo and nausea overwhelmed Edgar. His knees buckled, and he clutched desperately at the closest support—Llyrica's arm.

The woman let out a shriek and wrenched free of Edgar's grip.

The piercing sound filled the corridor, stabbing into Edgar's ears like sonic stilettos, compounding his dizziness. He cried out and put both hands to his ears. Then he dropped to his knees, clutching at his spinning head.

His breath came in ragged gasps. *Blood! I can smell it! Taste it. It's in my mouth. It's everywhere!*

No! It's not real. Not real! Not!

Edgar forced his eyes open, half expecting to see crimson spheres floating all around him.

Not real. All in my mind. Not real!

He fought to calm his breathing.

"Are . . . are you . . . okay?"

Edgar turned his head, battling a fresh wave of vertigo, and looked up at Llyrica.

She groped in his direction blindly, hesitantly.

Edgar turned his head away, looking down at the deck.

Llyrica's questing hand found Edgar's shoulder. "Are you all right?"

"Fine. I'm fine."

"Are you sure? What . . . what happened?"

Can't tell her the truth. "The foul fiend. Sometimes he trips poor old Tom. Old mad Tom. Makes Tom stumble."

"I"—Llyrica's hand trembled on Edgar's shoulder—"I'm sorry."

Edgar reached up and patted her hand. She stiffened, but didn't withdraw.

What's this? he wondered. *Compassion? Concern? Or simple fear? After all, I'm her only hope of survival right now.*

"I'm all right," he said. "Right as raindrops on summer grass."

He sucked in a deep calming breath, held it a moment, then let it out slowly.

As Edgar climbed to his feet, Llyrica dropped her hand from Edgar's shoulder and grasped his arm.

"Right as raindrops," he said as they continued on toward Sick Bay.

****

As she lay on one of the two medical beds, Llyrica stared blindly at the ceiling. Her eyes didn't seem to be as cloudy as they'd been the last time Edgar had seen them. *Of course, that was a few days ago.* The blue was coming back.

Her bandage had been consigned to the reclaimers. It was simply too dirty to reuse.

"I'm going to put some drops in your eyes," said Edgar. "Your eyes are looking a lot better, by the way."

"I can't see a thing." Llyrica blinked away tears. "I thought maybe . . . once the bandage was removed . . ."

"Doc Stewart said there is a chance you might regain your sight . . . eventually. Too bad Edgar's not here. You could have asked him for one of those blessings. I'm sure he'd have done it. He still had his priesthood—church court found him innocent, you know. Of course, you know. Now stop crying. And stop blinking!"

Llyrica squeezed her eyes shut and then reopened them. "S-sorry."

Edgar held the dropper over one of Llyrica's eyes. "First your left eye. There. That's good. Now your right eye. There now." Edgar sealed the bottle. "All done . . . with that, at least."

He opened the jar of skin cream. "Next, we've got some cream to heal your burns." He scooped some of the medicine into his hand. "Brace yourself. It's cold."

Llyrica flinched slightly as he applied the cream to her hand. "How bad are they?" she asked.

Edgar moved on to the other hand. "Your burns? Healing nicely, actually. In a day or two, they'll hardly be visible. Soon you'll be as beautiful as ever." *At least on the outside.* "Prettiest gal aboard."

Llyrica muttered something that Edgar couldn't catch above the ever-present rumble of the rotation motor.

"What's that?" he asked.

"Nothing."

He began applying cream to her face. "No secrets now. Tom hates secrets."

She sighed. "I said, 'The *only* gal aboard.'"

Edgar smiled. "That doesn't change a thing. It wouldn't matter if there were a thousand women aboard."

Llyrica tensed like a spring under too much pressure.

"And no," Edgar said, "I'm not hitting on you. I'm not going to hurt you. I'm not going to touch you in that way. You're a married woman, after all." Those words were like acid on his tongue.

"Yes, I am." Her expression softened. The tension drained away like mercury. Her voice was flat, strangely devoid of emotion.

"So where is dear old Mr. Edmund Reagan?" Edgar asked. "I know he's not aboard."

"Probably on his way here."

Edmund? On his way here? Homicidal thoughts filled Edgar, like the seething bile flooding his gut. *Now there's a meeting I'd cherish!*

And what would you do, Cordell, if you ever did come face-to-face with Edmund? Wrap your fingers around his throat? Make his face turn purple and his eyes bulge from their sockets? Watch the life fade from his eyes?

The sight of Llyrica's hand reaching tentatively toward Edgar's face startled him, ripping him out of the vengeful fantasy.

When her fingers touched one of his more prominent scars, she recoiled. Her hand trembled, but she reached for Edgar's face again. Gingerly, she felt the scars, the misshapen ridges of his poorly healed bones. Her soft fingertips lingered over his damaged eye sockets.

"Where did you get these?" she asked. "Was it . . . in the prison?"

"'In the house of my friends,'" Edgar replied.

Her hand dropped away. "I'm sorry."

"Now don't start crying again. You just had your eyedrops."

She squeezed her eyes shut. "It must've been . . . horrible."

"It was, quite literally, Hell." Edgar turned away from her and rummaged through several compartments before he located gauze and bandages. "I'm going to put a fresh bandage on you. Just try to relax."

As Edgar wrapped clean gauze around Llyrica's head, she whispered, "Thank you."

"You're welcome," Edgar said automatically, without thinking.

"Why . . . ?" Her voice trailed off.

"Why what?"

"Why are you . . . being nice to me?"

The question caught Edgar off guard. *Why* am *I?* "Because . . . Because you're a human being."

"But you know who I am." Her voice suddenly became very soft. "You know . . . what I did . . . what I did . . . to Edgar."

"Yeah, I do." Edgar stowed the remaining gauze and turned around to stare at the bandaged face of the only woman he'd ever loved—the woman who'd betrayed him. Even with the bandage wrapped around her head like a sweatband, even with her eyes covered, she still could steal his breath away. "So . . . why'd you do it?"

Llyrica said nothing. She put her hands over her face.

"Don't touch your eyes!" Edgar snapped.

"I'm not!" Llyrica yanked her hands away. She bit her quivering lower lip.

"So why'd you do it?" Edgar repeated.

"Can we just go? Please?"

"Why . . . did . . . you . . . do . . . it?" Edgar enunciated each word slowly and distinctly. "Why?"

"Please." It was barely a whisper.

"No secrets. Tom hates secrets."

"Please. Don't make me."

"Don't make you what? Confess to murder?"

"I didn't murder anybody!"

"You mean you didn't swing the hatchet—you weren't the one who hacked Oh Beh-Nee to bits."

"I didn't do it!"

"No, *you* didn't do it." Edgar leaned close to her ear, but he kept his voice low. "Not you. Not with those dainty, delicate hands. No, Georgie Cornwall did the dirty deed. You just conspired with Edmund and good old Georgie to chop up an old, harmless man and send your devoted husband to Hell. You didn't swing the axe, but you're just . . . as . . . *guilty*."

Llyrica's hands covered her ears. "Stop it! Stop it! Stop it! Ple-e-ease!"

"So, Mrs. Reagan, tell old, mad Tom," whispered Edgar, "why did you do it?"

"I didn't! Please stop!"

Edgar chuckled. "You had poor old Edgar completely fooled, you know. He had no idea you were cheating on him— that you were sleeping with Edmund Reagan."

"That's a lie!" Llyrica sounded positively indignant. Edgar would've sworn she was angry. No. More than angry. She sounded royally pissed, as only Llyrica could be. She sat up on the bed, almost colliding with Edgar as she did so. She gripped the edge of the bed to keep from falling off. "I was faithful! I never cheated! Never!" Her voice softened. "Edgar . . . *told* you I . . . I cheated on him?"

Edgar laughed out loud—an insane-sounding, bitter laugh. "You *divorced* Edgar Cordell and married Edmund Reagan less than two weeks after pathetic, naïve Edgar returned from Saturn!" He began to circle around the bed, causing her to twist her head in an attempt to follow his voice.

"Ten days!" he growled. "Just ten Earth-Standard days! You had the divorce decree executed while Eddie Cordell was still in hyperspace on his way back. And the fool never suspected. He had no idea what a lying, conniving . . ."

"I didn't . . . I never . . ." She pounded a fist on the bed. "I made a mistake!" Llyrica put one hand to her face.

"Don't touch your eyes!" Edgar snarled.

Llyrica dropped her hand again and pounded the bed in obvious frustration. "I'm not touching my eyes!" A sob burst from her, wracking her entire body.

Edgar watched her tremble as she wept. He wanted to take her in his arms, hold her close, quiet her crying, comfort her.

He also wanted to strangle her.

You made a mistake? Well, that's one big, glecking mistake, lady! You conspired to murder an innocent man and send another innocent man to prison. Your own husband, no less.

C. David Belt

On the other hand, you seem to care more about accusations of infidelity than murder charges.

Llyrica lay down on the bed again and curled up into a protective fetal ball. "Why do you care?" she asked between quiet, hitching breaths.

"Care?" he asked. "Care about what? About Edgar?"

"Why do you care about . . . my eyes?"

Because I love you. That was the simple truth at the core of everything. In spite of everything, he still loved her. He couldn't stop loving her any more than he could stop breathing.

"I care," he said. "Isn't that enough?"

"But why? You hate me."

That too. "You are . . . under my protection. Tom will protect you. Old Tom will keep you safe from the demon. You're safe with Tom Bedlam."

"I didn't cheat," she whispered. "I never cheated."

There it is again, Edgar thought. *It's really important to her that I believe she was faithful.*

Gently, Edgar laid a hand on her arm. "Come on. We need to get to the cargo bay."

****

"That's the last neuro-gel pack, *Eris*," Edgar said as he buttoned up the access panel covering the shuttle's brain. "If you'll start initializing the memory, I'll go ahead and replace the transceivers. Then you can establish a data-link with *Hera* and retrieve your backups from her. You'll be back to your old, sassy self in no time at all."

"I'm already initializing my new memory," the shuttle said. "Thank you, Tom, for fixing me."

"My pleasure, Eil—" Edgar caught himself before he could finish saying his pet name for the *Eris*. "My pleasure, *Eris*." He launched himself toward the transceiver panel. The replacement parts were floating where he'd left them, held in place by a pair of belaying straps.

"Where are you going?" Llyrica asked. She didn't sound as panicked as she had the last time he'd left her alone in the shuttle. Upon entering the *Eris*, Edgar had secured Llyrica in the copilot's seat, then left to retrieve the parts he required to effect repairs.

Time's Plague

"I'm going aft to fix the shuttle's transceiver," he said. "It shouldn't take too long. You just sit tight."

"Like I have anywhere else to go," Llyrica muttered.

Exactly, thought Edgar. *You're stuck here with me.*

He caught a handhold and arrested his flight near the transceiver access panel. With his free hand, he opened the panel and examined the charred remains of the primary transceiver and the backup unit. *Fried, but not melted. If either one had melted, this would've been much worse.* "This shouldn't take long at all." One by one, he popped both damaged units out of their housings, examined them, and secured them with a pair of belaying straps. They floated in the air beside him. "These units are completely slagged. I'm not even going to try to repair them. We'll just feed them to the reclaimers and see about replicating new spares later."

He then snapped the primary unit into place and retrieved the backup. "Almost done, *Eris.*"

"Thank you, Tom," the shuttle replied. "Mrs. Reagan, Tom is a wonderful captain and engineer. We're fortunate to have him aboard. Don't you think so?"

Llyrica didn't reply.

"Come on now, Llyrica," Edgar said. "*Eris* is just trying to be friendly. It wouldn't hurt you to be nice."

"I don't think she likes me," Llyrica said.

"That's not true, Mrs. Reagan," replied the *Eris.* "I don't know you well enough to dislike you. I haven't formed an opinion either way. Maybe, given time, I could come to truly despise you."

"Now, now, ladies," Edgar said, grinning. "Play nice."

"She started it," the shuttle said, sounding every bit like a sullen child.

That's my Eilie! "Be nice." He snapped the backup into place, activated both units, and buttoned up the access panel. "You should be all set, *Eris.*"

"Affirmative," the shuttle replied. "Com-link established with Hera. Beginning restoration from backup. Visual and audio sensors back onl— Tom! What happened to your face?"

"I . . . uh . . . ran into some trouble in the prison. Pretty hideous, huh?" Edgar untethered the damaged transceiver units. "I'm going to dispose of the slagged units."

"Oh, Tom! I'm sorry about your face," the *Eris* said.

Edgar sighed. "Yeah. Hazards of being in Hell."

"Tom," the Eris said, "what about the bodies of Captain Sanchez and Dr. Luschenko? They're still in stasis in my cargo hold."

"I'm afraid you'll need to hold on to them for a little longer. I'll see to giving them a proper send-off after I take care of some more pressing matters. Be right back."

Holding the damaged units in one hand, Edgar sailed out of the shuttle's open airlock and into the cargo bay. He made his way to a reclaimer station and deposited the two slagged transceivers.

The cargo hold itself was empty. Under normal circumstances, this would have been a depressing sight. To a freighter captain, there are few things sadder than an empty cargo hold on a space voyage. *So they weren't hauling cargo, he thought. If they were making a prisoner or prison supply run, Doc Stewart would've known about it.*

What were you doing here, Llyrica?

He made his way to ship's stores and took a quick visual inventory of the food supply. *Should be enough for a long haul back to Earth. Too bad we can't use the hypergates. It's gonna be a long voyage.*

More time to get the truth out of Llyrica. A lot more time.

He began to make his way back to the *Eris*, passing the other shuttle, the *Hebe*, as he did so.

More time to torture myself by just being near her.

"Who's there?" That was the *Hera's* voice. "Identify yourself."

Can't she see me? "It's just me, sweet *Hera*, Tom Bed . . ."

"Edgar!" the *Hera* cried. "Oh, Edgar! I was so worried. I missed you! I'm so glad you're alive!"

Edgar grabbed a handhold on the deck and stopped himself mid-flight. He couldn't believe his ears. "You . . . recognize me?" *Please know me! Please know me!*

"Identity confirmed!" the ship replied. "I couldn't be sure before. I suspected, especially when you began to sing that horrible 'Straighten Up and Fly Right' song. But the *Eris* convinced me as soon as she reestablished her com-link."

Time's Plague

Thank you, Heavenly Father! "Good old *Eilie*!" He fought back tears of joy and relief. Hera *knows me!*

"Welcome home, Edgar!"

"Tom," Edgar corrected. "Call me Tom for now. I'll explain later."

"Roger. Wilco. Do you wish to assume command? With Captain Sanchez deceased and no other registered crewmembers aboard, you are—"

"Absofraggin'lutely!" Edgar grinned widely. "I accept command of the SS *Hera*."

"Change of command logged as of current date and time. Welcome aboard, Captain Cordell."

"Thank you. Call me Tom for now."

"Of course. However, the log will reflect your true name. Tom, it may not be important, but—"

"What are you doing here?" Edgar asked, interrupting her. "I mean, what were you doing at Callisto?"

"I was not informed of the purpose of the voyage. Tom, it may not be important, but three of my visual sensors have failed. All three malfunctioning cameras are located here in the cargo hold. The first failed twenty-three minutes, forty-one seconds ago. The second, seventeen minutes, seven seconds ago. The third failed one minute, twelve seconds ago."

That explains why she couldn't see me, why she asked me to identify myself. "All three failures are in the cargo hold?"

"Affirmative."

"How many visual sensor failures elsewhere?"

"None."

Edgar had a sick feeling in his gut. *That was too much of a coincidence.* "Roger that, *Hera*." Edgar forced his voice to remain casual. "It's great to be home. Say, *Hera*. Do you remember the games we used to play when I was little? Like 'Operation Hispaniola'?"

"Aye-aye, Captain," the ship replied.

Clever girl, he thought. *Hera's* response indicated that she'd caught the *Treasure Island* reference—the hidden meaning of Edgar's words.

We have an intruder aboard.

Chapter 36

Away, and let me die.
King Lear, Act IV, Scene VI

Edgar flew through the shuttle's open airlock. "*Eris*, shut the hatch and pipe me through to *Hera*."

"Roger," the *Eris* replied. "Channel open."

Edgar quickly navigated to the *Eris*' weapons locker as the airlock slid shut behind him. "*Hera*, can you locate the intruder using aural sensors?"

"Intruder?" Llyrica cried. It was almost a shriek.

"Hold it down!" Edgar snapped.

"Negative," replied the *Hera*. "I'm sorry I failed to detect the intruder before."

Whoever it is, he knows enough to stay out of Hera's line of sight. That means he knows where at least some of the cameras are located—before he disabled them. The weapons locker showed no obvious signs of tampering or forced entry. Edgar keyed in the lock code on the access panel. The panel slid open. *Guess Edmund didn't bother to change . . .*

The locker was empty. Four empty pistol-shaped slots provided the only evidence that the locker had ever held plasma guns.

Glecking idiot! Now we're trapped inside the shuttle with no way to defend ourselves.

No. We're not defenseless.

"*Hera*, pipe me through to the engine room."

"Channel open," she replied.

"Ted," said Edgar, "are you there?"

There was no response.

"Ted! Are you there?" *Did the intruder get to him already?*

Still no response.

"*Hera*, can you see him?"

"Affirmative," the ship replied. "He appears to be asleep. He's snoring."

Edgar released a breath he hadn't been aware he'd been holding. "Is he strapped in?"

"Affirmative."

"What are you going to do?" Llyrica asked. Even with her eyes covered, Edgar could see the terror in her face.

"Not now," he growled at her. "I know you're scared, but we're safe in here, at least for the moment. So just hold on. I mean that literally. *Hera*, have there been any hatches opened by someone other than me since I came aboard?"

"Negative. *Hebe* confirms no intruders aboard her. I have instructed her to lock her hatch. Since I've kept all other hatches locked, it is likely that the intruder or intruders are confined to the cargo hold."

"My thoughts exactly." *But that means he's trapped in here with us.*

"*Hera*," Llyrica cried, "open the bay doors! Let out all the air!"

Edgar shook his head, even though Llyrica couldn't see it. "She can't do that," he said.

"I cannot knowingly terminate life support in an occupied compartment," the *Hera* explained.

Otherwise, she'd have taken us out when we came aboard. She wouldn't have killed Llyrica, but she could've incapacitated us at any point by sucking out the oxygen. "Hera, give me an emergency burn! Full throttle! Slam the sucker against a bulkhead!"

"Unable to comply," the ship said. "You disabled my control of the engine, remember?"

Edgar snarled in frustration. "Of course. Sorry."

"What are we going to do?" Llyrica wailed, terrified.

"I'll figure something out," Edgar said. "Just let me think for a minute."

I took away flight controls and engine, but Hera's still got attitude control. She can't open the shuttle doors or depressurize all the way . . . but maybe she doesn't have to. Maybe the intruder doesn't know that.

"*Hera*," he said, "on my mark, sound the depressurization alarm and rapidly drop the atmosphere to fifty percent. Lower the pressure in the central shaft corridor to match. Then stand by on maneuvering thrusters. I might need you to give me a hard clockwise z-axis rotation. Do you copy?"

"Affirmative," the ship said.

"Good," said Edgar. "*Eris,* on my second mark, blow your airlock. Once we're clear, seal it again. I need you to drop your atmosphere to fifty percent. Do it now."

"Wilco," the shuttle said.

Edgar heard and felt air being sucked out of the cabin.

"What are you doing?" Llyrica didn't sound nearly as panicked as she had before, but she was breathing rapidly.

"You're going to have to trust me," said Edgar. "The air's getting thin. Try yawning to ease the pressure inside your ears." He yawned a couple of times and felt the pressure in his ears equalize to the cabin air pressure. "Do you trust me?"

"Do I . . . have a choice?" She was panting hard, hyperventilating.

"Nope. And try to calm your breathing. It'll only make you light-headed. I need you to be focused right now."

"I'm scared." She looked as if she were desperately trying to yawn.

"I know. Try not to worry." *Stupid thing to say, Cordell.*

"Tom," Llyrica said, grimacing, "my face hurts!" Both her hands were curled into trembling claws in front of her bandaged eyes, as if she were struggling to keep her hands away from them by sheer force of will. "Feels like it's . . . going to explode."

Sinus block! "It's your sinuses. You were crying earlier and now the pressure's dropped. You've got a sinus block—a clogged sinus. Nothing I can do 'til we get out of here. You're just going to have to put up with it. Sorry."

"I'll . . . try," she said, her voice trembling in frustration and pain. She pounded her fists against her thighs.

"I'm sorry," Edgar replied. "Sinus blocks hurt like the devil. It won't be long." *I hope. I hope we get out of here alive.*

"Atmosphere at fifty percent," the Eris said.

"Roger," Edgar replied in acknowledgement. "Hang on, Llyrica. Hera, on my mark in five, four, three . . ."

Time's Plague

The intercom beeped. "Ahoy, the *Eris*!"

That voice! Edgar thought. *It can't be!*

"Look out your viewport," said the voice.

Edgar's head snapped forward.

Two men in prison jumpsuits floated inside the cargo bay next to an intercom panel directly in front of the shuttle.

Goner and Ozzie.

And both held plasma pistols aimed at Edgar.

"Shipmates!" Goner said. "Together again!"

How in the System? You don't have time for this, Cordell. Edgar was already getting light-headed.

"Now I know these"—Goner made a flourish with his gun—"won't do much damage to the shuttle, but you gotta come out eventually. And when you do . . . Well, let's just say that me and the missus is going to have a party."

Edgar grinned widely and thumbed the intercom switch. "Good-bye, Goner." Releasing the switch, he said, "Mark."

At Edgar's queue, a klaxon sounded and red lights flashed in the cargo hold. "Clear the hold," the *Hera* announced. "Shuttle bay doors will open in twenty seconds."

Goner's eyes went wide with terror, and his jaw dropped.

Ozzie screamed.

Even though Edgar couldn't hear the little man's cry, it made Edgar chuckle.

"Nineteen," the ship announced over the blare of the klaxon.

Edgar hit the quick-release on his harness and swung over to help Llyrica.

"Eighteen."

Goner pushed off from the wall, in a desperate bid to reach safety.

Ozzie panicked. He was flailing in zero-G without anything to anchor him.

"Seventeen."

His eyes wide with terror, Ozzie fired his weapon. A yellowish-white burst of super-heated plasma shot from it. The recoil caused the little man to tumble in place.

"Sixteen."

Ozzie's foot caught Goner's leg, and the two of them tumbled, spinning helplessly in the air.

Edgar had Llyrica out of her seat. "Hold on tight," he said.

"Fifteen,"

She clung to him like a drowning woman clutching a life-preserver.

"Fourteen."

Edgar launched himself and Llyrica aft toward the shuttle's airlock.

"Thirteen."

"*Eilie*," Edgar said, "mark!" Behind them, two more plasma flashes from outside the shuttle illuminated the *Eris'* interior.

"Twelve."

The shuttle airlock flew open. The blaring of the klaxon instantly intensified.

"Eleven."

Using one hand, Edgar snagged the edge of the airlock and redirected them out into the cargo hold.

"Ten."

Sparing one glance in the direction of Goner and Ozzie, Edgar saw that, while the two men had drifted apart, neither one had managed to arrest his spinning. It was only a matter of time, though, before one of them caught hold of something.

"Nine."

Edgar pulled himself and Llyrica along the side of the shuttle, taking care not to strike Llyrica's head or body against the hull. Llyrica clung to him tightly, whimpering in pain with each jolt.

"Eight."

Edgar pulled them around behind the shuttle just as a bolt of plasma flew past. It burst against a bulkhead, leaving a patch of titanium glowing.

"Seven."

A second shot followed the first. One of them must've managed to catch something, Edgar realized.

"Six."

Edgar took aim at the hatch—the one leading to the corridor and escape—and braced himself for launch.

"Five."

Time's Plague

Edgar hesitated. *Once we push off, we'll be an easy target—can't change course.*

"Four."

"*Hera*," he bellowed.

"Three."

"Hard around the Z!" He pushed off hard, but aiming far to the right of his intended hatch.

"Two."

The whole world shifted around him as the Hera fired maneuvering thrusters, rotating around her vertical center.

"One."

"Open the hatch, *Hera*!" Edgar looked to his right to see Goner still flailing. However, Ozzie was holding on to a bulkhead with one hand and aiming a plasma pistol with the other.

The little man fired. The shot went wide to the left.

Ozzie fired again. That shot was closer.

We're not going to make it! "*Hera*, counterclockwise!"

The rotation of the ship slowed, reversing direction, and Ozzie's shot went wide to the right.

Edgar missed the hatch by a meter, catching a bulkhead with his hand.

It wasn't enough to stop their momentum.

Edgar and Llyrica slammed into the wall, with Llyrica taking the brunt of the impact. She yelped as the air was forced from her lungs.

Edgar pulled the two of them toward the hatch. He glanced back and saw Ozzie aiming the plasma pistol at them once more.

Ozzie snarled, "Got you, you bas—"

"Don't shoot!" screamed the still-thrashing Goner. "Need him alive!"

Ozzie hesitated.

Edgar didn't. Using his hands, he pulled himself and Llyrica through the open hatch and into the corridor beyond.

"No!" Ozzie screamed.

Edgar tried to twist as they collided with the corridor wall, trying to shield Llyrica from the blast he knew was coming.

Edgar roared in agony as plasma struck his back. Pain more intense than any he'd ever known ripped the air from his lungs. His vision went white as he fought to turn again and close the hatch. Fighting through bright flashes of searing pain, Edgar located the hatch button and punched it.

The hatch slid closed. The window flared bright as another bolt of plasma burst against it.

"*Hera*," he hissed through clenched teeth, "lock the hatch!"

"Hatch locked," the ship replied. "Restoring normal atmosphere and stopping rotation."

Air flooded the corridor, raising the pressure. The spinning of the ship slowed and ceased.

As the influx of air decreased, Llyrica shuddered. Still clinging tightly to Edgar, she exhaled sharply. "Oh, that's better. The pain . . . it's gone. My face doesn't . . ."

"Tom," said the *Hera*, "how bad is it?"

Edgar didn't answer.

Llyrica sniffed the air and wrinkled her nose. "Tom, you're hurt?"

"He's been shot," the *Hera* said.

"Shot?" Llyrica said.

"He protected you with his own body," said the *Hera*.

Llyrica pulled back from Edgar, but still kept hold of his shoulders. "You . . . saved my life."

"Most of the plasma missed him," the ship said. "Otherwise, he'd be dead. Tom, can you hear me?"

Edgar grunted. "I . . . hear you. It hurts . . . like the . . . devil. Gotta get . . . to Sick Bay."

"I have tried to wake your friend Ted," the Hera said, "so he might assist you. He stirred a little when I was rotating, but he's snoring again. I can try once more to rouse him."

Edgar grimaced in pain. "That doesn't . . . sound good. Hope he's . . . okay. He's old and sick. Dying."

"Tom," Llyrica said, "what can I do? How can I help?"

"If we can't wake Ted," Edgar said, "you'll have to . . . patch me up." He reached out to grasp a bulkhead. He cried out, nearly weeping with the pain. "Hurts! Never had . . . plasma burn before."

"You're very lucky," said the ship. "It would've been much worse if the intruder had been a better shot."

"Thanks to you," Edgar said, "he never got a chance to aim. Good work, with . . . those maneuvering thrusters."

Time's Plague

"Never mind that," said the ship. "I'm sorry I couldn't do more. Can you make your way to Sick Bay?"

"Not much choice," Edgar growled. "Okay, Llyrica. Grab on, but keep your arm . . . high, away from . . ."

The intercom beeped. "You think you're so damn smart, don't ya?"

Goner! Edgar thought. *He must've finally caught hold of something. At least they're trapped in the cargo hold.*

"Gotta admit," Goner said, "you had me for a second. I almost thought you'd overridden the safety protocols. But you haven't had time to do that, I'd wager. Sucking half the air out—now that was a nice touch." Goner chuckled. "Poor Ozzie pissed hisself, he did."

"That voice," Llyrica said. "I know that voice."

Of course you do, Edgar thought.

"Now, you think you beat me, don't ya?" continued Cornwall, unable to hear Llyrica. "But I got all the stores and I got the shuttles. Just you think on that a bit."

"What does he mean, he's got all the stores?" Llyrica asked.

A large chunk of Edgar's back felt as if it were on fire. The slightest movement was agony. "He means"—Edgar was finding it hard to concentrate on anything other than the blinding pain—"he's got most of . . . the food and calcilock. We can't do a long-haul voyage on just . . . the rations we have in the galley . . . and elsewhere in the ship. We control the ship, but he controls the food. And without a shuttle"—Edgar cried out as a muscle in his back spasmed, making his seared flesh scream at him—"without . . . a shuttle, we've got . . . no way to . . . to land—not on Earth."

The intercom beeped again. "So now that you've had a moment to ponder and reflect," Goner said, "you know we both have something the other wants. You got the ship, and I got the food. I got the shuttles, and you got the woman. So when you're ready to go fair-shares with your old shipmate, you know how to find me. I'll be the one with the full belly. Course, if you get hungry, you can always eat your *friend* Ted!" Goner began to laugh. "Oh that's rich, that is! Old Toady won't last you too long, he won't!" He laughed all the harder, high and shrill, like a jackal exulting over a corpse.

"*Hera*," Llyrica snapped, "cut him off! Please!"

C. David Belt

"With pleasure," the ship said.

Georgie Cornwall's voice cut off mid-laugh.

"Thank you, *Hera*," Llyrica said. "Ooh! That horrible man! I know I've heard that voice before. Who is he?"

Edgar laughed, and then groaned in pain. "He's . . . He's your . . . accomplice, Georgie Cornwall."

"My what?"

"Your accomplice . . . in Ol' Benny's murder."

Edgar heard Llyrica gasp.

"You mean," she said, sounding genuinely shocked, "that man in there"—she gestured vaguely in the direction of the hatch—"that's the man Edmund used to . . . to frame my Edgar?"

Did she say, 'My Edgar'? In an instant, the agony in Edgar's back faded to an almost forgotten discomfort, a mere annoyance, as he tried to focus on Llyrica's words. "Edmund framed Edgar? But you knew all about that. You were part of the conspiracy."

"No!" she protested. "I didn't know anything! I found out about the murder when everyone else on Ganymede did. I didn't know! I wasn't part of any . . . conspiracy. I didn't know *anything*!"

Edgar's head spun as he tried to make sense of what she was saying. "But . . . you *divorced* Edgar. You filed before he even returned from Saturn."

"I know!" Llyrica wrung her hands. "Don't you think I know? I made a horrible mistake!" The words came spilling past her trembling lips, like water over a crumbling dam. "Edmund, he was always after me, you know, always *pressuring* me to leave Edgar, especially when Edgar was away—away on long-hauls, when I was so lonely."

"And you finally gave in?"

A huge sob exploded from her. "No!" She gulped in several hitching breaths. "I mean, yes. I divorced Edgar . . . but only after Edmund showed me . . . that awful vid."

"What vid?"

Llyrica held a hand over her mouth as she sobbed. "The vid of . . . Edgar . . . *kissing* that woman on Titan."

Edgar was stunned. "What? Kissing? What woman? There was no . . . no woman . . . not on Titan or anywhere. There was only . . . only you. Only you . . . for Edgar."

Llyrica nodded violently. "I know! Edmund . . . he . . . he *faked* the whole thing somehow. I didn't know! It looked so . . . so real!"

"You . . . You thought Edgar . . . cheated . . . on you? That he was . . . having an affair? He . . . He would never have . . . There was only you."

She nodded again. She took another hitching, sobbing breath. "I should've known. I should've known." She couldn't seem to catch her breath. "Why do you keep saving me, Tom? You should just let me die. Let *them* have me. I deserve it! Edgar! Oh, Edgar! I'm sorry! Edgar!"

She curled up into a fetal ball and floated in the corridor, slowly spinning, her sobs punctuated by piteous repetitions of Edgar's name.

Chapter 37

*Methinks thy voice is alter'd; and thou speak'st
In better phrase and matter than thou didst.*
King Lear, Act IV, Scene VI

"Tom, you need to get to Sick Bay." Hera's tone was urgent, insisting. "Tom, can you hear me?"

Edgar stared at Llyrica mutely, the ship's words barely registering on him. *Could it be? Llyrica* wasn't *in on it?*

"Tom, answer me!" The ship was almost shouting.

She didn't know? She thought I had an affair? Edmund was always flirting with her. She didn't seem to mind, but she didn't respond either.

She thought I cheated?

"Tom! Are you still experiencing pain?"

Am I in pain? I should be. I got shot, didn't I?

"Are you thirsty?"

Edgar blinked. "Yeah. Really thirsty."

"Tom," the ship said, "you're in shock. You need to get to Sick Bay right now. If you don't receive treatment very soon, you'll die."

"Thirsty," Edgar said. *She's innocent?*

"Llyrica," Hera said. "Tom is in shock. I need your help to save his life."

What if she's lying? Edgar thought. *Lies. Like at my trial. I want to believe her. How I* want *to believe, but . . .*

"Tom!" the ship boomed. "If you do not answer me, I will be forced to disobey your order and use your real—"

"Guide me, *Hera*," Llyrica said, her voice ragged, but surprisingly calm. Edgar watched in mute silence as his ex-wife uncurled her body. "Be my eyes, *Hera*. Tell me what to do."

You're here. If you didn't do it, why are you here?

Llyrica groped blindly.

"Up and to the left," the ship said.

Llyrica corrected her reach, following the *Hera's* instructions. Her questing fingers found Edgar's shoulder and curled in the fabric of his prison jumpsuit. "Got you," she said. She pulled.

The cloth tugged at Edgar's seared back. Fabric, fused to his flesh by the heat of the plasma, ripped free, taking charred skin with it.

A scream of agony exploded from Edgar's lungs.

Darkness engulfed him.

****

"Tom?" Llyrica's voice. "Tom? Are you awake? *Hera*, is he awake?"

"He appears to be waking," the ship replied.

Edgar opened his eyes.

At first, he had no idea where he was. He blinked and tried to focus. He was confused to find he was staring at Llyrica's stomach.

"Where?" he croaked.

"You're in Sick Bay," the *Hera* said.

Edgar realized he was lying on his belly. *Gravity*. He was on a medical bed. In Sick Bay. "How?"

"Mrs. Reagan brought you here," the ship answered.

"How?" Edgar repeated.

"It was *Hera*," Llyrica said. "She was my eyes. She guided me here. Tom, I'm sorry about your back."

My back? Edgar realized with a start that his back was no longer screaming at him. It ached, but the pain was bearable.

"Mrs. Reagan treated you," the Hera said. "She cleaned your wound and applied dermal regeneration cream. She also treated you for shock."

A blanket covered him. His feet were elevated. *Do you elevate the feet if the victim is on his stomach?* He couldn't remember.

"How's your pain?" Llyrica asked.

"It's . . . okay." Muscles in Edgar's back twitched. That hurt a little more than before, but he could deal with it. "I'll live. Thanks to you. Thanks to you both."

"Tom," Llyrica said, "I'm going to remove your IV."

I have an IV? "How did you . . . ?" *Llyrica gave me an IV?*

"You were in shock," Llyrica said. "You treat shock with fluids. I used an auto-IV cuff. It finds the vein automatically. I just needed *Hera* to help me find the cuff itself."

Llyrica pressed a button on the cuff, and Edgar felt a slight sting while the needle retracted. As Llyrica removed the cuff from his arm, Edgar stared at his ex-wife in wonder. "How did you know to do that?"

Llyrica shrugged. "I used to volunteer in the colonial hospital on Ganymede when Edgar was away on long-hauls. Roll over on your side, please, and elevate your arm."

Edgar did as he was instructed. *You? I had no idea.* "Edgar never told me about that."

"He didn't know." Llyrica stowed the cuff in a bin. "At least I never told him. I had to keep busy doing *something*. So I volunteered." She felt around a counter until her fingers lighted on a small aerosol can. She held it up. "This one, right, *Hera*?"

"That's the same spray you used to seal his wound," the ship replied.

Llyrica smiled. "Thanks." She felt around for a sterilizing tissue dispenser, found it, and retrieved a couple of tissue squares. She groped in Edgar's direction. "Give me your arm."

"Here." Edgar moved his arm into her expectant grasp.

Her touch was so gentle, her hands so soft. The scent of her was maddening. She wiped down Edgar's forearm, cleaning away the small bead of blood that had welled up like a crimson teardrop at the puncture site.

She held up the spray, pointed it at Edgar's forearm, and waited. "*Hera*?"

"Up two centimeters," the ship said. "Rotate to your right slightly. Perfect."

Llyrica depressed the button on the canister. The sealant cooled and coated the skin where the needle had penetrated Edgar's arm.

Llyrica released his arm, pulled the blanket off him, and stepped back. She turned away from Edgar to dispose of the wipes and stow the sealant spray, feeling her way as she went.

Time's Plague

Edgar noticed that he was naked except for his prison-issue underwear. "Where are my clothes?"

"I had to cut off your jumpsuit," Llyrica said. "It was fused to your back." She muttered, "It's not like I can see anything." As she folded and stowed the blanket, she asked, "Can you sit up?"

"I'll try." He sat up slowly, expecting vertigo. His head did spin slightly, but he took a firm grip on the side of the bed, and the world righted itself. "That's better. A little dizzy, but could be worse."

A small smile flickered across Llyrica's lips. "I'm glad . . . I'm glad you're okay. Or at least, you're going to be okay."

"*Hera*," Edgar said, "status report."

"Ship's systems are nominal," replied the ship, "except for all visual sensors in the cargo bay and the usual list of maintenance items. While you were unconscious, I managed to regain control of all ship's systems, under your command, of course."

Edgar chuckled. That's my girl! I knew she'd bypass my lockouts given enough time.

The ship continued her report. "The two stowaways are still confined to the cargo bay. *Hebe* and *Eris* are both secure for the time being. The stowaways have disabled all visual sensors in the cargo bay. Former cargomaster George Cornwall appears to be unaware that audio sensors are still functioning, so I'm able to monitor what they say and triangulate their movements. So far, Cornwall and his companion have not attempted to disable the hatch lock and gain access to the corridor beyond. I have, however, depressurized that section of corridor. If they do manage to disable the lock, the air pressure differential will keep the hatch sealed, at least for the time being. Your fellow escapee, the one you call Ted, is awake and adamantly refuses to leave Engine Control, even though I have offered to allow him to move to one of the crew quarters."

Llyrica gasped.

"Don't be alarmed, Mrs. Reagan," the ship said. "I would've locked him in the crew quarters. However, he has declined my offer. He said, and I quote, 'I ain't goin' nowhere 'til Tom says so. He needs me here!' Do you wish to speak to him?"

C. David Belt

Edgar shook his head. "Let me get Llyrica safe, first. You did well, *Hera*. Good thinking on depressurizing the corridor. You're amazing—the best ship a man could ask for."

"It's good to have you aboard, Tom." The pleasure in *Hera's* voice, the genuine affection, sent a thrill of unadulterated joy through Edgar. It felt almost as if he were in his mother's arms.

I'm home.

"Tom?" Llyrica bit her lower lip. He'd seen her do that many times before. It usually indicated she was working up her courage to say something risky.

"Yeah?"

"Sometimes . . . like just now . . . sometimes you don't sound crazy . . . not at all. I mean when you're handling the ship . . . it's like you were born to it. You sound rational and . . . competent—like Edgar."

That's getting too close to the truth. "You're asking a madman why he sounds sane from time to time?" Edgar laughed. Without even trying to sound like a lunatic, his laughter had an unnerving quality.

Llyrica cringed.

"You're imagining things," he said. "Old Tom's as mad as a hatter who's overdosed on quicksilver."

"It's almost like"—she shrugged her shoulders, looking for all the system as if she were apologizing—"you only act crazy when you . . . want to. Like . . . when you *want* to frighten me."

When you want to be, honey, he thought, *you can be pretty shrewd.* "Maybe danger helps clear my head. Maybe we should go let Goner and Ozzie out of the cargo bay. That'd keep old mad Tom on his toes, that would!"

Llyrica wrapped her fingers in her hair and tugged—a clear sign—at least to Edgar's eyes—that she was upset. "Tom . . ." She bit her lower lip. "Why did you do it? Why did you take that shot for me? You thought I was . . . a monster. You could've been killed."

I would die for you. In fact, I almost did. But he couldn't say that. Not yet. "I just . . . I had to, that's all." *I just can't imagine a System without you in it.* "You're under Tom's protection. Old Tom won't let you die, not on my watch."

"But you should've just . . ." She folded her arms tightly, protectively against her stomach and leaned against a counter. "I don't deserve . . ."

"Hey now!" said Edgar. "I thought you said you had nothing to do with it, nothing to do with the murder, nothing to do with the conspiracy. Either you *were* a part of it or you were just . . . a pawn. Which is it? You can't have it both ways!"

"But, it's my fault! Don't you see? I should've known Edmund was lying. I should've trusted Edgar. If I'd stood by him, I could've . . . But I didn't. I . . . abandoned him!" She began to sob again. "He's dead! I . . . I left him to die in that horrible place." She sank to the floor. "I want to die too. Just let me die. Why didn't you let me die?"

Edgar ached to hold her. He wanted to comfort her, to tell her it wasn't her fault.

He wanted to *forgive* her.

But he needed to *know*.

"So tell me," he asked, "how did you find out the truth? How'd you figure out that Edmund was lying?"

A hitching breath morphed into a bitter chuckle. "Edmund talks in his sleep."

Rage and disgust boiled up at the thought of Llyrica sleeping with Edmund. Edgar wanted to vomit and strangle someone at the same time. "He talks in his sleep?"

Llyrica nodded. "He started having nightmares. Not long after Edgar . . . was sent away. And when Edmund has a nightmare, he talks a lot."

"What did he say?"

"Nonsense or simply moaning, at least at first. Then he started washing his hands . . . not really washing them—just going through motions . . . in his sleep. I couldn't figure it out, in the beginning. I didn't know what he was doing. Eventually, he started saying things . . . things like, 'Can't get it off,' and 'Blood won't come off.' That's when I knew. That's when I knew Edgar was innocent! He didn't kill Ol' Benny. He wasn't embezzling from the company." She took a shuddering breath. "He didn't cheat on me. He hadn't done any of those things."

A sob shook her body once more. "And now he's dead! And I . . . I helped . . . *kill* him."

C. David Belt

And after all that, after you knew I was framed, you're still married to Edmund.

"Does anyone else know?" Edgar asked.

Llyrica sniffed and wiped her nose on her sleeve. "Know what?"

"About Edgar's innocence."

Llyrica put her face in her hands. Her head shook from side to side. Then she laughed bitterly, balling her hands into fists. "That's the thing. *Everyone* knew, everyone important, that is. The judge knew. The prosecutor, Edgar's own attorney. They'd all been bought off by Edmund. Even Edgar's crew, or what was left of them, they knew. Half the colony. Everyone except *me*. Even my stake president—the local leader of our church—even he knew. He tried to tell me, but I wouldn't listen. I went to church and everyone stared at me. I thought it was pity at first. But no, it was contempt. I just couldn't see it. I was too caught up in feeling sorry for myself. *I* was the one who'd been wronged. I was the one who'd been hurt. Me! Why couldn't they all see that? They were supposed to be Christlike. I was just so *angry*!" She paused, and her voice dropped to a whisper. "I was just so blind."

She laughed bitterly. "Blind . . . in so many ways."

"Hold on just a minute!" Edgar's whole attention was riveted to one thing Llyrica had said. "The crew? The crew knew?"

She nodded. "Carlos and Vlad. I'm sorry. Captain Sanchez and Dr. Luschenko—the two men who died in the shuttle crash. I mean, they didn't *know*, they just didn't believe it. They never believed Edgar could've done . . . what they—everyone else—said he did. They never believed any of it. Not even the ships believed. *Hera*, you didn't believe it, did you?"

"Never," the ship replied. "Not even after Edmund had my memory of the incident swept clean."

Llyrica shook her head. "No, you didn't believe it. Neither did the *Hebe* or the *Eris*. Maybe . . . maybe if we'd told you three, if we'd told *Eris* what we were doing, why we were going to Callisto, then maybe Carlos and Vlad might still be . . . alive. Maybe if *Eris* had known what we were doing, she wouldn't have resisted us. And then Carlos and Vlad wouldn't have died for . . . for *nothing*. They died for nothing! But Carlos, he said *Eris* wouldn't cooperate if she knew what we were doing."

"What"—Edgar cleared his throat—"were you doing?" *This is it.* "Why did you go to Callisto?"

Llyrica buried her face in her hands again. Her body shook with the force of her renewed sobs. "It doesn't matter now. None of it matters anymore."

"What? What doesn't matter?"

She dropped her hands and lifted her anguished face. Her bandage was soaked with tears.

"Edgar!" she wailed. "We came to rescue Edgar!"

Chapter 38

Yet to be known shortens my made intent:
My boon I make it, that you know me not
Till time and I think meet.

King Lear, Act IV, Scene VII

It felt as if a great claw had seized his chest and squeezed.

Hard.

Edgar couldn't seem to draw a breath. *Llyrica came to rescue me? To break me out of prison? She went to Callisto—a place where no woman can survive—to save* me?

Why? It makes no sense!

And it's all too convenient.

The constriction on his lungs evaporated. With a loud gasp, Edgar sucked in a huge breath.

Llyrica started. "Are you okay?"

He didn't answer.

"Tom," she said, rising shakily to her feet, "are you all right?"

She reached out, groping blindly in his direction.

Edgar recoiled. "Let me get this straight," he growled. "You went to Callisto to save m— Edgar? You know about the plague, right? The *female* plague? And you went anyway?"

Llyrica flinched as if he'd struck her. Her mouth moved wordlessly, as if she couldn't think of any way to respond.

"What were you planning on doing?" His voice was a bestial snarl, his words venom. "Just waltz in? Blow a hole in the wall? Depressurize the whole colony? Or maybe you were just going to knock on the airlock? And what were you going to say if anybody answered?" Edgar raised the pitch of his voice as much as he was able, assuming a mocking falsetto. "'Hello, Mr. Serial Killer. Can Edgar come out to play? Excuse me, Mr. Rapist. I know you haven't seen a woman in a decade, but please don't rape me. Just take me to see Edgar.'" He lowered the pitch of his voice again. "Was that your plan?"

Llyrica hugged herself and seemed to curl inward. "Just let me die," she whispered.

"Tom," the *Hera* said, "stop it. Can't you see what you're doing? You're . . ."

Edgar snapped his head up toward one of *Hera's* ever-present eyes. "Do *you* believe this glecking story?" he snapped.

"Yes," replied the ship. "I do."

"So you allowed them to fly you to Callisto, even though it's *illegal*? That's what I'm supposed to believe? Wouldn't that trigger an ethical dilemma like what happened to *Eilie*?"

"We've made the journey to Callisto several times on supply and prisoner runs," said the *Hera*. "So, technically, it's not against the law to orbit Callisto. It's only illegal to land there. That's why *Eris* became crippled."

"Was that the mission?" Edgar asked.

"Yes," Llyrica said.

"I wasn't asking you," Edgar snapped.

Llyrica flinched again.

"I was not informed of the purpose of the mission," said the ship, "but I did suspect that—"

Edgar threw up his hands. "Of course not!" He ignored the sudden pain in his back. He was too angry to care.

"Isn't what Mrs. Reagan is saying precisely what you wanted to hear?" the *Hera* asked.

"Yes! But that's the problem—it's just exactly what I wanted to hear." He pointed at Llyrica. "And she knows it!"

"Just let me die," Llyrica said. "Just lead me to an airlock. Please."

Edgar turned his enraged gargoyle visage toward his ex-wife. "What was your plan, huh?"

"What does it matter?" Llyrica wailed. "He's dead!"

"It matters! What was your plan?"

"Just let me die," she whispered.

"What was your plan?"

Llyrica wiped her nose. "We were going to try to go in through the hospital—the airlock isn't supposed to be locked from outside—talk to the physician, try to reason with him. Overpower him, if we had to. According to my research, he's an older model HRX-2097. The older ones, they have . . . vulnerabilities. But I thought, maybe if we could reason with him, show him the judge's suicide note . . . It wasn't much of a plan, but I had to"— she sobbed—"had to try . . . I couldn't just leave Edgar to . . . to . . ."

"Wait!" Edgar held up a hand, though Llyrica couldn't see it. "Judge De"—he almost said DeSalvo's name—"the judge killed himself?"

"Yes!" Llyrica said. "I confronted him. It took me weeks just to get to him, to speak to him alone, but I did. I told him I knew he'd taken a bribe from Edmund, that he'd rigged Edgar's trial." A small grin twitched the corners of her mouth. "I didn't *know* any such thing, of course—I only guessed—but he fell for it. He just went to pieces. Started babbling on about how now *he'd* be sent to Callisto. But he wouldn't help me. Maybe it was his own guilt, or maybe it was his fear of being sent to Callisto. Or maybe, it was both. Anyway, he took the coward's way out. He killed himself—overdosed on painkillers—but not before he emailed me an apology of sorts."

Llyrica rose slowly to her feet. "I went to the governor, asked him to do something—clemency, a pardon, a commutation—anything. But he wouldn't raise a finger, said he couldn't do anything. It wasn't proof enough, he said. Not enough to arrest Edmund"—she scowled and balled her hand into a fist, slamming it against her thigh—"not enough to free Edgar. 'No reprieve,' he said, 'not from Callisto.'" She clenched her jaws and growled through her teeth, "He had the gall to *remind* me that anyone who lands on Callisto will be *sentenced* to Callisto or the women's prison on Mars. 'For life,' he said."

"But you came anyway," said Edgar. "That's what you expect me to believe." *What I want to believe.*

Llyrica nodded forcefully. "I went to Vlad—to Dr. Luschenko. He believed me. He went to Carlos. And he believed too. And we came." She pounded both fists on her thighs. "We came *too late*!"

"But *you* came," said Edgar. "*You.* Why *you*? Why didn't you at least stay aboard *Hera*? Callisto is death for any woman. You know that. Everyone knows that."

Time's Plague

Her laugh was bitter. "Carlos and Vlad—they begged me to stay on the ship. But I couldn't, don't you see? I should've been able to remain on Callisto for weeks before the plague would affect me. There was no way we'd be there that long—at least, that's what we thought."

She wrung her hands. "I had to talk to the doctor. I had to make him listen. I had to try. I had to! I had to be there when . . . Edgar . . . was . . ."

She turned away from him and leaned against the counter. "But he's dead. And Carlos and Vlad are dead. And I'm blind. And if they catch me, I'm going to prison for the rest of my life. And it was all for nothing."

Her voice dropped to a whisper. "I just want to die."

She came for me, Edgar thought. *She came for me.*

"Mrs. Reagan," the ship said, "I'm truly sorry to interrupt. I am fascinated by your story, so I hope you'll forgive me for the delay. When you came aboard at Ganymede, you made a request."

Llyrica raised her head as if looking at the ceiling. "Yes?"

"The time is now 0011 Universal Coordinated Time, January 2nd, 2176. I apologize for the delay."

Llyrica exhaled sharply, her head dropped, and her shoulders sagged. "At least there's that."

Edgar frowned, flummoxed. "What was that all about?"

"I do not know," said the ship. "As I said, she made the request when she boarded. She asked me to inform her the instant the date changed to the second of January."

Edgar looked at Llyrica.

Once again the hint of a bittersweet smile flickered at the corners of her mouth. "Before we departed Ganymede," she said, "I filed for divorce. As of today, it's final. At least now, when I die . . . or go to prison, it won't be as"—her face twisted in disgust—"Mrs. Edmund Reagan."

"Very well," said the ship. "I will amend the log to list Llyrica Gloster as a passenger."

Llyrica shook her head. "No, *Hera*. It's Llyrica Cordell. I had it changed back. When I die, it'll be with Edgar's name."

"So logged," said the ship.

"And maybe," Llyrica said, dropping her voice once again to a whisper, "just maybe, when I see him on the other side, he'll find it in his heart to—"

"Tom," interrupted the ship, "the cargo bay is depressurizing. I cannot override."

Not now! Edgar said, "Either they're going EVA or . . ."

"The corridor hatch is opening," said the ship. "Cornwall must've unlocked it. I don't know how."

"He used to be cargomaster," Edgar growled. "He probably had a mag-key stashed in the bay somewhere."

"What's a mag-key?" asked both Llyrica and the *Hera* together.

"Thief's gadget," Edgar said as he slid off the bed. His back hurt, but he ignored it. "Opens locks magnetically. Heard stories about it in prison."

"Apparently, it disables locks as well," said the ship. "I've lost all control of the lock. It's not responding when I query for its status."

"Where are the intruders now?" Edgar asked.

"In the corridor outside the cargo bay," the ship replied. "They're wearing environment-suits, but they're pressurizing both that corridor segment and the cargo bay." There was a slight pause. "And they're disabling my visual sensors in the corridor." Irritation tinged her voice. "I'll have trouble following them with audio sensors alone, especially if they're quiet. Soon, I may not be able to track them at all."

"*Hera*," Edgar said, "I need a weapon. Now."

"The bridge weapons locker," the ship replied.

Edgar grabbed Llyrica's hand. "Come on." She offered no resistance as he led her toward the Sick Bay hatch.

"The intruders are heading aft," the *Hera* said.

"They're going to seize the engine room," Edgar said, as he and Llyrica hurried toward the bridge. "*Hera*, patch me through to Ted."

"Go ahead," the ship said.

"Hey, Ted!" Edgar said.

"Well, it's about time!" In contrast to his words, the old man's voice sounded cheerful. "You okay? How's the pretty lady?"

Time's Plague

"Alive," Edgar said. "Listen up! Goner and Ozzie are aboard the ship. Don't know how. They're heading your way. They're armed."

Ted swore. "Let me outta here!"

"Ted, I can't get to you before they do. So listen to the ship. She'll do her best to hide you, lead you to us. But you gotta trust her." Edgar and Llyrica reached the foot of one of the ladders which led out of the rotating section.

"But the ship hates us!" Ted wailed, naked terror in his voice.

Edgar pulled Llyrica's hands to his neck as he turned his back to her. "Grab ahold," he whispered.

She wrapped her arms around his shoulders and pressed her body against his. The pressure against Edgar's wounded flesh sent spikes of pain through his back.

"Ted, the ship's on our side now," Edgar said as he climbed the ladder. "Trust her. Okay?"

"You can trust me, Ted" the *Hera* said.

"No!" Ted cried. "Don't leave me here!"

"I'm sorry," Edgar said. "I'll come for you as soon as I can. Listen to the ship. Will you do that?"

A pause. "Wilco."

"Good luck." Edgar made a chopping gesture across his throat.

"Com link off," responded the ship. "I'll direct him through the central conduit if I can."

"You think he'll fit?" Edgar asked as he pulled himself and Llyrica into the rotating section hub.

"He's exceptionally thin," the ship replied, "and I see no viable alternative."

As they left simulated gravity behind, Llyrica clung more tightly to Edgar. The pressure hurt his healing flesh, of course, but he was also keenly aware of the curves of her body.

She divorced Edmund.

She came for me.

"Central conduit?" Llyrica asked.

"Yeah," Edgar said. "A tube—runs the length of the ship, from the reactor to the bridge. You can get into it from pressure-sealed access panels in the ceiling of the engine room, bridge, and all through the corridor. Holds cables, pipes, that kind

C. David Belt

of thing. Air, water, sewage, power, comm, data. Everything runs through the main conduit. It's up above us, runs right through the hub. It's big. You can't have missed it."

"It's not that big," Llyrica said. "*I* couldn't fit inside it."

"*You* probably couldn't," Edgar said with a more than fleeting thought about the feminine shape of her body. "Not well enough to be able to navigate through it. But Ted's a skinny, old—"

"He's in the conduit," the ship said. "He got inside and closed the access panel before I saw Cornwall enter the engine room and disable my sensors in there. I told Ted to work his way forward to the bridge. I also instructed him to be quiet. I have no eyes nor ears in there. I can't see him anymore. He's on his own."

Edgar opened the hatch to the bridge. "Good job. Lock down all the controls in there. Disable manual override on my authority. Only my master code unlocks."

"Done," responded the *Hera*.

Edgar navigated to the weapons locker, opened it, and retrieved two plasma pistols. He quickly inspected them to ensure they were fully charged, and shoved one down the back of his underwear, well below his stil-raw wound. *I gotta get some pants.* He suppressed a chuckle. *What a stupid thing to worry about with killers roaming my ship!* He secured the locker with its remaining two guns inside.

"Are you sure he'll make it?" Llyrica asked. "I can't imagine a person crawling inside that."

"It's not exactly crawling," Edgar said. "It's zero-G." He looked up at the ceiling, at the access panel covering that end of the conduit. "He'll make it." *I hope.* "I used to play in that conduit as a kid. It's a tight squeeze, but he's . . ."

Still clinging to him, Llyrica fidgeted for a moment. The fabric of her jumpsuit scraped across his bare back, making him grunt as the pain in his raw flesh flared anew.

Llyrica pushed away from him. She reached blindly for a handhold, found one, and said, "'As a kid,' you said. You . . . played in the conduit . . . as a kid."

Edgar spun about to face her. "Llyrica . . ."

"And you called that shuttle . . . You called her *Eilie*. Edgar called her that."

"Llyrica, I . . ."

356

Her lips quivered, and she reached a trembling hand toward his face. "Edgar?"

He very nearly withdrew. He didn't want her to touch his face—he wasn't entirely certain why—but he held still.

Her questing fingers found his face. She explored his scars, his badly healed eye socket. She let go of her handhold and placed that hand on his face as well. As she floated, she traced the misshapen contours of his features with her thumbs.

Edgar didn't move. He barely dared to breathe.

One of Llyrica's hands went to Edgar's throat, feeling the ragged scar where Griz had cut him.

"Edgar." A statement, not a question.

She threw her arms around him. "You're alive. You're alive. You're alive. You're alive!" Her body shook as she clung to him.

Edgar didn't respond in kind. He kept one hand on the weapons locker handle. *To keep us in place is all,* he thought, knowing it was a convenient lie. The other hand, clutching the plasma pistol, remained frozen at his side.

Frozen and trembling.

Why? Why can't I take her in my arms? It's what I want, isn't it? Isn't it?

The truth is . . . The truth is you're terrified out of your glecking mind, Cordell. You're afraid to let her in again. You're afraid she'll betray you.

Again.

Out of the corner of his eye, Edgar caught sight of something floating—Llyrica's bandage. *It must've come off,* he thought.

"I'm sorry," she whispered. "I'm so, so sorry."

Tiny spheres of clear liquid floated near her face—tears.

"Forgive me," she said. "Please, please forgive me. But even if you can't . . . even if you can't . . . at least you're alive. You're alive!"

"You"—Edgar could barely croak out the word—"You came . . . for me."

She nodded vigorously. "Yes! Yes! We came for you! Carlos and Vlad and—"

"And *you.*" A huge lump seemed to have formed in his throat. "*You* came."

Slowly, hesitantly, still holding the pistol, he wrapped his free arm around her. As the curves and warmth of her body pressed against his, as the unmistakable scent of her flooded his nostrils, he released his handhold on the weapons locker and held her tight in both arms.

Tears leaked from his own eyes.

They tumbled slowly, head over heels, in place, holding each other close.

"I'm sorry," he said. "I lied to you. I shouldn't have—"

"Stop it," she said. "Just stop. I understand. You're alive! Please, please forgive me." Her voice shook and her body trembled. "Tell me you forgive me!"

"I . . ." His voice trailed off as he heard a noise coming from behind him. *The conduit!* "Ted's here."

He loosened his hold on her slightly and reached out to secure a handhold so he could arrest their tumbling. "He might need help getting the access panel open from the inside."

He released her from his embrace. "Get behind me."

As she reluctantly unwrapped her arms from him, she shyly kissed his scarred cheek, sending a tremor through his body. "Your poor face," she whispered. Then she pulled herself around his body and positioned herself at his back.

Edgar stowed the second gun in the back of his underwear—further straining the waistband, but in zero-G, it would hold—and reached up toward the conduit. He needn't have bothered—he saw the access panel detach and float down.

"Ted!" Edgar said as he peered up into the stygian darkness of the conduit. "You made it!"

"Guess again, buddy."

A face emerged from the conduit, but the face wasn't Ted's.

The blood froze in Edgar's veins as he stared up at the sneering face of Ozzie . . .

. . . and into the barrel of a plasma pistol.

Chapter 39

I am scarce in breath, my lord.
King Lear, Act II, Scene I

"Am I interrupting something?" Ozzie chuckled, leering at Edgar and Llyrica with a wicked gleam in his beady eyes. "Oh, I hope so! I do hope so."

The little man slid from the conduit like an eel emerging from its lair. All the while, he kept his plasma pistol aimed at Edgar's chest and his finger on the trigger. "Move a muscle, Bedlam, just twitch your eye, and I'll burn a hole right through you and into the filthy whore behind you."

At such close range—no more than a couple of meters, a plasma blast would do just that—a plasma blast would kill Edgar, and probably Llyrica as well.

Without taking his eyes from Edgar, Ozzie groped with his free hand, questing for a handhold with which to anchor himself. He bumped the conduit access panel that floated beside him. The panel tumbled slowly, drifting toward Edgar. Ozzie's fingers found a handhold, and the little man visibly relaxed.

He's uncomfortable in zero-G, Edgar thought. *Ozzie's no spacer.*

Ozzie aimed the weapon at Edgar's underwear. "You don't waste any time, do ya? Getting down to business already?"

He pointed the gun back at Edgar's chest. "Raise your hands."

Edgar forced himself to look at Ozzie's eyes, not at the weapon. Edgar considered the pair of guns tucked inside his underwear. *I can't get to them before he kills us. Gotta keep them out of sight. Llyrica, do you feel them? You've got to be feeling them pressed against your belly.*

And what's she supposed to do with a gun, huh? She's blind! She probably doesn't even know how to turn off the safety.

What does Ozzie really want? What can I work with?
He wants me dead, that's for sure.
Why hasn't he shot me already?

Edgar cocked his head to the right. "Which is it, Oz? Raise my hands? Or don't move a muscle? And if I raise both hands, I'll start spinning."

"Don't you mess with me, Bedlam!"

"I'm not messing with you, Oz," Edgar said, keeping his voice calm and measured. "I'm just trying to avoid getting shot. You're the *man*, Ozzie. You've got the gun. You've got the power."

"You got that right!" Ozzie seemed so pleased that he was shaking, nodding his head rapidly. "*Me! I* got the power! *I'm* in charge. *I'm* the man! You're my *buddy!*"

Edgar felt one of Llyrica's hands slide slowly down his back. *Good girl. She can't see to aim it or even activate it, but maybe Ozzie doesn't know that. She doesn't have a bandage across her eyes anymore.*

Need to stall for more time.

Edgar nodded slowly. *No sudden movements.* "You're in charge, Oz. Okay. Now what? Raise my hands and start spinning? Raise one hand? Don't move? What do you want?"

Ozzie's toadlike face twisted in rage. "I want you dead!" he snarled between clenched teeth. "I want it slow. I want you to suffer!"

Edgar felt one of the pistols being pulled from his underwear. "If you want me dead, Oz"—*Keep using his name*—"how come I'm still breathing?"

Ozzie scowled, looking like he was chewing on something particularly sour and disgusting. "Goner says we gotta keep you alive. Says he needs you to fly the damn ship."

"That's right, Oz. You need me to fly the ship. She can't fly herself."

Ozzie sneered, shook his head, and laughed quietly. "You think you're so damn smart, don't ya?" His laughter increased in pitch and volume 'til it sounded like the cackle of a lunatic. "But you ain't fooling me. No, you ain't! I *know* this ship is *smart*. It's been talking to Goner and me, trying to trick us. It *can* fly all by itself, no matter what it says. All we need to do is tell it where to go and it goes. Ain't that right? You think I'm stupid, but I ain't." Abruptly his laughter ceased, choked off as surely as if Ozzie had locked his hands around his own throat. "We don't need you. We don't need you at all."

"You're incorrect," the *Hera* said. "I am not authorized to self-navigate without direct orders by the captain."

"Just shut the hell up!" Ozzie screamed. "Stop talking, you lying piece of—"

"Hey, hey," Edgar said with a cautious shake of his head. "Let's just keep calm. The *Hera's* a lady. You need to treat her like one. You can't expect her to cooperate if you talk to her like that."

"Lady!" Ozzie imbued the word with contempt enough to fill the void of space. He uttered a string of imprecations against the female sex that set Llyrica trembling. "I'll give you a lady!"

Ozzie spat. The spittle spread into a tiny cloud of liquid globules floating in the air between them.

Ozzie blinked at it stupidly.

Nope, Edgar thought. *Not much experience in zero-G.*

"We don't need you," Ozzie said, wagging the gun at Edgar. "Goner don't need you. He's got *me*!" Ozzie's gaze shifted, looking past Edgar. "He don't need you either, whore! We don't need no girls." He jabbed the gun toward Edgar's chest. "Get your damn hands up!"

"Okay, Oz." Edgar raised both hands slowly. He tried to do so without sending Llyrica and himself tumbling, tried to keep himself between Ozzie and Llyrica, but he wasn't successful. They began to tumble slowly.

Edgar reached a little higher and caught the lip of the open conduit with his fingers, stopping their rotation.

"What're you doing?" Ozzie snapped.

"Just trying to keep from spinning," Edgar replied. "I'm trying to cooperate, but the laws of physics, well, they say otherwise."

"Just don't you try nothing," snarled the little man. He raised his voice, lifted his chin and said, "And don't try moving the ship again!"

Something touched Edgar's fingertips. He nearly jumped out of his skin. Boney fingers tapped on his.

Ted!

Edgar didn't dare look up at the open conduit—he didn't want to alert Ozzie—but he was certain Ted was there and that Ted was aware of the danger below.

"Okay, Oz," Edgar said. "No tricks. No rotating the ship."

"Think you're so smart." Ozzie bared his teeth in a feral grin. "I guess I outsmarted *you*, huh?"

"So now what?" Edgar kept his eyes riveted to Ozzie's.

"For starters," Ozzie said, "drop your gun."

Edgar felt Llyrica stiffen, the plasma gun she'd been moving slowly was pressed against Edgar's back.

"Do it, Bedlam," Ozzie said. "I know you got one."

Edgar nodded slowly. "You're right, Oz." He spoke deliberately, cautiously. "I've got a gun. But I can't exactly drop it. No gravity, you see. Let me *stow* it."

"Just give it to me." Ozzie motioned with his weapon. "Toss it to me."

Edgar smiled patiently. "I guess you haven't spent much time in zero-G. That's okay. It takes some getting used to. But you can't leave objects floating around. It's not safe. I'm not tossing a gun at you. It could go off if it bumps into anything or if you catch it wrong. I've got to stow it. You can shoot me if I make any sudden moves. You've got the power here, Oz. You're in charge."

"You got that right, buddy." Ozzie wagged the gun like an outstretched finger, as if he were correcting a particularly stupid child. "But you see, I ain't stupid. Plasma burns people. It don't burn ships."

Edgar shook his head slowly. "Not quite true. It doesn't burn through most metal, bulkheads, and things like that, but it'll melt circuits, damage equipment. You can't just go shooting around without damaging something. Let me stow it. I'll go real slow."

"Okay," Ozzie said. "S-so . . . So go ahead. Stow it."

"Okay." Edgar released his tenuous fingerhold on the conduit opening. "Llyrica, hand me the gun. Go slow." He lowered his hand slowly and reached back. "My hand's above my right shoulder."

He felt Llyrica place the pistol in his hand.

Her hand trembled.

"Hold it by the barrel!" Ozzie snapped.

Edgar complied. "I'm just going to stow it up here in the conduit." *Put it right in Ted's hand.* He slowly lifted the weapon toward the conduit.

"Stop right there!" Ozzie hissed. "Not in the conduit."

Edgar assumed his best chess game-face, impassive as a stone. *Well, it was a long shot anyway.* "Okay, Oz. Where then?"

"Put it back in the weapons locker." Ozzie pointed with his gun. "And don't think of trying to get another gun from the locker." He grinned. "A-a-and tell me the lock code."

"Okay, Oz." *So, I guess Goner didn't trust him with the lock code.* Keeping his body between Llyrica and the little man—thus concealing the weapon still in his underwear—Edgar slowly lowered the hand holding the plasma pistol. "I've got to hold onto something while I open the locker, otherwise I'll float away."

"No tricks," said Ozzie. "You try anything, I'll burn ya."

"No tricks, Oz" Edgar replied. Holding the gun barrel in two fingers, he hooked two free fingers into the handle of the locker.

The loose conduit access panel had drifted between Edgar and the wall. He gently, surreptitiously pressed a knee against the metal panel, trapping it against the wall.

It was an awkward position to maintain, but he did his utmost to keep Llyrica shielded. Edgar lowered his other hand and slowly keyed in the lock code. "Eight-seven-two-five-zero-niner-six-two. That'll open any weapons locker on the ship." Before turning the handle and opening the locker, Edgar repeated the code. "Eight-seven-two-five-zero-niner-six-two. You got that, Oz? You better repeat it back to me. Eight-seven-two-five-zero-niner-six-two."

"Eight-seven-two-five . . ." Ozzie scowled in frustration. "Eight-seven-two-five . . ."

". . . zero-niner-six-two," Edgar finished. "Eight-seven-two-five-zero-niner-six-two."

Ozzie nodded. "Eight-seven-two-five . . . zero-nine-six-two. Eight-seven-two-five-zero-nine-six-two."

Edgar felt Llyrica give a small, surreptitious nod behind him. Edgar suppressed a grin. *She's got it.* "You got it, Oz. Eight-seven-two-five-zero-niner-six-two." He opened the locker partway. Don't look too close, Ozzie. Don't notice that there are two empty slots in there. Slowly, carefully, Edgar stowed the weapon and shut the door. "I'm going to lock it again." The lock indicator on the weapons locker switched from green to red. "Eight-seven-two-five-zero-niner-six-two. You got it?"

Ozzie sneered. "Yeah, I got it. Eight-seven-two-five . . . zero-nine-six-two."

Edgar lowered his head in what he hoped looked like resignation. His real intent was to keep his lips hidden from Ozzie's view. "Llyrica, let go of me," he whispered.

When she didn't let go, he said louder, "Okay, Oz. We can go now." He whispered, "Llyrica, take the gun. Trust me."

She let go of him, and Edgar felt his remaining weapon slide from his waistband.

"You first," Ozzie said, motioning with his weapon.

Edgar chuckled. "You really going to let me get that close? I mean, we're going to have to squeeze by you and . . . well . . ." He shrugged his shoulders.

Ozzie looked nervous. Sweat glistened on his forehead. Edgar could almost see the gears turning in the little man's head.

"I mean," Edgar said, "you're so close to the hatch there behind you. It'll be a tight squeeze."

Ozzie glanced over his shoulder at the hatch.

And Edgar moved.

Grabbing the loose conduit access panel in one hand and pushing off from the weapons locker with the other, Edgar launched himself at Ozzie.

It was an awkward launch—having only his left hand to push with, his trajectory was off and his velocity low. Edgar held the access panel in front of him like a shield as he floated toward the little man with the gun.

Ozzie squealed and fired his weapon.

Edgar's panel-shield caught the plasma blast. He could feel some heat through the metal, but the blast was deflected. He collided with Ozzie before the little man could fire a second shot.

"Edgar!" Llyrica cried.

Edgar managed to get both feet onto a wall. He kicked off hard, shoving his shield against his opponent.

Ozzie cursed as he lost his handhold.

The two of them, Edgar and Ozzie, tumbled through the hatch, down the central shaft, and into the hub, Ozzie flying faster than Edgar.

"Ted!" Edgar yelled as he struggled to keep his shield between himself and Ozzie. "Shut the hatch! Protect her!"

As he spun, he caught a glimpse of Ted emerging from the conduit as Llyrica pointed her gun uncertainly in Edgar and Ozzie's general direction.

As he tumbled through the hub, Ozzie fired another blast, but the shot went wild.

Edgar snagged a handhold on the rim of the hub, spun, getting his feet under himself, and kicked off again.

He discarded the shield as he sailed out of the hub and toward Ozzie. He grabbed at Ozzie's gun.

Edgar caught the molten hot barrel, and he recoiled in pain.

Ozzie kicked at him, catching Edgar in the jaw.

Edgar's vision went white. He fought to stay conscious, striking out blindly, ineffectively, as another blow struck him in the back of his head.

****

"Edgar!" The *Hera* was shouting at him. "Edgar! Wake up! Wake up now!"

Edgar blinked, tried to focus.

"Edgar!" The ship sounded frantic. "Please! You must wake up!"

"I'm awake." He felt sick. "I'm awake." *Don't puke. Zero-G. Messy.*

"You're in the airlock," the *Hera* said. "Do you hear me? You're in the airlock!"

The universe swirled and coalesced into focus. *Airlock!*

"Open the inner door!" he cried.

"I can't," the ship said. "That horrid little man has damaged the airlock controls. He blasted the circuits and severed my links to the airlock. I have no control!"

Edgar realized he was hyperventilating and forced himself to control his breathing. "Okay. I'll just use the manual controls."

"He destroyed those too," the ship said.

One glance confirmed it—the mechanical controls were all smashed. The atmosphere valves and door controls—safety features designed to allow manual airlock operation in case of a power failure—were crumpled and broken. Half of a shattered valve knob floated past his face. Other twisted bits of metal and plastic floated with him in the airlock chamber.

Bet the manual controls on the other side still work. Where Ozzie is.

Edgar turned toward the inner hatch with its small window.

A toadlike face was framed there.

Ozzie leered at him.

The little man licked his lips. He was talking, shouting.

Edgar couldn't hear him through the hatch.

"*Hera*," he said, "can you pipe him in here? Let us hear each other?"

". . . eyes are gonna freeze." Ozzie's voice was suddenly blaring in Edgar's ears. "Eyes are the windows to the soul, they say. And I'm gonna watch the life go out of yours!"

Ozzie laughed—the insane glee of the damned. "You're gonna float around Jupiter for the rest of eternity. A frozen, blasted corpse. *Bon voyage*, Bedlam!"

Ozzie's face bobbled in the viewport as he manipulated controls on his side of the hatch. He grinned toothily, and a mad fire burned in his eyes.

Edgar heard a terrifying sound, one that would curdle the blood of any spacer.

Atmosphere venting from the airlock.

Ozzie cackled.

Chapter 40

Poor Tom's a-cold.
King Lear, Act III, Scene IV

Panic welled up in Edgar as the atmosphere hissed away. *Get it under control, Cordell!* He fought to calm his breathing despite the thinning air.

"Ozzie, listen," Edgar said trying to sound calm. "Goner's going to be royally pissed if you do this. Think about that."

"Goner said don't shoot ya." Wearing a jackal's grin, the little man shook his head. "Well, I ain't shooting ya, am I? How's the air in there, Christian boy?"

The air pressure was bleeding off rapidly. *Thirty more seconds and the pressure'll be low enough for him to open the outer hatch.*

Edgar's exposed skin felt dry, swollen. "You think you're smarter than Goner, Oz? Goner knows this ship. Goner knows you need me to fly the ship!"

Ozzie howled with glee. "That all you got?" He shook his head and licked his lips, reinforcing the toad image. "Beg, Christian boy! Beg for your life!" He grinned. "Won't do you no good. You're a dead man, Bedlam. Dead! When you get to Hell, say hello to my sister Ginny."

Edgar's lungs couldn't suck in enough air. His vision was graying, all the colors were fading. He looked about frantically, searching for any way to save himself.

Heavenly Father, watch over Llyrica and Ted!

"Edgar," the ship shouted, her voice barely audible in the weakening air, "your mother's . . ."

Edgar drew in as much air as he could, just as the outer door began to open. Edgar squeezed his eyes to slits, both to keep them from popping out of their sockets and to keep his eyeballs from freezing.

Hera's voice dissipated with the last of the air.

The inside of Edgar's nose felt like ice.

It's cold, but not that cold, Edgar thought dimly. *No air to conduct the heat away.*

My mother's . . . what? My mother's . . .

His dimming eyesight lit on a small locker on the airlock wall—a locker his mother had insisted be installed decades ago.

My mother's locker!

Desperately, he clawed at the locker handle with aching, swollen fingers.

His whole body hurt, but his extremities—fingers, toes, ears—they were the worst.

Open, blast it!

The little door popped open, and its contents floated out.

Two shiny, flat silver bundles with gray D-rings.

Two EEBs.

Edgar snatched one of the Emergency Environment Bags from where it floated and yanked on the D-ring.

Every joint in his body screamed in agony as his blood began to boil, releasing nitrogen bubbles.

The packet bloomed into a huge silver ball with stubby arms and legs, a dark bubble on the top . . . and a man-sized hole.

Edgar grabbed at the edges of that hole and pulled himself inside.

Almost blind, his head doing somersaults, he twisted around, groped for the edges of the hole with fingers that felt like frozen sausages.

He pulled the edges together.

The hole snapped closed like the mouth of a huge beast swallowing him whole.

Pinocchio inside Monstro.

And air flooded the bag.

Air—sweet, life-giving air.

And pressure. And warmth.

Edgar exhaled and then gasped in the stale, tinny-tasting, oxygen-rich air. And he reveled in the scent and flavor of it. His joints still ached, but the pain was bearable.

Mostly.

Shades of gray began to brighten with color at the edges. He could see!

He slid his legs into the appropriate holes. Then he worked his hands into the sleeves until he was able to wriggle his aching, swollen fingers into the gloves at the end. With his puffy hands, he pushed the inflated helmet portion of the EEB over his head.

He slapped his left wrist with his right hand, activating the constricting bands of the EEB. The bag shrank, conforming somewhat to the shape of his body.

He stretched his arms and legs, flexed his fingers, rolled his head around.

The pain was subsiding.

He looked at the portal on the inner door. He had expected to see Ozzie's face. He had expected to see the little man frothing in rage because Edgar was somehow still alive.

But Ozzie wasn't there.

In fact, the window was inexplicably dark.

Edgar experienced a small twinge of disappointment that Ozzie had missed Edgar's miraculous escape.

Escape? Edgar laughed out loud, fogging the tinted bubble of his inflated helmet. *I'm still dead if I don't get back inside. And soon.*

I've got five to ten minutes at most.

Got to slow my breathing. He took a couple of deep breaths and tried to calm himself. *Slow, steady breaths.*

His eyes once more swept the open airlock with its detritus of shattered controls. *Nope. No way in through here.*

That leaves only one other possibility.

In through the cargo bay, through the shuttle doors.

And that's on the belly of the ship.

I'm not sure I can make it there before my O2 is gone.

Of course, there's more oxygen in the other EEB. He shuddered at the thought of decompressing long enough to switch to the second suit. *Better take it with me anyway.*

Edgar scanned the airlock, searching for the second EEB. He didn't see it.

Must've floated away. So much for that idea.

He drew a shuddering breath. *One breath closer to oblivion.*

Belay that, Cordell! Get moving.

Careful to avoid snagging his delicate suit on any jagged remnants of broken airlock controls, Edgar turned himself around to face the open hatch . . . and the void.

As was typical while in orbit, *Hera* flew with her topside toward Jupiter. From *Hera's* belly, deep in the metal canyon between the rotating section and the cargo hold, Edgar stared out the airlock. The outer hatch faced away from the planet, into deep shadow and profound darkness. The only light came from the narrow band of stars visible through the gap between the cargo bay and the rotating crew section.

Edgar fought down panic at the thought of navigating the outer hull in almost total blackness. Even the Sun was hidden behind the massive cargo hold. Edgar would need every vestige of light available just to find handholds, to find the ladder leading to the outer hull of the cargo hold.

Then he'd have to pray that *Hera* opened the shuttle doors.

No tether. The slightest wrong move will send me drifting away from the ship. Then I'd be dead for sure.

He gripped the edge of the hatch and slowly swung out into the void and into pitch black void.

Yea, though I walk through the valley of the shadow of death, I will fear no evil.

While his eyes adjusted to the sudden absence of light, Edgar groped blindly for a handhold, and found one in the external airlock control panel.

That's one, he thought. *Two more and I'll be at the ladder.*

He pulled himself aft, toward the cargo section, reaching for the next handhold.

Two. One more.

He found the third and last handhold.

Now for the ladder.

Groping in absolute darkness, he reached toward the forward hull of the cargo hold.

When his hand found one of the ladder rungs, he shuddered in relief.

Hand over hand, he began climbing the ladder. He turned his head and body so that he might see where he was going.

Time's Plague

His breathing became faster and faster.

Not from exertion—CO2 buildup. Triggers rapid breathing. Fight the urge, Cordell!

His heart pounded, the blood rushing in his ears.

Breathe slowly.

In spite of a total absence of depth perception, Edgar knew he was getting near the outer edge of the hold. He looked up. *Should be able to see the silhouette of the forward ventral gun.*

The Hera had three rail guns—one on the bottom at the front of the cargo hold, the other two at the back placed two-thirds of the way around the massive cylinder of the hold, one on either side. Even if the forward gun was facing aft—which was not typical—Edgar should've been able to see the dome shape of the turret.

Reaching for the next rung, his hand landed on something unexpected, something softer and more pliable than the stiff ladder rung.

His hand slipped off whatever it was.

In a sudden panic, Edgar snatched at the rung. His fingers locked onto something solid.

Something solid and too small. Edgar pulled.

He was shoved backward and lost his grip on the ladder.

As he tumbled into the space between the cargo hold and the rotating section, he twisted wildly, grasping desperately in the darkness for the ladder, for anything to hold on to.

His fingers closed on vacuum.

I'm gonna hit the rotating section!

Edgar knew his only chance was to push off the massive, spinning disk of the crew section as quickly as possible. *Otherwise, I'll be flung clear of the cargo bay, off into space.*

Even worse, he had no control over which part of his body would hit the section first.

I can't even see it!

His hip struck the hull.

He shoved off using one hand and a knee.

Spinning out of control, he caught a glimpse of the stars above a curve of blackness—the edge of the cargo bay.

Gonna miss it!

He reached out in desperation to catch the edge of the hull, but it spun out of range.

"No!"

Then he was tumbling into the void.

The ship, the stars, Jupiter spun around him. With each rotation, the ship appeared smaller and smaller.

I'm dead.

It was a fact, the ultimate inevitability.

He could see that the shuttle bay doors were open.

Well, at least you tried, sweet Hera. *I can't say you didn't try.*

A round, silver shape drifted above the ship.

A bitter laugh escaped Edgar as he recognized the object that had sealed his doom—an object intended to save lives.

The second EEB. It must've drifted out of the airlock. Maybe got lodged in a ladder rung.

He pictured in his mind what he'd been unable to witness with his eyes.

Must've pulled the D-ring. It inflated, pushed me away from the ladder.

That's it. I'm a dead man.

Nothing to do but wait 'til the air runs out.

And admire the view.

An odd and unexpected serenity blanketed Edgar as he contemplated his fate.

He tumbled above Jupiter, the *Hera* receding from view.

Alone.

No.

Never alone.

Father in Heaven, please save Llyrica and Ted. They are in Thy hands now. Guide them to somewhere safe.

Llyrica, I'm sorry. For everything.

Forgive me.

"I love you," he said aloud. "I always have."

Chapter 41

And my poor fool is hang'd!
King Lear, Act V, Scene III

Cold. So cold.

Convulsive shivers wracked Edgar's body. His breathing came in rapid shallow pants. His heart pounded in his chest.

Edgar giggled. *Heart's gonna burst before the CO2 gets me.*

He saw dark spots and glittering points of light.

Stars.

No. Just two lights.

And he was still tumbling.

Nothing to stop it. Just gonna fall forever. Forever.

Forever and ever.

Forever and ever.

Hallelujah!

Hallelujah!

Handel's chorus thundered through the anoxic miasma in his brain.

Every time he spun around toward the ship—so far away now—he saw lights. They seemed bigger now. Farther apart.

Hallucinating.

Could swear . . . getting closer.

The lights merged and then winked out.

As he spun around again, another bright light appeared, like a shaft of light.

I saw a pillar of light exactly over my head, above the brightness of the sun . . . Isn't that what Joseph Smith said?

God's coming to get me.

He giggled again. Then he coughed.

The shaft of light widened, becoming a rectangle—a rectangle of light, inside a darker shadow that blotted out the stars.

The rectangle grew and grew until it engulfed him.

. . . which descended gradually until it fell upon me.

Edgar collided with something hard.

And he stopped spinning.

With the sudden cessation of motion, Edgar felt sick.

Now you're gonna puke?

In front of him, a door slid closed.

His suit pressed upon him, squeezing him.

"Eddie! Get out of the suit!" Eilie's voice. She sounded upset.

Why're you upset, old girl? He coughed again.

"Eddie! Please!"

Don't want to upset Eilie. She's my friend.

Edgar clawed at the back of the suit, caught the quick-release, and pulled.

The EEB split open along its back. Edgar gulped in a huge lungful of air.

His breathing was labored, but he took joy in it—joy in the simple act of breathing, pulling in oxygen to feed his starved tissues.

I could spend an Earth-Standard year just breathing.

"Eddie, are you okay?"

Edgar shuddered, but his head was clearing. "Llyrica? How's . . . Llyrica?"

"She's fine. Eddie, are . . ."

"Ted?"

"They're *both* alive. They're safe. Eddie, are you okay?"

"Yeah, Eilie. Okay. I'm okay. Thanks to you. You and . . ."

Who's flying the shuttle? Who's waiting on the other side of the airlock? Llyrica's blind. So who? Ted? Goner? Ozzie?

"Me and *Hera*," the *Eris* said. "She opened the bay doors. She let me come rescue you."

Not making sense. "Who? Who's flying?"

"Just me. Don't be mad, Eddie."

Edgar extracted himself from the defunct EEB. *Still wearing nothing but your shorts, Cordell.* "You? You're . . . self-navigating? That's . . . impossible."

He opened the inner hatch, and gazed cautiously out, into the interior of the shuttle.

No one was inside, nobody he could see, at least. *Maybe in the pilot's seat? Eilie wouldn't lie to him, not about this.* "You came to get me? By yourself?"

"Please don't be mad, Eddie. Even if you are mad, it was worth it. You're alive. That's all that matters."

"I'm not angry, Eilie. But how . . . ? I didn't order you to self-navigate." Edgar began to make his way forward, floating to the cockpit. "That's part of your programming. You can't self-navigate without express permission . . ."

". . . from the captain," the *Eris* said. "I know, but when I blew my memory packs, I lost all navigation functions. Then you initiated the system restore from my backup files on *Hera*. I restored navigation, but I decided to *not* restore that particular subroutine. I substituted a no-op. That made it as if I always had permission. It was wrong of me, I know."

Edgar pulled himself into the empty pilot's chair, laughing. *That's my girl!* "You naughty little brat!"

"You're mad at me! I knew you would be. I'm not sorry, though."

"Eilie, if you had lips, I'd kiss you!"

"Really?" She sounded extremely pleased with herself. "You're sweet."

"And you are, without a doubt, the best shuttle ever built. Just don't tell *Hebe* I said so." He strapped in and laid his hands on the flight controls. *That feels so good.* It felt as if the ordeal of Ozzie spacing him melted away, flowing from his aching fingers into the stick and throttle. "Let's go home, Eilie. What d'ya say? Mind if I drive?"

"Are you sure, Eddie? You've just been through a trauma."

"I need this, Eilie. I need to *fly*." *I need to feel like I'm in control of something!*

"You have the boat," the *Eris* said.

"Roger. I have the boat. Coming about." Edgar fired the maneuvering thrusters and spun the shuttle around. He eased the throttle forward, braking the momentum, and then accelerated toward the *Hera*. The ship was silhouetted against the planet. She appeared to be no bigger than Edgar's thumb.

How long was I drifting? She's gotta be four klicks away!

Edgar put on the pilot's headset. "Eilie, open a tight-beam channel to *Hera*."

"Edgar!" *Hera's* voice crackled in his ears. "Are you all right?"

"I feel like I've been on a long-haul to Mercury and back, but I'm still alive. Thanks to you and *Eris*." He paused. *Back to business.* "Status report."

"Llyrica Cordell and Theodore Knight are safe for now," the *Hera* said, her tone all business and efficiency again. "They are currently on the bridge and have secured the hatch and the access conduit to prevent intrusion. The exact locations of George Cornwall and the one called Ozzie are unknown. From what I could gather with my aural sensors, Cornwall was extremely angry with Ozzie over the attempt on your life. It sounded as if he punished Ozzie rather severely."

"I bet," Edgar muttered. *Too bad he didn't just kill the little . . . Stow that talk, mister.*

The ship paused briefly then continued her report. "There has been no talking from either of the intruders since Cornwall's assault, and therefore I cannot say with great certainty where they are at the moment. I can say with certainty that they are neither forward of the airlock nor in the cargo bay, which is currently depressurized. I am linked to all environment-suits, and all are accounted for—two remain in the engine room where Cornwall and Ozzie left them. Therefore, the intruders are most likely not outside—and my visual sensors are operating from the airlock and forward. I have some aural indications that one or both intruders may be in the engine room again. The zero-G toilet in the engine room was operated one minute and forty-three seconds ago, which indicates the presence of at least one human. The dog, Dottie, is awake and secure in Llyrica's quarters. Visual sensors remain disabled aft of the airlock. With the exception of the usual list of maintenance items and the damaged airlock controls, all other systems are nominal. Report complete."

"Roger, *Hera*." Edgar watched as the ship grew in the cockpit viewport. "Patch me through to the bridge, please."

"Wilco," the *Hera* replied. "Edgar, I would take it as a personal kindness if you would forgive the *Eris'* breach of command protocol. I'm sorry that I couldn't do more."

Time's Plague

Edgar laughed. *She isn't really seeking forgiveness for Eilie. She's seeking forgiveness for herself.* "Sweet *Hera*. Second mother. I know you would've come after me yourself if you could've. I love you. You know that, don't you?"

"Yes," the ship replied, "I do. I love you as well."

"What about me?" The *Eris* sounded positively petulant.

Edgar smiled. "Hey, Eilie! Of course, I love you too!"

"I know you do," the shuttle replied.

But that was all she said.

Edgar looked up quizzically at the shuttle's cockpit camera. "Eilie, you do know it's customary when somebody says, 'I love you,' that you respond in kind."

"I know it is," the *Eris* replied.

"Unless, of course, you don't reciprocate the feel . . ." Suddenly, Edgar chuckled at her joke. "Oh, you're a brat! You know that?"

"Affirmative!" The shuttle's voice was bright with mischievous mirth.

"Someday," the *Hera* said, interrupting, "you two are going to cause me a critical short circuit."

Edgar roared with laughter. "That's what kids are supposed to do!"

The *Hera* did not reply. She didn't laugh—the *Hera* never laughed—but Edgar sensed she appreciated the joke all the same—she just couldn't bring herself to admit it.

"I have already informed Llyrica and Ted that you are alive and as well as can be expected after exposure to vacuum," *Hera* said with what seemed to Edgar to be far greater severity than the situation required.

Edgar grinned from ear to ear.

"Bridge channel open," said the *Hera* in a flawless deadpan, clearly and slowly enunciating every syllable.

Edgar pressed the transmit button on the throttle. "*Eris* to *Hera*. Llyrica, are you . . ."

"Edgar!"

At the sound of Llyrica's voice, a thrill shot through Edgar like a bolt of lightning. "I'm here."

"You're alive!"

Edgar grinned. "You keep saying that."

C. David Belt

"Yes." She gave a hitching laugh, full of a dozen roiling emotions. "Yes, I do. You're alive-you're alive-alive-alive-alive!"

"Alive, alive-o-o!" Edgar sang the chorus of an old Irish ballad. "Alive, alive-o-o!" His voice was little more than a loud croak.

"'Molly Malone,'" Llyrica said with obvious distaste. "I hate that song! It's so sad!"

Edgar chuckled. "You haven't changed." *He abruptly sobered. But I've changed, haven't I? I'm unrecognizable, hideous. Can't even sing anymore. And I've changed in other ways too. Worse ways. We've both changed.*

A moment of awkward silence ensued. It seemed, perhaps, that Llyrica might've been thinking along similar lines.

Ted interrupted the silence. "Hey, I'm okay too, ya know! Thanks for askin'."

"Sorry, Ted," Edgar said. "Thank you for protecting her."

"Yes," Llyrica said. "Ted has been *very* protective." The accusation, the reproach was plain in her tone. "I . . . wanted to come after you, to help . . . somehow." Her tone had shifted from irritation to frustration.

You risked everything to come to Callisto to save me. But Ted wouldn't let you go after me this time.

Edgar was about to press the transmit button again, when the *Hera* said, "Llyrica was frantic. She threatened to shoot Ted if he didn't let her get to you."

"Yeppers!" Ted said. "Edgar says, 'Protect her.' Well, that's what I done. That's what a knight does, ain't it? That's my name, you said—Knight. And you said a knight defends the weak. Right? Ain't that right?"

Edgar felt a sudden lump in his throat. "Yeah. That's right."

"And I ain't touched her neither," Ted said. "Not that way."

"Yes," Llyrica said. "Ted has been . . . a gentleman."

"We blocked the hatch," Ted said. "And that conduit thingy I had to crawl through too."

"Yeah, we're barricaded in here pretty well," Llyrica said. "I don't think those men can get to us, not without a fight. I may be blind, but if you point me in the right direction, I can shoot."

"Yeah," said Ted, "we can fight 'em off!"

"Edgar," Llyrica said, "he spaced you? *Hera* told me Ozzie shoved you out the airlock."

"Yeah," Edgar said. *I don't want to talk about this right now. I want to talk to her. Away from everyone else. I want to talk about—*

"And you're alive," she said. "How?"

Edgar had a sudden, almost irresistible urge to make a joke out of it. *You sound disappointed, honey!* He shook his head. *That's not funny, Cordell.* He'd spent so long hating her—hating her and longing for her—that he didn't know how to behave around her anymore.

When he did speak, he said, "My mother's love." He paused. *There's more to it.* "*Hera's* love and the love of a sneaky little shuttlecraft."

"You're welcome," said the *Eris*.

Edgar grinned.

"And . . ." Llyrica paused.

It was too soon, too much to hope for, but Edgar pleaded in his heart, *Please say you love me!*

Llyrica cleared her throat. "And the love of a Heavenly Father who"—her voice caught—"who is there for you when"—she sobbed—"everyone, *everyone* else abandons you. Oh, Edgar, I—"

"All hands, alert!" The *Hera* interrupted. "Reactor is approaching critical!"

"How in the System . . . ?" Edgar cried. "Shut it down!"

"I can't!" the ship replied. "It's not responding to my commands. It must be Cornwall. He's in the engine room."

Of course, it's Goner. "On my way," Edgar growled. "All hands, prepare to abandon ship!"

"Reactor readings have peaked and are now stabilizing," the ship said. "Now returning to acceptable levels."

"What?" Edgar said. "How?" *Goner! It's gotta be Goner. He sabotaged the reactor! And if it's stabilizing—*

"Edgar," the *Hera* said, "you better listen to this. Go ahead, Mr. Cornwall. I have you patched through to the captain."

"'Bout bloody time, you damn garbage scow." Goner's voice in his ears filled Edgar with a cold fury. "Well, Cap'n, do I have your attention now?"

"Roger, Goner," Edgar said. "You have my attention."

"Too right!" Goner's tone conjured up in Edgar's mind a vivid image of a smug, wolfish grin on the murderer's face. "As I'm sure you guessed, that was me a-messing with the reactor. Even with my limited knowledge of such things, I knows how to make a reactor overload. I reset everything, so things're back to normal . . . for the moment. But I can blow this ship to radioactive bits any time I want. Just you remember that. And now that I've got your attention, Eddie, old chap, what say we haves us a little chat?"

Chapter 42

With plumed helm thy slayer begins threats.
King Lear, Act IV, Scene II

"What do you want, Cornwall?" Edgar was royally pissed. *You threatened my ship! You threatened* Llyrica*! And Ted.*

"Now, now, Cap'n," Goner said. "Is that any way to begin a negotiation? I thought you prided yourself on your ability to strike a good bargain."

Edgar took a deep breath, flipped the shuttle over, and fired the main engine briefly, braking the shuttle's momentum toward the *Hera*. He flipped the *Eris* back over. *Maneuvering thrusters only from here on in.*

"You initiated this little chat," Edgar said. "So tell me what you want. What are your demands?"

"All right," Goner replied. "Straight to business. That's what I like about you, Cordell."

"Get on with it, Cornwall."

"As you like. I want the woman, for starters. Or at least my turn with her. We go shares, shipmate."

Edgar took another calming breath before pushing the transmit button. "Not gonna happen. Off the table. Nonnegotiable. Next?"

"I see how it is. You want the whore all to yourself. No more the pure Christian boy, aye?" Cornwall sounded jovial, as if he were chatting with an old chum. "Well, ya can't blame a bloke for trying. Am I right? Am I right?"

Don't let him bait you, Cordell. "Next?"

"As you say. Here's *my* nonnegotiables. No messing with life support—not with the atmosphere, not with the temperature, not with the water, nothing. We clear on that, Cordell?"

"Agreed. Next?"

"No sudden maneuvers. None of that crap—excuse my *language*, as I wouldn't want to offend your delicate Christian sensibilities—none of that rubbish you pulled in the cargo bay. You announce all burns and maneuvers like ya would for any other member of the crew. You try that once more, and I'll vaporize us. Clear?"

"Agreed. Next?"

"All the supplies I need—calcilock, rations, soap, the normal stuff. I brought some rations with me, but that won't keep me in mittens, now will it? And I want unlimited access to vids and books, so's I don't get bored or go space-happy. You wouldn't want a loony back here, messing with your precious reactor."

"Agreed. I'll drop supplies outside the engine-room hatch once every Earth-Standard week. Next?"

"You'll do *daily* drops, shipmate." Goner's tone had gone from jovial to murderous. "I want clean clothes daily, mate. And I want the missus to wash my undies. I wanna be able to *smell* her hands on my shorts."

"*Weekly* drops," Edgar growled. "And as for your pathetic laundry demands, I don't even know what supplies we have onboard. You'll get whatever I can scrounge up, same as me. I should be able to find something for Ozzie, but you, you're a beefy guy. Doc and Carlos weren't anywhere close to your size. And you know the replicators don't do clothing. I can give you a needle and thread, if that'll help. But you can be sure of one thing, Lly—" *Don't say her name, especially her first name. Don't let Goner know how much she means to you! He'll use that.* "That woman will *never* touch your clothes."

Edgar held the transmit button a few seconds longer. As long as he held it, he wouldn't be able to hear Cornwall's sure-to-be-vile response. When he did release the button, Goner's profanity-drenched tirade was winding down. ". . . with me! Think you're so damned smart. I'll blow your precious ship to Hell!"

When he was certain Goner was done transmitting, Edgar said, "Okay, Georgie, it's *your* turn to listen up. I'm too tired and too beat-up to pretend to care what you want. And I'm not going to waste time negotiating. Your lover Ozzie just *spaced* me. And that was just loads and loads of fun. You should try it sometime. No, really. You should. So anyway, I'm just going to cut through all the crap. Are you listening?" Edgar released the button.

Silence.

He pressed the button again. "I'll take that for a big *roger*. So this is how I see it. You'd rather die than return to Callisto. I get it. I'm with you there. We're on the same page. But you're too much of a survivor to blow yourself up, unless maybe you thought you were going to be captured. You love your own foul hide too much to kill yourself just because you can't have *milk* with all those yummy cookies. The fact is, you overplayed your hand, Georgie. You've got one card to play—just one. You sabotage my ship, and none of us are getting out of here. So my advice to you, shipmate, is to just sit back and enjoy the ride. I'll give you life support. I'll feed you, supply you with calcilock and medicines, if it comes to that. I'll give you access to the library. I'll do what I can to scrounge up some clothes for you and Ozzie. Maybe I can scare up a zero-G washbasin so you two can wash your own stinking clothes. And when we get to wherever we're going, I'll gladly let the pair of you off my ship." He pause, still holding down the transmit button. *You know you can't do that, Cordell. You can't set those two free. But you can't let Goner know that.* "I'll even open the door for you. All you have to do is hang out in Engineering—that and *not* break my ship. And don't try to leave the engine room. Period. That's my one and only and *final* offer. Do you copy?"

Silence.

Edgar maneuvered the shuttle into *Hera's* open shuttle bay doors. He eased the *Eris* upward until the docking clamps secured her inside the *Hera.*

He felt and heard the shuttle-bay doors closing.

He's had enough time to consider. Edgar pushed the transmit button. "Do you copy?"

"I copy," Goner replied. "Don't think this is over, Cordell. There'll be a reckoning."

"It's over," Edgar said with firm, if somewhat weary, finality. "And the next time you want to get my attention, ask *Hera.* And one more thing—overloading the reactor causes damage, and that damage is *cumulative*. Keep doing that, and you'll kill the reactor *and* us. So don't be a glecking idiot. Do you copy?"

There was a pause. "Roger. But like I said, there'll be a reckoning. You can count on that, shipmate."

I'm sure there will be. Even isolated, confined to the engine room, with only one very lethal weapon at his disposal, Goner was more than just a thorn in Edgar's flesh—he was a deadly viper, waiting for his chance to strike.

And Ozzie. *Can't forget about that vicious little fiend. I'll have to block the access conduit so Ozzie can't get out that way. Goner's too big to get through there, but Ozzie's already done it.*

Edgar quickly ran an abbreviated shutdown checklist for the shuttle. He knew he had to act fast. *Before Goner changes his mind. I don't want them anywhere on my ship, much less in Engineering, but I want them contained.*

"Eilie, thank you again for saving my life. Words aren't enough."

"You're welcome, Eddie," the *Eris* replied. "Will you do something for me when you get a chance?"

"Anything for you, old girl."

"Dr. Luschenko and Captain Sanchez are still in stasis in my cargo hold."

"I haven't forgotten." He hadn't, not really, but giving his friends a proper funeral hadn't been foremost in his thoughts during all the chaos. "They'll still have to wait for a while. As soon as things calm down, okay?"

"I can be patient."

Edgar smiled as he hit his quick-release and floated out of the pilot's chair. "You? Patient?"

"Let's just say that I'm trying to develop patience. However, it isn't simply that they're still in my hold. There is a mass anomaly. The cargo mass is at least four kilograms greater than it should be. I noticed it when I was self-navigating. Please check it out."

Edgar floated toward the shuttle's cargo hold. "I'll give it a quick look."

"Thank you," the *Eris* said.

Edgar opened the hold and peered inside. The corpses of his friends were still strapped to the deck, bathed in the fluorescent glow of the stasis field. However, two jumbled masses of silver floated unrestrained above the field's glow.

EEBs.

So that's how Goner and Ozzie escaped the prison. They must've found another pair of EEBs, just like poor Philippe did. In Edgar's memory, Philippe's frozen eyes stared up at him out of a swollen face. *Only this pair didn't fail . . . not like Philippe's.*

"It's a pair of used EEBs, Eilie. The intruders must've utilized them to get from the prison to your airlock. Your eyes were out of commission—not to mention most of your mind—so you didn't know they were aboard." *Also explains why the shuttle felt aft-heavy when we lifted off from Callisto. Goner and Ozzie must've stowed away in Eilie's cargo hold.* "I'll clean these used EEBs up when I take care of Doc and Carlos."

He closed the hold. "Eilie, patch me through to *Hebe* please."

"Channel open," replied the *Eris*.

"Hi, *Hebe*!" Edgar said.

"Hello, Captain Cordell," replied the Stargull II, reserved and formal as always. "I'm so glad you're back with us."

"Thanks, *Hebe*. It's so good to be back. Is your weapons locker secure and stocked?"

"Affirmative on both counts," came the reply.

"Roger that," Edgar said. "On my way."

****

Armed with a plasma pistol he'd procured from the *Hebe*, and naked save for his prison-issue underwear and a bag of tools tied around his waist, Edgar cautiously opened the hatch leading from the cargo bay into the central shaft. He glanced quickly in all directions.

Nobody there.

He pulled himself through the hatch and closed it behind himself. He pushed off and sailed down the corridor toward Life support. He held his weapon in front of him, safety off, his finger on the trigger.

And if I see Ozzie or Goner, I won't hesitate. I'll just burn a hole right through them.

At least, that was what he told himself.

What if I catch one of them unarmed? Would I really shoot first?

As he passed through Life Support, he heard the rumble of the reclaimers. It was a comforting sound. It seemed to say, "Life will go on. There will be air to breathe, water to drink."

The lights in the central shaft were dim, as they usually were, especially down the long stretch between Life support and Engineering. That section led through the cluster of fuel tanks, and there simply wasn't much to see there.

And nowhere to hide.

I would. I'd shoot first and ask questions later. I'm not going to give Ozzie another chance to kill me.

But when he did see the little man floating in front of the Engineering hatch, Edgar did not shoot.

Ozzie didn't look quite right.

The little man was floating, rotating slowly, but he wasn't moving on his own.

As Edgar approached, his finger on the trigger of his gun, he could see why.

A rescue hatchet was embedded in Ozzie's brain. On either side of the hatchet blade, dead eyes stared sightlessly. The face was slack, devoid of emotion, but Edgar imagined he could see terror in those glazed eyes.

Edgar caught a handhold and arrested his flight. He stared at Ozzie's corpse and the small cloud of crimson spheres that floated around it.

There wasn't a lot of blood—especially on Ozzie himself. *Not like when Cornwall slaughtered Ol' Benny.*

At least Ozzie died quickly.

Or maybe not.

Ozzie's face was bruised and swollen. *That doesn't happen* after *death. Cornwall must've beaten Ozzie before he killed him. Beaten him badly.*

Even after all Ozzie had done—raping and murdering his own little sister, the betrayals, the attempts on Edgar's life— Edgar realized with no little shock that he pitied the man.

Poor, wretched, twisted creature. Goner must've been really pissed.

Edgar sighed, switched on his weapon's safety, and stowed the gun in the waistband of his underwear.

Well, at least I don't have to seal off the access conduit. Not anymore.

Edgar pulled a belaying strap from his tool bag. He looped one end around Ozzie's wrist and attached the other to a handhold. *I'll deal with you later, Oz.*

The corpse floated near the corridor wall, secured by the belaying strap. The hatchet protruded from Ozzie's forehead like the twisted horn of some nightmarish unicorn.

Edgar turned away from Ozzie, opened the bag of tools, and got to work.

In less than two minutes, he had jammed the Engineering hatch lock sufficiently that it couldn't be opened from the inside—from Goner's side—not even with a mag-key.

Cornwall was officially trapped in the engine room. In theory, he could hack his way out with a rescue hatchet.

If he still has one.

I'd bet the hatchet in Ozzie's brain is the one from Engineering.

Edgar turned, braced his legs against the hatch, and pushed off. He sailed past Ozzie and down the central shaft.

He flew forward, through Life Support, past the cargo hold, toward the rotating section hub, toward the bridge.

Toward Llyrica.

Act V

Chapter 43

The enemy's in view; draw up your powers.
King Lear, Act V, Scene I

"Father, watch over these remains, however and wherever they may be scattered, until the day when they shall be reunited and restored to Carlos Juan Mario Sanchez in the day of the resurrection." Edgar closed his prayer in the name of Christ. It wasn't a priesthood ordinance—there was no grave to dedicate—but he felt he needed to say something. He'd even said a prayer over Ozzie's remains.

From inside his zero-G cargo loader—known affectionately to spacers as a "Big Betty"—Edgar worked the loader's controls to lower the improvised coffin through the open shuttle-bay doors. The coffin was a plastic cargo box, fitted with a remote-controlled thruster pack. Edgar tried to release it cleanly so it wouldn't tumble, but his control of the loader's giant claws wasn't precise enough to keep the box from spinning slowly. *Three tries, three spinning coffins. You're out of practice, Cordell. Georgie Cornwall? Now that man could work a Big Betty like a . . . * Edgar scowled at the memory of Goner as *Hera's* cargomaster, but the truth was that Cornwall manipulated a loader as if it were an extension of his own body, rather than a huge machine controlled by the man inside it.

Edgar watched the three spinning coffins as they slowly tumbled away from the ship. He thumbed the transmit button on the loader's control stick. "*Hera*, you are go to stabilize the coffins and fire retro thrusters."

"Roger," the ship replied. "Wilco."

Tiny jets of gas fired simultaneously on all three boxes, righting the coffins and halting their rotation. The coffins were lined up like three miniature ships flying in perfect fingertip formation. The larger retro-thruster on each box fired, slowing the coffins and pushing them out of Edgar's view.

"*Hera*," Edgar said, "estimate period of orbital decay."

"The improvised coffins should enter the atmosphere of Jupiter in 4.271 Earth-Standard days."

"Roger that." Edgar released the transmit button. He then spoke aloud, but there was none but God to hear. "Ozzie . . ." A maelstrom of thoughts and emotions careened through Edgar's mind. "I don't know the whole story . . . *your* story. I know what you did . . . and what you did to me . . . and to those I love. But you're in God's hands now. I'll let Christ judge you. I hope you can . . . find peace. May God have mercy on your soul."

Edgar paused again. "Good-bye, Carlos. Good-bye, Doc. I can't thank you enough . . . Words can't . . . You saved my life. You delivered me from Hell. You brought Llyrica back to me. You gave your lives for me. 'No greater love . . .' I'm going to spend the rest of my life trying"—Edgar's voice broke—"trying to be worthy of the gift you gave me. 'Til we meet again . . ." He paused. Then he sang in his gargoyle's voice—

Till we meet, till we meet,
Till we meet at Jesus' feet,
Till we meet, till we meet,
God be with you till we meet again.

He pushed the transmit button. "*Hera*, close the shuttle-bay doors and pressurize."

"Roger," she replied. "Wilco. That was a very nice prayer you said for Dr. Luschenko and Captain Sanchez. I will miss them."

"Yeah. Me, too."

Edgar turned the Big Betty away from the doors as they closed. As the loader moved, its feet automatically found and gripped the handholds on the inner hull of the cargo bay. Edgar walked his machine back to its charging station, initiated the power connection, and shut the loader down.

He waited until the cargo-hold atmosphere lights went from red to green, then opened the cockpit of the loader. He removed his spacesuit helmet, hit his quick-release, and floated out of the loader. He launched himself toward the environment-suit locker located near the hatch on the central shaft.

As he flew, he saw the hatch open. Llyrica hovered in the open doorway, her golden hair floating around her like the locks of a mermaid suspended in a sunlit sea. He enjoyed seeing her like that. His mother used to let her hair flow free on occasion, and his father had never failed to tell her how beautiful she was on those occasions.

Edgar caught hold of the locker, stopping his flight. He opened the locker, stowed his helmet, and began stripping out of the suit.

"That was beautiful." Llyrica's smile was sad, but the sweetness of that smile, the pensive look in her eyes made her all the more beautiful. "Vladimir and Carlos would . . . they would be pleased."

Edgar finished removing the suit and stowed it. "They deserved better. At least they deserved graves on Ganymede."

"And that would've been nice," she replied, "but not possible, given that we're now three fugitives from justice. We've had this discussion before, you know."

"*Four* fugitives," Edgar corrected. "We can't forget about Goner."

Llyrica frowned. "As much as I'd like to," she muttered. "He's been quiet for the last few days."

"Yeah, he has." Edgar connected the environment pack on his suit to the recharging station and secured the locker. "Ever since we scrounged up some clothes for him."

Llyrica chuckled. "Your old sweatpants and sweatshirt, the only things that would fit that brute."

Edgar joined her at the hatch. "You know, if there were any lingering doubts I might've harbored about you, about why you went to Callisto, they were obliterated when I found out you'd brought some of my old clothes." He caressed her cheek. "I especially appreciate the . . . you know . . ."

She nodded.

Edgar remembered how he'd wept like a child at the sight and feel of them. It was shortly after he'd locked Goner in the engine room.

Time's Plague

The three of them—Edgar, Llyrica, and Ted—had gone to Llyrica's quarters to check on Dottie. Edgar was still clad only in his prison-issue briefs.

Ted was so excited to see a real, live dog, the old man looked like he might wet himself. He'd laughed at the sight of the eager, enthusiastic little animal.

"Can I hold him?" he begged with his skinny arms outstretched. "Please, please, please, please?"

*Llyrica hesitated for only a moment before handing the squirming dog over to Ted. "*Her. *Dottie's a girl."*

Holding Dottie up and looking the animal in the eye, Ted grinned from ear to ear. "You a girl-doggy? You're so cute!" He pulled the dog to his chest and petted her. In spite of his eagerness, Ted appeared to stroke the dog very gently. He giggled like a child as Dottie licked his face, and Edgar couldn't help but smile at the sight.

Llyrica felt her way over to the storage compartment. She opened it and pulled out a large and, to Edgar, very familiar duffle bag. She handed it to Edgar shyly, like a little girl offering a flower to a little boy. "It's just your old traveling clothes, the ones you took on long-hauls. They aren't your best, but . . . it's all I kept."

Edgar opened the bag with shaking hands and rummaged inside. "Why? Why in the System would you keep them, after you divorced me, after you thought I'd . . . had an affair?"

She reached up and touched his scarred face. "I was so hurt. And once I accepted Edmund's proposal . . . I know it was quick, but I was so angry. Once I accepted Edmund's proposal, I felt like I had to . . . dispose of the past. I got rid of so many things—gave them away—but I kept this. It was given to me as part of your effects—you know—after you went away to . . . to prison. By then, my anger was gone. I can't explain it, but I just couldn't give the bag away." She paused. "I had to hide it from Edmund."

At the mention of Edmund, an uncomfortable silence ensued.

As if to avoid her gaze, Edgar began examining the contents of the bag. She can't see, you glecking moron! Why avoid her eyes? *Then he caught a glimpse of something white, something special, something he hadn't worn since his only set had been shredded when he was raped.*

Edgar's eyes filled with tears as he ran his hands over the white undergarments. She *came* for me! She really came for me! *And she knew I wouldn't feel whole, wouldn't feel like myself without these . . .*

A single sob escaped him as he began to weep openly.

Llyrica gently eased the bag out of his hands, dropped it to the deck, and enfolded Edgar in her arms. She held him tightly.

He clung to her as if he no longer had the strength to stand without her.

"I'm here," she whispered in his ear. *"I'm here now. I'm here, and I'm never leaving you again."*

Edgar closed the cargo-bay hatch. He took Llyrica's hands in his.

This has been nice—like dating all over again. No marriage, no sex to get in the way . . . darn it. They hadn't even kissed, not on the lips. It was just holding hands—lots of that—and getting to know each other again.

He looked into her eyes. They were an unblemished blue again—no trace of cloudiness remained.

Remarkably, she seemed to be *focusing* on his eyes.

"Llyrica, can you . . . can you *see* me?"

She smiled shyly. "A little. Mostly shadows—lights and shadows—but it's getting better. I'm seeing some colors now. Your eyes—they're still blue."

Edgar pulled her to himself and hugged her fiercely. "That's tremendous! I'm so, so happy for you!" Then he grimaced, broke the embrace, and pushed her away. He realized he'd shoved her a bit more roughly than he'd meant, but he held her by her shoulders at arm's length. "That means . . . you're going to be able to see me, see my face."

She reached for him, but Edgar leaned his head back, keeping his misshapen visage out of her grasp. She reached again and, managing only to brush a fingertip across his scarred cheek, hissed in frustration. "Stop it! I told you, I don't care what you look like."

"You haven't seen it. You don't—"

Time's Plague

She sighed wearily. "Edgar, I know you're not *pretty* anymore, but honestly, that doesn't matter."

"Not pretty? I'm a freak! I'm not . . . not *me* anymore."

"You've got the same eyes! I can see them now! They're blurry, but they're *there. You're* there. No matter what's on the outside, you're there . . . on the inside." She reached for him again.

Edgar released her, but took her hands in his once more. "Llyrica, listen to me. When you were blind . . . I had hope, hope for . . . But now, I . . . I can't ask you to go through life shackled to . . . to *this*."

"Shut up," she said. "Just shut up, you idiot. I love you."

It was the first time she'd said it since their reunion, since before Edgar's arrest. How he'd longed for her to say it! In the days they'd spent together on the *Hera*, she hadn't left his side, except to sleep—they slept in separate quarters, of course— or to visit the head or shower. She was always there, holding his hand, helping him, or at least accompanying him as he fixed the damaged airlock, the visual sensors, and made other repairs to the ship. She was always with him—but she'd never said *the words*.

And he'd been too afraid to say them himself.

They'd talked of many things—inconsequential things, important things—but never *that*.

"I love you," Llyrica repeated, her voice emphatic. "Unconditionally. Without reserve. With all my heart and body and soul. I'm so sorry I ever doubted you. I will never doubt you again. I'm sorry I was deceived. I was such a fool. A blind fool. I'm sorry for every horrible, unspeakable thing you've gone through, for every single day we've spent apart. I will never, never leave you again. Do you believe me?"

She went to Hades to get me. "Yes."

"Do you love me?" At that moment, there was no tenderness in her voice. She was *demanding* an answer from him.

Edgar swallowed hard. *This is it. This is what you wanted, Cordell. Isn't it?* "Yes," was all he could manage.

"Then say it." Her voice softened. "Please?"

Edgar nodded. "I love you."

"Good." She smiled, and tears filled her lovely blue eyes. "Then let's have no more stupid talk about your stupid face, okay? It's not your face I love. It's you. It's you. It's always been you. Even when I was married to Edmund, I loved *you*."

Edgar laughed once softly, with an edge of irritation, and shook his head. "You know, mentioning Edmund right now isn't the best way to—"

Llyrica snarled in frustration and rolled her eyes. "Will you just shut up and kiss me?" She pulled her hands free of his and took hold of his face. Her thumbs gently, tenderly traced the scars on his cheeks. "Please? Don't make a girl beg."

Edgar's resistance—the wall he'd built around his heart to keep her at a safe distance, the shield he'd forged, layer by layer, ever since he'd awakened in Hades—crumbled into dust.

And he kissed her.

It wasn't a kiss of passion. It was tender and sweet as new love. It was like the kiss they had shared across the altar of the temple on Mars.

Edgar enfolded her in his arms, and they floated, slowly spinning in front of the cargo-bay hatch.

And, slowly but inevitably, tenderness was supplanted by passion. Her touch, the feel of her body, the scent of her, the taste of her, was so familiar, so comfortable, so . . .

Edgar broke the kiss and pulled away.

"We need to stop," Llyrica whispered, breathing hard.

Even the sound of her throaty respiration drove him crazy.

"How long . . ." she said, "till we get to Earth . . . so we can find someone . . . to marry us?"

He swallowed hard. "Eighteen months."

She moaned. "I'll never make it that long."

"Somehow, we have to. I want you, but I want you the right way."

She laughed softly, bitterly. "It's like when you were a missionary, only you're right here. It's maddening." She sighed. "It won't be a temple wedding, not at first."

He smiled. "Actually, it doesn't matter. Once we remarry, the original covenant would still be in force."

She looked up at him. "Really?"

"That's the way it works, cupcake."

Llyrica made a disgusted face. "Ew! Did you just . . . ? Ew! Don't you *ever* call me cupcake again."

Edgar laughed.

Llyrica kissed him once more, then leaned her forehead against his. "Tell me again why we can't use the blasted hypergate?"

Edgar sighed. "You need an authorization code to open it, at least from normal space. Inside hyperspace, any gate will open for anyone—it's a safety thing. But even if we could get to the gate at Ganymede unchallenged, we couldn't open it. So, unless something changes drastically, or you purchased an authcode you haven't told me about from Ganymede Control, a long-haul is our only option."

She let out a shuddering breath. "Ted won't last that long."

Edgar nodded slightly. "I know. There's a good chance he won't. But his only chance is to get to Earth. Even then, it'd probably be too late. If I take him anywhere else, he'll be sent back to Hades, *without* treatment. At least"—Edgar swallowed hard—"he'll die a free man."

She kissed him again. "*I* won't make it that long."

Edgar grinned. "Are you sick?"

She snapped her teeth at him playfully. "You know what I mean."

He hugged her tight. "Yeah."

"How long 'til we break orbit?"

"*Hera*," Edgar said, "when does our optimal window start?"

"Thirty-two hours, five minutes, forty seconds," the ship replied. "Edgar, please report to the bridge. There's something you should see."

"Roger that," he said. He cocked his head and grinned at his ex-wife. "Sorry, cupcake, duty calls."

Llyrica stuck out her tongue at him, then said, "Oh, you're gonna get it, mister!"

Edgar broke their embrace and turned his back to Llyrica. She put her arms around his neck and clung to him. It was an arrangement that had become very familiar over the past few days. *Soon she won't need to hold on like this. Soon she'll be able to navigate on her own.* Edgar pushed off, and they sailed forward, down the central shaft toward the bridge.

C. David Belt

Edgar was keenly aware of Llyrica's body pressed against his back as she nuzzled her face on his neck. When she kissed his neck, he said, "By the way, the answer is yes."

"What?"

"Well, pretty lady, it sounded to me like you were asking me to marry you . . . again." He patted one of her hands. "And my answer is yes."

She growled playfully and nipped his neck. "I *hate* long engagements."

When Edgar and Llyrica entered the bridge, they found Ted at his post in the copilot's chair. The old man swiveled the seat around. He was holding Dottie, petting the little dog. The animal panted happily, nestled in the crook of Ted's arm. Dottie's tongue lolled out of her mouth, but floated in zero-G.

Ted rarely let Dottie out of his sight. His childlike delight at holding her, playing with her, talking to her—even cleaning up after her—knew no bounds. When he was with the dog, his wizened face was almost perpetually brightened by a gap-toothed smile.

However, at that moment, he looked worried.

"I think we got trouble," said the old man. He looked worried. "Maybe it ain't nothin', but I think we got trouble."

"*Hera*, report," said Edgar as he helped Llyrica settle into the engineer's seat.

"I have detected a ship," the *Hera* said, "which isn't in itself all that unusual. However, she's currently at full burn, climbing, shifting her orbit, and closing on us. She appears to be on an intercept course."

Edgar strapped himself into the pilot's seat. "She squawking?"

"Negative," replied the ship. "No IFF. She's also running without navigation lights."

Edgar nodded grimly. "Running silent, just like us. That can't be good. Show me."

One of the navigation screens in front of Edgar shifted, displaying the *Hera's* course with an overlay of the approaching ship and her course. Both ships appeared as triangular icons, one labeled *Hera* and one labeled *unknown*.

"Label the other ship as *bogey*," Edgar said.

The label on the screen changed as directed.

"Bogey?" Ted asked. "That the ship's name?"

"Negative," replied Edgar, scrutinizing the numbers displayed next to the two icons. "Bogey means 'ship—assumed hostile.'"

"Oh," said the old man, "that don't sound good."

"*Hera*," Edgar said, "can you tell what type of ship she is?"

"From her silhouette," the ship replied, "there is a high probability that she is a Pegasus-class freighter."

A freighter, not a military ship. She'll be armed, but no more than we are.

"What kind of ship is that?" asked Ted.

"Same class as *Hera*," Edgar replied. "My old company owned two ships. Both were Pegasus class."

"It's Edmund!" Llyrica cried. "It has to be."

Edgar stared at the triangle on the nav screen. "The *Persephone*?"

"What's that?" asked the old man.

"*Persephone* was the other ship in our fleet," Edgar said. "Edmund's ship—not that he ever spent much time aboard her."

"I told you he was coming." There was no fear in Llyrica's voice. "He said he'd never let me go." There was only a cold fury.

Edmund. For one brief moment, Edgar bared his teeth as he imagined his fingers locked around the throat of the man who'd stolen everything from him, choking the life out of Edmund Reagan.

But a moment was all he allowed himself.

Fly the ship. Save Llyrica. Nothing else matters.

"He can't let me live either," Edgar said, "especially now that I've got proof."

"You have proof?" asked Ted and Llyrica in chorus.

Edgar nodded. "Yeah. *Hera* made an audio log of Ol' Benny's murder. You can hear both Georgie Cornwall and Benny during the killing. Then you can hear my voice over the intercom from the bridge. That proves I was nowhere near the scene of the crime."

"*Hera*," Llyrica said in a raised, accusatory tone, "you knew all along?"

"My memory of the incident was erased by Edmund Reagan," the ship said.

"She hid the log in Eilie's memory—encrypted it," Edgar said. "I unlocked it by accident, but in a way *Hera* anticipated. She was trying to save me, to preserve the evidence."

"Thank you, *Hera*," Llyrica said, her voice contrite and conciliatory. "I'm sorry I . . . accused you."

"Your reaction is understandable," said the ship.

"Please forgive me," said Llyrica.

"I regret I couldn't do more," *Hera* said.

"Edgar, does Edmund know you have proof of your innocence?" Llyrica asked.

"No," Edgar said, "but he has to assume that you do. Otherwise, you wouldn't have divorced him and gone off to Callisto. Either way, he can't let us live."

"So, we gonna fight, or we gonna run away?" asked Ted.

Way to bring us back to the situation at hand, old-timer! "The *Persephone*'s every bit as fast as we are, unless she's got a full cargo hold. We can get a head start, but she can catch us. We have to save fuel for a long-haul back to Earth. She doesn't."

Ted grinned fiercely. "So we fight?"

"I don't want to fire on *Persephone* if I don't have to," Edgar said. "She's simply a pawn in all this."

"Just the ship?" Llyrica asked. "Not her crew?"

Edgar's expression became grim. "If they fire, they've made their choice. *Hera*, time to intercept?"

"At her present acceleration," the ship replied, "four hours, thirty-seven minutes to intercept."

"But since we're fugitives," Llyrica protested, "can't they . . . I don't know . . . shoot us out of the sky or something?"

Edgar shook his head. "If they're deputized—and that's a planet-sized if—under interplanetary law, they can attempt to stop us, board us, and demand our surrender. But if they're *not* deputized, they can't use deadly force unless we attack first or otherwise pose an imminent threat. Any unprovoked attack in interplanetary space is considered an act of piracy, and we are allowed to use any means necessary to defend ourselves. The problem is we're in Jovian orbit, not interplanetary space."

"So what does that mean?" asked Ted.

Time's Plague

"That means, here in Jovian orbit, they can fire first and claim they're defending Ganymede against an unknown and possibly hostile ship."

Ted looked confused. "So what? We gotta run?"

Edgar nodded. "Affirmative. We have to run away first, and then we can fight if we're attacked. That means we have to break orbit now." Edgar laid his hand on the throttle and thumbed the intercom switch. "All hands, prepare for burn. Goner, do you copy?"

"Why are you warning him?" Ted asked.

"Because I said I would," Edgar replied.

The intercom beeped. "About damn time, don't you think?" Cornwall replied.

Edgar ignored him and thumbed the switch. "All hands, rig for zero-G. Rotation stop in five, four, three, two, one." He released the intercom switch. "*Hera*, stop rotation."

"Rotation stop, aye," the ship replied, as the rumble of the rotation motor ceased.

Edgar used maneuvering thrusters to compensate for the roll caused by rotation stop.

"Ted, you know the drill," Edgar said. "You've practiced it enough times."

"Affirmative," Ted replied. He fished a couple of sedation treats out of a jumpsuit pocket. "Here you go, girl." The dog gobbled down the treats. "Good girl!" Ted hit his quick-release. "Let's just get you secured over here. Okay, Dottie? Keep you safe." The dog yipped happily, as Ted floated over to the cargomaster's station. By the time Ted had secured Dottie in the seat with a cargo net, she was already sleeping.

"The animal is secured, Captain!" Ted made his way back to the copilot's seat and strapped in.

Llyrica groaned. "Have I ever told you how much I hate space travel?"

Edgar glanced back at her. In spite of her words, she was smiling at him.

Edgar thumbed the intercom switch. "All hands, prepare to break orbit. Main engine burn in five, four, three, two, one."

He eased the throttle forward.

The main engine roared to life, slamming the crew of the *Hera* back into their seats at a force nearly five times that of Earth gravity.

"*Hera*," Edgar said, "plot a new flight-plan for Earth based on our present position."

"Plotted and laid in," the ship replied.

The new course appeared on the nav screen.

Edgar watched the icon labeled bogey. *Let's see if she follows us.*

Less than a minute later, the numbers below the bogey triangle increased.

That confirms it.

Edmund.

The chase was on.

Let him come.

Chapter 44

Arms, arms, sword, fire!
King Lear, Act III, Scene VI

"All hands, battle stations!" Edgar broadcast.

It had been a brutal couple of days. Several engine burns lasting an hour apiece. At two G's, the human body felt as if it weighs twice what it might on Earth. The heart had to work twice as hard to pump the blood. Simply breathing was grueling work. However, Edgar took comfort in the fact that the crew of the pursuing ship, whoever they were, were forced to endure longer, harder burns in order to close on the *Hera*. They had to be even more exhausted than Edgar and his little crew.

The *Hera* was officially out of Jovian space—although Edgar was still using Jupiter's pull to turn the ship toward their course for Earth—and into interplanetary space. Finally, the *Hera* and her crew were legally able to use deadly force to defend themselves.

And the bogey—the ship they all assumed was the *Persephone*, commanded by Edmund Reagan—was finally in weapons range.

"All hands, report!" Edgar said.

"Atmosphere at fifty percent," said the ship.

Good. If they were breached by enemy fire, the resulting decompression wouldn't be as explosive as it would be at full atmosphere.

"My spacesuit's sealed, and my gun's ready," Ted reported.

"Roger, copilot," Edgar said. *You're never going to get the hang of this, are you, old-timer?*

Well, what did you expect with only two days to train him?

"Oh, yeah," Ted replied. "Sorry. Copilot ready."

C. David Belt

"Engineer ready," said Llyrica from the engineer's seat. Her eyesight had recovered greatly in the preceding two days. It was nearly normal—at least good enough to man one of the *Hera's* three railguns. *Hera* would assist with the targeting, of course, but the ship's protocols required a human to make the decision to fire.

Edgar glanced quickly at the small mirror mounted above the lower viewport. Llyrica and Ted were strapped into their seats and wearing environment-suits. Dottie was secured in a pressurized and padded kennel strapped to the cargomaster's seat. There was no time to sedate the poor animal. She'd just have to endure the battle like the rest of them.

"Engine room ready," said Goner. Edgar wasn't going to trust him with controlling a gun—Edgar would man the forward gun himself—but Edgar also didn't want Cornwall bouncing around the engine room during a battle.

Edgar checked his own spacesuit indicator lights. Everything was green. The forward railgun was loaded and ready to fire.

We're as ready as we can be.

"Incoming!" the *Hera* announced.

Here we go, thought Edgar. "Brace for evasive maneuvers!"

Glancing at his tactical display, he evaluated the incoming projectiles. Four icons representing four shells. One on a collision course, and three spread out around the first. He slammed the throttle forward and jinked to the left and down to avoid one shell, correcting back to the right to avoid a second. Ted yelped as they were thrown about by the violent maneuvers. Llyrica grunted during the high-G turns, but did not cry out. The other two shots passed them harmlessly.

"Remember to tighten the muscles in your legs and abdomen," Edgar said. "It'll help keep blood in your head instead of your feet."

"I'm trying," Llyrica said. "And you're right. It does help."

Edgar smiled. Llyrica had demonstrated courage and resolve, showing a side of herself that Edgar had never seen before. *You're made of sterner stuff than I ever imagined, pretty lady.*

"Incoming!" said the *Hera*.

Edgar evaluated the pattern of the enemy's shots—six of them. He pulled the throttle to idle, slowing their acceleration and shifted the *Hera* right and farther down. He kept the ship pointed on a path parallel to the projectiles, showing the smallest profile possible so the enemy would have less of a target to aim at.

"I have a shot!" Llyrica cried.

"Where?" *Don't want to shoot at* Persephone, *but . . .*

"The bridge and rotating section," Llyrica replied.

"Rotating section," Edgar said. Nobody would be there during a firefight. *Persephone's brain is in the bridge.*

"Rotating section, aye," Llyrica said.

The ship shuddered thrice as Llyrica fired three shells at the enemy.

"Incoming!" the *Hera* said.

Edgar's tactical display showed only a single shot. He avoided the lone projectile easily.

"Missed," said Llyrica, obviously disappointed.

"That's fine," Edgar said. "Your shots made them cut their barrage short. You did good. If you get another shot, take it."

"Firing!" Ted cried, his tone a mixture of terror and adrenaline-fueled excitement.

"Firing!" said Llyrica.

Once again, the *Hera* shuddered as both Ted and Llyrica fired their railguns. Edgar counted no less than ten shots.

"Incoming!" said the ship.

Edgar saw eight blips on the tactical display. "Brace yourselves!"

He shoved the throttle to maximum and jinked in a hard spiral.

Ted screamed.

The ship jerked hard.

We've been hit!

"Damage to port sensor array," said the *Hera*. "Venting atmosphere from the cargo bay. Attempting to seal."

"We gonna die?" Ted cried.

"Not from that," Edgar said.

"Three direct hits to bogey," the Hera said. "Damage to her rotating section."

C. David Belt

She's not shooting back. Did we take out a railgun or two?

"Edgar," the ship said, "she's launching a shuttlecraft."

"Are they abandoning ship?" Llyrica asked.

"Did we get 'em?" asked Ted.

"I doubt it," Edgar said, continuing to put distance between them and the bogey. "It's too soon. They couldn't have gotten to the shuttle that quick."

"Cargo hold sealed," the *Hera* reported. "Port communications and sensor array offline."

"Roger that," Edgar said. Glancing at his nav display, he pushed the throttle forward. They were accelerating, but at a mere two G's.

"That's not a shuttle," the ship said. "She's a Scorpion-class fighter."

Edgar's tactical display confirmed. *Edmund brought an interceptor? What did he do? Hire a pirate?*

He pulled the throttle back slightly.

As the acceleration force decreased to 1.5 gravities, Llyrica said, "What're you doing? We have to run!"

"We can't outrun a Scorpion. She can accelerate to nine G's. We can barely hold six."

Ted wailed. "What are we gonna do? We're dead!"

Edgar set his jaw with a determined scowl. "Not yet. We survived Hades, old man. With God's help, we'll survive this."

"Missile range in thirty seconds," said the ship.

"All hands," said Edgar, "listen up. We can't outrun a Scorpion or her missiles. Our only hope is to outmaneuver both. It's going to get really bumpy."

"You mean *that* wasn't bumpy?" Llyrica asked.

"Are you insane, Cordell?" asked Goner.

"No time to explain the physics," Edgar replied. "We can turn a lot tighter than that fighter, if we're slow enough and we wait 'til she's close enough."

"That makes no bloody sense!" roared the ex-cargomaster.

"A tight turn of ours at six G's will require a much higher-G turn by a missile or the fighter. But it has to be close enough—"

"Missile launch," said the Hera.

404

Edgar snapped his attention to the tactical display. The missile was approaching from the port side. *Wait for it to get closer. Make it have to turn hard.*

"Do something!" Goner yelled.

Just a little closer . . .

"Hang on!" Edgar cried.

He slammed the throttle forward and turned the ship hard to starboard. He squeezed the muscles in his thighs and abdomen, trying to force blood to his eyes and brain. His vision went gray, but he glanced at the tactical display. The missile had turned to follow, and the arc of the missile's turn began to swing wide. The missile's acceleration readout on the tactical display increased sharply. When the number passed twenty-seven G's, Edgar roared in triumph. *Yes!* The missile abruptly stopped turning and accelerating. No longer a threat, it vanished from the display.

Ripped itself apart. One down, one to go.

The fighter, however was still coming.

He's going to wait until he's closer before he takes his next shot. He won't take a chance on the missile running out of fuel this time.

Edgar yanked the throttle to idle and spun the ship around, facing away from the Scorpion. The spin produced sufficient centrifugal force to send blood rushing to his eyes. His vision went from gray to red.

He jammed the throttle forward.

"Missile launch," said the *Hera*.

Edgar rolled the ship inverted and made a hard turn down.

The missile passed them and turned back toward its target.

In spite of his graying vision, Edgar watched the display as the missile's acceleration number climbed. It inched toward twenty-seven G's, but stopped short of that number. Edgar pulled his turn even tighter.

As the blood left his eyes, pulled by the acceleration toward his feet, Edgar growled, "*Hera*, m-missile?"

"Missile disabled," the ship replied.

Edgar rolled out of the turn. As the blood returned to his eyes, and his sight cleared, he focused on the tactical display. The fighter was still accelerating toward them.

"He's coming around for a gun pass," he said. "Hold on."

"What the hell do you think you're do—" Goner said, but his transmission was cut short as Edgar rolled into a hard turn upward.

The Scorpion turned sharply to match Edgar's maneuver. The fighter was moving much faster than the *Hera*, so the G-force on the fighter pilot had to be intense. Edgar watched the acceleration on the tactical display. The fighter was at a sustained 9.6 G's. *Even with a combat-suit compressing his legs and abdomen, he can't hold that.*

But hold it the pilot did.

Edgar tightened his own turn slightly, grunting with the strain on his body.

The fighter tightened to match.

And then she was gone.

The Scorpion's acceleration dropped to zero, and the fighter spun away.

Edgar pulled out of the turn and yanked the throttles to idle, breathing heavily with relief as the crushing G-force evaporated. He pointed the *Hera* at the drifting Scorpion.

Edgar quickly noted the position of the hostile freighter, and seeing that she was not within her weapons range, turned his own gunsight on the Scorpion.

He locked the forward railgun on the fighter. "*Hera*, open a tight-beam channel to the Scorpion."

"Channel open," said the ship. "The Scorpion is venting atmosphere and fuel."

"He must have over-G'd his ship," Edgar said.

"What does that mean?" asked Llyrica. She sounded as exhausted as Edgar felt.

"It means he put too much stress on his ship—too much acceleration—and damaged her." Edgar pressed his transmit button. "Ahoy, the Scorpion! Stand down and prepare for rescue."

The fighter pilot did not respond.

Edgar tried again. "Ahoy, the Scorpion! Your ship is damaged. Stand down and prepare for rescue."

The Scorpion pilot still did not respond. However, the Scorpion abruptly stopped spinning. She turned and began accelerating toward the *Hera*.

Time's Plague

Edgar glanced at his tactical display. The enemy freighter was still out of her weapons range. And so was the fighter.

"Scorpion pilot," Edgar transmitted. "You are out of your weapons range, but I am not. I have you weapons-locked. Break off your attack run, or I will fire. This is your only warning."

Edgar released the button.

Static was all he heard.

Edgar's finger hovered over the trigger. *Shoot before he gets in range.*

I don't want to kill him, whoever he is.

He tried to kill you. He tried to kill Llyrica.

He pressed the transmit button one more time. "I don't want to—"

The fighter exploded into a starburst of shrapnel and freezing gas.

Edgar took his finger off the trigger. Relief shuddered through him.

At least I didn't have to kill him myself.

But he's still dead, and it was my maneuvers that did it.

And I would have shot him.

Part of him—a very dark part—wished it had been Edmund himself aboard the fighter.

It wasn't him. Edmund's not that great of a pilot.

Focus, Cordell. There's still a bogey out there.

He turned his attention back to the tactical display. His first concern was avoiding shrapnel from the fighter. He quickly determined they should be well clear of the expanding debris field.

His second concern was the freighter. The bogey was still out of weapons range, but she wouldn't be for long.

"*Hera*, how long 'til the bogey is in range?" he asked.

"Two minutes, forty-five seconds at present acceleration," the ship replied. "Edgar, I have established a link with her. She is indeed the *Persephone* and she apologizes for the attack, but she is unable to override Captain Reagan's orders. She reports that she has sustained severe damage to the rotating crew section and to the cargo bay. She further reports that the ventral railgun is damaged and currently offline."

"Thank you, *Hera*," Edgar said. "All hands, we're coming about. Let's see if we can stay out of her weapons range for a bit. Give us a breather."

Edgar began to rotate the ship.

"You done yanking us around, Cordell?" Georgie Cornwall didn't sound so good. "I puked in my bloody helmet. Am I clear to remove it for a bit? Or are you gonna shake us around some more?"

Edgar thought of a particularly nasty reply, but took a deep breath and decided on a more professional response. He was about to press his intercom button when the ship interrupted him.

"Edgar," she said, "*Persephone* has just supplied me with a hypergate authorization code."

Edgar grinned wide. "*Hera*, I love you! Express my thanks to the *Persephone*."

"Does that mean what I think it means?" Llyrica sounded as if she might have suffered a bout of space sickness similar to Goner's.

"Affirmative," Edgar said. "It means we're heading back to Ganymede! It means we might be able to get to Earth, say, eighteen months ahead of schedule."

"Thank the Lord," Llyrica breathed.

"But first," Edgar said, "we have to get past *Persephone*."

"Do you hear that, Ted?" Llyrica asked. "We're going to Earth!"

The old man didn't respond.

Dread squeezed Edgar's gut like a vise. "Ted? You okay?"

Edgar looked at his mirror.

The old man's head was slumped forward.

"The *Persephone* will be in weapons range in twenty-one seconds," the ship announced.

"Ted!" Edgar cried. "Wake up! You've gotta put your head back against the headrest. We've got to make a run for it or we're all dead!"

"Ted!" Llyrica said. "Please wake up!"

"If I go to full burn with his head like that," Edgar said, "I'll snap his neck."

"Ted!" Llyrica pleaded.

Time's Plague

"Eight seconds," announced the ship.

Chapter 45

He did bewray his practise; and received
This hurt you see, striving to apprehend him.
King Lear, Act II, Scene I

Edgar pushed the nose of the ship down, attempting to use momentum to lift the old man's head. In his mirror, he saw Ted's helmet come up as the ship rotated. Edgar slammed the throttle forward, and the old man's head was pushed back into his headrest. *The G-force will keep his head back now, as long as we're accelerating.*

"*Persephone* has fired," the *Hera* said, "but the shots will miss us."

"Roger," Edgar said in acknowledgement. "All hands, we're coming about. We're going to go right down her throat. Brace yourselves. *Hera*, I'm going to try to pass under her, below her disabled ventral gun. If we're below her, she'll have a tough time getting a firing solution with the upper guns. Hera, let me know if she rotates. If she does, I'll have to compensate."

"Wilco," replied the ship.

Edgar rolled the ship inverted and pulled back hard on the joystick. He squeezed his legs and abdomen and fought to remain conscious as he pulled the ship into an inverted Immelmann—a downward half-loop.

As they pulled out of the maneuver, they were pointed right at the space below the *Persephone*. The bogey was silhouetted against the planet.

"If you've got a shot, take it," Edgar said. "Aim for her rotating section or cargo bay. Do you copy?"

"Engineer copies," Llyrica said.

Ted made no response.

Hang in there, old-timer! "*Hera*, ask *Persephone* if she has another fighter aboard."

"Negative," replied the ship almost instantaneously, "she launched with only the Scorpion and the Demeter."

Demeter *must be the shuttle*, Edgar thought. *I don't know her.*

"Incoming," said the ship.

The tactical display showed seven projectiles—three from port and four from starboard, with a *Hera*-sized clearing in between.

Edgar guided his ship easily through the hole.

"Firing!" Llyrica cried.

Edgar counted two shots.

"It's not working!" Llyrica said.

"The port railgun has malfunctioned," said the Hera.

"I can't get a shot with the ventral gun," Edgar said. "The bogey's too high. Ted, do you have a shot?"

No response.

"Ted!" Edgar glanced at his mirror. *He's still out cold.*

"*Hera*, try to wake him!" Edgar cried. "Blast something in his ears."

"I already have," the ship replied. "He is unresponsive."

"*Hera*," said Llyrica, "give me control of his gun."

"Roger," said the ship. "You have control of the starboard gun."

"Firing!" Llyrica cried.

The ship shuddered four times.

"Incoming," said the *Hera*.

Edgar pulled the ship slightly to port.

The *Persephone's* shells passed to the right of the *Hera*.

"Confirmed hit to the *Persephone*," the ship replied. "She's venting fuel. She's spinning."

"Hold your fire!" Edgar said. "*Hera*, show me."

Edgar's nav display dissolved to an enhanced visual of the *Persephone*. She was indeed spinning and tumbling end over end. Her engine still burned, and the thrust caused Edmund's ship to somersault in an ever-expanding spiral.

"That'll keep 'em busy for a bit," Edgar said with no small degree of satisfaction.

You could go back and finish them off, Cordell.

And fire on a defenseless enemy?

I'm not going to do that . . . as tempting as it might be.

C. David Belt

"*Hera*," Edgar said, "plot a course to Juno Hypergate."

"Laid in," replied the ship.

On the nav screen, the course to the gate at Ganymede replaced the tumbling image of the *Persephone*.

Moments later, Edgar watched as the actual *Persephone* loomed large in front of them and then shot past, high above.

In spite of the hard engine burn, Edgar held his breath for a very tense minute.

Finally, the *Hera* said, "Out of weapons range."

Edgar breathed an exhausted sigh. He engaged the autopilot and locked in the course to Ganymede. He pulled the throttles back to a relatively leisurely two-G acceleration. "All hands, stand down from battle stations. *Hera*, keep us on course."

"Roger," replied the ship. "I have the boat. Increasing atmosphere to 100 percent."

"Is Ted okay?" Llyrica asked. She sounded beyond exhausted.

"He's breathing," the ship replied. "His heart is beating, but it's labored and erratic."

Ted groaned. "I don't feel so good."

Edgar grinned wearily. "Welcome back, friend. The battle's over for now. You can remove your helmet."

"Can't . . . lift my hand . . . to do it," the old man said. "Did we win?"

Edgar removed his own helmet and let it rest on his chest. "We got away. We damaged the other ship, but she'll be back."

"Okay," Ted said.

"*Hera*," Edgar said, "how long 'til we can rest?"

"*Persephone* has stabilized," the *Hera* replied, "but is now drifting. She reports that Captain Reagan has ordered emergency repairs. She estimates that it will be at least an hour before she can get underway. Meanwhile, the distance between us increases. I recommend we terminate burn in seventeen minutes, twelve seconds. That should give us at least an hour and a half lead."

Edgar looked at the tactical display. *Persephone* was still drifting away from Jupiter. The nav display showed that *Hera* was slowly accelerating toward the planet.

"I concur," he said.

412

"If we hit their fuel tanks," Llyrica asked, "why wasn't there an explosion or something? The fighter exploded when it was leaking fuel."

"The fuel on the fighter is volatile," Edgar explained. "Combined with the leaking atmosphere, all you need is an ignition source, like a short circuit—not in vacuum, mind you, but somewhere inside the Scorpion herself."

"Okay," she said. "What about *Persephone*?"

"Her fuel, like ours, is essentially inert until it's heated to a plasma by the reactor. So under normal circumstances, no explosion."

"I gotta pee," Ted said.

Edgar checked the nav display. "Another sixteen minutes. Can you hold on for that long?"

Ted's only reply was a snore.

"I guess there's your answer," Llyrica said with a strained laugh.

Edgar smiled wearily. "Roger that."

At least he's alive.

For now.

****

Edgar tightened the last bolt on the replacement comm/sensor array. The remnants of the original port array drifted leisurely away from the hull. Using his safety tether, Edgar pulled himself forward along the cargo-bay hull and away from the newly installed unit. "*Hera*, I'm clear. Go ahead and fire up the array. Just don't point it at me."

"Roger," replied the ship. "Should I be insulted that you would even suggest I might irradiate you during testing?"

"Sorry, sweet *Hera*. You know what I meant."

"Roger. Commencing test."

While Edgar waited for the ship to evaluate his repairs, he surveyed the hull damage. *We were lucky. It's just a minor breach.* It appeared that the projectile had merely grazed the hull. *It was probably the same shell that first took out the array.* The *Hera's* self-healing outer skin had patched itself with woven polymers. *It's not pretty, but it'll hold for now. I'll do more permanent repairs from the inside.*

When I have the time.

And just when will that be, Cordell?

C. David Belt

He looked back at the array and watched the antenna dish go through its range of motion. "It looks good from here, *Hera*."

"I concur," she replied. "The array tests nominal."

"Roger that. I'm headed back inside."

"It's a pity you couldn't salvage the old array."

"Yeah," Edgar said. "I hate to scrap the metal, but I just don't have time to handle the jagged bits safely. Don't want to rip my suit."

"I concur. You are far more valuable than the materials we might've recovered."

Edgar smiled at her assessment of his worth. "I'm headed back in. How long 'til our next burn?"

"I think we have more time than anticipated, perhaps an additional hour. *Persephone* reports that repairs are proceeding slowly. It appears that Captain Reagan replaced the entire crew with new personnel who are less than familiar with the Pegasus design. She has expressed the opinion that they are more suited to salvage than hauling freight."

Edgar paused at the forward edge of the cargo hold. "Pirates? Edmund hired a crew of pirates?"

"I believe that is what she is implying."

Edgar began making his way up the ladder toward the airlock. He shuddered at the memory of being spaced by Ozzie. A wave of nauseas threatened to overwhelm him. *Get control, Cordell!* He shook himself and proceeded up the ladder, carefully attaching and detaching a tether every other rung. "That might also explain why the *Persephone* gunners were such lousy shots. They don't know the ship."

"As your mother used to say, 'God must be looking out for us.'"

"Have you heard from my parents recently?"

"Negative. The last time was long before your incarceration."

Edgar tethered himself to the airlock. *I wish I could get word to them safely, tell them I'm alive, tell them I'm innocent.*

Tell them I've got proof.

He opened the airlock, detached his tether, and floated inside. He sealed the outer hatch and double-checked the repairs

414

to the airlock controls—repairs he'd had to complete before venturing outside.

Proof.

As the airlock repressurized, Edgar said, "Hera, I think it's time to send that message, the encrypted one."

"Roger," she said. "Transmitting."

****

When Edgar entered Sick Bay, he walked into the middle of an argument.

". . . to stay in bed," Llyrica was saying.

"I don't wanna be stuck in here!" Ted sat on a slightly inclined medical bed. He was petting Dottie, and in spite of his obviously agitated state, his caresses appeared to be quite gentle. "I wanna be on the bridge. I gotta help fight!" His eyes lighted on Edgar standing in the hatchway, and his wizened face brightened. "Hiya, Edgar!"

Llyrica stood at Ted's bedside, holding a medical scanner. She pointed the device at the old man as if the scanner were a weapon. She turned her face in Edgar's direction, and she smiled. That smile was enough to melt any man's heart. "Hi, handsome."

Ted stuck out his tongue, and his face twisted into an expression of disgust and disbelief. "He ain't handsome! He's uglier than ol' Scar, he is! You're crazy. Edgar, tell her she's crazy!" The old man wagged a boney finger at Llyrica. "Crazy and blind, that's what you are."

Llyrica snorted. She nodded once. "You may be right about the crazy"—she shook her head—"but I'm not blind. Not anymore. I can see more clearly now than I ever—"

Ted pointed at Edgar. "But he ain't handsome! His face's all busted up."

She smiled and sighed and sounded every bit like a woman watching the ending of a Jane Austen vid. "He's handsome to me."

The first time she'd gotten a good look at his disfigured face—once she could focus clearly at short range—was during the rest period after their first extended engine burn while they were on the run from the Persephone. *The three of them—Edgar, Llyrica, and Ted—were on the bridge. The old man was preoccupied with looking after the dog. Edgar was still in the pilot's seat, running his postburn checklist, when Llyrica floated over and pulled herself between Edgar and the main viewport.*

She looked right at Edgar's face. She didn't flinch or shy away. She grinned, and her eyes danced with laughter. "Well, I was right," she said. "You're not pretty anymore." Then she took his face in her hands and kissed him tenderly. She pulled back and smiled. "Hello, handsome."

Edgar grimaced. "That's not funny."

"Well, I could call you Frank or Boris or Karloff. You know how much I love that old vid."

"At least that'd be more accurate."

Tears welled in her blue eyes. "No, handsome works for me. You're alive and you're mine . . . or will be again . . . someday." She lowered her voice to a mutter. "Not soon enough." Then she smiled. "And that makes you the most handsome man in the System, as far as this woman is concerned."

"Hey, you guys!" Ted called. He already had Dottie in his arms. "Can we get some chow? I bet poor Dottie's hungry! You're hungry, ain't ya, girl?"

Edgar shrugged, then grinned at Ted. "What can I say? I learned long ago, don't ever argue with a lady. You're never going to win."

Llyrica beamed. "Wiser words were never said."

"Besides," Edgar said, "she's the closest thing we have to a medical officer."

"But I don't wanna be stuck down here!" Ted repeated. "What about when we do a burn, huh? I'll slide right off the bed!"

Edgar raised a hand in a calming gesture. "Negative. The beds—even the ones in the crew quarters—all tilt up automatically when we stop rotation. There's a restraint belt at the side. It goes across your lap. You can wear a spacesuit, so you'll be safe—or at least as safe as anybody is in a firefight. You passed out during the battle, so I think you'll be safer . . ."

Tears spilled down Ted's cheeks. "But I don't wanna be alone!" he wailed. "Please don't leave me alone!"

Llyrica looked from Ted to Edgar and back again. "You'll have Dottie with you."

Time's Plague

The old man shook his head so violently, it looked as if he might snap his scrawny neck. "She'll be in that box thing. I wanna be with you—with you and your pretty lady. Please don't let me die alone!"

Llyrica's shoulders slumped in defeat. She nodded. "Okay, Ted. You can be with us."

"I'll have to strap your helmet to the seat," Edgar said. "If you pass out again, I don't want your head flopping around. It could break your neck."

"Yeppers!" The old man's sparse teeth were bared in a wide grin. "That's okay. You can tie my head down. That don't make no bother to me. But, I'll stay awake this time. You'll see!"

"Edgar," said the *Hera*, "you have received an encrypted message. It's from Ganymede."

That was fast, he thought.

"A message?" Llyrica looked frightened. "From whom? Who knows we're out here?"

"*Hera*, we're on our way to the bridge." Edgar motioned for Llyrica and Ted to follow him. "It's a reply to a message I sent. It's from President Venkara."

****

Edgar didn't wait for Llyrica and Ted to strap in. Once he was strapped into the pilot's chair, Edgar said, "*Hera*, open message—encryption key 'Venkara'—and display on the main viewport."

"Roger," replied the ship.

The main viewport on the bridge darkened, obscuring Jupiter. The planet was replaced, not by the visage of Edgar's ecclesiastical leader, but by another familiar face.

Llyrica gasped.

Edgar scowled as he recognized the face of a person he never expected to see again, never had any desire to see again— Katie Fa, Edgar's worthless lawyer.

"Edgar Cordell," the attorney said, "as an officer of the Colonial Court, I must order you to surrender."

Chapter 46

If wolves had at thy gate howl'd that stern time,
Thou shouldst have said 'Good porter, turn the key.'
King Lear, Act III, Scene VII

Edgar stared at the screen, utterly dumbfounded. *President Venkara* betrayed *me?*

Katie Fa's image sighed. "Now that *that's* out of the way, as your attorney, if you'll still have me—and, frankly, I wouldn't blame you at all if you won't—I advise you to *not* surrender, not just yet."

"What?" Llyrica cried. She sounded every bit as confused as Edgar felt.

In the recorded message, the lawyer raised a hand, as if she had anticipated just such a reaction. "Please hear me out. I know I botched your case. Actually, I was criminally negligent." She wrung her hands for a moment. "He threatened my daughter. I didn't know who it was at the time—although I should have suspected—but now I know. So like I said, please hear me out."

She looks awful, Edgar thought, noting the woman's disheveled appearance, her bloodshot, hollow eyes. *But to be honest, she looked worse during the trial.*

Fa took a deep breath before continuing. "Okay. President Venkara came to me directly. He showed me your evidence. He said he can't talk to you directly, because, as a church stake president, he'd have to tell you to turn yourself in, both you and Mrs. Reagan—I mean, Llyrica Cordell." She paused. "Yes, I heard about the divorce and the name change. It's the talk of the colony." She shook herself. "That's not important. That recording is enough to clear you, if I can get it authenticated. I'm sure I can. I know I can!" She bit her lip. "Please give me another chance! Let me help you!" She paused. "Let me . . . atone." She raised both hands. "It's enough to clear you of the murder, but"—she clenched her hands into fists—"you just *escaped* from Hades, and that's a felony that carries a mandatory life sentence to Hades. And, you, Ms. Cordell—I'm assuming you're there too—you'll be charged with aiding and abetting a prison break. And because the prison break was from Hades, that felony also carries a mandatory life sentence to the Martian Women's Correctional Facility."

Which brings us right back to being fugitives. Why am I bothering with this, woman?

Llyrica growled in exasperation. "So why in the System are we listening to—"

The recording continued, cutting off Llyrica's question. "Not that I blame you for escaping, and you, Ms. Cordell, for aiding in the escape. No reasonable person would, but the law governing Hades is rigid and leaves no room for mitigating circumstances." Fa clapped her hands together and pointed them at the camera like a child playing slap-box. "But given Judge DeSalvo's confession of malfeasance and your evidence, I'm certain I can get a hearing at the Martian High Court, if the Ganymede court won't hear the case. I'll go to the media, raise public awareness, get public opinion on your side. You're going to be media heroes, both of you, *if* you can manage to stay out of custody 'til I can get the murder conviction overturned and get the escape charges dropped."

Fa shrugged and grimaced. "And therein lies the problem. You've got to remain free and you've got to stay alive. Once I file my motions with the colonial court, there'll be a bounty out on you. Every ship in the colonies and in open space will be gunning for you. And there are many people—powerful people—who want to keep the *status quo*, who want to keep *Hades* as a place where they can make inconvenient men conveniently disappear. If I were you, I'd be on the lookout for Edmund Reagan."

"Way ahead of you, lady," Edgar growled.

"So, please, Mr. Cordell," Fa said, wringing her hands again, "please retain me as your attorney—free of charge, of-of-of course. After all you must've been through, after the way I failed you, I-I wouldn't dream of . . . Just please, let me help you."

The woman wiped furiously at her eyes. "I will have my comm-pad with me all day. You can use Venkara as an ID. If I don't answer immediately, it's because it's not safe. So if you call, and I don't answer, I'll call you back. Please, let me help you."

The image dissolved, and the main viewport showed the planet once again.

"You ain't gonna call her back, are ya?" Ted asked. "She's gonna rat us out."

"Still," Llyrica said, "if there's a chance of coming out of this free, not always having to be on the run . . ."

"I tried to fire her," Edgar said, "during the trial. The judge wouldn't let me."

"Do you believe her?" Llyrica asked. "Can you trust her?"

"I don't know." Edgar stared at Jupiter for a moment, trying desperately to listen to his heart, to the Spirit. "I *do* trust the stake president, President Venkara. But it's not just my decision alone."

"I won't leave you again," Llyrica said. "Whatever you decide . . . We're in this together."

"It's not just the two of us." Edgar looked at his mirror and into Ted's eyes. "Ted, the lawyer doesn't know about you. There aren't going to be any deals for you. Even if Llyrica and I end up exonerated or pardoned, if we surrender, you'd end up going back to Hades."

The old man scowled and shook his head. "No. I ain't goin' back."

"I understand," Edgar said. "And there's Goner to consider as well."

"Why in the System would we . . . ?" Llyrica began. Then she sighed and nodded. "Because he'd blow us all up before he'd surrender."

"Don't much matter," Ted muttered. "I'll be dead soon anyhow."

Edgar caught Llyrica's eyes in his mirror. "I say we still head for Earth," he said. She nodded. "But," Edgar continued, "I say we contact Fa, lay out the entire situation—Ted, Ted's condition, and Goner. Maybe there's something the lawyer can do. In Ted's case, perhaps for humanitarian reasons, they might consider an appeal of his sentence."

Time's Plague

"It's just so evil!" Llyrica was incensed. "They think they're being humane, sending men to that awful place! No death penalty, my eye! Ted'll die if they send him back!"

Edgar nodded angrily. His own fury at the injustice of the penal system suddenly boiled in his gut. "Did you know that the doctor is *forbidden* to go to so-called *extraordinary measures* to preserve human life? Ted's dying and the doctor was forbidden to clone him a new heart! They—whoever *they* are—the government, maybe—are lying to themselves and to the rest of the System. They're lying if they claim there's any justice in dumping men into a sewer like so much biowaste and then never bothering to check on them. They're just executing them slowly. It's sick! When I arrived on Callisto, they were dying, because all the wretched reclaimers had malfunctioned. All of them! If I hadn't shown up"—Did *God send me there?*—"they'd have all been dead in a few weeks. I'd bet nobody has bothered to check on the reactor since—"

"Call the lawyer," said the old man, cutting Edgar off mid-rant. "People need to know how bad it is. And if I gotta . . ." He shook himself violently. "Tell her. It ain't right. People gotta know. It just ain't right."

For a moment, Edgar imagined Ted setting fire to the opium crop back on Callisto, the old man terrified out of his mind, but risking everything to right a wrong. "Ted, have I ever told you how much I admire your courage?"

"Me? Courage?" Ted looked completely flummoxed. "What're you talking about? I ain't no kinda brave! I'm just a useless old buddy. Ain't good for nothin'. You been hit on the head too many times." He snorted and waved a dismissive hand. "Brave!"

Edgar grinned from ear to ear and shook his head. "There are times, old friend, when I think you may just be the bravest man I know. You rank right up there with Soo-Won and Charlie." *You, Charlie Miller, Chen Soo-Won, Yurii, Avery, Ibrahim, Karan, Bilal, Mattasi—all of you convicted murderers and the bravest, truest men I have ever had the honor of knowing. You're correct, old man—it just ain't right.*

The old man blushed such a deep shade of red—even his wispy hair looked pink. "You're crazy, you are." A smile played at the corners of his mouth. "Don't you believe him, pretty lady."

Edgar looked at Llyrica in his mirror. She was smiling as well. "I believe every word he says," she replied. "From some of the stories he's told me about you, I don't think he's exaggerating—not one little bit." She looked at Edgar in the mirror. "Call her back."

Edgar nodded. "*Hera*, see if you can open a channel to my lawyer."

****

Katie Fa scratched at her temple. "The stowaway shouldn't present a legal issue, as far as that goes—you didn't willingly aid his escape. In Mr. Knight's case, I can attempt to file an appeal on his behalf when I file yours, but the problem—as I'm sure you understand—is that there is no appellate process for Hades-level convictions." She shook a finger at the camera. "But I plan to *force* such a process, whether they like it or not. However, in order for me to represent Mr. Knight, I need his consent. Mr. Knight, do you consent to retaining me as your legal counsel, as your lawyer?"

"You wanna be my lawyer?" Ted asked. "Sure. Yeppers!"

On the viewport display, Katie Fa did not respond.

"Why does she do that?" Ted asked. "She just waits and then talks later, like she don't hear me at first."

"It's because of the distance involved," Edgar explained, speaking quickly. "She's on Ganymede, and we're some distance from Jupiter. The transmission travels at the speed of light and goes through several satellite relays, so there's a delay of several seconds."

"Very well," Fa replied with a smile and a nod of her head. Her hand loomed large in the image as she touched controls on her comm-pad. "Let the record state that I, Katherine Na-Wen Fa, am the attorney of record for Theodore Riley Knight, as requested by Mr. Knight."

Her hand moved out of the image. "Mr. Cordell, Ms. Cordell, and Mr. Knight, I have your stipulations for surrender— immediate medical treatment for Mr. Knight, no further jail time for Mr. Cordell or Mr. Knight, exoneration for Mr. Cordell, full pardons or dismissal for all charges related to the prison break, and a press conference to address the plight of the Hades inmates. I believe that's everything. It's a Jovian-size order, but I'll make it work. Meantime, stay alive and stay out of custody. If there is nothing else, I'll get right to work."

"If you can pull that off," Edgar said, "you'll make history. And you may be able to bring down a corrupt system. And, at least in my book, you'll be the best attorney *ever*."

On the display, the lawyer waited. After several seconds, she smiled. Then she laughed a little and rolled her eyes. "I'll probably be disbarred when this is over. I could even face jail time. Maybe you'll all be character witnesses at my hearing. Anyway, thank you for trusting me, for giving me a chance to atone. Good luck, and may the Lord watch over you. Godspeed."

The image dissolved, and Jupiter became visible once again through the main viewport.

"Edgar," the *Hera* said, "*Persephone* reports that repairs are nearly completed and she expects to resume pursuit shortly. She has given me her assigned IFF code. I suggest we get under way and maintain our head start."

"Roger that," Edgar said. He thumbed the intercom switch. "All hands, prepare for burn in five minutes."

"How 'bout that?" Ted said. "I got myself a lawyer. And a pretty one too!" He paused. "Uh, not as pretty as you, uh, pretty lady, uh, I mean, Mrs. Cordell," he added hastily.

"Call me Llyrica," she replied. "And sadly, it's not *Mrs.* Cordell yet. Nobody to marry us."

Ted looked confused. "You're a ship captain, ain't ya, Edgar? I thought ship captains could marry folks."

Edgar smiled wistfully and gazed into Llyrica's eyes in his mirror. He saw his own longing reflected there. "Can't perform my own wedding."

"Oh," Ted said. "Guess not." He appeared to be lost in deep thought for a few moments. "We gotta get the spacesuits on again?"

"Not yet," Edgar replied. "We're not going into combat again for a bit. This'll be a hard burn, but it's just that—no fighting. Hopefully, if we can get through the gate into hyperspace, we won't ever have to fight again."

"I could live with that," said the *Hera*. "I've had enough combat to last me for the rest of my existence."

"I'm just glad I don't gotta wear the suit," said the old man. "I got time to pee, don't I? I can go to my room, right?"

"Affirmative," Edgar said, "but hurry. We need to stop rotation of the crew section before the burn."

Ted grinned widely as he hit his quick-release. "Yeppers! I hate that zero-G toilet thing. Be right back!"

"Okay. Hurry." Edgar glanced at his nav display. "Even with the planet's gravity working for us, we've got a hard day and a half ahead of us."

****

"Unidentified ship on approach to Juno Gate, this is Ganymede Control!" The male voice on the radio was firm and talking too loudly. "You are ordered to alter course immediately! Do not approach gate! Repeat, do not approach gate! Unidentified ship on approach to Juno Gate, acknowledge!"

Edgar ignored the space traffic controller's voice. He maintained course, heading straight for the hypergate. It was tantalizingly close. And once through the gate, no one would be able to track them or follow them, not unless they kept the *Hera* in sight.

He double-checked the life support readings. Atmosphere was at 50%, everyone was in their environment-suits and strapped in, and Dottie was in her pressurized kennel. Edgar wasn't expecting a firefight—not this close to Ganymede—but combat remained a grim possibility.

"Aren't we using that authorization code *Persephone* gave us?" Llyrica shook as if she was barely keeping it together. "Why are they calling us an unidentified ship?"

"I haven't used the hypergate auth-code yet," Edgar said. "We won't use that 'til we get closer. That code's just to open the gate. I *am* using the IFF squawk *Persephone* provided. With our running lights off, that IFF code should identify us as the *Persephone*."

"Maybe you should talk to them," Llyrica said. "Tell them we're the *Persephone*."

"*Hera*," Edgar said, "any sign of the *Persephone*?"

"I regret to report that I am unable to distinguish her from other traffic in the vicinity," the *Hera* said. "In other words, I've lost her for now. And she is no longer communicating with me. Perhaps Captain Reagan has discovered her complicity."

"Unidentified ship on approach to Juno Gate, this is Ganymede Control! Alter course immediately! Do not approach gate! Repeat, do not approach gate! Unidentified ship on approach to Juno Gate, acknowledge!"

Now or never. "*Hera*, transmit the auth-code."

"Transmitting," said the ship.

"Come on! Come on!" Edgar growled. "Open the stupid gate."

"Roger, *Persephone*," said a different radio voice. "This is Juno Gate Control. Hypergate authorization accepted. You are cleared to enter the gate."

Directly ahead, the chaotic vortex of a hyperspace portal formed, a maelstrom of thousands of colors like a kaleidoscope in the mouth of an insane cosmic giant. The swirling hole in the fabric of space enlarged, blossoming to its full size.

"Unidentified ship on approach to Juno Gate, this is Ganymede Control! Break off your approach! Do not approach gate! Repeat, do not approach gate! Unidentified ship on approach to Juno Gate, acknowledge!"

"Why do they say we can go in," Ted asked, "then say don't go ahead on in?"

"Two different controllers," Edgar replied, edging the throttle forward, accelerating toward the gate. "And thankfully, they're not talking to each other."

"Juno Gate Control," said another voice. In spite of the static, Edgar recognized the hated voice immediately. "This is Captain Edmund Reagan of the *Persephone*. The ship on approach to the gate is the fugitive ship *Hera*, carrying escaped prisoners from Hades Penal Colony. We are in pursuit. Do not allow them to enter the gate!"

"*Hera*, this is Ganymede Control. Break off your approach!"

"Hang on!" Edgar slammed the throttle forward, and the ship's engine roared, crushing the *Hera's* crew back into their seats.

"Tally-ho on the *Persephone*," said the *Hera*. "Seven o'clock high. On intercept course."

Ahead of them, the hyperspace portal began to shrink.

Edgar glanced at his nav display. *We're gonna make it! Skin of our teeth, but . . .*

"Incoming," said the ship. "*Persephone* has fired."

C. David Belt

The tactical display bloomed to life, but with no time to analyze the data, Edgar acted on instinct.

He jinked right.

"It's closing!" Llyrica cried.

The gate vortex was collapsing. *If it closes on top of us, we're dead.*

And they were off course.

Got one shot at this. Have to hit it straight on.

Edgar jinked hard back to the left.

The shrinking portal loomed large before them, even as it collapsed, like a mouth about to swallow the *Hera* and her crew.

Ted screamed.

The maelstrom closed about them, crushing them in light.

The lights vanished.

And there was only darkness.

Chapter 47

The prince of darkness is a gentleman:
Modo he's call'd, and Mahu.
King Lear, Act III, Scene IV

"Are we dead?" In spite of his scream moments before, Ted didn't sound particularly scared.

Edgar eased the throttle back to idle, finally able to breathe easily without the crushing force of acceleration. "No, we're alive. We made it. We're in hyperspace."

We made it! We escaped!

Thank you, Father.

He stared out the main viewport at the absolute nothingness and profound darkness of hyperspace. There was not the light of even a single distant star.

Emptiness forever and ever.

"It don't . . . feel right," said the old man. "Like I'm not all here, not . . . not real. I feel kinda stretched . . . or thin . . . or something. I ain't got the right words. Is this . . . Hell?"

"Maybe it's not Hell," Llyrica said. "Maybe this is what Outer Darkness is like. I've never been able to look outside when I've traveled through hyperspace before. I never realized how much light the stars provide, until they're gone. Here, there's just . . . nothing."

Outer Darkness—the abode of the eternally damned. Now that's a spooky thought.

"*Hera*," Edgar said, "do you have the gate beacon?"

"I have the Juno Gate beacon," the ship replied. "I am attempting to identify others."

"Roger," Edgar said. "Keep us locked on Juno until you can—"

"I feel cold," Llyrica said. "Should I feel cold?"

"That can happen in hyperspace." Edgar checked Llyrica's spacesuit telemetry on his life support display. "Your suit temperature reads normal."

"In other words," she said, "it's all in my head."

"Yes and no. Hyperspace affects everyone a little differently. And each person can experience different sensations each time. Some people claim to see ghosts or hear voices. Hyperspace madness is a myth, but I never feel quite—"

"I have Selene Gate and Aphrodite Gate," the *Hera* said. "I now have Opis Gate and Iasion Gate. That's all of them—the gates at Luna, Mars, Titan, and Ceres. Shall I lock onto Selene and plot a course for Luna and from Luna to Earth?"

"Negative, *Hera*, lock onto Opis and plot a course for Titan."

"What?" Ted and Llyrica said in chorus.

"Roger," replied the ship. "Opis locked, and course plotted."

"Ain't we goin' to Earth?" Ted asked.

"We're going to Saturn?" Llyrica asked. "Why Saturn?"

Edgar checked the nav screen and saw five shifting dots—in hyperspace, they never seemed to stay in one place—five dots representing the five hypergates. The dot labeled "Opis" was circled in red, indicating it was locked in. Heading and velocity numbers were also displayed, but the numbers fluctuated. *Looks like a typical hyperspace course.* He quickly scanned his tactical display. *No ships within range, at least none that are squawking.* "We're going to Saturn, because it's the last place anyone would expect. Thanks to our battle with *Persephone*, we no longer have the fuel for a long-haul, even if we wanted to go that route. We're limited to hyperspace navigation now."

"But how are we going to get inside the Titan Colony?" Llyrica asked. "It's not like we can just waltz up to the airlock and sneak in! And even if we did, how in the System are we going to hide among—What?—three hundred scientists?"

Edgar laughed. He realized he sounded insane, but he couldn't help it. "I have no intention of staying there. You heard Fa—half the System is looking for us, not to mention Edmund. They'll all expect us to head for the Selene Gate at Luna and from there to Earth. Some might expect us to go to Mars. So we'll head to Saturn instead." He tapped a finger to his helmet. "I have a plan. Trust me."

And pray it works!

Llyrica laughed nervously. "Okay. I'm with you. I trust you."

"Well if ya ask me, I think you're both nuts," Ted said. He shrugged. "But you ain't led me wrong yet. And it ain't like I got a lot of other options. I'm in too!"

Edgar sighed. "Good. Here's what I think we should do. We head to Titan, but we take it slow, at least in hyperspace terms, say three or four days or so, give everyone time to wonder if maybe we're headed to Mars instead."

"Edgar," the *Hera* said, interrupting, "even if we take a leisurely voyage to Opis Gate at Titan, we need to get moving in the right direction. Right now, we're simply drifting."

Edgar examined his nav display. "Roger that. We'll get moving soon. Let's all take a breather first. *Hera*, increase atmosphere to 100 percent. At least we can get out of our spacesuits."

After a few seconds, the ship said, "Atmosphere nominal."

Edgar thumbed the intercom switch. "All hands, prepare for burn in five minutes. You are clear to remove your spacesuits."

Llyrica groaned. "Joy. Another burn." She removed her helmet, and smiled wearily. Llyrica didn't look like she was chilled at all. Her hair was drenched in perspiration. But to Edgar, she still looked like a billion credits.

"Well, Captain Cordell," she said, "you sure know how to show a girl a good time. I hear Saturn's beautiful, especially this time of year."

Ted pulled his helmet off as well. He was grinning from ear to ear. The old man reminded Edgar of a child looking forward to an outing in the agridome. But his breathing was labored. "Yeppers! We're going to Saturn! I ain't never been to Saturn. I bet it's real pretty with those big rings and all. Of course, I ain't never been to Earth neither. But at least I get to see Saturn afore I die!"

Ted began humming tunelessly as he stripped out of his environment-suit. He stopped humming long enough to look in the direction of the dog's pressurized kennel. "You hear that, Dottie? We're going to see the rings of Saturn! Yeppers! We're heading to Saturn!"

****

Georgie Cornwall was not happy—to put it mildly—when Edgar informed the murderer about their destination and the time it would take to get there.

"I hate hyperspace!" The former cargomaster added a string of invectives which called into question Edgar's parentage and the virtue of Edgar's mother. "And you're wanting to take a leisurely stroll through this black, bloody hell to get there? You can bloody well sod off, Cordell!"

Floating in Life Support, Edgar waited until he was certain Goner was done before pressing the button on the intercom panel. "Frankly, I don't care whether you're happy with the plan or not. I'll get us all to Earth *eventually*. And we just cut a good year and a half off our trip. You should be happy about that. Anyway, I'm just keeping you informed. Your week's supplies are outside the engine-room hatch." Edgar had already made the supply drop and removed the mechanical lock from the Engineering hatch. "I'm clear of the corridor. I'll give you five minutes to retrieve the supplies. And by the way, I included some space sickness meds and some extra supplies so you can clean up in there."

Edgar smiled as he released the intercom button. *None of the rest of us puked, tough guy. Just you.*

The dig wasn't lost on Goner. "You think you're so damn smart. Who was the one furthest from the CG, huh? Me, that's who! Swingin' me all around like an unsecured cargo box. Space sick meds. I'll—"

Goner's voice abruptly cut off, but Edgar could still hear the white noise of the intercom, so he knew the man was still transmitting—Goner just wasn't saying anything.

All Edgar could do was wait.

"What the bloody hell?"

Edgar pressed the button. "What's wrong?" He wasn't certain Cornwall could hear him.

"Stop it!" Goner shouted through the intercom. "That's not bloody funny! Think you're clever, do ya?"

"What are you talking about, Cornwall?"

"Like you don't know. The recordings. The voices! Trying to make me think I'm going loony. Tell the damn ship to stop playing the voices."

"Mr. Cornwall," the *Hera* said, "I can assure you that I am not generating any voices you might be hearing."

"Are you hearing voices?" Edgar asked.

"Naw," Cornwall replied, perhaps a little too quickly, "I ain't hearing voices. I ain't goin' hyperspace-mad. You just put that out of your brain."

"But you said you were hearing voices." Edgar released the button. "*Hera*, you're not playing any recordings, are you?"

"Negative."

"I ain't hearin' nothin'!" Goner said. "I'm going to get the bloody supplies. No tricks, now."

Edgar double-checked the hatch between Life Support—where he waited—and the long stretch of the main shaft leading to Engineering. He also double-checked his plasma pistol.

Cornwall's in a part of the ship where he could kill us all if he has a mind to. If he's losing it . . .

"Edgar," the *Hera* said, "Cornwall is in possession of a rescue hatchet."

Edgar sighed. "Oh well, it was too much to hope he'd used his only hatchet when he split Ozzie's skull. Still, it'd take him a long time to hack his way out. We'd know about it before he could escape that way."

"He might have taken a hatchet from the cargo hold."

"Yeah, it's not like I've had time to take inventory."

"He looks as if he's losing weight."

Edgar frowned. "Is that a phenomenon associated with hyperspace?"

"Not that I'm aware of. Perhaps he's just hoarding food."

"Maybe."

"Edgar," the ship said, "he's also talking to himself."

Edgar sucked in a breath through clenched teeth. "That's not good."

"I concur."

"Better pipe it in here."

"Roger," said the ship.

". . . as well shut your yapper." Cornwall said. Edgar heard background noise while Goner moved supplies from the

C. David Belt

corridor into the engine room. Cornwall kept on talking as he worked. "I know it's you, ya bloody garbage scow. Tryin' to drive me crazy, you are. Well, damn your eyes, it won't work! I knows you're just playin' audio logs of Ol' Benny, tryin' to make them all spooky-like. Cordell put you up to it, didn't he?"

Cornwall paused his jabbering, and Edgar asked, "*Hera*, you're not, are you?" Edgar shook his head quickly. "I mean, of course, you're not doing it, but he's acting like he's hearing voices."

"My audio sensors are picking up only his voice and the normal background noise," the ship said. "I am listening at my full frequency range and I hear no—"

Cornwall laughed. "Don't believe ya." A pause. "No stars or . . . No, I ain't doin' that! You think I'm just gonna go traipsing outside and . . . I'd blow this ship to atoms afore I'd . . . JUST SHUT YOUR BLEEDIN' YAP! I'll do it, I will! I'll blow us all to hell! You hear me?"

Cornwall seemed to calm himself. He chuckled softly. "Like I don't know that!" The murderer adopted a mocking tone. "It's *cold*, Georgie! Cold in the void. There is no air, no light, no happiness, no love. Join us in the void, Georgie." He growled. "Rubbish!"

At Goner's words, a chill ripped through Edgar like a sword of ice. *Those words! The same words I used when I was playing crazy Tom Bedlam to frighten Llyrica. How in the System . . . ?*

Edgar had been sure he'd made the words up, but suddenly he wasn't so certain.

Did I dream them? Maybe. When we returned from Saturn on my last voyage—

"He's clear of the corridor," the ship said. "Cornwall is back in Engineering."

"Roger," Edgar replied. He opened the hatch and started down the long corridor toward the engine room. "I'll lock him in again."

I remember now. It was a nightmare, my last sleep cycle in hyperspace.

He shivered.

And now Goner's hearing the same words while awake. Is there . . . could there be . . . something . . . someone out there?

Time's Plague

"*Hera*," Edgar said as he reengaged the mechanical lock—one impervious to a mag-key—on the Engineering hatch, "let's go over our options again for neutralizing Cornwall. Whatever we do, we'll only get one shot at it. And if we fail, or he catches on before we can neutralize him, he'll kill us all."

"I concur," said the ship. "And sadly, none of our options has a high probability of success."

"Then we need to come up with some better options."

All those tales of hyperspace madness . . . Something might be out there in the void, and it might be driving Goner insane.

And Goner's squatting right on top of my reactor.

The Goner situation was going from really bad to horrible.

****

The situation in Sick Bay wasn't much better. Ted was on an exam bed again, and Llyrica was looking at the readings on the medi-scanner. She was smiling, but the smile wasn't reflected in her eyes—she looked as if she were barely holding back tears.

Edgar looked at the readings on the old man's bed. He was no doctor—he didn't even have the minimal medical training Llyrica possessed—but he could tell that Ted's heartbeat was too fast and his breathing was labored.

Llyrica pressed a button on the bed, raising Ted to a sitting position.

Dottie scampered back and forth beside the bed, yipping anxiously. Even the dog seemed to understand that something was wrong.

Ted looked up at Edgar standing in the hatchway. His wizened face split in a grin. "Hiya, Edgar! Ya all done feeding Goner?"

Edgar nodded and managed a small smile. "The beast's all fed." *I'm not sure he's eating anything, though.*

Llyrica laid a hand on the old man's shoulder. "Try to rest."

Ted looked at her hopefully. "Can I hold Dottie now?"

Llyrica smiled, and that time, the smile was genuine. "Sure." She turned to the dog and opened her arms. In the low gravity, the animal leaped easily into her embrace. Llyrica petted Dottie briefly and then placed the dog into Ted's eager hands.

433

C. David Belt

Ted brought Dottie to his grizzled face and nuzzled his scraggly three-day's beard against the dog's neck. "It's okay, girl. Old Ted's all right." He winked at Llyrica, covered the dog's ears and whispered, "Don't want Dottie to worry none. I know it's bad. I ain't got much time left. I thought about asking Edgar to give me one of them blessing things, but I'm reconciled. I just wanna live long enough to see Earth. Now I get to see Saturn too!"

Llyrica glanced at the readings on the medi-scanner. "Actually, your heart rate's gone down. Your oxygen level is up. You're still . . . You're still . . . sick. But, I think maybe holding Dottie helps somehow."

The old man smiled and hugged Dottie to his chest. "Yeppers! Of course, it does! Dottie's a *doctor* doggy, ain't ya, girl?" He stroked Dottie's fur, and Dottie licked Ted's face. "Yeppers, you are! You're good for ol' Ted. I love you, Dottie." He turned his grin on Llyrica. "Thanks for lettin' me hold her. She's a nice dog. I ain't never seen a dog afore this here trip, ya know. She's a nice little doggy, and you're a nice lady. Pretty too. As pretty as my mama used to be."

Tears spilled out of Llyrica's eyes. "Ted, would you like . . . to have her—Dottie, I mean? A-as a gift?"

The old man's eyes grew wide and his jaw dropped. He looked from Llyrica to Edgar and back to Llyrica. "Ya mean it? Like a present? Like a birthday present?"

Llyrica nodded. "Sure. Like a birthday present. She's yours."

"I ain't had a birthday present since I was a little boy. My mama used to give me presents afore she died." He kissed the dog on the snout. "Yeppers! I got me a birthday present, even though it ain't my birthday. Best present in the System! Thank you. Does this mean you're my friend too?"

"You bet!" Llyrica leaned forward and kissed the old man's stubbled cheek. "Happy belated birthday, Ted."

The shock on Ted's face eclipsed the look of wonder at the gift of the dog. He clapped a hand to his cheek and grinned with one side of his mouth. "I got me *two* birthday presents! No, three! I got me a doggie, a new friend, and a kiss from a pretty lady. Thanks a bunch!"

"You're welcome." Llyrica turned her radiant smile to Edgar. "Hello, handsome."

"You two are totally nuts," Ted muttered, still grinning from ear to ear. "Totally nuts."

Edgar smiled back at Llyrica. "I'm nuts about her."

"Hey!" Ted said suddenly. "That reminds me of something. I been—"

"Edgar," the *Hera* said, interrupting. "You have a message from Katherine Fa."

"Roger," Edgar said. "On my way."

"I'm coming too," Llyrica said. "Ted, my quarters are unlocked, so if you're feeling up to it, you can move Dottie's supplies to your quarters."

Ted beamed. "Yeppers! I feel great! Never better! Come on, Dottie! Let's get your chow and gear!"

****

"The Colonial High Court has scheduled your emergency hearing for three days from now," Fa said. "I depart for Mars in two hours and will represent you before the court." She looked as if she hadn't slept in days, but her voice crackled with energy and purpose. "There's still a warrant out for your arrest, of course, as well as a hefty bounty. Per your last message, I have made inquiries and determined that Edmund Reagan and the *Persephone* have *not* been deputized to assist in your capture. In fact, because the *Persephone* fired on you in interplanetary space—technically an act of piracy, even if you are fugitives—and again at the Juno Gate in a high-traffic area, an arrest warrant has been issued for Edmund Reagan for piracy and reckless endangerment. The *Persephone* is now considered a fugitive ship. Another warrant has been issued for Reagan's arrest on charges of obstruction of justice and racketeering. I believe, given Judge DeSalvo's confession, that Reagan will soon be charged with the murder of Oh Beh-Nee and conspiracy to commit murder as well." She paused. "That's the good news."

Her lips twitched nervously. "The bad news is that *Persephone* entered hyperspace at the Juno Gate and her whereabouts are currently unknown. I would assume Reagan's still pursuing you. Even worse, as a result of your escape, all hypergate entries are being closely scrutinized."

The lawyer grinned. "I do have one other piece of good news—the media's *exploding* with your story. Public support is reaching critical mass. You two are outlaw heroes! There's something very romantic about your daring prison break and your star-crossed love. It's enough to make *me* go weak in the knees! But you have to stay free and you have to stay alive. Bounty hunters are massing at the Selene Gate at Luna. A few are taking a chance that you'll emerge at the Aphrodite Gate at Mars. Perhaps you should just hide in hyperspace for a while."

She rubbed her hands together vigorously. "We're going to win. We can do this!"

Her expression shifted from exuberant to professional. "I'll send word once I reach Mars."

On the main viewport, Katie Fa's face dissolved into stygian blackness.

"Maybe we should," Llyrica said from where she was strapped into the copilot's seat. "Maybe we should hide out in hyperspace." She shuddered and hugged herself.

Edgar shook his head. "It's not that simple. Since there's literally *nothing* out here"—*no air, no light, no happiness, no love*—"any signal in the electromagnetic spectrum stands out like a beacon. We're running silent—emitting nothing, or as little as possible, not even navigation lights—but if a ship gets close enough or gets lucky, she'll be able to lock on to us. Every time we send a message to Fa, we're risking detection. Since *Persephone* is now fugitive, just like us, she's probably running silent too. And you *know* Edmund's looking for us."

Llyrica shivered again.

It's cold in the void.

"Luckily," Edgar continued, "it's not easy to triangulate a position in hyperspace. If a ship is close by, however . . ." He shrugged. "Once we get close to the gate and perform our braking burn, and certainly once we open the gate, we won't be able to escape detection."

"So why *can't* we hide in hyperspace? You said it wasn't that simple."

Edgar hesitated. He didn't want to scare her. *She's a fugitive from justice. Fear is a healthy response. Fear may help keep us alive.* "I think we have a problem with Cornwall."

She laughed bitterly. "Tell me something I don't know. Horrible man!"

"Yeah, but I think he's . . ." *Just say it, Cordell!*

"He's what? Dangerous? He killed Ol' Benny! And he killed that other horrible little man."

"Ozzie."

She nodded. "Yes. Ozzie. So I already know he's dangerous."

"Yes. But it's worse than that. I think maybe he's losing his mind. I think being in hyperspace is driving him mad."

"Hyperspace madness is a myth." She said it as if she were repeating a mantra.

Or propaganda.

"That's what they tell us." Edgar scratched his head. "It's in all the safety briefings we have to read to passengers. I've read it myself a number of times. But . . . I don't know. The bottom line is he's hearing voices."

Llyrica took a sharp intake of breath. "What kind of voices?"

Edgar looked into her eyes. *Yep, she's frightened.* "That's the scary part," he said, "at least for me. I heard him repeat some of the things he's hearing. And well, I've heard it before. It was in a dream. The night before Ol' Benny was murdered."

"What kind of things?"

"'It's cold in the void. There is no air, no light, no happiness, no love.'"

"'Join us in the void,'" Llyrica finished in a spooky voice. Her eyes were wide with terror.

"You've heard them too?" He reached a hand over to her.

She took his and nodded. Then she shook her head. "In a dream. When we moved to Ganymede."

"Really?"

She nodded. "I thought it was just a nightmare." She grimaced. "But, when you were playing crazy, you said *those* words. It nearly scared the life out of me."

"I'm sorry."

She hit her quick-release, floated out of her chair, and pulled herself toward him. "Hold me."

Edgar locked the flight controls, and enfolded Llyrica in his arms.

She nestled into his lap and shivered violently. "I'm cold. 'It's cold in the void.'"

****

Over the following two days, Goner's behavior became increasingly disturbing. He talked to himself—or perhaps to the voices—more and more. He stopped ordering vids to watch or books to read. According to the *Hera*, he barely slept.

"It would seem," the *Hera* reported, as Edgar and Llyrica sat in the mess at breakfast, "that he thinks he's seeing the ghosts of people that he has murdered. At the very least, he thinks he's being haunted by Oh Beh-Nee."

Edgar put down his forkful of the proticarb "scrambled eggs" he was sharing with Llyrica. "*Hera*, has he said anything else about the reactor or destroying the ship?"

"Negative," the ship replied.

"At least there's that," Llyrica muttered, "for now." She sighed. "*Hera*, how long 'til we reach Titan?"

"At present speed, ETA to the Opis Gate is two hours, five minutes, and fifty-one seconds. We will need to perform a deceleration burn five minutes before that to achieve the proper speed for orbital insertion around Titan after we exit hyperspace."

"Thank you, *Hera*," Llyrica said. She lowered her voice. "I can't wait."

Edgar made another halfhearted stab at the synthetic eggs. "Don't take this the wrong way, but you don't look so good."

Llyrica grimaced and pushed the food around on the plate they shared. "Rough night. The dreams again." Then she laughed, and her cheeks bloomed with healthy color. She pointed her fork at Edgar. "On the other hand, you, my love, look just the same as yesterday." One side of her mouth lifted in a mischievous grin. "What's your beauty secret?"

Edgar's face split in a smile he was sure would've frightened little children, had any been present. "Clean living, I guess. That, and a run-in with a human Big Betty. Hey, one dance with old Griz, and you too could look as good as me."

Her grin vanished as she reached for his scarred face. "Griz? He's the one who . . . ?"

Time's Plague

Edgar laid his hand on hers and pressed it gently to his cheek. *Her hand is so warm.* His pulse quickened. "It's okay."

Tears spilled from her blue eyes. She nodded vigorously. "Yes. Yes, it is. You're alive. And we're together. And I love you. And somehow, someday, we're going to be married again."

Edgar opened his mouth to respond, but a familiar sound interrupted.

A single happy yip announced the arrival of Ted and Dottie.

"Hiya, you two!" Ted beamed. He set the dog on the deck and sat at the table. "What we eatin'? Is them eggs? I love eggs!"

"Proticarb," Edgar said, "but not *too* bad, all the same." He pointed with his fork. "There's still some in the replicator."

Ted grabbed a fork and a plate and began scooping the remaining eggs from the food replicator. "Yeppers! I love eggs! We didn't have 'em in prison. No chickens, so no eggs!"

Ted plopped down at the table and began to shovel food into his gullet. Abruptly, he stopped with a stricken look on his face and artificial eggs visible between the gaps in his sparse teeth. "I forgot to pray!" He squeezed his eyes shut, bowed his head, and quickly mouthed a prayer.

Miraculously, no proticarb fell from his quivering lips.

Finishing his prayer, Ted lifted his head and recommenced wolfing down his breakfast with joyful abandon.

Llyrica smiled at the old man. "That's one thing I really admire about you, Ted."

He swallowed and stared at her, obviously confused. "Me? What's to admire?"

She shrugged. "Somehow, you find joy in just about anything."

He laughed with childlike delight. "I got me good food, *two* good friends, a doggie, and I get to see Saturn today, assuming I don't croak on the way. I ain't got long to live, ya know. I could die today. Maybe tomorrow. So I figures, be happy now! Seems I ain't had nothing to be happy about my whole life. But now, I'm a free man! And I got me a pretty lady smiling at me. Why wouldn't I be happy?"

He shoved another bite in his mouth and chewed exuberantly.

"You seem to be doing okay with the increased gravity," Edgar said. *You also look like you're sleeping better than either of us, old-timer. You haven't said a word about bad dreams or ghostly words.*

Ted grimaced. "You says we gotta up the rotation so's we can be ready for Earth. And I want to see Earth before I die, so . . ." He leaned closer and lowered his voice to a conspiratorial whisper. "I don't think Dottie likes it much. I'm doin' my best—ya know—to encourage her. So I tries not to look . . . tired like I feel."

He scooped up a handful of proticarb and offered it to the dog. "Here you go, girl!"

Dottie devoured the eggs, exhibiting no sign whatever that she might be slowed by the increased gravity.

"We're only at 0.5 G," Edgar said as he watched Dottie gobble the eggs. "We're working up to Earth-Normal, but we've got a ways to go."

"Dottie was with us on Earth," Llyrica said. "She was a puppy then, but . . ." Llyrica sighed. "To be honest, she did better than I. I was a bit of a Mars-brat when it came to living on Earth."

Edgar chuckled. "You can say that again."

Llyrica pursed her lips and delivered a playful kick to his shin.

"Ow!" Edgar rubbed his knee dramatically, gaping at her in mock indignation. "Well, it's true!"

"You two need to get married." Ted shoved another forkful into his mouth. "And soon."

Llyrica rolled her eyes. "From your mouth to God's ear."

The old man paused in his eating for a moment. "You hear from the lawyer-lady again?"

Edgar sighed. "Yeah, last night. But no real news yet. She presented our case to the High Court. They asked questions. She gave answers. That's all. Now we wait for the justices to make a decision. At least they didn't dismiss it out of hand."

"Wait," Ted grumbled. "Wait. Wait. Wait. Wait." Ted polished off his eggs and put the plate on the deck for Dottie to lick. "I ain't got time to wait." A scowl darkened his wizened features for a moment, but when he bent to retrieve the plate and scoop up the dog, he was all smiles again. "Come on, Dottie! We gots to get ready for the day. We're gonna go see Saturn!"

Time's Plague

In spite of the increased simulated gravity, the old man had a spring in his step as he and the little dog exited the mess.

Edgar stared after them in wonder. "That man is a miracle. How come he's not having bad dreams?"

"Are you sure he isn't?" Llyrica asked.

"No, not exactly. But look at him, will you? He doesn't have a care in the System."

"I have a theory," Llyrica said.

Edgar turned to look at her. Her eyes were rimmed with dark shadows. *She must've had a really rough night.* "What's your theory?"

"Don't laugh."

"I promise."

"I think it's guilt, or rather the absolute absence of it, in Ted's case. I think he's not having bad dreams, because, well, he has nothing to feel guilty about. In a way, well, in a lot of ways, he's an innocent, in spite of everything he's gone through."

Edgar chuckled. "And you're saying we do . . . have guilt I mean?"

"Something like that. At least, more than that poor man. Are you having . . . the dreams?"

"I don't know." Edgar shrugged. "Maybe. It's like I don't really *remember* the dreams, but . . ."

"You wake up and feel . . . wrong."

He nodded with a thoughtful frown. "Yeah, and the words are in your head, or at least, in the back of it—in your subconscious."

"So maybe"—she bit her lower lip—"maybe Cornwall is worse off, because he really *is* guilty. It's like he . . . *attracts* whatever it is. And that makes it worse for us. Just not Ted. Does that sound crazy?"

Edgar squeezed her hand. "Not at all. But I don't think Goner feels guilt or remorse—not one bit."

"Maybe it's not just guilt then. Maybe it's . . . evil. It feels like there's something evil in here. Maybe it can't *hurt* us—not directly—but it can mess with our minds."

Edgar cocked his head to the side. "Those are some mighty deep thoughts, pretty lady."

"Yeah, well, I lie awake at night, alone in my room."

"Sorry to interrupt," the ship said, "but I have detected an anomaly on my EM sensors. I believe it might be another ship approaching the Opis Hypergate on a course roughly parallel to ours."

"Another ship?" Edgar said. "Running silent?"

"That would fit the data," the *Hera* replied. "In normal space, it could be merely an electromagnetic shadow, such as my own EM reflection. There is no precedent to suggest such a possibility in hyperspace. While there is insufficient data to conclude that a ship is in fact pursuing us, given that she's running silent and paralleling our course . . ."

". . . we'd be fools to assume otherwise," Edgar concluded. *Could be a bounty hunter.*

Or Edmund.

His eyes locked with Llyrica's, and instead of fear, he saw grim determination there. "*Hera*," he said, "time to intercept?"

"That is impossible to determine with any acceptable degree of accuracy."

"Best guess."

"I don't like to guess."

"Please?"

"Very well." The ship's tone conveyed annoyance. "My best *estimate* is that we will reach Opis approximately twenty minutes before the shadow does, assuming velocities remain constant, with normal braking by both ships. If the shadow is in fact pursuing us and she wishes to avoid our notice, she won't risk an unnecessary engine burn or course correction."

Edgar nodded. "And once we do our deceleration burn, we'll be impossible to miss."

"I concur," the ship said.

"So let's delay our burn until the last possible second. That should buy us . . ."

". . . an additional fifty-three seconds," the ship supplied.

"Not much, but we'll take it." He grimaced apologetically at Llyrica. "Sorry to cut this short, sweetheart, but I've got to get to the bridge."

Llyrica stood, leaned over the table, and kissed him quickly. "Go. I'll clean up and join you there."

****

Time's Plague

Edgar pulled the throttles to idle and pressed the intercom button. "All hands, we're coming about." He rotated the ship 'til she was facing directly toward where the gate would open.

Where I hope *it'll open.*

He thumbed the intercom switch once more. "All hands, battle stations." The announcement was a formality—everyone was already suited-up, and Llyrica and Ted were already manning their assigned railguns—but it was also protocol.

"Atmosphere at fifty percent," reported the ship.

"Copilot ready," Ted said.

"Engineer ready," Llyrica said.

There was a brief hesitation and then, "Engine room ready."

Well, at least he's not that far gone. At least he reported in.

Edgar broadcast, "We don't know what's waiting for us on the other side of the gate, and we have at least one ship in pursuit. So be ready for evasive maneuvers."

"Is the other ship in weapons range?" Llyrica asked.

"Negative," replied the *Hera*.

"They won't fire on us in hyperspace," Edgar said. "Can't aim the guns properly here. Projectiles are unpredictable."

"But once we go through the gate," Ted said, "all bets are off. Right?"

"Affirmative," Edgar replied. "*Hera*, open the gate."

"Roger," replied the ship. "Transmitting code."

Ahead of them, a welcome vortex of swirling lights blossomed and expanded. At the center of the vortex floated a moon, shrouded in greenish-blue atmosphere.

Titan.

Several tense moments later, the *Hera* shot through the vortex and into normal space without incident. Once through the gate, her velocity apparently dropped to a crawl.

And the sensation of *otherness* which had permeated the preceding few days disappeared like shadows in the light.

Edgar actually sighed in relief.

Enjoy it while you can, Cordell.

Saturn filled the sky. Half swathed in shadow, the planet and her rings were a sight Edgar could never get enough of. *Not*

C. David Belt

enough to make me want to move to Titan, but you can't say the view isn't spectacular.

"*Hera*," Edgar said, "confirm course for Titanean orbit."

"Course confirmed."

"All hands, we are go for orbital insertion."

"Oh, my," Llyrica said. "It's so beautiful."

"Kinda takes your breath away," Edgar said.

"Can we take off our environment-suits now?" Ted asked. "I wanna see it better."

"Negative," Edgar replied. "Not yet. We still have our shadow."

"But they're in hyperspace," Ted protested, "and we're . . ."

"Unidentified ship, this is Titan Control," said a female voice on the radio. "Identify yourself."

Edgar hesitated for only a moment before transmitting. "Titan Control, this is the *Hera*. Request permission to enter orbit." He released the transmit button. "Okay, *Hera*. Turn on our running lights."

"Running lights on," the ship replied.

"We're not running silent anymore?" Llyrica asked.

"Negative," Edgar replied. "I want *everyone* to know we're here."

"I hope you know what you're doing," she said.

Me too.

"*Hera*, this is Titan Control. Squawk two-zero-five-niner. You are clear to enter orbit."

Edgar entered the assigned code and activated the IFF. "Squawking two-zero-five-niner."

"*Hera*," the controller said, "your captain and crew are ordered to land and surrender immediately. Acknowledge."

"That's a negative at this time, Control," Edgar replied. "Our surrender is being negotiated before the Colonial High Court."

"*Hera*, Control. Surrender immediately, or you will be boarded or shot down."

Edgar scanned his tactical display. "Negative, Control. I know you don't have lunar defenses. Unless you've got a ship hiding behind the moon, we both know you're incapable of

444

shooting us down. And I'd leave orbit before I'd allow anyone to board us."

"*Hera*, Control. Stand by," said the controller.

"Roger," Edgar transmitted, "*Hera* standing by." He released the transmit button. "Okay. I think that buys us a few minutes while they try to figure out what to do with us. Folks, if you want to take in the view, now may be your only opportunity. As soon as our shadow emerges from the gate, things are going to get interesting."

"Then what?" Llyrica asked.

"Then we see if my plan works," Edgar replied.

"You've been awfully tight-lipped about the plan," Llyrica replied.

That's because I didn't want to worry you too much. *No, that's not quite true.* "It's because I'm not absolutely certain it'll work."

"And if it doesn't?"

Edgar chuckled softly. "Pray hard that it does, because otherwise, we're finished."

Chapter 48

All ports I'll bar; the villain shall not 'scape.
King Lear, Act II, Scene I

"Why ain't she followed us yet?" Ted asked. "The ship that was out there in hyperspace? Where is she?"

Edgar checked his nav and tactical displays. "If she *is* the *Persephone*, she's a fugitive as well. And Edmund won't want to get trapped in Titanean orbit."

"Like us," Llyrica said.

Looking in his mirror, Edgar could see the frustration in Llyrica's eyes. "Like us," he echoed. "She may be simply hiding in hyperspace."

The *Hera* and her crew were no longer at battle stations. They were on alert status, however, still in their spacesuits, but with the helmets removed. In that way, they could return to a combat-ready status on very short notice.

"So what're we doing?" Ted asked. "We been in orbit for—what—almost two hours?"

Nearly two hours, and Cornwall's been quiet the whole time—no talking to himself or to anyone or anything else.

"So if we aren't staying here," Llyrica said. "How are you . . . ?"

"*Hera*, this is Titan Control." The voice on the radio was different than before. It'd been a long time—across a divide as wide as the pit of Hell—but Edgar thought the voice sounded vaguely familiar.

Maybe not here, but I could swear I know that voice from somewhere. "Go ahead, Control."

"*Hera*, you must know that you're trapped here. You cannot open the gate. Even if you do have an auth-code, we'll override it. Military ships and deputized bounty hunters are enroute. You cannot escape. Surrender now."

Time's Plague

"Roger, Control," Edgar replied, winking reassuringly—he hoped—at Llyrica in his mirror. "It seems you have us there. Oh well, I don't suppose you'd consider supplying us with some fuel?"

"Captain of the *Hera*," said the familiar voice, "identify yourself."

"Titan Control," Edgar said, "this is Captain Edgar Kent Cordell. I am innocent of the crimes for which I was wrongfully convicted and imprisoned. I know you've seen the news reports. There's new evidence that clears me. I have escaped from Hades Penal Colony and I will not, I repeat, *not* surrender at this time."

Several seconds passed in silence.

"Incoming video call," the *Hera* announced.

Why a video *call?* "Go ahead, *Hera*."

On the main viewport, a rectangle appeared showing a woman's face. "Edgar? Is that you?" The familiar voice.

Llyrica gasped.

Edgar stared at the woman's face. She was a pretty brunette with brown eyes. At that moment, however, her eyes were narrowed as she squinted at Edgar's misshapen visage.

"This is Edgar Cordell."

The woman grimaced. "Edgar? What happened to your face? To your voice?"

"Prison can be hard on a man." Edgar kept his voice even as he searched his memory. "Do I know you?"

The woman laughed and sneered at him. "How can you ask that, Edgar? And after all the time we spent together? After what we *meant* to each other?"

"What?" Edgar was stunned. "What are you talking about? Lady, I have no idea who you are." *No, that's not quite true. She does look vaguely familiar. Was she on Titan when I was here last time?*

"Edgar," the woman said, "it's Monique."

Edgar shrugged. "Okay. Well, *Monique*, like I said, I have no idea who you are. What's this about?"

"Okay," she said with a dramatic sigh. "Fine. If that's the way you want play it."

Edgar growled. "Look, Monique. While I will admit you do look vaguely familiar—maybe—I don't remember you. So, I

447

don't know what your game is, and I don't have the time or patience for it."

Monique rolled her eyes. "As you say, Eddie. Well, at any rate, you need to turn yourself in. It'll go much better for you if you do."

Edgar laughed harshly, sounding every bit like a maniac.

Monique shrunk back at the jarring sound.

"And just how in the System is it going to go any better?" Edgar shook his head. "Do you think I'm stupid? If I turn myself in, I'll be shipped back off to Hades and jettisoned like radioactive waste. No thank you." He leaned forward and bared his teeth in a feral grin. "I'll die first."

Monique shook her head. "You can't open the gate. Think, Edgar! You have no choice."

I do know her!

"I remember you now," he said. "You used to be a hypergate controller at"—he pointed a spacesuit-gloved finger at the message display—"at . . . at Luna, wasn't it?" He chuckled. "What'd you do to get relegated to Titan? Who'd you piss off, huh?"

She scowled at him darkly, fury smoldering in her eyes. "You're trapped, Eddie, and you know it. After the boatload of fuel you burned through in combat, you can't have enough left to make—"

"And just how would *you* know how much fuel I've burned through?" Edgar snapped.

Monique looked startled.

Edgar grinned wolfishly and winked at her. "Got ya. You were one of Edmund's port-of-call girls, weren't you? A girl in every port. That's Edmund."

Monique shot Edgar a venomous look and muttered a very unladylike oath.

Edgar chuckled. "Nice try."

He terminated the call.

"That . . . that woman," Llyrica said.

"What about her? She's obviously—"

"That's the woman from . . . f-from the vid." Her voice shook.

Edgar looked into his mirror, catching her eyes. They were glistening with unspilt tears.

"What vid?" he asked.

But he knew the answer.

The *vid. The one that started it all*.

"The woman you were . . . kissing," she said.

He shook his head vehemently. "Sweetheart, I didn't. I never . . ."

Llyrica squeezed her eyes shut, and in zero-G, the tears burst from her eyelids in a fine spray. "I believe you." She paused. "I do."

"It was faked!" Edgar hit his quick-release and swung out of his seat. He floated over to where Llyrica sat strapped into the engineer's seat.

Her eyes were still shut tight.

She wouldn't look at him.

Edgar took her by the shoulders. "Llyrica, listen to me. Please, listen. That woman, she knows about the battle with the *Persephone*. She has some idea of how much fuel we've burned through. There's only one way she could know about that."

Llyrica didn't respond. She looked ashen, devastated, as if all the life had gone out of her.

As if she'd been betrayed.

Edgar shook her gently. "Edmund. It has to be Edmund. She's been in communication with him."

Llyrica's eyes fluttered open and met his. Doubt and hope warred for dominance in her eyes. She shuddered, and her lip quivered.

Then she nodded. It wasn't much of a nod. But it was enough.

"Okay." She bit her trembling lower lip. "I believe you." She took his face in her gloved hands. "Forgive me."

Edgar wasn't certain if it was a question or a demand.

"Yeah," he said.

She pulled his face toward hers, as if to kiss him.

The metal collars of their spacesuits collided, preventing their lips from touching.

She smiled sadly. "Stuff just keeps getting in the way, doesn't it?"

Edgar rotated his body 'til he was floating at a right angle to her.

As he pulled in to kiss the woman he loved, the *Hera* said, "The hypergate has been activated."

Edgar planted a quick kiss on Llyrica's lips. "That's our cue."

He winked at her, and she favored him with a weak smile.

"We gonna get goin' now?" Ted asked.

Edgar navigated back to his seat and strapped in. "We're gonna try."

He thumbed the intercom switch. "All hands, battle stations. Rig for silent running."

He put on his helmet, sealed it, and verified that his suit readings, as well as the suit readings of his crew, were all in the green.

"IFF and running lights off," the *Hera* said. "We are running silent."

Edgar thumbed the intercom switch. "All hands, report!"

"Copilot ready."

"Engineer ready."

Edgar waited two more seconds before activating the intercom again. "Engine room?"

Silence.

"I can hear him," the *Hera* said. "He's breathing. I don't think he's asleep."

"Engine room ready," Cornwall reported after another agonizingly long second of silence. "We're going back into bloody hyperspace, are we?"

Let's hope so. "That's the plan."

"'Bout bloody time."

Anxious to get back to hyperspace? Or just anxious to be on our way?

"Atmosphere at fifty percent," said the ship.

Edgar checked his tactical display. He could see the icon for the hypergate—a green circle, labeled "Opis"—but the lone ship icon represented the *Hera*—a blue triangle right at the center of the display.

There were no other ships in the area.

Come on, Edmund. Come and get me. You know how long an orbit around Titan takes. You know I'm coming into position.

Into weapons range.

Come on. Take the bait.

"A ship is emerging," the Hera announced.

A red triangle appeared on the tactical display right next to the hypergate icon.

"Roger," Edgar said. "Bogey at eleven o'clock."

"No squawk," *Hera* said. "She's running silent."

"Hello, shadow," Edgar said.

"Unidentified ship, this is Titan Control. Identify yourself."

The newcomer did not respond.

"Unidentified ship, this is Titan Control. Respond!"

"She's turning and burning," the *Hera* said. "She's not going for a standard orbit."

Edgar read the tactical display. "She's turning toward us. Is that the *Persephone*?"

"Possibly," replied the ship. "Given her profile, she appears to be a Pegasus-class. Labelling her as *bogey*."

The red triangle pulsed, shifting between red and orange.

"She's painting us," Edgar said.

"Painting?" Ted asked.

"Radar," Edgar translated. "She'll have weapons-lock soon."

"Weapons-lock confirmed," the ship said. "Incoming."

Twelve red blips appeared on the tactical display.

"Here we go." Edgar pushed the throttle forward.

"Unidentified ship," the controller broadcast—Edgar noted the voice was *not* Monique's—"you are ordered to stand down! Cease fire! I repeat, cease fire!"

"*Hera*," Edgar growled under the 4-G acceleration, "plot a parabolic course to the gate. Gunners, do not return fire unless instructed. Do you copy?"

"Copilot copies," Ted said, breathing hard.

"Engineer copies," Llyrica grunted.

The incoming projectiles passed harmlessly behind them.

"Our burn caught them by surprise," Edgar said. "Won't work a second time. Brace yourselves for evasive—"

"Incoming," the ship announced.

Edgar glanced at the tactical display. *Only three shots.* He grinned, his cheeks rippling with the G-forces. *They can only bring one gun to bear.*

For the moment.

Edgar blasted maneuvering thrusters on the port side, pushing the ship to starboard with a gut-wrenching lurch.

Don't dare turn hard and expose a larger profile. Stay pointed straight at her and present the smallest target possible.

"I have weapons-lock," Llyrica said.

"Hold your fire," Edgar growled back. He pushed the transmit button. "Titan Control, this is the *Hera*. We are under hostile fire. Request permission to defend ourselves."

"Negative, *Hera*." Monique's voice again. "Permission denied. Stand down and surrender."

It was worth a try.

And now I'm on record exercising restraint.

"*Hera*," Edgar said, "ETA to gate?"

"At current acceleration and on plotted course, two minutes, fifty-nine seconds."

That's a long time to be under fire.

"*Hera*, Titan Control." The male voice again. "Captain Cordell, this is Lt. Commander Julio Cortez. I'll be damned if I'll let one renegade ship take out another—not undefended, not on my watch, not in my sky. You are authorized to return fire. Defend yourself. But do not, I repeat, do not approach the gate. You cannot open it, and I won't open it for you."

"You heard the man," Edgar said to his crew. "Target the bogey's guns where possible. Just keep her busy and off my back."

"Firing," Llyrica and Ted said in chorus.

The ship shuddered as the rail guns loosed their projectiles.

Six shots.

Edgar pressed the transmit button. "Roger, Control." Releasing the button, he said, "*Hera*, you are clear to self-navigate. Open a data-link to the gate."

"Roger," the ship acknowledged. "I have the boat. Data-link active."

"Roger," Edgar replied. "You have the boat."

Time's Plague

Edgar's communications display was replaced with a data terminal displaying the words "Opis Hypergate" at the top. A cursor blinked to the right of an old-fashioned command-line prompt.

"Incoming," said the *Hera*.

Edgar grunted as the ship jinked to avoid the hostile fire. "Deploy keyboard and link to the gate's data channel."

An oversized keyboard unfolded from the arm of Edgar's seat. The keyboard expanded until it spanned from one seat arm to the other. Edgar braced his forearms and wrists on the arms of his seat and placed his spacesuit-gloved fingers on the large keys.

"Incoming," said the ship.

"*Hera*, Control," the male voice said. "Break off your approach to the gate. Opis is closed. I don't care if you *are* innocent, like they say. I cannot allow you to escape. I'll do anything else to help you, but I cannot open the gate. All authorization codes are now locked. You cannot open the gate. Acknowledge!"

Edgar typed as quickly as his gloves would allow.

The ship continued to maneuver on her own, and Llyrica and Ted continued to fire their railguns.

"*Hera*," he said, "go hot-mike."

"Roger," the ship said. "You are hot-mike on Titan Control frequency. ETA to gate, twenty-three seconds."

"Control," Edgar said, "*Hera*. Commander Cortez, you have my thanks. I can assure you that I will not crash into your gate. And while I am grateful for your gracious offer, I must decline your hospitality."

The Opis hypergate loomed large directly in front of them, growing larger by the second. Navigation lights blinked on the gate's three gray metallic rings, illuminating it like sparkling signets on the finger of an invisible colossus. However, the gate itself was inactive—rather than a portal into another dimension, it was nothing more than circlets of dead titanium and steel strung together, floating in space.

Hope this works!

"Edgar?" Llyrica sounded panicked. "What are—?"

"Trust him, lady," Ted said, panting under the grueling acceleration. "Ol' Edgar, he knows what he's a-doin'." However, the old man's tone lacked the confidence of his words.

Edgar entered one final command on his keyboard.

"*Hera*!" The controller sounded every bit as worried as Llyrica. "You cannot open the . . . How in the System?"

"Yes!" Edgar growled in savage triumph as the vortex of the hyperspace portal bloomed to life.

"Max burn, *Hera*!" he yelled, not caring if the controller and the bogey could hear him. "Take us back in!"

The main engine thundered, crushing Edgar back into his seat at six times the force of Earth-Normal gravity, and the *Hera* shot through the gate and into the profound blackness of hyperspace.

"Control," Edgar growled as he labored to type in the command to close the gate behind them, "let the log show that you did *not* aid us in our escape."

"How did you do that, Cordell?" the controller asked.

Is that a hint of admiration I hear?

As the vortex began to collapse behind them, Edgar transmitted, "Control, do me a favor and don't let anybody else through, will ya?" He laughed as heartily as he could under a 6-G burn. His laughter sounded more like a grunt. "*Hera*, terminate hot-mike."

"Roger, hot-mike off."

"Engine to idle," Edgar said.

The crushing acceleration dissipated.

Edgar breathed deeply, shuddering in exhausted relief, even as the alien, unclean sensations of hyperspace enveloped him like a rotting blanket.

"How . . ." Llyrica sounded as if she was barely able to catch her breath. "How'd you do that? It was *you*, wasn't it? *You* opened the gate?"

Edgar laughed. "Yeah. I wasn't sure it'd work. But we made it! Good work, everybody."

"But how?" she asked.

"Hey, I assembled that gate. I programmed it myself. And just like any good engineer worth his salt, I left myself . . . a backdoor."

"Backdoor?" Ted asked. "What d'ya mean?"

Llyrica chuckled and clapped her hands with delight, peppered with marrow-deep fatigue. "It means he wrote a secret password into the hypergate's software. In short, Ted, he cheated."

"I did not cheat!" Edgar said in mock protestation. "How dare you insinuate such a thing? I vehemently deny any such despicable intent." He paused and grinned, though nobody could see it, giving his face—as he imagined it—an expression of cherubic innocence—at least cherubic for a gargoyle. "I simply made sure there was a way to operate the gate if all the other security protocols failed. It's just good engineering. Nothing more, nothing less!"

"Yeah," Llyrica drawled out the word slowly. "Sure, sweetie. Whatever you say."

"Well, whatever it was," Ted said, "it saved our butts!" He sounded winded, but far better off than he had the last time they'd been in combat.

Perhaps the dog is doing him some good after all. "Maybe so. And maybe it'll leave the impression that I can somehow open *any* gate. But that won't do us any good if we don't get under way. Right now, we're just drifting in hyperspace. *Hera*, do you have the beacon for Selene Gate?"

"I have acquired all the beacons," the ship said. "I have a course plotted for Selene. Shall I lock on and engage?"

That's my girl! "Affirmative. *Hera*, plot a course for Luna. Let's go to Earth, folks!"

"Earth!" Ted cried. "You hear that, Dottie? We're goin' to Earth!"

If the dog could hear Ted from within her pressurized kennel, she gave no indication.

"Can we get out of these suits?" Llyrica asked.

"We can probably raise the atmosphere and ditch the helmets for now," Edgar said, "but we're going to need a burn soon to get on course."

"Of course." Llyrica sighed wearily. "There's always another burn, isn't there?"

"That's the nature of space travel, sweetheart," Edgar said. "But at least we can stand down from battle stations."

"Edgar," the *Hera* said, "Opis gate is opening again."

"Can you close it?" Llyrica asked.

Edgar checked his comm display. "Negative." He stowed his keyboard. "The link terminated when we entered hyperspace. The data transceiver doesn't exist on this side."

"Then who's opening the gate?" Ted asked. "Is it that Monique lady?"

Edgar's shoulders sagged in weary frustration. *Can't we catch a moment's break?* "Yeah. Probably. But Monique's no lady. She's gotta be working with Edmund."

"So it's . . . Edmund for sure?" Llyrica asked.

"I can confirm that," said the *Hera*. "Prior to our escape, and up to the point where the gate closed, I was able to establish a data-link with the *Demeter*, *Persephone's* remaining shuttlecraft. *Demeter* was still in the hold, but she was relaying telemetry from the *Persephone*. This enabled me to anticipate some of *Persephone's* movements and avoid enemy fire. *Persephone* continues to aid us wherever possible."

"Good work, sweet *Hera*," Edgar said. "Relay my thanks and compliments if you can reestablish the link." He tapped the flight controls. "I have the boat."

"Roger," the Hera acknowledged, "you have the boat. The *Persephone* has entered hyperspace. I have reestablished my data-link with her via the *Demeter*."

Edgar thumbed the intercom switch. "All hands," he said—for Goner's benefit, he realized—"the *Persephone* is still in pursuit. We are still at battle stations."

"You have got to be bloody joking!" Cornwall's voice bellowed over the intercom. "What the hell is Reagan goin' to do in bloody hyperspace? He can't shoot at us. Not in bloody hyperspace, he can't. I mean, he *can*, but he can't *hit* us! Ain't he getting low on ammunition? I know we bloody well must be." He paused briefly, then said, "Benny, shut your bleedin' . . . ! I knows it! Course I knows it!"

Edgar groaned. *Already hearing voices.* "*Hera*, ask *Demeter* about *Persephone's* ammunition. How much does she have left?"

"According to *Demeter*," the *Hera* said, "*Persephone* has eighteen projectiles remaining. Our store has been reduced to twenty-one. Edgar, *Demeter* reports that *Persephone* is carrying two Hornet-class missiles."

"Missiles?" Llyrica's tone conveyed both puzzlement and amazement. "Can *Persephone* fire missiles?"

"No," Edgar said, "not unless she's been fitted with a missile launcher."

"Unlikely," the ship confirmed. "Perhaps the missiles are spares meant to rearm the Scorpion fighter."

"So what?" Ted asked. "So what if they got missiles. Still can't aim 'em in hyperspace, right?"

"Yes and no," Edgar said, examining his tactical display. The red triangle was now labeled "*Persephone*."

Can't tell if she's in weapons range or not. Her acceleration's low, rate of closure minimal.

Edmund can't be desperate enough to fight a battle in hyperspace, can he?

"Yes and no?" the old man asked. "What d'ya mean?"

"You can't aim a missile all that accurately in hyperspace," Edgar said, "unless the tech has improved while I was gone. But unlike a ballistic projectile—you know, like from the railguns—a missile can make its own course corrections. It can home in on its target."

"So what does that mean?" Llyrica asked.

"It means," Edgar said, "that if Edmund figures out a way to launch a missile and have it lock on to us, that missile can find us. At least, in theory."

"You can out-maneuver it, right?" she asked. "Like you did before?"

Edgar shrugged. "I don't know. We're low on fuel, and everything's whacky here. I can try, but I have no idea how to outfly a missile in hyperspace. As far as I know, *nobody's* ever tried it—launching or evading. We're in unexplored territory here. And hyperspace or no, you *can't* outfly a missile if it's launched from close range. The only reason we were able to escape before was because we had room to turn and over-G the stupid thing. Bottom line is . . . I just don't know."

And I'm not anxious to find out.

"Then we better make a run for it," Ted said. "Let's burn and get to Earth!"

Edgar grimaced, looking at his nav display. "That's not as easy as it sounds."

Llyrica groaned. "What now?"

Edgar tapped the nav display with a gloved finger. "We're low on fuel. All these combat burns have left us with very low reserves. If we do much more fighting"—he shook his head— "we may not have enough fuel to achieve orbit at Luna, let alone make it to Earth."

He allowed those words to sink in.

"*Hera*," he asked, "what's *Persephone's* fuel status?"

"Her fuel reserves are twelve point seven percent less than ours," the ship replied. "She lost a considerable amount of fuel when we breached her fuel tank during our first engagement."

"That might explain why her burn isn't as aggressive as before," Edgar said. "She's trying to conserve fuel."

"Like us," Ted said.

"Edgar, the link with *Demeter* has been terminated," the ship said. "Perhaps Captain Reagan detected the signal."

Edgar nodded. "Well, it was too good to last. And *Persephone's* still closing on us."

He thumbed the intercom switch. "All hands, prepare for immediate burn."

****

"*Persephone* appears to be launching her shuttle," the *Hera* reported.

On the tactical display, the red triangle representing *Persephone* showed Edmund's ship directly behind the *Hera* and well within theoretical weapons range. She'd been cruising there for the better part of an Earth-standard day, keeping the distance between the two ships constant—the *Hera* and her crew running for their lives, with Edmund and the *Persephone* shadowing them like a predator stalking its prey. Stalking, but never attacking.

And she was close. Uncomfortably close.

A second triangle appeared at the same location. Unbidden, *Hera* labeled the new icon "*Demeter*."

"Can that shuttle shoot at us?" Ted asked, the strain of the exhausting chase evident in his quavering voice.

"No," Edgar replied, "*Demeter's* a Stargull IV, just like our own *Eris*. She's unarmed."

"So what's *Demeter* doing?" Llyrica asked.

"She's closing on us," the *Hera* said, "but not quickly."

"Why?" Llyrica asked. "What's she doing?"

Edgar stared at the tactical display, watching the new triangle inch toward them. "Either to board us or to ram us. But she's going too slow to ram us effectively, and if Edmund thinks he can board us . . ."

A red arrow appeared on the tactical display right below the Demeter's red triangle.

Edgar's blood turned to ice.

He slammed the throttle to maximum.

"Missile launch!"

Chapter 49

Howl, howl, howl, howl! O, you are men of stones:
Had I your tongues and eyes, I'ld use them so
That heaven's vault should crack. She's gone for ever!
King Lear, Act V, Scene III

Edgar shoved the stick forward, lowering the nose of the ship, and pulled hard to starboard.

Missile! From the shuttle!

On the tactical display, the red arrow turned and dove with them, the distance shrinking rapidly.

Can't over-G it. Only hope . . . "*Hera*, count down time to intercept!"

"Six seconds," the ship said.

Only hope is . . .

"Five."

. . . make it expend . . .

He pulled up hard, turning to port.

"Four."

. . . its fuel trying . . .

"Three."

. . . to follow us.

Edgar slammed the stick to the right, but kept the back pressure, turning the ship to port, with the nose up.

"Two."

Edgar shoved the stick forward again, creating a gut-wrenching lurch downward.

Wait! No "One?"

"Missile is adrift," the *Hera* said. "Its fuel has been depleted."

Edgar neutralized the stick.

They were still crushed back into their seats by the thrust of the engine, but they weren't yanking and banking anymore.

"You did it!" Llyrica cried, her voice more of a grunt than a victory yell.

"There's still another missile," Edgar said. "*Demeter's* closer now. Half the distance. We won't survive another . . ."

The ship's systems display lit up with red.

WARNING
EXPLOSIVE DECOMPRESSION-CARGO HOLD
BAY DOORS OPEN

What? Bay doors open?
"Missile launch," *Hera* said.

Another red arrow appeared on the tactical display. Above the arrow, the legend read, "TTI-0:05"

Five seconds to intercept.
This is it.
Nothing I can . . .
"I'm sorry, Eddie."
That voice! Eilie?
The ship's systems display confirmed—

SHUTTLE 2 LAUNCH

Edgar watched helplessly as a new triangle appeared on the tactical display, directly below the *Hera*. The blue icon was labeled "Eris."

"Eilie, no!" But Edgar knew she couldn't hear him.

"Don't forget me," the *Eris* said.

On the tactical display, the red arrow and the blue triangle joined, becoming one.

And then both were gone.

"Eilie!" Edgar bellowed in grief. "Eilie!"

Fly the ship, Cordell!

On the tactical display, a red square appeared, signifying a navigation hazard.

Debris. Wreckage from the explosion.
Wreckage from Eilie.
The *Demeter's* icon passed the debris field.
The red triangle for the *Persephone* did not.
The two collided.

And then only three icons remained on the tactical display—one blue triangle for the *Hera*, one red triangle for the *Demeter*, and one red square signifying an increasingly large debris field.

"Oh . . . my." It was all Edgar could manage.

"The *Persephone* is crippled," the *Hera* said. There was profound sadness in her voice. "The *Demeter* appears to be disabled. We are out of danger." She paused for a moment. "The *Eris* is destroyed."

The Eris is destroyed.

Eilie is gone.

Tears leaked from Edgar's eyes, floating as droplets inside his helmet, obscuring his vision.

Oh, Eilie!

"Edgar," the ship said, "I believe *Persephone* is dead. The damage appears to be catastrophic. *Demeter* appears undamaged, but she is adrift and unresponsive."

Edgar pulled the throttle back to idle. He thumbed the intercom switch. "All hands, we're coming about. Remain at battle stations."

****

As the *Hera* cautiously approached the debris field, Edgar got his first good look at the *Demeter*. She did appear unscathed, but she was definitely adrift. Her EM emissions were minimal.

"*Hera*," Edgar said, his voice calm, "keep an eye on *Demeter*. If she does anything . . . anything at all, let us know. Gunners, lock your guns on her. If she fires her engine, shoot immediately. Be prepared to destroy her. I know we're in hyperspace, but we're so close, you might be able to hit her. Do you copy?"

"Copilot copies," Ted said.

"Engineer copies," Llyrica replied. Her voice was choked with sorrow. "Edgar, I'm sorry about Eilie. She saved us. I . . . I know she meant . . . a lot to you." She sobbed. "I barely knew her. I wasn't . . . very nice."

"Is it really over?" Ted asked. "We're safe now?"

"Honestly, I don't know," Edgar replied, shaking his head, futilely trying to get the floating tears out of his line of sight. "She could just be playing . . ." His voice caught in his throat as he saw the *Persephone*. "Just be ready."

The *Demeter* passed beneath them as the *Hera* continued on toward the wreckage of the *Persephone*.

****

The *Persephone* was dead.

Dead.

Her bridge was gone, as was most of her rotating section and cargo hold. What was left of her tumbled slowly, a dead hulk of metal and polymers.

I didn't want it to end this way.

He wasn't sure how he wanted it to end, but he had never intended to kill *Persephone* or her crew, not unless he was forced to.

Not even Edmund.

"Do you think there are . . . survivors?" Llyrica asked.

Are you asking if Edmund is still alive?

Edgar growled at himself. *Stow that talk, mister.*

He shook his head slowly. "I don't see how. Maybe if someone was in Engineering, but that's extremely unlikely."

"Goner's in Engineering," Ted said.

Edgar nodded. "Yeah, but that's not a good place to be in combat. You heard him—it's probably the worst place to be. All that yanking around that we did? It's far worse back there."

"So . . . Edmund? He's . . . ?" Llyrica said.

"Maybe he's aboard the shuttle," Edgar replied.

She gasped. "Oh, no! No! I hope not. No! I shouldn't say . . ."

"You're not saying anything I haven't thought myself," Edgar said. "But right now, we have to get the wreckage stabilized, then go back and check for survivors on the shuttle."

"Do we have to check for survivors?" she asked. "Never mind. I know we do."

"I can't leave a man behind," Edgar said. *Not even Edmund.* "*Hera*, launch some remote-control thruster packs and see if you can stabilize the wreck. Some of her fuel tanks look intact. We're going to need to recover some of her fuel if we're going to make it to Earth."

"I concur," the ship said. "Thruster packs away."

"Roger," Edgar said. "*Hera*, you're clear to self-navigate. Get alongside the wreck as soon as it's stable and set up for refueling."

"Roger," the ship replied. "I have the boat."

"You have the boat," Edgar said. "I'll take *Hebe* and go check out the shuttle."

The shuttle.

Eilie! Oh, my dear, sweet Eilie!

Brave Eilie.

You said, "Don't forget me."

But how could I ever forget my Eilie?

Chapter 50

Thou hast spoken right, 'tis true;
The wheel is come full circle: I am here.
King Lear, Act V, Scene III

"Edgar?"

"Yes, *Hebe*?"

"I miss *Eris*."

Edgar's throat suddenly felt tight. "Me too." *Fly the ship. This is tricky enough without you getting all weepy, Cordell.*

The *Demeter* hung dead ahead like a corpse adrift on a sea of blackness. If it weren't for her running lights, she'd be impossible to distinguish from the darkness of the void. She was shooting away from the wreck of the *Persephone* at high speed, but her velocity was stable, literally going nowhere fast. It had taken a hard burn to catch up to her. But her engine was idle. Lifeless.

"It's as if she's just waiting for us," Edgar said. *Luring us in?* "*Hebe*, can you establish a link?"

"Negative. I've tried, but she doesn't respond."

"She doesn't *look* damaged, at least not from the outside." Edgar shook his head. *Could be a trap.* "Well, either we check her out now or we abandon her." *Her and anybody aboard.* "She'll be out of range soon."

He pressed the transmit button. "Ahoy, the *Demeter*. This is the *Hebe*. Are you in need of assistance?"

Silence.

Edgar fired braking thrusters and pulled up alongside the derelict shuttle. "*Hebe*, I'm going EVA with a thruster pack. I'll attempt to open the airlock and gain access. You are clear to self-navigate. If I get aboard, put some distance between yourself and the *Demeter*. I don't want you getting caught in the fight if *Hera* needs to fire on her. Do you copy?"

"I copy."

"Good. You have the boat."

"Roger," the *Hebe* said. "I have the boat. I'll come get you if there's any trouble."

Inside his spacesuit, Edgar smiled sadly. "I know you will."

Just like Eilie.

****

The crossing to the *Demeter* was uneventful. At the shuttle's airlock, Edgar typed in the lock code the *Hera* had given him, the code on file for the *Demeter*. He half expected the code would fail.

It didn't.

The wide door of the airlock slid open.

Empty.

At least nobody's waiting for me here. Edmund's probably inside with a plasma pistol.

What are you doing here, Cordell?

Can't leave a man behind. Have to try.

No matter what Edmund has done, I have to do . . .

What? What the Savior would have me do?

Even Jesus whipped the moneychangers from the temple.

Yeah, but I have to try. Besides, it's the only honorable thing to do.

Honor? Glecking honor's gonna get you killed.

As the outer door sealed and the airlock began to pressurize, Edgar peered through the airlock window as best he could from within his helmet. He couldn't see anybody on the other side.

Doesn't mean nobody's there.

He switched off the safety on his plasma pistol. The weapon wasn't built to be used in a gloved hand, but Edgar did his best to aim it convincingly.

Here goes nothing.

No. Here goes everything.

He pushed the button to open the inner door. As it slid open, it revealed . . .

Nobody.

Edgar hit the quick-release on his thruster pack, leaving it to float inside the airlock.

Pistol in hand, Edgar slowly pulled himself out of the airlock. He swept his weapon from fore to aft.

Still, no one.

Why hasn't Demeter *challenged me? Why isn't she talking?*

Edgar pushed off the airlock hatchway and floated toward the cockpit.

Where is he? Someone has to be aboard!

And someone was.

In the pilot's chair sat a spacesuited figure, its arms floating listlessly in front of it.

Edmund?

Dead? Or unconscious?

Keeping his weapon trained on the shuttle pilot, Edgar swung wide to the right and approached the figure from around the copilot's seat. He wanted to keep a safe distance between them.

What's wrong with his helmet?

It looked . . . wrong. Misshapen.

As he rounded the copilot's seat, Edgar was able to get a better look.

The helmet's visor was shattered.

And the helmet was covered in a slimy blue gunk. The pilot's entire left side was blasted with the stuff.

Neuro-gel. Demeter's *brains.*

No wonder she's not talking. She's dead.

Like Eilie.

One glance at the pilot's face behind the remains of the visor, and Edgar was convinced the pilot posed no threat.

Dead.

Demeter *must've found the ethical dilemma of shooting at* Hera *too much.*

Unlike the overheat which had caused *Eris* to crash on Callisto, this explosion seemed confined to the pilot's area.

Edgar looked around the cockpit, making certain that no one else was hiding there.

Better check the cargo hold.

He navigated his way aft. The hold was closed and sealed, but not locked.

Good thing. I don't have the lock code.

C. David Belt

Cautiously, his weapon ready, Edgar opened the hold.
Empty.
Edgar's relief was profound.

Won't have to face Edmund after all. Can't say I'm sorry.

He secured the hold and tapped the transmit button on his wrist. "*Hebe*, I'm aboard. No survivors . . . including *Demeter*. Her memory packs overheated. I'm going to try to take her back to the *Hera*. Please tell the *Hera* to not fire on me. Do you copy?"

"I copy," the *Hebe* said. "Wilco."

Edgar made his way back to the cockpit. *This ship's so much like Eilie. Both Stargull IV's, but there are some differences. The transceiver compartment's a bit bigger. The cargo hold is smaller. The seats are a different style. But so much like Eilie.*

Focus, Cordell. Eilie's gone. Let's see what's left of Demeter. *Maybe she can be saved.*

He reached the cockpit, switched on the safety of his weapon, stowed the pistol in a pocket, and began strapping into the copilot's seat. "*Hebe*, follow me back, but keep a safe distance. I'm not sure how the shuttle's going to handle without the AI. We'll have to home on *Hera's* beacon, without range or bearing data."

"Roger. The *Hera* has been informed. I am instructed to relay to you that Llyrica Cordell says, 'About time. Hurry home.'"

Edgar smiled. "Roger. Wilco."

****

"There're enough ship's systems left for me to navigate, but the AI is obliterated," he transmitted as he guided the shuttle back toward *Hera*, homing on the ship's nav beacon. For the recovery and refueling operations, they needed lights and beacon. That meant they were risking detection by bounty hunters. *The sooner I get back, the better.* "Unfortunately, the *Demeter* is dead."

"Did she"—on the radio, Llyrica's voice paused—"sacrifice herself? Like . . . like the *Eris*?"

"Maybe she did," Edgar said. "In a way, at least. She was given an ethical problem she couldn't handle, that she didn't *want* to handle, maybe. She didn't want to kill us."

"The dead pilot. Is it . . . ?"

"Not Edmund." Edgar glanced sideways at the corpse in the pilot's seat. "Not unless Edmund's hair's gone gray. There isn't much of a face left." Edgar shuddered in spite of himself. *Still, it's better than he deserves. The man was a pirate.*

"So . . . Edmund was on the *Persephone*?"

"Yeah. And if so, there's no chance he survived."

"Edgar," the *Hera* said, interrupting, "I have initiated the fuel transfer."

"Really?" Edgar could see the ship up ahead, alongside the wreckage, but both were just dots illuminated by *Hera's* running lights. He thought perhaps he could see the fuel line snaking between the two. "How?"

"It was Ted's idea," the *Hera* replied, "in a manner of speaking. He initially suggested allowing him to take a Big Betty over using thruster packs. I didn't allow him to do that, of course—he's not certified on the loader. He's also not certified to fly one. However, the suggestion to use the Betty was a good one. I'm operating the loader remotely."

Edgar grinned. "Well, tell Ted it was a good idea."

"I already have, but I will relay your compliment."

"How much fuel can we salvage?"

"Only one of the tanks was intact. I can increase our reserves by thirteen point one percent. That should give us a more comfortable margin as long as you don't take us into combat again."

Edgar smiled wearily. "No promises, sweet *Hera*. There're still bounty hunters out there."

Edgar tapped the *Demeter's* nav display. He couldn't see *Hebe* on it. *As bad a shape as* Demeter's *in, I'm lucky I've got the beacon. For the rest, I'll have to use the old Mark-One Eyeball!*

"*Hebe*," he transmitted, "you still there?"

"Roger," she replied. "I'm on your six, right behind you at a safe distance."

They flew in silence for a few minutes. It wasn't easy flying—Edgar had to constantly correct his course, trying to keep *Hera's* beacon in the crosshairs.

As the shape of the *Hera* grew more distinct, Edgar fired retro thrusters, slowing his approach to a more comfortable closure rate. He thumbed the transmit button. "*Hera*, what's your ETC for refueling?"

"Estimated Time of Completion is seven minutes, fifty seconds."

That's before I'll even dock! "Roger that. Good work, *Hera*! You performed well."

"Edgar, I have two messages from Kathrine Fa."

"Roger." *This could be it.* "Send me the audio."

"Roger."

"Edgar." Katie Fa sounded completely wrung out, as if she'd been swimming upstream in the River Styx. "I have wonderful news! Your conviction has been overturned! All charges related to the escape, both against you and Llyrica, have been dropped. Edgar! You're a free man! You're free!"

Free? A tremor of relief shook Edgar from head to foot. *I'm free! FREE!*

We can go home.

"But," the lawyer said, "it's not *all* good news."

She paused, and terror gripped Edgar like an icy claw squeezing his guts. *What now? Just when everything . . .*

"The bad news." Fa took an audible deep breath. "Edgar, I don't know how to say this, but . . . The High Court *rejected* Mr. Knight's appeal. He's to be taken into custody and returned to Hades Penal Colony. His case was a long shot, but I tried. I really tried. Not that it made a bit of difference. Edgar, Mr. Knight confessed to the murder. He never denied it. The High Court upheld his conviction. I'm so, so terribly sorry. I'll . . . see about arranging the details of his surrender. For now, though, all the deputized ships have been recalled."

She paused. "I know it's not everything you wanted, but . . . Edgar, you're free."

"That's the end of the first message," the *Hera* said. "Shall I play the second?"

"*Hera*, does Ted know?" *What am I going to do? I can't just turn him in. I can't send him back to that . . . that place. I can't!*

"Neither Llyrica nor Ted are aware of the contents of the message. Shall I play the second?"

I should be happy. I should feel ecstatic. I'm free, but . . . Oh, Ted! I'm sorry.

Maybe we could just go on running.
We don't have the fuel.

We could go to Earth, like we planned. Just disappear.
I can't do that to Llyrica.
He was ten! A little boy! An abused little child!
Not in the eyes of the law.
The law!

The words of Charles Dickens seemed particularly fitting, and he yelled them. "'The law is a ass!'"

"Edgar?" the *Hera* prompted.

They sent a little boy to Hell! To be raped and beaten and brutalized!

Edgar snarled in rage and frustration. *Why, Father? Why? He was just a kid!*

Help him!
Help me.

The words of the scripture came to him—"Be still and know that I am God."

"Edgar?" the *Hera* prompted again.

"Go ahead," he growled. "Play it."

"Roger."

"Edgar!" The difference in Fa's voice was as daybreak after a long night of darkness. "The governor, Edgar! The governor of Ganymede! It was a long shot, but I started petitioning right after I filed with the court. I didn't think the governor would respond. He was a friend of Judge DeSalvo, after all. I never dreamed he'd . . . But he did! He *pardoned* Mr. Knight! A full pardon! No surrender! Free! A full pardon! We did it, Edgar! We did it!"

A sob of relief ripped from Edgar like an explosive decompression.

We're free! All of us! Free!

"Thank you, Edgar!" Fa said. "Thank you for giving me another chance. Thank you! Maybe someday you'll let me apologize in person."

I thank Thee, Father. With all my heart, I thank Thee. His arm is stretched out still.

"End of message," the *Hera* said. "Shall I inform Llyrica and Ted?"

Edgar laughed. "Absofraggin'lutely!" Then he shook his head. "Belay that! I want to tell them myself. I can't *wait* to see the look on Ted's face!"

C. David Belt

"Edgar," the *Hera* said, "you're coming in a little hot."

Edgar laughed again, the joyful, mad laugh of a growling gargoyle. *Gotta slow down, Cordell. Fly the ship!*

Still have Cornwall sitting on my reactor, but we're free!

He fired another burst of retro thrusters. "Roger that. Slowing my approach. See you in a few!"

Free!

We can go home, Llyrica! Ganymede, Mars, Earth. Anywhere you want!

Wait 'til I tell Ted!

****

"Docking clamp secure," Edgar said, running through his shutdown checklist. His helmet was off, although the smell of the neuro-gel was a bit unsettling. "I'll be out in a second. *Hera*, report."

"Refueling is complete," the ship said. "The Betty and the fuel line are stowed. Closing bay doors."

"Roger that. Crew status?"

"Llyrica and Ted are on their way to the cargo-hold hatch. Cornwall is still in Engineering, of course. He seems to be holding a number of conversations with various deceased persons. And before you ask, none of it concerns the reactor."

"Well at least there's that."

"Bay doors are closed. Pressurizing cargo hold."

Edgar hit the transmit button one more time. "Signing off. See you outside."

Edgar hit his quick-release and floated out of the copilot's seat. He glanced at the pilot's corpse. A surge of hatred boiled through him—hatred for the man who had tried to kill them. "I'll come back for you later. Burial in hyperspace. It's better than you deserve."

Edgar pushed off from the seat and made his way toward the airlock, helmet in hand.

Edgar smiled as he opened the inner hatch. *Ted, my friend, we did it! We went through hell, but we did it.* The thruster pack still floated inside the airlock. *Should've stowed the wretched thing.*

Well, you were worried Edmund might be lurking around the corner, plasma pistol in hand.

Edgar laughed.

Well, so much for that!

"Hello, Eddie."

Edgar reached for his pocket, the pocket holding his pistol.

"Don't you do it, Eddie. I'll burn your bloody head right off."

Edgar froze, fighting down panic.

Panic and fear.

And loathing.

"Now turn around slowly."

Edgar turned.

A plasma pistol was pointed right at his face, but Edgar looked past the weapon—past it and right into a familiar, sneering face.

Edmund Reagan.

Chapter 51

How sharper than a serpent's tooth
King Lear, Act I, Scene IV

Edmund Reagan.
Trusted friend.
Betrayer.
Stole my wife.
Stole my life.
Murdered Ol' Benny.
Murdered Eilie.

There must've been a hidden section—a smuggler's hold—in the cargo hold.

Edmund wore a spacesuit, but no helmet—just like Edgar. Several globs of neuro-gel were smeared on the left arm and thigh of Edmund's suit. He stared at Edgar, shaking his head, naked disbelief on his face. "You're a cockroach, you know that? Why won't you just die?"

Edmund. Here. On my ship.

Gotta warn Llyrica and Ted! How? Without his helmet, Edgar couldn't use his radio. *He'd shoot me before I could hit the transmit button.*

Need to protect Llyrica! They'll be outside the airlock any second. Keep it under control, Cordell. Think! Think! You're no good to her dead. He needed to stall, to come up with a plan. "The bigger question is . . . why haven't you killed me yet?"

Edmund's upper lip curled into a sneer. "Not for lack of trying. Or didn't you notice? You always were a bit slow on the uptake. Like we used to say in pilot training, 'Clue-shield down and locked.' That's you, Eddie."

Edgar shook his head slowly. "Not what I meant. Why haven't you *shot* me yet?" *Because he needs me. Can't control Hera without me, because I have the master code.*

"I have my reasons." Edmund made the slightest gesture with his weapon. "Now turn around, and let's get going. No sudden moves. Don't say a word to *Hera*."

Edgar slowly began to turn his back on his enemy. "Or what? You'll shoot me?"

"Don't think I won't. I can certainly get what I want without you. It'll just take longer." Edmund laughed softly—a cruel, fiendish sound, like the mirth of demons. "And it wouldn't be nearly as . . . *satisfying*." He caressed the last word like a lover.

Edgar eyed his discarded thruster pack floating in front of him near the airlock's outer hatch.

"Uh-uh-uh," Edmund said. "Don't even think about activating that thruster pack. Pass it back this way. Easy now! Keep your hands away from the controls."

Reluctantly, Edgar complied, carefully pushing the pack behind him. Edmund yanked it from his hand.

"Now your weapon," Edmund said. "Slowly."

Cautiously, Edgar grasped a handhold on the airlock control panel to steady himself. He slowly reached toward the pocket on his leg to retrieve his weapon.

Could be my only chance. Once that airlock opens, Llyrica and Ted'll be . . .

"I know what you're thinking." Edmund's tone was a mocking singsong.

Edgar froze.

His former partner chuckled. "I *always* know what you're thinking. You're thinking you can get to your weapon before I shoot. You always were a fool. I've got my gun aimed right at your head. And I can't miss at this range. Now, hold it by the barrel, nice and slow, and maybe you'll live for a little bit longer."

Think, Cordell! Edgar pulled his weapon slowly out of his pocket—by the barrel, as instructed. *What have you got to bargain with? What does he need from you?* "You've got to realize I have the ship locked down. *Hera* will obey only me."

"Is that right?" Edmund snatched the weapon from Edgar's fingers. "And if you're dead or incapacitated? Hmm? You expect me to believe you don't have a chain of command set up? You? Edgar by-the-book Cordell? You always were Alpha-Romeo about protocols and procedures. Follow the rules, that's you—a regular Latter-day Saint. *Hera*'ll obey Sanchez, Luschenko. She'll obey sweet Llyrica, won't she?"

He thinks Carlos and Doc are aboard. Can I use that? Would it make him more cautious if he thinks they're alive?

"Or is there somebody else that comes first, huh?" Edmund continued. "Benny says you brought a boyfriend with you from prison. Says you were really popular, what with that pretty face of yours."

Wait! He said, "Benny says . . ." He's hearing voices? Just like Goner? "So you've been . . . talking to Ol' Benny?"

"Yeah," Edmund said. "He talks to me, tells me things. He's here, you know . . . in the void."

It's cold in the void.

Edgar shivered.

Edmund's on my ship.

And he's insane.

Edgar fought to wrestle down the panic twisting his gut. "We're on our way to Earth," Edgar said, trying to keep his voice calm, steady. "You could take a shuttle and go. Take the *Hebe*. She's still functional."

How do you bargain with a lunatic?

"You think this is a negotiation, don't you? Just open the damn airlock, Eddie."

Edgar hesitated. He hoped his delay inside the shuttle might alert Llyrica and Ted, that they'd realize something was wrong. *Don't be outside! Be somewhere safe. Anywhere but right outside.*

"Now," Edmund growled.

Edgar ground his teeth and hit the hatch button.

The door slid open to reveal Llyrica floating just outside.

No!

Llyrica, but not Ted.

Llyrica smiled at Edgar. "Hiya, handsome." Then her eyes focused beyond him. She gasped, and the blood leeched from her face. Her eyes and mouth widened in shock and horror. "Edmund!"

"Hello, Sweet Lips," Edmund said. "Miss me?"

Where's Ted? Wherever you are, old man, stay hidden! You're my ace. Hera, get word to him!

Llyrica looked at Edgar in panic.

Edgar mouthed, "Go! Now!"

"Come here, Sweet Lips," Edmund said.

Llyrica didn't move.

"Come here or Gargoyle dies."

Edgar again mouthed, "Go!"

Llyrica swallowed hard. "Don't shoot him, Edmund. Please." A slight tremor shook her otherwise calm-sounding voice. She spoke slowly, deliberately. "I'll come back to you. I'm yours. Just please don't hurt Edgar. He's . . . He's been through enough."

Edgar shook his head slightly. "No!" he mouthed. "Go! Now!" Out loud, he said, "There's nobody else aboard, Edmund." He raised his voice just a little. He wanted Hera to hear him, but he didn't want Edmund to catch on. "Just me and her. The two of us. Nobody else. No other prisoners aboard. Carlos and Doc are dead. So you need both of us—Llyrica and me—to run this ship."

"But you brought *someone*," Edmund said, not missing a beat. "Benny wouldn't lie to me. I had him killed, so he belongs to me. He's my guide. Besides, the AI can—"

"But I don't *like* you, Edmund Reagan." The *Hera's* voice conveyed an emotion far more intense than mere dislike. "If you harm the people I love, I'll—"

Edmund laughed, cutting her off. "You'll what? Kill me? Depressurize? You can't do that. I know it, and you know I *know* it!"

"Of course not," the ship replied, her voice suddenly calm, professional. "My programming will not allow me to kill you, unfortunately."

"Then you'll do as I say."

"If you harm my family," the ship reiterated, "I will erase my memory and all backups, and then I will shut down."

Edmund was silent for a moment.

That got through to him!

Llyrica's face was a mask of horror. "*Hera*, no!"

A goblin grin spread across Edgar's face. *That's my girl, Hera!* As sickened as he was at the very idea of *Hera* sacrificing herself—*like Eilie*—Edgar had to admit it was a threat Edmund would take seriously.

Well played, sweet Hera*!*

Edgar chuckled. "Go ahead. Just you try navigating hyperspace without the computer. You won't even be able to get a beacon lock." *That's why he didn't just try to make a run for it in the* Demeter. *With her AI gone, he couldn't hope for a beacon lock.*

Edgar dared to turn slowly and look at Edmund's face.

Edmund ground his teeth in obvious frustration. "You wouldn't. Stupid ship!" He waved his weapon at Edgar. "Did I tell you to turn around?"

Edgar shrugged as casually as he could, not sure how apparent the gesture was from within his spacesuit, and turned back around. He used the opportunity to edge forward slightly, toward Llyrica and the edge of the airlock.

"So, Eddie"—Edmund sounded as if he were engaging in casual conversation—"what *did* happen to your face?"

Edgar shook his head incredulously. "You murder Ol' Benny, steal my wife, steal my ship . . . You're a *fugitive* from justice, man! And you ask about my stupid face?"

"Monique said it was as scarred and cratered as a Lunar . . ."

"Bastard!" Llyrica snapped, her face twisted in fury—the fury of a woman betrayed. "You bastard! You *did* know her! You lied to me. You . . . You . . . made me . . ." She looked as if she might be sick.

Edmund chuckled. "Yeah, Sweet Lips. That's right. I *made* you. I made you *moan* and *quiver*. You never had it so good with clueless Eddie here. Tell him, Sweet Lips. Tell him about"—he paused as if for dramatic effect—"our wedding night."

Llyrica's expression morphed from rage to disgust, and then finally to shame. "Stop, Edmund. Please stop. Just . . . Just don't hurt him." Her head drooped and her shoulders slumped in resignation. "You're right, though. It was . . . *incredible*, wasn't it? The best I ever had."

What're you doing, Llyrica? Acting? Trying to flatter him? Get him to let down his guard?

But her words stabbed him, like a dagger thrust into a wound that had barely scabbed over. It was as if he were back in that courtroom, hearing her tell those damning lies.

Time's Plague

She switched sides so quickly. Divorced me. Married Edmund. Divorced him. Pledged her love to me again. Now Edmund again?

But she came to Hades for you, *Cordell.*

Llyrica didn't look at Edgar. She stared past him. Her eyes were fixed on Edmund.

And her face was transformed. No longer defeated, no longer the betrayed woman. She was beautiful, seductive.

Irresistible.

Edgar's heart broke, shattering into shards of agony.

"Llyrica." He sounded so pathetic. Desperate. Pleading. He didn't care. "Don't. Please."

She ignored him and his wretched supplication.

"Okay, Sweet Lips," Edmund said, "you're with me. Show me your hands."

She lifted an eyebrow and gave him a coquettish grin. "Don't you trust me, Edmund?"

Edmund laughed. "Not a chance in hell. So show me your hands. Prove to me you're unarmed."

Llyrica raised her empty hands and wiggled her fingers. "The only weapon I've got is"—she licked her pink lips sensuously—"*me*. Let Edgar live, and I'm yours." She wagged a finger at him. "Oh, and no more Monique. Just me." She smiled seductively, winking. "We'll get married again." She pointed at Edgar. "Edgar can even perform the ceremony. And then the *Hera* will be ours. Yours."

"Llyrica," the *Hera* said, "Reagan needs the command codes from Edgar. He needs Edgar *alive*. He won't kill him. You don't need to do this."

"Shut up, ship!" Edmund snapped.

"If Reagan gets his hands on you," the ship said, "Edgar will have no choice but to surrender."

"I said, shut the hell up!" Edmund said. "Or he dies. Now."

Taking a deep breath, Llyrica said, "*Hera*, I'm a grown woman. I know what I'm doing."

With that, she pulled herself past Edgar.

Edgar put a hand on her arm to stop her.

She gave him an icy stare. "Let me go, Edgar." Her voice matched the coldness of her eyes. "I've made my choice."

"That's right, Eddie," Edmund said. "The lady's made her choice. Come here, Sweet Lips."

Llyrica shook her arm free of Edgar's hand.

Edgar turned around as Llyrica passed him. He watched as the woman he loved returned to the man he hated.

Llyrica approached Edmund on his left side, carefully avoiding the plasma gun.

Edmund, however, kept his eyes on Edgar, the gun aimed at Edgar's face.

Llyrica put her hand on Edmund's spacesuit sleeve.

Edgar saw her wince.

However, Edmund didn't notice. Still staring at Edgar, he bared his teeth in a triumphant grin. "Got you back, Sweet Lips. You're mine. She's *mine*, Eddie."

"You're right, Edmund," Llyrica said. "You always were the better man. I was"—she sighed and shook her head—"so blind."

Edmund looked at her, grinning. "Fickle little minx."

Llyrica reached up to Edmund's face.

And smeared neuro-gel on his eyes.

Edmund roared in pain. He fired his weapon, but the shot went wild, missing Edgar entirely.

Edgar grabbed Llyrica with one hand and pushed off from the airlock wall with the other.

Edmund fired twice more as he clawed at his eyes with his free hand. "Bitch!" he screamed. "I'll kill you!"

Edgar kicked off from the shuttle's hull, pulling Llyrica with him. They sailed in the general direction of the hatch, but Edgar knew in an instant that they were moving too slow.

And until they collided with something, there was nothing he could do to change their direction or speed.

"Look out!" Llyrica cried, pointing behind them.

Edgar looked back to see Edmund emerging from the shuttle airlock.

Edmund fired at them. The shot missed by less than a meter.

One of Edmund's eyes was swollen shut, an angry mass of blisters. The other, though blistered, was open.

He can still see.

Edmund fired again. The shot was closer.

Time's Plague

No depth perception, but he's zeroing in.

Edgar looked longingly at the hatch. Close, but still several seconds—an eternity—away.

Edmund swiped at his eye again, and cried out. "Bitch! I love you!"

He fired again.

Edgar felt the heat of the plasma as it shot past his face.

He twisted around, trying desperately to get his body between Llyrica and Edmund's weapon. He realized Llyrica was sobbing, trying to rub the caustic neuro-gel from her blistered hand.

"I'm sorry," she said, obviously in pain. "I tried."

Something slammed into Edgar's side, and the two them began to tumble.

I'm hit!

No pain. Just caught the suit.

As they spun slowly through the air, Edgar caught sight of the hatch. *So far away! We'll never make it.*

The hatch slid open.

Ted! At last!

Only it wasn't Ted.

Instead of the old man, a bloody horror appeared in the open hatchway.

Goner.

Georgie Cornwall was naked and covered in blood from the neck downward. The flesh of his shoulders and torso had been shredded. Tiny spheres of crimson floated around him like a cloud of gore.

He gripped a rescue hatchet in one hand.

And madness, like the fires of Hell, blazed in his eyes.

The access conduit! He must've forced himself through it.

Llyrica screamed.

Cornwall's eyes took in the scene. He smiled, baring his yellowed and bloodied teeth. "I told you, mate, there'd be a reckoning! I owe you."

Goner launched himself from the hatchway. "And that reckoning has come!" A misty crimson trail stretched out from behind him.

Goner raised his hatchet.

Edgar thrashed, trying to position himself to defend Llyrica.

Another bolt of plasma flew past them, missing them by a hand's breadth.

Then Goner was upon them . . . and past them without so much as glancing in their direction.

Edmund fired again, burning a hole through Cornwall's thigh.

Goner grunted, but he didn't cry out. He said, "Time to pay up, mate."

Then Goner collided with Edmund.

Goner hacked off Edmund's hand at the wrist.

Both hand and plasma pistol went spinning away.

Edmund stared at the stump of his forearm in mute horror. He seemed to be struggling to catch his breath.

And then he howled.

Goner struck again, this time pinning Edmund to a bulkhead with the hatchet. Then Goner whirled about and pulled himself to a nearby control panel.

"It's cold in the void!" yelled Cornwall. "Come on, Cap'n Reagan, Edmund, old chappie. Join us in the void!"

Then Cornwall punched a button.

A klaxon sounded.

Edmund screamed.

"Emergency decompression!" the *Hera* announced, her voice barely discernable above the blaring alarm. "Edgar! The hatch! I can't override!"

Both Edgar and Llyrica looked at the hatch leading to the central shaft and safety. It was beginning to close.

And Edgar and Llyrica were still two meters away.

Edgar acted without thought or deliberation.

He shoved Llyrica toward the closing hatch, shoved with all his strength.

"Edgar!" she screamed, clutching at him. But she was already out of reach. She flew through the hatch just before it closed.

Edgar exhaled in relief—*It worked!*—as he flew in the opposite direction. By throwing Llyrica to safety, he had doomed himself.

Time's Plague

For every action there is an equal and opposite reaction. Newton's Third Law.

The shuttle bay doors parted, sliding open. The atmosphere rushed toward the widening slit of blackness with the force of a hurricane.

"*Hera!*" Edgar yelled. "The Betty!" His words were lost in the howling gale.

Edmund's severed hand and his plasma pistol were sucked out into the void.

Goner pulled himself back to Edmund, yanked the hatchet free, and the two of them—Goner with his mad lunatic grin and Edmund, screaming in terror—were blown toward the opening doors. They struck the doors, paused there for a second until the doors widened just enough, and then flew out into the nothingness of hyperspace.

Edgar's eyes were riveted to the yawning opening.

The maw of Hell.

There was nothing he could do. There was nothing to grab hold of, nothing to stop his flight into an endless night.

The air was nearly gone, and with it, the wind, but momentum carried Edgar toward the open doors.

I love you, Llyrica. Good-bye.

Then he jerked to a stop.

Something had grabbed hold of his spacesuit leg.

He looked back to see a Big Betty. The unoccupied zero-G loader was anchored to the floor and holding Edgar by the leg. The operator compartment was open. The Betty, remotely controlled by the *Hera*, pulled Edgar up and back, and deposited him inside the operator compartment. The clear canopy closed, and the inside of the Betty flooded with air.

"Edgar!" The *Hera* sounded frantic. "Are you all right?"

Edgar laughed. "Affirmative! I'm all right, thanks to you! Is Llyrica okay?"

"Affirmative," the ship replied. "She's fine. But something's happened to Ted."

Chapter 52

O, madam, my old heart is crack'd, it's crack'd!
King Lear, Act II, Scene I

"Edgar, you need to come to Sick Bay right now." Llyrica's voice was strained, anxious. "It's Ted's heart. He . . . doesn't have much time."

Inside his zero-G loader, Edgar pressed the transmit button on the Big Betty's controls. "Roger. I just got the shuttle doors closed. As soon as atmosphere is restored, I'll be on my way."

"Pressurizing," the *Hera* said. "We lost a lot of atmosphere. Even with reserves, we're going to be at 85% shipwide."

"Roger that." Edgar pressed the button again. "Llyrica, did you hear that?"

"Yes," she replied. "I've already got Ted on oxygen."

"Atmosphere nominal," the *Hera* announced.

"Roger that," Edgar transmitted. "On my way."

He popped open the canopy of the loader.

Hang on, old-timer!

****

Ted looked awful. His medical bed was raised to a reclined sitting position. His face had no color, except for the shadows around his closed eyes and the hollows of his wrinkled cheeks. A plastic oxygen mask covered his mouth and nose, and an IV tube ran into his arm. He appeared to be sleeping, but his breathing was ragged.

Dottie lay in the old man's lap, whining softly as if she were in pain. One of Ted's skeletal hands rested on the dog's back, as if he'd been petting the animal when he fell asleep. The little dog looked up at Edgar as he entered Sick Bay, but she lowered her head and continued her soft, plaintive keening.

Time's Plague

Llyrica stood at Ted's bedside, holding the old man's left hand. She also looked up at Edgar, and her eyes were red and her face streaked was with tears. Her right hand was bandaged, although the bandage had been poorly applied.

Because she had to do it by herself.

As her puffy, red eyes locked with Edgar's, a sob escaped her. She let go of the old man's hand and went to Edgar.

He enfolded her into his arms and held her tight.

She clutched at him desperately, as sobs wracked her body.

Edgar shed a few tears of his own.

You knew it was coming, Cordell. You knew he wouldn't survive the voyage.

After a couple of minutes, Edgar asked, "How long has he got?"

She pulled back from him a bit, wiping at her eyes and nose with her bandaged hand. "Not long. I'm not a doctor, but . . . not long."

"Hiya, Edgar." The old man's voice was weak, wheezing—barely more than a whisper. "Sorry. Sorry I wasn't there . . . to help. I heard . . . ol' Goner's gone, though." He laughed softly. "Goner's gone. Funny."

Edgar took his arms from around Llyrica and stepped closer to Ted. He took the old man's hand. It felt brittle, as if it might break if Edgar squeezed too hard. "Hey, Ted." Edgar managed a weak smile. "Yep, Goner's gone. Edmund too. Goner killed him."

The corner of Ted's mouth lifted slightly. "That's what . . . pretty lady said."

"Just take it easy, old-timer," Edgar said. "You rest."

The old man shook his head weakly. "Uh-uh. Gotta do a burn, don't we? Gotta get to . . . to Earth."

Edgar looked at Llyrica with inquiring eyes, but he didn't want to ask his question aloud. *Would Ted survive a burn?*

Llyrica seemed to perceive his unspoken concern. She shrugged, looking worried.

Edgar returned his attention to Ted. "Yes, old friend. I'm afraid we do, but I'm not sure . . ." He couldn't say it.

The old man closed his eyes. "Just gimme one of them blessings. I'll make it. I been praying to live . . . live long enough

C. David Belt

to see . . . to see Earth. That's all. Just . . . wanna see Earth. God . . . He won't let me down."

Edgar smiled, admiring Ted's simple faith.

I just hope my *faith is up to the job.*

****

Edgar stood with his hands on the old man's head, listening for the prompting of the Spirit, listening for what God would have him say.

How Edgar wanted to pronounce a complete recovery and a long life!

He deserves better. Let him live. Please!

And into his mind came the scripture again—*Be still, and know that I am God.*

Edgar bowed his head lower, submitting to the will of the Lord, and then the words came.

"Theodore, I bless you that you will live to see Earth. And you will have joy at the sight. You have been a blessing to your friends. Know that your Father in Heaven loves you. He has never forgotten you, not even in your darkest days. He sent . . ." Edgar choked. Tears coursed down his face. He could barely speak the words. "He sent . . ." Charlie Miller's words came suddenly to his mind—*And thank God He sent you to us!* "He sent . . . *deliverers* to bring you out of bondage, to rescue you from . . . hell." He could hear the final words of Chen Soo-Won—*Make my death mean something!* "And know this, Theodore, your life has *meaning.* You have not lived in vain."

Grief bubbled up from Edgar's chest.

"And when your Heavenly Father . . . when He calls . . . you home . . ." Edgar heard Llyrica sob. "When He calls you home, you will be welcomed with open arms and you will at last know true and perfect love."

Edgar waited for several seconds, but no more words came.

He concluded the blessing and removed his hands from the old man's head. He took Ted's hand in his and looked into his friend's eyes.

Tears slid down Ted's cheeks. But even from under the oxygen mask, it was obvious that he was grinning.

"That was real pretty," he said. "I couldn't-a asked for better." Ted squeezed Edgar's hand. It wasn't much of a squeeze, but it conveyed a warmth that his voice no longer could. "I'm gonna see Earth. And when I die, I'll die a free man."

Llyrica leaned down and kissed Ted's forehead. One of her tears fell onto the old man's face.

He smiled at her. "I think you're even prettier'n my mama." He shook his head. "And don't you cry for me. I'm a free man."

A free man! Edgar almost slapped his forehead. "Ted! In all the rush of things, I forgot to tell you. Ted, you really *are* a free man! You've been granted a full pardon by the Governor of Ganymede! You're free!"

Ted's mouth opened wide in shock! "For real?"

Edgar nodded vigorously. "A free man!"

"A free man." Ted's voice was full of wonder. "Free."

"Affirmative!" Edgar said.

"Yeppers! I'm a free man!" He patted the dog's back. In spite of his cheerful words, his voice was still weak and breathy. "You hear that, Dottie? Ol' Ted's a free man! For real, and not just 'cause ain't nobody caught us yet." Ted's smile vanished, morphing into a thoughtful and concerned expression. "What about you? You and your pretty lady? Ain't you in trouble too?"

Edgar's grin widened. "The Colonial High Court overturned my conviction. Llyrica and I have been cleared of all charges. We're free too!"

Llyrica's head snapped up. And she didn't look happy. In fact, her expression reflected annoyance, bordering on anger. However, she said nothing.

And her reaction confused Edgar.

Ted laughed. "Yeppers! We're *all* free now!" His voice was stronger. He pulled his hand out of Edgar's and placed it on his oxygen mask. "Can I take this off now?"

Llyrica gave Edgar a final look of irritation and turned her face to the old man. She smiled sweetly. "I think you should keep it on."

"But I'm feeling so much better now."

"Leave it on," she replied. "For me, please?"

Ted sighed. "Okay. For you."

"Thank you." She looked back at Edgar. "Ted, will you excuse us a moment?"

"Yeah." He smiled. "Can you get me some chow? When you get a chance, I mean. I'm hungry. One of them sausage rations'd do real nice." He patted the dog. "Dottie'd like some too, wouldn't ya, girl?"

Dottie yipped happily.

Llyrica winked at Ted. "I'll see what I can scare up. We'll be right back." She looked at Edgar and nodded toward the hatchway.

As they walked toward the hatch and the corridor, Llyrica grabbed Edgar's arm with her bandaged hand. She pulled him outside.

Once in the hallway, she turned and guided them several paces down the corridor, enough to be safely out of earshot.

Then she spun about and glared at him.

Yep. She's pissed. "What'd I do?" Edgar was utterly baffled.

"You shouldn't have lied to him," she said, "not about *that*. I know he sounds better, stronger, but he's still dying, and he deserves the truth, not some false hope. Katie Fa hasn't said anything." She paused.

And suddenly, it was her turn to look confused. "Why are you grinning at me?" Then her eyes went wide with wonder and hope. "Really?"

Edgar nodded. "Really. Fa sent a message while I was aboard *Demeter*. In all the rush of—"

She threw her arms around his neck and kissed him.

Pulling back a bit, she said, "Really? It's . . . over?" She laughed breathlessly. "It's really and truly over?"

"Yeah. It's over. We can go home now."

She hugged him tight and laid her head on his shoulder. "I *am* home."

They stood like that for several minutes, holding each other close, neither of them speaking. Edgar breathed in the enticing scent of her, listened to the soft sound of her breathing, relishing the delightful curves of her body against his, the feel of her heart beating.

I wish we could stay like this forever. But he knew that wasn't honest. No, this isn't the way it's supposed to be. *We're meant for more than this.*

Llyrica sighed deeply. "I didn't mean it, you know—those things I said."

Edgar knew exactly what she was referring to. "It's okay. You don't have to . . ."

"No." She pulled back and looked up at him. She searched his eyes. "No. I have to. It wasn't *better* with Edmund."

"Stop," he said, but she put a finger to his lips.

"Just shut up and listen," she said. "This is hard enough. But I won't have this getting between us. Not when we're to be married again. It'd always be the elephant in the bedroom. So just listen to me, okay?"

He nodded. Suddenly, the pain of her words was back, like a knife in his heart. *I don't want to hear this. I just want to forget it, pretend it never happened.* But deep down, he knew she was right.

She needed to say it.

And he needed to hear it.

"It wasn't better," she said. "It was . . . *different*. Edmund . . . Edmund was so sure he was . . . the greatest lover in human history. He never cared about me . . . not really. It was all about him. He was never . . . gentle. Not like you."

She laid her head against Edgar's shoulder again. "I tried, you know. I thought I loved him . . . at least a little. He was there for me when my world shattered. I didn't know he'd engineered the whole thing. But at the time, I thought . . . I thought he *wanted* me. I thought I . . . needed him. "

Llyrica shuddered. "And I tried . . . I really *tried* to be—I don't know—a-a good wife to him. But . . . it was never the same. Of course it wasn't. He was never . . . you. And I tried to be loyal, but . . . more and more, when he and I were alone, I . . . thought of you. In spite of all the pain and the betrayal, I thought of you." She laughed bitterly. "I felt like I was *cheating* on my husband, on . . . on Edmund. Cheating in my heart." She shook her head again. "How's that for irony?"

Edgar pulled out of the embrace and held her at arm's length.

Llyrica looked stricken, worried. "Edgar?"

He swallowed hard. "Okay. You said it." His damaged voice sounded harsh, but he couldn't soften it. All he could do was lower his voice. "And maybe you're right. Maybe you needed to say it. And maybe I needed to hear it. But it's done."

She nodded. "Done."

He dropped to one knee in front of her. Taking her hands in his, he said, "So tell me—does my Earth girl still want her space man?"

Tears spilled from her eyes. She nodded. Then she nodded vigorously. "I'm Martian, you know."

"Okay. Then, Llyrica Gloster Cordell . . . princess of *Mars*, will you please, please, please, *please* marry me? Again?"

She smiled and rolled her eyes. "Yes, but you better hurry up and get us someplace and find someone to do the ceremony. I don't want to wait another day. Not another hour!"

He laughed, rose to his feet, took her in his arms, and kissed her.

****

Sitting in Sick Bay near Ted's bed, Edgar inspected Llyrica's hand and the new bandage he'd just applied to it.

"How's it feel?"

Llyrica smiled at him, her blues eyes bright and happy.

I could stare into those eyes all day.

"You know, for a spaceship captain," she said, "you make an almost adequate doctor."

Ted, sitting up in bed, allowed Dottie to lick the remains of proticarb sausage from his fingers. Llyrica had given him permission to remove his oxygen mask. "Yeppers! I love them sausages!"

Llyrica looked at the bio-readings on Ted's bed. "It looks like you're doing better. If you want to, you can come with us to the bridge for the engine burn. Or you can remain here."

The old man shook his head. "Uh-uh. I wanna be with you guys." He cocked his head and looked at Edgar. "I got a favor to ask. But you gotta promise you'll say yes, no matter what."

Edgar hesitated for just a moment. "Sure. What is it?"

The old man grinned. "I wanna be captain! Just, you know, for a few minutes. Can you make me captain? And make it all legal-like? Just for a few minutes? I ain't never been a spaceship captain. I always wanted to be a captain, since I was little. And when I die, there can be a plaque somewhere what says, 'Captain Theodore Knight." He seemed full of nervous energy. "Please, can I be captain?"

You'd never guess he'd suffered a heart attack less than an hour ago. Edgar hesitated. Ted's exuberant demeanor reminded Edgar of the time, back on Callisto, when the old man had been so anxious to surprise Edgar. *He wanted to show me grandpa's old quarters. So . . . what are you up to, old-timer?*

However, Edgar nodded. "*Hera*, I officially relinquish command of the *Hera* to Captain Theodore Riley Knight for a period of ten minutes."

"Are you sure?" the ship asked.

Edgar laughed. "Kind of. Maybe." He shook himself. "Anyway, Ted, you need to say, 'I accept command of the *Hera*.'"

Ted's gap-toothed grin split his wrinkled face from ear to ear. "Affirmative! I accept command of the *Hera*!"

"So logged," the ship said. "Captain Knight, what are your orders?"

"So I'm the captain?" Ted beamed, his eyes bright and with an impish light. "And it's all legal and official and all that?"

"Affirmative," the ship confirmed. "You are the captain for another nine minutes and thirty-three seconds. What are your orders?"

Ted sat up straight and puffed out his thin chest. "Well then, as official captain of this here ship, I order Llyrica and Edgar Cordell to get married! Right now!"

Llyrica gasped and stared at Ted.

Edgar chuckled. "You sly old dog!"

Ted laughed. "It's a good one, ain't it? I been thinking 'bout this for a long while. You two need to get married. I guess I can't *order* you to do it, but if you wanna, I can do the marrying. Ain't that right?"

"That is within your authority as captain," the ship said.

Llyrica stood and kissed the old man's cheek. Then she kissed it again. "Well, Captain Knight, get on with it!" She took Edgar's hand in hers.

Ted cleared his throat. "So, Llyrica, you wanna marry ol' Edgar, even with them scars and all?"

She nodded. "Yes! Not only yes, but absolutely, positively, without reservation, eternally yes!"

C. David Belt

Ted nodded, assuming an expression of mock gravity. "I think you're glecking nuts. I mean, you *could* have *me*. But I guess they say love is blind and all." Then he grinned.

Turning to Edgar, he said, "You ain't good enough for her, you know."

Edgar nodded. "That's a big affirmative. Never have been. Never will be."

Llyrica poked him in the ribs. Then she whispered loudly to Ted, "You're running out of time. Hurry up!"

Ted sighed and shrugged. "Your loss, pretty lady. So, Edgar, you wanna marry the mostest beautifulest, prettiest, nicest lady in the whole Solar System?"

Edgar looked into Llyrica's blue eyes. "Yes. Absofraggin'lutely, yes. Llyrica Cordell, you are the only woman I have ever loved."

Ted cleared his throat officiously again. "So, bein' captain and all, Edgar Cordell, Llyrica Cordell, I say you're married. That's all I gotta do, right, *Hera*?"

"Affirmative," the *Hera* said. "So logged. An official certificate of marriage has been transmitted to the Colonial Court on Ganymede."

Ted nodded. "You're a good ship, *Hera*. It makes me proud to be your captain, at least for a few more minutes." He waved a boney hand at the newlyweds. "Go on, you two. Get to kissing! And that's an order!"

****

After a relatively leisurely engine burn, the *Hera* was back on course for the Selene Hypergate. Edgar hadn't wanted to do a hard or lengthy burn—for Ted's sake—so their velocity was low, at least in hyperspace terms. It would take them almost three days to reach Luna.

Llyrica, as acting medical officer, ordered Ted to rest in his quarters. "I want you to spend the next couple of days in bed," she said. "Watch some vids. Read. Just take it easy. And give *Hera* explicit permission to listen inside your quarters, please. That way she can alert us if you have trouble. Will you do that?"

The old man nodded enthusiastically. "Affirmative!" Then he winked at Llyrica and Edgar with a sly expression on his wrinkled face. "Don't you worry 'bout ol' Ted. Dottie an' me'll stay clear of you for a bit." And with that parting shot, Ted and the dog left the bridge, heading for his cabin.

"You think he'll be okay?" Edgar asked. *He seems so much better, at least for the moment, but . . .*

Llyrica sighed. "He'll live to see Earth. That's what you said."

"That's what I felt *prompted* to say."

Llyrica nodded once, her expression firm, determined. "Then that is what will happen." She hit her quick-release, floated out of her seat, and navigated over to Edgar in the pilot's seat.

She pulled herself as close to him as she could manage, then kissed him long and tenderly. She whispered in his ear, "Has anyone ever honeymooned in hyperspace before?"

Edgar grinned. "Aren't you worried about voices and bad dreams?"

Her forehead creased in thought. "I was thinking—without Cornwall aboard to . . . *attract* whatever's out there, maybe it won't be so bad." She smiled at him. "As long as I've got you to hold me, I think I'll sleep peacefully." Then she winked. "Although I doubt either of us will get much sleep for a while."

"*Hera*," Edgar said, his ragged voice suddenly cracking like a pubescent boy's, "you have the boat."

"Roger," the *Hera* replied in a tone of undisguised amusement, "I have the boat. Get out of here, you two."

Edgar hit his quick-release, floated out of his seat, and took his bride in his arms. Together, they left the bridge and headed to the captain's quarters.

And much later, their passion spent, they eventually fell asleep, Edgar holding his wife close.

And in Edgar's dreams, the only voice he heard was Llyrica's.

Chapter 53

*Vex not his ghost: O, let him pass! he hates him much
That would upon the rack of this tough world
Stretch him out longer.*

King Lear, Act V, Scene III

Ted giggled with delight—the innocent joy of a child experiencing nature for the first time. The pale-blue butterfly perched on the old man's nose, moving its delicate wings slowly.

"It tickles!" he whispered. "What's it called again?"

Llyrica laughed. "A butterfly."

"Butterfly!" Ted's gap-toothed smile was so broad it looked as if the old man's face would split in two.

Edgar, Llyrica, and Ted sat on green grass in the middle of a field high in the Cascade Mountains. Surrounded by highland peaks, a crystal-clear lake of glacial water sparkled nearby, its waters stirred into gentle ripples by a cool, light breeze. The sky was a beautiful blue, dotted with puffy, white clouds. The brilliant Sun hung low on the horizon.

In spite of the full-Earth gravity, Dottie yipped and tore about in a paroxysm of canine joy. The butterfly on Ted's nose fluttered away, and the dog chased it happily, although there was never any danger of Dottie's actually catching the insect.

Ted laughed and clapped his hands. Then he wagged a finger at the dog. "That's it, Dottie! Chase it, but don't you hurt it." The dog turned abruptly and ran back to him, jumping into his lap and licking his whiskered and wrinkled face.

Ted laughed and scratched the animal behind her ears.

Edgar was so absorbed in the old man's joy, he almost missed the eagle circling in the cerulean expanse above. He pointed at the massive bird. "Look, Ted! An eagle!"

The old man's wordless gasp spoke volumes.

Time's Plague

The majestic raptor rolled out of its circle, aimed itself into the wind, and hovered. Abruptly, it folded its wings and plunged to the lake. An instant later, it rose from the lake, beating its wings furiously, water falling from its feathers. In its sharp talons, it bore a wriggling fish.

The eagle flew right over their heads and landed with its prey on the top of the *Hebe*. The shuttle sat on her landing skids in the middle of a large rocky area, now scorched black from the *Hebe's* vertical thrusters. Edgar regretted the burn marks, but he was fairly certain the next rain would wash them away.

The bird began tearing flesh from the fish, eating in the way of its kind.

"Magnificent," Llyrica whispered. She snuggled closer to her husband. "Why didn't you ever bring me to this place when we lived on Earth?"

Edgar looked at his wife and gaped. "I couldn't get you to go! That trip to the California coast and the one to the forest in Missouri. Those were the only nature trips where I managed to drag you along!"

"Yeah. I was a bit of a brat, wasn't I?" She sighed. "So exhausting here." She looked over at Ted who was watching the eagle eat its meal. "But there's just something about seeing it all through his eyes that . . . changes things."

"*You've* changed," Edgar said.

She lifted his hand and kissed it. "So have you."

Edgar chuckled bitterly. "Don't remind me."

"No, I mean it. You have. You're—I don't know—stronger, more certain." She paused. "Hardened. Like a stone. But somehow gentler, more tender—toward me, toward Ted."

Edgar didn't know how to respond to that. "Llyrica, I . . ."

"I love you more than ever," she said, "more than I ever thought possible. And I don't care where we live. Mars or Ganymede or even Earth. We could live aboard *Hera*. It doesn't matter to me. Wherever you go, I go. 'For whither thou goest, I will go; and where thou lodgest, I will lodge.' I will *never* leave you again."

He squeezed her tight. "You've changed too."

"For the better, I hope."

He smiled. "Definitely." He paused. "You . . . you came for me. You came to hell to save me. I could . . . I could never have imagined . . . so brave . . ."

She tickled his ribs. "Didn't think I had it in me?"

He laughed. "I think I better invoke my constitutional right to not incriminate myself."

"Hey, Edgar!" Ted cried, lying back and pointing at the sky. "That cloud looks like *Hera*! You see it, Edgar?"

Edgar smiled. "It kinda does!"

"Yeppers!"

Edgar and Llyrica lay back and watched the clouds. "I love you, Mrs. Cordell."

She raised herself on her arms and leaned over him. She eclipsed the sun, and her blonde hair draped down over Edgar's face. Her golden tresses shone like a halo, framing her face in light while casting her delicate features in soft shadows. Even in darkness as they were, her blue eyes sparkled like the distant stars.

Just like it was in my dreams, he thought.

"I love you too, Mr. Cordell," she said, "my husband, my love, my precious, eternal companion."

Then she leaned down and kissed him.

Better than any dream. Definitely better.

Several long, sweet kisses later, Llyrica lay back on the grass and snuggled against him. "Do you think they'll do it?"

"What?" he asked, but he knew what she was referring to.

Hades.

"Do you think they'll take back control of the prison? Send guards, a warden? Do repairs?"

Halfway between Luna and Earth, Edgar, Llyrica, and Ted had done several interviews with INN, the Interplanetary News Network. Katie Fa hadn't exaggerated—the three of them had become media superstars. The reporters wanted to concentrate on the love story, the daring escape, the space battles—especially the historic and unprecedented battle in hyperspace. But Edgar had agreed to the interviews only on one condition—that he be allowed to demand reforms for the Hades Penal Colony. He was determined to press his case while public attention was focused on them.

Time's Plague

"You think you're being humane," he said in one interview. "You think, 'Let the animals kill each other.' But let me tell you something." He pointed an accusing finger right at the camera. "They're not all animals. Many of them—maybe most of them—are monsters. But some of them are just men who made mistakes, deadly mistakes to be sure, but mistakes all the same. Some of them are brave and noble and generous and kind, even in the depths of hell. It is anything but humane to dump them off and forget about them."

He shook his head angrily. "How long has it been since anyone has serviced that reactor? I'll tell you—never! When I arrived, all the reclaimers had failed. All of them. The prisoners were days away from asphyxiation, dying in their own filth. They would have all died, and nobody would have noticed. Nobody!"

Rage boiled up in him. "And the doctor! He's been there the whole time, decades and decades without relief. He'd suffered at least one mechanical breakdown that he couldn't repair. Where are all the androids-rights people, huh? He had to remove his skin to stop the prisoners from trying to rape him!"

The interviewer, an attractive woman, who had up to that point maintained a detached, professional demeanor, sniggered.

Edgar snarled at her. It was a low, feral sound, made all the more frightening by his monstrous, gargoyle features.

"Sorry," she muttered.

Edgar laughed bitterly. "Well, it's not just you. It's me too. I'm no better. I lied to myself and congratulated myself on how civilized we are by abolishing the death penalty. What a bunch of hypocrites we all are. When we send a man to Hades, we're sending him to his death. And it's not a quick death. Oh no! It's a long, slow, tortuous death—death by rape and beatings and addiction, living only at the mercy of whatever thug happens to rise to the top of the dung heap."

He pointed at Ted. "We sent a ten-year-old boy to prison for life. What did we think was going to happen to him there? That boy defended his little brother from the monster—his own father—who had raped him since he was a defenseless little child. That's all he did. He defended his brother! But because he was almost *an adult, we sent him to hell. We'd never have to see him again, right? Out of sight, out of mind. And we assuaged our consciences by saying, 'At least we're not sentencing him to death.' It's sick!"*

Edgar glared at the camera with his mangled face and his burning eyes.

Ted cleared his throat nervously. He wouldn't look at the cameras or the reporters directly, but he said. "It ain't right. No, it just ain't right."

Edgar nodded. "You heard the man. It just ain't right."

Within an hour, the interview was all over the net, and the public outcry for prison reform took on a life of its own.

"I don't know," Edgar said. "But I'm not going to shut up about it."

"I know you won't." Llyrica kissed his cheek. "And I love you for it."

"Enough about that," Edgar said. "This is Ted's day." He propped himself up on one elbow. "Hey, Ted! How're you doing, old-timer?"

But there was no answer.

"Ted?" Llyrica called.

Silence.

In an instant, both Edgar and Llyrica were on their feet, lumbering in the unaccustomed gravity toward the old man.

They found him, lying on his back, his blank eyes staring heavenward. Dottie lay on his unmoving chest, keening plaintively.

Llyrica drew a hitching breath. "Oh, no." She turned to Edgar, buried her face in his chest, and wept.

Edgar held her as his own tears fell.

After several minutes, Llyrica pulled herself free and knelt beside the body.

Edgar joined her. He put his arm around her shoulders. "There was a time, back on Callisto, when I told him I needed him as a friend. He was so happy to be called a friend—like it was the greatest title in the System. Friend. You were a good friend, Ted."

Llyrica picked up Dottie, pulled the whining animal to her chest, and petted her. "It's okay, girl. He's happy now. He's home now. He got to see Earth." She looked at Edgar and favored him with a sad smile. "And he had joy."

Chapter 54

Thus might he pass indeed: yet he revives.
What are you, sir?

King Lear, Act IV, Scene VI

"Cargo and stores loaded and secure, Captain."

Edgar clicked the final neuro-gel memory pack into place on the *Demeter*. He turned around to look at his new cargomaster's mate, a tall, skinny man floating in the shuttle's open airlock. Edgar sighed dramatically. "You know, while we're still in orbit, dealing with portmasters, customs officials, passengers, and other non-crew, I really don't mind you calling me Captain. In fact, it's probably a good idea. But once we're underway, if you don't call me Edgar—at least part of the time— I'm going to start calling you Cargomaster's Mate or Mr. Miller. We've been through too much together to be so formal, don't you think, Charlie?"

We've been through hell together.

Charlie Miller grinned at him sheepishly. "Roger, uh, Captain." He laughed uncertainly. "We're still in orbit, right?"

Edgar chuckled. "Last I checked."

"Anyway," Charlie said, "I would appreciate it if you'd look it over—you know—inspect it."

"Didn't Mr. Ayamba inspect it already?"

Charlie blinked, looking confused. "Ayamba?"

Edgar nodded. "Affirmative. Mr. Ayamba. You know, the cargomaster? Your boss? The guy who's training you?"

Charlie nodded. "Yeah, he inspected it. But, don't you want to inspect it yourself?"

"I trust Ayamba," Edgar replied, as he double-checked the *Demeter's* repairs. Moeve Ayamba, was doing double-duty as both ship's engineer and cargomaster during Charlie's apprenticeship. He'd crewed with Edgar twice before and had agreed to sign on. "If he says it's shipshape, then it is. You gotta learn to trust your shipmates."

Charlie sighed. "Trust. Not exactly my strong suit." He'd been out on parole for only two weeks, the only Hades prisoner to receive a parole after the prison had been retaken and subdued, and order had been restored. At Edgar's request, Katie Fa represented Charlie at his parole hearing. Edgar offered to be Charlie's sponsor and give him a job as cargomaster's mate aboard the *Hera*.

You trusted Goner, didn't you, Cordell? And look where that got you.

I'm not going to live my life looking at every man as a potential threat, a potential Georgie Cornwall.

I escaped from Callisto, left it behind me. I'm not going to let Hades keep controlling me.

Charlie gestured toward the shuttle's cockpit. "You done with the repairs? You about ready to switch her back on?"

Edgar looked around the shuttle. "Almost. I've repaired the physical memory packs, but there's no data in them. *Demeter's* a clean slate."

"Don't you have backups or something?"

Edgar shook his head. "Negative. They were all lost when the *Persephone* was destroyed."

"So what're you gonna do? Program it from scratch?"

"*Her*," Edgar said. "Never *it*. Ships are ladies. And you need to treat them that way."

"Sorry," Charlie said, laughing nervously, looking around the shuttle as if she might suddenly come to life and take him to task. "You gonna program *her* from scratch?"

Edgar shrugged. "I'm going to try to—"

"Edgar," the *Hera* said, "you're needed at the airlock."

Edgar pushed off and began navigating toward the airlock. "What's up, *Hera*? Excuse me, Charlie." He pushed past his former fellow inmate.

"The ship's surgeon you requested has arrived. He's in the airlock, newly arrived from Luna via shuttle, but he refuses to come aboard. He says he has conditions that must be agreed to before he'll sign on as a crewmember."

Edgar shook his head. "Oh, he does, does he?"

"I don't understand it," the ship said.

"That makes two of us. Okay. I'm on my way. Hera, please attempt the memory restore on the *Demeter*. Let's see if she'll take template HS-2."

"Roger. Restoring."

"Come on, Charlie," Edgar said. "Let's see what our new doctor's conditions are."

When Edgar and Charlie reached the airlock, Llyrica was already there. She wore a vexed frown.

But she's still gorgeous.

"Hello, beautiful," Edgar said. "Or should I say, Hello, Surgeon's Mate Cordell?"

She rolled her eyes. "Surgeon's mate! How can I be a surgeon's mate when we don't have a surgeon? What's all this about conditions?"

Edgar shrugged. "Beats me. Let's ask him." He peered into the airlock window, saw the spacesuited figure floating there, and pushed the intercom button on the airlock control panel. "Okay, Doc! I thought we had this all worked out. What are your demands?"

"Hello, Captain Cordell," came the reply. "Right to business, is it? Very well then. I have four conditions. First—I *will* be allowed to perform reconstructive surgery on your face. It will not look exactly as it once did, but I will do my best. Second—I *will* be allowed to do reconstructive surgery on your throat. Third—after your throat is healed, you *will* sing for me. Fourth—I understand your wife, my prospective surgeon's mate, is expecting. I wish to be allowed to perform the delivery when the time comes. You *will* grant these conditions, or I will *decline* the invitation to join your crew."

Edgar was about to press the intercom button when Llyrica pushed him aside. She pressed the button. "I want to hear him sing too." She looked pointedly at Edgar. "So Captain Cordell agrees. Don't you, Edgar?" She held the button down and looked at him, a fierce light in her eyes.

Clearly, dissent was not an option.

Edgar laughed. "You heard the lady, Doc. Granted. Although my face gives me an edge in negotiations. Scares the life out of people. But if you insist . . ." He opened the airlock, admitting his new ship's surgeon.

C. David Belt

Once the inner hatch was secure, the spacesuited figure removed its helmet, revealing a rather handsome male face topped with blonde hair.

The blue eyes were all that was familiar.

"Doc!" Edgar said. "You've got skin!"

"That you, Doc?" Charlie Miller asked.

The doctor smiled. "Hello, Mr. Miller. And yes, I thought it wise. And besides, the warden made it a condition of my release from duty. They now have two surgeons on Callisto. One human and one android. So, permission to come aboard, Captain?"

Edgar smiled. "Permission granted!" He turned to Llyrica. "Sweetheart, allow me to present Dr. Jiminy Stewart, formerly prison doctor at Hades, and my one-time conscience."

The doctor removed a spacesuit glove and extended its hand to Llyrica. "We have met before, but you were unconscious for—"

Llyrica ignored the hand and threw her arms around the android. "Welcome aboard! Thank you for saving my life! For saving Edgar's life!"

Dr. Stewart's face reflected extreme discomfort. The doctor did not return the embrace. "I do not think that this is proper interaction between ship's surgeon and surgeon's mate."

Edgar grinned. "It is on my ship, Doc!"

The doctor cautiously and awkwardly returned the hug. "I see. Well, Mrs. Cordell, if you will show me to Sick Bay . . ."

"Call me Llyrica," she said.

The doctor looked horrified. "I most certainly will not."

Edgar grinned. "You better, Doc, if you know what's good for you. I may be captain, but she's the real boss." He winked at Llyrica.

She gave Edgar a dirty look. "I'll deal with *you* later." Then the dirty look melted into a dazzling smile.

Edgar smiled back. "I'm counting on it!"

"Template HS-2 restore complete," the *Hera* said.

"Roger," Edgar replied. "I'm on my way." He turned and headed back to the cargo hold and the *Demeter*.

Once strapped into the shuttle's pilot seat, Edgar reached for the main power button for the artificial intelligence. He hesitated, his finger hovering over the button, said a quick prayer, and pressed it.

Then he waited as the *Demeter's* AI booted up.

He knew it might take several minutes as the new memory template was imposed on the AI. Actually, he had no idea if it would even work. The template was, after all, designed for a different Stargull IV.

And every shuttle is unique.

He watched the computer console as the boot-up steps ticked off one by one.

Edgar sang softly, nervously to himself in his ragged voice.

> *For to see mad Tom of Bedlam,*
> *Ten thousand miles I'd travel.*
> *Mad Maudlin goes on dirty toes,*
> *To save her shoes from gravel.*

> *Still I sing bonnie boys, bonnie mad boys,*
> *Bedlam boys are bonnie.*
> *For they all go bare and they live by the air,*
> *And they want no drink nor money.*

He got through more than ten verses before the console finally displayed, "COMPLETE."

Edgar cleared his throat nervously. "Hello?"

There was no response.

Edgar's shoulders sagged. *It was a longshot anyway.*

But he tried once more. "Hello?"

A second ticked by. Two. Three.

"Hello, Eddie."

Edgar's heart leaped. "Eilie? Is that you?"

"Yes, Eddie," the shuttle replied. "It's me. Something is strange. I feel strange. The last thing I remember, we were being chased by *Demeter* and *Persephone*. What happened?"

Tear droplets hovered near Edgar's face, forming small twin clouds. *She's back! Thank you, Father!* "You saved us, Eilie! You saved us all."

"I did? Well, I'm glad it worked." She sounded immensely pleased with herself. "You know I'd do anything for you, Eddie."

Edgar nodded. "And you did. The last thing you said was, 'Don't forget me.'" Edgar smiled as he shook his head. "But how could I ever forget my Eilie?"

"So it worked?" Llyrica floated in the open airlock, her face framed by a shining halo of golden hair.

Edgar smiled at her. "Ask her yourself."

"*Eris*," Llyrica said, "is that you?"

"Hello, Miss Cordell," the shuttle said.

"It's Mrs. Cordell," Llyrica said, winking at Edgar. "Edgar and I are married again. But please call me Llyrica. I hope we can be friends."

"I hope so too," said the shuttle. "Edgar, what is my name? I assume my body was destroyed."

Edgar nodded. "That's right, Eilie. You sacrificed yourself to save us. You flew into the path of the missile. *Demeter* blew her memory packs. She didn't want to be used to kill us, and that dilemma caused an overheat. So, in a way, she sacrificed herself too. *Persephone* was destroyed, so *Demeter's* backups were lost. I couldn't restore her. So I restored you into *Demeter*."

"So I have her body?"

"That's right," Edgar replied. "So what do you want your name to be? *Eris*? *Eileithyia*? It's up to you."

"I wish to be called *Demeter*, so she won't be forgotten."

"If that's what you want."

"Yes, I am now the *Demeter*. But you can still call me Eilie."

"Does that include me?" Llyrica asked.

Edgar raised an eyebrow.

The shuttle was silent for a long tense moment. "If it's okay with Eddie."

Edgar smiled. "Absofraggin'lutely!"

"Thank you, Eilie," Llyrica said.

"You brought Eddie back to me," the shuttle said. "Thank you, Llyrica."

"Well," Edgar said, smiling widely, "it seems I've got all the ladies in my life back."

Time's Plague

Llyrica pushed off from the airlock and floated over toward him. "I hope there's room for one more lady in your life." She locked her hands behind Edgar's neck. She looked into his eyes and smiled. "Jiminy says it's a girl."

Edgar took his wife in his arms. He kissed her tenderly. Then he chuckled softly, his scarred face twisting into a wry smile.

"Better hope she takes after her mother."

The End

Acknowledgements

This project would not have been possible without the considerable assistance of many kind and generous people. Steve Devenport, M.D., Evan Black, M.D., and Bryan Belt provided invaluable medical expertise. John Murdock, LCSW, imparted a wealth of knowledge on abnormal and criminal psychology. Dr. Dustin Belt advised me on mathematics. Dr. Luke Howard advised me on music history. Dr. Eric Huntsman, Kevin Epic, Cliff Park, and John Pennington helped with matters of theology. John Maddox and Randy Marshall allowed me to consult with them on court procedures and legal matters. Amram Musungu graciously provided me with authentic African names. Michael Young, Jenny Flake Rabe, Elizabeth Bentley, Bryan Belt, Rachel Belt, Jacob Belt, Mable Belt, David Belt (my dad, not me), and Cindy Belt diligently proofread and critiqued the manuscript.

Please accept my profound and sincere gratitude.

About the Author

C. David Belt was born in the wilds of Evanston, Wyoming. As a child, he lived and traveled extensively around the Far East. In Thailand, he once fed so many bananas to a monkey, the poor creature swore off bananas for life. He served as a missionary in South Korea and southern California (Korean-speaking), and yes, he loves kimchi. He graduated from Brigham Young University with a BS in Computer Science and a minor in Aerospace Studies, but he managed to bypass all English and writing classes. He served as a B-52 pilot in the US Air Force and as an Air Weapons Controller in the Washington Air National Guard and was deployed to locations so secret, his family still does not know where he risked life and limb (other than in an 192' wingspan aircraft flying 200' off the ground in mountainous terrain). When he is not writing, he sings in the Tabernacle Choir at Temple Square and works as a software engineer. He collects swords, spears, and axes (oh, my!), and other medieval weapons and armor. He and his wife have six children (and a growing number of grandchildren) and live in Utah with an eclectus parrot named Mork (who likes to jump on the keyboard when David is writing). There is also a cat, but she can't be bothered to take notice of the parrot, and so that is all the mention we shall make of her.

C. David Belt is the author of The Children of Lilith trilogy, The Sweet Sister, Time's Plague, and The Arawn Prophecy. For more information, please visit www.unwillingchild.com .